Rose Quinlan

By the same author

Women are Bloody Marvellous!
Jude
Jaen
Women of No Account
Hard Loves, Easy Riches
The Consequences of War
Goodbye Piccadilly
Long, Hot Summer

ROSE QUINLAN

Betty Burton

HarperCollins*Publishers*

HarperCollins*Publishers*
77–85 Fulham Palace Road,
Hammersmith, London W6 8JB

Published by HarperCollins*Publishers* 1994

A catalogue record for this book is
available from the British Library

ISBN 0 246 13925 0

Set in Linotron Bembo by
Rowland Phototypesetting Ltd
Bury St Edmunds, Suffolk

Printed in Great Britain by
HarperCollinsManufacturing Glasgow

ROSE QUINLAN
is for
Mary Shanley
of Boreen Point
Queensland

PART ONE

Television • Suez • Korea • Israel • Cyprus
Iran • Mau Mau • Burgess • Maclean • Philby
South Bank • Festival of Britain • LPs • Juke-box • Rock
'n' roll • Helsinki and Melbourne Olympics • Blue jeans • Dior
Stilettos • The Goons • Under Milk Wood • The King and I • Singin'
in the Rain • Space • Espresso • Alabama • H-bomb • CND
Notting Hill • Castro • Teddy boys • Elvis • J.F.K.
HRH Elizabeth II • Jackie Kennedy • Ruth
Ellis • Marilyn Monroe • Grace Kelly

1951

Rose Quinlan pulled Anoria's rain-hood further down over her damp, smooth baby-pink forehead. Anoria at five was a most amenable, watchful and uncomplaining child. Rose's instinct was to kiss the forehead, but withheld – as would have most women of her class and age – from a display of spontaneous affection in public. And in any case, Villette was already forming her mouth to have her say.

Villette, eleven, was neither amenable nor uncomplaining, and not given to putting a brave face on it. Her grandmother described her as 'spirited'. Villette liked things to be happening – or rather happening! She hunched her shoulders crossly at the rain. 'Oh do let's move, Mummy.'

Rose said, 'You want to see the king and queen, don't you?'

'No, I don't. I've seen them. She was so *terribly* stodgy and old-fashioned, and he was just a man in a sailor's cap. They weren't much cop.'

Jonathan, well on in his teens, laughed. He didn't really mind much what happened; he was easy-going and would fall in with most plans. He liked his sisters best when they left him out of their squabbles.

Rose said, 'Jon, you are old enough to know better. I thought I could rely on you not to encourage her.'

By way of explanation he hunched his shoulders and smiled charmingly at his mother.

'You see? Jon doesn't want to waste his time on a mouldy old king, do you, Jon?' Villette said. 'Jon doesn't want to see them, Becc doesn't, I don't . . .' She looked meaningfully at Anoria, but Anoria looked blank, not wishing to get into the bad books of whoever won. 'So it's only you that wants to see them, Mum, and you're only saying . . .'

'Not democratic, Mum?' Jonathan said.

Rebecca, who, although younger than Jon, was top-dog of the family and liked to be shocking, said, 'Papa said that he wouldn't even get off his backside if the queen went by the window. I agree with him. Who needs them?' Great-grandfather, known as 'Papa', was their father's grandfather, always a Liberal, now in old age moved much to the left and republicanism.

'Becc, I wish that you would learn to speak without raising your voice to such a pitch,' Rose said.

Anoria said, 'It is Mummy's birthday, she should be the one to choose.'

Villette indicated, by crawling her fingers at her young sister, what she thought of a creeper.

Although it was May-time and in the London parks bloomed the pastel shades of lilac, prunus, magnolia and sorbus, today was more March-like: chill wind, flurries of rain, and an all-pervading drippiness on the starkly aggressive, post-war architects' dreams-come-true in bare, reinforced concrete, which not even the flags and tubbed flowers could lighten. Not easy to persuade anyone that this was a morning to stand about to wait for anything, let alone a small dull king, and a queen wearing an ordinary hat and coat.

Rose, seeing their point, decided that there really wasn't a great deal of point in getting wet and spoiling the rest of the day. 'Well, all right then, what are we hanging about here for?' and took them away from the entrance to the 'Dome of Discovery', and the wet but loyal crowd, and off to one of the new pavilions where, although coffee cost ninepence for a cup, they all had coffee and Smith's Crisps whilst they made plans, each of the children laying claim to part of the Festival and part of the day.

The father of these four children, and husband of Rose, was Ballard Quinlan, MP, Member for Covington. The idea of this Festival of Britain, this spree, this joyful reward to a war-weary country, had been the heart-love of Labour, his own party. But Ballard Quinlan had opposed it from the beginning, and had agreed openly with the Conservative Opposition argument that the 'Poor Old British Taxpayer' (of whom Ballard often spoke in the House of Commons) did not want to make an eleven-million-pound contribution to the Festival. Since his election in 1945, Ballard's problem had always been, and still was, that of an MP with a small majority; one of the smallest in the country. His constituency of Covington was fairly evenly divided between left and right, with a small floating vote keeping him on his toes. And, as the Covington left were hardly recognizable as Labour, and the right still thought like man-trapping landowners, he spoke up for the Poor Old Taxpayer, which showed that he always had his voters at heart.

In spite of a carping minority, many of whom still hankered after the repressions of wartime Britain, the Festival went ahead, and promised to be the most joyful event since before the Great War over thirty years before.

'All right,' said Rose, 'we'll see as much as we can today and come back tomorrow. Just so long as we all keep together.'

'Mother!' Jonathan protested. 'We'll have to split up. I'm old enough, for God's sake.'

Rose capitulated easily. Everything would be much less fidgety if she wasn't going to be called upon to arbitrate on their choices. 'Oh, very well, but we absolutely must meet up at four o'clock. I don't want any lost children announcements.'

'This isn't an end-of-the-pier show, Mummy,' Villette said seriously.

Jonathan accepted the proviso, and the spending money his mother handed him, and Rebecca put the case for herself. 'I'm even more responsible than Jonathan,' which was true, so she was given a similar amount of money, and licence to have as much fun as her brother.

'And before you ask, Vee,' Rose said, seeing Villette lining up her plea, 'the answer's no. You and Nora and I will stay together.' She winked at Villette, still a child in Rose's eyes, yet already she was the second of her three daughters to have joined the women. Rose knew, of course, that there were countries in which girls of Vee's age were married, but she wanted her daughters to hang on to childhood longer than that. For Rose herself had gone almost straight from girlhood to marriage.

Vee accepted with good grace, knowing that being with her mother would probably be more fun than being treated as a kid by Jonathan and Becc. If she stuck with Mother, it would be Nora who was the kid, and, when Daddy wasn't around, Mummy was a good sport and terribly good with spending money.

Rose felt elated. In having brought her children to the South Bank site, she had won a minor victory over the combined forces of Ballard and his mother, Winifred. Charlotte, Ballard's grandmother, had supported Rose against him. 'Ballard, you just think a bit about the time we took you on holiday to Germany. We didn't agree with Hitler, any more than you agree with this Festival, but you aren't sorry we took you, are you, Son?' Ballard hated being called 'Son', but he had to admit that the pre-war visit had often stood him in good stead when making speeches on international affairs.

Ballard had been Member of Parliament for Covington (Lab.) since the 1945 Labour landslide when he rode into Covington on a very dodgy majority. His real income came from a small but very lucrative 'head-hunting' agency specializing in top jobs in industry and commerce. His two professions were well grafted: he knew useful men of whom many were, one way or another, indebted to him. Ballard's skill was in knowing just when to call in those debts.

He loved being in the Palace of Westminster. Not merely for the idea of it: Mother of Parliaments, Hub of the Empire, Birthplace of Democracy, and all that. Not only for the pomp and circumstance of it: His Majesty, Black Rod, Mr Speaker, Honourable Members, My Honourable Friend; but he loved being physically there in the Corridors of Power where the very smell of the fabric of the building as well as its sights and sounds evoked a sense of one having a place in history. Green upon green row in the Chamber, red upon red row in the Other Place; dust, stone floors and polished wood; echoing archways, secret stairways and respectful attendants; wigs, robes, silk stockings and tradition.

He was speaking in the House today. Whenever Ballard made a speech – a proper speech with notes and try-outs in front of a looking-glass – his mother did her best to be in the Strangers' Gallery. He would give her tea.

'Good old Mum,' Rebecca said to Jonathan as they went off together, each with five one-pound notes which, as Winifred would have pointed out, had she known, was more than some skilled men earned in a week.

Rebecca found the freshness and new ideas that rushed at her from every side absolutely thrilling, and the prospect of her own future set out, as it was here at the Festival, almost overwhelming in its possibilities.

'Makes you think, doesn't it, Jon? Makes you wonder what it's going to be like when the bomb-sites have gone and there's lots of lovely things about.'

'It'll probably be like this, I suppose. A lot of concrete and glass. Sky-scrapers, I should think. London will look like New York.' Jonathan, having dealt with the subject of Future, was more immediately interested in the present and his imminent entry into university life.

Rebecca said with great enthusiasm, 'I think it's going to be wonderful! When people see all this nobody's going to want old chintz and squashy armchairs, they'll want all these lovely plain colours and clean lines to go with the buildings.' As they pushed their way around the exhibitions and displays, they discovered more and more of their future, as foreseen by technocrats. Technocrats and designers were hitherto quite unknown in Britain. Jon looked on with interest and let Rebecca chatter on about her vision of homes that followed these new contemporary designs.

It was all so different from anything that had gone before when the majority of people liked most things to last and not show the dirt. The pattern on fabric and wallpaper was called 'the design'. Design was something quite new. Rather awesome too. A new language – form, line, proportion, and primary colour. 'Antelopes' and 'Springboks', new chairs with stiff, splayed skeleton metal legs and undulating seats, cutlery where blade and handle were as one, plates and saucers which were unadorned discs of pure colour, unfussy cups with large handles; whole dinner sets made of a glass that was said to be heatproof; taps with levers; soap dishes set into bathroom walls; and television sets that would make everyone's sitting room into a family cinema.

Rebecca said happily, 'I think that homes will be just like Hollywood film sets and people will be happy.'

'I thought you were going to live on a houseboat.'

'You always have to make difficulties, Jonathan.' It *was* difficult to see how the new contemporary style fitted in with her intended Bohemian life on a houseboat, but she would work it out. 'I am talking about *trends*, *design*. Anyhow, when I've been through art college, I shall know how to do it.'

'If you've still got that idea about going to art college, you'd better start work on Dad now. Give him time to get used to the idea.'

She laughed; she often did. 'I've sown the first seeds. He quite likes the idea of a daughter who is a portrait painter.'

'Portrait painter? Ye Gods. That's a crummy idea.'

She grinned at him. 'I said that Daddy likes the idea. I never said that I did. When I get to art college, I shall slide over into design – fabric, fashion, something like that; maybe even furniture. But in some field where I shall have influence on how things look.'

Jonathan had a high regard for this sister. She had always known exactly what she wanted, and how to go about getting it. Even now she managed to look different from other frumpy schoolgirls, her plastic mac flung round her like a cloak, her hair bunched up in a long floating scarf, the hank of hair dragged to one side and hitched over her ear.

'In ten years, all this –' indicating the lamps, chairs and tables of the Embankment and the shockingly stark exterior of the Festival Hall – 'will be old hat. Ernest Race and Hugh Casson will be O-U-T. People will be ready for somebody new.'

'And the new style will be dictated by Becc Quinlan?'

'Why not? Somebody has to dictate it. I know what label I shall sell under – "Rebel!" With an exclamation mark. So that it will be a message too. Re-*bel*! You have nothing to lose but your chains.'

Jonathan smiled. Becc couldn't help hamming anything up. 'Who will have nothing to lose but their chains?'

She looked up under her brows at her brother. '*Jon*! "Workers of the world, unite – you have nothing to lose but your chains." Basic Marx.'

'Communist Marx?'

'No, Groucho, idiot! Of course Communist Marx. Great-gran told me – don't tell Dad, but she went to Southampton to hear Harry Pollitt speak. Isn't that a great phrase?' Standing atop one of the concrete walkways she looked down at the damp crowds. '"Workers of the world unite . . ."'

Jonathan pulled her arm. 'Come *on*, Becc.'

Rebecca had a high, trilling, infectious laugh. 'Just think, there will come a day when we'll be able to do anything we like. Fuck Parliament, fuck the Party.'

Jon blushed. There were times when Becc was just too much.

Winifred too was in London at the time of the Festival but, like Ballard, had forsworn the 'acres of folly' (a phrase from a speech of his that had caused a furore within his own Party but had delighted the Tory Opposition). As her taxi went over Waterloo Bridge, the Festival of Britain site was laid out below. She knew that somewhere down there her daughter-in-law and grandchildren were pushing their way round the exhibits. The Festival Hall was a monstrous concrete box. 'Contemporary?' as she often scathingly said, 'I should call it contemptible.' And, as Ballard had said when he had joined the Labour Party: they'd had plenty to say about the housing shortage, yet they had gone ahead and sanctioned concert halls like palaces – and, as for the nonsense of the Battersea funfair, foolishness knew no bounds. People walking through the branches of trees, and hundreds of pounds' worth of fireworks going off every evening. And, quite apart from anything else, Winifred thought, the sheer tastelessness of it all!

But that was typical of the people with whom Ballard had allied himself. Even though he was now 'My son, the Member of Parliament for Covington', she still found it hard to swallow his allegiance to the Labour Party.

As she had said of the Festival ages ago to her friends at the bridge and canasta club: 'Of course, none of it will be finished on time. Walk-outs and strikes. All this closed-shop business . . . Workmen these days don't want to work; all they want to do is to drink tea for a fat pay-packet. As my son was saying only last week in the House . . .'

Her son saw himself as the scourge and conscience of his Party. He loved that role. Several of his Honourable Friends saw him as a right-winger who would feel a lot more at home on the Opposition benches. But as Ballard had foretold, some of it had *not* been finished on time. Little gangs of men were still down there finishing the place. And, as for the Festival Hall – they had got the acoustics wrong, which meant more money for the poor old taxpayer to find.

Above on Waterloo Bridge, the lights changed and Winifred's taxi moved on, so she had no chance of spotting the fat pay-packeted, unionized men drinking tea instead of putting in a decent day's work.

After a while Jonathan and Rebecca had agreed to split up, Rebecca to go and look at some exhibition or other, whilst Jonathan went to look at the new technological wonder of a mechanized brain that could work out calculations a hundred (or was it a thousand?) times faster than a human brain. He had hoped that somewhere in all of those fantastic dreams-about-to-come-true on exhibition in the Dome of Discovery, he would find the answer to his own future.

He watched with scores of other fascinated visitors as a totem-pole of metal cones poured water one from another, catching, brimming, tilting, cascading on to a ledge and waterfalling into a pool, over and over and over again. He wondered if Becc had seen this: she would know if there was any significance to it or whether it was just for pleasure. Certainly the futuristic design would appeal to her. But was it art? Jonathan knew that he was destined to be a plain and ordinary sort of a man who would never know the answer to those clever sort of questions. Becc would know. Vee would know.

His gaze wandered off across the piazza to an enormous, solid sculpture of a man and a woman. He thought that he understood this because the figures were recognizably human. It too was very modern, but although they were heavily booted and wearing working clothes, one could tell that this was a couple with a vision. Their eyes were directed way above the heads of people, across the roads and traffic, over the tops of buildings, their gaze fixed on a distant point. Perhaps they were Becc's workers uniting.

Jonathan followed their line of sight. There is something out there. If only I knew what. He wanted to do something, to be something, to have a purpose as men of his father's generation had. But not another war. God, no, not now there were nuclear bombs. He had been eleven when the doodlebugs had come. All over London, even now, six years later, there were still huge areas of rubble with nothing but flame weed and butterfly bushes. Imagine a whole world like that but without the flame weed and buddleia.

The waterfall stopped. People watching, not knowing whether it was supposed to, looked at one another, then moved off to find something else that was new and did the unexpected. Their places were taken by a new crowd who, having taken the fountain to be a static work of art, were moved to breathe 'Aah!' when it started cascading water again. Jonathan found his ability to make observations like this very pleasing, but was there a market for that kind of skill when it came to making a living? Becc had once introduced him as, 'My big brother who's up at Cambridge reading Daydreaming.'

One reason for his going to university was to see if he could find what career there might be that would define Jonathan Quinlan. Sometimes when he awakened in the morning, he felt that in his dreams he had been about to know what it was he was searching for, but as soon as sleep cleared from his mind, he felt the answer slip away. Had he been at all religious, then he might have gone as a missionary, but he wasn't and, in any case, he did not see that people who threatened one another with nuclear bombs had anything to teach anybody.

If only he could be like Becc. She knew exactly where she was going. People like her were the ones who got there. He was sure that his father must have been like that: bags of ambition. Men like Dad never seemed to have doubts, and Nan would have reinforced his self-assurance – she believed in him totally. Dad had probably been praised from the time he gooed his first goo.

Jonathan had doubts about himself which were reinforced by his father at every opportunity.

'Daydreaming again, Jonathan?'

'Only eighty percent marks, Jonathan?'

'Now buck up, my boy, this is just not up to Quinlan standard.'

Mum would stand up for him, which did nothing for his self-assurance. 'Not everybody's a Ballard Quinlan, and your old school was a very swatty kind of school.'

'I know that you did your best with him, Rose, but things might have been very different had I not been a soldier.'

Poor Mum. Jonathan was sorry that she seemed to get the flak for his own failure. Mum had been great when Dad was in the army. He knew that she had hated living in rented accommodation in Sandhurst. When they had moved into the old house left to Mum by some old relative, it had been great. Jonathan had loved living at Longmore, and had never understood why Dad had wanted to move to the country, and why Mum had given in to him and let tenants rent the old home. His happiest memories were of when he and Becc went to the tiny school in Bosham and Vee was little. That was before 1945; before Dad left the army and went into politics.

The current questions, if not on the lips then on the minds of his family, were, 'What are you going to *do*, Jonathan?' 'What are you going to *be*, Jonathan?' 'Don't you *know*, Jonathan?'

He would have liked to say, 'Tell me what to be.' 'You just tell me and I'll try to be it.'

But not a soldier, not a politician, not any sort of a person who has to give orders or tell anybody what to do. Becc, of course, had been right: in a way he *was* reading Daydreaming.

★ ★ ★

'I thought there were supposed to be tree-walks with animals that lit up,' Anoria said.

'Silly,' said Villette, 'that's not here, that's at the Battersea funfair.'

'Oh.' Anoria, who knew that coming here was special and that she would remember it for the rest of her life, had brought with her a quite different picture of what a festival would be. 'Festivities' were what Nan called Christmas parties, and last year Anoria had seen a carnival and wondered if it might be like that. 'What's this for then?'

Rose, loving her youngest child for being so uncomplaining and stalwart, said, 'It is a kind of celebration, to let people see that the war is really over. And to show what the world will be like when you are grown-up.'

The war was something Anoria had heard about all her life, but she had never grasped it. She did know that, because she was born just when it was all over, she was a post-war baby boom. Great-gran had said that meant that babies were the fashion the year Anoria was born.

'But can we go to the Tree-Walk and the fireworks?'

'Poor love,' Rose said. 'We will go there and see everything, but not today.' She squeezed Anoria's solid little hand. 'We'll wait for Aunt Monica and her lot; it will be more fun doing the fair together.'

Vee pulled her mouth down. 'Oh, drippy Kate.'

'Not drippy Kate,' Anoria said. 'Drippy *James*.'

'That's unfair,' Rose said. 'There's not much wrong with James, and Kate is lovely.'

'But everybody thinks that just because me and Kate . . .'

'Kate and *I* . . .'

'. . . because we are the same age, that we want to be best friends. Well, we don't.'

'You were best friends last week.'

'That was last week.'

'You'll get back as you used to be; all friendships go through rocky patches. Anyhow, we will all be going to Battersea together, and the idea is to have fun.'

'*And* a walk in the tree-tops,' Anoria said.

'We will do everything.'

Anoria, satisfied – now that her mother had said so – that they *would* go to the funfair, trudged on round this place where you really needed to be able to read the notices to know what it was about. But she liked the working models, and eating in cafés and walking along eating ice-cream. She didn't like the coal mine – even though it wasn't working – because it was black and in a tunnel, and seemed so real. But at least now she understood what Jean meant about her da having the coal in his chest. Men would. She hoped she wouldn't dream too much about it. The next time Jean came in to clean the house, Anoria would tell her everything she could remember about the Festival coal mine. She would take home a souvenir for Jean from the funfair.

When Winifred reached the House of Commons, her son was called by a man-at-arms. Today Ballard was dressed as she liked him best, in a dark Savile Row three-piece suit. 'Darling.' Winifred put up her cheek for a kiss, hoping that visitors milling around would appreciate that not all Members of Parliament are brash self-seekers, but there were men who welcomed their war-widowed mothers with a kiss.

He smiled, his eyes crinkling in the way that Jack Buchanan's did. He did that smile so well. People often remarked that Ballard did so remind them of Jack Buchanan. 'Mother, old faithful, you always turn up trumps.' He took her elbow and guided her through doors.

She teased him. 'You know that I only come to get free tea on the terrace. And not so much of the "old".'

Ah, tea on the terrace of the House of Commons. 'Taking tea on the terrace.' The phrase rolled off the tongue like a familiar line of poetry. Winifred Quinlan simply loved the opportunity of using it. 'Oh, darling, a new suit?'

'Like it? A chap I know.' He gave her the old nod and a wink as he fingered his lapel. '"Export Only".'

Winifred looked up from under her lashes. 'Darling! A bit more discretion.'

He laughed. 'Mother dear, of all the places in England, this is one of the few where a fellow can safely admit to acquiring an "Export Only" quality length of worsted. Everybody does it – except for the old Leviathan. I swear he gets his suits at the fifty-bob tailor's.'

'Well, it's your Party, Ballard. They wouldn't be my first choice, as you know.'

Although she had never liked to ask the question, Winifred had often wondered how it was that there were so many obviously high quality suits here, when the best of everything that the country produced was not permitted to be sold in Britain, but was licensed only for export, mostly to America. She had, of course, seen the odd bottle of malt whisky in Ballard's study, but "Export Only" Isla Scotch used discreetly at home was not the same as the blatant wearing of the "Export Only" finest worsted suiting. Winifred preferred not to know. It would only worry her. Knowing the fickleness of the Covington electorate, the trap of her mind always snapped shut on any marauding thought of possible scandal.

'Well, darling, if anyone deserves the best quality, then it is those who appreciate it.'

* * *

Rose Quinlan was happy. She and her children met up again as planned, and around the café table there was a rare mood of sibling generosity and co-operation and willingness to be nice, creating a Rupert Bear atmosphere of clean and honest adventure in a secure but slightly magical land where she need not be her everyday self.

Which was? Middle-class, unqualified and responsible for the welfare of four children, a husband, his mother – who still specialized in her war-widow role even though the more recent war had created a new crop, whilst Korea looked like providing some more – and his sparky grandparents.

'What did you see?' Villette asked the two older ones.

'We saw television.'

'So did we,' said Anoria. 'And stars.'

'The Dome of Discovery, and an electronic brain.'

'And the planets, and a coal mine.'

'And we saw a hypnotist.'

And Anoria, not really understanding what she had seen, said, 'Mum had her photo taken under the . . . thing . . . and the man said she had a perfect . . . something. What was it?'

Vee said, 'It was under the Skylon and he said she had wonderful colouring and a perfect profile. And Mum blushed.'

'I did not,' said Rose with a nice warm feeling.

'It's true,' Rebecca said. 'It's just that you don't do anything with yourself. Most women would give anything for your classy face.'

Rose, unused to being the focus of attention of her four children, looked back at them with amusement as they scrutinized her. 'Anybody would think you had never seen me before.'

Vee said, 'Well, I never even thought about it before . . . But you have got quite a nice profile.'

'What's profile? Why does nobody tell me nothing?' said Anoria, sounding like her father.

'Anything,' Vee said.

Becc said, 'It's just the way people's chins and noses stick out and things like that. You've got one, but it's all soft and babyish.'

'And it's beautiful too,' said Jonathan – who got along with Anoria better than any of them – picking her up for a carry.

'Jonathan is the best one of all,' said Anoria.

'Of all *what*?' said Vee. 'You'll have to explain yourself better than that when you start school.'

'Of Quinlans, silly.'

'Better than Mum?' said Vee. Scoring points off Nora wasn't difficult.

'Of course not,' said Anoria from her lofty position on Jonathan's shoulders. 'Mum doesn't count.'

Out of the mouths, etc., thought Rose wryly. 'Come on, do you want to try one of these hot dog things?'

'Natch!' said Becc.

'The American ones with ketchup and onions?' said Vee. 'Super fantastic!'

'Or hamburgers,' said Rebecca. 'I saw a hamburger stand just like in the films.'

'This is supposed to be the Festival of *Britain*,' said Jonathan.

'OK,' said Rebecca. 'You go and eat your old scones; Vee and I will eat American.'

And so, on the wet, chilly, first great day of the rest of their lives, the youngest members of the Quinlan family were given their first taste of their future with ketchup and onion rings.

Ballard Quinlan took his mother through to the little office and to a PA (not provided by the Party, funds did not run to that, but a voluntary worker with ideals and time on her hands), whom he shared with two other Members. 'Mother, you've met Miriam? Miriam, you know my mother, Winifred, don't you?'

Miriam Corder-Peake (of top-drawer society and red-book, monied family, a species not too thick on the ground in the Labour Party) skipped up from her typewriter eagerly and took Winifred's bag and scarf. Since she had discovered that the Party needed her, and that she could be useful, her three MPs had become her raison d'être. It was not often she was privileged to be here; usually she did her stint for a better Britain in a room at Transport House, the power-house of leftish politics.

Miriam Corder-Peake spoke breathlessly and with scattered emphases. 'Mrs Quinlan, of *course*, how nice to *see* you again.'

'My son tells me that you have become a Londoner.'

'A place of Daddy's *really*.' Covering her lips with two fingers as though she had been indiscreet. 'A teeny flat not *far* from the House, well Petyt Place . . . not *very* far.'

Winifred felt slightly irritated, as she always did when she came face to face with people who had money, played bridge, spoke familiarly of schooldays at Eton and student days at Oxbridge, yet professed to be *Socialists*! How could one have a Belgravia address or a Petyt Place flat and work for this collection of caps, tweed jackets and northern accents? Yet there were those who did.

'Oh, off Chelsea Walk, of course, I know it.' And Winifred did. To a railing she knew which parts *were* and which parts were not. Petyt Place *was*.

'Tea, Mrs Quinlan? Something stronger? A gin? I said to Ballard

– Mr Quinlan – only recently, that it has been simply *ages* – and now here you *are*.'

Winifred noted that 'Ballard'. Top drawer or not, the House was not the place for familiarity, but Winifred knew that social mores were greatly changed by wars, and so long as there was no disrespect . . . And young Debs had to be made allowances for. Oh, if *only* this had all been going on within her own True Blue natural party of government, which she could no longer openly recognize since Ballard . . . well, be honest, *defected*. She had heard it said that towards the end of the war there had been some kind of Russian plot to send young men home dissatisfied with their lot and their heads stuffed with revolution. It was probably all true.

'I should quite like a small gin, plenty of tonic.'

Ballard grinned happily at his mother and at Miriam. 'You're an old soak, Mother. I know, I know – not so much of the old. Ha, ha.' He took one clear and one green glass bottle from a locked filing cabinet and poured a Johnny Walker and two Gilbys. Miriam split a bottle of Schweppes tonic water between the gins.

'No lemons, I'm afraid. Even *Fortnum's* had none. I don't *believe* them, of course.'

'You should have mentioned my son's name,' Winifred said, smiling archly. 'That would have produced one or two, I'll be bound.'

Back in Hampshire, where the Quinlans lived scattered around in the beautiful Meon Valley area, Charlotte and Sidney Quinlan (Nan and Papa) argued amiably over today's runners. They themselves had a clear field – no Winnie to outwit; no Ballard pretending that his visit was a pleasure and not a duty; no Rose calling in to see what she could get from the shops to save their legs. Neither of them wished to have their legs saved.

'Here,' Charlotte handed him a much-folded note. 'Tippy Tree. Ten bob on the nose.'

'You'll lose it, Lotte. Tippy Tree hasn't done anything all season.'

'The going's soft. You spend your money, and I'll spend mine.'

'I'm going half a dollar each way on Duck Drummond, and you'll be sorry you didn't listen to me.'

With the two folded notes for the bookie's runner and another ten-shilling note for a beer and a couple of Guinnesses to bring away, Sid Quinlan, retired draper and haberdasher, within sight of being a hundred years old, made his surprisingly sprightly way to the Three Tons. Charlotte took bread to ducks who roamed freely around their garden.

* * *

Winifred raised her glass. 'To your speech at Covington.'

Miriam raised her glass too. 'Amen to that. And it is a *fine* speech, Mrs Quinlan.'

Winifred felt a minute pang of hurt. At the '45 election it had been Winifred who had typed up his speeches. She was no trained typist, yet she had managed to type his election speech over and over again, each with separate and highlighted alterations to suit the particular town or audience he was addressing. But there it is, as Winifred often said, one must not try to live one's life through one's children; one must never be tempted to hang on. Let them go. Generously she said to Miriam Corder-Peake, 'Don't tell me, then I may listen to his rehearsal with a completely open mind.'

Ballard Quinlan laughed and Jack Buchanan's eyes crinkled at his dainty, upper-crust assistant. 'What can a man do with a mother who is not only automatically on his side, but also listens to his speeches with an open mind?'

Miriam Corder-Peake, whose home was in Ballard's constituency, joined in her Member's gentle ribbing of his mother. 'Poor Ballard, if Mrs Quinlan's mind is so *open*, then you may *yet* lose her to the Member for Ebbw Vale.'

Winifred Quinlan's shudder was not entirely jocular. Aneurin Bevan, Member for Ebbw Vale, was, to Winifred Quinlan and many of her kind, the *bête noire*, the bugaboo, the highwayman who would order her class to stand and deliver. 'Don't mention that man.'

'What about the *wife*, then?' Miriam Corder-Peake knew Mrs Quinlan's love of a good controlled tirade against the worst excesses of Labour.

'Well, of course, she is worse. She is not only a woman socialist, but an educated one at that. And look how shameless she is in always hogging the headlines. What a *pair*!'

'Oh, she is no *fool* when it comes to self-publicity,' Miriam said.

Winifred offered her usual solution to the revolutionary reds. 'If I had my way, those people with such communistic views should be put on an island and told to build their socialist state there. *Then* we should see where their equal shares for all would get them.' It was *very* difficult for Winifred to realize that, in theory at least, Ballard too would needs be joining them on their island, for although he was not a convinced socialist, he went with them through the voting lobbies.

Ballard laughed. 'Our Nye and Jenny would soon elect themselves king and queen.'

Winifred smiled, and surrendered her glass.

A friendly tirade and plentiful gin had brought such a pretty glow to Winifred Quinlan's cheeks that when Miriam Corder-Peake led the way to the terrace, Winifred felt ten years younger and prettier than when she had passed over Waterloo Bridge earlier.

Although she often chided Ballard for having chosen a wife who needed to be dragooned into doing constituency work, in truth Winifred Quinlan was grateful that it was she herself who was so often seen walking these Corridors of Power in this Mother of Parliaments.

If London's South Bank was the place where war-dulled Britain was reminded that it had enterprise, initiative and inventiveness, then the Pleasure Gardens reminded it that it was OK to have fun. And it was at this frivolous part of the Festival of Britain that Rose and Monica Wilkinson planned to give their total of eight children a holiday they would remember.

There was no way that Ballard's pied-à-terre could have accommodated ten, so Leo Wilkinson had arranged the accommodation in a friend's flat. So, following their visit to the South Bank, the Quinlans decamped and joined the Wilkinsons – Monica and her four children – at Chiswick.

For more than ten years, Rose Quinlan and Monica Wilkinson had lived as neighbours in the small Hampshire village of Honeywood in the beautiful Meon Valley.

Rose and Monica's houses (or rather their husband's houses), were the only two in Shaft's Lane. Neither Rose nor Monica did any paid work.

The Quinlans lived at Shaft's, a big fourteenth-century farmhouse, beamed and crooked and no longer belonging to a farm. Shaft's sat low in the valley, at one time the fast little stream had run through the farm, but now it was separated from the house by the narrow, winding road that ran between the A27 and East Meon.

At one time the house had been the hall where master, mistress, hands, servants and beasts had shared warmth and shelter. But over the centuries it had known many variations on this shelter theme, so that floors and walls and windows and doors and outbuildings and barns had been added to allow for the need to compartmentalize and classify as the social order changed. When Quinlan money settled its hash (probably for all time) by restoring and refurbishing it, Shaft's became what an estate agent would recognize as a fourteenth-century farmhouse – and a fourteenth-century farmer would recognize as the most important house in the valley.

The Wilkinsons lived in Ludd House, a pretty Regency-style building that was thoroughly out of place in a Hampshire village. It was barely a hundred years old, and had been built by a novelist who, whilst living in a cramped London house, had made his pile by writing about farm hands and shepherds' lives. When eventually he came to live the rural life in Honeywood, amongst the people he thought he knew so well, he couldn't stand their curmudgeonly rejection; or the cow-pats outside his front door; or the pitiful exchanges between cows separated from their calves, who were being prepared for the veal market. So he returned to London and wrote no more of hedgerows and fieldfares.

Rose and Monica were close friends whose children were pretty much of parallel ages.

The men, Ballard and Leo, hated one another's guts in a neighbourly way.

They were both ex-Forces, and had both returned from the Second World War avowed socialists. Ballard's allegiance to the Labour Party was stamped on to his skin, and was always in danger of being washed off in a downpour. Leo's convictions ran through him like letters through seaside rock. By the early fifties, Leo Wilkinson's small engineering and steel erection company (WESCO) was beginning, after six years of hard grind and getting his own hands dirty, to become profitable. Ballard was a professional politician; he had not been able to keep his hands entirely clean either. Ballard had other irons in the fire.

In marriage Monica was brave and bold. When she saw Leo (already married to Shirley) for the first time, he was dressed in tennis shorts, having just come off the court where he, as he usually did, had won his match. Ages before they made their relationship legal, Leo and Monica discovered that they were mutually able and healthy, roll-in-the-hay types.

In marriage, Rose was submissive. Which is not surprising as, until she met her husband, Rose's experience of men came from the wide variety of novels she read avidly, and from Hollywood films, wherein even the most brooding, dark and passionate of men (who were soothed in their torment and softened by the love of a gentle woman), kept one foot on the ground in bedrooms, and wherein married couples slept in twin beds with space (and often a locker and a teetering lamp) between them. The most dangerous these screen heroes got was to loosen their neckties and allow a single lock of hair to fall on to their brow. Their most devilish action went only as far as to grasp their lover tightly, breathe heavily, and look handsomely dissolute as they forced a hard, three-second, closed-lip kiss upon her. When Rose Weston saw Ballard Quinlan for the first time, he (dark and brooding and masterful) might have stepped from the silver screen. Had she, at seventeen, known that Clark Gable, whilst masquerading as Rhett Butler, would take out his dentures to wash them, she might have wondered for a moment whether her own dark and brooding suitor Ballard was flawed. Probably not.

Over ten years as neighbours, Rose and Monica and their eight children had spent some of their happiest times on jaunts together. But nothing had ever come up to the days they were to spend at Battersea Park, the great funfair which was part of the Festival of Britain.

Jonathan being, at eighteen, a couple of years or so older than Rebecca (and than Tom and Helen, the two eldest Wilkinsons), was able to take a lofty enough attitude to really enjoy the most ridiculous entertainment. The three sixteen-year-olds were less able to live with the spectacle of seeing their mothers making fools of themselves by giggling before distorting mirrors or eating cotton-candy against the breeze.

Kate Wilkinson and Villette tried to keep their distance from all of them. In showing solidarity for one another they became best friends again.

The youngest, Anoria and James, had no complaints. They had coins for their pockets and had been given all the badges, trinkets and souvenirs that the others didn't want. Anoria's only complaint was her usual one, that James was allowed to pee into the bushes whenever he felt like it and did not have to think about going in plenty of time to queue for a smelly toilet. When they gathered for lunch, they took up three tables, Vee and Kate insisting on eating separately.

Monica flung down her various bags and trophies and flopped into a chair. 'Phew, Rose, I haven't enjoyed myself so much since the Yanks hit town in 1944.'

'Did they have a funfair, Aunt Mon?' Anoria asked.

Monica grinned at Rose, 'Not your actual fair, Nora, but we did have a ball.'

Nora liked Aunt Mon. A lot. She liked the way she would grab hold of you and give a hug, or flip your bottom in a friendly way as you passed and say, 'God, what a smashing bum', the same as Uncle Leo said to Aunt Mon. Aunt Mon could say rude things and nobody seemed to take any notice. She was also cuddly, which Nora liked. But not always. Sometimes she went down like an old balloon and would look quite crotchety. Helen said it was because she was trying to get thin. Those times she would turn her head away from something really luscious and say, 'Don't tempt me! A moment on the lips, a lifetime on the hips.' She had nice hips; they went up and down in her swimming costume. Nora wished that children could do patting and say, 'God, what a smashing bum.' In the end, Aunt Mon always said, 'Oh, what the Hell!' and had a big slice of birthday cake or something like that, saying that she had 'given up dieting for Lent.' Nora loved it when Aunt Mon gave up trying to get thin. She wasn't a thin kind of person. Mum was. Aunt Mon was always saying that it wasn't fair that Mum could eat devil's food three times a day and angels on horseback for snacks and keep as thin as a rake. Nora, who Nan said was 'pudgy', suspected that she would grow up more like Aunt Mon than Mum, and made up her mind that if she did she would just enjoy chocolate cake and potato crisps and eat them whenever she liked. She would also eat condensed milk straight from the tin. Mum did that when she was making her own special sort of tea, and if she was caught would give Nora a spoonful and say, 'Not a word to the enemy.' Mum never went up or down, which wasn't as interesting as Aunt Mon. Vee was like Mum.

A waitress came and took a disdainful order from the ten people spread annoyingly over three tables.

Whilst they were all preoccupied with plates of soup, Monica said, 'We could do it again, whilst we are being grass widows. We could have a bit of a ball . . . well, a dance. It's ages since I've been to the Hammersmith Palais. Is it still open?'

Rose laughed. 'With all this lot?'

'Of course not. The top four are old enough to keep control, and they all take notice of Jonathan – he's terribly good with them, isn't he? I can't see Tom ever being like that. What do you say? We deserve a night out. They've had days of our attention. (Oh God, look! Apple pie and cream. What the hell, this is an occasion. I'll start again when we get home.)'

Rose's eyes flicked over the eight children. It seemed a dangerous thing to do to leave them to fend for themselves, to say nothing of what Ballard would have to say. She had never left the young ones unless her cleaning help or Winifred was in the house.

'She who hesitates is lost,' said Monica. 'If it's not the Palais, then somewhere. Just a night out in our glad-rags. Have you got any with you?'

'Only that sun-top with the bolero.'

'You can go without the bolero. That's settled.' She got up and went over to the table where the four eldest were eating and trying to outdo one another with ecstatic descriptions of Bill Haley's new record – or 'disc', as they called it. Money changed hands. She came back fastening her wallet. 'I don't know who told me that there isn't any palm that cannot be greased, but it was good advice. A fiver for Jonathan, three quid for each of the others.' And, giving the wink that is as good as a nod, added, 'I said that we would like a night out at the theatre.'

'But you don't intend going to the theatre. We couldn't . . .'

'Don't start fussing. If you like we'll just tell Jonathan.'

Rose said, 'Nearly twenty pounds!'

'If you are going to bribe, give the most you can afford – it binds them to you. I had to include permission for the six to see *The Seven Year Itch* without a parental presence. I suspect they wouldn't enjoy getting a glimpse of Marilyn Monroe's crotch with their mothers there . . . I did a deal. I said they must go to a matinée, but they insisted on an evening performance. Your Becc's good: drives a hard bargain.'

'That sounds like Becc,' Rose said. 'So the price of a night at the Palais is twenty pounds plus cinema tickets.'

'And a 3-D film for the young ones – but we are allowed to go with them to see that.'

'We could have hired a royal nanny for that kind of money.'

'We should still have had to have paid hush money to the kids.'

Rose felt at a distinct disadvantage. Leo never made a murmur whatever Monica decided to do. Ballard was quite different, and Rose would rather go without than live with the suggestion that she was doing something he would rather she did not. She knew she should stand up for herself, but she had never learned how to explain herself without feeling guilty and appearing so too.

Anoria and James followed the whole thing with expressions that made grown-ups believe that they were intent on picking cherries out of their pudding and that the grown-up conversation was above their heads – which, of course, it was not. It is the means by which little children gather the material that keeps parents in check. Almost as soon as they returned home, James said, 'Daddy, we were good when Mummy went to the ball so she took us to the pictures and we all had to wear glasses that made arrows come right out of the picture and there was a lion too.'

Leo Wilkinson, looking over his newly acquired glasses at his wife, raised his eyebrows questioningly.

'Rose and I went out but that's not good news in the other camp. And you, James Wilkinson, owe me a quids' worth of chores.'

When, at midnight, the two friends had one last drink at the Palais bar before going out into London's spectacularly active night-life to find a taxi, Monica said, 'Well, wasn't I right?'

Rose nodded. 'As usual, you were right. I loved it.'

She had. In such a large gathering of dancers there were plenty of men who had come solo. Rose quite enjoyed their smoky, panting breath and warm, damp hands on her bare back. In such a crowd she had felt anonymous, almost to the point of invisibility, so that she found herself saying to a younger man with whom she was dancing, 'Look, I've never done this kind of dancing, but I'd love to learn.' At once he sent her spinning away from him, then clutched her fingertips and brought her back until, hips touching, they dipped their elbows towards the floor in time to the fast beat of the loud music. 'I can do it, I can do it,' Rose said, and he had nodded, pleased with himself. She only learned about three movements, but it was as much as most other dancers seemed to be using and, after watching from the balcony, she tried some variations. 'Well, well,' Monica had said, 'if you aren't the dark horse, Rose Quinlan.'

Rose had blushed, as she often did. 'It's such good fun.'

'So it was worth twenty quid from the housekeeping?'

'Infinitely worth it. Just as long as you don't think you've finished paying. Becc has probably got them hatching further pleasures to squeeze money from us. But it was super. I understand why the kids are all so excited about rock-and-roll music. I never realized . . .'

'We should do it back home – an evening on the town . . . Southampton pier,' Monica said.

Taxis went by with their 'For Hire' lights off, so they walked arm in arm away from Hammersmith in the direction of the Chiswick flat.

'Do you mean go dancing on our own?' Rose said. 'Without –'

'Without the balls and chains? Of course. Rock-and-roll with your husband? Not on your Nellie.'

Rose laughed in a low-down way that only Monica was ever privileged to hear. Monica could picture her lips lifting at the corners showing the tips of her top teeth. It was the equivalent of her own great whooping responses. 'You're terrible, Mon. Wives and mothers, and you are trying to get me to go rock-and-rolling at our age. Jonathan and his girlfriend go to the pier anyway.'

'Well, maybe not the pier. Anyway, I think they only have wrestling there now . . . I say, do you fancy wrestling?'

'Hasn't it got through to you, after all these years, that I am the wife of a conservative Labour MP?'

'Rose, my sweet love, why don't you tell the bugger that he's not your keeper.'

Rose fell silent.

Monica guessed that she had overstepped the mark. Rose and Ballard had a very different kind of relationship from their own, it was not a bit of use trying to force Rose into situations that scared her off. Hating the awkward silence, she said, 'Didn't the kids just love Battersea? I do like to see them enjoying themselves. It takes me back to when I was young and my mother and father took the family to Wickham Fair. Isn't it always the gaudy and trivial things we remember from childhood?' If Monica had hoped to draw Rose into talking about her own childhood, she was unlucky. She knew hardly anything about Rose's life until she had appeared in the big house next door twelve years ago.

Rose had no memories of outings to gaudy fairs, except those filmed sequences of a scene at Coney Island, or a frontier town set with a genial rogue selling patent medicine. No family except for her elderly, slightly batty aunt and her aunt's companion.

Ballard had come into her life at a social event in Chichester – Rose's first. Having recently become seventeen, she had been bowled over by the darkly handsome young man, as masterful as Mr Rochester and as heady and awesome as Heathcliffe. When Rose first saw Ballard she said nothing, but she did long for him to notice her.

He did notice her – how could he fail to with that face? – and they were married.

The thing about Rose – quite apart from her strange upbringing and her belief that a masterful man may be transformed and made a caring partner for life (from the number of times she had read *Wuthering Heights* she ought to have known better) – the great and astonishing thing was that she had no idea that she was a 'stunning' beauty. In this case the adjective is not used carelessly; on meeting her for the first time it took most people a pause of seconds to think of anything but her appearance. 'Icy', 'perfect', 'cool', 'serenely beautiful' sprang to mind. Because she was unable to think of her face as anything other than another bit of her body that needed the attention of soap and water, she was not vain.

Coolly, serenely beautiful, Rose Quinlan's face was a slim oval in which were widely set large, bronzy eyes almost always partly hidden beneath slightly lowered lids; fine cheekbones; a narrow nose with neatly placed nostrils; a wide mouth with thin bowed lips which flicked-up and had little commas that suggested a smile; and a pointed chin. The face had a fine, creamy complexion and a drape of pearl-coloured hair which fell thick and straight, partly hiding her right cheek. Ah, but it is ludicrous to try to describe the phenomenon of beauty, for one finishes up rummaging around in the cliché drawer, and comes out with the setting of the eyes and placement of the nostrils, and when that fails one resorts to the bag of adjectives.

You must take it that Rose Quinlan had rare looks.

And because we all tend to have our prejudices triggered by stereotypes, people automatically assumed that she was cool, superior, distant, self-controlled, solemn, and even wise.

And that she was good. None of this was difficult to believe.

Not a woman to swear, smoke, romp, cry or growl with sexual gratification.

Surprisingly, Monica took Rose's hand and held it between both of hers. 'I'm always so thankful that it was you who came to live in the old farmhouse.'

1955

Rose Quinlan opened her eyes as soon as she awakened, but the dream did not go away. She had never before dreamed in colour. She had been back on that holiday in 1951 spent with the children at the South Bank and Battersea Festival Gardens.

In her dream, as in an out-of-body experience, she had seen herself, standing in the crowd waiting for the hand of the 'Guinness Clock' to point to three, six, nine or twelve. This extraordinary clock drew a crowd of people who waited for the moment when the big hand reached the quarter and triggered into life the whole amazing spectacle of moving figures. In Rose's dream, she saw Rose Quinlan from the point of view of the moving figures looking down upon a Rose Quinlan looking up. The Rose in the crowd watched as the animated Rose was triggered into life, a thin, sharp-featured woman with pale hair parted on the side, smiling up as well as smiling down. That vision had suddenly dissolved into the vertiginous Tree-Walk where she had been with Anoria. Then the colour had vanished from her dream as she – with her rain-cape undone and her flowery dress showing – stood directly beneath the Skylon looking up at the great lace-bobbin and looking down at the Rose who was having her picture taken. She had even seen the face of the photographer who had made her blush.

'You have the most beautiful profile I've ever had in my lens,' he had said.

In the dream she had responded without blush and panic, but with sophistication. 'It's just the one I was born with.'

Suddenly she could remember the incident as it had been. What he had actually said was, 'With such wonderful bones you should always wear your hair up and away from your face; you should show the line of your neck.' He had taken her silk scarf and looped her hair back before he had photographed her.

It had been an erotic dream that had left her moist and at ease, a dream that she would have liked to have continued. The man's hands had touched her intimately as he tied the scarf. The sensation had been joyful and wholly pleasurable. Just at the point of awakening, everything had dissolved into the Skylon which stood steadily erect on air without even its guy-ropes. She had forgotten his face, but he had taken the picture when she had been thinking, 'I wish we didn't ever have to go home.' Like a child at a funfair.

Stripping off her flowered cotton nightdress, Rose went to the window and pushed it open a few inches to let in the May early morning air and the thrilling, trilling bars of the dawn chorus. Quietly she gathered up her gardening clobber. Ballard didn't stir: he had had a week canvassing in Covington. Quite unlike the typically English middle-class male he claimed to be, Ballard, who had actually come from a long line of shopkeepers, liked windows closed at night, calling her a fresh-air freak. He was probably right – he usually was about such things – but when he snapped the window shut on balmy nights she felt a pang at being cut off from her garden, whose scents and perfumes now entered on a dawn breeze that puckered her dark nipples and goose-bumped her pale skin. Quietly she closed the window so as to keep the spring morning away from Ballard.

This was the blossom month, and this, when the sun was rising, the best bit of the day. She savoured it and hoped that she would not have to share it with anyone. This was also the month when Taureans celebrated their birthdays. Rose Quinlan was Taurean, and today, Friday 6 May, was her birthday.

In the bathroom she sluiced her face and neck (using the cold tap so that the hot pipes would not knock and awaken anyone), pulled on corduroy slacks over cotton pants, and one of Ballard's old jumpers over flannelette shirt.

The jumper, a ten-year-old felted and shrunken khaki number, was a relic from his wartime army days. The shirt, too, dated from the war years, a time when British women were told to be proud of their make-do-and-mend efforts. This same shirt (together with a couple of little blouses in which Jonathan started junior school, and several pilch-pants for Rebecca, to say nothing of any number of decent dusters), Rose had made from the good parts of an old and worn green flannelette sheet. The dusters, little shirts and pilches were long gone, as was the original green colour. Even so, Rose liked her gardening shirt, and although the war was ten years behind them, English women who had brought up a family on unpicking and patching, shortages and rations, would never get used to throwing anything away. Rose still smoothed out and saved paper bags, margarine papers and brown wrapping; she unknotted string and kept it wound in handy balls; she reused unravelled knitting yarn, trimmings and buttons. As Ballard said, British industry wouldn't get fat if it were left to the Roses of the world.

* * *

Disturbed from sleep by Rose rustling around the bedroom, Ballard looked at his wristwatch. God almighty! The last thing he needed was to be awakened at the crack of dawn. He needed rest: the next three weeks were going to be murder. Yet, even as he thought of it, the prospect of the election aroused him. Anticipation in his loins and entrails. His brain began to tick over. This one would be a fight.

There was a lot of goodwill for Churchill – now that he had at last resigned. A tax-cutting budget. Eden hadn't had time to make any mistakes. He rolled on to his back and unwillingly opened his eyes. This time, whatever else went on in the country, Ballard must increase his personal majority. The old fear of failure rose to the surface. This could prove to be a dirty, mud-slinging campaign. Ballard Quinlan could pass muster as long as nobody dug too deeply. His business interests were all out in the open. He had never pretended to be one of the flat-cap faction, nor had he allied himself to the intellectuals.

A socialist by conviction. 'To secure for the workers, by hand or by brain, the full fruits of their industry.' And he could remember three verses of 'The Red Flag', which was more than most could. Not born to it, but convinced of it. That was his public line. 'In those last euphoric months of army life, I, like thousands of others, became convinced that the natural political condition for a civilized nation was socialism.'

He was, too, a political pragmatist. A line he didn't publicize, but which suited his constituents very well. All along the coastal part of Covington spread great flat reed-beds, their nine-foot fronds thriving where all else perished. If one ever found it necessary to bend with the wind, Covington was the place in which to bend.

Five past five! Why in hell's name couldn't Rose stay in bed like any normal woman, instead of going off out growing stuff she could very well afford to buy.

The question was rhetorical. He knew why it was. She couldn't cope with his virility. Bitterly. He'd had his allocation. As usual he felt anger and desire rise simultaneously. Even in the dark, he never failed to see her dead-pan expression as he spent himself within her, to the accompaniment of the biblical phrase that always came into his mind: 'spilled his seed on to the ground' – and about as satisfying. That was how he thought of it, not making love. The act was a kind of allowance by her of conjugal rights. Safely and without pleasure – without even a woman present was how he often felt . . . always that bloody barrier of rubber. The French letter wouldn't have mattered had she shown a bit of enthusiasm . . .

Mr Speaker, sir. Will the Honourable Gentleman explain the

nature of Conjugal Rights? Do the rights of the husband allow access to his lawful wife? (Laughter in the House.)

For Christ's sake, after all this time . . . If only she saw it as any normal woman would, she would have taken it as a compliment . . . What normal woman doesn't want to drive men over the top with desire? These days she behaved as though she didn't like it, but he could remember a time . . . Perhaps if they hadn't had Jonathan so quickly after they married . . . She had liked it enough at one time. There were times when he caught a glimpse of her looking up from beneath that lock of hair, and remembered.

She had looked like a sexy angel.

It was always at times of early-morning sleeplessness that he returned time and again to the two highlights of their most furious passion. He had never expected that such a calm woman could become so demented. She had said some terrible things that night. Her face had had a terrible, vicious look as she had tried to pull her torn dress round her. He had never realized how easily she bruised. Of all the women he had had during the war, he had never ravished one.

She hadn't cried. He could have understood that, expected it even. Men did make women cry, and then they made it better for them. He had tried hard to make amends with that beautiful watch, Swiss, the kind that was almost impossible to get hold of at the time. She had never taken it from the box, not even when she had got over it.

Miriam cried. She sometimes made errors with his work, and in his frustration he occasionally shouted and threw things across the room. And Miriam cried. Then, when he had dried her eyes and taken her to lunch, she was twice as sweet.

'Men are such beasts you know, Ballard.'

'But you always forgive us.'

Miriam was good with men. But not Rose.

In '45, she had all but withdrawn, but had put on a face for the election, had worn a Party rosette and sat on platforms by his side. Once the Swiss watch had failed, he had no idea what to do or say. Obviously the memory had faded with the bruises, for when Anoria was born Rose doted on her. He did not doubt that he understood women, but there was something different about Rose. For all her apparently fragile appearance, and what seemed like timidity, he felt vaguely intimidated. Once he had called her a prick-tease. Not only had she not understood what he meant, she was clearly quite unaware that that was what she was.

He drifted back into a half-sleeping state and, as happened so often, he went over the old ground of that night of the regimental Victory dinner. God, how beautiful she had been at thirty. And she still was, underneath that scarf and all the awful clobber she always put on in the mornings – he sometimes wondered whether she dressed like that when he was away. She could do nothing about her face, though; her face was as beautiful as when she had been a girl of seventeen and he had first seen her. Perhaps more beautiful now that she was a woman.

He gave up the idea of sleep and lit a cigarette, sinking back into the pillows and letting his mind drift on, knowing that, even after ten years, it could still tear him apart. But it did him good; he had come to appreciate that. Going back over it was like sifting again and again through a junk cupboard, each time finding it possible to get rid of something. It wasn't only sorting through this disaster of a marriage they had, but other areas of his life too came under the scrutiny of these early-morning confrontations. He had recently discovered that he could throw away his chagrin at having shop-keeping ancestors. Retailing was honourable, in a party full of shop-stewards and miners' sons. Earlier he had thrown away his resentment at a father who had never been able to be at the school sports' day because he had been killed when the '14–'18 war was practically over. If only he could sort out in his mind just what sort of a marriage theirs was, but that particular junk-hole needed drastic attention. He knew it; she knew it. Some dreadful, fearful, suppurating stuff that he never looked at if he could help it had to be dealt with before they could ever pick out the bits that must be saved, prime of which were the children and their entangled finances.

Rose had been not much more than a schoolgirl bride, and when Jonathan was born she became a schoolgirl mother, but the war had made a woman of her. The summer of '45. The first regimental dinner – with trophies, silver and all the trimmings – since 1939. She had been wearing a ladylike style of dress that didn't hide a bloody thing. He would remember that bloody dress till the day he died. White; a high-necked, slinky silk affair that buttoned down the front with dozens of tiny covered buttons, and was gathered softly at all the places a man wanted to touch. His fellow officers skinned their eyeballs to see what she had, and fell over one another for a dance. None of them had a woman to hold a candle to her. He had watched as they had behaved like wolves in red jackets, not really bothering to disguise their desire and slavering mouths.

What had she supposed she was doing? What did she expect would happen if she exhibited those bloody breasts in cradles of gathered silk? Didn't she know what a dress like that did to a man? High neck, fitting where it touched, looking as though she was wearing nothing beneath it, feeling like it, too; the silk had slithered beneath his hands, feeling like lubricated gossamer rubber. The first time in full evening dress since before the war. Later he discovered that she had been wearing something under it, but only cami-knickers. Christ, what were those things for if not for easy access? And no stockings. All right, women had got used to bare legs, and stockings were difficult to come by. But respectable women covered their legs, only tarts and whores did not. For God's sake, she had practically offered herself.

In the early part of the evening he had enjoyed pride of possession. He had felt good, watching her dance with his friends, sardonically watching their hands as they tried discreetly to manoeuvre a better hold. But Rose always smiled and moved to a 'Don't Touch' position. It was only later, when the whisky turned sour on the wine, that his mind kept returning to red hands feeling around the white silk, knowing that she would provide some of them with better ideas than they ever got from paper pin-ups. No man could blame another for trying, but the thought of what she might have been getting out of it flared up inside him.

She was so bloody naïve. She had expected moonlight and roses, whilst he had wanted – more than that, had needed – the frequent and unadorned gratification that was the due of a man recently returned from a bloody war. What the hell did you do with a woman like that? She flirted without realizing that she was flirtatious, seduced without knowing that she was seductive. What you did, if you could, was to stop hankering after her and go looking for a woman who liked it.

He lit another cigarette. It was all still unhealed, but he could not help reopening the wound, probing the memory which could give him a kind of angry satisfaction.

After the dinner, he had stopped the car on the road out of Winchester. She had been fine until he tried to go further than kissing. She had pulled his hand away. He had said, 'I'll be careful.' He knew that these days he could control himself much better than when he'd made her pregnant with Villette. 'No!' she had said, 'I won't take any chances. I don't want any more babies.'

'I promise . . . I can be careful, darling.'

She had sounded both brave and afraid. 'You said that once before. Anyway, it isn't a good time of the month.' That had been a tale, unless she had meant that it was one of those days when she was at her peak and most likely to conceive.

As much as anything, it had been her trying to put him off gently and the anxiety in her tone that had riled him up. She had no business being afraid of him. He had wanted her there and then. He had been through six years of war. He had got used to women responding. Women did. When you were a soldier it was a case of anywhere and everywhere, get what you can now, you'll be a long time dead. 'Well, sweetheart, if it's not a good time for you, it's the best bloody time for me!' And if fifty buttons were not intended as an invitation to open up, then she should have worn a blouse and a long skirt like most of the other regimental wives. He had never seen the dress again, not even cut up and made into something else as she did with everything.

That had been ten years ago, yet he had only to think of it now for arousal to surge through him. The puck-puck-puck sound, probably twenty or thirty times as the little buttons gave way. The panting moments as he mastered her struggles and pinned her down with his weight. She was surprisingly strong, but he was stronger; she was fit and wiry, but he was much heavier. He had heard his own groan almost at the moment he penetrated her. She had not made it easy for him, but in the very strength of her tightened muscles he found stimulation. It had almost been like having a virgin.

And Anoria had been the result. Anoria, the good child. He had never understood why it was that Rose still held on to the idea that he had forced her into something she didn't want. She appeared to love Anoria more than the others. Couldn't she reason that, if he had not used his strength to give her Anoria, she would have missed something great?

It wasn't often that he went this far in letting everything up from the depths of his mind, but whenever he did, he longed to experience that same ecstatic, powerful moment again. The only thing that ever came close was raising his arms in triumph after being declared Member of Parliament for Covington – except that it lacked the explosive physical climax which was what sex was all about. If it wasn't for that, who would want it?

In Rose Quinlan's life there were no bounding dogs to greet her mornings, no cats to sidle up, cupboard-loving, for milk. She feared dogs and loathed cats. In strategic places about the garden she kept jars of water handy for any hole-scraper or sprayer who hadn't learned the lesson that the Quinlan garden wasn't the best place to come for that purpose. Still they came, sneaking in during the night, the bane of Rose's horticultural life.

A pair of brand-new Wellington boots stood in the back lobby, suedy-black still, their fresh, rubbery interiors still felty and white, their ribbed bumpers unclogged. Real *Vulcan* boots, none of your surplus-stores stuff, these. That showed how things were beginning to look up.

Rose Quinlan knew that she was rather a crazy woman to want a new pair of scarce boots in her own size rather than a box of scarce nylons. For years and years, both during the war and after, anything made from rubber (except for 'protection' for men going to war zones in hot countries where there were unclean women) had been difficult to obtain – unless you were in the know or could do a deal with the nodders and winkers. But Rose was the kind of woman who never was or could be, for no other reason than she would have been too embarrassed to try in case she should be rebuffed. She took her share and awaited her turn, so that when it came to getting something like new Wellingtons, which were not guaranteed by rations, coupons or allocation, it had been a case of doing without or managing, as she had done till now, in second-hands.

But, for her birthday today, her children had bought her a pair, adding new green land-army socks from a government surplus store. Her gardening feet had not felt so wonderfully pampered for years. She did a little tap-dance, ending it with a professional wide smile and dancer's finale lunge.

The tin kettle boiled and rattled. Tea with condensed milk – a taste she had acquired during wartime. More seductive than sugar. Bad for your teeth according to Ballard, bad for your complexion according to Becc, bad for your insides according to Winifred. As it was her birthday – and she was Taurean, anyhow, wasn't she? – she put one bulging dessert-spoon of Fussell's Unfit-for-Babies sweetened milk into weak tea, then scooped up another which she took into her mouth, its sticky tail dripping down her chin and on to the felty jumper. Oh, the ecstasy of that unique sweetness. She cleaned the spoon with her tongue then, having considered greed for a brief moment, took another and drizzled it on to bread. Funny thing was, Ballard had troublesome teeth, Rebecca was often plagued with acne, and Winifred was a martyr to acidity. Rose's only ailment was a dry scalp which she put down to washing her hair with bath soap. Her teeth were certainly unblemished. Shampoos were back in the shops, but old economies died hard. Perhaps Becc was right; she should take more care of herself – if only to please Becc. She took her breakfast into the fresh air of a beautiful May morning, which prompted the song she hummed to herself as she made her way to her secure place.

As I rode out on a May morn-ing
A May morning right ear-rly,
I overtook a handsome maid . . .

She paused to drop in a few crumbs for the koi carp which had once been Jonathan's obsession, now forgotten by him, and left to grow large and sleek and beautifully patterned without his schoolboy attentions.

I am seventeen come Sunday . . .
With my rue-dum-day . . .

The herbs were showing plenty of new growth. She pinched in turn rosemary, sage and mint, and bit on a sprig of ground-cress, hot to the tongue.

I dare not, for my Mammy,
With my rue-dum-day . . .

The bit of the garden at Shaft's which composed Rose's private world was a slab-stoned area enclosed on three sides by weathered brick and stone walls, spindly birches, bamboos, and rambling roses supporting evergreen clematis. The area had at one time been the stabling yard, and her present shed had been the tack-room. On the fourth side there had once been a gate and four low steps down to the garden proper. The gate had long gone, and these days Rose used the steps as the best place to bring on her large pots of lilium before dispersing them in bud into the garden borders. Whilst the rest of the garden was planned and controlled, this place had an air of rambling wildness that was deceptive, for whilst Rose let climbers and ramblers have more head here than she would have done elsewhere, she knew what she was doing. She was creating, indeed had created, the kind of leafy, tendrilled and fallen-petalled bower that a member of the pre-Raphaelite school might have arranged. There had been such a bosk in the grounds of Longmore, where she had lived until she met Ballard, and again for a while during the war. There she had built a stone 'shrine', decorated with shells and bits of coloured glass and china, in which she had installed a statue (art deco from the house), honouring elegance, perhaps, for the statue had that quality.

The Shaft's Farm bosk had no shrine, but it did have a collection of old stone sinks and troughs, each of which held a miniature terrain – scree, bog, moraine; each with rocky outcrops and flora in believable proportions.

Opening the tack-room door, Rose savoured the smell of its interior, of Jeyes fluid, a mildewy collection of old mats, drying seed-heads, and sharpened and cleaned oily tools. She took her tobacco tin from a shelf close to the door. Another small pleasure she had picked up during the war and clung to, was a roll-your-own of moist tobacco, best smoked, as now, sitting on any make-do seat, preferably in the sun. In public she used a tortoiseshell holder and smoked Players. She sometimes wondered how the Covington constituency workers and voters would react if she brought out her Rizla papers and oiled pouch at a fund-raising dance.

Inhaling the aromatic smoke, she idly wandered about. It was a funny thing about Ballard's supporters, they were all Equality and Fraternity, yet whenever someone appeared with letters after their name, or a title, or an Oxford accent, they reverted to the modern equivalent of forelock tugging. That their MP was public school had a kind of shameful kudos. Rose had observed this in Jean, her domestic help. Rose was too insecure to voice her own opinions aloud, but spent hours whilst working in the garden pondering what made people tick. From an early age, children were shown that there was something special about class and privilege, and although Jean, who was Welsh, was fiercely against class distinctions, even she had grown up understanding how it operated the levers and switches of society. The wife of an MP was, of course, supportive and circumspect beyond anything. At the moment he was an official candidate. At the reselection meeting, the constituency chairman, who had publicly awarded himself the privilege of being on first-name terms, had dubbed them 'Ballard and Rose, the best team (and the best-looking team, ha-ha)'. In so conservative an area (conservative in spite of its tendency to vote Labour), the best team could not afford to be less than happy and united, with no hint of scandal or eccentricity attached to it. Women's complicity was the buoyancy jacket that kept men afloat. Women presented whatever image was wanted. No one would ever see her smoking roll-ups, savouring cheap sweetened milk, or tap-dancing in rubber boots.

Rebecca was still fast asleep. Last night she had sat late in her room, sketching and sketching as a stream of ideas came to her. Only an hour or so before Rose had leaned out and listened to the first thrush of the dawn chorus, Rebecca had fallen into a sleep of satisfaction and exhaustion. She felt that it had been like sipping a hard drink, the first sketch or two had made her cheeks glow, others following raised her mood until, by the small hours, she felt like those drunks who are sure that they can walk on water and climb towers.

She had speculated for a short while. She had been studying costume and current fashion magazines. She considered the work of the big fashion houses, the St Laurens, the Diors and Chanels, and sketched their direct antithesis. Houses! Houses! Why are they all so pretentious? Chanel is a woman who has an eye for a good line and sells it: it's no different from selling cabbages. Any woman knows a good cabbage. If cabbage-growers could label their goods and so create the same kind of mystique as top designers, then there would be women ready to make farmers rich. She must remember that. When she did her first collection, perhaps she would call it 'Cabbage'. She liked that. All night she sketched. Where fashion-house skirts were full and flounced, she sketched hers short and tight; where gloves were long, she chopped them at the wrists; French-pleated hair and hats were exchanged for bare, closely sculpted heads. Discreet fabric shades that 'went', went, in favour of plain, over-stated colour. She named them 'Shrimp', 'Goddam Red', 'Oil', 'Tar', 'Prickly Pink', 'Gunk Green' . . . Her models were flat and straight and narrow – as their heads were sculpted, so would their bodies be. Her sketches sang Young-Young-Young, in colours that would scare the pants off the 'houses'. Older women with bums and tits would look ridiculous in 'Cabbage' fashions. 'Cabbage' was for a very specific age-group, sixteen to twenty . . . maybe fourteen to twenty-five. There would be nothing that would, in the slightest, associate them with their mother's style or their mother's fashions. Dior – leisurely feminine! Hartnel – regal! Chanel – suits for ladies in middle age. Barbara Golen – modelling fashions for women in the bath-chair. Didn't any of them see that her own generation wasn't going to have any of that élitist stuff? Becc Quinlan's generation weren't going to be real women. Her generation had money to spend, their own money, not an allowance, or a bit pinched from the housekeeping. If they earned good money then they would spend it on clothes to suit themselves. Why would they want to teeter to work on four-inch heels that forced them to throw out their tits to keep balanced?

Four years ago, at the Festival, when she had first seen the use of white with bright, clear colour, Rebecca had assumed that everyone would want it. Yellow dresses, bright blue shoes, red coats. Women loved colour, why were they so afraid of it?

Nan was typical: 'Don't you think Villette is a little old for such a very loud sort of blue?'

'Rebecca, darling, you weren't think of wearing red slacks *out*?'

'I thought you liked them, Nan.'

'I do like them, dear. They look very cheerful about the house and garden.'

They had been brought up to be afraid of things. Of bare legs and arms, of unrestricted bodies, of luscious tastes and smells, of bright colours, and most particularly of sex. They thought it a compliment to say that a woman looked as though she'd got out of a band-box, meaning that she was arranged perfectly, untouched and untouchable. To wear red (no respectable English woman ever wore red), was to suppose that there must be some 'dago' blood somewhere, or that she must have a loose sexual inclination – 'red hat and no knickers'. Rebecca was beginning to understand how such things connected, and how subtly women had their inclinations curbed. Nan was typical: a woman should be 'nice'. A nice polite girl. Nice and fresh with nice manners, wearing nice matching clothes in nice unobtrusive shades. Rebecca thought that once girls began to wear strong colours and not feel ashamed of doing so, then their liberation from stultifying 'niceness' would follow.

Within the circle of girls of her own age, she had already observed the urge to rebel against girdles and bras, and the beige and dusty pinks and 'Gor-Ray' skirts where a pleat never got out of place. In her own set 'Gor-Ray' was used in place of 'passé'. She felt sure that things were on the move, and she dreamed of what her part in that movement would be. A design student could not hope to launch a collection of her own, yet she absolutely must get her name noticed now so that by the time she had completed her training she would be on the way. There was no time to waste, she was already twenty. She noted an outline plan of action, then fell asleep with the light on, surrounded by her startling and brightly coloured sketches.

Rose did not relish the speed with which her birthdays seemed to come round. Probably half of her life had gone and she felt that she was still waiting for it to begin. But then she thought about her mother-in-law and Great-gran. And look at Papa, not far off one hundred. Winifred too, sprightly and well cared-for. Rose shivered as a goose walked over her grave. Where would all the old Quinlans be when Rose was Charlotte's age? Still all tottering around, living here? Was that to be the other half of her life? Old women broke their hips. Would there be any time between Anoria breaking away and Charlotte and Winifred becoming dependent upon Rose?

She snapped out of it and sipped her cool, sweet drink. She drew on her shaggy cigarette, lit it again, and pinched off a shred of hanging tobacco. This was her secret life. No one could approach without scrunching noisily along the gravel path. Not that her family were wont to come to this part unless they needed her for something. Certainly not at five-thirty in the morning.

Ballard was too much a man at the centre of things to want to visit a vegetable garden, and in any case he was away much of the time, either in the House or working in his constituency, tickling his small majority. The smallness of his majority would give him an ulcer if he didn't watch out, particularly now that Covington had a new Tory candidate who was young and ruthless and working like mad to take the seat away from Ballard. The prospect of Ballard without his seat was something Rose pushed into the Pending tray with things such as old ladies with broken hips.

Jonathan hardly ever came into the vegetable garden. He was a young man still too close to his years of potato-picking holidays and Dig-for-Victory school allotments. Winifred, a mother-in-law who fancied herself of the old, formal school, was not likely to call unexpectedly. If she did she would always send someone to find Rose rather than trust her high heels to shifting gravel. And as for Rebecca and Vee, they were amused by, and probably a little ashamed of, a mother whose hobby required horse-manure, which they often came home to find dumped in the drive. Anoria, who was still only a girl, didn't mind a mother who wore Wellies – she would sometimes even show willing and help with raspberry picking; but Anoria did find vegetables so awfully and absolutely *bor-ing*! Rose smiled; Anoria was still nice and unaffected.

Rebecca, Villette and Anoria. These names had come about because, with one of those giddy gestures that young couples make when they realize what they have caused in that moment of reckless rapture, Rose and Ballard had, when Jonathan was in the offing, each insisted that the other should choose the names. Rose could choose for the sons, Ballard for the daughters. In the event, Ballard was a little put out that Rose had not agreed to call their firstborn Heracles, which had been a Quinlan family name until some time in the early nineteenth century. When it was his turn to choose, he had searched his family archives for memorable Quinlan women. But of course things were different by then; there was no giddiness in their relationship, and rapture was the last word appropriate to Anoria's conception. Now, although both Rose and the girls themselves preferred Becc, Vee and Nora, Ballard always referred to his children by their correct names.

Rose, having finished her tea and roll-up, took down her cared-for, sharply bladed draw-hoe, and went to where her beautifully straight rows of potato haulms were ready to be drawn up.

A grown woman, and all I know is how to grow prize vegetables.

As Rose started the hoeing, the village of Honeywood was beginning to show signs of life.

The driver of the IRF works bus, which circled four villages collecting young men and women to serve the rubber factory, was peeping its horn, signalling that locals had fifteen minutes before he came back through the village.

The hunt's yelping pack was being let out into the estate's pound.

The milkman was delivering bottles with a clatter, the milk a little less fresh than it was when taken from the Willses' Friesians a day or so ago.

A railway train passed with a hollow rumble across the bridge over the main road.

Young Teddy Wills put his foot down and roared the Willses' old Fordson along the main road, whilst his father 'Young' Ted (for 'Old' Ted was still alive and kicking) was 'Yip-yip-up'-ing the Willses' herd of Jerseys from Top Meadow to the milking sheds.

In the Old and Young Teds' day, the Willses had lived here at Shaft's Farm, but in Young Teddy's day, now that they could afford to, they had built a large, modern, centrally-heated red-brick house, and sold off to the Quinlans their old beamed house with its bulging walls, picturesque chimneys, peculiar drains and inadequate cesspool. The Quinlans didn't seem to mind pouring money into a place that had been built four centuries ago – before damp-proof courses were developed. The Willses' new house was named Connemara, but their fields and meadows were still known as Shaft's.

Connemara was built on a plot sold to the three Ted Willses by 'The Estate'. The Estate (Merrion Park – a name never used locally) occupied and owned a disproportionate amount of the village. For some reason, Honeywood folk were extraordinarily proud of the Estate, which was odd – as Leo Wilkinson liked to point out – when one took into account that most of the Estate lands had, before being enclosed by the Estate, belonged to the villagers. The Willses were the only people ever to get back a bit of the old field strips. But of course, unlike the Estate, they didn't get it for nothing.

In subtle ways the village was changing, and in some less subtle also. A row of prefabricated white houses had been put up during the time that Ballard's party had been in power. There had been a gradual selling of the older properties to people who had no connection with the village; two of the oldest thatched places were now occupied only at weekends.

The village shop had a delicatessen counter.

The newsagents and tobacconists now offered a delivery service, this service being at present James, Monica and Leo's eleven-year-old. Underage but cheap. Leo didn't like it, but Jack had made out a case for his independence.

The police house was no longer a police station: it was the home of Police Sergeant Carver-Flett and his family, who had been in the area for twelve years. The nearest actual station was now in Petersfield, six miles away. Not that the village had ever really needed a station. Pete Carver-Flett dealt with village crime in his own way. In return for keeping one eye on known poachers, he was given free range over Estate land with his own shotgun, and in return for making sure that the eye he kept on local poachers was blind, he was never without good game on his own table, as well as on the tables of anyone from whom he might one day want a favour. The Carver-Fletts were 'Old Village'; had been there for generations.

The church, fearing for its silver, had taken to locks and bolts, and for the first time in its life was administered by a youthful vicar with a young wife who wore slacks and had a motor fixed to her bicycle.

Whilst the Quinlans were not truly Old Village, they had lived hereabouts for a long time. 'Quinlan's of Winchester' was a departmental store of the old 'emporium' kind. 'Quinlan's' had supplied good bedding, furniture and clothing to the people of Honeywood for generations. It was in Over Meon (a mile away, where Sid and Charlotte lived) where the Quinlans were truly Old Village.

It was this perhaps, more than anything else, that had made Ballard decide that he must make his home in the area. He could have bought somewhere closer to Covington, but he had never really seen that area as the one in which he would *belong*. The Quinlans were southerners, and Covington was situated in what had been to him, until he had secured the nomination in '45, unknown territory that bulged out into the North Sea between Ipswich and Peterborough. Ten years on, he was still clinging on to Covington. It had caused not a little speculation and interest in the village when it had been learned that it was Sid Quinlan's MP son who had bought the Willses' old place and was bringing in builders to do all kinds of things to the old place.

It was a queer thing to do, Ballard being a Labour MP and coming to live in the heart of a Tory constituency, the one with the largest majority in the country. People knew that the lady who had held the seat was ill at ease with a troublesome member such as Ballard Quinlan living in her constituency. Truly her constituency, for she had held the seat for so long and with such a large Tory majority that it was felt to be hers by right. People loved it when the two of them had a go at one another in Parliament, but only the locals understood the underlying animosity. Ballard was a true local, born and bred in the constituency. If he hadn't made the mistake of standing for the wrong party, he might have had that seat.

Of course, Ballard would have loved to have been offered one of the safer seats, but few ever came up for grabs, and because most of these were in the industrial north, it was the sons of those towns and cities who were always in the running. Covington, being not very industrialized, was more suited to the image Ballard presented: posh accent, ex-officer, good-looking. But his time would come. It was a pity he hadn't been a Tory, for most of those who owed him favours were in that party.

It was Sid's boast that the Quinlans had been here when the royal family were still a bunch of foreigners. (Sid was a Liberal and a bit of a republican.) Winifred, like Rose, having no real home town or family of her own, had come to accept the Meon Valley and the Quinlans as substitutes for their own sparse (or embarrassing) antecedents. It suited Rose. You could put names to faces. And, although Old Village was incredibly nosy (they saw it as looking out for themselves), they were nosy in a keeping-yourself-to-yourself way. Nobody thought that there was anything special about meeting an MP in the village shop.

Leo and Monica Wilkinson. Leo a little younger than Ballard and Monica, a little older than Rose. Leo, a lean-faced, lean-bodied engineer, on his way to forty.

On that same May morning, Monica sat revving the car whilst Leo rushed around grabbing jacket, sports bag, rackets, wallet. 'Come on, come on, come on, Leo.' She had never been the sort to stand in the hall, holding his jacket, brushing his shoulders and seeing him off calmly.

'Right!' Leo jumped in as Monica drew away.

'You do cut it fine, Leo.'

Jonathan was just coming out of the Quinlans' back gate as Monica sprayed gravel turning into the road. 'Lift, Jonathan?'

He waved her on, smiling. 'In training,' he called, punching the air like a boxer and waving them on.

'Reminds me, we're eating with them this evening. It's Rose's birthday. And you *will* be back in time?'

'I remember. The match will be over by four o'clock.'

'That doesn't mean a thing.'

'I'll *be* back. I wouldn't disappoint Rose. I suppose the Hon. Memb. won't be able to drag himself away from his voters?'

'Well, actually he's home now. Needed a break.'

'Oh, poor lamb.'

'Leo!'

'Late night then. They always eat so bloody late.'

'Nine o'clock isn't late, and if you will be friendly with this class of person, then you must expect late dinner.'

'This class of person eating late gives me the pip, but I'd suffer a sleepless night any day for Rose.'

She drew up outside the Red Lion, where the single-decker was waiting. 'Go on, get out, the coach is ready to go.'

He gave her a brief kiss. 'See you about four o'clock.'

'I'll give you till six,' she called after him. 'Then you won't have to find excuses for being late back.'

She watched him run lightly across the road, as he did every other Saturday when the badminton team was playing away. He was fit from racket games, still tanned from last summer's tennis, and he had a neat, high backside and good legs which looked fantastic in white ankle socks and shorts. A feature that had played its part in their affair and Leo's divorce.

Jean Thompson threw open the back door and the kitchen windows of her council house to let out the smell of fried bacon and egg that permeated the house every workday morning.

'Anything in your paper about Mr Cue, Stanley? I'm goin' round there this mornin', it's her birthday and I said I'd give her a couple of hours just to help out.'

'There won't be anything now until the election's over.' Stan and Jean were staunch Labour – not that they thought much of Ballard's sort of politics.

Jean's da had been a miner from the Valleys, and her ma had never liked to know her man without a good lining to his stomach. Her da had never grown an inch fatter, but Jean's Stanley in his forties was a plumber and not a miner, so that Jean's breakfasts and teas showed up about his waist and neck. Even in the war, Jean always managed to put on a good table for her family.

'Ah well, I'd best be making tracks.'

'It's no good, Stan,' she said, sizing him up, 'you goin' to have to go on a di-yet. It was saying in my *Woman* that eggs is fatt-nenn. I never knew, I thought it was only potatoes and bread. My da had eggs every day till he died. Eggs never did him no harm, he just died sudden when his heart stopped.'

Stanley, who knew that an article in *Woman* was as good as Moses's tablets, surmised correctly that it might be some while before his working jacket would again be permeated with the smell of a good fried breakfast.

'OK then, love, perhaps it's as well. I been finding it a bit puffy getting under some of them new sinks.' It was no good going against what Jean said; she was a little fiery Welsh dragon – which was why Stanley had fallen for her.

Jean put the gas stove together again and gave a final polish to the row of tiles behind the gleaming brass sink taps. 'There!'

Stanley put on his fried bacon jacket and, before he put on his outdoor shoes, went through to round up David and Cliff who went for football training on Saturdays. The boys pounded down the stairs two at a time. 'Watch your fingers on that paintwork, your mam's only just finished wiping it down.'

If anyone had asked Jean why she got up at six every weekday and cleaned through her already immaculate-looking home, she would have said, 'You don't expect me to go out and clean somebody else's place until my own's been done, do you? When else would I do it?'

Winifred, as she did every morning, examined her face in the mirror as she nourished her skin with gentle, circular, upward movements, lightly tapping her lids, patting her eye area and stroking her throat. It was only at this stage of applying cosmetics that the brown spots on her cheeks and temple were visible; for the rest of the time they were covered by blended dots of Leichner cover and a film of Max Factor fluid.

She had bought cosmetics for Rose's birthday. A box made up in the Harrods cosmetics department, containing an expensive night-time nourisher, a pore cleanser, astringent splash and day-time protective creme. Winifred hoped that Rose would use it all. She was younger than Ballard, it was true, but Winifred did have a nagging worry that, in another twenty years, when Ballard was a silver-haired diplomat or Cabinet Minister, Rose might have become weather-beaten and homely. One could never consider the plain Eleanor Roosevelt as a suitable consort for a world leader; she was not in the same league as the elegant Clementine Churchill.

Apparently they were having the Wilkinsons in this evening. Winifred hadn't wanted to be asked: she wasn't very comfortable in their presence. They were obviously pretty well-heeled, and he did have a degree – engineering and not arts – and his business was quite large; but they were people who had never had the corners knocked off them. They flaunted their origins in a manner that was positively *de trop*. Who wished to know that Leo's father had been a farm labourer and Monica's an engine driver? Winifred knew very well that the Wilkinsons did know better, because they were always being invited to sit at top tables in places where Winifred herself would have given much to be invited. Rose and Ballard seemed to like them well enough, though, and Winifred supposed that being on good terms with one's neighbours was what one liked if it were possible.

The basic face cleansed and bare, she began the pleasurable daily task of painting on that of Winifred Quinlan, war-widow, bridge player, mother of the Hon. Member for Covington.

Jean came in at nine.

''Ello then? You there then, Mrs Cue?' Jean's smoke-harsh Welsh voice penetrated the far corners of the house at nine o'clock on three days a week. Mondays, Wednesdays and Fridays, with a bit of extra, as today, if required. And she would also, if needed at the Quinlans, leave her own two boys in Stanley's care and stay in the Quinlans' house on those occasions when Rose was needed to do her bit for Mr Cue's constituency.

Rose and Jean got on well. Jean was fussy about who she worked for. Bein' Welsh. From the Valleys, y'know. Her pin-up and hero was Nye Bevan, the Member for Ebbw Vale, Mrs Winifred's troll and bugaboo. Although Mrs Winifred never actually *said*, Jean was pretty sure that, if Mr Cue wasn't a Labour MP, his mum would be out working for the Tories. Jean wondered how she would feel if Cliff or David was to put up for the Conservatives. It couldn't be very nice for the old girl, but there, she should stick to her guns. Jean's other criteria when choosing her employers were status and non-interference by anybody at all. When Jean took on a house, it was she who did the interviewing. Everyone knew that Mrs Quinlan must be an absolute gem to have been given Monday, Wednesday and Friday mornings, plus occasionals.

''Ello then? You about, Mrs Cue?'

Rose, renewing the washer on the outside tap called back, not words, but just a hallo so that Jean would know where she was, because Jean hated to find people in places where she did not expect them. They made her jump, and jum-pen made her cough, which would only stop if she sat down and had a fag. By the time Rose came into the house, Jean had all her cleaning equipment sorted and the lavatory brush whizzing around the bowl, under the rim, back of the seat, good old-fashioned Jeyes fresh, and the wooden seat slippery and smelling of lavender polish.

Later, Jean fiercely cleaning and Rose scrubbing and peeling garden produce, they carried on their usual exchange of news. 'What d'you think, then?'

Rose joined in the guessing game.

'I don't know . . . You're going to take up golf?'

'Aw, Mrs Cue, that's a terrible thing to say, my mam'd kill me. She'll never forgive me for leaving the Valleys as it is.'

'What then?'

'My Stanley's getten' us a tele-vision.'

Rose, stepping back from the sink so that her voice carried into the cloakroom, said, 'A television! Lord, Jean, I can't think what gave him that idea.'

Jean laughed her low laugh. 'No more can I. You don't think it was nothen I said, do you?' She leaned back on her knees so that she could see through to the kitchen, shaking with laughter at Rose, who was grinning.

'You've never mentioned it to him, have you?'

'Especially I haven't since them next door to me got one. But when Stanley saw theirs he said, "Don't you fret, Jeannie, we don't want no rubbish. When we have a telly, we shall have quality – one of the new Fergusons".' She hissed Welsh esses, relishing the name of quality in tellies. 'He put a deposit down – there was a waiting list – and now we've come to the top of the list ages before they said. It could arrive any day now. You'll have to come round.'

'Lovely,' Rose said.

'You'll have to get Mr Cue to get you one. Stanley said that if you got one you might have to get the top sawed off that big cedar to get good reception, but you'll have to get one.'

Jean and television had fallen for one another on Coronation Day. People were getting them, even in the Valleys. Her mam had one and, in the ways that some people know every dog, Jean knew every set in the village. There were parts of Honeywood where the signal was interrupted by the Downs and no picture at all was possible. They were lucky in the council houses at the top of the hill. Jean wanted a telly and she wanted a Ferguson.

And Rose knew that, if they were to keep Jean's evening services for child-minding, then the Quinlans too would indeed have to get one, preferably a Ferguson also.

Over their fifteen-minute cocoa break, Jean passed on village news, and scandal about the London people whose lives were a source of wonder to Jean and her neighbours. Rose returned that gift of gossip with the attentive ear that Jean liked to have for her uninterrupted stream.

Jean lived in the midst of a small cluster of red-brick council houses where feuds, affairs, quarrels and friendships, where tales of rivalries, debt, pools wins, dead cats flung over fences, and farm accidents sometimes made Rose feel that her own life was not touched with anything like the same purpose as the lives of those in the council houses. Real life was lived in the red-brick enclave with which she kept in vicarious touch via Jean. Among the middle-class inhabitants of Honeywood, the acquisition of a television set would be more a question of whether it was a 'Good Thing' and 'Educational', rather than whether it could be afforded, or how long would it take to pay off on the never-never, or which was best, Rediffusion or Radio Rentals?

'Just fancy, we might even see your man if they do the opening of Parliament.'

'Oh, we might, but he's got to win it yet.'

'He increased his majority last time.'

'He needs a boost this time.'

'He's quite a dish your man, the cameras would be sure to go on him.'

Rose handed Jean a roll-up in exchange for the Craven-A she had accepted earlier from Jean.

Jean tapped it and pinched off the end. 'I don't know why you don't buy yourself some decent cigs.'

Rose smiled. 'I might get to enjoy smoking.' She flared her old wheeled lighter at Jean who drew and coughed. They parted and Rose went back to her acre.

When Monica appeared at the back door, Jean said, 'I was just going to start on this floor, so you had better go and find her down the garden.' Jean worked for Monica too, and because she quite liked her because she treated Jean decent, Jean was thinking of giving her another few hours.

Rose recognized Monica's tread upon the gravel and called, 'I'm here.'

'Home-grown peas tonight?'

'I'm not sure whether they are pea-less pods or mange tout.' She held one up to the light. 'Mange tout on the menu.'

'Happy birthday.'

'Oh Mon, thanks.' Rose took the book-shaped parcel. 'A book?'

'You'd never guess from its shape. Leo brought it back from the States, he swears you haven't read it.'

It was a slim volume. '*Catcher in the Rye*, wonderful! Leo's right, I haven't read it.'

'He says it's selling in thousands, is it spicy?'

'No.'

'Leo said it was your kind of book, and he brought it all the way back from the States without reading it.'

'He deserves a kiss for that when I see him.'

'You do that. Make his day. I wouldn't be surprised if that's what he had in mind when he bought it.'

Leo was the only man, except for Papa, with whom Rose felt at ease.

'What did your old man buy you?'

'A crocodile sort of make-up case, and Winifred a load of expensive beauty products to go in it.'

'Nice.'

'Mmm. Very.'

Monica and Rose, keeping out of Jean's way whilst she went fiercely through the house, settled down companionably for half an hour of feeling pods and picking for tonight's birthday dinner.

'Don't you just love May mornings, Mon?'

'I do if I know I don't have to prepare a meal.'

'Dare I ask, what about the bananas and milk?'

'Bloody hell!' She smoothed her breasts and patted her stomach. 'Can't you tell? Seven pounds in a week.'

'I thought you must have. Don't lose too much.'

'It's always the thin ones who tell you that.'

'What about tonight?'

'The diet? What the hell, I've lost half a stone.' She made a face and hunched her shoulders, singing, 'Clot the cream and cherry the gateau, fala, lala, la, la, la, la, la.'

'Is going down to the pub still on?'

'Far as I know. Rose, don't let me get dragged in to drinking anything fattening. I'm absolutely on the wagon until I've lost another stone.'

'You won't take any notice of me.'

'I will! This time I will.'

Meanwhile, having driven over in her neat and shiny Morris, Winifred was looking in on Charlotte and Papa. It was the old man's centenary soon. Winifred thought that they should do the thing properly because, no matter that he was old and had been retired for a quarter of a century, the Quinlans' business had been quite prestigious in its day. Of course, it still was prestigious, and even though it was now one of a chain of shops, it was still called Quinlan's.

Winifred wanted a nice gathering at the Coach House. Charlotte wanted to give Papa a family party in their big front room, and Rose too tended to think that might be best. Ballard was too busy, asking them to just let him know before they went ahead with anything, but definitely no village halls. Vee said, 'It's going to be summer, why don't we have a garden party?' 'In a *tent*!' begged Anoria. Winifred tidied up their idea slightly and said, 'Why not? A small marquee and caterers, and a trio or something, an outdoor celebration would be very nice.'

For all her airs and graces, the old Quinlans quite liked the girl Henry had married. Actually, they had always felt quite sorry for her.

Winnie Mayhew had not been anybody very much. Her father (as Winnie had it) had been 'an officer in the Mercantile Fleet – very handsome with his beard and peaked cap and brass buttons'. This (very) ordinary merchant sailor had been lost at sea at a crucial time in Winnie's development, and she had fantasized a father who had over the years become elevated to captain.

Mrs Mayhew, Winnie's mother, having nobody left except her daughter, had encouraged Winnie in the idea that they were quite Somebody. Winnie became Winifred, and was sent to elocution lessons and dancing classes. She learned how to enter a room and walk its length, stepping with toes before heels. Fortunately for Winnie Mayhew, she met Henry Quinlan of 'Quinlan's Drapery, Shoes, Ladies & Gentlemen's Wear, Linens, etc.', who gave her Ballard and then disappeared before the dying German guns. Had he not, then the naming of the child might not have been left to Winnie and Mrs Mayhew, and Ballard might also have been Henry.

Charlotte and Sidney had been distraught at losing their only child, but when Winnie brought little Ballard to live close at hand, they felt that they were being given a second chance to have a son. Unfortunately, having enjoyed a dead-father fantasy, Winnie easily took on a dead husband – not that she had not loved him, for indeed she had. But to be brought up with a fantasy father and grandfather had not been good for little Ballard Quinlan, for, what with his mother's terrible class awareness, reinforced by the petty snobbery fostered in his boarding school, little Ballard grew up with the idea that there was a natural ruling class, and that he belonged to it. Thus Winifred was just succeeding in preparing him for the Conservative Party when the plebs took over.

No one had ever put on a braver face than Winifred when Ballard, ex-public school, ex-officer, announced in his deep, resonant, well-tuned accent that he had joined the Labour Party and been selected as one of their 'khaki candidates'. Her face had been saved by Lord Mountbatten, the great aristocrat and war hero, cousin to the king, no less. At the '45 election (Ballard's election, in Winifred's terms), Lord Louis had declared that, if only he had a vote, he would be a Labour supporter.

Privately she longed for the old days when one knew just where one was.

Charlotte and Papa were ever-thankful that Winnie had given them Ballard, and thankful that Ballard had given them Rose and the great-grandchildren. Two well-off, race-going, beer-drinking old Liberals, they were aware of their good fortune. Not many have got what we've got, Sid. And Sid always agreed: You're right there, Lotte, and no mistake.

Because of sentiments such as these, on the morning of Winifred's visit to her in-laws to settle Papa's birthday arrangements, Charlotte instructed her husband, 'Now, you don't be awkward with her, Sid. Let her do it her way. She means well and it's not going to matter much to me and you.'

And as it turned out, it did not.

The early May evening was as fresh and mild as the morning had promised as they walked beside the stretch of the River Meon that belonged to Shaft's Farm. The air seemed to be so clear that Ballard's coins could be heard chinking in his pockets, the crunch of the dry road-surface and the sounds of the rill's clear, fast-running water sounded as sharp as on a frosty night.

'We are so lucky, don't you think?' Rose said.

'Luck had nothing to do with it. This was hard earned.'

She didn't argue, she had meant being alive on such a beautiful evening, and they walked in virtual silence through the village towards the pub where they were going to meet Leo and Monica, speaking only to greet people working their gardens.

They were lucky. Honeywood was one of the prettiest villages in the south.

It had photogenic thatch, cat-slide roofs, long cottage gardens, knapped-flint walls, front porches with honeysuckle and clematis, and several houses as old as Shaft's, all of which made painters and photographers want to capture bits of it and frame them to take away. Meandering little lanes, leading to the Rec., the school, the sub-post office and shop, the church and the two pubs, kept villagers safe from the fast traffic. Honeywood was on the floor of the valley where the river ran, and where the air was almost always moist, which kept vegetation green and fruit plump. A short railway train tooted, ran across the bridge over the road, and followed where its rails plunged into the wooded furrow between two slopes of downland. London was not much more than an hour by rail; several buses a day went between one town and another and back again; yet on evenings such as this, one could easily picture the same scene – two people ambling along in apparently companionable silence – a hundred years back.

Leo was limping when he and Monica arrived in the lounge-bar of the Lord.

'Poor Leo,' Rose said. 'Put your foot on this stool and rest your leg.'

Monica said genially, 'Take no notice, Rose, you'll only make him worse. He plays damn badminton as though it paid the mortgage.'

Ballard handed them their usual drinks: a Whisky-Mac for Monica and a beer for Leo. 'None of us getting any younger, ol' man.'

Rose knew that Ballard knew that Leo couldn't stand being called 'old man' in that public school accent which Ballard used when he fancied.

Leo did not react. 'You might not be, old man, but I'm not a day over twenty-five. Ask my woman.'

'I'll give you that . . . He's got some way to go before he matures, hasn't he?'

Rose said, 'I won't hear a word against Leo. He flew all the way to America just to buy me the very book I wanted, and then flew back with it in time for my birthday.' Giving him a quick, dry, friendly peck.

'Nnnh!' He held on to her hand, which she had rested on his shoulder, and caressed her fingers until he saw that Ballard's eyes were fixed upon them, which prompted him to kiss her hand loudly. 'You like the book? I resisted temptation to read your copy. I actually bought my own.'

'That's really noble of you. It's an extraordinary book. I read pages and pages in the bath . . . the water went cold.'

'What is the great epic this time?' Ballard asked.

'You know very well, I showed you when I opened it - *Catcher in the Rye*.'

Leo said, 'It will win awards.'

'What's so special about it?' Monica said.

Leo answered. 'It gets inside the head of modern youth. That right, Rose?'

'It *does*. Amazingly it does. Under the skin, right into the boy's bones.'

'God preserve us from the minds of modern youth,' Monica said, handing her glass to Leo whose turn it was to order.

Rose said, 'Do you want me to remind you, Mon, or are you on your own?' She blew out her cheeks and indicated fatness with a spread of her hands. 'You were supposed to be on a . . .'

Monica tapped her forehead and threw her hand away in the 'I blew it!' sign. 'I'll have a two-day fast starting tomorrow to make up for it. Anyway, I need my own mind numbing if we are going to hear about this masterpiece of literature.'

Ballard said, 'Don't start Rose and Leo off on books, or we shall never get a game of darts.'

Behind the practised geniality which was Ballard's political stock-in-trade, Rose heard irritation, and felt her own irritation that he should practise it here where he had no business to. He was probably going to behave badly and it was her own fault for asking him to be at home. Too often a Quinlan/Wilkinson supper or dinner was one Quinlan and two Wilkinsons, and it wasn't often that she asked him to come home during election time. Mostly she did her duty by going round Covington playing the supportive wife. A thing she never forgave the Party was their public laying claim to a belief in equality of the sexes, and a record in office that did not bear examination. In the reverse situation, Ballard would never be expected to drive north for three hours on Fridays so as to appear smiling and silent at Rose's side at meetings. But then, would Rose ever have got past the dreadful sexual prejudice of the constituency selection committee? Some had. Sharp, smart, Barbara Castle, whom Rose liked, and sexy Jenny Lee who usually scared Rose into inarticulacy. Both were childless. Ballard had four children. Where was equality of the sexes there?

Percy and Marge, licencees of the Lord, came to the other side of the bar. Percy said, 'Have a drink on us, Mrs Quinlan. Cheers, happy birthday.'

Rose, genuinely pleased, said, 'That's really nice. Ballard, isn't that nice of Percy and Marge?' and flushed with pleasure.

Ballard, addressing no one in particular, but indulging in the small pleasure of sniping at Leo, said, 'This literature business is all so false, I don't see how it's possible to award prizes for books.'

Marge said, 'It's true that they're all so different.'

Ballard nodded at his ally. 'How can anyone judge a love story against a political book? Who has the say-so?'

'Academics,' said Leo, 'and professionals in the literature game.'

'I'm glad you call it a game,' Ballard said.

Percy, whose only real interest outside his pub was following the hunt on foot on Boxing Day, indicated that he must get back, and went behind the bar where he was safe from customers who wanted to talk rather than chat. Marge liked the Quinlans and the Wilkinsons because they did actually talk. Not when it was politics, though; whenever anybody started on politics, Marge retreated along the same route as Percy. If you kept a pub, you couldn't afford to talk politics, especially in Honeywood which was the heart of one of the Tory blue areas. Even so, Ballard Quinlan was a local, and he was an MP, so Marge said, smiling to show her interest, but making her way towards the other bar in case he should say something controversial, 'I thought we wouldn't see you this weekend. Thought you'd be off up North.'

'Special dispensation for my wife's birthday.'

'Aah, that's nice . . . Isn't that nice, Percy?'

Monica, who although she wasn't really interested in the book argument, still felt prompted to keep it going, said, 'I'm inclined to side with Ballard. I mean, an award for medicine or an invention – like the iron lung – I can see that you could decide to give an award to somebody for saving lives. That's something you can see, it's cut and dried. But a book's only a good read . . . or not, as the case may be.'

'Careful, Mon,' Leo said. 'Start getting in deep and you'll leave us all standing.'

Monica grinned and made a punching movement in his direction. 'I'm not just a pretty face, you know.'

'Is there something I don't know about, then?'

She gave Leo a funny, intimate little smirk.

Rose, quite envious of their relationship in which they could take a dig at one another and not leave bruises, said, 'Films get Oscars.'

Ballard said, 'My point really . . . Nobody takes film awards seriously, but literary buffs are always so po-faced. If you want to give prizes, then give it to whoever sells most. Any other criterion is élitist.' He smiled. Any stance against élitism was usually Leo's.

Rose had meant that, if it was possible to select a best film, then it ought to work for a book as well, but she did not pursue it because he wasn't really interested in the discussion. It wasn't a subject at which he could shine or dominate; he had none of the political bons mots or anecdotes or scurrilous gossip with which to hold his audience.

'Good literature isn't élitist,' said Leo, moving to get back his own patch on the moral high ground. 'Anyone can enjoy it.'

'They can't, Leo,' Monica said. 'Jean couldn't. Take away her *Woman* magazine and give her – I don't know, one of those deep things you and Rose get so stirred up about – *Animal Farm*, I mean . . . if you hadn't told me what it was about, I might not have got it. Jean certainly wouldn't.'

Leo said, 'That doesn't mean that it isn't a great book. Or that women's magazine readers can't enjoy it.'

'But, Leo old chap, if they don't get out of it what you and Rose seem to, that's élitist!'

Leo felt the discussion was going down a slippery slope, as did most discussions in which the four of them were involved. 'Rose, come on, don't desert me.'

'I admired it, I can't say that I enjoyed it. I've never liked animals who talk.'

'But it is a great book; you'd agree to that, wouldn't you?' asked Leo, leaning in her direction.

'Not his most important.'

'There you are then,' Ballard said, 'that shows how impossible it is to award prizes for so-called literature. If you two buffs can't agree about two books by the same writer, how can anybody – I don't care if they are academics, Leo – how can they judge books that are totally different? It's got to be personal preference.'

As usual, Leo and Ballard took charge of the discussion. They never agreed about anything. Rose tried to keep out because whatever comment one made, it was taken by one or the other of them as siding-with or sniping-at. Once they took their positions it seemed impossible to make a simple contribution. Even if one wished to put a stop to it, it meant giving one of them the last word. Monica rolled her eyes at Rose, and went to sit beside her on the other sofa.

'Of course,' Leo said, 'personal preference is bound to come into it.'

'OK, so what if that week one of the judges feels down and prefers the light-hearted book and not the heavy tome . . . that comes into it too?'

'Judges are only human.'

'So if it came to a majority vote, the light-hearted book might get the award because one of the judges had a cold?'

'I say,' Rose said, 'if we don't play darts now, the roast will be over-cooked.' A well-judged moment. The wrangling stopped.

'She doesn't look any different from when you came here to live,' Leo said, following Rose with his eyes as she went to claim the darts. 'How many years ago was that?'

'About ten, I suppose,' Ballard said.

'I can tell you exactly,' Monica said. 'Nine years and five months, and I could probably work it out to the day if you like.'

'Crumbs,' said Leo, 'you must have been impressed at the prospect of getting an MP for a neighbour instead of the Teds.'

Monica grinned and winked at Ballard. 'Nah, MPs are ten-a-penny where I come from down in Railway Cuttings.'

Rose came back, unruffled and looking cool and perfect in a tightly-belted plain black dress worn with Ballard's last expensive birthday gift: a string of pearl beads almost the same colour as her hair. She threw the darts, one-two-three, quickly. 'There! Double straight off. Forty, fifty-two, seventy away.' She handed the darts to Monica.

'Rose knows why I remember. Blast!' One dart bounced from the surrounding car-tyre and another ricocheted from a wire.

'What is it that you remember?' Rose watched as Ballard took his dead-eye aim.

'The exact length of time that you've lived in the village.'

'Should I?'

'Shut up!' Ballard said, 'I can't concentrate with a lot of chat going on.'

'No special treatment, Ballard, just chuck the damn darts. Your Nora and our Tom were born in the June of '46. So it must have been January, because when Rose and I met the day after you moved in, we both had bumps of equal size. Five months gone with our Victory celebration mistakes. Right, Rose?'

Ballard threw two wild darts and then scored a double 'top'. 'Forty away! Follow that, Leo.'

Rose flushed. 'I remember that it was endlessly cold and the fish were frozen in the pond.'

Leo took the darts. A deceptive player who did not appear to take aim and, like Rose, threw one-two-three, quickly. But he was a haphazard scorer who was as likely to get a five and two ones as to hit three treble-twenties. He scored fifty-seven, forty, and one off the board.

Monica took the darts. Her intense concentration did not stop her talking. 'And about the first thing I said was . . . is that three or sixty? Damn . . . ! I said, "Hello, glad to see somebody else had too much to drink on VJ Night", and you blushed . . . Fifty-seven, nice one Monica . . . And I thought to myself: If she can blush, then she can't be all that bad, even if she is married to an MP. There, fifty-seven, sixty and double-top . . . one hundred!'

They played best of three games, which Monica and Ballard won.

Rose said, 'I'll skip on home just to check on the roast. You come on when you are ready.' Waving goodnight to people she recognized, she left.

In seconds Monica had caught her up. 'I thought I'd come on. I should only have had another one if I'd stayed there with them.'

'I wasn't much help with the diet, was I? Sorry.'

'You don't have to worry, nobody's much help. I've thought of having my lips sewn up just leaving a space for a straw. God, Rose, that smells wonderful!' They had reached the house where the aroma of good beef roasting was expelled across the courtyard from a fan in the kitchen wall. 'Anything I can do?'

'Absolutely not, you're guests. Anyway it's ready; nothing to be done until I hear them coming, and then I'll pour in the batter.'

'Did I put my foot in it?'

Rose, dashing ice-water over the pea pods, didn't look up from the sink. 'Put your foot in what?'

'I don't know. But you seemed . . . anyway, if I did, I'm sorry. I have a big mouth.'

Rose came near to actually taking Monica's square and capable hand. 'Of course not. What makes you think that?'

'I did, didn't I? I have a big mouth.'

'Mon, don't go on about nothing. Now come on through to the dining room. This is cream of chive and lemon soup, and it's supposed to be eaten chilled.'

As Leo and Monica were preparing for bed that night, and he was trying to manoeuvre his good foot under her slip whilst she was putting a cold compress on his ankle, she said, 'Stop getting all worked up, this terrible injury won't stand it. When I was pulling Rose's leg about getting pregnant on VJ night, did you notice how flustered she got about it?'

'Perhaps it's a sore point?'

'Well, that much was obvious, but why? It's ten years . . . if Nora was a mistake . . . For God's sake, they should've been over that by the time she was born. You don't think maybe that Ballard's not Nora's father?'

'Oh come *on* . . . Rose?'

'Why the hell not?'

'Because . . . she's not like that. I mean, can you imagine . . . ?'

'Like what?'

'The type.'

'What type?'

'I don't know. She's the remote, untouchable type . . . She's not even a type: I've never met a grown woman who looks like that. She's got this look of virginity . . . *Don't laugh*!'

'I wasn't going to.' She laughed. 'The Angel Gabriel descended upon her in a tongue of flame . . . *four times*!'

'You're . . .'

'I know. The woman of a man taken in adultery. It's written all over me. I look the type. All this hair, these . . .'

'These are fantastic.'

'Hold still.'

'Och! No need to cut off my blood supply. You're becoming a real old village gossip.'

'I'm not!'

'So why are you trying to draw me into speculation about how Rose became pregnant? Do you know, you have wonderful Italianate breasts.'

'Fat.'

'Generous. Soft to the touch. Stop trying to starve them.'

'And when did you last have a handful of Italianate bosom?'

'I have them all the time – two-handed jobs, like yours.'

'I need to lose a stone.'

'Oh Mon, not *again*. You know dieting makes you crazy.'

If she promised she was bound to break it, and then suffer twice: first for her lack of self-control, second for not keeping to her word. She knew that there would inevitably come a day, after days or weeks of being good, when she would suddenly be unable to stop herself going 'hunting'. Then the Good Monica, who had been living on bananas and milk, would break out and go in search of something to satisfy her rage and her raging hunger. Good Mon usually broke out after a breakfast, as she scraped the remains of fried egg and bacon fat from *their* plates, her mouth watering at the sight of the crisp curls they despised, her gorge rising at their cavalier attitude to her efforts. Crashing the plates into the sink, she would begin calculations. Six breakfast plates times seven days is forty-two plates times fifty-two weeks for ten years. Twenty-one thousand eight hundred and forty. And this was just one plate at one meal during the school years. All her diets ended more or less in this way.

'Mon? Promise me you won't start again.' He held and caressed her breasts. Their love-making usually started in this way.

When she did not respond, he went on. 'It was what you said about getting drunk on VJ Night . . . That hit a raw spot with Rose.'

'I noticed.'

'God, that's cold.'

'Cool your ardour. Get your hand away until I've finished.' She pinned the elastic bandage into place. 'I don't like to think that I hurt her feelings. She obviously didn't want to talk about it. There! Now that your wounded soldier act has set me on the road to ruin, you'd better do something about it. Go and put on your tennis shorts – the really short ones.'

He laughed, but did as he was told. 'In my youth, I had no idea that the human female came on heat – or so frequently. I was so innocent, in spite of having read Huxley and Lawrence.'

'If you'd left the theory alone and gone more for the practice, you might have lost your innocence when you lost your virginity.'

'You don't have much in the way of inhibitions, do you? Not a lot makes you blush.' His ankle had suddenly become amazingly flexible as he leaped into bed.

'Next time put on the knee-socks too. You have such a smashing bum on you.'

'It was the first thing you said to me that wasn't to do with the election.'

'It could be. It's what I thought, anyway.'

'It's what you said.'

'That's hindsight or whatever. I don't believe I actually said it.'

'Hindsight?'

'No, but it would have been witty if I had . . . Never mind, forget it.'

'This delicious female came up to me in the clubhouse and said, "You're Leo Wilkinson, aren't you? I'm Monica Dowling," and I said, "I saw you at Horace King's meeting, you asked a question," and she said, "I really enjoyed watching you play . . ."'

'And you said, "I didn't think I was that good, but I'm glad you enjoyed the game."'

'And you said, "I didn't notice the game, but I liked the way your backside moves when you serve."'

'And you went all red.'

'Me, blush?'

Monica smiled down at him, her mass of frizzy hair hanging like bulky curtains. 'You know you did, and for a second you were so nonplussed that you didn't know what to say; then you shook hands with me and said, "That's the nicest thing anybody ever said to me. Pleased to meet you."'

'And you said, "Nice meeting you, Leo. When you know me better, you'll know that I never say things I don't mean."' And, rolling over to gain the dominant position, Leo looked pleased with himself.

'It does, you know, it moves beautifully . . . It's these muscles here . . . and here . . . and here. It's no wonder the team will hold the bus for you every time you turn up late for an away game. I think that's why the ladies team is so keen. Honour said, "Leo's an absolute peach." She actually looks as though she'd like to sink those great British teeth into something pink and downy.'

'They're loyal to me as team captain and coach.'

'Mmmm.'

He looked down at her and shook his head as though he still could not believe his good luck. 'Love you.'

With a coarse, quiet laugh. 'All night if you like, coach.'

After they had made love, satisfyingly as they always did, Monica lay awake, her arms crossed and her hands cupping her breasts. They *were* large. *Fat!* She felt ambivalent about them, but then women did. Kate and Helen and their girlfriends seemed obsessed by the subject of bra size. Listening to their confused tales of womanhood, it had occurred to Monica that nothing had changed since her own puberty. Once girls had 'developed', they had the problem that, at one and the same time, they were expected to hide and reveal their femininity: nice girls didn't flaunt their figures in tight jumpers, yet they could not open a magazine or newspaper without receiving the message that flaunting breasts is the way to the high life. The way to the best men and success.

The butt of jokes and cat-calls. Advertising images. Male trophies. A woman's breasts were never allowed just simply to *be*.

Monica slid her hands over her own soft mounds. She actually did like them, even though they were so overblown, and they aroused Leo. Not only her own did that: she had often seen the way his eyes followed the lean women he coached at tennis, as their pectorals lifted curves much more 'pert' than Monica's. 'Pert' was now the favoured shape in breast language. Monica felt that she too could be pert if she only had enough self-control to get down to nine stone.

During the evening, Monica had made herself promise Rose that she would go back on her diet tomorrow. Rose had said: Oh, Mon, why on earth do you punish yourself like that? You're just right. The kind of thing said by people who were not afraid of food.

She thought about tomorrow, and nothing in the prospect pleased her. But it wasn't tomorrow yet. She crept out of bed and went downstairs.

Hunting.

Even as she opened the pantry door, she knew very well of course that there was nothing in there that would satisfy her. She could go endlessly from pork pie to chocolate biscuits, from tinned fruit to bowls of cereal, and nothing would fill her. She had often tried to locate the space. Somewhere between her throat and her midriff, and on the left side of her brain.

Even as she took out the biscuit tin, she knew very well that she would be furious with herself, be guilty, be angry, be miserable; until at last she would start on another crash diet. Then she would become elated, and Good Monica would be back.

Sometimes she was quite afraid of the amount of eating she could do. After a recent 'hunting trip', she had put matters right with fingers down her throat. This remedy was immediate and less debilitating than Epsom salts or a mustard emetic.

When she returned to bed, shivering from the regurgitation and guilt and fear that it would get worse, she wished that, instead of sleepily pulling her to him, Leo would ask her what she had been doing. In the anonymous darkness and with his warm arms around her, she might have found the courage to tell him.

All that she needed was to tell *someone* that she did these crazy things. Yet, even as she longed to tell, she knew that, when it came to the point, she would be too mortified and ashamed to put it into words. She was on a treadmill that was speeding up. Soon she would not be able to jump off.

Leo's divorce years ago – in the days when divorce was rare and socially unacceptable – had been an unpleasant affair. His wife, Wendy – even though she had had a series of lovers during the war years – divorced Leo for infidelity – which he could not deny, as Wendy had employed an agency which presented the necessary proof, and Leo and Monica had not been very secretive.

Like thousands of other young people, the war had made them political activists. Throughout Britain there was an electric atmosphere. A kind of peaceful revolution was being fought in a fine midsummer. A ration of petrol was allocated to political parties and Leo, being one of the few Labour workers with a car, drove all over the constituency, ferrying speakers and handbill distributors.

Being self-employed, the divorce did not harm Leo's career, but Monica was forced to resign her hospital post. In any case, Wendy had gone away with a lover and left Leo and Monica to start their married life with little Tom. The years since had been a succession of days and nights of the most joyful life any couple could wish for. The thing was, neither of them tried to change or to have any control over the other. Although Monica had seen nursing as a 'calling', she discovered she liked domesticity and motherhood, and found herself to be very good at it. Leo was good at engineering and made a decent income. Monica had her amateur dramatics and operatics, and Leo had his badminton. She supported his important league games and he went to her first nights. They were everybody's favourite guests. Monica and Leo, Leo and Monica. They were the most unshackled couple imaginable, yet bound securely to one other. Those who knew their entire love story waited for it all to come crashing down: 'It will all end in tears.' But it had not. In 1955, theirs was still a truly happy marriage.

Winifred and Rose put a lot into making Papa's party something special. Nineteen fifty-one, the Festival of Britain year, had been something of a watershed. The colourfulness and daring of that event had lifted spirits. Now, four years on, women's skirts billowed out, men no longer wore hats in the streets; indeed many young men stopped having mere haircuts and went in for hairstyles; furnishing fabrics came under the influence of Picasso, kitchens went red or orange – often both – and had amusing features such as ropes of onions and strings of imitation fruit. Recently 'in' and 'contemporary' were the imitation aubergines and large red capsicums – soon known as peppers – because quite ordinary people were now holidaying abroad and they wanted to show that they knew an aubergine or a capsicum when they saw one.

For those who were young, who were always one step ahead of a coming trend, black winged-settees with angled legs, designed by Ernest Race, were absolutely 'in', as was the word 'in' itself. To be fashionable and up-market was to eschew every colour except those in the *House and Garden* range: lemon peel, aubergine, cerulean blue and guardsman red. For the first time, young couples had money to spend; they had joint incomes and were prepared to pay high prices to achieve the 'contemporary look'. A square of guardsman red carpet on black tiles: rooms in which three walls were painted with the fourth as a 'feature' – covered in expensive paper that drew the eye and admiration of the onlooker. Picture-rails were removed, and there were no flower motifs anywhere – absolutely none. Certain house plants of the ficus genus became known as 'architectural' and thus desirable, rubber and cheese plants were longed for in every modern home. Plates and saucers no longer had rims, and cups were really bowls of heavy ceramic – ceramics were very 'in'.

For the avant-garde, the desire was for shocking colour and simplicity. A simplicity of the William Morris school, but in skeletal metal. The first shoots of the throw-away tree was planted in the fifties but would not begin to show its exuberant nature until the sixties, then, like the rubber plants, would begin to get out of hand.

For the mass-market, simple red was not enough, so a red

carpeting with 'skate marks' criss-crossing it – acres and acres of it – was produced and was snapped up as soon as it arrived in the shops. In 1955 people living in terraces and council houses aspired to wall-to-wall, instead of lino or carpet squares that could be turned to hide the wear. And when red became tiresome, there would soon be acres and acres of orange swirled with black to follow.

Things were looking up, so, in early July, four years on from the Festival, Winifred and Rose prepared for the first big party since the war that did not have the dull hand of 'shortages' laid on it.

'Super, Mum! Absolutely super.' Vee, whose idea had been the springboard for the garden party, squeezed Rose's arm.

'I do feel it's turned out rather well, though of course –' turning to Winifred – 'most of it is due to Nan's organization.'

Winifred was flushed with the satisfaction of having something purposeful to do and with having done it well. 'All we need is good weather.' She had rejected the *House and Garden* colours Rebecca had suggested for the drapes, cloths and serviettes, in favour of a safe shade of blue with white cloths and red carnations on the tables.

Rebecca's soul, when she had heard what her grandmother had arranged, had been seared by such want of taste. 'It will look like a Tory fête, Mother, it will look like a Tory fête!' Rose warned. 'Not a *word*, Becc, not one single word. She has worked her behind off.'

'Whatever will Nan do if Daddy loses his seat?' Rebecca asked gaily.

Villette scoffed. 'Daddy lose?' It had never occurred to her that all the talk about Daddy's narrow majority had such relevance. She had supposed that it was a thing that *was* possible, but not very likely. Only now did she wonder: what *would* Daddy do if he didn't win? He had his 'head-hunting' but Villette had never been really sure what it actually was, or whether they would be able to live on that.

In the event she need not have worried, for although the Conservatives were elected under Anthony Eden, Ballard retained his seat with a slightly increased majority. The Covington electors' motto being, 'Better the devil you know', and knowing that he was not really a dangerous sort of socialist, voted him in for another term.

The guests at Papa's party were a strange mixture of some of Ballard's more house-trained politicos; some of Winifred's bowling club friends, and some of her bridge and canasta partners; various villagers, such as Jean and Stanley Thompson, Percy and Marge from the Lord, the Wills family, and a few of Papa's friends, plus Monica, Leo and all of the old Quinlan's Draper's and Outfitter's staff. And Aunt Ellie. Actually, being Papa's little sister, she was the young

Quinlans' great-aunt, who had arrived in England from California only days ago, and whom they had seen only briefly last night before she disappeared into the best room at the Coach House 'to catch up with things'.

She fascinated the three girls.

Rebecca was envious of her deep tan. 'It's not fair, she's too old for a tan like that.'

'But she looks younger than Nan,' Anoria said. 'Lots younger.'

'That's because she has face-lifts,' said Vee knowingly.

Nora didn't ask the question Vee waited for, so Vee had to offer the information. 'Face-lifts are when women have their spare skin stitched up behind their ears.'

Nora's face said, 'Pull the other one, it's got bells on it.'

'OK, if you don't want to believe me, then don't, I don't care. But I heard Nan said to Great-gran that Ellie wouldn't be able to put up her hair because of the stitches.'

Anoria didn't know whether to believe it or not. She had laughed at Vee when she had said that babies came out between your legs and not out of your umbilicus. Nora still did not see how, but apparently Vee was right about that, so she decided to wait and watch, which she was good at doing. In the meantime, she concentrated on listening to the way Aunt Ellie talked. She certainly didn't sound old either. She refused to suppose that you could have something stitched to make your voice young.

Ellie had brought boxes of candy for the four children, and was amazed that Becc and Jonathan had not stayed at seven or eight years old as they had in her mind. The candy turned out to be boxes of chocolates, the size of which Anoria had never known existed, and Vee and Becc had seen only on the screen. And, oh, absolute bliss, they were all cream centres and they had a box apiece. Aunt Ellie knew kids, liked kids, spoiled kids. She especially liked these great-grandchildren of Sid's that she had scarcely known existed. It was great discovering that you had real family. The only ones she had Stateside were a mixed bag, acquired over the course of three marriages, none of which had a drop of Quinlan blood in their veins. 'I'll change my will,' she thought. 'Yeah. I'll see these kids all right.'

Now she was seated in animated and flirtatious conversation with Leo, perched on the raised side of the lily pond. A marquee for the food and drinks had been erected in the garden, with its flaps rolled up along one side because it was so warm and sunny. People sat around in the garden using assorted garden seats, cushions, low walls and blankets.

Miriam Corder-Peake had volunteered to do 'Anything at all, Mrs Quinlan, *anything*. I'm *used* to being Mr Quinlan's dogsbody.' Which was meant as a joke, except that it was the truth: Ballard Quinlan hadn't been able – or perhaps willing – to function without a dogsbody since the first day he acquired a batman. So Miriam saw to it that the caterers did their stuff, leaving Mrs Winifred and Mrs Rose to do their hostess thing.

Jonathan caused a stir. He had said that he would like to bring a girl, and in those regulated and formal days, young men invited only 'serious' girls home. Although he said, 'Don't make a great thing about it. She's just a girl I know . . . It's not a romance or anything', inevitably the family buzzed with anticipation.

A girl he worked with?

No. Just a client. She found it difficult to find accommodation and Jonathan was able to fix it. Her name was Elna and she was a nurse.

'Gosh!' said Anoria, 'she's not –' she knew that there were certain things that one did not comment upon openly – 'really Englishy!'

Not only was she not Englishy, she was not even whiteishy.

'I am not surprised that she could not find accommodation,' said Winifred to Ballard as soon as she could take him aside. 'More than just a touch of the tar-brush there. What on earth is Jonathan thinking of? If you ask me he's trying to rebel against something. I was reading an article about young people . . .'

'Mother,' said the Member of Parliament for Covington, 'these people have been invited here by us. We need their labour. We are all going to have to be more broad-minded and tolerant. If we persuade them to uproot themselves from their homes to come here and do the work that our own people can't or won't do, the least that we can do is to behave decently towards them.'

'Not in our *homes*, Ballard; that is taking duty to a ridiculous extreme.'

'Mother, we must move with the times. I served with Ghurkas. They were very decent fellows.'

Later, to one of her bridge partners, Winifred had confided, 'But the girl is not a Ghurka, she's half nigger.' Give Winifred her due, had she known that Jonathan was within hearing distance, she would not have said such a thing.

Jonathan turned pale. 'And if you ever find yourself in an operating theatre, it is more than likely to be a "half nigger" you will be relying on to see that you don't die, because if it wasn't for "half niggers", the health service would grind to a halt.' No one had ever heard Jonathan speak with such anger.

The relationship between Jonathan and his grandmother was never the same. Winifred didn't have it in her either to apologize or change her views. People were either 'right' (in all senses of the word) or they were 'very much mistaken in their opinions', and if they were mistaken then there was nothing wrong in pointing this out. Jonathan was mistaken, and should not have embarrassed the family; certainly he should have been open about her colour so that they might have prepared themselves.

Villette and Anoria didn't mind what colour she was. In fact they thought that she was very beautiful, with her black curls and skin with a permanent tan. What they minded was that their brother was behaving in a very un-Jonathan-like manner, being, as Vee said, 'Awfully, terribly sloppy. Did you see him light *both* their cigarettes in his own mouth? Ho-hum. Bumfrey Hogart himself.'

Rose welcomed the girl, Elna, feeling a little hurt that Jonathan obviously knew the girl much better than he had led his mother to believe. 'Jonathan never told us he was bringing such a pretty girl,' Rose said.

'That's really sweet of you to say that, Mrs Quinlan. I was doubtful about coming, you know, it being a family occasion.'

'We love our children to bring their friends home,' Rose said.

Merry was the only word for Elna's smile. 'My parents are like that – they like to know what is going on.'

'Parents worry.'

'I'm not complaining. I am pleased that they care so much.'

'Have you met the birthday boy?'

'He is such a remarkable man. No one would think that he could be a hundred.'

Rose was pleased that Jon's girlfriend had such good manners. She made Vee's disregard for the niceties and Becc's need to be shocking appear very poor in comparison.

'Jonathan, you must introduce Elna to Monica. Monica's our next-door neighbour. She used to be a nurse. I expect she'd like to ask you things.'

Rose and Winifred spiked the lawn with their stiletto-heeled shoes. Rose uncomfortable in the prissiness – to say nothing of the difficulties – that accompanied this new fashion; Winifred loving the way they flattered her slim ankles. Rose and Winifred had colluded in getting Papa a surprise present and, against all Papa's requests, Ballard and Miriam Corder-Peake had colluded in getting *Country Life* magazine interested. Proper photographs were to be taken of Papa Quinlan undoing his present.

Rose answered a ring at the front doorbell.

'Mrs Quinlan? My name's Trevelyan. I hope you're expecting me . . . you know, to do the magazine photographs.'

'Of course, yes, come in. For a moment I thought you were a guest, and I couldn't remember who . . .' Rose blushed a little because she felt that this was a rather gauche thing to say. 'Come through, I expect you'd like something to drink . . . It's so hot. There's iced wine cup, fruit juice.'

'Tea?' He raised his eyebrows and smiled. He had the most beautiful teeth, something Rose liked very much in a man – in anyone for that matter. She flushed again, finding her gaze fixed upon the smiling mouth. 'Excuse me, I'm all at sixes and sevens today. Tea, yes. Would you like to come through to the kitchen?' Again she felt that she sounded like the lady of the house directing a workman who had not used the tradesman's entrance. 'Everywhere else is overflowing.'

'Quite harassing these dos. I dare say you could do without a photographer, but I promise you won't find me intrusive. Mind if I have a look around?'

'Of course, then come back and get your tea.'

When he returned he was carrying the photograph of Rose beneath the Skylon. 'I hope you don't mind. I wanted to look at it in natural light.' He held the photo at arm's length and considered it.

'It was a very happy day for me.'

'I'd say you were daydreaming.'

'But I *was* happy. I and my children had spent a week there and at the Pleasure Gardens.'

'It's quite a decent shot considering: nice contrast, flowery femininity against the new technology, though I prefer the lady to the Skylon. Do you know who took it?'

'Oh, yes. Look.' She took the photograph and turned the glass to catch the light on the name embossed across the corner. '"W. J. Trevelyan, Shaftesbury".' She looked up to see him grinning. 'Didn't you say . . . ?'

'Yes . . . Wes Trevelyan, but I'm no longer at Shaftesbury. I thought I had seen you before. Never forget a face, though I don't always get the details right. Thanks.' He took the tea she had made him. 'I often wondered whether I would ever come across you again . . . in a professional capacity.'

'Why would you do that?'

He firmly turned her head and looked at her against the light of the kitchen window. 'Because of this. Well, Mrs Quinlan, I'd better not get settled in, I want to get this job done and get the prints in the post.' He stood the photo on the dresser and considered it. 'It's a good picture. I put an enlargement of it in my shop window during the Festival year.'

Rose, embarrassed, said, 'I'll show you where to go.'

She led the way through the empty house and into a hallway, where she replaced the photo on its shelf.

'I must tell the truth and shame the devil. Not long after I took the Skylon picture, I saw you at the State Opening and then realized who you were, so was really pleased to get this commission when I heard that I'd be coming to your home. I'm not one for deviousness! I hoped I could persuade you to sit for me.'

'Oh, I don't know . . . I'm not much of a one . . .'

'I know. You keep a low profile, as they say. Not much in the limelight.'

'It's my husband's world out there. This is mine.'

'And you prefer this?'

Rose shrugged her shoulders. 'To politics? Yes. I have a nice garden.'

'Right! Which is where I should be.' He snapped some pieces on to his camera and looked around him. 'Could I take one of you? Here?'

Rose looked a bit startled. 'In the kitchen?'

He smiled disarmingly. 'Not to worry, I am trying to do a collection – people in unexpected settings. People tend not to think of a Member of Parliament having a kitchen with a pretty wife in it.'

'Especially if they are women members, I suppose.'

Raising his eyebrows and pulling down his mouth, he said, 'Touché. I deserved that for thinking stereotypes.'

Rose said, 'I'm glad you get the point. Maybe you could come and photograph me and my compost heap one day.'

'Would that be more typical?'

'Yes, it would be of Rose Quinlan being herself.'

'And not the Honourable Member's wife? Good.'

His humour and easy manner reminded her of Leo.

Rebecca came into the kitchen. 'Mummy, Dad says we ought to do the present soon.' She flounced, swishing the fabric of her black skirt with its yards of taffeta. When she had come down ready for the party, Winifred had said, 'Heavens, dear, how did you manage to get your cardigan on the wrong way round.'

'It's not the wrong way round, Nan. And it isn't a cardigan, it's a sweater.'

'But darling, the buttons are down the back . . . and sweater is such an ugly word, don't you think?'

'Nan, it is the way I wear it, and so do my friends. Black cashmeres buttoned down the back are "today".'

'Back to front?'

'No, Nan,' Rebecca insisted. 'Back to front is when it is a mistake. This is back-buttoned and intentional.'

Winifred really did not know what was happening to young people, doing strange, untidy things to their hair – all of these things coming out of Hollywood and the art colleges. Marilyn Monroe,

Jane Russell, and women like that. Then there was the influence of strange men like this Bratby, who painted pictures of cluttered kitchens which would have shamed any normal housewife; and the peculiar Sutherland man – one suspected that there was something very nasty hidden away there. Sutherland's pictures were *really* disturbing. One did not know why they disturbed, because there were no objects in them, but the fact remained that the effect was unwholesome. Secretly she guessed that it was all part of the Labour years. No wonder young girls took to wearing their cardigans back to front and calling it fashion. Thank the Lord the Party was back in the Government seats once more. Nightly she prayed that Ballard would leave that terrible mob and cross the floor of the House to sit with gentlemen.

'This is my daughter, Rebecca.'

'I like to be called Becc,' she said.

Wesley Trevelyan shouldered his gear and framed Rebecca in his fingers. 'I hope that this is the young lady who is going to make the presentation.'

Rebecca knew how to take a compliment. She flounced her skirt and hooked herself upon one of the new, high kitchen stools, her skirt draping and her stiff-pointed breasts emphasized by the tight, black top. Rose thought that Winifred was probably right: young girls were changing. They wanted nothing more than to get as far away as possible from their mothers' fashions. But what was wrong with that? Becc looked very pretty. Trevelyan snapped a quick picture in that pose. Rose was proud of her.

Rebecca said, 'We haven't decided who's going to give Papa the present. I think it should be Nora, she's the baby.'

'Don't let her hear you say that,' Rose said.

In the end it was of course Ballard, as Winifred said it must properly be, who must give Papa his present. Not so much actually give it to him, as to take Papa to it. The great secret was hidden within a very large box, wrapped and beribboned and exhibited just outside the marquee, and it was around this that Trevelyan arranged an informal family group.

'Nice,' he said from behind his camera. 'Look at each other if you like, don't look at the camera.'

At the moment when the Member of Parliament for Covington released the clips holding the box together, Wesley Trevelyan fired off with his camera a whole series of shots.

Jean Thompson's smoke-harsh Welsh voice said, 'Oh Stan, just look at that: a twelve-inch floor-model Fergussson! Walnut cabinet. Oh, thass a real lovely mo-dell, Stan.'

The Aahs and Oh Nices covered the sound of Charlotte saying,

'Oh, Sid, it's a television. We'll be able to watch Newmarket and all the other gees. What's wrong, Sid? Sid, are you all right?'

It was Wesley Trevelyan, with his eye to the viewfinder, who saw the slow slide and the strange expression on his face as Papa Quinlan fell sideways.

'Sid?' Charlotte said.

'OK, Papa?' Ballard asked.

But Papa Quinlan was not – or was, according to how one saw a sudden and painless death in the bosom of one's family and friends at the age of one hundred – OK.

Without at first really appreciating what was happening to his subject, Wesley Trevelyan had click-click-clicked as the old man collapsed, click-clicked as he was laid down on the lawn, click-clicked as two women, one coloured one white, felt his wrist and neck as though they knew what they were doing, and shook their heads almost imperceptibly at one another, and had obtained a series of pictures of the last seconds of the life of a man who had been born on a July morning in 1855 and had lived for a hundred years.

Within a fortnight of the birthday party, many of the same people were again at Shaft's Farm, again taking wine and cake.

It was only Rebecca who wore the same clothes, this time with a large, black bow that substituted for a hat.

This time Jonathan did not bring the girl, Elna Birdham, even though Rose knew, from the hint on his clothes of the spicy perfume that the girl used, that he was still seeing her frequently. About the only conscious idea she had about child-rearing was 'wait and see if they grow out of it. If they don't, then it is part of their character', and she was certainly not confident enough to try to do anything about that. So she neither pried nor commented, except to say to Jon that he must not think his grandmother spoke for the rest of them. He had nodded and looked regretful. 'I know, Mum, it's a bloody shame she even speaks for herself.'

Although in agreement, Rose's only comment was, 'Don't swear, Jonathan.'

This time, when they gathered in the garden, Miriam Corder-Peake did not come with an offer to do anything, absolutely *anything*. She had been very affected, so Ballard said. 'She had never seen a dead person before.'

'Oh dear, poor *her*,' said Villette, who recently had begun to show a very vinegary tongue in the third week of her cycle. 'The rest of us are used to it, of course. We see our great-grandfathers keel over dead all the time.'

Her father had said, 'All right, clever Miss, one day your sharp tongue is going to cut your lip.'

Villette would not give him the pleasure of seeing tears, but forced them into her sinuses which made her nose run.

Behind her father's back, Anoria had stuck out the tip of her pointed tongue just enough so that, if she was caught, she could ask indignantly if a person couldn't even lick their lips now.

Ballard, Rose thought as he mingled with the mourners, looked very handsome in his black suit, stiff-collared shirt and black tie. He really was as handsome now as he had been when he had flicked a lighter at her cigarette twenty-odd years ago. Perhaps more so, for the hint of white at his temples softened his thick, black mane of hair. In the twenties and thirties, he would have been called a matinée idol or a ladies' man. There were always a lot of them in the public eye – John Gilbert, Clark Gable, Ivor Novello, Noel Coward, Jack Buchanan, Anthony Eden: suave, charming, and looking, as Ballard did at his father's funeral, as though formal black and white had been invented for them.

Jean, who was helping with the making of tea and coffee, said, 'Have to watch your man, Mrs Cue, or you'll have me runnin' off with him. Oh, he's so hansome I could eat him. He looks like Alvar Liddell sounds.' (This being a radio announcer with a particularly smooth and perfect accent and melodious voice.)

Thank God for Jean. Rose was glad to be able to smile again; the last days had been an absolute strain. There had had to be a post-mortem because, for all that it was his hundredth birthday, Papa hadn't seen a doctor for years and his death had been so sudden. It had turned out to be the simplest of deaths, switched off between one heartbeat and the next – except that there had been no next.

Charlotte had gone silent and become strangely acquiescent. She had not cried. Very occasionally an odd tear would well up in her eyes, brim over, and make its way down through the channels of her soft, lined face. Rose found that silent kind of grief so heart-rending, but she understood it better than anybody because her own emotions were always dealt with within her. Visible emanations of grief, anger, love or jealousy were frightening, and might get out of hand. Much better to set one's face in a pleasant mould and swallow them down. They might stick like acid-drops in the gullet, and rest like pebbles in the solar plexus, but at least in there they were not threatening.

'Do you want to go upstairs and have a rest, Gran?'

'No, Rose dear, it's my place down here. It's best to do things in the way you're brought up to do. In my day funerals were always very important occasions, people knew the rules and kept to them. My place is down here.'

'I wish I could help you, Gran.'

'You did very well. Sid would have been proud of you. Sid always liked you.'

'I know he did.'

'He was one who could always let people know things like that. If he liked you, he didn't mind saying. Same thing if you crossed him, he always liked things out in the open.'

'He did, but he never seemed to hurt anybody though.'

'Some people find it easy, letting people know that they like them.'

Rose briefly took the old lady's thin, dry, cold hand. 'And some of us find it a bit hard.'

A crack appeared in the dam that was holding back Charlotte Quinlan's grief, allowing tears to stream silently down her face. She whispered, 'I loved my Sid for over fifty years, nobody else ever. Only Sid.'

Rose wanted to put her arms about the old lady, to hold her and let her weep, and to weep herself. Everything that Rose felt about her own marriage was bound up in the old lady's declaration of love for the man she had married. Ever since Rose had stood under the Skylon at the Festival, and not wanted to return home, she had come to realize that she had never loved Ballard. Never. She had been smitten by him and, having been such a tender age when she had been bowled over by his handsomeness, she had thought that love was what she had found.

At seventeen years of age, she had been glad that there was somebody in the world to whom she could belong again, perhaps somebody who would become as close as Ayah had been, a man to take over the problems of her father's will and settle the need for her to have to do something about a career. I never loved Ballard in all these years. Not for a minute. Grateful, yes. She had enjoyed his love-making then, and they had had Jonathan, and in having a husband and son she had attained a place in the world. Once, whilst sitting in her own secluded bit of the garden, it had occurred to Rose that she supplied the face for one of those seaside façades behind which one stands to be photographed as a can-can dancer or flower girl. Rose had stood behind the façade of wife of a Member of Parliament. She felt grieved and cheated and angry, and swallowed all of those acid-drops. There would never be a day when she might say, 'I loved my Ballard for fifty years.' Offering a handkerchief, she said, 'How about a cup of sweet tea, Nan, with a good dash of whisky?'

Charlotte blotted her face. 'Thank you, Rose dear, that'd be lovely. You have one too, a really good dash.'

And Rose did. Several really good dashes.

Later, in the late hours of the night, Rose lay awake beside a relaxed and sleeping Ballard, trying not to roll into the dip his heavy body made in the mattress. Close your eyes and think of home. It had been rather like that. She almost smiled, wryly. Protected by half a tube of spermicide, she had not tensed when he came inside her: it had been quick and rough as usual, but that had hardly seemed to matter anyhow in the shadow of Charlotte's great unhappiness, and now that the cream had been sprayed down the bidet, all that remained of that conjugality was sleeplessness.

Sleeplessness and a kind of anxious tension she always experienced when she allowed her mind to drift back and back to thoughts of home – to South Africa, where she had been born. She allowed her mind to find its own way along the path to her early childhood where she had been before, a journey that went nowhere, because there was nowhere to go. The outcome would be the same as ever – frustration that the images of herself with her parents before she was orphaned were lost. Stacks and stacks of blank memory cells.

To Rose, South Africa was a place as strange as Alice's Wonderland or Dorothy's Oz, except that Alice's place was generously filled with characters, and Dorothy's yellow brick road was going somewhere. Rose's South Africa was an almost empty wilderness where occasionally an image would lead her along a track, only for her to discover that it was a cul-de-sac or a barred track. The only person she was sure to find was Ayah.

South Africa, in spite of having spent the first years of her childhood there, was a place which consisted only of fleeting, meaningless memories, and those perhaps not even true ones, perhaps made for her by Aunt Fredericka or Threnody Chaice. Certainly she could not remember her mother or her step-mother. Her memory began at the time when she went to live with Aunt Fredericka. For the rest she lived with it sometimes nagging at the back of her mind. Scents, the smell of leather car seats and petrol (gasoline it had been then); an image would begin to form, only to fade like Alice's Cheshire cat until only the grin was left. Rose's grin was always that of being in a car, comforted and rocked by Ayah. Gasoline and flower scent.

Certainly she could never bring forth her parents. She did not even know whom she resembled, for she had not a single likeness of any kind of her mother, and only a couple of photographs of her father, George. These had been Aunt Fredericka's, and taken before her father sailed for Johannesburg. George Weston, in a foxed sepia photographic mist, might have been any young man posing in a hard hat, stiff collar and narrow, high-buttoned jacket.

It was only in later years that she had grown more curious about her origins; until then her mind was never left alone for long enough, nor given space enough for it to be used for anything except the thousand-and-one details that went with everyday life. Six of them plus Winifred, Charlotte and Sid to attend to. Ballard's constituency, his Party, his career, and the general running of Shaft's with its six bedrooms, three bathrooms, toilets, passageways, open fires. And often there had been forgotten hamsters, fish, newts and tadpoles. Only when she was in her own bit of garden or, as now, sleepless, did she ever consciously wonder what it had been like, what had little Rose been like. Did they love her? Had she known about them dying? Once she had opened up her mind to curiosity, she wondered why it was that she had so unquestioningly accepted the history given her by Aunt Fredericka; even that was mostly filtered through the romantic storytelling of Rose's tutor, Miss Chaice.

Threnody Chaice was (according to Threnody) a romantic story in herself; she often referred to her position as governess as being in the tradition of many well-educated, handsome heroines of literature.

When Threnody Chaice was forced to look for employment – having burnt her previous boats – and went as housekeeper to Miss Fredericka Weston, she had not bargained for the inclusion of a girl in the household. Still less had she expected to become the child's tutor. But as it turned out, for the period when Rose lived at Longmore she became the warm and bright centre of Threnody Chaice's life. And Threnody became practically the only source of knowledge for Rose.

Fortunately, Threnody had been given an education equal to that of her brothers, so that she was able to teach Rose a certain amount of arithmetic, history, geography, and a lot about literature and films. Rose picked up, by practical application, the art of good cooking from Mrs Mason, Aunt Fredericka's cook, who was inclined to adventure and experimentation in the kitchen. From Aunt Fredericka she learned the art of gardening, almost by osmosis, because she loved the huge Longmore garden and hot-houses in which her aunt, together with Mason the gardener, spent most of the day. Rose was welcome to spend any amount of time with them.

Even so, the education Miss Threnody Chaice was able to give the orphaned child was, academically, a pretty threadbare one compared to that of a good school, but perhaps no worse than she might have received had she lived in Honeywood village in the twenties. Threnody did not know how to teach art, or biology, or home economy, and not even the most elementary science. Nor could she give her youthful companionship. She made up for it by taking Rose to the cinema once or twice a week, and up to town whenever there was a new film with good reviews.

And during all those seven years, when the schoolboard was laying in wait for truants who were helping out on market stalls, no truancy officer enquired into the quality of Threnody Chaice's teaching methods, presumably because the system did not cater for a child living within the walls of a large rambling mansion in a small village.

Threnody Chaice's story, although a sad one, was romantic, and so it was told many times to the abandoned child in her care. 'Ah, Rose, he was such a *manly* man, a man who loved adventure, and if I live to be a hundred I shall never hear a word of blame laid against him.' She would smile indulgently at this point, 'Of course he was a rogue, I knew that he was; it was his very roguishness that was so appealing. If he *did* sail without me, wasn't I just asking to be taken in by him? Wasn't I just asking him to run off home to America without me and take my ticket money and what little savings I had? But I don't think that is what occurred. I have spent five years speculating and have thought of so many things that might have prevented him from coming back from the steam-packet company, so many ways in which we may still be reunited. Ah, Rose, my dear, any woman who can say at the age of thirty that she has had a romantic adventure with a man as manly and roguish as Arnold Rigg, can say that she has had something worth having lived for. And waiting for? Do I *know* that he will not return? I do not. Do I know that, even as I speak, he is not on the high seas having made his fortune? I do not know that.

'We have a strange life here, me and you. You lost to your homeland, I somehow mislaid by my lover. But think of the remarkable women in fiction who have led stranger lives. Poor Tess who loved all the wrong men, Maggie Tulliver, Jane Eyre, and Cathy, who loved that terrible rogue. Didn't Heathcliffe disappear as Arnold disappeared? And did he not return with a fortune? Be sure, Rose, if any such romantic adventure should ever come your way, count yourself as fortunate. You know how I love the resolution of a novel. Time and again I am pleased at the outcome for Jane Eyre. But for poor Heathcliffe, to return and discover that Catherine is married to that milksop of a husband . . . Have you never speculated on those years when Heathcliffe disappeared, Rose?'

Heathcliffe's sudden departure and return, and his transformation from poor gypsy to wealthy man, was inspirational to Threnody. She would never lose faith in Arnold Rigg.

And so, it was from this romantic woman that Rose learned what events led to her being in England and in the care of her aunt, Fredericka Weston. The story comforted both Rose and Threnody Chaice. From time to time, details were changed and Rose would correct, and Threnody would look up and ask, 'Did I say that, Rose?

Perhaps you are right, yes . . . of course it was a water-melon.' Then she would return her gaze to South Africa. Rose learned her own story as she had learned all the others Threnody either read aloud or related, but because they were not her own memories, Rose always thought of her South African childhood as

The Authorized Version

Although both of George Weston's wives were known to Rose the child as 'Mother', there was no confusion in the child's mind. It was May who had given birth to Rose, and so May was, 'My Mother'.

Phillis, who came later, had taken on Rose when she married the bereaved George Weston. Phillis Weston was 'Mother'.

May was a true English beauty. Her bone-structure, complexion and colour bespoke breeding. As well as being beautiful, May was a strong-minded and intelligent young woman who, once having met George Weston, was determined that she should marry him.

Now George, having made a success in banking in London, was offered the opportunity of opening branches in South Africa. He and his wife would live in Johannesburg and settle there for a good many years. George did not yet have a wife, but he had been engaged for two years to Molly, and so they would marry before he set sail, and arrive in Cape Town with his bride.

Molly, poor creature, was mortally afraid of the sea, and nothing, absolutely nothing, would persuade her to venture upon it, not even to take a ferry-boat to the Isle of Wight. Poor George. It went without saying that any bank manager must have a wife but, catch as George Weston was, his fiancée returned his ring and set him free.

But, of course, this presented a problem if he was to set up in Johannesburg as a respectable bank manager. Bachelors are all very well in certain professions, but banking, doctoring and law are not among them. However, the Fates are ever-watchful and ready to work on such situations. So, whatever Fate was caring for George put him in the way of Molly's best friend, the beautiful May. Without hesitation, and to his astonishment and amazing good fortune, she (on hearing that Molly had returned his ring) proposed to him. What an outrageous action! But such a romantic and practical one. George at once saw that not only was it an offer he could not refuse and one that few men receive, nothing in the world would suit him better than to start his life in that raw and new frontier town of Johannesburg with a bold and beautiful wife.

So he arrived to take up his position in Johannesburg as the husband of a most desirable and now, pregnant woman. For all its frontier town privations, May Weston found Johannesburg to be wonderful, romantic and exciting – in much the same way as she found handsome George.

To assist her with the coming baby, May took on a young Asian woman, Fatima Kalim, whom she proposed training as an English-type nanny. The child was born and she was named Rose.

The several branches opened by George for his bank throve, and May and George became as much of a social success as it was possible to be in that fast-growing city. But, May, who boasted an iron constitution and *would* eat water-melon, without enquiring as to their origin, was laid low from eating one such fruit that was contaminated, and tragically did not survive.

At this point of the story Rose remembered how Miss Chaice would always pause and ask with concern, 'Rose, my dear, don't you recall anything? Nothing at all of those years?', to which Rose would truthfully reply that she remembered nothing except little jumbles of feelings, but these were mostly to do with Fatima, who Rose remembered as Ayah. Threnody would reply, 'I always hope that in telling this story something will come back to you. It is my opinion that we all need our memories, the bad ones quite as much as the happy ones. How else can we measure happiness if it is not against the other? Perhaps one day you will remember. It may not be pleasant, but you will be glad because you will then possess everything of your past that is rightly yours.' Then she would take up the story again.

So, May Weston was dead, leaving George with a household to run, a full complement of servants with whom he had seldom had any dealings, and, of course, the child Rose, about whom he knew very little, except that she had a sunny nature.

Then (and here come the Fates again) came Phillis Dartington into George and little Rose Weston's life. Phillis Dartington was a client of George's bank. She had been widowed only weeks before May had died, and was thus an understanding companion to the bereaved George. She had gone to consult him about her finances as she was about to return, reluctantly it would seem, to England. Quite out of the blue, she asked George whether he had not considered taking a temporary housekeeper, and offered herself in that capacity. It was not done like that, of course; Phillis did not have the audaciousness of May. This arrangement was made more informally – as these things are between expatriate English people – over sundowners and sympathy at the British Overseas Club.

Within the year, the widow Dartington had become the second Mrs Weston. She liked George's child well enough, but did not particularly relish having babies of her own. Soon Phillis and George became true 'Club' people. Bridge, dinners, sundowners, G and Ts, talk of Home, talk of plantations, talk of trouble and incidents. And, of course, talk of servants. Fatima Kalim continued as Ayah.

At this point the Authorized Version seemed to run out of steam. It is possible that Threnody had gleaned no facts or detail from Aunt Fredericka about her brother's sudden death, other than that, not many months after Phillis became George's second wife, she again became a widow, who despatched her deceased husband's child by way of the *Southern Star* to Southampton in the care of a Scottish engineer and his wife. At Southampton, Rose was met by Aunt Fredericka and Threnody Chaice and taken into their care behind the high walls of Longmore, the old Weston home.

In theory Rose was in the care of Aunt Fredericka, but in practice in the care of the extraordinary Threnody Chaice who, with Fredericka Weston, lived untouched by the real world – a little like Miss Havisham, but without the mice and cobwebs.

What seventeen-year-old girl, given such nurturing by such women, would not have felt her heart leap at Ballard Quinlan, the handsome man of the world who, almost as soon as he saw her, asked her to marry him. He had whisked her away and into his world so completely that she had never returned to Longmore until it became hers on the death of Aunt Fredericka, and it had been years since she and Threnody Chaice had exchanged Christmas cards.

Had Arnold Rigg come back? Was Threnody reaping the rewards of her steadfastness? Or was she creating a colourful piece of jigsaw to fill some other blank space?

Rose, at seventeen, had been drawn to Ballard's life as a comet to a planet, and from then on had orbited him.

These then, were the thoughts that occupied Rose the night of Old Sid's funeral. When, just before dawn, she drifted into sleep, she dreamed of the graceful, brown woman who wore a sari. Rose's sole contribution to those lost years. This time she saw the sari in vivid colour: it had been red with gold threaded bands at its edges.

Rebecca Quinlan, at coming twenty, had started out as a fine arts student of the Not At All Bad school, studying at the Royal College of Art. In her first year, following her own career plan, she 'ditched' portraiture and slid over into design and, as she had predicted, her father had not noticed.

Rebecca herself recognized that she did not have the extreme talent of some of her fellow-students, but knew that she had flair, which they did not. The kind of flair that had made her wear her cardigan back to front to emphasize the thrust of her breasts and to surprise with the long row of buttons at the back. It had only needed the idea to be used in a fashion magazine for the style to catch on; for a while every young woman under the age of twenty-five turned up in the office or factory wearing a black cardigan buttoned down the back.

She was, too, the first of her set to find a pair of the spike heels which were like six-inch nails, the wearing of which became *de rigueur* and which, if not fitted with little plastic shields, were banned in public buildings.

Much of her flair was for sensing a trend. Once young women began to abandon the notion that they should dress like their mothers, the world of fashion – where Rebecca was already heading – blossomed, finally recognizing an age between girlhood and womanhood. The put-down description 'in-between' was dropped, and the word 'teenage' crossed the Atlantic. No sooner the word than the deed: teenage fashion exploded. A small coterie of designers and art students, of which Rebecca was one, became influential in the new teenage fashion market. Recognizable Rebecca Quinlan fads were immaculate white cotton gloves cropped almost to the base of the thumb, black stockings and flat bopping shoes, bags like plastic buckets and slim, tight blue jeans worn with high heels. The latter flash-fashion caused women of Winifred's age to wonder how much sillier young women could get – nothing they wore 'went' any more. High heels and labourer's trousers!

Rebecca was known among London's young fashion leaders as Quinney. There was a 'Quinney' style which seemed to spread like wildfire through the girls of her generation. She loved clothes and she set her mind on becoming a designer. And getting herself noticed.

Ascot was the place where a new fashion designer must be seen.

'Mummy, do you remember that man who photographed Papa's birthday and did that super pic of me on the stool?'

Of course Rose did.

'Where did he come from?'

'He's a freelance man. Why?'

Rose was planting out lettuce for maturing in late summer, and Rebecca was following along with the water can, an indication that she was hoping to soften her mother up.

'Well, I need some pictures. The ones he did are really avant-garde.' Rose had long-since seen that it was a need of Becc's to be at the front of a trend or fashion. 'Avant' was much in the vocabulary of Becc and the people who surrounded her.

'Pictures of what?'

'Of me, Rosey love, of me at Ascot, for instance. Do you think he'd do it?'

'How do I know whether he'd do it – not so heavy, dear, you'll wash them out of the ground.'

'Oh, *Mum*! Don't you ever think of anything except your precious garden?'

Rose smiled, 'Of course . . . occasionally I remember my precious daughter.'

'Who was he? Where can I find him?'

'Wouldn't one of your friends be . . .'

'Juvenile!'

'Don't tell me that youth is out?'

'That man is good. I mean, those photos of me . . . us, at Papa's . . . they are so absolutely *right*. His angles, contrasts . . . I mean, the man is just so good. I mean, who was he, where did he come from?'

'He was commissioned by *Country Life*.'

'And?'

'I don't know. He lives . . . I think I remember he said he was somewhere on the Hamble River . . . a houseboat.'

Rebecca put her head slightly back in the expression of the moment and said, 'Wow. Really?' To live on a houseboat in the country was almost as smart as living on a Thames houseboat. 'What's his name?'

'Mr Trevelyan, I think.' Rose knew perfectly well; she saw his name on the Skylon photo every day. 'Wesley Trevelyan. He did that one of me at the Festival of Britain.'

'Of course. I simply must have him. Mummy, darling Rosey,

please do this one thing for me and I'll never ask you to do another thing.'

'Becc! You sound just like Nora. And you know as well as she does that it's a great big lie.'

'But do it, Rosey.'

'I hardly know the man.'

'Oh come on, Rosey, when I came into the kitchen that day, he was practically eating you, and you were blushing.'

'Don't talk so silly, Rebecca.'

'And you wouldn't have minded being eaten by him.' Rebecca laughed gaily and flipped the water playfully over the mother's feet. They had reached the end of the row. Rose sat on the grass path and took out a pinched-off cigarette and re-lit it.

'In any case, I wouldn't know where to begin looking. There's a lot of Hamble River.'

'Oh, you don't have to worry about that stuff. I'll find out the exact address now that I know the area and his name. All you have to do is go there, turn on the charm, and get him to do some pics of me at the races.'

'You could do that better than . . .'

'Darling, you really don't know men all that well. He just isn't the type to fall for my ice-cream cones. He's a real melons man, and you've got the fruit.'

'Becc! Stop it! You really do get worse. And I wouldn't dream of . . .'

'Flaunting your fruit?' She giggled girlishly and, taking Rose's roll-up, took a drag at it. 'Stap me, how do you smoke this stuff?'

'I was going to say I wouldn't dream of asking him to follow you about. He's probably got important commissions for Ascot week. Even if I did agree to asking him, which I certainly should not . . .'

'All the better. If he's working for one of the big mags, he'll be able to slip them some shots of me along with the ones of Debby girls. I know who I'd pick if I wrote a fashion column.'

'So would I, sweetheart, your ideas are so . . . colourful.'

'Listen, Mummy, I'm serious. I am determined to make my name in the fashion world. Making your name means getting everyone who's anyone to remember it. They've got to see what I'm like and what I wear.'

'Darling, I'm not saying that you shouldn't aim high, but isn't Royal Ascot a bit out of your league?'

'Rosey-posey, I shall not be aiming at fuddy-duddy ladies in hats. I'm aiming at their daughters, and eventually I'm aiming at everyone's daughters. Classless fashions. I want to design for young people like me. I don't want to look as though I'm wearing your clothes. Young people these days want to look totally different from older people.'

'I thought that they did.' Rose looked meaningfully at her own roomy cords and then at Rebecca's blue-jeans, so tight that the seam dipped between her buttocks. 'Rebecca, what kind of undies are you wearing?'

Rebecca slapped her own behind, quoting like an advertising slogan, 'The Quinney G-string. Undetectable in wear', then quickly flicked up the hem of her cotton top, which looked like a tennis shirt minus collar and sleeves, and revealed her naked young breasts.

'Rebecca! Is that the fashion too?' said Rose, feeling that she ought to protest, but not quite knowing at what.

'It soon will be.'

'You'll not get anywhere near the Enclosure like that.'

'I know, so I'm thinking of not wearing a top at all. Prince Philip isn't the mature type like your Trevelyan; he'll take one look at these pretty ice-cream cones . . .'

Rose could half believe that she might do it. Art college had not improved Rebecca's tendency to outrage, and her friends encouraged her. 'Well, that's certainly put the stopper on asking Mr Trevelyan.'

'Ah thank you, thank you, I knew you'd do it. If that's all that's stopping you asking him, then I promise, promise that I will do nothing to spoil your relationship with sexy old Trevelyan, and I shall appear on Gold Cup day so respectable that Jean won't mind speaking to me.'

Yes, he was that. Not that women like Rose used such descriptions aloud. 'Very manly' was as explicit as women of her generation went. And now she would not be able to think of him except as . . . well, sexy. 'Don't knock Jean.'

'I'm not, Jean's OK. It's just that she's Welsh and born with her knickers on.'

Rose knew that it was best not to rise to Becc's bait, so she started another row of lettuces, and Rebecca's assistance with the water can petered out.

If Becc thinks houseboats are romantic, Rose thought, then she should come and see this one. This one was not much like a house, and very little like a boat; quite unlike the others tethered close by. Those were mostly painted white and green with tubs of flowers and prettily painted bargees buckets.

Rose wondered how on earth one called on people who lived on boats. Walking aboard seemed rather pushy; perhaps one called 'Ahoy!'? There seemed to be no alternative to stepping on to the deck. As she was dithering, Trevelyan himself appeared through a narrow plank door. 'Hello. Hello. Come over, it's quite safe.' He helped her aboard and shook hands with the same movement.

'You do look nice. Rust with a touch of black – very original.'

Her flush didn't bother her. 'Thank you. It's ages since anyone said anything nice about my appearance.'

'Shame on them I say.'

'Nobody's fault but mine: I tend to wear clobber.'

Trevelyan unhooked two canvas chairs from the side of the boat. They were of the kind film directors are seen using; he hooked up a little green canvas awning over them. 'The sun's about to come around that building. Lemonade?' He poured without waiting and clinked lumps of ice in. 'I'd offer to gin it, but I ran out. I could rum it for you?'

Rose handed him back the glass. 'I'll go along with that suggestion.'

'White rum.'

'Even better.'

He took a half-bottle from a bag that was slung behind the door and poured generous tots into each of the glasses.

She sipped and said appreciatively, 'That's very nice.'

He sat opposite, stirring his own drink with his finger. 'Well, well, I would have taken you for a true G and T lady.'

'Why?'

'Those two rows of pearls you wore with your black dress, the Home Counties address, Elizabethan farmhouse, marquee on the lawn, garden parties with caterers.'

'You wouldn't make a very good Madam Arcati.'

'Tell me that I am wrong.'

'You are not right, and if I remember correctly, our first conversation was about your tendency to stereotype.'

'Absolutely. You told me off.'

Rose felt the rum flow from her warmed heart into her arteries and veins and then into her capillaries. 'How lucky you are to live like this.'

He grinned and reached across with the rum bottle. 'Let's drink to that, but come back in February and tell me again. Should I apologize?'

'For what?'

'For believing in your two rows of pearls?'

'Yes.'

'Then this I do –' he got down on his knees before her, and bowed his head – 'unreservedly and humbly.'

'Fool,' Rose said, laughing gaily.

He did not rise again, but sat easily at her feet, leaning back against the wooden wall of the cabin.

'I'm sorry if I'm taking up your time but I came to . . .'

'No don't, not yet. Let me go on anticipating for a bit longer. I was most intrigued by your note.'

'I can't see that there was much intrigue contained in a few lines asking for ten minutes of your time.'

'Ah, but the intrigue was in that you had written at all. I have thought about you a lot since that day when the old gentleman died. It was an awful thing to have happened on such an occasion.'

'It was. Poor Papa, he would have loved the television set.'

'I meant rotten for you, his family, looking on, giving him such a good time, and then it happening like that.'

'Don't you think that is how we should all go? Quickly, at a time when we are happy.'

'Maybe you are right.'

Rose felt relaxed with this man about whom she knew next to nothing. It was as she still felt with Anoria, as she used to feel with Vee, Becc and Jonathan, before they became ever more sophisticated and judgemental. They had grown up, and she felt that she had not. They knew so much. Nora had not yet got to the stage of making such comments as, 'Mother! You weren't thinking of wearing *that* to sports' day?' Rose, insecure and afraid of doing the wrong thing, let them all sweep her this way and that, like a sea anemone in a current of water.

Wesley Trevelyan was not as tall as Ballard, not as handsome as Ballard, certainly not as suave and clean-cut as Ballard; yet, Rose guessed, he too was a ladies' man. Ladies' man: what an odd phrase when one came to analyse it. A ladies' man was what Ballard was: they loved to fuss around him, helping in committee rooms, canvassing, organizing fund-raising raffles and fêtes. Wesley Trevelyan was more . . . ? She searched for the description . . . He was a man who liked women. There was a world of difference. He was as interested in what she had to say as though he was listening to another man. She remembered how he had listened attentively when Becc told him about her course, and to Winifred when she had told him about being a war widow. He had appeared genuinely sympathetic to the way war widows were treated. Becc had said he was sexy. He was interested in the opposite sex, that's what it was. Interested in women as people.

'A penny for them?'

'I can't imagine you depressed,' she answered.

He rolled his drink around in his glass, watching it swirl, then putting the cool glass to his cheek. He had a nice face: his eyes were grey and he had hair that was not cut short at the back and sides, but worn long enough so that it curled at the nape of his neck. His neck and forearms were heavy and brown, as was the bare part of his leg, which showed between his rope-soled deck-shoes and canvas slacks. Her eyes travelled back up his body until she saw that he was watching her. He grinned.

'I'm sorry,' she said, 'there I go again . . . miles away.'

'Oh, how sad, I thought that you were right here.' He indicated himself with his glass.

She felt herself blushing. If only I could stop doing that. Proof that I haven't grown up. 'I, ah, was saying that I couldn't imagine that you ever get depressed.'

'It's only too easy since the last election.'

Rose looked at him very directly. 'You don't like Mr Eden?'

'I can't *stand* Mr Eden.'

'Oh.' Rose really did not know what to say. She had lost her way politically and floundered dreadfully when an opinion seemed asked of her.

'Ladies are supposed to like his looks, aren't they?'

'Not my type, too stuffy.'

'What type is yours, then? How about Nye Bevan? You can't get much different from Anthony Eden than that. You must have met him?'

'Bevan? Yes, many times. I've met them all.'

'No, I mean the prime minister.'

'Goodness, no.' She laughed. 'He's the enemy. I really don't have a great deal to do with Ballard's political life. The only real live person I know who talks politics is Jean, my char. She has no option but to vote Labour, you see: "Well, I'm from the Rhondda, you see, we're all strong Labour in the Valleys." It's as though she can't help herself. Oh yes, and the milkman's Labour.'

'There must be other disreputable leftists in your life.'

'Leo and Monica who live next door. And of course there are our two eldest. They're given to sniping at the Party for being weak. As they can't bring themselves to rebel by going to the right, they have gone quite red, but Ballard will point out that it is the milk-sop Party they rail against that puts the bread in our mouths. Which is not strictly true; it's his agency which does that.'

'Will any of them follow their father into politics?'

'I can't see it. I suspect that Becc has been helping one of the mature students who is standing for the communists in a local council election. I'm afraid I'm a poor wife for a politician. It all seems so complicated. I shut my mind to it half the time. To be honest, there are times when I wish that it would all go away.'

He took her glass and made fresh rum-laced lemonade for them both. 'Did you teach your kids to share, or did you let the big ones take what they could grab and let the little ones have the crumbs?'

'Well I certainly didn't bring them up to be smash-and-grab merchants.'

'So you know about politics, that's all there is to it. One party shares, the other grabs.'

'I hate politics!' She stood up and went to lean on a guard-rail on the water side of the mooring. Wesley Trevelyan came up beside her and handed her the drink. 'I'm sorry, very boorish of me.'

Rose wasn't unused to drinking spirits, but three rums in the middle of the morning? She was silent, and aware only of the regular sound of his breath.

'You are quite right,' he said. 'I deserve to be sent to Coventry.'

The longer she was silent, the more difficult it became to think of something to say that would not sound tetchy or petulant, so she turned a little, smiled, and shook her head. She watched the current moving the tresses of green weed just beneath the surface of the water. Another of those tricks of memory which, since the night of Papa's funeral, she had been subjected to. An image of a small pool with goldfish. Rose had no idea where or when the reality of it had existed, but Ayah was allowing Rose to dangle her feet in the cool water.

She saw the feet, plump on the instep; fat, well-separated toes; straight-cut nails: the feet of a four-year-old.

She felt the mouth as it closed over her toes in the way that she had closed her own mouth over the toes of each of her babies, hearing their giggle. Several times over the last weeks something, vivid like this, had flashed upon her retina, clear and in colour, superimposed upon what she was looking at. It was as though someone had slipped a photographic slide before her eyes and said, 'Look. You must remember this.' And often she did, but only as a snippet, and always out of context. There was never any meaning to the scene, no continuance.

She remembered the fish, the coolness of her feet in the water, and the sun beating down upon her head, and the feel of her toes in Ayah's mouth.

A pang, and a longing to be back there.

More visions. Brown skin, thin dusty legs and ankles, and Rose's head nodding against the soft young breasts of Ayah, and the feel of the large soft nipple against her lips. Was that true? A soft hand holding her chin, turning it, a soft kiss. Sweet child, my sweet child.

His hand rested lightly on her shoulder and Trevelyan's voice broke into her thoughts.

'What did I say? What on earth did I say?'

'I'm sorry, I was miles away again. It was nothing to do with you at all. Nothing, believe me.'

'Can't you tell me? I long to know about Mrs Quinlan. Tell me about her.'

'What's to tell? I am as you see me. The lady wife of the MP for Covington, mother of four, hobby gardening – no, gardening is my *obsession*. There is nothing else to the lady.'

'Mrs Quinlan, you disappoint me. They say that the camera never lies. It does; it's the greatest liar there is. But not the eye, the eye never lies, the eye you can trust. My camera sees a great beauty, with a terrific figure, but that's not what she is. She is intelligent, compassionate, loving and . . .'

Rose, with her usual expression back again, interrupted him. 'I'll come here again if I go home with a bag of compliments like that. Anything else?'

'I was going to say "and very afraid of life".'

'I should say, still too immature to mix with the grown-ups.' Rose met his gaze for a second, then withdrew it again and took a piece of ice from her drink to suck. 'Goodness, aren't we serious all of a sudden? Actually, I came to see you to ask you a favour on behalf of my scatty daughter. To take on a commission.'

'The one who doesn't wear . . . ?' He twirled a forefinger in the direction of Rose's breast.

Rose's hand went there instinctively. 'It's a phase she's going through.'

He nodded. 'Art school.'

'I wouldn't blame that entirely. Rebecca was a born rebel.'

'Without a cause?'

'I don't know. I would say that she is a rebel with all too many causes, most of them to do with promoting Rebecca Quinlan.'

'That's no bad thing in women. For sure we men aren't going to do it for you; we've had it far too easy for far too long. But I think that we shall soon have had our chips. The Rebeccas of this world are going to give men one God-almighty shove, and we shall tumble from our high horses.'

'Actually she wants you to photograph her, and she thought I could persuade you.' Embarrassment caused her to rush it out.

'Does she really? What's wrong with Snowdon?'

Rose looked blank.

'The society photographer? Deb's delight?'

'Oh, I don't keep up much with that kind of thing. Becc says that you are the best – you are avant. It's the word of the moment: they pronounce it avanty.'

He smiled broadly. 'When an art student says you're avant, it's a compliment and you go running. What does she want, a portfolio for a model agency?'

'No, she's hoping that you will have a commission at the Ascot Gold Cup meeting and you would photograph her there. She plans to be a fashion designer when she leaves college, and she thinks that, if you photograph her, then she might get herself into one of the gossip columns and then one of the fashion magazines might take her up. I'm afraid it absolutely has to be you, which is why I have come to plead her cause.'

He blew out his cheeks. 'She doesn't want much, does she? Every woman there will be trying to get themselves into the gossip columns.'

'I told her that it was impossible.'

'Oh, it's not impossible. But I'm curious, why doesn't she go with you and your husband? She's got much more chance of making *Country Life* or *Queen* with the famous handsome daddy in the frame.'

'If you knew Becc, you'd know why. I told you about the red rebellion in the family. Becc's not Royal Enclosure material, but she's shrewd and a self-publicist.'

'Most of these young girls long to be in Snowdon's sights . . . I know Rebecca isn't most young girls. If we're playing stereotyping, you guess what my father does for a living.'

She guessed that he was trying to catch her out, so she said, 'Stockbroker?'

He threw back his head and wagged it at the sky. 'The woman's a marvel.'

'Do you mean that he actually is a stockbroker?'

'Lives in Egham. Old enough and rich enough to retire, but can't bear the thought of letting go. Am I transparently the son of a stockbroker, or do you get the jackpot prize?'

'You are nothing like any stockbroker's son I ever met, so I think that I should get the prize.'

'Photos of Rebel Rebecca?'

'Would you, oh would you really? Becc would so absolutely love it!'

'And you?'

'I'd be most grateful, of course.'

'Enough to wipe out my series of blunderings about the Quinlan family?'

Rose laughed easily, now that the dangerous moments had been got over. 'More than enough. Becc says that you "cost", is that right?'

'Depends on who is paying.'

'I will be paying, and I am not asking for favours. This would be my birthday present to her.'

'Then you'd better do me the favour of having lunch with me so that we'll be level-pegging the next time we meet.'

Rose panicked and looked hastily at her watch. 'Oh, I don't . . . I'd better . . .'

'Better sit down and let those three rums disperse. I'd never live it down if I heard that you were picked up in the street for being D and D.'

'D and D?'

'Drunk and Disorderly. Have you never been it? There, you see I'm a reformed character: I did not automatically assume either that you did not know the meaning of D and D, or that you had never been in that state. Do you want to wash your hands or anything whilst I cut us up some pie?'

Rose took the opportunity to go inside, not necessarily to wash her hands or anything, but to see what the inside of his houseboat was like.

'Why, this is wonderful! Becc says that everybody who is anybody lives on the river these days. She's absolutely mad to leave home and get something like this.'

'Is she prepared for the rats and effluent?'

'There aren't . . . ?'

'Not inside. But where there are humans and water you get the other things.'

'I have a feeling that she would take things like that in her stride. She calls herself a "tough cookie".'

'Where would you prefer to eat – in here, or out in the sun?'

'Oh, in the sun. Shall I take something?' She reached for the tray of plates and forks laid out ready. Two of everything. He'd been pretty sure of himself . . . and of her, apparently.

'Wise choice.'

'Why?'

'Less chance of me losing my head and . . .'

She thought for a moment that he was going to kiss her, so that with a momentary flash of desire, her thighs automatically contracted.

And she was right.

Taking the plates from her and putting them down again, he encircled her with his arms and pressed his lips gently, warmly, firmly against hers.

No man except Ballard had ever kissed her on the lips. His mouth was warm and soft and dry. She stiffened, but only momentarily, for more than anything at that moment she wanted him to go on kissing her. His tentativeness over, he drew her closer to him, pressed his lips more firmly. She did not know why she put her arms around his neck, pulled him closer and opened her mouth.

But of *course* she knew; her whole body responded to the romantic scene, a casual, illicit kiss; she wanted it not to stop. When they drew their mouths apart, they did not release one another, but stood close, each looking at the other in surprise, his hand moving, pressing her into even firmer contact with his arousing body. She was loving it.

'Well!' he said, his eyes searching her face. 'What's going on here?'

The wet on her lips from his felt cool, her cheeks hot. He wore a bright red smear of lipstick. She reached up to wipe it away with her fingers, but he caught them and took them in his mouth, weaving in and out with his tongue, circling the palm of her hand, her wrist, her inner elbow. It was wonderfully, terribly erotic. Sometimes Ballard kissed with his tongue in her mouth, its thrust in unison with his body and breath, moving, pushing, sounding like a piston, but those contacts felt not at all like this warm, sensuous erect tongue with which Trevelyan now made contact with her.

Breathlessly she escaped his arms. 'You've got lipstick on your mouth.'

'I shall never wash again.'

Smiling, she again picked up the tray. 'If the offer to lunch is still on, I really do think it would be advisable for us to sit outside.'

He grinned at her. 'Where I shall be safer?'

Half smiling, she bit her lip, unsure of herself. On the one hand she felt panic at having lost control, yet on the other she felt more aroused than she had felt in twenty years.

Surprisingly the moment of sudden passion did not intrude awkwardly into the meal they shared. They sat on cushions on the deck, their backs against the warm board of the deckhouse, his brown arm brushing hers as they lifted food, his knee casually in contact with hers. If they caught one another's eye unexpectedly they smiled, and once, to emphasize a point, he touched her hand and, although he left it there over long, she did not withdraw it. Their talk drifted from one unimportant topic to the next with the ease of two people who had known one another for a long time. Occasionally, the fact that she had lost control to the extent of kissing a man she didn't know came into her mind, but she ignored her conscience. She did know him, perhaps not the detail of his life, but she felt that she well knew what it was that made him tick. Perhaps that she had never known anyone so well.

It was mid-afternoon when she eventually said, 'I must go, I have to be home for Anoria, she'll be back from school in an hour. Thank you for agreeing to do that for Rebecca.'

He walked her to her car. Holding out her hand to shake his she said, 'I want you to know, I have never done anything like this before.'

Perhaps mistaking her gesture, he held on to her fingers with both hands. 'Like what? You haven't done anything . . . I wish that you had.'

'I don't usually go around kissing other men.'

'I know you don't.' He patted her fingers. 'Perhaps you should. I'd say you have quite a talent for it.' He grinned.

'My conscience will pounce on me once I'm away from here. I shall probably get nightmares.'

'I hope not, only sweet dreams. May I see you again? I should like to.'

She looked down at the water, the waving weed, the dabchicks, then back at him. And she would like to see him again . . . and again. She did not want this to have been the only time when she would feel his lips soft and firm on hers, his hard and arousing body adjusting to the contours of her own. She knew very well why she felt like this, why she was so close to telling him. Her most natural response would be to go back into the cabin and . . .

'I hardly think . . . It would be so complicated.'

'It would be worth it.'

She knew that he was right. But to go further might have consequences that were serious. 'I think I'd better go.'

He let her, but she wished that he would not.

On the drive back to Honeywood, old, stored phrases were twitching.

Ayah? Perhaps not, yet who else? 'Ah child, if you grow to be a woman who likes to be with men it is trouble, trouble, trouble. You are a girl now only, but there will come some day when you wish nothing more than he will stay with you for ever. And some day when you want only that he goes away far.'

Aunt Fredericka. 'Now then, Rose, there may well come an occasion when you find yourself out of your depth, or a thing may happen that you do not feel sufficiently experienced to sort out . . . Well, my dear, I am afraid that I have to tell you, it is not the slightest use coming to me. Miss Chaice, she is the one. Miss Chaice is a woman of great experience.'

Miss Chaice. 'It is as well to be armed with the knowledge of men from a very early age, Rose . . . I mean rather, knowledge of their ways. A man has but one natural instinct (and in that he is no different to a buck or a drake), which is to secure females for himself. It may appear not to be so, but this is my experience and I hold to it. Once you have fixed this piece of knowledge in your mind, then you will have no difficulty in sorting out their little ploys to secure you.'

Rebecca. 'That day when I came into the kitchen, he could have eaten you.'

Rose looked at her hands gripping the steering wheel, and teased and tempted herself by trying to imagine what they had looked like when his rigid, expressive tongue had made a kind of love to her. Here she was, married twenty years to a man who thought himself virile and long-suffering, yet until today she had had no idea that her hands could respond in that way. She knew that he would not leave it there, which was quite a frightening prospect, but one she knew that she would welcome.

When she arrived home, Anoria had cut herself doorsteps of bread and spread them with Marmite. Rose hadn't told the truth about having to collect her: I didn't have to tell him a lie, I could simply have said that I was going. But she knew that without her Anoria excuse, she might just have sat on and on.

'I couldn't wait, I was starving, Mum.'

'I'm sorry, darling, I had quite a few things to do in town.'

'Did you get my new tennis socks?'

'I'm sorry, darling, they were out of your size.'

Fiercely tackling the vegetables for supper, she wondered at herself. Why had she not told Anoria that she had forgotten? Guilty conscience. No, thinking it through, she decided that she had done nothing very bad. An encounter, a stolen kiss, a sweet memory. Rose recalled Madame Bovary. Miss Chaice had once said that Madame Bovary was intended to illustrate the iniquitous unfairness that was women's lot in a society where they were supposed to have lesser emotions than men. Rose now wondered whether this meant that Threnody knew this supposition to be flawed. She knew what had become of Madame Bovary, but not what had become of Threnody Chaice.

Ballard, who had been away for a few days working in his constituency, was pleased that Rose was willing to let him make love that night. But Ballard should have known, from his own experience, that nothing over-compensates as much as a guilty conscience.

Rose and Ballard had always taken a summer holiday with the whole of the Quinlan family, a tradition that had begun during the war when Rose and Winifred had taken the babies to whatever quiet place they could find close to where Ballard was posted. After the war, they had rented country cottages, and Winifred always went with them. Once the children had become civilized, they had gone to hotels in English coastal towns – 'resorts' was the word Winifred preferred: Weymouth, Bournemouth, Lyme Regis. This year, though, there were changes.

Charlotte, as yet not functioning very well without Sidney, said that she would come with them. 'Just this once. Next year I shall have sorted myself out. I'll do something stimulating: a WEA study tour, or some residential course.' Jonathan said that he could not possibly get away. Rose saw that this was a stage of letting him grow away from them. 'I expect he wants to get away on his own.'

'On his own? Ha, do you want to bet!' said Anoria. 'He's got a piece of crackling he's going to take away.'

Winifred being there at the time, Rose couldn't ignore it. 'Nora, where on earth do you pick up such rubbishy slang?'

'From the wireless, Mummy.' Anoria was a past mistress at wide-eyed innocence. At school she had become the girl in the playground who knew all the answers. Partly her knowledge was gleaned from Rebecca, who didn't mind answering questions about men and women and sex and bodies; but Anoria was also a great reader and listener to the wireless. Wide-eyed, 'Is it rude to say "crackling"?'

Rose knew all about Anoria, and treated her very much in the way that she treated her other two daughters – she tried not to rise to their bait. But when Winifred was present, it was always difficult. It was Winifred's opinion that children must be put down or argued down, and that Rose was too soft with them. Rose said, 'It is disrespectful to women.'

Winifred had added, 'It is a vulgarism, as I suspect you very well know. In my day, I should have made your father write out one hundred times, "I must not be vulgar".'

Rose willed the girl not to say, 'It didn't work, did it, Nan? Daddy uses vulgar swear-words all the time', which was surely hovering on Anoria's lips.

'Sorry, Nan. I just heard it on the wireless. I think it was Jimmy Edwards who said that June Whitfield was "a piece of crackling", I thought it was all right if it was on the BBC . . .'

Which was only reasonable. You can't blame children: we only know what we learn from grown-ups. It was never a good idea to tangle with Anoria's quick wits unless one was in a mood to sharpen one's own. And another thing, several times of late, Rose had heard, in the midst of a huddle of other ten-year-old girls, Nora's coarse little laugh and the giggle of her friends.

Villette and Anoria knew that they could not get out of the family holiday. Not that they minded going, because they had always quite enjoyed it when Daddy was with them for two weeks, buying all sorts of amusements, toys and books, going to Pierrot and Pierrette shows and band concerts, and fishing about in pools. It was just that they always went to such dull places. So they presented a united front and some persuasive literature gleaned from an advertisement in the *Observer* illustrating 'private family villas in Spain'. As an alternative they suggested a Pontins or Butlins holiday camp, knowing full well that, although Daddy had not thought of Spain, an advertisement in the *Observer*, and a brochure showing empty beaches and whitewashed villas with geraniums, would win him over.

Rose let her mind dwell upon that image rather than that in which she and Ballard would be thrown together for two or three weeks under the eye of the family, and quite likely with no secluded garden corner for her to slip away to. Family holidays had always been a nightmare of false cheer and perkiness until, with relief, Ballard was called back before time to deal with some urgent business at the agency. Maybe with the sun and the geraniums and with no Becc and Jon to kick their boredom around on chilly beaches, a holiday in Spain might not be so dire. And she could read endlessly. Three or four weeks' uninterrupted reading on a sunny beach, somebody to cook and clean and wash, al fresco eating, plenty of wine.

Maybe it wouldn't be so bad.

Rose had saved three cheap edition Lorna Lammente romantic mysteries, her favourite page-turners, and she wanted to read yet again *Catcher in the Rye*, perhaps to see whether there was a clue in the text that might indicate where she might be going wrong with Becc who, as far as Rose could tell, rebelled as a matter of course. Perhaps, as she hoped, she had not gone wrong with Becc – young people of today were just different. They were so much more knowing than herself. She wondered whether her own upbringing by an unmarried recluse of an aunt and Miss Chaice was faulty. Ballard thought so, particularly because Rose did not respond to him sexually as and when he needed it. 'Any normal woman would . . .' said too often over the years for her to believe anything other than that she *was* flawed. So, whenever she could, she picked up a crumb of reassurance that she was not – such as that she had perfectly normal children growing up in the 1950s. *The Catcher in the Rye* put Becc and Nora's little outrages in perspective.

Maybe he *was* right about her sexuality though. Certainly Monica enjoyed sex. But then maybe Leo had a different attitude to Ballard's. She could not imagine Leo bruising Monica, frightening her, ripping her clothes from her and then forcing himself into her so that she had to bite her lips to stop crying out at the burning sensation. But then it was likely that Leo had never had to do so. They were like street pigeons who displayed their mating instincts all year round. Often, when they had all been out for the evening, Rose imagined them going home and falling upon one another, enjoying one another. Enjoying sex in the way that she and Ballard had done a long time ago. In the early days of marriage when she had been an eager bride of seventeen, with life about to unfold as it usually did in Universal Films or a Boots library book. Handsome lover, attentive husband, a new home, a new baby. Monica and Leo appeared to have been able to hang on to their attraction for one another. Maybe Monica had never refused him. Time and again Rose had wished that she could ask Monica.

Rose could not imagine Leo using his strength to overpower Monica.

Not overpower, Rose. Rape. The word is rape.

Husbands can't do that.

They can insist.

They can force.

They can overpower and claim conjugal rights.

She had once looked up the definition of 'conjugal'. '*The privilege that husband and wife have of each other's society, comfort and affection.*' But nowhere had she found a mention of the right to the use of another's body. He could have felt no comfort in those painful grindings; he had lost her affection and destroyed all hope of society. Yet she knew that he had felt pleasure at having taken possession of her. Not mere gratification. She had seen from the way his body arced triumphantly as he climaxed that he had gained pleasure from the ripped fabric, from his show of greater strength, from his ability to do what he wanted, no matter what. If it hadn't been for that, she might have felt less resentful. But he had used her body with no more consideration than he might use his car, or any other of his possessions that had its particular function.

She looked for reasons; not excuses, reasons why he treated her with such lack of understanding and subsequent antagonism. Perhaps the war had to do with it. Men in general did seem to be stimulated by any kind of combat, using anything from cricket bats to bayonets. Trevelyan could never be like that . . . she felt sure that he was not. And from the gentleness of that kiss and his sensuous, pleasure-giving tongue, she knew that he could never be. But Ballard had given her something: she had security and children. Much to be thankful for. All that was required in return was that she give Ballard reasonable conjugal rights, supported him before his constituents, and put a family face on things.

A villa with geraniums and a Spanish beach. She would manage that.

Rebecca refused point-blank to go anywhere where she could not dash to London. 'I can't possibly go to Spain, Daddy, I must be here. Mr Joffe has put three machines aside for me.'

Surprisingly, Ballard had accepted that she must attend to her business arrangements. 'Just be careful, Rebecca. The man may be decent, but he's still a Jew.'

'Daddy! What a foul thing to say.'

He had looked hurt, as any politician does when his unguarded moment is seized upon. 'Good God, Rebecca, you don't think I meant Jew in racial terms? I have every admiration for them. I meant that the man is a natural Jewish businessman, part of his make-up . . . it is part of his culture to make the best contract for himself.'

She stared at him. Nail-hardness in her look, as she said, 'I suppose you mean that you would trust a Gentile to handle my first business affair with the same consideration with which you'd trust him to handle my untouched maidenhead? Trust an Englishman to be a gentleman? That's crap, Daddy. You either trust somebody or you don't. I trust Mr Joffe, and I don't care where he comes from. Mr Joffe is a good man. Put your money on it, Dad.'

Ballard had backed off. Somewhere in his subconscious he was probably aware that she was a young woman to be reckoned with. Still as yet only in his subconscious, but he had no appetite for locking his eldest daughter in a fight that involved the questioning of his moral integrity. His subconscious was aware that his everyday weapons – those with which he inveigled executives to swap their loyalty to one company for a contract with another, or with which he attacked other politicians across the floor of the House – were inferior to those weapons which Rebecca would wield. She didn't play by his set of rules. Maybe it would do her no harm if Joffe taught her a lesson about trusting no one in the world of commerce and business. Ballard never did. He was growing rich on the fact that nobody had any loyalty to anybody else in the world of rich pickings. 'You've never had it so good.' One thing you could say for Prime Minister Macmillan, he had summed up the mood of the British people.

Since Ascot, Mr Joffe and his wife had become very important to Rebecca.

Aisa (Aze) Joffe was the son of a poor Jewish tailor's cutter. Aze Joffe was one of the post-war rag-trade tycoons who had seen the potential of the 'pile 'em high and sell 'em cheap' philosophy. As well as producing petticoats and aprons, he had cornered the market in cheap contemporary furnishings – cushions, curtains, table-mats, lampshades, table-cloths and tea-towels. Aze Joffe's brightly patterned fabrics were sold on market-stalls from Aberdeen to Plymouth. He knew that people who lived in long terraces, on council estates or in rural villages, had had enough of the wartime 'Utility' brand – which was for plain goods that lasted – and so he produced goods that were not only cheap and cheerful, but cheap enough to be disposable when the next novelty came along.

Sally Joffe, unlike Aze, had never been poor. To her step-father Mel Adler, a successful Jewish jeweller, she was a princess. To her step-mother, although Sally was a princess, she was also a problem with a mind of her own. Sally refused to be matched, and brought her own chosen one home.

Aisa Joffe had only two of many qualities Mrs Adler had hoped for in a son-in-law – he was Jewish and he was going places. Fortunately these two qualities were at the top of the list of Mrs Adler's requirements, so she was willing to forgo the profession, the youth and the good looks she would have wished for her daughter. As far as giving her grandchildren was concerned, many middle-aged men were putting children into their wives.

Rebecca had thought that her mother had been unnecessarily reticent after her visit to Trevelyan's houseboat. 'How did you manage it, Mum. Did he make a pass? Look, you're blushing.'

Rose controlled herself and said levelly, 'If I'm doing anything, Rebecca, it is showing annoyance. Why is that you always seem to see something . . . suggestive in everything?'

'There *is* sex in everything. When men and women are together it's a sexual occasion. Leave any man and woman alone together for a week – it doesn't matter if he's twenty and she's forty – and they'll begin to eye one another and wonder what the other one's like in bed. Even I could see that there was a great male inside those awful clothes he wears . . . and I mean, when you've got your glad-rags on, you certainly put all your goods in the window.'

'Becc!'

'And quite often,' she continued, knowing perfectly well that her mother was so straight that she just begged Becc to be outrageous, 'it's a sexual occasion when there are men and men, and when there are women and women. Human beings can't help themselves. Our primary object in life is sexual gratification; the only reason we work is to get the wherewithal to keep going. And if we were all left alone to get on with it we wouldn't half enjoy our lives.' Her sophistication was a bit self-conscious. 'I intend to.'

There were times when Rose didn't know what to make of Becc's allusions. It wasn't true that Rose was a prude, but Rose, like so many women of her class and her era, knew little about any sort of love except the Hollywood ideal. She knew about homosexuality because of Oscar Wilde, but could not imagine, even after she had looked up the definition, what he and Alfred Douglas could have done that was so criminal. She had understood from an early age just what she could ask Miss Chaice and just what was taboo, just as she knew how much of her body might be displayed 'fetchingly', at what point it would become 'titillating' and when it would reach the point of, 'Cover yourself, Rose, you have no idea who might be looking.'

Rose was not alone in her ignorance. And Rebecca was not alone in not understanding how ill-informed a grown woman born before the Second World War could be. In the era when Rose was growing up, although there were pockets of enlightenment in certain large cities, the Shire counties were mostly still living with the legacy whereby pamphlets on sex, contraception and even mildly explicit literature led to the criminal courts. It was no wonder that Rose felt embarrassed when Rebecca, who had 'been through the State system' and then spent a couple of years studying art history, spoke so easily about sexuality.

There were times too when Rose felt that there were things going on in the world that, had she not been sent to England, she might have known more of. As it was she had had to rely on Threnody Chaice and what she learned from novels and films. Miss Chaice had not the slightest knowledge of how to be a mother-substitute – and who could blame her: she had been engaged as Fredericka Weston's companion-housekeeper and nothing more. There were times when Rose felt like an innocent in the presence of her knowing children. They had a nudging way of referring to things that Rose often found incomprehensible. From Ayah to Aunt Fredericka and Miss Chaice, and then directly to Ballard and marriage.

Taking a strange (but perilous seeing as it was Becc) pleasure in hearing his name mentioned, Rose said, 'Trevelyan is just a nice, generous man.' Rose, touching her lips with her fingers, heard herself being false. How easily she did it. Becc was right, as soon as Rose had stepped on his houseboat and he had smiled at her, it had become a sexual occasion.

'Oh, it's "Trevelyan" now.'

'It's the name he answers to.'

Rebecca smiled, 'OK, you don't need to be defensive.'

'I should say he is generous. He's got a commission so he'll be at Ascot on Gold Cup Day, and he'll try to do something about taking your photo if he can, but I'm beginning to wish I hadn't asked.'

'Oh, come on, Mummy, I'm only teasing. As old men go, I think he's rather a dish.'

'Well, those sort of suggestions can lead to misunderstandings. I didn't tell Daddy or he would have made some kind of fuss. He hates owing people favours, and you know what Nora is like these days, she sees double meanings everywhere . . .'

'Hell, Ma, you're talking like Nan. The only thing happening to Nora is that her sex buds are bursting . . . And, anyway, I'll bet Daddy makes passes all the time – Members of Parliament are known for it. Lloyd George laid every woman he met. Anyway, if your nice, generous old Trevelyan didn't make a pass at you, then you'd better ask if that's socks he keeps in his pants. You're a very sexy lady if you only knew it – which you don't, do you?'

The sexy lady description left Rose feeling very aware of herself for days, and caused her to look covertly at her reflection in the mirror.

But she saw what she had always seen: a woman of average height, with a slimmish figure, pale hair bleached light on top from spending so much time in the garden. She saw hard arm- and leg-muscles, the convex abdomen of a woman who has carried four babies, and breasts whose muscles gravity and age had loosened and softened and whose nipples were an inch lower than when, in the first flush of marriage, they had given her and Ballard so much pleasure. And her face was so familiar that, in the deep-set eyes, straight brow beneath silvery hair, narrow nose, straight mouth and small chin, she saw only the everyday Rose Quinlan. And, if she ignored the beginnings of crêpe and crinkles, she could still see young Rose Weston who years ago had had an ayah, a father, two mothers – and Threnody Chaice, who did not know how to be any of these, but who, in filling a gap in her own life, had drawn Rose through from childhood to womanhood virtually untouched by reality.

Was a sexy lady like a vamp? That would be dreadful. Surely one couldn't be a vamp and not know it. Ballard had said that she was a 'prick-tease'. Was that true? Trevelyan had become aroused when he kissed her, but it was not Rose who had made the pass.

Oh, but she *had* responded. Put her arms about his neck, opened her mouth, let him draw her close – and then backed off.

The difference was that Trevelyan had accepted that that was as far as she was prepared to go. Becc and Vee talked about girls who 'went all the way', a favourite phrase of the moment. How did girls like Becc, who presumably did not go all the way, signal how far they were prepared to go? Rose knew that the legacy of her strange upbringing was a strange bag of knowledge and a mixed set of morals. She had been as honest and open as she knew how in telling her children 'the facts of life', but Rose suspected that because of her and Ballard's failed relationship, her children's knowledge must be badly flawed. Monica had said all parents felt like that, but the human race still managed to find out which bits went where, and was always on the increase.

One thing that Monica did agree was that, when eight pounds of newborn child was handed in a towel to any mother for the first time, she had not the slightest idea of what she had been let in for.

Becc was no fool. As Rose had recently discovered, the human sexual motive *was* strong. It led normally quite truthful women into telling half-truths and inventions. It encouraged supposedly cold women to become suddenly flooded with sensation, making them perfectly willing to rush out at a moment's notice to keep an assignation with a man about whom they knew hardly anything – expect that he excited them. Sexual motive could cause the damaged libido of a woman to recover miraculously.

When the telephone had rung one morning about a week before the Gold Cup meeting, and she answered, 'Rose Quinlan speaking', and Trevelyan's voice at the other end had said, 'That's who I want', her instinct was to crash the receiver back on to its hook. Instead, she said, 'It's you. Hello.'

And he had said, 'Hello, Rose', and waited. Confusingly.

His disembodied voice brought back the smells of river water and warm, tar-washed wood, and lemon; and the sounds of raucous ducks and distant traffic; and the gentle seductiveness of the house-boat, rocking in the wake of passing craft. And it brought back the smell of his shirt, dried in the sun, and the sharp eau-de-Cologne of his shaving soap when their mouths had made contact.

'Hello,' she said. 'I hope that you're ringing about Rebecca. She's been pestering me to . . .' Ahead of herself she let it peter out, seeing what his reply might be if she said 'pestering me to get in touch with you again'.

'I thought you might like to come too . . . You know, moral support.'

'You don't know nineteen-year-old art students. She'd die with shame having a mother in tow. And actually, I shall be there, you know . . .' she was glad that he could not see her blushing. 'It's part of my husband's . . . ha-ha, I was going to say "circus" . . . you know, there are things we just *have* to attend . . . social *circuit*, that was the word.'

He had laughed, and she had remembered the reason for its resonance. His firm, hard chest beneath the sun-bleached cotton shirt. 'In the Enclosure?'

'Yes, I'm afraid so.'

'I'll keep trying, Rose.'

She had stood gripping the buzzing handset minutes after he had rung off, her hand trembling, her own pulse sounding in her ears.

On Gold Cup day, they had gone to the races, Rose, Winifred and Ballard; and yes, in the Enclosure. Winifred in a Hartnell frock, a gift from Ballard; Rose in sea-green Dior and a fashionable flower-band that passed as a hat; Ballard immaculate in his own morning dress, his grey topper a hint rakishly tilted, sufficient to be flattering but not too much. In the second half of the fifties, the Quinlans were doing very nicely.

Rose, on tenterhooks, not wanting to see Wesley Trevelyan, yet her eyes were drawn in the direction of every clicking camera. She had known nothing of the incident that led to Mr Joffe until Jean came to work with a copy of Stanley's paper. 'You seen it, Mrs Cue?' Confident that Rose had not, Jean had spread the tabloid on the kitchen table. 'Mr Cue know?'

'He didn't even know that Becc was at the races.'

'Ah well, he probably won't get to know then. See it says in the reading that they don't know who she is. Calls her "A young rebel". Anyway, it's not his sort of paper, is it?'

At the time when Rebecca discovered the Joffes, they were favourites of the jollier element of Fleet Street. Sally Joffe, who knew the value of publicity to her husband's business, usually gave the press what they wanted. So it was that, when this girl in an outrageous frock approached Aze Joffe in the car park and asked if she could sit on the bonnet of his car and be photographed, it was Sally who took over and gave Wesley Trevelyan the scoop that other press photographers hoped for, which was first sight of Sally Joffe in *the* hat which this year was trimmed with a replica of the Gold Cup trophy and reputed to have cost one thousand pounds. It hadn't cost that much, but it was a figure that looked good in print and added something to the 'Princess' Joffe legend.

Consequently, the Trevelyan photographs which appeared in newspapers and magazines were pure 'Princess': Sally Joffe and Rebecca posed together on the rear seats of the famous convertible Rolls-Royce with the rattan panels and heart-shaped passenger windows.

> 'Princess' Joffe in her Gold Cup hat with the new fashion designer 'Rebbel' wearing her own-label 'Peephole' design, and ready to take London by storm. The Princess's gold-leaf-covered hat outshines the other madcaps made specially for her. And what about the 'Rebbel' number? Panels of matt white and lime green. More peepholes than dress? It might not have endeared Miss Rebbel to the stewards of the Royal Enclosure, but will surely put 'Peephole' fashion ahead of the rest.

Not for the first time, Rose had realized that bringing up daughters was nothing at all as the books and district nurses suggested it would be, which was to put a nipple in their mouths, give them gripewater, put zinc and castor oil on their nappy area, take them regularly to a good dentist, send them to a school with religion, discipline and good examination results, and get them through their infectious ailments as early in life as possible. And there they were, grown-up and ready for the altar.

Jean had taken away the newspaper and folded it. 'I'll just pop it away. You never know, somebody very posh might come in.' Alluding to Winifred.

'Yes, pop it as far away as you can. Least said, soonest mended. At least with her hair hanging down like that you can't see much of her face.'

Jean, always ready with the tea-caddy, had handed Rose a large breakfast cup. 'Why don't we have a spoonful of condensed to keep up our strength?'

Rose had sipped the hot, sweet drink that tasted nothing like tea and thanked the Lord for giving her Jean's good sensible help and friendship.

Jean got on with her routine. 'You sit there five minutes, Missus Cue. And lissen, you don't want to worry yourself none about your Becc. She's got her head screwed on all right. She's just a girl that likes things happening. And you got to admit, the dress turned out a treat, didn't it, and she got a bum that I'd give my high teeth for.'

Trevelyan's picture of Rebecca started Rose thinking about him.

Imagined phoning him or him phoning her, thought about his nice voice, so that when the telephone did ring she jumped guiltily, yanked the earpiece from its hook and said, unaccountably harshly, 'Hello!'

'Rose?'

It was him. 'Yes, it's me.'

'Are you alone?'

'Not really,' aware that Jean's clatter in the downstairs cloakroom had quietened. Jean liked to listen.

'I'm working in the New Forest. I thought . . . Could you come?'

'Of course not, and that's miles away.'

'You could be there in an hour.'

'I'm in the middle of packing.'

'Much better be in the middle of the forest enjoying the weather. You don't need to answer if it's difficult. I shall stop off at the Jack o' Lantern at about eleven. I'll wait. I shall be disappointed if you don't come.' From experience, Rose knew that Jean was very adept at assuming the other side of a one-sided conversation. How much had her answers given away? She was no good at untruths. Even her children could read her face. She went out into the old stables and rooted around until she felt able to make something up for Jean.

'I've just remembered, Jean. I need some more bone-meal.' (Bone-meal! In the middle of packing?) 'So I think I'll kill two birds with one stone and get some odds and ends from the chemist's whilst I'm at it. Will you be all right?'

'What shall I say about when you'll be back, if some posh body calls in?'

'Ah, tell her . . . just tell her that you have no idea.'

'She won't believe me.'

'I know. But she doesn't have to know everything I do.'

'That's right, Mrs Cue, you should tell her.' Even Jean's laugh seemed to have a Welsh accent. Rose was sure that Jean knew that she was going out to do something she ought not to. Innocent friendship. Quite innocent. A morning in the New Forest with someone whose company she enjoyed and who had done Becc a great favour.

In the bedroom – as she flung off her trousers and shirt, stepped into new pink silk knickers, tightened a belt around the tan skirt he had liked and knotted a loop of amber beads so that they rested on her sleeveless silk top – she knew quite well what she was doing. Why else should she think of Threnody Chaice and of Madame Bovary? She knew that the silk clung, knew that the knot of heavy beads fell between her breasts, separating them.

Why was she doing it?

Because Rose had not forgotten his lips and tongue and the warm pressure of his body. And because on several nights she had awoken breathless and with her heart thumping as the result of an erotic dream. The desire to see him overrode anything Jean might make of her suddenly dropping the holiday preparations and rushing off out.

When she looked, Rose saw in her mirror a reflection that momentarily halted her. The circular tan skirt with its widely belted waist, the black top, opaque yet concealing nothing, looked striking and alluring. A grown-up woman with a knowledge of herself, of her worth. Valuable. Her own desire making her desirable. Rose had seen Monica look like that. When Monica entered a crowded room, even men who had not seen her enter were somehow drawn to look in her direction. 'Monica putting on the old-fashioned "here-I-am-boys-come-and-get-me",' Ballard said of Monica's entrances. Was this how Monica felt all the time, wanting to be got? On heat. Yes, like street-pigeons that displayed twelve months in every year. Although Rose could not bring herself to look into the reflection of her own eyes, she noticed that she did not blush at this moment of self-knowledge.

When Mrs Cue had gone and she had finished the cleaning, Jean made herself another cup of sweet tea, lit a proper, factory-made cigarette, took out the newspaper, and studied the picture of the lady with the daft hat and Becc, both smiling. No flies on you, girl. You just let them have a bit of a look through your peepholes and bash their 'ands if they so much as think of trying anything on. I bet *you* never sat up there on that car with no pink French knickers on. You could teach your mam a thing or two. People might laugh at Chapel girls being made to wear their 'lastic tight, but it do make you think twice. With French knickers there wasn't nothing between you and a barrel-load of mischief.

How did Jean know about the pink silk beneath Rose's skirt? She missed nothing. Before the phone call, the pink silk had been on the table ready for packing, and afterwards gone. And upstairs, when she cleared up, Jean had found only Mrs Cue's old cords and shirt thrown down with her cotton bra and white cotton pants. She riffled through the clothes on the kitchen table. The pink silk bra was still there. Well, well. She told Stanley most things. She wouldn't tell Stanley this. He'd always said that Mrs Cue was a real lady. Trouble with Stanley was that he hadn't never mixed with no real ladies. But Jean, she had been in service till she got married. If you went out looking for the kind of real lady such as Stanley meant, you'd be gone from home a damn long time.

★ ★ ★

Rose had sped towards the New Forest until she saw his car, parked where he said that it would be. He had drawn off the road opposite the Jack o' Lantern tea-house. Trevelyan was sitting watching the approach of every car. A shot of adrenalin surged into her blood when she saw him, made her feel breathless, and she wished for a moment that she had worn a bra to conceal the aroused state of her breasts. At least she had a clutch-bag to hold. She was convinced that she had never had any intention of deceiving Ballard, yet here she was, secretly meeting a man with whom she had touched tongues in the most intimate way. No other man than Ballard had ever kissed her except in the brotherly way that Leo did. No man had ever tried. She had never expected them to.

It seemed to take ages for him to get out of his car, walk from the car park and wait for a gap in the stream of fast traffic. He was more attractive than she had remembered, longer-legged, more loping in his stride. His hair was still outrageously long, his skin more tanned, his jawline . . . As she watched him she had a brief flash of memory of the last time and the rasp of his nails when he had apologized for having used a blunt razor, and another of the feel of his bristling jaw against her face.

He dodged the traffic and arrived panting a little as she stepped from her car. 'I knew that you'd come,' he said.

She smiled, 'I knew that I would come.'

He took her elbow, and together they dashed through the holiday traffic on its way to Bournemouth.

They talked in a friendly way about the work he had been commissioned to do, and about the villa the Quinlans had rented in Spain. Their eyes locked and said other things. Rose parked her car and they drove into the New Forest in Trevelyan's big estate car. There he photographed ponies, wild flowers, and great oak trees, a commission for a Hampshire Scenes calendar. He asked if she would pose for him, but she would only agree if he would sit her so that her face was hidden by her sunhat. He took careful romantic shots where sunlight rayed through the branches of the great oaks.

At about midday they called at an hotel, where he bought rolls, some thick-sliced ham, and two bottles of beer, which they shared seated where King Rufus was reputed to have been killed; here they speculated idly on what the place had looked like before Henry VIII had thought of planting a forest.

Trevelyan watched the most lovely and enigmatic woman he had ever encountered in all his years as a photographer. Every time Rose turned in his direction she caught him speculating on the body beneath her skirt and top. That's what he was doing; more than that, he was wondering how long it would be until she allowed him to discover it. Her naïvety excited him as much as her face and figure; she was his own age, a woman with four children, yet she seemed to have a virginal aura. That was ridiculous, of course, for virgins aren't given to swallowing tongues at a first kiss.

He studied her physical beauty. Wonderful head and neck. Full-face and profile it was perfect. It also had to do with the impression she gave of hauteur, which Trevelyan knew masked surprising insecurity. Head erect, she gazed at the world down a fine, straight nose; often when she smiled, only the outer corners of her mouth lifted, as though she might be misunderstood and have to retract and quickly pull it back in place. When she sat, she sat still. When she stood, she stood straight. When she walked, it was with an unhurried, even pace that Trevelyan had often admired in water-carrying black women and sari-wearing Asian women. It was not possible to imagine her rushing about, fidgeting, tripping. Superficially, a cold beauty. Trevelyan knew otherwise. He had seen her giggle, watched passion flare behind her gaze, and known her response to a kiss.

He often moved in the same circles as Ballard Quinlan, and knew him to be a bigot. What had this god-given woman seen in a man like that?

There was no justice.

He watched as she walked across the grass and into the hotel. A small breeze belled out her skirt, but she did not brush it down as she had on that day a few weeks back when she had stood looking down at ducklings. Her hips swayed smoothly, her hair was flicked by the breeze. As she mounted the steps, she seemed quite unaware that the eyes of every person eating out on the terrace were turned in her direction.

He had had a few idle thoughts about a seduction scene. He knew the forest well; there were perfect places: dells with dewponds and rosy banks, where such a lovely woman should be seduced. But although he had not abandoned that setting, he realized that it would be the easiest thing in the world to be too hasty and cause her to take flight.

Since that day when she had stepped gingerly aboard and accepted his plea that she eat lunch with him, he had wanted her more than he had wanted any woman before. But, as he now knew from long hours of thinking about what to do, he wasn't totally sure that he wanted her whilst she belonged to Ballard Quinlan and slept with him. Trevelyan was not jealous, but it was that, if she let him make love to her, he couldn't bear the thought that he might be following Ballard Quinlan.

Twice he had had a married mistress; and times without number in many countries he had enjoyed prostitutes, sharing them with God knew how many men. What troubled him was that he had imagined what might be going on in her head if she should give herself to himself after being taken by Quinlan. That was how he thought of it – Trevelyan making love, Rose giving herself, Ballard taking her. Whichever way he looked at it, Trevelyan came to the same conclusion: they would be two men sharing the one woman in the world who should not be shared.

He would get her, of that he had no doubt. If he had arranged this outing today to find out something about her, the fact that she had come, and her expression when they came face to face again, and the fact that she had been aroused ever since she had got out of the car and had given up trying to hide it, assured him that she was interested in him. He could afford to wait for a time when Quinlan was off on one of his trips abroad. He longed to know every inch of her, but until she came to him unshared, he would be willing to make any kind of love with her except that!

I love her, he thought. God Almighty, I love her. Just that thought, just for a moment, dissolved everything he had just thought about not wanting to share her. His desire for her, as she walked back down the hotel steps, again followed by a dozen pairs of eyes, overrode everything.

Later they had wandered deeper into the dappled sunlight of the oak trees, crunching oak-apples beneath their feet, sending up pungent wafts from the crushed mycelium of fungi, spore-clouds of fern-fronds and mosses. Stiff-legged New Forest ponies crossed their aimless path, then disappeared into the undergrowth of hazels; a fawn and white goatling followed them and posed prettily before Trevelyan's lens.

Just after the sun had reached its apogee, they had lain together in the shade of the ancient trees, where they gave in to the long and passionate kiss that had been held back all morning. Looking down at her, watching her response, he sensuously and at length re-learned the contours of her mouth, lingeringly running the tip of his tongue across and between her lips and, dallying like some young lover deep in a forest glade with his maiden, he kissed her eyes, her ears, her neck, her tongue. She had kissed him, had learned him, had watched his expression as she had eased her blouse from the anchor of the wide belt, and listened to her own intake of breath when his lips touched her breast with a sensuousness that had nothing to do with Ballard's kind of prurient insistence, but everything to do with tenderness. As he bent over her, his long hair brushed her shoulders. They had kissed long and wonderfully.

And that was all.

But it was indeed not all that they wanted.

They had parted in a state of mild bewilderment, surprised by ramblers. The moment had come, they were alone and almost intoxicated with their desire for one another. Each of them had wanted it, yet neither of them had made that one small move where in a moment they would have become lovers. He had made up his mind that he would only respond, and she expected the move to come from him.

She ached for him. She thought: I'm really attracted to him. What am I going to do? I want to be with him again.

Rose Quinlan was awakening. Trevelyan had done something to her that had acted like switching on a light for her to see clearly. Rose Quinlan was coming to life.

With these events as the precursors to the annual family holiday, Rose was surprised to find herself enjoying Spain. Both Charlotte and Winifred agreed that Rose hadn't looked so bright and sparkling for years. Spain certainly suited her.

Except for Ballard, who was used to foreign travel, it was an adventure for all of them. In Britain, before the Second World War, it had been only salary earners who took proper vacations. Wage-packet workers with few paid holidays, if they left home at all, expected no more than to stay with relatives in another town one year and return the compliment the year after; railway workers taking advantage of ticket 'privileges' might take day trips around the area in which they lived, or go to the next town – where there might be a cinema, a market or a pier – for a special treat. Vast numbers of people never went anywhere. Now, however, wage earners were getting big ideas. Holiday camps were thriving. People were getting a taste for going away, small numbers venturing to Jersey or Guernsey, and a fair few to France and Spain. There was a curb on the amount of money a person could take out of the country, but the combined allowances of a family such as the Quinlans permitted them to take enough sterling to rent a nice roomy villa on the Costa del Sol, where they were to live for a month.

Villette was enraptured by the house. Before they had been there for a week, she had picked up a good smattering of Spanish, and could communicate better than her father who knew a little of the language, and went about with an English/Spanish dictionary and a lot of charm. At first Rose managed very well, with a small essential vocabulary of nouns, plus politeness and smiles; Winifred made do with gestures and a raised voice.

'It seems very rude,' Rose said, 'to have to point at what one needs.'

'Continentals don't mind,' Ballard said, 'so long as they sell you something.'

'But I should like to talk to people.' So she bought a simple phrase book and did something about it, amazing herself and the rest of the family by discovering that she had a flair for the language. By the end of the first week she was able to go into the kitchen and hold a halting conversation with Maria ('Well, aren't they all Marias?' said Villette), who was a kind of cook-general who went with the house ('Villa,' corrected Rose). Rose's obvious effort pleased Maria no end, causing her to smile and warm to the English woman who, Maria thought, had the look of high birth and the nature of a deer. Whenever they were together, Maria spent time offering Rose new words with the gesture of a conjurer pulling silk scarves from her own mouth.

Ballard took Anoria on expeditions to places of interest, whilst Villette and Rose mostly swam and sunbathed. Winifred read novels, and Charlotte wrote pages and pages of a journal that she had been keeping since she was a young girl. When Rose wasn't soaking up sunshine on the sand, she was poking about in the extraordinary garden which slid down a rocky slope to join the beach.

'There's no soil to speak of, yet just look at the flowers.'

'You wouldn't know what to do with your time if you had a garden like this,' Ballard said. 'You'd make heaps and heaps of compost, I suppose.'

Rose's compost heaps were a family joke. She hated even a single eggshell or a bunch of carrot-tops to be put into the refuse bin. 'We owe it to the soil. If we take goodness out, then we have to put back. I think that I would be a totally different person if I had a garden like this. I should grow red geraniums in oil-jars and let the rest ramble to its heart's content and buy all my vegetables from the market. Honestly, I couldn't compete with the stuff they sell there.'

Rose stretched luxuriously in the sun, her pale streaks now very white and the hairs on her arms and legs glistening against her suntanned skin. Villette, with her fists supporting her chin and elbows resting in the warm sand, had been watching her mother. 'You like it here, don't you, Mummy?'

Rose looked up from her book and took in the sea and the gently shelving white sand, then rolled languidly on to her back facing the amazing blue sky. 'I do. Yes, I like it very much.'

'You seem different. Younger.'

'Perhaps it is Nan's sun-cream.'

'Brylcreem! How can you use it?'

'It is supposed to give one a dark tan – I want to show off to Monica.'

'But haircream! Ugh!'

'All the models use it. Nan said she read it in –'

'– Don't tell me . . . *The Lady*.'

'Brylcreem doesn't sound very like *The Lady*, does it?'

Vee giggled. 'She reads *Titbits* and *Weekend*. You can always find them under her cushion. I don't know why she doesn't just read them and enjoy them.' She pondered a moment. 'Maybe reading them secretly is what she enjoys . . .' In a stage whisper, 'Illicit magazines. She probably gets them under plain wrapper.'

Rose's brow gathered as she wondered how it was that her daughters had become so knowing in spite of Rose's potted puberty talks. 'Your body is preparing itself for when you are a woman. It's going to go on doing this until you have had all the children you want; then when you are about forty or fifty it will stop. It is nothing to worry about, it happens to all girls of your age. You wear this belt and these. If you feel any discomfort use a hot-water bottle and aspirin. It doesn't take long to get used to it all.'

This was not news to any of her daughters. They would not experience the trauma of believing that they had some dreadful terminal disease. But she didn't tell them anything about how it could all go on for years and years after a woman had had more children than she ever wanted, had overflowed with them.

Nothing about the getting of children.

Nothing about not getting them.

Nothing of the part their husbands would need to play.

Time enough for that. But they knew. Perhaps, she thought, we all know it instinctively. Certainly it had been unsurprising to Rose when seeing zebras mating at Whipsnade Zoo, and she had been told by Threnody Chaice that the animals were making baby zebras. Of course. Hadn't she seen pretty much the same in the bird and animal population in the gardens in Johannesburg, and later those at Longmore? Had she? Or had this notion somehow crept into the Authorized Version of life before she was orphaned?

Observant Villette was right. Rose did feel different.

What Vee could not know was the reason for her mother's calm and luxuriant voluptuousness – not that Villette would have used that description. What she saw was her mother stretched out on the sand, looking into the far distance and smiling faintly, everything going on inside her head. She was like one of those small white balls found in hedgerows that appears to be a knot of silk until suddenly it explodes as a thousand minute spiders. Vee, not realizing that she was growing more like her by the day, envied her mother's looks. It was not often that anyone except Ballard saw Rose in a state of undress; she was so often wearing gardening clothes that it was always a surprise to her family when there was a special occasion and she appeared in high heels and a silk dress, when Anoria would make her usual joke, 'Gosh, look, Mum's got legs!'

Vee, inspecting her mother now at close quarters, wondered what it must feel like to have a real Venus's cushion – which was what Mrs Daish, her biology teacher called it – and to have breasts that moved as though they were two creatures. Her own, although she was now fifteen, were still insignificant and too firm to be mobile. And, as she often did since she had seen it happening a few weeks ago when she was out in Ludd Meadow looking for flowers to press, she wondered what it was like to have a man lying on top of you. Why didn't the heaviest person lie underneath the light one?

She had seen it happening, and had watched briefly until it came to her that this was probably spying and she ought to stop. Vee had left the meadow quietly and with the knowledge that the purpose of 'the act of coitus' (as Mrs Daish referred to it) was not only to 'beget children'. There had been a lot of fun going on in the meadow. She hadn't been shocked, just surprised and interested. Until then she hadn't liked to think that quite oldish people did it, especially in daylight in a hayfield. But it had been quite smashing.

The incident in Ludd Meadow had pushed Vee a bit further through the course of understanding her own developing sexuality, for now at nights, as well as having the arms of Elvis the King, she had Uncle Leo . . . *Leo* to fall asleep on.

And Rose had Trevelyan.

Warm nights and plentiful wine and images of love in the New Forest helped Rose to feel relaxed when Ballard turned to make love to her at night, and to feel tranquil during the days when she lay becalmed at the water's edge. Habit got her up at the crack of dawn, when usually she took her tobacco and coffee and went to sit amongst the craggy rocks that composed the Spanish garden.

All through these days, Trevelyan was loving her. At night she heard his breathing in the regular lapping of the waves below the villa. In the pearly morning light, he suddenly appeared on the cliff path. On the beach it was his footsteps she heard coming towards her, pressing into the wet sandy beach. A whiff of his warm shirt in the basket of washing Maria was sorting, and the wine that lingered about his lips on the neck of a bottle. And she lay, her eyes half closed, looking at the waves, looking at the sky, looking at the pale sand, working out all the possible and probable ways that might bring him coincidentally to this stretch of beach.

Vee sat up and tied her halter more tightly, preparing to swim. 'Come on, Mum, get some of that grease off you.'

They high-stepped into the warm water and then sculled easily with the waves. 'Lovely,' Vee said. 'Poor old Becc, she doesn't know what she's missing.'

'I went on a seaside holiday when I was a child in South Africa.'

'Can you still remember it?'

'I'm not sure. I remember Ayah taking me to buy a sunhat, I think.'

'Poor Mummy, it must have been awful, having to be sent away from your home.'

'I'm sure it was preferable to being an orphan in Johannesburg. I really had a lovely time growing up at Longmore. Miss Chaice was such a strange, interesting person. We kept in touch at one time. I'd really like to know what she is doing now.'

As Rose was dutifully oiling her skin again after her swim, down the steps from the villa came Anoria, returned from her excursion with her father, Winifred and Charlotte with rolled towels, Maria carrying a basket with the food, followed by Ballard carrying another. Maria, endowed with the womanly qualities and relaxed movements of her race, Winifred burdened with those of her race and of the class to which she now belonged, Charlotte and Nora, unendowed and unburdened and unself-conscious. Ballard, watching the movement of Maria's buttocks and the way her unrestrained bosom moved as her foot alighted on every step, was constrained to remember that there wasn't a cat in hell's chance, and that anyhow Maria's uncle was the village priest.

'I always hope that one day I shall be able to go back,' said Rose, a little regretful that having Vee to herself was over.

'To South Africa?'

'Yes, where I was born.'

'Which means that you are South African? How weird.' She withdrew for a few seconds. 'I could tell people that my mother is a South African. Isn't that funny?'

'Is it?'

'I can't think of you as being anything except English.'

'And I am English.'

'I dare say if I went to live abroad, I should like to come back to England when I was older. I'm sure that you will go back one day, Mummy . . . Just for a holiday. You wouldn't want to stay.'

'No, darling, I'd never want to stay anywhere except home.'

Vee said, 'I'm glad. I love all this. I love the sun and the hot weather, but I like home.' Villette, needing to touch her mother, began to plait Rose's hair. 'I wish that I had inherited your hair and not Daddy's.'

'Don't wish that, Vee, black hair is so positive. Everybody thinks that blonde hair grows out of empty heads. Can you think of one important person who has blonde hair?'

'Marilyn Monroe, Betty Grable.'

'I mean important, not famous. When I went to listen to Daddy speak in the House, I don't remember seeing a single fair-headed person there.'

'There might be if they let in more lady members.'

'I don't see what lady MPs have to do with it. Nobody keeps lady members out, Vee. Any woman over twenty-one can stand if she has the ambition.'

The others came and disturbed the quiet atmosphere. Villette asked at once, 'Mummy says that any woman can stand for Parliament. Is that true, Daddy?'

'Yes, it's true. Why? Are you planning your future?' He sat beside Rose and patted her with unusual familiarity, 'Or is it your mother who is thinking of standing?'

'Why not?' Villette said. 'The first blonde in the House of Commons.'

'I shouldn't mind,' said Anoria.

Winifred said, 'I believe Lady Astor was fair . . . but then, maybe not, she was never without a hat. Anyway, Anoria, who do you suppose would run the house and cook dinner? It is a very demanding vocation. You know how hard Daddy works.'

'I didn't mean Mummy, I meant that *I* shouldn't mind being an MP like Daddy. But if Mummy did want to, then Jean could do the housework. She's always glad of a few hours extra, isn't she, Mum?'

That it was Charlotte who interposed was surprising, as generally speaking she did not often air her views these days. 'And who do you suppose is going to see to the Thompson family if Jean is looking after the Quinlans?'

'Oh, the Thompsons' house is only small, and they haven't got things like bathrooms to clean. She could easily do it in her spare time.'

'And David and Cliff could . . . ?' But Anoria, with her mouth full, considered, came to no conclusion and dropped the subject.

'Now, Mother,' said Winifred, 'we shouldn't be getting into the realms of politics in this beautiful place.'

Charlotte said, 'That's not politics, Winnie, it's feminism.'

'What's feminism?' Nora said, her interest again engaged.

'Something you don't hear a lot about these days. Everybody got so fired up about equal shares in your father's election that they forgot it was women as well as men who were supposed to be equal. That's feminism when it's at home.'

Rose said, 'I imagine that this place must have a great history of politics.'

Charlotte said, 'I was thinking about that this morning, I was thinking of the Civil War. It was at the time when Rebecca was born. I remembered thinking at the time that I was so thankful that Rose was not a Spanish mother with a toddler and a baby.'

'Is that politics?' Anoria asked.

Ballard laughed, 'No, sweetheart, it is your great-grandmother being a suffragette again.'

'A suffragette?' Villette asked. 'Were you, Gran?'

'I was not.' She prodded Ballard genially in the back, 'as well your father knows. I was a suffra*gist*. Try to remember the distinction.'

'We did suffragettes at school. They chained themselves to railings and tried to stop the Grand National to get votes for women.'

'I suppose those two memories are doomed to be the sole history of a great movement,' Charlotte said. 'Now you girls listen, and the next time somebody tells you that story, you tell them that suffragettes were trying to get votes only for a few women, not women like Jean. It was *we*, the suffragists, who wanted votes for *everybody*.'

'And now everybody has a vote,' said Winifred, trying to wind up a topic that had always given her trouble. She had married into a family of Liberals, and she had hoped that, under her guidance, Ballard would turn from their views towards the views of people who came from the top drawer. Nobody who was anybody wanted to know Liberals. The only time she had felt Ballard safe from the liberal notions of the Quinlans, was when he had been in boarding school. It had never occurred to her that as an army officer he would meet any men with less than sound views, yet it had been within the armed forced that the leftists had had free rein. And what had come of that? Young officers with public school and university behind them joining Labour.

'Come on, you girls,' said Ballard, ending the conversation by pulling off his shorts and shirt, 'beat you down to the sea.'

Anoria followed in her woollen swimsuit, her legs round and sturdy, her waist still thickly childlike, but her chest showing the first tiny buds of the womanhood that Rose had had to face up to with Rebecca and then Villette – the old story of a girl's body preparing itself to become a woman. Rose guessed that Nora would initially resent the restrictions, as had Rebecca. She guessed also that there wasn't much that she would be able to tell Nora.

Winifred called, but controlled and polite, 'Not in above the hips, Ballard, not above the hips: the child's meal isn't digested.'

Rose watched Ballard's neat buttocks in his fashionable pale blue swimming-trunks as he ran lightly between the few other groups lazing in the sun. She had not seen a more handsome man since they had been in Spain, and this in spite of many Spaniards having good profiles and the same heavy, wavy dark hair as Ballard's. But the presence that was always with her, reminding her, arousing her was, of course, Wesley Trevelyan.

Villette did not move except closer to her great-grandmother.

Winifred said, 'Perhaps we should go down too, Rose. You see, Ballard is already letting Anoria go out of her depth. He thinks that I am a fuss-pot, but then maybe I am.'

Rose went to sit with her mother-in-law at the tideline, where curved waves broke over her legs and sucked at her heels in their undertow. Looking back over her shoulder she saw Villette lying in a listening attitude within the shade of Charlotte's great green golfing umbrella, and Maria climbing up to the villa with the big round picnic basket. 'Oh dear, poor Maria,' Rose said, 'I feel quite guilty lazing around here whilst she has to go back to wash up and start supper.'

'It is what Ballard is paying her to do, Rose. In any case, these people are used to their life. And I imagine that she is looked upon as very fortunate to work in such a beautiful villa. I am sure that they must sleep six to a bed in those little huddles in the village.'

Rose took a sideways glance at her mother-in-law. She is always so sure of herself. How easy things must be for her. She says that things are such and such, and to her that is then how they are. In many ways she was ageless. Her stomach was flat and her breasts did not draw attention to themselves. She looked after herself with creams and isometric exercise. Before she had come out today, she had obviously shaved her legs and armpits, and her body appeared to have been poured into her swimsuit by somebody who knew when to stop.

Not so Rose, whose abdomen was a gentle mound and whose breasts were rather too heavy for her swimsuit of ruched satin. It was hardly a swimsuit proper, but a brassière top and brief shorts joined at the sides with a gilt ring, leaving an open midriff. In the cubicle of the leisure-wear department, she had said, 'I hardly think so', but the assistant had said, 'If I were fortunate to have a figure like yours, madam, I shouldn't mind showing it, not a bit.' 'But you are younger than I am,' Rose had said. 'Well, madam, if you ask me, I think it's us women that think about our age; men just think about our figures.'

The girl must have known something of the psychology of men and women, for Rose had bought the small but expensive piece of elasticized satin and Ballard had said that she looked absolutely stunning in it.

Maria had reached the top of the climb where she stopped, as Jean would have stopped and said, Must have a bit of a blow and a fag now. If the Marias and Jeans didn't look after themselves, who would? Rose, still following her own train of thought said, 'And I quite often feel guilty about Jean coming in to clean.'

Winifred, sounding irritated now, said, 'That kind of thought leads nowhere, Rose.'

'I can't help it. I have never worked for a salary, I have produced nothing, I contribute nothing. Why should I have all this?' Her gesture encompassed everything around her. 'Jean is the one who deserves holidays in Spain.'

'You are the right hand of an important member of the most important government opposition in the world, and the mother of his children. Of course you have contributed. Four bright and healthy children? Who knows what they will become?'

So, presumably, Winifred's justification for her own place in the sun was Ballard. And Rose's justification was Ballard and his four offspring.

And Rose saw that she, too, in her turn, must be the grandmother and sit on the tideline. And would she in her turn have sixteen grandchildren to give her her reason for having existed?

And that is *it*? Rose thrust the maverick thought back into that part of her mind which was Pandora's box. The trouble was that it was crammed full and it had a very dodgy catch.

Ballard came running out of the water and grabbed a towel, perhaps conscious that the pale blue trunks rather clung to him. Anoria splashed out after him, giggling and dripping everywhere, her knitted swimsuit stretched and sagging from the weight of water it had absorbed. Rose determined that she must get her something a bit less childish.

'Come on, Rose, walk to the village with me. I want to get a few more bottles of that nice white wine.'

'I'll come,' Anoria said.

'You stay with the grannies. We shan't be long.'

'Bring us back something nice to eat then.'

Rose did not want to stop lazing, but when Ballard hauled her to her feet she acquiesced, not wanting to put a stop to the good mood he had been in since they arrived, and with towels thrown about their shoulders, they climbed the rough stone steps.

In the cool, shaded house, Rose said, 'I'll have to change my frock. Ten minutes?'

He ran his hand over her back and let it slide between the satin and the dip at the base of her spine. 'We have oodles of wine. I just wanted half an hour in bed.'

'But . . .' She had been about to mention last night, but he said, 'Daytime, I want to do it in the daytime.'

On the rare occasion when he was like this, romantic and gentle, it was hardly possible to believe in the truth of those other times, of hurt and brutishness. He had been gentle in the early days. Why had he spoiled it all by making her body sullen and resentful of his? He always excused himself by saying that he was a passionate man. But then so was Trevelyan, of that she was sure. A passionate man did not have to use force and brutality. Trevelyan hadn't even gone on to the end that had seemed inevitable. It had been he, and not Rose, who had pulled away first.

'Shower off all that sand and let me put some sun lotion on you.'

The bedroom walls were slashed with sun and shadow thrown by the shutter laths. The sound of the breaking waves entered on a breeze that carried with it the smell of the sea and the scent of flowering shrubs. Rose glanced at Ballard as he lay watching her drying herself after showering, his hair tousled, his parted mouth red and full in his desire. It was his mouth above all that always brought back those times when he had forced himself into her. It was true that over the years he had become less insistent, less urgent. She had been able to treat her resentment like a patch of oil on to which handfuls of sand had been thrown. Slowly absorbed and hidden. There, yet not there, sometimes forgotten, at others the original stain seeping through. There for ever.

'I sometimes forget how beautiful you are, Rose. Do you know what I'm thinking?' He laughed, half closing his eyes.

'How could I possibly?'

He laughed again. Mature, urbane, handsome. A bit of the army captain showed through, a bit of the Ballard who had swept her off her feet when she was terribly young and innocent. 'I'm thinking a kind of secret. I think that secrecy is one of life's pleasures.' He ran his hands up and down his own body sensuously; along his arms, over his shoulders, neck, face. Finally dragging his fingers through his heavy hair, he lay back with hands behind his head. 'I think to myself sometimes, when we are at some function, that there is no one here except me who knows what you look like when you are being fucked.' He laughed. 'It's even come into my mind when you've been beside me on an election platform.'

He was in a strange mood.

'Yes.' The thought obviously excited him. 'I give them half my mind and think of this with the other.' He kissed her. His eyes closed and a faint smile touched his lips; she watched as they pressed against her skin. He seemed inflamed at the thought and kissed her in a way that he had never kissed her before, descending her body even to her lower abdomen. Acute sensations raced along routes of pleasure that had not been much used in recent years – until her encounter with Trevelyan.

The white candlewick counterpane, freshly washed and dried in the sun, had the same smell of soap and being dried in the open as Wesley Trevelyan's cotton shirts. Remembering that, Ballard's mouth became Trevelyan's mouth that was arousing her, making her feel desirable, making her want to be involved in this new way of making love.

She felt poised on a kind of precipice.

He kept looking up at her and saying, 'My God, Rose!'

If she could only launch herself then she could fly, and if Pandora's box flew open and her rogue thoughts and fantasies flew out, perhaps they would no longer cause her any problems.

'My God, Rose!'

She felt outrageous. She wanted to be the one to be looking down, to be the one to take control, to be above him and let her hair hang down on to his shoulders, to be the one who made the rules.

For the first time she felt healthy, female sexual assertiveness. It was powerful but frightening, yet it gave her a confidence she had never known. On the warm white counterpane, with her eyes closed and a faint smile on her lips, she made love to Trevelyan.

'Rose!' His shout as he climaxed with her brought her back from the depths of the New Forest and the houseboat, out of the hard brown arms, the sinewed fingers, the tongue and soft mouth, away from the lean hard torso and the long hair – and into the room with the slatted sunlight where she heard the tail-end of a long, heavy exhalation of breath which she realized was her own.

In the bathroom, she did not like to meet her own eyes. In taking that great, thudding pleasure, she had colluded with Ballard and allowed him to believe that she had given him backdated permission for those times when he had hurt and bruised her into submission. When, even though he knew that he could have done so, he had made no attempt to withdraw safely from her. And it had been his right to do so. Was it that uncivilized attitude that she had resented the most? He had taken her violently on more than one occasion, and twice she had become pregnant. Not this time though. This time, even though she took the best precaution money could buy, she still moved away from him at the last moment. He had shouted 'Rose!' in protest, but it had been too late.

In the next room, Ballard lay on the rumpled bed, watching the smoke of his cigarette being drawn across the room, and dragged back that image of her lolling with the waves breaking around her, hoping that before they went back to the beach he could have her again. This time he would not be fooled into enjoying her perverseness. When he had come up the beach towards her, he could easily have taken her there and then, perhaps if they had been alone he might well have. The tantalizing memory of those times when he had done just that still came back to him, but he was surprised to discover that it did nothing to arouse his interest.

Suddenly he realized that he had had enough of a houseful of women who knew him too well and a maid who had the dark, silky facial hair, and the sweat and body-shape of the passionate Latin type of woman. She was aware that he quite fancied her, but she made more fuss of Rose and her Spanish than of the man who paid her wages and fancied her hips. He had done as much sightseeing as he could do in one go, the taverns and cafés had lost the charm of the first days here, and the beach was boring.

He had decided to go back.

At breakfast next morning, after reading the mail from England, he said, 'I'm sorry, darling, but I'll just have to go back.'

He had wondered whether Rose's sudden storm of excitement might have changed her. He didn't know what he had expected, but when she had come from the bathroom, her hair tied back severely and that disdainful expression back, he understood that nothing had changed. She despised him for being what he was – a red-blooded male whose deep-down prime function was to impregnate females of his own kind. Years ago, he had read the most mind-expanding article he had ever had the luck to pick up: 'The Nature of the Human Male.' The argument contained in those few pages had left him totally assured that his instincts were normal; not only normal, but desirable for the improvement of the race. Thereafter he rarely felt any sense of guilt at his desire for power, authority and wealth, for these were merely the modern means of outdoing other males for the best females. As the author of the article argued, this had been going on since the dawn of time, when the most dominant male in the tribe was the one who took charge by whatever means he could, and thus had the pick of the women. It explained everything from football to war, from common theft to the Stock Exchange, from chest-expanders to rape.

For a few minutes on the bed, dominance had shown on her face. She had become masculine, temporarily seducing him by her surprising tactics; he had even been lulled into expecting that she intended plunging herself down on to him to achieve the ultimate satisfaction. But she had not: at the moment of his climax she had left him. It had been stimulating, but it was submissive women that excited him most. And he knew where to find them.

So he said, 'I'm sorry, darling, but I'll have to go back.'

'Oh, Nora will be disappointed. Weren't you going to take her to see the young bulls or something?'

'You can take her.'

'Bullfighting? Not a chance.'

'Not fighting, just a hacienda where the animals are bred. In any case, it can't be helped, I really can't be swanning around here whilst the abolitionist camps are getting their heads together again, ours and theirs. They mean to try using the Ruth Ellis thing to put an end to hanging.'

'Not before time, Ballard. Hanging that woman was appalling, dreadful, shameful . . .'

He had risen from the table and gone to sit on the low terrace wall to smoke a cigarette, not really wishing to discuss the matter with Rose. She had never known how to argue: she was simply too emotional. That was perfectly all right within the home and family – like the time when she had gone to the head-teacher like an avenging angel when some boys had bullied Jonathan – but gut feelings were no substitute for rational discussion. She could go off in all directions, bringing in totally unrelated topics. 'She was a murderess, Rose, she killed a man. Penalty for murder? Death. End of story.'

She had followed him to sit on the wall and brought from her skirt pocket one of her awful hand-rolled cigarettes, which he had taken from her, thrown out on to the rocks, and had lit her a firm tube of Craven A.

'Obviously not end of story, Ballard, or you wouldn't be flying off home in the middle of your holiday. Ruth Ellis might be dead, but she is not going to lie down.'

'I suppose you think that she should have been reprieved because she was a woman? Or maybe because she was a beautiful blonde?'

'I don't think that she was beautiful, I think she had a hard face. She did a dreadful thing. She shouldn't have been hanged because hanging is barbaric. Killing is uncivilized – killing in cold blood the most hideous of all crimes – and that's how I see capital punishment: the state killing in cold blood for revenge.'

'You don't understand, Rose.' He drew deeply on his cigarette, grimacing with his jaw as he did so and then forcing out the smoke in a long stream, something he did when irritated. He really did not want to get into a wrangle with Rose; on the other hand he did not want her to go opening her mouth and giving an opinion that was directly opposed to his own. It was the kind of thing that always got back to Party officials and Whips. And he was still smarting from the way she had used him yesterday. 'The death penalty is the only weapon the state has to defend ordinary, decent people against the killer.'

'Her lover wasn't a decent person, he had played about with her for two years and was going to dump her.'

'And you think he deserved to die for that? And because it's a woman who kills him, she should get away with it?'

'Oh, Ballard! Why do you always twist my words into meanings I don't intend? I'm not the Opposition. Of course he didn't deserve to die for abandoning his mistress, and she most certainly shouldn't have got away with it. But they *had* had a passionate affair, and he *had* told her that he was going to leave her. There should be more understanding of a crime of passion.'

He had given her a strange, wry look that she entirely failed to comprehend, then said, 'How would you feel if some woman took a gun and shot Jonathan?'

'I should think in my grief and fury I might easily pick up a gun if there was one handy and want to shoot whoever did it. That's understandable, and so would it be if David whatever-his-name's mother shot Ruth Ellis. It would be horrible but it would be understandable. But carrying out the death penalty means complete strangers arranging to strangle someone to death.'

Ballard had felt extremely uneasy. Rose was not given to airing opinions and seldom voiced any of importance that were not his own. He knew men in his Party who almost feared having their wives let loose in the constituency in case they opened their mouths and put their foot in it. Not Rose: she smiled and looked lovely and only said how pretty the flowers were, or what nice parks the town had. Imagine the field-day the abolitionists would have championing her.

'That's Monica talking.'

She had ground her cigarette out, not neatly stubbing the lighted end until it went out as she usually did. He had smiled to himself. Oh dear, Rose at her most violent. 'Darling, listen. The Wilkinsons can have whatever outlandish opinions they like, but for me that's dangerous talk. Leo is not part of the Establishment, I am. We always have to be watching our backs – there are people out there with long knives.'

'Ballard, there are times when you might be a right-wing Tory.'

He frowned. 'There are times, like now, when I think that may be no bad thing. Now, I'm going to pack a case and go to the village to book a taxi and reserve a seat on the London plane.'

He went indoors, and she had picked up a beach-towel and gone off down the cliff path. Five minutes later he had seen her, arms and feet splashing, as her strong overarm stroke carried her quickly along parallel to the shore. Later she had seen him into the taxi. He had not felt impelled to say much about what his movements would be once he reached England. 'I'll try to get over again, darling. If not, pack the rest of my things. If you can't get me at home or at the flat, liaise with Valerie.'

When Ballard arrived back at the house, which he had supposed would be quiet and uninhabited, he found the place in uproar. On every surface were bits of cut-out fabric and the floors seemed to be knee-deep in scraps and card templates. Two young women, wearing black ski-pants and frilly blouses in different colours, were working at sewing-machines in the breakfast room.

'Oh, Daddy, it's you.' Rebecca too wore the ski-pants uniform. 'Sorry about the shambolic mess. I thought you wouldn't be back for another two weeks.'

'That's pretty obvious. What is going on?'

'Daddy, you'll never believe. It's darling Mr Joffe. He loves my stuff. These are samples of our new range . . . well, mine actually. Mr Joffe wants the samples pronto.' She laughed, elated with the prospect of success. 'For last week if we can work fast enough. He's a slave driver, but he's my absolute angel in disguise. Do you like this?' She pulled at the elasticated neck of her blouse to expose her shoulders. 'Two styles in one. Show Daddy Mark II, Pet. Daddy this is Petronella, and that's Franke (actually Frances). This is Daddy Quinlan.' Petronella displayed the versatility of two cords that could bare her tanned midriff.

Ballard smiled. 'It's very nice. Pretty.'

Rebecca rolled her eyes at the other girls. 'They aren't intended to be pretty, they're meant to be fetching. Goes with the tight pants.'

Ballard took away the scissors which she was using to point out the features of the ensembles, and steered her by the shoulders down the hall. At his study door he hesitated. 'Dare I look?'

'Absolutely yes, Dad. Holy ground and all that. I told Franke and Pet, no Daddy's study – pain of death.'

Ballard felt that he was being sucked into a whirlwind. He was used to sudden changes in Rebecca's appearance and style of speaking, but with these changes, he had the impression that Rebecca had quite disappeared. He was amused, and impressed by her air of confidence, but he did not like the assumptions she was making that she could do what she liked with no advice from her own father.

'What happened to your hair?' It was chestnut-coloured, centre-parted, straight and flicked up just above her shoulders. 'It makes you look like the Jack of Hearts.' He withheld any comment about her eyelids, which were heavily outlined in black, the outer edges flicked in the same upward curve as her hair. It was quite disturbing the way some of the young women of Rebecca's age seemed to be more interested in pleasing themselves and each other, rather than in pleasing young men. Ballard had never seen his mother unless she was wearing at least powder and lipstick. He pushed things around on his desk. 'Now, what is going on? Who are those young women in the breakfast room?'

'Pet is going for hair fashion, Franke is the notions woman – you know, crazy buttons and stuff. The "Rebbel" look will be a total concept. I say, don't you think Rebbel rather good – it plays about with the idea of Rebecca and rebellion. Good, isn't it?'

True, they had not invaded his study.

'Sorry, Dad, but I'll have to track.'

'No, sit down and let me have a really good explanation in language I can understand, with good reasons I can believe, for having arrived home to find the house looking like some backstreet factory.'

'Daddy, darling, that is what it is. Mr Joffe, as it turns out, had just become "Pretty Miss Fashions", he bought somebody out . . .'

'Mr Joffe?'

She tried to smile winningly. 'Yes, Daddy, old Aze Joffe, and I know what you think – well Aze and Princess – she's Sally Joffe his wife – the Joffes have put up cash to back us. Princess adores my designs, and I showed her Franke's notions, and she and Aze love them, and Aze wants to get a whole bundle of Rebbel "looks" out on the street to fill a between-season gap in his end of the market.'

In spite of the new way of speaking, Ballard saw what was going on. 'Which is what?'

'Small shops in the London area – and possibly the market trade. He has spare between-season factory capacity on his machines. And he knows the small shop and market trade like nobody's business. I say, Dad, you do look lovely and tanned, was it super? You can see now why I didn't dare go to Spain. And I *will* have all of it out of the house before Mum gets back. I mean, if you hadn't come back before you said you would, we'd have been out of here and no one the wiser.'

Ballard Quinlan lit a cigarette and, without asking, Rebecca helped herself and took his cigarette to light her own. He did not know how to handle this. A slight gripe of apprehension contracted in his stomach, something he seldom experienced these days. She had done something wrong, but he could not decide what. He had to deal with her but did not know how, or why, he should. She was sparkling with vitality and enthusiasm.

'I warned you about getting in deep with these people.'

She swallowed her rising anger well. 'Listen, Dad, I know you're a bit bugged about this, and I can understand you don't like me going off and doing my own thing, but it's all really-really legit. I did tell you weeks ago about this company which was interested in my designs, but I don't think you really took it in. Anyway, the company was one of Aze and Princess's. They are really-really big in the rag trade . . . you know, mass-production women's clothes. It's really Princess who is behind the buying out of the Pretty Miss business.'

'That girl who wears the ridiculous hats?'

'She's not a girl and she *does* wear some amusing things to Ascot, and she wears them because all the toadies take it so *seriously*. People always remember her hats. Nobody ever seems to remember that she started all those places for latch-key children, or that she started a fund for free legal advice for the poor, it's always the Ascot hats.' She spread her hands and shrugged her shoulders. 'Anything else you want to know?'

'Yes, about this whole thing with you and them. When I agreed that you should go to art school, I did not expect that I would come home unexpectedly and find you setting up shop with cheap clothes.'

She held on to sweet reasonableness in her tone. 'I must admit that I would never have thought about selling through market traders and the cheap-jack shops, but it's perfect for my scheme. I want to create a style from scratch. To give it a special look that people recognize, you know – like Dior's New Look – except that our market is going to be really-really cheap and directed entirely at girls of my age. Young styles that aren't copies of their mother's clothes. Daddy, the market here is hardly tapped. We are going to be an absolute success.'

'Rebecca, listen to me, I don't want to stifle your enterprise . . .'

'No, Dad. You absolutely couldn't.'

'What do you know about these people? What do they want from you? They aren't in business to grant wishes to young would-be designers.'

'I'm not would-be. I *am* a designer. Look at this. It's mine, I thought of it, created it and I made it something real. It's not just pie in the sky . . . I'm actually wearing it.'

'Yes, and it's pretty, but you are talking about business. You say Joffe has just bought . . . a factory, is it?'

'*Another* factory. It's minute of course, but his others are quite large. He also does, you know, household stuff: cushions, curtains and things.'

'Well then, he must be a man with his head screwed on the right way, so he is not going to bring you into his business for nothing. He knows who you are, of course?'

'He's not hoping for any favours from you, if that's what you are thinking. It was ages before I admitted that my name was Quinlan.

I mean, they know now, but they didn't know when Sally asked me to meet them.'

'But I dare say he expects me to invest in this scheme.'

'No. Sally is putting up the money. You have never been mentioned.'

'But a man like that is nobody's fool. I can't see what other angle he's got except a direct line to me – he probably wants a contact in the Department of Trade. He'd be a fool not to see how useful I could be.'

Rebecca suddenly saw where he was leading, and her cheeks turned an angry red. 'He sees no such thing. You don't even know them. They're super people.'

'And they are Jews, and Jews always have an angle where business is concerned.'

'Of course they have an angle, it's the same as mine, to find an empty niche in the fashion market and fill it before anyone else does.' She felt herself about to slip down a slope with no hand-holds.

Who was he to talk about angles? Even if she had never put it into words, she knew how he operated, half truths, insinuations.

She swallowed a longing to shout and clench her jaw at him. He was supposed to be *for* minorities and the underdog. She was not going to let him browbeat her. With her best attempt at mature control, she said, 'Look, Dad, I know what I am doing. Mr Joffe has spare machines, Mrs Joffe is putting up cash for the fabrics and I am putting in my designs. We are a tripartite. If it doesn't work, then I come out of it with everything I've got now, plus the experience of having been in business.'

'You are talking to a businessman, Rebecca. There's never something for nothing.'

'I'm not nothing. I'm putting in flair for knowing fashion trends, maybe even shaping fashion trends in girls of my age, and my ability to come up with the designs. There are plenty of dabblers who can come up with fancy creations for end-of-term displays – totally impractical on the street – but I can do it, do the whole thing. I've got imagination, but I'm practical with it. You've never believed an art-school training is anything but a joke, but you're wrong, Dad. The way a country looks, the way its people dress – you know, buildings, cars, clothes – all matter terribly to the way we all behave. Art is important.'

'As it was in Germany and Italy? A lot of art and design there.'

'I'm not saying that the influence was always for the *good*, I'm saying that it is *important*. It's not just the frivolous thing you think. OK, this stuff is frivolous, but if it works it's going to be fun, it's going to make young women feel happier, more independent. That makes my work important.'

Ballard crushed out his cigarette. 'Rebecca, this is all beyond me. I have to say what I believe, and I am saying it for your own good. You have got yourself into a gimcrack kind of business, and I don't like the sound of these Joffe people. I don't suppose you have even got a contract with him.'

'How can I get through to you? He is a totally nice man, Daddy.'

'Totally nice men have been known to sew up other totally nice people with totally nasty arrangements. You haven't signed anything?'

'We have established a good relationship, he uses my designs and I get a percentage of the profits.'

'How much?'

'Ten. Plus a straight amount per garment. It is a very good deal.'

'For whom?'

'Everybody.'

'And you have given him a binding contract?'

'Dad, couldn't you even *try* to think that it might be Sally and Aze who might need some protection? For me, it is a chance to have my own label right at the beginning of my career. It is a fantastic opportunity. And if I turned out to be the one who wasn't totally *nice*, I could let them invest in me, launch my label, distribute my stuff, and then I could leave them high and dry. But I won't do that. They believe that I won't; they think I'm honest. And I think they are.'

'You are young and naïve and trusting, Rebecca.' He stood, adopting a dominating attitude, but she was aware what he was up to, recognizing the technique of using physique to control. She was a tall girl who almost levelled with him in height. Changing tack, he said, 'What sort of people are they?'

'The sort who have already made a fortune trusting their judgement I expect. The sort who'd take a chance on buying a painting by somebody like Graham Sutherland before anybody else had heard of him.'

'But this kind of thing?' He waggled his fingers at her clothes. 'This isn't an investment, it won't last and you couldn't even hang it on the wall. Why haven't they been open and come to me?'

'Aze would have, but I wouldn't have it. This is my thing, I want to do it on my own without anyone judging or interfering.'

He was about to say something, but turned away and sorted through a pile of unopened mail in silence.

'OK, Dad, why do you think they're making me this offer?'

He flung down the envelopes. 'Don't ask me to get into the minds of people like these, I wouldn't know how to. If they are offering money, there's bound to be an angle and I don't see what it is. And . . . furthermore, I have no intention of allowing you to become involved.'

'Allow me? You can't allow me or stop me.'

The muscles around his mouth tightened and his jaws worked. 'You are my responsibility, I refuse to let us be made fools of.'

'What will you do, send for the cops?'

He raised his voice, 'Don't be childish,' and made a motion as though to bang one fist into the other, but drew back as he had trained himself to do when somebody in the House got under his skin.

Rebecca still stood her ground and faced him, 'Don't you try that on me, Dad.' Ballard Quinlan felt panic rise at her hostile tone. 'Don't think you can intimidate me the way you do Mum, and your own mother.'

It is easy to lay blame at the door of the mother, and say that she should not have allowed him to dominate her, and that being male it was right that he should do so. But that would not be fair to Winifred, who did as mothers usually do. Untrained, and faced with rearing a child, she did the best she could in the circumstances. And it would not be fair too, because Ballard was now a big grown-up man capable of making his own decisions, and controlling his own actions, but as had been proved with Rose more than once, when it came to a woman standing up to him, his response was panic that quickly turned to aggression and rage.

Nothing worse than sudden rage rearing up to bring to the surface that which is most dark and shameful.

'How dare you speak to your father in that tone.'

'Father? Aze Joffe has taken more interest in my work and future than you have ever done, Father. You didn't even notice when I dropped out of art college.'

His face darkened, 'But I suppose your bloody Jew-boy . . .'

'You racist.'

The slap across his face, the first he had ever taken, was stinging, loud and final.

And shocking.

He did nothing.

Within the hour she was out of the house, gathering on her way an astonished Petronella and Franke, and all their paraphernalia. They drove out of town in the little van Aze Joffe had loaned them, and headed for London.

A cigarette calmed Ballard. He had witnessed his fiery daughter storming off since the time when she was two when she clashed with everyone who tried to help her do something she wanted to do for herself. She would come back. The next time he saw her she would laugh and dismiss the spat with a hug and a kiss. Then, if she was still determined to go on with the scheme, he would go and see the Joffe couple and get the thing properly drawn up. It was more than likely, once they realized the sort of people they were dealing with, they would get out from under and Rebecca could get herself into some proper fashion house with a name. That shouldn't be too difficult; he would talk it over with Miriam: the Corder-Peakes knew everybody.

Or maybe he could persuade her into one of those Commonwealth schemes for youngsters. Get her away. There was something rebellious in this generation of youngsters. They were becoming wild, uncontrolled. Except for his son. Jonathan was indecisive and wishy-washy, and had not the slightest idea of what he wanted to do with his life. An estate agent! All that decent education wasted, no ambition, no career, just a job that any council estate boy with a state education could do.

He dismissed the matter from his mind, and went to look through his wardrobe for some of his London suits. He packed his new white dinner-jacket which he was pleased his tailor had persuaded him into. Then he stripped off, thrust his cast-off clothes into the laundry-basket, and showered away any remaining sand from his hair. In his dressing room he took off his robe and inspected himself, turning sideways to see whether any signs of age had crept up on him. He was pleased: all the swimming and walking had toned him up.

He ran his hands appreciatively over the hair on his chest and his own familiar nipples, patted the natural mound of his belly, satisfying himself that his virile nature had not been damaged by his pater familias interlude. He had naturally dark skin and thick, black hair, but he quite liked the way that the area that had been shielded from the sun by his beach shorts was pale in comparison to his tanned chest and legs. He had pretty good legs; he had been told that by scores of women. He smiled at himself. He had pretty good everything, and he was about to take it to Miriam where it would be appreciated. Where his own solidity and her dainty fragility never failed to suit them both equally. The image of himself as she would see him aroused him and hurried him on with his dressing.

It was quite late when Ballard called in at his office, but Valerie, his secretary, was still there. His intention had been to slip in, sift through his mail and leave her a note. 'Just passing through, Val. Nothing here you can't handle. You won't be able to get hold of me, I have some Party business to attend to.' He rocked his spread hand back and forth, conveying that it was early days yet to say anything about what was going on. 'I'll try to ring you each morning. Give you time to sort the mail first. If Rose rings – I don't think she will, there isn't a telephone at the villa, but if she does – tell her, if it's urgent, I'll . . . Damn, I don't know, if there isn't a phone, I can't ring her anyway . . . Just take a message. Rebecca might ring. Tell her you think I'm with a foreign delegation and you can't get me.'

He was trying to avoid telling Valerie that he could be reached at the Corder-Peake's estate. Valerie was a very conventional woman who ran his business affairs like a dream, but, like his mother, she did have the knack of making him feel like a naughty child if he wasn't entirely honest with her. She liked to know what was going on. Fair enough. Things in the agency would soon run down without Valerie. Even so, he had no need to make excuses to his secretary. He could have said, 'Valerie . . . I, ah, I'm going away on my own for a few days', but he needed Val.

Life at the agency would be less complicated if only Valerie did not feel that she must know almost from hour to hour where her boss would be. If he told her that he would be staying with the Corder-Peakes, he would then have to explain why his wife should not be able to reach him there. Certainly she would not understand him leaving his family in a villa in Spain to go off weekending in the Lake District. And he could not plead 'abolitionists plotting' with Valerie: she knew only too well what was going on in that direction. Valerie kept tabs on everything. She believed him to be a great family man, but one inclined to sacrifice himself to his cause. He quite liked her to have that image of him.

In fact, his knowledge of Valerie was considerably less than was hers of him. She guessed, quite rightly, that had he not feared losing her, he would have had his hand up her skirt long ago. She knew that she was attractive; she knew also that she was not his type: she was too Amazonian, too intelligent. She was quite aware that hers was one of the most successful heads he had ever hunted. She was good at her job, had been granted considerably more responsibility than most secretaries would be allowed but, like most secretaries, could have done her boss's job with much less fuss than he – in fact, this is what she did. To all intents and purposes the agency was run by Valerie Newly.

It was whilst driving north to what (among some of Ballard's colleagues) was known snidely as the Corder-Peake district, that Ballard, having relaxed into the comfort of his impressive new, low-bonneted Jaguar car, began to mull over the row with Rebecca. For as he now realized, even though he had sat on in his study and listened to her packing up and leaving, it *had* been a row. Hypocrite. Racist. Jonathan had not accused him of racism, with Jonathan it had been colour prejudice.

Which was ridiculous. The party he represented was a broad church, he had plenty of Jewish colleagues. He harboured no racial prejudice, had no feelings one way or another. Jews and Blacks, he did business with them all the time; he'd even do business with the Japs if it came his way. He had got on well with black Yankee soldiers during the war. He had been on numerous visits to Commonwealth countries. He liked the black races, they knew how to enjoy themselves. He really had had no objection to Jonathan having that same pleasure he had had himself with a black woman. His own first experience of a fine, black body had been unforgettable, in the days when you could still have a black woman in Durban without finding yourself in trouble. She had called him 'baas', even as she clenched him with muscles he had never realized women possessed. She had said, 'Right, baas? OK, baas?'

He would drink and eat with a black man any day, and sleep with a black woman any night. Thin, bony legs topped by wonderfully generous behinds, soft bellies like round cushions, heavy swinging breasts that looked as though they had been black-leaded and tipped with hard ebony. In December he was going with a trade delegation to Nigeria to discuss a dried milk deal. As he piloted his powerful car, speeding along the Great North Road, he thought of how absolutely *un*prejudiced he could be. Perhaps, on reflection, that should have been his approach with Jonathan. He should have said that he was not opposed to a mixed-race affair – only just be careful that it does not become serious, or result in half-caste babies.

Perhaps he should have got Valerie to see what she could discover about Rebecca's Jews. On second thoughts, Miriam would find out for him. He'd ask her to look for something that might bring Rebecca to her senses.

What Miriam *would* discover without much trouble, for they had never hidden their allegiance, was that Sally and Aisa Joffe had good, unionized workshops, and had contributed generously to the organizations and parties of the left. Nothing there for Ballard to quarrel with.

Rose, in another new swimsuit, a minimal black two-piece, looked suntanned now, and elegant.

It was two days since Ballard left for home. She was glad now that she had not given in to her feelings; although she might easily have – if she had wished – recalled the anger she had felt at his 'that's Monica speaking'. Thanks to her rare upbringing, Rose knew how anger could be dealt with. As a child she had often been sent to knock hell out of some old velveteen cushions, so, on the morning he had left, sensing that Ballard was watching her from the terrace, she had thrashed and banged the warm coastal water, giving it a good cushioning for half an hour, and had then basked in the early sun, encouraging it to soak up any bile she had not rid herself of.

Several times in recent months she had thought of Threnody. Threnody Chaice. Such an evocative name. During the war years they had exchanged birthday and Christmas cards, short letters and bits of news, then one year Rose's card had been returned 'Not known', and Rose had heard no more of her. Until lately, Rose had not thought of her for years.

And now, soaking up the sun with small pleasures of tobacco and the Lorna Lammente pulp-fiction romantic mystery she had saved for the holiday, Rose prepared to enjoy an idle morning. Charlotte was on the cool veranda reading, Winifred and Vee away for a couple of days in Granada to see the famous water gardens, and Nora was happy as a lark, having rumbled off on a little cart with Maria and an elderly man, who turned out not only to be Maria's uncle, but also the village priest. Her uncle, according to Maria, was an authority on bulls, and would be pleased to take Nora to see where the best bulls in Spain were bred. Rose wondered whether breeding techniques were just the thing for Nora at the moment, but she was with the patently honest Maria and a priest.

Free of everything, she could surrender herself to thoughts of Wesley Trevelyan, allowing them to ramble over the houseboat, the tea-house, the picnic in the New Forest, the feel of her tongue in his mouth and his tongue between her fingers and how alive he had become in the fantasy with Ballard. Guilt plucked a little at her stomach: was infidelity only practised with the body? She had taken Trevelyan into her mind, and had created a temporary world in which she was taking him into her. Where was the harm? She surprised herself by concluding that, if the price of fantasy was an attack of conscience, it was cheap at the price. Somewhere in her mind she was preparing herself for the day when it would be Trevelyan's climax in reality, and she would bear down instead of arching away as she had done with Ballard.

Wesley Trevelyan picked up his phone in his studio. 'Trevelyan.'

'This is Rose.'

'So I hear.'

'I hope I haven't disturbed you.'

'Not my work. Only me.'

'I'm sorry.'

'Don't be. You are the kind of disturbance I can do with. You're a disturbing woman.'

Rose laughed. 'Just a deep-fried woman. My shoulders are peeling.'

'Have you no one to massage them? I could fly out at once. Where are you?'

His voice was deep and wonderful, with its suggestion of amusement and complicity in their secret which, except for erotic fantasies, was pretty innocent. Just a couple of meetings, a bit of petting, and a few passionate kisses. Rose felt a momentary breathlessness. This is the beginning of an affair. Is it the way affairs start? It was so easy to do, so uncomplicated. Everything about it was positive, exciting. Nobody hurt so long as it was secret.

'I'm calling from a public phone. In the village.'

'Still in Spain, I assume?'

'Oh yes. There's no telephone up at the villa.'

'A pity, because now that I've at least got your voice, I can't bear that you'll suddenly say that you are running out of coins.'

'Well, actually I haven't got that many. I was just idling around and I thought I'd ring somebody. Perhaps I'm experiencing the effects of withdrawal from a telephone.'

'I'd prefer it if you said that you were suffering from the effects of withdrawal from me.'

'Perhaps that's nearer the truth.'

'I'm glad. I wish somebody had invented a televisual phone. I long to see you. Are you very brown?'

'Quite tanned.'

'All over?'

'Well, not entirely.'

'That's English prudery. I should like to see you with a full body tan. I'd photograph you with your white hair in a pigtail and wearing nothing but a frayed sombrero.'

'And sell me for an engineering works calendar.'

'I don't do that stuff. This one would be real exhibition material. No, I'd keep it for myself.'

'I've never heard you talk like that before.'

'That's probably because of the state you've got me in. There's a lot you don't know about me, and even more that I don't know about you.'

'What would you like to know?'

'The things I'd like to know about you, Rose Quinlan, I could hardly ask over the telephone. What are you wearing?'

'The skirt and top you like.'

'Did you choose it specially because you were going to ring me?'

'Probably. Yes.'

'What else? Sandals?'

'Gold ones. And my new black swimsuit.'

She could not decide whether the groan of desire was real or an attempt at jokiness. She fell silent, wondering whether she should have indulged herself to the extent of making such a long trunk call. Although she had pretended to herself it would only be a minute or two, she had gone into the bank and obtained a large number of small coins.

'You're wasting your coins. Let me have that number and I'll ring you back.'

'No, it's the only public phone. I just wanted to say hello.'

'Are you having fun?'

'Ballard has been called back: some crisis in his office, I think.'

'Am I supposed to take that as a yes or a no?'

Rose laughed. 'Neither. Well, a "yes" I suppose: it is fun being with Nora and Vee. The villa is a woman's world at the moment. And the sea and sand are marvellous, and the villa is wonderful, so are the flowers. There's a nice housekeeper called Maria . . .'

'I keep dreaming about you, Rose.'

'Do you?'

'And not just at night. And not the kind that I'd tell anyone but you.'

Could she say: Then why don't you come here? She longed to. Couldn't she say to Winifred that she wanted to go to Barcelona and go there alone.

'Rose?'

'I'm trying to learn a bit of Spanish, and I've a suspicion that I speak it with a very rural accent.'

'I like that.'

'I'm coming to the end of my coins.'

'Rose. There is a place in Seville – "Cantina Rosa", most appropriate – I could be there the day after tomorrow at about noon. Like our rendezvous in the New Forest, if you come, you come; if you can't make it, then I shall understand. I shall be in pain with disappointment, but I shall understand.'

'I can't just abandon the girls.'

'What about the other women?'

'They are old ladies, I'm responsible for them.'

'Please, Rose. Just come there for a day. I just want to put my arms round you, I want you to kiss the way you did it the first time. Christ! Rose, it's bloody agony knowing that you won't be back for weeks. I can't do my work for thinking about you. You know the shots I took of you in the forest? They are wonderful. I've blown them up and have them standing all round my studio. I'd fly to the moon if I thought there was half a chance that you wouldn't throw me out when I arrived.'

'Trevelyan, you're talking as though I was free. I'm a married woman. I can't just do as I please.'

'You can if you have the will to. I haven't forgotten what you did to me before I had hardly got my lips on you, Mrs Married Woman.'

'I've got four grown-up children.'

'None of that has a single thing to do with my wanting you. And it's nothing to do with you wanting me, and I know you want it as much as I do. Who would be harmed if we slept together for a single night in Seville?'

Who would be? Rose really could not counter that. She wanted it, he wanted it. Two people happy and no one harmed.

'Rose, you know I'm not playing fast and loose with you. If it was just a roll in the hay I wanted, I come across those opportunities almost daily in my job. If I hadn't thought so much about decency, and about all that wife and mother stuff, we would both have done what we were bursting to do that day at my place. I don't think you would have held back. You were waiting for me to do the seduction thing, weren't you?'

'Then why didn't you?'

'Because we had been sloshing all that rum into our drinks. I've never had much of an opinion of men who give women a couple of gins and then try to lay them.'

'Was that what you hoped would happen in the forest?'

'It almost did, didn't it?' He sounded amused at the memory.

Rose paused at her memory of that moment when they had teetered on the brink. No one could blame too much rum that day.

They were drunk on their own desire for one another. She leaning over him, kissing him fiercely, and he with his hand sliding beneath her halter. 'Almost, but not quite,' she said.

He laughed, breaking the tension. 'Lust lost at the sight of forty ramblers in khaki shorts and studded boots doing a march-past.'

'They brought me to my senses.'

'Rubbish!' You took flight because you looked at your watch and suddenly realized that you were supposed to have gone shopping. Another fifteen minutes' grace and you'd have flung me down again and had your way with me. Don't blush like that.'

She blushed. Smiled. 'Then be thankful you got away.' She put in her last coins. 'I'd have liked Seville.'

'Liked? I promise you – you'd have loved it.'

'I know, I'm sorry. It really isn't easy. Winifred would absolutely insist that at least one of the girls came with me, and if I balked at that, she would be suspicious. I'm no good with Winifred. And I feel that I can't leave Charlotte alone just now. She's grieving most terribly for Papa, and Winifred would only tell her to pull herself together.'

'I know. I know. It's one reason why I want to go to bed with you.' This was the first time either of them had been explicit about their intentions. 'You care about people.' He laughed, and the sound went directly to the mysterious place where desire begins, never the same place twice, always changing, and soaked her whole body with need of him. 'Not that you care about me.'

'That's not true, Wes. You aren't the only one who is having erotic dreams.'

'Good,' he said.

'Just be patient.'

'Don't hang about too long, Rose, or I'll burst at the seams.'

When Rose emerged into the sunlight, she suddenly remembered the thing that Ballard had said: Women who look as though they're asking for it should either put up or shut up when they get it. Ballard could be so coarse. Trevelyan could be direct, but would never be purposely offensive like Ballard, and he would never hit out.

Wandering through the village with its thick, stone-built houses with their purple-shadowed interiors, she bought a few bits and pieces here and there: peppers, and the sweet oval tomatoes which only ever reached England in a tin. She wondered whether Maria ever wore any scarf but a black one, and bought a black one with an embroidered edge which could double as a table-centre if Maria couldn't bring herself to bedeck herself with stitched flowers.

The thing was, with Trevelyan she did want to put up. With

Trevelyan she longed to. But she felt all at sea. Three times since she had found herself engaged in this madness with him she had been ready to throw her cap over the windmill. Only the timing of the ramblers had stopped her in the New Forest. What had stopped her when she was so close to rushing off to Seville?

She tried to stop thinking about Trevelyan. In her halting Spanish (quite obviously, from the smiles, dropping clangers left, right and centre), she bought flowers for Charlotte's room, and thus laden she made her way back towards the sea.

Perhaps she had not rushed off because she really was the naïve village woman the girls regarded her as. Romance and erotic love had suddenly flung themselves down in the middle of her life and told her to get on with it. But how did one? What were the rules? Certainly she had never discovered what these were from any of hundreds of novels and films. Unless it was that there were no rules because only men are supposed to play. Becc would know, quite likely Nora too. No, it wasn't only a man's game – look at Monica, look what she and Leo had gained from their affair. But things were different with them: although Leo had been married, he had already lost his wife to another man. Although Monica didn't know that when, if it is true what she said, she made explicit advances to him. 'I felt him up, didn't I, Leo?' Monica made up all her rules as she went along.

The sea came into view, so she sat on the roadside verge and looked over at the tranquil view of the blue sea with white rims washing the strand, a sprinkling of sunbathers and swimmers and the red tiles of the villa set on the rocky promontory. She could see the patches of purple bougainvillaea, probably left to its own devices because of its devilish thorns, so that it grew on in great wild mounds, much in the way that brambles and wild roses would be growing in the fields behind the house.

She hadn't thought of the place in days and days.

Jean would be in there today; and then going to Monica's. Jean would feed the cats and pick up the mail, sifting through to see what was interesting. Then she would open all the windows to let out the bad air and bring in some good. English fresh air never really satisfied Jean. 'Iss too bland, you see, the coal back 'ome give the air a kind of taste. I always miss it.'

Monica and Leo were also on holiday with Helen and Kate; James was camping with the cubs. Tom, like Jon, was probably off sowing wild oats somewhere. Tom Wilkinson was very much like Becc: knowing and sophisticated beyond his years. Tom Wilkinson never left anyone in any doubt that he knew how to conduct an affair. Monica said it was all talk, but Rose didn't think so. He was one of those boys females of all ages found attractive, one of those boys over which old ladies shook their heads indulgently and said, 'He's going to break some girl's heart.' Rose remembered a time when Leo had responded with a friendly slap on Tom's back saying, 'But he'll have given them a thrill of a lifetime first, won't you, Tom old lad?' Tom hadn't been at all embarrassed. Jon would have been. Her mind drifted back willy-nilly to its earlier thoughts.

In recent years, marriage vows had not seemed to be meant to be taken too seriously. Separation was on the increase, and divorce was not scandalous. It was obvious from what one read in the papers that people were having affairs all the time.

But she wasn't thinking of anything so drastic as divorce. She was merely contemplating making love with a man she found extremely desirable and who found her to be so too. The only real sexual satisfaction she had had in years was here in Spain, when she had fantasized that she was with Trevelyan, but it had been short-lived, and she had felt afterwards that she would never be able to sleep with Ballard again. But then she had felt that on other occasions. It passed, she got used to him again, slept lightly, and slipped out of bed in the early morning as soon as he showed signs of arousal, or gave him what he wanted. Or perhaps not that, but as much as she could bring herself to give him. In her subconscious, she held that he had long ago forfeited the right to expect more. What were marriage vows worth when Monica and Leo had something much more enviable than Rose and Ballard? Rose had done everything society asked: a formal engagement, a church marriage, and a bride who had gone to the altar with her hymen intact.

If only she had known then what she knew now.

As the five Quinlan women were living their unstructured days in warm idleness, Rose was in the minds of two women back in England: Monica, as she returned to Honeywood from holidaying in Yorkshire, five pounds heavier in spite of all the climbing and walking, and Mona Birdham, Elna's mother, as she stood with other women of her church, all raising exuberant voices in rehearsal for the Sunday service.

Mrs Birdham, wearing white summer gloves, shoes and hat with a starched cotton dress, was considering the possibility of writing ('Amen! Amen!') to Mrs Quinlan, whilst her spirit ascended in the form of her good singing voice. She toyed with the idea of having a mother-to-mother discussion with her regarding Elna and the Quinlans' son, feeling sure that Mrs Quinlan would no more wish her son to marry into a black family than Mona Birdham wished Elna to marry into a white one. (Alleluia!) Her spirit drew her palms heavenward in automatic response. She had even considered the possibility of making her approach to the father, but men were difficult: they were self-indulgent, and quite capable of being obtuse, especially when it came to their sons. It was even likely that he might condone his son's liaison with a coloured girl. He was a liberal and quite likely saw nothing wrong in mixed marriages. At least ('Praise be!') it had not gone that far – yet.

No, Mona Birdham reasoned, it was the mother who was far more likely to look ahead to the possibility of their stubborn and unreasonable young people talking of love and making an unsuitable marriage. How could she? How could her own daughter, who had been brought up in a good Christian family, be doing this brazen thing? When Elna had brought him home, and Mona Birdham had seen the nature of her daughter's thoughts about the white man, she had realized that she must act before Elna did something they would all be ashamed of. She must act both as a Christian and a mother to prevent all kinds of sinning.

Reverend Revelation Alma, whose severe eye she now met, had called upon her to pray with him when the meeting was over, and let the Lord provide the answer using Reverend Revelation as the vehicle. It was he who had broached the subject of Elna's behaviour after he had seen the white man kissing her as they waited for a bus. Kissing in public was not the action any decent mother could condone. Mona, having received from her husband, Frank, very little encouragement to crush Elna's 'little affair', as he called it, had been relieved when Reverend Revelation had offered guidance.

At the time that Rose and the other Quinlan women were sitting at their evening meal on the geranium-scented terrace, Mona Birdham was back in her own home, full of determination, removing her church-going hat. The Reverend Revelation had said that it was Elna herself who must see the wrongness of her liaison with a man of another race. It was Mona's job to bring Elna to church to hear for herself the Bible's own words on that subject.

Monica, Leo and the girls had returned to Honeywell from the moors of Yorkshire, where they had hiked and tramped, watched predatory birds plummeting, and fox cubs playing on a terrain that was in stark contrast to the Meon Valley. Monica wished that she could be returning to Honeywood to find that Rose was back home.

Having come from the Cleveland Hills, which in places were only half clothed in a prickly moorland that left bare, large expanses of cracked and difficult crags, and arriving home in Honeywood where the sprung turf of the southern downlands sloped easily away from the village, Monica felt stifled and uneasy. With a refreshed perspective, she began to look upon her home territory with a kind of irritation. Although, on the higher slopes of the Hampshire Downs, there were places where some knuckles of white showed through bent-grass, lower down, on the lush and well-nourished sheeplands she could see from her kitchen window, no part of the county's calcareous skeleton had scarred or rubbed the turf thin.

In comparison with the vigorous air that had never stopped moving for the fortnight they were in Yorkshire, the mild, vaporous air of the Meon Valley was muggy. Mugginess seemed to suffuse the village. On the sunless side of the railway viaduct, one could walk knee-deep in verdant sphagnum moss, whose fronds grew as long as ferns. On timber signposts and live trees, green algae flourished. On stone grave-markers, lichens had condiment-coloured age-spots. In her mood of dissatisfaction and condemnation, Monica saw spurges as vomiting, bindweed as strangling, and the vast variety of fungi as infecting.

Monica's freshly blown mind concluded that the year-long vapours and summer-long humidity had caused the community to stagnate. They did not protest, complain openly or even vote in any numbers; the best they did was grumble amongst themselves.

Whereas before the change of scene and the high elevation had altered her view of her neighbours, she had still always defended the stoicism of the rural people. Now she believed the community to have become as stagnant as the air that carried the spores of the mosses, algae and lichens. Perhaps this was the reason that the birthrate was falling. Perhaps these phlegmatic country people no longer knew what to do; instead they waited for the odd, lucky sperm to be carried on the spore-laden air to find its way to a suitable recipient.

Not that Monica would ever have thought of her dissatisfied mood in such terms. Leave that to the likes of Rose and Leo!

Monica did not like to discuss angels on the head of a pin, or landscapes in literature. Monica liked action and practicality. She decided to try to return to her old career of nursing.

Techniques and equipment might have changed since she last worked in a hospital, but the fundament of nursing had surely not. A person was sick and, being sick, was at a disadvantage, and so needed reassurance and care – that basic element in nursing would never change.

Monica had gone into nursing partly because she had been brought up in Embley, a village in the south of the county which was where Florence Nightingale had lived, and partly because it had still been the era of large white muslin head-squares and stiff apron bows which made the uniform both nun-like and coquettish. Not particularly sound foundations, but careers and professions do tend to be built upon images. As it turned out, Monica made a good nurse. Not so much at theatre work, where the patient was merely an interesting section of organ, gut or muscle, but good at the ward work, the bathing, the jollying along, the teasing out of stitches, the gentle unplugging of internal dressings, the administering of food and medication.

She had quickly learned to live on institution food, swear, smoke, walk on aching feet, keep awake in the small hours, deal with other people's pain and grief, share their relief and happiness and receive their gratitude. It took longer for her to learn to swallow her resentment at the exploitation, snobbery and petty unfairness that existed within the system. She never learned to enjoy being known only by her surname, or not to run in a crisis or to talk quietly: she was too extrovert for that.

She had never had any regrets at having given up her nursing career, just when it was about to take off, because of Tom, but it was regrettable that when she found herself able to return, the career ladder had been taken away. People tended to believe that a nurse must make a good mother, but Monica had not found the caring and tending side of motherhood very rewarding, perhaps because there had not been the same day-to-day drama that was to be found in a hospital ward, perhaps because children don't express gratitude. Or perhaps it was the dress: no Gor-Ray skirt or shirtwaister dress can come up to crackling cotton, blue candy-stripe and red-lined cloaks.

'A bit sudden, isn't it?' Leo had said when she told him that she was thinking of applying for retraining.

'Not that sudden. I've been thinking about it off and on ever since I talked to that nurse Jonathan brought to Papa Quinlan's birthday. She was telling me about the new treatments, and new drugs, and things like polio being a thing of the past. It all sounded so purposeful and so *fair*, all those twopence-a-week hospital clubs are gone, and the convalescent homes aren't run by the churches and charities any more. Even the career structure is being geared towards a more normal life. I began to think, well, what am I *for* these days?'

'Nursing's hard work.'

'Do you think I don't know that? Not as hard as servicing you and the other four animals.'

'I mean . . . well, you aren't twenty any longer.'

'Neither have I got one foot in the grave. God alive, Leo, what do you want me to do: become another Winifred Quinlan, hanging on to Tom and Helen, patting skin-food on my wrinkles and bleach lotion on my age-spots?'

'Of course I don't. It's good that you are thinking about outside things. All I mean is, what about all the rest of the stuff here . . . at home?'

'I don't know. I can't see that there's anything that we can't sort out. This is the 1950s, not the dark ages. We've got a washing machine; we could get one of the new Canadian Bendixes with a drier as well as a spinner. It ought to be easy with just a bit of organization and everybody pulling their weight. Most of our food and stuff is delivered. I never see the laundryman as it is, and we could pay Young Ted for the milk any time. I know that there are things like the coke deliveries and meter readings, but they aren't insurmountable problems – nothing that I need to stay home all day for.'

'And what about James?'

'Jean says he can go round to her house the times when there's nobody here. We'd pay her.'

'Won't you find it a bit much, two jobs?'

'I'm hoping it isn't going to be two jobs. I had thought more on the lines of one job plus my home and family – just the way you do. You have a job and a family, don't you?'

'Yes, but . . .'

Monica always supposed that he had been going to say, 'But that's different', but stopped himself in time when he saw that she was waiting for him. In theory and argument he was a committed egalitarian and feminist. In practice he was a male of the twentieth century. Family, home and outside job would be too much for her, but he would not stand in her way.

'No harm in finding out,' he said. 'The kids won't like it, they've been used to having a mum about the place.'

'Tom and Helen are twenty and aren't here half the time.'

'Kate? She'll be having a lot of homework for the next –'

'It was Kate who was actually the one to point out to me that I was a "wasted resource".'

Leo smiled without much behind it, and held up his hands in a way that suggested capitulation. 'OK. OK. You do it, Monica. Organize the kids and tell me what to do, but you just be absolutely sure you know what you are doing.'

Monica drew breath to stand up for herself, but thought better of it. She would do it. If they could not manage to live without her being a servant to them, then they would just have to do the other thing . . .

And so their conversation, as it so often did, changed direction. The question of how they would manage with Monica as a working mother was never talked about again to any purpose. Monica would have to forage for time on her own.

She had not applied to the little Petersfield cottage hospital which was close to Honeywood, but to the large one at Winchester which had special units dealing with cardiography, neurology and urology, as well as a large maternity wing. The idea of belonging to that sort of establishment, with its bleepings, its oscilloscopes and its machines with flashing lights, appealed to her. In cottage hospitals there were no skin-graftings, no impressive monitoring machines, no pale babies taped to little crucifixes having their own blood slowly drained and replaced by donor-blood that made them pink and lusty – these miracles were performed in the great new National Health multi-purpose hospital.

She guessed that the shortage of nurses must be serious, for she received an immediate reply and, by the time Rose had returned from Spain, an interview had been arranged.

'Come with me, Rose?'

'Want somebody to hold your hand?'

'Something like that.'

On the morning of the interview, they set out together in Rose's new Ford Popular which had been a gift from Charlotte. 'My Sid's insurance loot to spend as I like.'

Rose said, 'Go back and put on some blush, you look white as a sheet.'

'God,' Monica said, actually feeling pale and agitated in spite of having taken a pep-pill and a small Scotch, 'I feel as though I've been called to the head's office to answer for myself.'

'You'll be all right. They need nurses.'

'I know, but I'm *old*.'

'Mature, experienced.'

'It's a lifetime since I was interviewed for anything.'

'I'll treat you to lunch at the Saracen's afterwards.'

Having reached the hospital car park, Monica felt much as she had when she had sat her first interview board. 'God, Rose, aren't I an absolute wet!'

'It's not wet to want to succeed at something important to you.'

Monica felt a surge of sentimental thankfulness sweep through her. 'Thank the Lord for you, Rose.' Rose was the only one who realized how important this interview was. It was not a test of capability: Monica knew well enough that, even if They did not appreciate the fact, she could still handle any ward they would like to put her on. Their heels echoed on the polished plastic tiles. 'It's a test of me as a person, Rose. It's daft, I know, but I want somebody to give me a seal of approval. I want a label that says that I am *something*. I'll even be a bloody probationer again if necessary, just so long as I don't have to keep on being the Lady with the Shopping List.'

'There's a buffet on the next floor. I'll wait for you there. You'll be fine.' Monica thought that Rose's hand felt hot, but that was only because hers was cold and clenched as Rose gave her a squeeze.

She walked off into the world of polish and carbolic overlaying the human odours that are not usually so concentrated or so numerously exposed as in a hospital. Rather than dwell on the future that lay a couple of minutes ahead, she went over the immediate past.

'Why are you so het up?' Rose had said.

'Because I lied about my age.'

Would they find out? Would they check back on old qualifications?

It was a door like any other office door.

She knocked firmly.

Tiny, and with rice-coloured hair and almost invisible eyebrows, the interviewing sister, Madeline Stringfellow, waited behind Matron's desk.

Stringfellow thought about the immediate past, present and future as one. Thrown in at the deep end. This interview with a woman who wanted to return to nursing was only a preliminary examination of the applicant's suitability, but Stringfellow knew that it was a test of herself both as a sister and as a woman with high ambition. For a week she had been charged with administrative work that would not normally have come her way had it not been for the bug that had floored half the staff including Matron.

Shake hands or not? Stand up or not? One was never trained in this kind of thing, one learned it over years of assisting and watching. This candidate was mature, with teenage children: it would be like interviewing Mother. Sister Stringfellow heard the purposeful stride from way down the corridor, then the sharp double rap which sent perspiration trickling down her sides. She answered with a 'Come in' that came out soundless, so that she hastened to open the door herself.

The woman standing there was large and confident and dressed in a beautiful grey suit, white blouse and low court shoes, an outfit that must have cost a month's salary for a nursing sister. 'Please come in.' She held out her hand and the woman, whose hand was as cold as her own, shook it confidently and sat full square in the seat facing what was normally Matron's desk. 'I'm Monica Wilkinson,' she said. 'I hope I've come to the right office.'

Money and maturity could give women that kind of confidence, Stringfellow thought. Stringfellow was forced to rely on a few puffs of the potent kind of cigarette that was becoming not only popular but necessary to many nurses. 'I'm Sister Stringfellow. I'm afraid Matron's laid low at the moment. I'm filling in.'

'Oh dear,' Monica Wilkinson said. 'I am sorry . . . I mean, you know . . . not that you are filling in . . . that Matron is not . . .'

Stringfellow felt a little of her own confidence return as she observed that moment of floundering. But they always had the advantage, these women who looked like women, with their thick definite hair and eyebrows; this one also had good teeth and a straight nose. Had their positions been reversed, Stringfellow would have felt very nervous.

Monica's hands were trembling. So much so that her knuckles were white from trying to control them within her gloves, yet still she appeared relaxed and poised. Stringfellow turned her attention to the application forms. 'Wilkinson. Monica Joan. Ludd House, Shaft's Lane, Honeywood?'

'That's right.'

'Isn't that that lovely little village just outside Petersfield?'

'Yes.'

'But you did not apply to the hospital there?'

'No. I wanted to come here.'

'Why?'

And so for twenty minutes, fearful little Madeline Stringfellow lifted her chin and interviewed a confident and assured applicant – one of the lucky ones. And for twenty minutes Monica Wilkinson, stressed and anxious in her need to succeed, sat upright with her knees together and tried to appear confident and assured, envying the crisp and efficient little sister in her starched collar and prim white cap who knew it all.

'Hell's teeth, Rose, she was like one of those clever little terriers they train for music hall turns. She made me feel like some great St Bernard trying to jump through hoops.' Monica drank off her gin and tonic and signalled to a barman. 'Again, please. She didn't look much above twenty-two or twenty-three and she sat there, cool as a cucumber. She was one of these white-haired, albino-ish sort of girls, all kind of pink because they seem to have this transparent skin . . . About five feet tall, thin as a rake, and her belt pulled in till her belly touched her spine.'

'But you did the trick all right.'

'I don't know. She said that the final decision wasn't hers, but I got the impression that it would be on her recommendation whether they took me or not. I think she was impressed; she seemed to be: I did do rather well in my training years. I think she thought I was a waste of a good nurse. After about ten minutes she seemed quite affable. "Of course," she said, "you are rather above the age we normally think of taking . . . it's a long time to be away from nursing." So I said, "It takes a long time to bring up four children." I didn't say it sharply like that, I smiled quite a lot, and she said, "Yes, I suppose it does, I hadn't really thought about it like that."'

'Well it does,' Rose agreed. 'I mean, Jon and Tom might be men, but Nora is still just a girl.' She shook her head at Monica's offer of a cigarette.

'Oh, go on, you can't make a roll-up in a place like this.'

'I don't fancy it at the moment.'

Monica lit up, adding nicotine to alcohol, feeling the tension drop away. She raised her eyebrows. 'Don't tell me Ballard's been and gone and got you up the spout. Holidays abroad will do it every time.'

For one awful moment, Monica thought that Rose looked as though it might be the truth. But she quickly proved it not to be the case by helping herself to the packet and lighter. 'Don't even suggest it,' Rose said. 'Not just as I'm beginning to see Nora getting pubic.'

'Pubescent.'

'Oh, Monica, you are so educated.'

'But not well read. I feel like a lout when you and Leo are together.' When settled at their table, the gin and relief that her interview was over put her in a skittish mood where she flirted openly with a waiter who seemed to enjoy it. Once, looking up from her plate, she caught Rose's gaze, which was quickly withdrawn and replaced by a bright look and a comment about the food. What was up? What was it that Rose looked as though she wanted to say? Now wasn't the time to ask, not with three gins on an empty stomach and two glasses of white wine on a nicely filling one. She had been so preoccupied with herself that she had scarcely asked about Spain.

The waiter brought the pots and jugs, discreetly flirted around a little and left Rose to pour. Monica watched her. How naturally elegant she was. Leo had once said that if porcelain could be had in a block, and it could be carved by a master, that would be the only way Rose's face could be attempted by an artist. A bit arty, but she had known exactly what Leo was getting at: Rose had the finest features of any woman Monica had ever seen. She did not envy her friend: to have that kind of beauty was too precious for an ordinary woman. Helen had got somewhere near it when she said that looking like Aunt Rose all day must be like having to wear a coronet at breakfast. Monica would have chosen Monroe's or Rita Hayworth's less precious looks. Although Monica knew differently, it was as though Rose was constantly serene.

After their extravagant and splendid meal, they were sitting in a lounge with their coffee. Rose was smiling and Monica watched the smile as it stretched the red bow of Rose's lips, showing her small, even teeth. 'How do you manage to get through a three-course lunch with your lipstick still intact, Rose? Make mine strong and black – I know I should never mix gin and wine in the middle of the day.'

'I'll let you off today, Mon. I should have hated being turned over by a trained terrier.'

'Oh, she was all right really. I shouldn't be unkind. Stringfellow, isn't that a curious name? Rose, what's up? I've been wanting to ask you for the last hour.'

Rose smiled, quite composed. 'Up?'

'Up. You keep sort of disappearing.'

'Don't be ridiculous. I wish Spain could have gone on. Come with us next time.'

'God! Can you imagine Leo and Ballard holed up together for longer than a single evening?'

'Just ourselves, and the four young ones. Wouldn't it be great?'

'I might be doing my Florence Nightingale thing by then.'

'Of course. You'll be a career woman. But career women get holidays.'

It dawned on Monica. Is that what is up? It had not really occurred to her what a difference herself taking a job would mean to Rose. It was not often that either of them went out without the other, even with other women friends. Monica always felt that something vital was missing if Rose was not there. Even more so in their children and toddler days: they were more like a couple with a family of eight.

Rose raised a finger at the waiter who came at once and took away the plate with the money. 'Ready? Shall we make a day of it? Have a look round the shops. Marks and Sparks' socks for Ballard.' Monica thought that she must have imagined the preoccupied expression.

'Lovely. Let's have a walk up as far as the Castle, shall we?'

It wasn't often they lunched at the Saracen's, but when they did, they usually took this walk up through the town gate and into the castle to look at the bogus medieval round table, where they read out the names of the knights which Rose always said were as bogus as the table. They couldn't have said why they did this, it was one of the small rituals that reaffirmed a relationship, in the way that lovers will go to 'our tree'.

'This hill gets steeper,' Monica said.

'It's having the wind against us.'

'It'll sober me up before we get back.' They stopped as usual in the great hall where the table of Arthurian legend hung, each segment divided and allocated to a knight like a fairly distributed cake.

'When you think about it, they were real buggers, weren't they?' Monica said in a voice that made a bunch of tourists look sideways and a uniformed attendant shuffle and rattle his keys.

Straight-faced, Rose said, 'With each other, do you mean?'

Monica's face displayed drop-jawed schoolgirl shock. Her reaction was not entirely put on; Rose simply did not make such remarks. 'Rose Quinlan! Fancy even thinking such a thing. They were like the England cricket team in their day, instead of going after the ashes, they grested for the holy quail.'

Rose heaved gently with quiet laughter.

Monica gave a little giggle. 'Oh, I like that better, don't you? "Farewell, sweet Guinevere, I go gresting for the holy quail."'

The tourists were aghast at this whispered irreverence. They had not paid coach fares to have a good legend mocked.

The attendant took a threatening step from his niche, hoping that he would not need to take another, for that would mean that he would be forced to pinch out his sneaky drag.

Rose suddenly noticed that they were the focus of attention, and pulled at Monica's sleeve. 'Come on.'

Obediently Monica followed. Fresh air hit her. 'Christ, Rose, am I half cut? I don't know why I'm laughing, it wasn't that funny.'

'We'll walk it off.' And Rose took her arm and they walked down the backstreets and into the cathedral close.

'Hold on to me, Rose, or we'll get arrested for being drunk and disorderly. Can you imagine Ballard?'

They sat beneath one of the old trees and lit cigarettes. Rose said, 'Are you all right?'

'I will be. I had far too much.'

'It was the stress of the interview.'

'Thanks. You always know how to save faces, Rose.'

A couple of seedy men with weathered faces halted momentarily. This was their bench, where on dry days they came to drink draught South African sherry from brown paper bottles, but they made no fuss and moved on to one on the far side. Their brief contact with the women soon passed, but the sight of them was enough to flatten Monica's mood.

'Do I really want this, Rose?'

'Want what?'

'All the hassle it's going to mean. Suddenly, being at the beck and call of a dedicated young woman like Stringfellow doesn't seem so hot.'

'Of course you want it. You know you shouldn't drink gin, it never agrees with you. Let's walk back and get a nice cup of tea at the Buttercross.'

'Maybe they'll uncover my lies and turn me down. They are sure to. The Stringfellow woman was one of those with highly developed integrity.'

'Stop whittling away at yourself. They will accept you and you will be great.'

Monica looked sideways at her. 'What's been happening to you, Rose? It's been six weeks since we did anything together. Is it that, or what?'

'It's or what. Drinking at lunchtime.'

Monica's attention drifted again. There were always women with high moral principles at the top of the nursing profession: they would never condone deception. Stringfellow would have no trouble in working out that her application was a tissue of false statements. She would stay home and settle down to the next part of her life, servicing her family and having outings with Rose, eating too much fattening food, going on starvation diets then bingeing again and drinking too much. The men with the brown-paper bottles couldn't always have been like that.

'She was terribly slim.'

'Who?'

'Stringfellow.'

Rose said, 'I know what you are thinking. I forbid you to start feeling guilty about having had that chocolate fudge cake.'

'But I always do, don't I?'

'Who cares?'

'I do! Not you, Rose. And not flat-ass Stringfellow with her twenty-inch waist.' She thrust her bag and jacket into Rose's hands and, diving into the ladies toilets, said, 'I have to pee, just hold these.'

In the gloomy cubicle, with practised technique, she thrust two fingers far down her throat. It was better than worrying as the chocolate fudge cake wended its way down. But not much better. She still felt as guilty as hell for not having the willpower to say no. Why was chocolate such a bloody comfort? Why couldn't women get hooked on celery sticks?

Madeline Stringfellow went once more through the details of the application form completed by 'Wilkinson, Monica Joan', and came to the conclusion that the dates didn't add up. She was older than her d.o.b. suggested. Why had she tried to juggle the dates? Wilkinson had probably thought that so many years away from the profession would disqualify her. Yet the woman was obviously terribly keen, a nurse to her fingertips. Stringfellow had liked Wilkinson, liked her pleasant, mature face and confident voice; she had visualized her capable appearance on a ward where there were too many curtained-off beds for comfort, imagined being able to call, 'Wilkinson! Quick!' and hear the prompt rush of her apron to the bedside of a haemorrhaging d & c.

The profession could not afford to lose women like that. Who would check on a list of dates and ages if she OK'd the application? Who had the time with staff shortages at every level? Wilkinson must want to get back very much. Stringfellow imagined what it must have been like for her all these years, drudging around after some man and a houseful of kids, and all the while longing to be back amongst the orderly wards she herself loved. Rows of identical beds, lockers, lamps, clipboards. And there was the clean smell of Dettol and the polished floors and the white mounds of pillows from where eyes followed every movement the nurse made.

Stringfellow could not bear to be the one to prevent Wilkinson from using her training. Matron was unlikely to check the details of the application. Stringfellow thought that Wilkinson was worth taking a chance on.

Jonathan now lived in a small basement flat in easy reach both of his job with an estate agency just off Kensington High Street, and of the delightful open space of Kensington Gardens. Jonathan was happier than he had ever been. He saw Elna frequently. His delight with his life was such that he wanted to tell his mother the whole story and get her blessing, because he intended buying Elna an engagement ring. But although his mother was obviously terribly pleased to see him, he felt that she was preoccupied, so he had decided to wait until she was more with it. Instead he went to see Charlotte. 'Gran, is there anything wrong with Mum?'

Charlotte said, 'I haven't noticed. Don't worry, lad, she was full of beans when we were in Spain. It's not easy for her, running that great place practically single-handed. Our Ballard's hardly ever home these days, and apparently Monica Wilkinson's decided to go out to work . . . and you know how those two have always been in each other's pockets, it's a big thing for both of them. They're bound to be touchy till they are used to it.'

'I didn't think she was so much touchy as not quite with it. Anyway, I decided to put off talking to her right away. But I wanted to talk to her without Dad there. *You* liked Elna, didn't you? There wasn't time for anybody to really get to know her that day, poor old Papa. I haven't got used to thinking of him as not being here.'

'I haven't myself, Jon.'

'Poor Gran. Are you OK?'

'There's a hole in my life but I'm gradually putting things into it. I've joined an archaeology group, I may go on a dig next summer. It's a big hole . . . ?' She laughed and looked her old self. 'No pun intended. I was only thinking the other day, I was only about Vee's age when I first went to live in Sid's house.'

Jonathan looked blankly at her. 'Fifteen!'

'About that.'

'I was their servant – Sid and his first wife's.'

'Papa was married before?'

'Yes, for quite a few years.'

'I didn't know.'

'No, I don't suppose you would. These things don't always come out – not that there's anything to hide. Honoria she was called . . . nothing to do with Anoria getting that name. She was good to me, they both were. It was a real tragedy when she died. Sid was heartbroken, they'd built up the business, got a nice house, and then this lovely little baby boy. It was having Henry – your grandfather – that did for her: it could be risky in them days, having a baby.'

Jonathan looked inwardly for a long moment. 'Then you aren't . . . ?'

'No, I'm not, my dear . . . not your actual blood great-grandmother, no.'

Charlotte took two cigarettes from a packet and handed Jonathan one. It was her way when she offered cigarettes, a relic from the days when her sort could only afford to buy two or three loose Woodbines or Black Cats which they shared and shared alike.

Jonathan lit them automatically. 'I never had a clue.'

'Don't make any difference?'

'No, of course it doesn't . . .' He held her hand and smoothed it reassuringly. 'Of course not, it's the relationship that counts, and I do love you, Gran.'

She nodded. 'And I couldn't have loved you all any more if Henry had been my own son . . . nor could I have grieved more when he was killed, because by then he really was mine.'

'Aren't families strange, they talk about everything under the sun but not a thing like that. Chap I work with has just found out that his aunt is really his mother, and his mother is really his grandmother . . . It didn't bother him, except that all these years everybody has known except him.'

'It won't bother you none, knowing that I'm not a blood relation?'

'Oh Gran, how could it? It's never been your blood-line that you had going for you. I love you because I love you.' He had always been able to be unembarrassed with his great-grandmother. On the other hand, if Winifred were to say, 'Come and give Nana a big kiss, darling', Jonathan would freeze at the thought of having to make a show.

'I thought so, but I'm glad to hear you say it. I'm going to get us a sandwich if you aren't going home yet.'

'Right-o.' He followed her into the kitchen which seemed now to be filled with Papa's absence. 'Will you get another house?'

'I shouldn't think so. This is a nice old place.'

'Good. I'd hate to see strangers living here.'

'There.' She slid across the kitchen table a plate of sandwiches that she had had ready-made in the refrigerator. 'Let's sit here and have them, the kettle's boiled.'

'This is like when I used to come in from school sometimes.'

'Not quite like – it won't never be quite like, without Sid.'

Jonathan nodded and, to her satisfaction, devoured the pile of sandwiches hungrily. 'Do you mind talking about Papa's first wife?'

'Not a bit. She was good to me in more ways than anybody can count, because when you think about it, I wouldn't have had you and the girls, or Ballard and Rose or Winnie. And she gave me all the years with Sid.'

'You've given us plenty, Gran.'

She lifted the corner of her sandwich, inserted more mustard, and said casually, 'Honoria wasn't quite white, you know.'

'Was she black then?'

'Mulatto they used to say she was, but Sid always said she was Lebanese . . . is that Arabic? I'm never quite sure on these things . . . I never really thought it mattered that much. Anyhow, she had this heavy black hair and her skin was really a kind of deep-dark suntan, really like your girl, except that Honoria's hair was straight.' She added thick mustard to her crusts and ate them as though they were spread with honey. 'I thought Honoria was the most beautiful thing that ever walked on two legs.'

'So Dad's twenty-five per cent what . . . ? Lebanese?'

She shrugged her shoulders.

'What does that make me?'

'Hundred per cent human mongrel, like all the rest of the English.'

He passed her a cigarette in his fingers. 'How come I've missed all this?'

'Sid was the sort of man who thought people made too much of things like nationality: where you came from, what colour your skin was. He always said that, whatever anybody said about Honoria, it didn't stop her being Henry's mother. But, as it turned out, she did stop being Henry's mother, because once we were married, Sid would never mention her – so she stopped existing at all.'

'Not now. You've told me, so she exists again.'

'That's true.'

'Shouldn't Dad know?'

'No. You're doing just what Sid said, you're making her into a Mulatto woman. And in any case, I want to keep Ballard as my own grandson.'

'Knowing about her hasn't changed me, in fact I think it makes me love you even more than before.'

'But your father is not you. Ballard didn't have the advantages of having a mother like Rose. That's not being disloyal to poor Winnie, it is just a fact. What with that school, and what with Winnie thinking she had to be somebody she wasn't, because she thought the

Quinlans were class, your poor father didn't have a chance. You should think on that if it looks as though there's trouble brewing over you and your young woman.'

'Elna and I are going to be married.'

'I thought you might . . . well, at least I thought it was getting serious.'

'Is that why you told me about Honoria?'

'I suppose I was really telling you about Sid. You two must try to be like Sid and never to let anybody say that she married a white man or you married a coloured girl. You're going to marry a pretty young woman and she's going to marry the best young man in Christendom.'

'Her parents are as prejudiced as Nan.'

'Sid said it would get worse before it got better.'

He stubbed out his cigarette. 'We'll call the first baby Charlotte.'

'Only if Elna has a great-grandmother called Charlotte, and only if the baby's a girl. I like to see the female line get some credit.'

'Put next Easter Saturday in your engagements book, or will you be off digging up old burial sites?' He gave her a light kiss as he left. 'It really isn't the blood, Gran.'

'Go and see Winnie on your way home.'

'I can't forgive her for talking about Elna as she did.'

'You can, I know you can. It's Winnie who can't forgive herself . . . not unless you help her.'

He tucked his bottom lip up under his top lip, showing his willingness to be stubborn over this. 'I can't stand that kind of snobbishness, Gran, it makes me feel ashamed.'

'Listen, lad. I'm not one to say I'm an old lady and have got the wisdom of the world, but one thing I know: Winnie is like she is because she's afraid people will find her out. She's got a very low opinion of herself and she's spent her whole life trying to be a Quinlan – or at any rate her idea of what a Quinlan should be. I hate to say this about your grandmother because, no matter what, she's always been my daughter-in-law and that's meant a lot, but she threw out the nice bits that Henry fell for, and filled up the spaces with stuff that was useless. When Henry brought her home, she had a lovely Bristol accent.' Automatically, as she had always done whenever Sid left the house, she took a clothes-brush from the hall stand and flicked at Jon's shoulders. 'We're all she's got, Jon, and she can't afford to lose any of us.'

When he got to his grandmother's, he found her in a classic frock, two rows of pearls and pearl studs, high-heeled street shoes, and a minute apron, making tiny canapés in the shape of playing-card symbols for her bridge friends. He sat down and ate two or three of the morsels, as though there had been no rift. She beamed beautifully. 'Jonathan, darling, do let me make you something a touch more substantial.'

Although he had eaten his fill at Charlotte's, he let Winifred cut him some dainty slices of Battenburg cake which she always said everybody except Jonathan loathed. He wouldn't put it past her always to have one in the house so as to be able to offer it.

Poor Nan. Gran was right. What *was* Nan except whatever it was she was playing that day – guest, host, bridge-player, widow, MP's mother?

On his way back to London, his thoughts drifted to his father, and by the time he reached the flat he had come to the conclusion that his father was very much modelled on Nan, and that, contrary to what everyone claimed, Ballard Quinlan was far from being the substance and heart of the Quinlan family: it was in fact their mother who was that.

From his deliberations, one thing more than anything else puzzled him now. This was how it was that he had become a socialist when he had been brought up by Nan in all the traditions of a Tory – even to the public school and the London clubs. He would talk to Becc about it, and bet himself that she had sorted all that out years ago. Which, of course, she had.

'Oh, Jon, you are such an innocent sometimes. Dad's not a socialist, he's Jack the Lad, the bloke with an eye to the main chance. He couldn't care squat about socialism, equality, or any of that stuff. He weighed things up in 1944, saw how the land lay with the soldierly hoi polloi and jumped on the bandwagon. If he had thought that either the Communists or the Conservatives would win the '45 election, he'd have put up for them.'

When they were children, it had always seemed to Jonathan that his younger sister knew everything. Now that they were grown, he was fairly sure that she did.

It was not only Monica and Jonathan who sensed that Rose was preoccupied, possibly worried. Trevelyan had phoned her in the middle of the day when he knew the House was in session. Waiting, he dwelt on imagining her lips drawing back in her restrained smile, just showing her small, cared-for teeth.

Recently he had studied an enlarged photograph of her trying to discover what were the elements that composed her beauty. Her mouth was not at all generous, but she had a most perfect nose and beautifully evenly arched brows. Her head was oval and her face had the heart-shape that was pleasing to Western eyes. Her complexion was always glowing and fine. Eyes of such clarity and fineness. Kindly? He was not sure. Guarded, certainly.

He was eager to show her the proofs for the calendar, and the prints he had made of her sitting in the clearing where they had picnicked. He had never before allowed himself to become so emotionally entangled with a married woman. Sex with them was fine, yet from the first he had seemed to do his best to become involved. Hadn't she done the same? A kind of rushing headlong for one another. Where were they going from here?

'Oh, it's you,' she had said.

'Is it all right? Not inconvenient?'

'No, no. I was just clearing away my lunch plate.'

'Are you well?'

'Yes, I'm fine. Why? Don't I sound all right?'

'You sound crotchety; I've never heard you crotchety.'

'I'm sorry, I didn't intend to be.'

'Rose, it's me, the man you drink rum and lemon with, the bloke you have picnics in the New Forest with, the one who makes you laugh, the one who wants to take you to bed.'

There was silence at the other end.

'What is it, Rose?'

'Why are you ringing me?'

'Because I want to talk with you. To see whether I had remembered your voice. Was it you cut me off from Spain, or . . . ?'

'I knew it was crazy even as I was asking for your number. It seems even crazier now.'

'Meet me somewhere.'

Her 'No!' was overly sharp.

'Has your . . .' He found it so difficult even to say 'husband', because by mentioning him the man existed. It was immature, and he knew it, but hell, it was how he felt. 'Has anybody said anything to upset you?'

'No, no, everything's fine.'

It didn't sound fine.

'Jonathan is going to get engaged . . . You remember the girl you photographed trying to resuscitate Papa?'

'The pretty nurse?'

'Her parents aren't very happy. Jon doesn't say much, but there's been a rift in her family. It's a racial thing.'

'And you?'

'I'm happy for them, but not about the prejudice you can be sure they're going to encounter. Marriage is hard enough as it is without all that going on as well.'

He let it pass. 'Let me buy you lunch somewhere.'

'No. I'm sorry, Trevelyan, but . . .'

'Look, that's not being fair. You phoned me from Spain all sweetness and light, then the next time we speak you are telling me to get lost.' Again he heard only the murmur of her breath in his ear. 'Please, Rose. If we aren't going to remain friends, at least let us part like sensible adults.'

He imagined her drawing the linked boxes she had told him she always drew on telephone pads. 'Anywhere you like. A drink? Lunch? You make the terms and I'll stick to them, but just say that you'll meet me.' He saw his own anxiety showing in the whiteness of his knuckles. If she did not agree to see him, he could see himself driving down to her village and . . . He didn't know what. He could not think straight for the thought that their affair was ended before it had hardly begun.

They met on the muddy foreshore at Emsworth. He was there first, standing leaning with one elbow on his car roof, looking at but not seeing nodding wading birds and swooping gulls. It was high tide on a day more like winter than autumn. Shallow sea covered the mud-flats, and the gusting wind shook it into triangular waves. Only days ago the foreshore had been burning hot; it might be again tomorrow, but today was depressing and chaotic.

He saw the black Ford Popular draw in, but did not realize it was Rose driving until he saw her slide out and walk towards him. She was half-hidden in a cloak with a monkish hood. The breeze caught the cloak, swirling it and blowing back the hood. Trevelyan had never experienced anything like this. He had a great desire to take her in his arms, bury his head close to her ear, and tell her that he loved her. He would have loved to capture that image of her, but only for himself. He felt as he had done when he had been eighteen and had taken a girl away for a weekend for the first time. He was so apprehensive in case it should all go wrong that his insides were churning, and so full of desire and anticipation that he was afraid he wouldn't be able to contain himself. He had never expected ever to feel like that again, certainly not twenty years after that first time. He hadn't blown it then, he must not blow it now. So, controlling his hands by thrusting them into the pockets of his cord jacket, he went to meet her. He smiled cautiously. 'Rose.' He took her hand and tucked it under his arm, but did not attempt to kiss her.

She looked pale and apprehensive. 'What on earth are we going to do?'

She stopped, turned towards him and, tightening her arms about his waist, pressed her body against his and buried her face in his chest. He was sure that she felt as deeply as he did. Indeed, what on earth were they going to do? When he looked down, her marvellous mouth was turned up towards his own. He freed his hands and held her hard to him as they exchanged their first true lover's kiss.

'I love you, Rose.'

Life is one long series of events that coincide, but we think nothing of it unless the events happen to result in our crossing a road at the same moment that a driver's attention is distracted and we end up with a smashed leg. It is then we think of the chain of events that brought us and the car together at that moment and the difference it would have made had we, or the driver, left one minute earlier or later . . .

That same morning, the wife of an engineer whom Leo Wilkinson was to have met on site, went into labour. It being their first child, the engineer did not turn up for the meeting, apologizing to Leo and leaving him with a free couple of hours which he decided to spend having a quiet pub lunch and a look round the Chichester bookshops. Thus, when he left the site of a half-erected tower at Bosham, a chain of events was set in motion that led directly to the White Hart close to the cathedral.

Coincidentally the lives of three locals and a confectionery rep. brought them to the same place at the same time as Leo. But these four had nothing much to do with Leo's life. The meaningful coincidence was when Trevelyan and Rose, Trevelyan with his arm proprietorially around Rose's shoulders, came into the same bar. Trevelyan took charge of the cord that held Rose's cloak in place and, in helping her out of it, brushed the tip of a forefinger across her lips. Rose reached up and took off the driving glasses he had forgotten to remove.

Leo sat rigidly in his corner, and wished himself anywhere but here when Rose saw him. She hesitated, glanced away and then back again. He looked back at his plate, but it was no good, they were like two people trying unsuccessfully to side-step whilst passing. The room was small, with nowhere where one might dissolve into the background. They could not even begin to pretend that they had not seen one another.

He raised his knife-hand in brief acknowledgement, then returned to his cheese and pickle and buried himself in some papers. They were only a dozen feet away from him, so that even though he did not look in their direction, he could not help but be aware that Rose was leaning towards the man and saying something in a low voice, at which the man turned and glanced towards Leo. He was lean and with a narrow face, glasses on a long straight nose – the same sort of face as Rose's – and quite longish hair. Vaguely familiar.

Leo drank from his pint tankard. He had been on too many away-contracts, been to too many conferences and too many badminton tournaments not to know the signs of a couple trying to appear nonchalant in circumstances when they felt anything but that.

Rose took the initiative and came across. 'Hello, Leo. Of all people . . .'

'Right. On my way back . . . we've got a tower site . . .' He indicated somewhere out there with a brusque, friendly air. 'Cancelled appointment.'

'Oh, right. I was just . . . ah . . .' Trevelyan, holding two drinks, stood waiting.

'Leo, this is Wesley Trevelyan . . . He came to Papa's birthday to do the photos . . . You remember . . .'

Leo stood up, still holding his buttery knife.

Trevelyan nodded, moving the drinks slightly, indicating that he would shake hands if it wasn't for them.

'I remember,' Leo said. 'Yes. Nice to see you again.'

'And you . . .'

'Leo lives next door to us.'

'Oh right . . . Honeywood . . . Nice place to live.'

'It's my neck of the woods.'

'Oh . . . very nice.'

Leo put down his knife and rubbed his hands together. 'Well.' He looked at his watch, 'Lord, is that the time? I'll have to go, have to be in Gosport in an hour . . . dockyard . . . naval contract . . .' He picked up his mac and newspaper. ''Bye, Rose. Nice meeting you again, Mr Trevelyan', and ducking his head to miss the low beams, he left, abandoning his half-finished meal.

Of course he had no appointment in Gosport, but drove fast on the A27, then turned off in the direction of the Portsdown Hills, where he had a legitimate excuse to be because a tower he had designed long ago was erected close by. He stopped and switched off his engine and gazed unseeing at the expanse of coastline and harbour far below. Strong winds buffeted his car and pressed at the end-of-summer wild flowers and ripening grasses, but here the sun was out, turning the entrance to Portsmouth Harbour into a glittering mirror.

Why the hell had he scuttled off like that? He visualized the table he had left: half-drunk beer, a buttered chunk of bread, half-eaten pork pie. He had rushed off as though he had been caught out at something. He had been embarrassed and had shown it. Why in hell's name had he been embarrassed?

If they had a legitimate reason to be out together, what would they think?

They would think he suspected them of something.

Which he did.

And if they *were* up to something, he had only made matters worse by behaving as though it was his business.

He felt a fool.

That was his own two-timing mind at work. Rose wasn't like that . . . He could better believe it of Monica than of Rose.

But then he visualized them as they were when they had come into the bar, in that short space of time when Rose was still unaware that he was there. The chap had pushed open the door and had stood aside to let Rose pass, but had taken the chance to catch her round the shoulders. Leo recalled that brief hug. Rose had looked up at him and smiled and he had given her a kind of tentative wink.

That action had been nothing – and everything. Every move they made indicated that they were aware of one another. The way she stood when he undid the cord, the way he had smiled when he realized that he had not taken off his glasses, the way she had tucked them familiarly into his breast pocket, the way he didn't have to ask her what drink she wanted. They knew one another, were familiar and sure of one another, looking for any excuse to touch. Leo had known it all. Twenty years ago he had been exploring that territory with Monica.

Rose? Cool, lovely, perfect Rose? He felt almost sick at the knowledge. Rose and a long-haired arty type? Had he been a smart-suited city type, it might have appeared more appropriate. They looked as though they did not belong together. It was a long time since he had given a thought to the contrast between Monica's plump bouncing sexuality and his own athletic, exercise-hardened body; her down-to-earth way of seeing, against the alchemy of his own view of things seen through literature and science.

He remembered what it was like – the distant pub, the kind of tension built up by the controlled excitement, the momentary revealing lapse because you wanted to make contact, and the subsequent almost relief at being caught out.

But caught out in what?

With himself and Monica they did know that they were having a serious affair with lies and complicated arrangements. What was there to indicate that this was what was going on with Rosc and that chap?

The hug, the exchange of smiles and his wink. Nothing less than sex explained their actions.

Looking from high on the downs on to the scene in front of his windscreen was like looking at an architect's model of the great panorama from Chichester Harbour to Gosport. He let his gaze follow the irregular, complicated coastline of creeks, inlets, sand-bars and harbours, with working model cranes, miniature railway systems, ferries, and toy naval vessels in the dockyards. Whenever Leo was in the south of the county, he made a detour so as to spend half an hour at this vantage point. It was as restful a place as he had ever known. But today the breeze, bird sound, the great visual feast did not register with him. As he sat on in his car with the windows down, he felt his spirits fall and wondered why.

Not because he had made a fool of himself.

Not because he had behaved with such gaucherie.

Not because he had long ago buried a sexual yearning for Rose himself. Not because he was angry that Rose had gone down in his estimation nor because he wanted to be in the other man's shoes.

Of course not. The pain he experienced when the two of them repeatedly performed their little tableau of intimacies, was something else entirely.

He had never before analysed his feelings about Rose. He liked her. He admired her. She was uncomplicated. Apart from her physical beauty, she was a very nice sort of person. Nice. How, '*nice*'? She was a quiet woman, her politeness and good manners always put people at their ease – always with that faint smile. Until you knew her she could appear a bit disdainful, remote, but that was because she did not find it easy to give an opinion for fear it would not be acceptable; yet when she could be drawn out, what she had to say was always worth hearing. And steadfast and loyal. Steadfast . . . There was an old-fashioned word, yet it did apply (had applied) to Rose. How many times had he said to Monica: How has she managed to stand him all these years? Or had Monica said to him: Why on earth does she stick with that man?

Yet the first time he had seen a hint that it might happen, he had scuttled away.

He couldn't stand it if Rose got hurt.

He would say nothing to Monica. It is no one's business but Rose's. And what was there to say?

Back at the pub, Trevelyan, seeing Rose's confusion, nodded in the direction of Leo's exit. 'What was that all about?'

'He was embarrassed. I've disillusioned one of my best friends. He thinks that I am Rose the Good Woman. He has a reputation for not knowing too many good women . . . At least . . .' Why had she said such a thing? It was total disloyalty to Leo to speak of him in that way, something she would never have dreamed of doing had she not felt confused and embarrassed herself.

'He's a womanizer?'

'No!'

'OK, OK. I thought that's what you implied.'

'It was a silly thing to say. Village gossip. He's an attractive man and because he runs a badminton team, he comes in contact with a lot of young women. He inspires loyalty from them.'

'No smoke without fire?'

She turned her head and inspected a framed fake map of old Hampshire. 'Look how few roads there were then.'

Their order for pies arrived. Rose's appetite had gone, but their attention to the food did at least make a firebreak in their conversation.

Some men who, from their conversation, seemed to be local Rotary club, came in and gave further interest to the bar, and before long the lunchtime office workers filled the place, leaving no room for Trevelyan and Rose to talk, which had been his purpose in persuading her to meet him.

He wiped his lips and balled the paper napkin. 'Let's go. We'll get some coffee somewhere quieter, shall we?'

Rose was glad to get away.

By the time they were back on the streets again, the sun had come out, bringing back the Indian summer of the past weeks. They had coffee brought out to them in the garden of a pretty café.

He reached across the table to touch her fingers. 'I said "I love you".'

A poor, false smile foundered out. 'Well, here's a pretty how-de-do.'

'Rose.' He clasped both her hands. 'I love you and I think I want to start a chain of events that will get you out of his bed.' He released her hands, put his head back and thrust his fingers through his long hair in a kind of desperate action. 'It's the thing I just can't cope with . . . thinking of you and . . . you letting him –' he found it profoundly difficult even to say it – '. . . you having intercourse with him.' He held up his hands, an action to reject whatever it was she was about to say. 'I know, I know. That's unreasonable and immature. A man who sets out to seduce a married woman knows what the score is. There have been women in my life, women who have never pretended to be faithful to me. But this – with you – this is different. I have fallen in love.' Now he lowered the barrier of his hands, but she did not reply at once.

Then she said, 'I've just told you about Leo's illusion about Rose the Good Woman, and now you are making up the same story about me. I'm just a woman, not an icon, not some representation of purity.' She knew then that she was not going to stop, that there was a compulsive need to get herself out into the open. If he really did love her, then he must love her and not the image of her he held in soft focus.

'I don't know how it happened. I flirted with you a bit that day you came to take Papa's photograph, I admit that. I was flattered that I had carried out my intention. The thing is, Trevelyan, I have no illusions about you. You have affairs, of course you do. I would not expect anything else.'

He shook his head in denial, but she continued. 'You attracted me . . . you do attract me. I think about you a lot, and I was thrilled at the thought of meeting you today. I had intended not to. I wish that I had carried out my intention. The thing is, Wes, I have no illusions about you. You have affairs, of course you do. I would not expect anything else.'

'But to be faithful?'

'Not if you had a . . .'

'But I would never want another woman if I had you.'

'If you had me on your terms.'

'I can't bear thinking of him having you.'

'He's my husband. You aren't suggesting that I leave home and live with you. What do you expect?'

She saw herself pulling out the petals one by one until he was left with the stark message, 'She loves me not.'

Perhaps if Leo had not been in the pub to catch her off-guard; perhaps if he had not left in such an odd manner; perhaps if she had not been in the vulnerable state in which she now found herself, then she might not have said, 'I might not like it, you might find it hard to accept, but he's been my husband for a long time and I can't pretend that he doesn't and won't sleep with me.'

Wanting him, yet wanting him to see that she was Rose the Ordinary Woman and accept her, she plunged on, 'I'm pregnant.'

She saw it in his eyes. He had really wanted her to be a virgin.

They returned to their cars in heavy silence, Rose's vision blurred by tears that she was determined she would not shed, for fear that she would not be able to stop.

She never did know what happened to her cloak. All that she could recall later of their parting was that she drove as far as South Harting, and then at Turkey Island turned into a gateway and sat listening to the silence.

Now she had no option but to face the fact that she had not menstruated in ages, not since she had returned from Spain at the end of August.

That evening Ballard sat with some drawings of the house spread out before him. For several months he had been working on some quite grand renovation and restoration plans for the house. He wanted Rose to sell Longmore, but for some reason that she didn't seem to be able to explain, except that she was attached to the place she had grown up in, she would not agree to do so. She said that he was welcome to use whatever money had accumulated from Aunt Fredericka's shares and the Longmore rents, but he wanted to extend Shaft's Farm and put in a swimming pool which was going to cost a lot more than Rose's investment income.

Whilst he dwelt on the possibilities of stage-by-stage upgrading of Shaft's Farm, Rose tried to focus her attention upon her new Hillier's Trees and Shrubs catalogue. Villette and Anoria were in the next room in front of the television. As usual reception was poor because high downland between Honeywood and the Isle of Wight transmitter interfered with the signal; even so they joined in with the weekly rock-and-roll music programme with the same ecstasy and fervour as the teenagers in the studio.

'You're quiet.'

'Not really. I don't feel quiet. I'm sorry,' smiling brightly at him, to compensate for what had been going on in her mind, 'you know how I get when I get my head in a new catalogue.'

He had been thinking of getting away. A weekend of peace and quiet, away from his Covington problems, away from his involvement with the pro-capital punishment group. He hoped that Rose would now be persuaded to put Longmore on the market. He hated the place, and thought that she must be holding on to it for some nefarious reason, perhaps planning that they should go back there to live. But they wouldn't. Chichester wasn't bad, but it lacked the sense of place that Honeywood had. One could never attain the same kind of social status in a place like Chichester as compared to a real village. Chichester was all Church. 'I can never understand what else you hope to find in a catalogue. All the same. A tree is a tree is a tree. Some have cones and needles, some don't.'

She closed the Hillier's. 'It must seem terribly boring to someone not interested in gardens, but I do find it terribly interesting.'

Apropos of apparently nothing, he said, 'Have you thought about standing for the county council?'

Rose looked startled. 'No!'

'You could do worse. The Independents are putting up a woman, the local Party thinks it would be a good move to oppose her with a woman of our own. The women's vote is quite important.'

'No, Ballard. I should hate it. Just the thought of it scares me to death. I know nothing about council politics . . . I know nothing about any politics, really. You told them no.'

'Of course not, I said I couldn't answer for you, but that I'd talk to you about it.'

'But you know I couldn't do it.'

'There is nothing to council work. You go to the meetings and you take the Party line.'

Ballard had expected that she would be difficult to convince. But once the idea had been put to him, it appealed to him. It wasn't as though the rest of the council were all so bright that she had any need to be scared. But it was a tricky one. He knew that it would be, which was why he had started to work on her now, months before the next election. Gentle persuasion. He made G and Ts, lit two cigarettes and gave her one. The action made him remember that afternoon in Spain when she had shown him the kind of passion that, years ago, when they were first married, he had expected would develop.

She had seemed mopy since Spain: she probably had too little to do with only Villette and Anoria to look after. The council would be ideal. He didn't want a mopy wife. He liked a relaxing and untroubled scene when he came home. And he wanted to get her away from that damned garden.

She sat in a pool of light from a red-velvet-shaded standard lamp, ill at ease, fidgeting with the corners of her catalogue, drinking the gin and smoking the cigarette in little puffs, as though it was distasteful. He could almost feel her apprehension, and assumed that its cause was the idea of becoming a candidate. Her silence felt sullen, her bowed head was passive. There were times when he thought that the best thing would have been to have let her go on as she had been when he found her, living with her dotty old aunt and that dykey woman who wallowed in the tragedy of her lost lover. There had been a time when he had seen himself as Rose's rescuer, but she wasn't really much good at being married. If he had been less smitten by her looks, her youth, and the virginity she appeared very ready and willing to surrender, she could have gone on living her life inside the Longmore high walls for ever.

Untouched by human hand.

Even before their wedding night (he had even been prepared to wait for that), he had known what sex would mean to her. He sometimes thought that he was the only one who was not fooled by her looks. He had known the first time he took her out that, inside her, the pretty porcelain figurine was burning up with hunger for sex. And he had not been wrong. In the early months she had seemed to be insatiable, and willing to do anything he wanted. She seemed to have forgotten that. Mostly, he preferred not to think of it himself because he could still not believe she would become so bitter about a bit of insistence on his part. She knew his appetites well enough. She had had her own. Then, because of a couple of episodes when he had wanted her so much that he couldn't hold back, she had turned against him. Turned herself off – that's how he saw it. If she had chosen to turn her sex drive back on, he could have saved himself a lot of hassle and intrigue over the years. After the episode in Spain he did wonder whether that was what she had done, but no. In any case, it was too late now. But that didn't stop him looking at her sitting in the pool of light, arousing him.

Suddenly his thoughts got out of hand, forcing him into action; forcing him to press his lips hard upon hers as he unzipped; forcing him to lift her skirt and yank at the crotch buttons of her cami. 'Come to bed, Rose. Do what you did in Spain. You can be fantastic when you want. Please, Rose. Come upstairs. You really love it, you know you do. I have . . . protection, I won't let you get pregnant.' He needed three pairs of hands to do everything he wanted to do. He wanted to carry her upstairs.

He tried to lift her, but her automatic reaction was to pull away. He tried to get a grip on her skirt whilst trying to manoeuvre his fingers into her with the other hand. She twisted and turned violently, hissing the words, 'Stop it! Stop it! The girls!'

'They're watching the television.' Her struggle aroused him to such a pitch that the earlier idea of Spain, when she had taken the dominant position, faded, and his mind slipped back into wanting her to be submissive. She was his wife and he could bloody have her. She had made him a fool. Messed up his life. Made it a misery.

When at last his hand made it to her soft skin, he found her dry, not melting and accessible as she had been in Spain. He held on, gripping with his strong fingers, determined that he would get her to that same receptive state. He would make her receptive. If he could hold her down and get his mouth to her . . . The more she hissed at him to stop and the more she struggled, the greater became his determination to prove that she had no choice. She would like it. Needed it.

They slipped to the floor in their struggle, almost silent except for their stertorous breathing.

As they fell in a tangled heap, compelling desire washed over him and became transmuted to lust and malevolence. Without any order to his thoughts, the whole bloody mess that she had got him into flooded his mind as he struggled angrily to penetrate her.

She had made him pay over and over again for those two measly quick tricks. He had paid for Villette, and paid again for Anoria. She hardly needed to be touched to get pregnant: first there'd been Jonathan, then Villette and Anoria from those short bursts of ecstasy. He had paid for his mistakes by all the times when a look from her had made him feel like some dirty rapist.

He wanted to have her, wanted her to want him, wanted to pay her back for all the women he hadn't really wanted.

'I'm good at it, damn you. Why can't you enjoy it?' he said through gritted teeth. He tried to kiss her but she struggled. Holding her face, he put his mouth over hers and weighed her down with his twelve stone solid body. He felt triumph surge up and he realized that he had won. Suddenly the hall flooded with light from the kitchen. There was a sound like a sob as he sprang away from her. The sound had come from himself as he had reached a premature and incomplete climax in the struggle.

From the kitchen at the far end of the hall, Anoria, her mouth and hand full of apple pie, saw nothing more than the flash of blue skirt colour as her mother ran out of the sitting room and up the stairs. Momentarily, as she passed the hall mirror, she glimpsed her father in the sitting room, facing the window and combing his hair in its reflection. He sounded out of breath. Something had happened, and she felt instinctively that if she was not careful she might find out what.

She felt ravenously hungry, and went back into the kitchen to find some crisps and chocolate biscuits.

In spite of Leo's earlier resolution not to say anything to Monica, that same evening he said, 'Mon?' Monica glanced up from her book, one of a number of new nursing textbooks she was studying. 'Is Rose having an affair?'

Monica pulled her glasses down her nose and looked over the top at him, blinking in an exaggerated way. 'Rose? As in Rose the Immaculate next door?' Then saw that it wasn't a joking matter.

The hours between lunchtime and now had been disturbing to Leo. Monica had said, 'You're quiet', and he had passed it off as being nothing new when he had spent the day driving round the sites. No matter how he tried to concentrate on *Moonraker*, a new novel he had bought that morning, his mind would keep sliding back to that moment when they had come through the door of the pub. 'I saw her today. She was with that photographer chap – you remember? The one who kept on taking pictures when Old Sid keeled over?'

'Wesley Trevelyan. Why shouldn't she be with him? She knows him. He did some photos of Rebecca that got in the *Mirror* or somewhere.' She knew Leo well enough, he hated gossip and speculation. He sounded quite worried. Her stomach turned over. Rose?

'Oh.' Leo returned his eyes to his book.

'Hey, come on, you can't just say a thing like that and then go back to your book. You must have seen something to ask a question like that.'

'I'm an old hand at trysts and assignations, remember? It was just something about them, I don't know . . . It was only a fleeting moment . . . Just the way they came in together, smiling, the way he touched her. Familiar, proprietorial . . . you know?'

Monica took off her glasses and closed her book and went to sit beside him. Usually he liked to sit like this in the quiet of the day, but now he found Monica's presence irritating. He rose and went to refill their glasses, going back to sit opposite when he had handed Monica her drink.

Monica said, 'She has been a bit . . . well, a bit sort of preoccupied lately. I thought so the day she came with me to my interview at the hospital, but I didn't take too much notice. I thought it was because she had just come home from Spain and had post-holiday blues, though I was too interested in myself that day to take much notice. I pulled her leg about having got herself pregnant.' She sipped her drink thoughtfully, her brows drawn.

Leo looked up sharply. 'She's not, is she?'

'No, of course not. You've got to be wrong about the photographer chap.'

Leo longed for Monica to come up with something that would put his mind at rest. He had blurted it out because he wanted to put a stop to the image of Rose's pleased smile as they had come into the pub. 'Don't you think I want to be bloody wrong?' he said.

Monica didn't reply but stared pensively into the fire.

Why? he asked himself. Why in the hell he was so concerned? Rose was too good for a man like Ballard Quinlan; she should have an affair with some nice chap.

Monica said thoughtfully, 'I do think there's trouble going on there, so I put her touchy mood down to that. Ballard and Becc had a row about Becc getting in with some people who are going to help her get started. Apparently he said something about them being Jews and Becc took her stuff and left.'

'You didn't tell me about that.'

'Well there's been so much going on here, what with James acting up about school . . . Anyway, I just put it down to Ballard being Ballard and it would blow over.'

'Jon gone in a row with him about colour, and now Becc in a row about race. Makes the rows with our kids seem trivial.'

They fell silent again until Leo said, 'I'm sure I'm right about Rose.'

He did not notice how closely Monica was watching him. He didn't see the faintly troubled look she was giving him, until eventually she knocked back the rest of her whisky in one and returned to staring at her nursing textbooks.

'Don't say anything, Monica.'

She looked sideways at him over her glasses. 'What the hell do you think I am?'

A few days later, when Leo played a really stinking doubles game, his partner wondered whether Leo had something on his mind or was at last coming to the time when he would have to drop his own name from the team and stick to coaching. Shame, Leo was such a sweet partner. She hoped he wouldn't stop playing altogether: he had such a smashing bum, and the movement of his racket-hand shoulder as he brought his racket to meet the shuttle . . . One of those great, naturally athletic bodies nobody likes to see go to seed.

After Anoria had waved Daddy off in his super-swish Jag that she absolutely loved, she went down to her mum's garden and found her sitting on an upturned bucket padded with a sack, rolling a cigarette. Just sometimes, but not very often, she would look at Mum and really see her. All of Anoria's friends said that her Mum was so beautiful, but how could people see their own families? Somebody had once said that Becc Quinlan was an absolute fire-cracker. Anoria knew what they meant, but could not see Becc like that: Becc was a bossy older sister.

Daddy was quite famous because of his job, but you could only see a daddy as he was really: cleaning his teeth in his pyjamas, or bending over with his foot on the shoe-box. Even when his photo was in a magazine or newspaper, it wasn't possible to think of him as somebody people wanted to read about. She had wondered whether James Dean's mother only saw him as her Jamie.

Mum was miles away, gazing up at the old apple tree, rolling her cigarette. She hadn't even heard Anoria's footsteps until she was close. For a second or two, Anoria saw a stranger: she was, as everybody said, really pretty.

Rose held out a hand and smiled. She must appear perfectly normal. Children should grow up feeling secure. Although Rose did not consider herself damaged by her odd childhood, she was sure that a normal and stable home were essential for the development of children into balanced adults. 'Nora, it's you. I didn't even hear you.'

'I've just seen Daddy going. I thought he was going to be here the whole weekend.'

'Well, you know what it's like with Daddy. There is always something important he has to see to.'

'You'd think we were important.'

Rose gathered her solid youngest on to her knee, feeling a bit like a mother sparrow with a fledgling cuckoo. She loved the feel of Nora's tightly filled skin, and the smell of her hair. 'Oh sweetheart, I do love you. Of course you are important. Children are the most important things in life. It might not always seem like that when you are a child, but it is true.'

Last night Rose had slept on a couch in what Ballard called his dressing room. She didn't know what would happen now. Ballard had gone off without saying where, or when, or even if he was coming back, but whatever might be going on between him and herself, Nora and Vee must not lose their sense of security. When Rose had run upstairs last night, she had caught a glimpse of Nora coming out of the kitchen, apparently unconcerned and absorbed in eating, but you could never tell with children. When she was quite young, Rose had come upon the man who came every year to pick the apples. He'd been pulling the blouse out of the waistband of Threnody Chaice's skirt, something that made sense to Rose only much later; but at the time Rose had sense enough to know that it would be better if she had not seen, so she had behaved as though she had not.

'Mum? Don't get cross at what I'm going to ask you. If you don't promise, I won't ask you.'

Rose swallowed down her apprehension. 'OK.'

'Most girls have done it, Mum. Could I have a go at your cigarette? Please, Mum?'

Mentally, Rose wagged her head. If one didn't know what was going on inside the heads of one's own children, then how on earth was one to sort out the rest of the world? 'I'm not cross, Nora, it's a perfectly reasonable request for you to make. But the answer is no. And, as you have a lot more common sense than I have, you will never try it.'

'I bet Jilly Johns that that'd be what you'd say and she said you were the sort of mother who isn't always stopping their children trying out things.'

'Why should she ever think that?'

'Because you're pretty, and pretty mothers are kind.'

'What about Snow White's wicked stepmother?'

'Oh, Mum, you aren't like that. You are just nice.'

Rose was very moved at receiving such a testimonial from a child who, being the youngest of four, had not really had a great deal of attention from either parent. She couldn't bear the thought of hurting her overblown, chunky baby who, for all her giggling in corners, and the buds of a woman's breasts swelling on her stocky chest, was still not lost to the pubescent tribe in which Vee now existed and through whose rituals Becc had progressed, and from which she was now beginning to return as a woman.

Sitting on her upturned bucket, watching the blue smoke of her autumn bonfire trail straight up into the morning sky, her vision leapt ahead ten years or so, when they would all be women. Poor Jonathan, he had never measured up to the targets Ballard had set for him. She hoped that he would never become alienated from herself and his sisters – they all liked him, needed him. Rose needed him . . . needed all of her children.

Rolling the wet end of her cigarette so that it become bitty and shaggy, she put it to Anoria's lips.

Anoria drew tentatively, not taking in much smoke, then spat explosively. 'Mother! That is disgusting.'

Rose agreed. Since Spain she had lost all satisfaction with her small early morning pleasures of sweet tea and a cigarette. No, she was not pregnant. She was not nauseous, nor were her breasts tender.

But she was pregnant, of course she was. The only safe method of birth control was celibacy.

In the lounge bar of a Petersfield hotel where Rose and Monica often met on a Saturday morning after they had done their weekend shopping, Monica waited for Rose to say what she had obviously come to confess. She was sure that it was a confession. About the affair that had knocked Leo for six and pained Monica severely. She had never known Rose's face to express such anguish. She was pinched and pale and looked ill.

From behind the shield of the gin and tonic she was sipping, Monica said, 'Ready to tell me what's up, Rose?'

Unhesitatingly, and raising her eyes to meet Monica's, Rose said steadily, 'I have to get an abortion Mon.' Then, close to tears, she took a cigarette from Monica's packet and lit it, shuddering at a wave of nausea.

Equally unhesitatingly, Monica said, 'OK.'

'Do you know a good man?'

Monica nodded. 'Excellent, but she's a woman, she'll do a d and c; but she's not cheap.'

Just a wry turn of the lips, not even near a smile. 'I don't want cheap, I don't care what it costs. I don't want to die from it, but I want it done . . . quickly.'

At the bar, as she waited to ask for more ice, Monica puzzled at Rose's fierceness. Why didn't she care if she was bankrupted? Was Leo right about the Trevelyan man? Back at the table, as casually as she knew how, Monica said, 'How many weeks do you reckon you are?'

'It happened in Spain, so I suppose I'm . . .'

'Spain?'

Rose heaved a great sigh. 'God forgive me, yes.'

'What does Ballard . . .'

'It's no affair of Ballard's.'

Monica felt her own face blench. 'It's not his?'

Momentarily, Rose looked puzzled. 'Of course it's his. Who else . . . ?' Her eyes met Monica's, causing her to look away. Rose smiled wryly and, patting her stomach said, 'You can't catch this from a couple of kisses and a picnic in the woods. That's all it was. It's over. Not that there was anything to get over . . . I expect Leo thinks there is . . . but there is not.'

'I didn't mean . . .' But Monica really didn't know what it was that she didn't mean.

Money can so easily buy the best there is in the gynaecological world, and Rose had money, quite an accumulation from years of leasing Longmore. It was all done on a theatre trip to London. Monica drove them, booked into an hotel opposite Green Park, and then watched over Rose during the critical hours once she had left the clinic and thereafter during the days of inevitable depression, guilt and anguish that followed. By the time Christmas was in sight, the worst of it was over.

* * *

Christmas and the end of 1955 were approaching. Monica had started her retraining in the big Winchester hospital, and once she had the scent of the wards in her nostrils again and the echoing corridors in her ears, she felt as though she had never been away.

Monica going out to work changed lives other than her own. Jean Thompson 'saw' to James after school and undertook a few hours more of cleaning at the Wilkinsons'; Tom, who was at Sussex University, found himself in charge of his own laundry; Helen, who was a research assistant in the laboratories of a chemical adhesives manufacturer was supposed to see to the washing machine but paid Kate to do it for her; Leo went about with shopping lists propped against his car windscreen. Kate took to appearing more and more often in the Quinlans' kitchen, something Rose did not mind at all. Villette and Kate seemed to be more permanently on a best friend basis these days, and usually disappeared into Vee's room to mourn the death of James Dean whose pictures covered the walls. Although it was in fact Nora who had been most devastated by the dreadful death of her first passion, Vee and Kate thought her too young to be a real fan, so they excluded her until they suddenly both went mad for Elvis Presley and let Nora have the mementos of James Dean to whom she remained true.

Even though she had expected to miss Monica, Rose felt very much more disturbed than she had supposed she would have. She felt so isolated. When Trevelyan phoned she answered abruptly, firmly refusing to meet him. Every time she heard his voice, her resolve weakened but did not break. She wanted someone to talk to: had she been a Roman Catholic, then she would probably have haunted the confessional. Instead she brooded. She needed to ask someone what they thought about Ballard . . . Were these incidents her own fault? She could not talk to Winifred, certainly not Gran, neither could she see herself actually saying to Monica, 'The thing is, he tried to rape me with . . . with the girls in the next room.' Would Monica be incensed, or would she suggest her usual treatment for deviant men: that they should have it tied like a wart until it dropped off.

Right up to the week or two before Christmas, things were at an impasse between Rose and Ballard. He had phoned a few times, been coldly polite, but had not come home nor made any mention of his behaviour. Because he had the little flat in London, it did not appear that he had left home as it might have done in other circumstances. Rose did not know whether he had actually left, or even whether he proposed leaving permanently. He had just filled the boot of his car with some of his belongings and driven off. It was a very unsettling state in which to be. She might have asked him, Are you coming back? or written to him, even; but to do so would mean actually disturbing the status quo. Though of course it would have to be disturbed: the House was already in recess for Christmas. On the phone, they had managed to talk fairly normally in a stilted way. He always had a word with Nora and Vee, telling them how awful it was that he always had to be in the London flat or staying in Covington. Then one Sunday evening, the problem had at last been faced.

'But you will be home for Christmas, won't you, Daddy?' Anoria had said.

'I sincerely hope so,' he had said, 'but I don't exactly know yet whether I am to be part of a trade delegation that is going to America.'

'At Christmas! Oh, Daddy, even Americans have Christmas.'

'Well, maybe not their Senators. The House of Commons isn't Woolworth's, we can't shut shop on Christmas Eve . . . well the shop shuts, but we still have to go to work.'

'But you will try.'

'Sweetheart, of course I will try. Now will you put me on to Mummy please?'

From which Anoria deduced that he knew already that he would be in America for Christmas, and was just building up to tell them. Which was more or less what he told Rose. Then, 'By the way, Rose, I should warn you in good time, Khrushchev is planning to come to this country next year. There will be an official reception – a "black tie and ladies" occasion, I should think, though it does appear an odd thing to suggest to a Bolshevik leader who looks like a peasant . . . Rose. Are you there?'

'Yes, Ballard, I'm here. Does this mean that you expect me to go with you?'

'Naturally. It would appear odd if you did not.'

She was bewildered and fell silent for a few moments. 'I'm afraid all this is beyond me.'

'We can't discuss matters by telephone. Neither of us can walk away from our duty.'

Monica would have said: 'Balls!' Rose had never learned the satisfaction to be had from giving vent to feelings crudely. 'Then I suggest you come home where we can talk reasonably. You have been away for weeks now.'

'I have kept away because I did not want the girls being involved in any contretemps we might have.'

'Contre . . .' She stopped herself, aware that Nora might perhaps be somewhere at hand.

'Then I will come to London. Will you be in tomorrow?'

There was a pause. The line sounded dead but still open: he had his hand over the mouthpiece. 'I was just checking my diary. I can be in the flat tomorrow about midday, or we could meet somewhere.'

'Thank you, Ballard, I'll come to the flat,' she said with an acerbity quite alien to her. 'Perhaps you can fit me into the lunchtime slot?'

Vee was very touchy sometimes, so Nora did not put her head round her sister's door without thinking twice. Vee was swotting over her books.

'What do *you* want, Nora? I have this project to finish.'

'I just wanted to ask you a bit about Daddy and Mummy.'

'What about them?' Vee stopped writing, but did not look round at Nora, who had placed herself on Vee's bed.

'Do you think they are breaking up?'

'What do you mean, breaking up?'

'You know what I mean, so don't pretend.'

Vee heaved a sigh, but still did not change position or speak.

'Oh come on, Vee, you're a lot older than me, and even I know that there's something up with them. That last time Daddy went away, he went off without saying anything to anybody. I know he didn't say goodbye to Mum because she was out in the garden, and I only saw him because I happened to get up early that Saturday. He didn't say goodbye to you, did he?'

'So what!'

'So he always says goodbye, even if he's going at the crack of dawn, he says goodbye the night before – and this time he didn't.'

Vee turned slowly and looked at her young sister. 'So you take that one piece of evidence as Mum and Dad getting a divorce?'

'I didn't say divorce. I didn't mean divorce, that's a terrible thing to say.'

'Well, what's breaking up then?'

Nora, shocked by the brutality of Vee's suggestion and the can of worms she may well have opened up, said, 'I don't know, it's kind of not being happy like they used to.' Vee looked angry and contemptuous. 'I only asked,' Nora said. And when Vee still didn't offer the reassurance she had hoped for, Nora went on, half hoping to justify having disturbed Vee and half hoping that Vee would have a resolution. 'The night before he went, you were watching the end of a programme, and I went into the kitchen to get some supper, and I heard some noises, and somebody sort of shouted. I thought it sounded like they were fighting, then Mummy rushed out of the sitting room and ran upstairs, her hair was all pulled about and she was crying. And Daddy was very funny too . . . I mean "odd" funny.'

Vee stubbornly refused to let herself be drawn into talking about anything that would make her fears come into being, forcing Nora to go ploughing on, 'I think Daddy probably hit her.'

'Don't say such a thing!' Vee suddenly flung herself in Nora's direction. Nora thought that she was about to be attacked, but Vee landed on the bed beside her and sat glaring. Not knowing what to do, Nora did nothing except sit and wait. Eventually, Vee drew in a deep breath and said, 'Listen, the best thing is to pretend everything is the same as always. If you start asking, it only makes them tell you lies, and that's worse. You can't make anything better by asking. If they don't have to say anything, it might blow over.'

'I can ask you though.'

'I can't do anything about it, can I?'

'But I can tell you, and you needn't do anything, but I just want somebody who knows more about things than I do. I don't like having to keep horrible things inside me.'

Vee, who these days usually found Nora and all her eleven-year-old friends irritating and embarrassing, suddenly felt quite protective of her trusting young sister, and actually gave her a squeeze. 'All right.' Then, after steeling herself, 'Do you actually know anything?'

'Daddy isn't coming home for Christmas. He says he is going to try, but I could tell by the way he was saying it, about having to go to America, that he was making excuses. And I heard Mummy say, "All this is beyond me . . ." And then she asked if she could see him, and she would come up tomorrow if he would be in. I think he must have said yes, because she said in a really nasty way, "Well, fit me in for an appointment."' She looked sideways at Vee to see how she had taken it.

'I don't suppose it means anything. It's just how me and Kate are when we stop being best friends. It doesn't last, and we get back together and everything is all right. I expect that's why we don't ever tell everybody when we aren't being friends. If people kept asking us about it, then it would be hard to get it mended again. Do you see what I mean?'

'Yes, I do see. I might be only ten, but I'm not stupid, Vee.'

'Well, let me get on with my project.'

Nora jumped off the bed and, by fussily straightening the bed-cover that she had crumpled, acknowledged her gratitude for the time Vee had given her. Before she reopened the door she said, 'It must be awful having divorced parents.'

'You are doing just what I said don't do,' Vee said.

Winifred was no fool; even if there was a long stretch of road between her own house and Honeywood, she knew about the comings and going at Shaft's Farm, and she was aware that there was trouble between Ballard and Rose. But she mentioned it to no one. Least said, soonest mended was all well and good, but it pained her to know that there was a rift and that, not only could she do nothing to help mend it, she was excluded from knowing just what was at the back of the trouble. Of course, Rose kept up her bright and smiling pretence, and Ballard confided in her latest bits of gossip about the Hon. Membs., all as though everything was as usual, but they could not fool Winifred into believing that they had not had some sort of big quarrel.

When Rose phoned to say that she was going up to London to do some Christmas shopping, and would Winifred mind giving the girls their tea if she was not back in time, and did Winifred want anything or have any message for Ballard whom she was meeting for lunch, Winifred thought that it would not be long before the trouble was sorted out.

'You might try to discover what I can get Ballard as a gift, Rose. I never have any idea.'

'But you always get such lovely, imaginative things, Mother.'

'He does seem to have everything.'

Rose took the plunge by saying lightly, 'I expect he's already told you about the trade delegation to America.' She did not wait to hear the embarrassment in Winifred's voice indicating that Ballard had not already told her, so she rushed on, 'Isn't it just like them? So inconsiderate, and just at Christmas.'

Winifred was quite taken aback; she certainly knew nothing about any delegation. 'He takes on too much, Rose.'

'Perhaps he will enjoy it if he does stay in the home of that Senator.' Even as she said it, Rose realized that it was all falling apart.

Even as Rose said it, Winifred felt that the story – well – lacked a certain authenticity. 'Of course, the children will be upset . . . and of course so will you, Rose. I certainly don't like us all not to be together, especially this year, with Papa not being here.' She longed to know whether Rebecca and Jonathan intended coming home. They did both speak to her by telephone, but neither of them would actually talk to her.

Rose, in thinking only of the unspoken estrangement between herself and Ballard, had entirely forgotten everybody else. Poor Gran, she and Papa had enjoyed Christmas so much.

'Rose? Ah, I thought we had been cut off.'

'Don't think too much of it yet, Mother, it might not happen. Ballard did say that it was only a possibility.'

'Oh, well, we must just hope for the best. But do ask discreetly if Ballard likes these new kind of electric razors. I had thought I might buy him one.'

'I should think he would love one.'

'What do you think about the Khrushchev visit, Rose?' Here was something that Ballard had told his mother.

'I said to Ballard, how incongruous it appeared, to have a black tie reception for a communist.'

What *was* going on over in Honeywood?

The London flat was really far too small for the row they had. Their first honest-to-goodness row, for Rose did not capitulate before his aggression but stood her ground, half smoking furious cigarettes, then grinding them into ashtrays. He banged things, slammed down books and papers, and shouted, but Rose held up.

Suddenly his rage no longer frightened her; she had an assurance that was new; perhaps a confidence come from just that morning starting her first period since the d and c, and from having taken a hand in arranging her own life instead of letting it roll over her. It was she who had decided to finish with Trevelyan, and it was she who had made the decision to have the abortion, and now she was standing up to Ballard.

'You can rant and rave as much as you like, Ballard. I don't care if you do hit me. I shall never again hide a bruise, I should use it as I should have done years ago. You can do this thing my way or not at all.' She directed a look at him that said: I have as much right to anger as you have. He appeared smaller. He was a bully and – not that Rose would have thought of it in these crude terms – she had him over a barrel. She had had him thus for years, had she only realized. A member of the House of Commons was as vulnerable to Fleet Street gossip as any deviant vicar. Members might be involved in a shady money deal and get away with it but, if they had any ambition to achieve high office, then there must be no hint of immorality, deviation or marital misdemeanour.

Ballard's career (not entirely in the field of Party politics) was about to take off. For the next month or two he could not risk the slightest hint that he was not 'sound'. The first mistake he made was to fire that information at Rose, 'A separation? Just when I'm about to meet Congressmen and Senators? I'll damn well see that you don't queer my pitch like that.'

'How will you do that Ballard?' It was at this point that he had deflated, and Rose, for the first time, saw that she didn't have to go on putting up with everything he handed out.

1956

For Rose, 1955 ended with a noisy party at the Wilkinsons', where most of the guests were members of the badminton club. At midnight, Leo, who was fair, pulled on a black knitted fishing-hat to be the dark man with the coal and bread, entering his own house and receiving first-footing kisses from Monica and Rose. 'Happy New Year to my two favourite women,' he said.

'And to you two,' was all Rose could manage, feeling so charged with emotion and gratefulness. She wished that she could tell them how important they were to her, how much she loved them for being open, loving people, how reassured she had felt since they had become neighbours. Instead she gave Monica a brief, strong hug and brushed her cheek against Leo before the entire party crashed out of the house in a fairly inebriated conga line which, when the frosty air hit them, had a sobering effect and soon broke up the party, leaving Monica, Leo and Rose in a quite pleasing mess of party debris.

'Quick, Leo,' Monica said, 'freshen our glasses before the effect of all the rest wears off. God, I'm glad that lot has gone. I don't know how you stand badminton players week after week: they're all so full of themselves.'

'The circumstances at the club are quite different. Anyway, they don't know it, but it was my swan-song as captain. Time for a younger man.' He was brisk; he had captained the team for a good many years. It had not been easy to decide that it was time to go.

'You'll still play, Leo?' Rose asked.

'Of course he'll play,' Monica said. 'His does would never survive without their twice weekly look at the way his legs go all the way up to his shorts.'

'Of course I'll still play, Rose. Take no notice of the coarse comments from the chorus. I'll probably enjoy it more not having to sort out all the team politics – they're a lot of bloody prima donnas. Now, where are some clean glasses? I hope you are all right till the early hours, Rose,' Leo said.

'I'm a free woman for once,' she said, flushing at what had remained unsaid between herself and Leo since the episode in the

Chichester pub. It was unsaid because there seemed to be nothing that she could say without making something out of nothing; it was nothing because she had pulled up just in time and saved herself from the bolting horse of a serious involvement with Trevelyan by refusing to see him. She thought that she had never experienced such painful deprivation, and expected any day to find herself, as she had in Spain, ringing him just so as to hear his voice. But so far she had desisted, her determination buttressed by the trouble between her and Ballard.

'We were only saying – weren't we, Mon? – all the years we've known you, we have never seen you pie-eyed.'

'And if you stand there with empty glasses, we aren't ever going to . . . And no more punch, fetch the brandy bottle,' Monica said. 'That's better. Now, Rose, let's settle down to some serious, maudlin remembrances of times past. Now that's what I call a drink,' she said, holding up the large glass balloon to the light. 'Happiness, Rose, lots of it.'

'Amen. To happiness, wherever it may be found,' Leo said.

Rose could not decide whether there was some kind of allusion in the latter part of his toast, so she simply said, 'To happiness. If ever it is to be found.'

Leo and Monica flicked a look at each other. They had not heard Rose say that, had they?

Rose was, for this evening, a free woman. Anoria and Villette were upstairs, sharing Kate's room quite amicably. Vee was touchy about having Nora mixing with her own friends, but as James had to be there too, and they needed four to play the 'Monopoly' with which they had suddenly all become obsessed, and which anyway belonged to Nora, they were all behaving like well brought-up children. Tom and Helen had gone off to London to bunk down with Becc and Jon for a couple of days so as to be in Trafalgar Square for New Year celebrations. Jonathan and Rebecca had gone back to London after spending a surprisingly jolly few days in Honeywood with a traditional dinner at home and formal Boxing Day morning drinks at Winifred's.

Winifred had been proud of her grandchildren when they were courteous and smiling with her canasta friends (canasta being the game in Winifred's circle which for the moment was ousting bridge), from whom she received condolences at the absence of her well-known son who had such a sense of dedication. Charlotte had mostly sat by the fire with great dignity and received the attentions of Winifred's acquaintances, whilst Rose circulated in her polite and smiling role of junior Quinlan woman.

All in all, Winifred thought later, when her best crystal was returned to its cabinet, and the little porcelain dishes that had contained politely minute snacks were back on their display stands, it had been a most satisfactory interlude; for, in spite of not having Ballard there in person, his reputation was enhanced by the reason for his absence. 'Can you imagine, Cape Cod at Christmas . . . A working break I'm afraid, but the Senator does have a beautiful holiday home there, and it snows in winter on that part of the seaboard. Of course, nothing compensates for not being at home at Christmas . . . Ballard is such a family man, such a traditionalist . . .'

So, following the long tolling of twelve, and with the aroma of Leo's cigar mingling with her own and Monica's Sobranie smoke on the dry, chill air, and with her children settled in various beds, Rose was quite happy, once the Wilkinsons' guests had departed, to be the grass widow, to talk and savour the strange feelings of apprehension and excitement that the first hours of each New Year brought to her. Particularly the first hours of 1956. This was going to be a tough year.

'Sheer heaven,' said Monica. 'I can sit here till the early hours, and sleep in tomorrow. I'm off for the next three days.'

Although she had been working for only a short while, Monica was waiting for a transfer. She had changed her mind about working in a big institution in a lowly capacity, and had secured a job with 'real' nursing in the small, local hospital. What had helped her decision along was that, for all the lists and memos about who was to do what at home, and the ad hoc arrangements for when she was kept late or had late or early duties, the house had gone to pot. They had all got into a never-ending state of accusation and counter-accusation. 'I can't stand it!' she had said, 'but you will not wear me down. I want to work and I mean to work.' She compromised her ambition – which had been to learn all the most up-to-date techniques – and opted for a hospital with no highly technical miracles, secretly relieved at not having to drive miles home at the end of each round of duty when she often felt dead-beat.

'Tell her she's mad, Rose,' Leo said, refilling their glasses. 'She moves heaven and earth to get herself a job where they work her like a navvy, and then says how great it is when she doesn't have to do it for three days.'

Making a face at him, Monica said, 'How naïve of me, I thought that's what one did. It's what men do.'

Leo spread his hands and raised his eyebrows at Rose. 'She's getting above herself.'

'Rose knows all about that,' Monica said.

'I think it is suddenly having all the money they pay her,' Leo said.

'Not just that, darling, don't forget, I have all that power too. People hoping that I will remove their stitches painlessly or bring a bedpan quickly. But you are right, there *is* that huge pay-packet at the end of it.' Making light of her capitulation was the best that she could do.

Rose thought how philosophical Monica was about having to give up the prestigious hospital after having won such a prize in spite of the odds against her. She was surprised that Leo hadn't been stricter with the children and seen to it that they kept their part of the bargain. Realizing that her own family would probably not behave any better, she dismissed those thoughts. Monica and Leo were such easy, warm people to be with. If a silence fell, no one felt obliged to fill it for the sake of politeness, and one could be controversial without aggravation. She sat next to Monica in the low-lit sitting room with her feet curled under her on the deep settee, warmed by the glow from the hearth and the kick of the brandy, for the time being almost content.

'How was Christmas dinner?' Monica asked. 'Did you manage to carve the turkey without your man?'

'Actually, Jonathan carved. He was surprisingly good. Winifred, of course, wanted to know who had taught him. He said, "Twenty years of watching Dad, I've always wanted to try." He did it beautifully.'

'Old Jon's a sweetie, Rose, we've always said so.'

'He still is, although she says it what shouldn't.'

Leo had covertly watched Rose throughout the evening, and saw no sign that she was perturbed. This was their first real meeting since the day in Chichester. They had seen one another as close neighbours do, and he and Monica had had a quick drink in her house on Christmas Eve, but all the children had been there exchanging presents, and so he hadn't really had a chance to observe her properly.

By two o'clock they had slumped low down into the soft cushions with their shoes off and had reminded one another of incidents that were part of the Wilkinson/Quinlan history, and had now got on to picking over the year that had just gone and competing for events that would stay in the memory.

'Ruth Ellis hanging, James Dean being killed and Churchill resigning?' Monica said. 'Ruth Ellis will be gone from people's minds in five months, but Churchill will be canonized,' Leo said. 'And for God's sake, who is James Dean?'

Rose said, 'There speaks a really old, old man.'

'You give us some,' Monica said.

'Marilyn Monroe with her skirt over her head, Princess Margaret giving up her lover . . . ?' She had not intended saying that. 'Good Lord, hasn't anything else happened? Oh, and what about skiffle? No, probably not skiffle, not for five years. Autobahns, or whatever they're going to be called in this country.'

Leo said, 'This bloody government will still be talking about autobahns in five years – sorry, Ballard, wherever you are.'

'Language.' Monica pushed a toe at him. 'Not when he isn't here to defend himself. I agree with Rose about Marilyn Monroe,' and went on to discard Cyprus, *Lolita*, diplomats with communist associations, the state of emergency in Cyprus, the death of Thomas Mann.

'His books will last,' Leo said.

'So will television advertising,' Rose said.

'Television advertising! Oh, poor old future,' Monica said.

'President Eisenhower?' Rose offered.

'Nah,' Monica said. '*General* Eisenhower, but not as President, especially if he pegs out, which looks likely.'

Leo went round with the brandy bottle yet again. 'Come on, Rose. If you pass out I'll sling you over my shoulder and carry you home, or you can sleep on the settee.'

'Is this to toast the great events of 1955?'

Leo ticked off on his fingers, 'Toothpaste adverts on TV; *Seven Year Itch*, *Death in Venice*, Churchill . . . James Dean?'

'You're right, Leo,' Monica said, 'it's not been a vintage year.'

Leo said, 'So let's be sentimental and drink to what will endure for us: five daughters and three sons between us.'

They didn't actually raise their glasses, but with Leo seated between them, they nodded and drank. Monica held his hand briefly and said, 'Isn't he a sentimental old thing, Rose.'

The long-case clock whirred and chinged. 'Three hours of the year gone already,' Leo said. 'That's how we get old so quickly. Time never knows how to relax and slow down.'

Rose said, 'Monica's right, it was a rotten year. I'm glad it's over.'

Rose and Monica looked deeply at one another, being aware of something more momentous to them than any world event; something that they, and only they, would remember in five years – and in ten, and in twenty.

Mona Birdham's voice soared with thanks for the presence of Elna in the congregation. A good omen for the coming year.

There had been a period recently of raised voices and tears, but Mona was confident that the problem with the white boy was over. Under those modern-day ideas she had picked up at grammar school, Elna was really a good girl, made with the same good qualities that made the McKenzies and Birdhams the God-fearing families they were. The Lord looked after his own. Her shining eyes slid from Frank to Elna and to Manley (Mona's cousin Manley McKenzie's eldest boy, known as 'Mac', but not to Mona), who had come visiting and was now seated next to Elna.

Boy? Manley had been a boy when Mona had last seen him, but that was long years ago. Here he was a mature man, the answer to any mother's prayer. Big and masculine, with the pale brown skin that was prized, that got on better than the berry-black in the white world. And he had neat features . . . no, not merely neat, Manley was handsome. Pale-skinned and handsome, the kind that does well for himself. And he was working close by in the kitchens of a big London hotel – learning the business, so he said. Well that was good, showed good sense and ambition.

Visiting with the Birdhams over the Christmas holiday was exactly the lever of family loyalty Mona had needed to prise Elna from the white boy. Manley was really good company; Elna liked him, and they'd been going places together. Everybody liked him. And there he sat, a great, mountainous West Indian, head and shoulders above anybody in the congregation, singing his heart out. It was as well that she had done nothing about seeing the white family in person; as the Reverend Revelation had advised, it might well have pushed Elna further into her wrong-headedness. As it was . . . ? Mona saw the future, and was thankful.

At midnight in Trafalgar Square, Jonathan and Helen with Rebecca and Tom were in high spirits. Earlier they had been to a party that did not appear to be given by anyone, in a flat whose owners appeared to be away; not that it seemed to matter, most people there knew

Rebecca. The entire party had gone as a crowd to Trafalgar Square, but inevitably in the crush had got separated, leaving Jonathan clinging to Helen and joining clusters of people they had never seen before to sing and dance.

'We should phone home.' Helen, grown to a neat and pretty young woman who had inherited Leo's nice facial structure and Monica's broad teeth and abundant hair which, unlike her mother, Helen kept cut and under control, was hoisted on Jon's shoulders. She was often told that she looked like Doris Day, which she did not take as a compliment, for Helen, in much the same way as Rose, knew that the girl-next-door image she presented was nothing like the woman trying to escape.

'All the phone boxes will be full,' he shouted back. 'D'you think we can possibly find Becc and Tom?' Rebecca and Tom had always been two of a kind, competing, daring one another, showing off, vying for leadership, Becc often wresting it from him even though Tom was the elder of the two at a time when every month counted. Now they were good friends, but still making daring bets with one another.

Jon jumped Helen down and they pushed their way through the singing, dancing crowd towards the fountain, which was the direction in which Jonathan had seen Tom and Rebecca go.

'I wish I lived in London,' Helen said, clinging tightly to Jon as the crowd got thicker. 'It's all so dull at home.'

'It isn't always New Year.'

'But there are people. We miss you and Becc: nobody to go to the pictures with, or go for a swim at the drop of a hat; nobody to moan to even.'

Jonathan hugged her in a brotherly way. 'Find yourself a job up here. Becc and I would put you up till you got settled.'

Somebody let off a crackerjack close at hand. There was some screaming and shouting. When Helen jumped, Jon put his arm about her shoulder and drew her to him.

'Sorry,' Helen said.

'They're idiots. Every year somebody does that, every year somebody gets burned. Hold tight, we're nearly there.' The gush and fall of the fountains, a whistling and cheering crowd obviously urging somebody to climb the lions or something equally traditional. Now that they had reached their goal, the shouting almost drowned Jonathan's voice. 'Can you see them?' He pushed Helen to the front and squeezed in beside her. Sprays of water were drifting over them.

Helen laughed, putting her face up to the mist. 'Thanks for suggesting we come, Jon. It's great.' She tugged him to give him a peck on the cheek, but as he bent towards her, she moved her head and gave him a long, unsisterly kiss full on the mouth.

Jonathan, taken by surprise by the usually quiet Helen, stayed in the position in which she had caught him and smiled, 'That was nice. Why didn't I think of that?'

'I'd hoped that you might.'

'You can bet I would have . . . it's just that we – all of us – we're like the same family.'

'We were, but we're big grown-up people now.'

He felt quite confused. Not only had he never been sexually excited by her, she had always been the quiet one, willing to go along with what the others wanted, content to remain unnoticed. All around them people were pushing and moving, but the two of them remained close, face to face, Jonathan still looking down at Helen with a pleased, amused look as he ran his hands down her body. 'Absolutely grown up. I missed the full force of it, do you think you could do it again?' This time, he made the move. They were pressed as close together as they could be by the crowd, so that when he kissed her he could not disguise the fact of his arousal. 'Sorry,' he said with a wry smile, 'it's an uncontrollable creature with a life of its own.'

Helen tucked her arms beneath his, moving even closer to his creature. 'You shouldn't apologize,' she giggled. 'I've known that creature since it was willie wee. Bend down so that you can hear me.' Then, in his ear, 'Would the two of you like to come into my bed tonight?'

'Helen Wilkinson! You dark little horse.' He looked down at her smiling, but with a quite startled expression. 'How much did you have to drink at that place?'

'I was stone-cold sober when I made up my mind I'd be bold. My New Year resolution.'

He laughed, threw back his head and spread his hands in a joyful expression, his suppressed anger at Elna's capitulation under her family's pressure – to say nothing of his suspicion about Mrs Birdham's plans for Elna's McKenzie cousin – suddenly dissipated. Now he became even more thoroughly aroused at the prospect of having sex tonight with Helen. Helen of all girls: it seemed audaciously akin to an incestuous relationship, the kind of experimental sex that to Jonathan seemed to be being enjoyed by everyone except for him. 'You've made me an offer I can't refuse. Let's go!' And, taking her hand, he pushed a way through the crowd. 'Becc and Tom will have to find their own way back.'

He led, not thinking clearly, except of this tantalizing turn of events so soon after Elna had broken with him. That Elna had capitulated under the prejudices of her parents, when he had stood up to his own father over the very same racial prejudice, had hurt him very much. Now here was sweet and reasonable Helen actually offering to sleep with him, as though she understood how he needed her to soothe his sore heart and pride. In a way he hoped to find that she wasn't a virgin, and that she would know what to do, so that the responsibility would not be wholly his, because his desire was growing and he was afraid that he would not be able to hold back for her. Yet, in another way, he wanted to be her first lover. He hadn't been first with Elna, but it hadn't mattered because she had learned how to demand her pleasure whilst giving out to him. It mattered with Helen. Pushing a way through as far as the perimeter of the fountain, it soon became almost impossible to move because of a crowd that had gathered to watch the usual exhibitionists and drunks who were trying to scale the lions and paddle in the icy water.

They hadn't seen Becc or Tom or any of the crowd they had come here with, and they were stuck, so they turned, facing one another, touching, feeling, caressing one another, trying to interpret one another's expressions. This contact which, in the midst of the whistling, singing, dancing throng, had a frisson of exhibitionism, was changing everything between them that had gone before. No matter how it ended, her lips on his and their automatic response to one another had finished them for ever as pseudo-siblings.

His hands were inside her furry-lined coat. Beneath her silky party dress, she was slim and warm, and more womanly than he had noticed before. He moulded her breasts, easily because she was not wearing a bra, and felt that she was aroused. 'When did you get these?'

'Five or six years ago. You were too busy looking at blue-stocking girls to notice.' They had known one another since he was ten and she was eight, and as children they had seen one another naked many times; his hands slid down and felt the curve of her buttocks. 'You aren't wearing . . .' She held and drew him to her, kissed him open-mouthed, then drew back and smiled almost conspiratorially. 'That's right . . . no anything.'

'Christ, Helen, you're a surprise package.' Earlier, when she had been on his shoulders and he had held on to her legs, he had wondered at her not wearing stockings on such a cold night. Helen. Christ! Becc was supposed to be the outrageous one, you were prepared for her. At that moment his attention was caught by someone calling Jon.

'Did you hear that?' Helen said.

'It's Becc.'

'Where is she?'
Becc's voice. 'You two. Hey. Jon. Over here!'
Jon saw her. 'There she is! Oh God . . . she always has to do something.'
Helen was giggling now. 'Isn't she the absolute limit? Where's Tom? Can you see Tom?'
'If he's got any sense he's cleared off.'
'I wouldn't be surprised if he didn't dare her to. He wouldn't go and leave her like that.'
'Like that' was barefoot and bare-breasted, posing like a triumphant naiad in blue-jeans, paddling in the icy water of the fountain whilst two policemen – one minus his helmet which had disappeared into the crowd – tried to reach her without actually stepping into the water, and two press photographers popped off flash-bulbs as she posed for them. In turning and spreading her arms, one of the policemen managed to grab her and then haul her in an undignified manner to the side, whereupon the other one flung his cape around her. Neither of the constables appeared to be too put out; Becc's disturbance was easier to deal with than incidents in other parts of the square.
Even so, they cautioned her. Each year the Trafalgar Square New Year 'incident' figures increased in number. There were suggestions about turning off the fountains and even boarding the whole thing up. Tonight's charges were an attempt to try to bring home the fact that breaches of the peace would not be tolerated.
As they were clearing a path for Becc, a cheer went up, and a second water-spirit sloshed its way towards the edge. This one was Tom, fully-clothed, soaked, and grinning. Even so, he came forward with his wrists held out, and the two of them were sent to join other exhibitionists in the Black Maria.
'Can I go with her? I'm her brother,' Jon asked.
'No, we got a full load, without any volunteers. She'll probably be bailed. You can come to Bow Street.'
Jonathan and Helen followed in the wake made by the policemen, and watched as Tom and Rebecca were given heavy grey blankets with which to drape themselves and were driven away in the Black Maria. For a moment Jon held Helen close, his ardour only slightly dampened but easily rearoused. 'Shall we go home and let them stew in their own juice?'
'I'm tempted,' Helen said. 'I'm afraid the moment might be lost.'
'There's all the rest of the night.'
'Well, don't let's waste any more of it.'
Jon grinned. 'God, what a hussy's been hopping through the fence to play in our garden. I think we should go to get them out of

trouble and off our minds, so that I can give you my full attention.' He kissed her again, so aroused by the new experience of her short, spare body against him, but unable to separate the new sensation from the memory of the soft, enveloping brown curves, and Elna almost dominating him. Before they started walking to try to rescue their errant sister and brother, in the shadow of the National Gallery, and by the thousand lights of the tall, narrow, perfect Christmas tree, Jon held Helen tightly, urgently. Mouth to mouth, hands clasping one another, they got as close as they could, each wanting to make up to the other for having this delay in their first experience of having sex together.

When, breathlessly, they released one another, Helen said, '"Next year in Jerusalem." Isn't that what Jews say?'

'It's already next year.' He tucked her arm in his and they headed out of the square. 'We'll squash up together just for tonight, but you've got another two days in London, so tomorrow I'm going to book into a swish hotel in Kensington, we'll have lunch and make love, then tea and make love, then I'll take you out to dinner, and we'll spend the night making a lot of love.'

'Kensington?'

'Why not? I've got money now; I get all sorts of bonuses and commissions. Where shall we go? Somewhere really posh. If we're going to do it, let's do it in style.'

'Somewhere with decadent satin sheets and red lampshades.'

'This from the little girl who was so careful that she would never bite off the end of her ice-cream cornet and suck the ice-cream through the hole. OK, we'll opt for decadence. Can you wait?'

She laughed, her eyes shining with excitement. 'Hardly.'

'Hang on, sweetheart, it's going to be *great*!' He swung her round, 'What a way to start 1956.' Sweet, surprising Helen. She had placed herself as a cobweb over the wound that Elna had made. With luck it would now begin to knit and heal.

A church clock, with a cracked and tinny bell, sounded a speedy one, two.

'We'll have to forget phoning home tonight,' Helen said. 'They'll all be in bed by this time.'

Winifred and Charlotte together before the old-fashioned fireplace in the old Quinlan house, sat through the last minutes of 1955. Charlotte had made a jug of egg-nog from her own recipe, and they had already had two drinks each.

'Come on, drink up, Winnie.'

'Do you remember what Papa used to say?'

'Of course, "Lotte's egg-nog recipe is that strong, a whiff of the paper it's written down on will knock your hat off." The secret is using best Napoleon. When I'm gone you can call it Winifred's egg-nog, and then you can pass it on so that it can be Rose's egg-nog.'

Winifred smiled, and accepted a third glass beaker of the aromatic blend. Her cheeks were flushed and, because she was alone with Charlotte, whom she did not have to impress, she was relaxed and quite enjoying herself, talking over old family occasions, remembering those few years when Henry was Winifred's good-looking bridegroom. The only two people left on earth who remembered the son of a provincial shopkeeper who had had the bad luck not to get through the last few hours before the 1918 Armistice.

'You always were a pretty girl, Winnie. A pity Henry couldn't see you now.'

'A pity he can't see his whole family.'

Charlotte lifted her beaker, 'Let's hope he can.'

'So many young men. So many. Only Jonathan's age – even younger – giving their lives for a country where many people don't even remember that they gave them.'

Charlotte said, 'I'd better switch on the wireless.'

It was an old valve set that needed persuading to an exact spot before it would stop its crackling. 'There!' The preliminary ding-dong, ding-dong of Big Ben came through clearly. 'Do you think that Jon and Beccy can hear that in Trafalgar Square?'

'I should think that there is far too much noise going on there.'

'Beccy said they would telephone; I told her that you'd be round here.'

'The lines are always busy directly after midnight.'

'You aren't in a hurry to get home?'

'No, I shan't sleep . . . I never do these days. I do a lot of reading, but the words get fuzzy after an hour.'

'Get yourself some stronger glasses, Winnie.'

The first stroke of midnight rang out at full volume, and Charlotte fine-tuned again. 'Happy New Year, my dear.' She gave her daughter-in-law a rare kiss which was returned with a similar light kiss.

'Thank you. I hope 1956 will be better for you, Mother.'

'Could hardly be worse, dear. Still, as they say, "Time heals." I don't reckon it heals, but at least it don't hurt quite the same after a bit.'

'Not *quite* so much,' Winifred said.

'Winnie, I know it's a bit late in the day, but I never much liked being called Mother. Do you think you could call me Lotte?'

Winifred looked slightly puzzled. 'Of course I could, I always thought you would like me to call you Mother as you had lost Henry.'

'It's just that, now my Sid's gone, there isn't nobody to call me Lotte, which is the first name I answered to.'

Winifred had always thought that Charlotte had a more superior ring to it than Lotte, but Henry's mother was old now and one humoured the aged. 'Then would you call me Winifred? I think that Winnie always sounds a bit common.'

'Of course, dear. You should have said before. Why does this family always keep things bottled up? I never used to when I was young – in fact I couldn't keep anything to myself – but it just seemed to grow on me once I got into this family.'

They sat meandering from one topic to another, from one memory to another, reaffirming what they knew about 1955 and all the years they held in common that had preceded it. The hall clock struck one . . . half-past . . . two. Winifred said, 'You were going to get out the old photograph albums.'

'And so I did, Winifred. They are ready in the hall. I've got to fetch the pork pie and pickle, I'll bring them in . . . No, you sit there, this is my do, I'm going to make us a nice pot of tea – you can't drink egg-nog with pork pie. I'll bring in the photos at the same time.'

Winifred, who enjoyed her mother-in-law's succulent hand-raised pies, but seldom indulged because of her figure, had promised herself a day of relaxation from some of the more irksome rules she imposed upon herself. She had not stripped and properly cornered her bed-sheets that morning; she had left dishes in the sink and, knowing that she would be with Charlotte for the day, had left the clearing-out of the ashes from her grate until tomorrow. By tomorrow there would be a two-day layer of dust on her polished dining-room table, and her underwear was still soaking in the bathroom hand-basin. Such sluttishness unnerved her – one never knew – but she had discovered long ago that the occasional day or two of relaxing her self-imposed rules could be quite beneficial.

She had allowed Charlotte to persuade her to slices of ham and buttery mashed potatoes at luncheon, and to tinned salmon and cucumber sandwiches and a bowl of tipsy-cake at tea-time. During the evening she had smoked several Sobranie cigarettes, and drunk sherry and quite a lot of the thick, creamy egg-nog. She had always been pleased that she had such a good digestive system which, she claimed, was as a result of not imposing upon it.

Charlotte had the tray ready in the larder, so she had only to collect the photograph albums which were ready in the hall-stand drawer. She had planned this weeks ago when Winnie had said that she would spend New Year's Eve with her. There were several very old albums, but it was only the oldest of them that she took through to put on the tray.

It was faded, and the cover frayed at the corners. The binding glue had deteriorated, so that some of it cracked and crumbled to dust. It had lain packed away and unopened for many years. As she waited for the kettle to boil for the tea, she opened the cover.

The first photographs were daguerreotypes, showing dream-like figures in faded sepia. Even the stiff young man with a bowler hat tipped over one eye had an air of romance about him as he loomed out of the fawn and faded past. Sid at nineteen. Turning the pages as she waited for the kettle to boil, she saw again the Quinlans before she had known them, and then in sequence when she had first known them: Sid wearing white trousers tied with a striped tie, a blurred Sid on some seafront arm in arm with a blurred young woman wearing a nipped-in waisted dress and a wide flowery hat. Sid outside a church, with the young woman formally surrounded by posed bridesmaids, women in large hats and complicated dresses, and men wearing high collars and formal suits. A studio portrait of the young woman. A beauty, almost smiling, her large eyes dark and appearing larger because of their deep setting, sooty lids and long dark lashes. That's where Ballard got his eyes and hair. Her heavy hair was lustrous and black. She had broad nostrils and a luscious sensual mouth which held a hint of a smile kept in restraint. This was not a Lebanese face as Lotte had told Jon – as she had always believed it to be. This was a beautiful woman of mixed race.

This was Honoria, who had been kept in the Quinlans' attic since she died, out of sight like some ghost of Mrs Rochester. Since she had talked to Jon about her, Charlotte had changed her mind. Now that Sid was gone, she decided, it was time for Honoria to come out of the attic and take her proper place in the family. If Sid had not been ashamed of her colour, then why should they not all know her and look at her? Except for Charlotte, there was now no one left who had known Honoria, had known what a kind and lovely lady she had been, had known about the trouble Sid's mother had caused because of Honoria's colour, had known how much Sid had loved her, and how much they had both longed for the child that had been the death of her.

This was Honoria, whose secret had been kept by Sid so wrong-headedly. What did it matter to anybody if Henry had some coloured blood in him. Sid had said, 'They don't ever forgive you for having a touch of the tar-brush. It don't show in Henry, so why drag it all up? If she had been here, then it would have been different, but she's gone, so I can't see any reason to complicate matters.' And, of course, it hadn't come out in Henry. If you knew you could see it a bit in Ballard, the same handsomeness as his grandmother.

Lotte wanted them to know. There wasn't anything to be ashamed of in Honoria, but by hiding her true origins, it made it seem to be shameful. The first person to be told must be Winnie, and it was Winnie's place to tell Ballard.

Her decision to tell Winnie came from reading an article about how, in South Africa, there were white families into which – because one of the parents had descended from a long-ago mixed marriage – a child could be born coloured, and consequently categorized differently from the rest of their family. If both white-skinned parents happened to have black genes, then there was an even greater chance that children would not be white. It was all right *saying* that England was a tolerant country, but she could imagine the shock to Ballard and Winnie if Honoria's blood came out now that Jon was engaged to Elna.

She put the tray down on the low table between her own and Winnie's chair. 'A good pie, if I do say it myself.' When Winnie did not stir, Charlotte looked up and saw that she had dropped off, still holding her beaker by its handle, letting the greasy egg-nog spill on to her blue silky dress. 'Oh, Winn, look what you've done to your pretty dress. Give that glass here and I'll go and fetch a sponge.'

When she took the glass from Winifred's hooked finger, Charlotte knew at once that there was no more life in that finger than in the rest of her daughter-in-law's body. Winnie was dead. In exactly the same way as Sid, she had gone slipping off without a word to anybody.

Charlotte sat down on the low table and took Winifred's soft, warm hand. 'Winnie. Oh, Winnie. It was my turn next.' She had no idea of time passing as she held the beautifully manicured and elegantly ringed hand, but by the time she released it, the teapot had lost much of its heat. The hall clock struck the three-quarters. Quarter to three. She went to the telephone and rang Rose's number. There was no reply. There was no rush: another half-hour here or there didn't matter now. As she made up the fire to keep them both warm until somebody came, Charlotte thought: If she had to go, it was as well she went before she found out what was going on over at Honeywood.

The young constable couldn't keep his eyes off that nice pair of breasts that kept escaping from the blanket, but the duty sergeant had seen it all before. He took her details. She'd be dumb if you took her hands away. Why did they do it? Two of them, together by the seem of things, wet as babies at the seaside, not even shivering yet.

They would soon. He should deal with them first so they could get their wet things off before they caught their death.

'Let's get shot of these two mermaids, Lovejoy.'

He entered brief details.

'Quinlan. Rebecca. Charlotte. 43 High Grove Flats, Hammersmith. Wilkinson. Thomas, Tom? Just Tom? University of Sussex . . . You have to give your home address. OK. 43 High Grove Flats, Hammersmith.

'Right, Lovejoy, find 'em a jumper or something and get 'em processed and out of here quick as you can . . . What's that racket, Lovejoy?'

'Reporter, Sarge.'

'Get him out of here, I don't care if he's from the *Financial Times*, just get him *OUT*!'

'Her father's an MP, Sarge.'

'Oh Christ. Why the hell couldn't you arrest some nice girl out of Woolworth's who won't do anybody any harm except get her mum down here to sort us out?'

'You, miss. Come back over here.'

What he had to say to Rebecca he said in a lowered tone.

'PC Lovejoy. They're yours, so you get down to the pool and persuade somebody that you need a car . . . Tell them it's for Jack the bleeding Ripper if you have to, but get these two dying ducks in a thunderstorm out of my station.'

And so, when Jonathan and Helen came to enquire of the desk what they must do to secure the release of Miss Quinlan and Mr Wilkinson, they did not understand why he seemed so particularly fierce in his reply that they were probably sleeping it off.

Rose left the Wilkinsons' at three-thirty. The air was icily fresh and the sky clear. Although it was only a few hundred yards along Shaft's Lane from the Wilkinsons' to the Quinlans' house, Leo insisted on walking home with her, their footsteps crackling the frosting on the mud and shallow puddles. She was wearing a mink jacket, into the pockets of which she thrust her hands deeply, whilst Leo tucked his hand into her warm minky armpit, an action intended to be neighbourly but which nevertheless physically stirred him.

For years he had enjoyed their relationship, which he would have described as uncomplicated but with a certain kind of loving. But for several weeks now, he had had pushed under his nose some evidence that, on his side, that relationship was not at all uncomplicated. He had been as jealous as a lover of Trevelyan. And if he was at all honest with himself now, his motives when insisting on walking with her were not innocent. He had no intention of trying anything, but he was enjoying having acknowledged that he was sexually attracted to her. As he had been for years, but sublimating it in all the hours of discussion. They had talked openly of birth and death, passion, sex and love, in a way that people of their generation and status usually did not.

After the party, when the three of them had been seated together at ease, he had thought, 'A perfect ménage-à-trois', which had led him to think that with 'his' two women he would have the best, the very best, of all worlds. Forthrightness, reticence, impetuosity, tranquillity, voluptuousness, daintiness . . . Between Monica and Rose he would get those characteristics, plus slim legs, plump buttocks, small breasts, a marvellously tempting bosom, coarse pillow-talk from one, love poems from the other. Of course, he'd had a fair amount to drink, but the general idea appealed to him, until impetuous Monica had, with her usual good-humoured forthrightness, pushed her glass towards him and asked him if he intended sitting there mooning or must she see to the booze as well as everything else.

'Beautiful,' he said, pausing to look up at the stars, and drawing Rose down to sit on a low wall at the front of the Quinlans' house. 'Every New Year it's the same: I never get over the childish idea that you can keep starting again, push the mistakes behind you and start with a clean slate.'

Rose, still keeping her hands in her pockets, and feeling more pleasantly drunk than she knew she deserved in view of the mixture she had accepted, looked at him. 'I never associated you with such sweet, childish ideas, Leo.'

'Oh, Rose, if only you knew.'

She waited, but he did not offer to let her know. 'Leo the Lion, always so assured and adult, not like me. I've never grown up. I don't think I know how to. And Becc, they're real women, they know what it's all about out there . . . Me? I have to wait to be told what to do. I could never bring myself to want to do something and decide to go for it in the way they have done. If I hadn't been put on a boat and sent here, I'd probably still be in Johannesburg, and if Ballard hadn't wanted to marry me, I'd still be living in Longmore. I expect I would have become as batty as my Aunt Fredericka. She was born there and I believe she stayed there because nobody told her not to. Never became a grown-up, you see? My only hope is that I'm like a sloe-bush in a blackthorn spring; I shall bloom late when all the frosts are over.'

'If that's true, then you fool everybody, but I don't think it is true. It's not only that you are beautiful, your face shows all the good adult virtues – sensitivity, discrimination, composure, tolerance, honesty . . . I'm a coarse and vulgar blockhead in comparison. Rose Quinlan is the epitome of refinement and elegance and adultness: she never makes a wrong move. Does she?'

Rose felt his grip on her arm tighten slightly.

For long moments she did not respond.

'You know she does, Leo . . . You caught her making one.'

He took her hand. 'And I behaved like a clodhopper. It isn't even any of my business, and who am I to talk?'

'It really was nothing, Leo.'

'Was?'

'It was a very short story.'

'I think I was almost glad to see you having a bit of a fling. I was only sorry that it was him and not me.' He laughed to show that he was joking.

'I mean it – it never was anything. He was nice to me, we had a few drinks . . . you know how drink always goes to my head, and for a little while I lost it. It really does something to you to know that somebody thinks you are special. He was great company, interesting . . . and I think I might have made a fool of myself if you hadn't happened to be there that day. I wouldn't be much good at having a secret lover.'

Putting an arm round her he patted her comfortingly. 'You would never need to, your face is so honest and open. Who would suspect you of ever doing anything at all base?'

'It's all rubbish, Leo. All my adult life, people have been telling me about my good looks: how lucky I am, how ageless, how beautiful is the profile, how photogenic . . . Oh yes, and the bone structure, and the complexion . . .'

'Why not? Looks like yours are few and far between.'

'But nobody ever gets it right. This face tells lies. It just happens to look this way because it is just the way it happened to grow . . . with my eyes just happening to be placed a certain distance apart and in balance with my mouth. The outline of my chin and nose just happens to have been drawn neatly. I'm like Dorian Gray: my face has never told the truth of who is inside. Monica seems to be the only one who knows that stupid Emma Woodhouse and the Wife of Bath are both behind this mask.' She shivered. 'Maggoty Rose, that's who lives in here.'

'Come on then, Emma, you maggoty old Wife of Bath, it's too cold to sit here.' He got up and offered his hand to help her up. 'I shall be in trouble with Mon if you take a chill.'

The deep gravel crunched like crushed ice as they walked slowly towards the house. She had left yard and houselights burning, so when they reached the back of it, the lovely Elizabethan house, frosted in the moonlight, with its tall, decorated tree and abundant trimmings of holly branches and mistletoe boughs, looked inviting and festive, especially after the party debris they had just left.

'This place is so beautiful, I think I'd give my eyeteeth to get my hands on it.'

'It needs a pit of money to keep it going. Ballard has never minded what he spent on it. Prestigious, that's what this place is now. It's not a home, it's a Grade 2 listed Desirable Residence.'

She unlocked the back door and he followed her into the kitchen.

'Hardly seems worth going to bed now,' she said. 'Would you like some coffee?'

'Not worth it for you, maybe, you're such an early bird. How about tea instead?'

She filled the electric kettle and opened up the Aga, which responded at once with a crackle and some heat. He plumped heavily down into the comfortable old couch that had been used for everything from children's sick-bed to imaginary worlds, and put his feet on the oven bar.

'And an owl too, I'm afraid.'

'You shouldn't be; it means that you get a longer day than most people.'

'To what purpose, though?'

'Oh, Rose, Rose . . . don't tell me that you've got the "purpose" bug too. Not the damned forty-year itch to go out to work like Mon? It was talking about "purpose" that started her dissatisfaction, which has ended up with her driving off at the crack of dawn to take temperatures of sick people who would rather be left asleep.'

Rose had never before heard him express any resentment, unless it was tempered with understanding and jokiness. She said, 'I would imagine talking about "purpose" was not the start, but the end. Monica caught the itch long before she mentioned "purpose" or anything as positive as that.'

'You aren't going to get started on sexual politics at four in the morning on New Year's day?'

She laughed. 'I shouldn't think so. I don't even know what sexual politics means. Unless it's about saying that housework is a low-grade, low-paid, repetitive but highly skilled job that women get themselves into because our instinct will eventually get the better of us. We get this overwhelming desire to feel a man on top of us and a baby at our breast.'

He raised his eyebrows at what, for Rose, was coarseness, but she was not looking. 'You see, you do know about sexual politics.'

As she spooned tea into the pot, she went on without even looking round at him. 'It's my party piece when I'm drunk. I expect that when I grow old I shall shame everybody by saying what I think in company.'

'I'd like to be there.'

'OK, then. This is what I think. Women are just like all other female mammals, we come on heat. And when we do there's always a male somewhere around waiting to see that we are served: that's the correct term, "served". Rams serve ewes, bulls serve heifers, lions serve lionesses. We females send out our signals and they are there, the males. For once in their lives they are ready and eager to do the females' bidding. He serves her and she, satisfied, would like to trot off quite happily. But the human male? He doesn't let her take what she wants and go; she's not going to get off as easily as that. He knows that if he can keep her he gets himself a free housekeeper – a replacement for his mother who's beginning to wear out by now.'

Leo had known Rose since she arrived in Honeywood twelve years before, pregnant with Anoria; yet he had never heard her speak with any strength and authority, except when giving her opinions on certain novels that she happened to know very well. Was she trying to prove to him that what she had said about her face being a mask was true?

She stirred the tea vigorously, poured it into two mugs, and searched around for milk. Now she turned and looked at him. He took his tea and she drew up a chair so that her feet too rested on the warm oven-door bar. 'Free nurse, a free errand-boy, a free laundry-maid, cook, bath-cleaner . . . and all the time there's all this free sex, wherever, however, and whenever he wants it. All free. He possesses rights to her labour and can penetrate her body every morning and every night if he wants to, and on the kitchen table at lunchtime if he has a mind to. But if *she* doesn't want to give up her body to *him* – that's her hard luck! Even if the law was not on his side, he's stronger and heavier and he will make her have it whether she wants it or not. But the law *is* on his side. In law, her body belongs to him – she may not give it, or even lend it to anyone else. If she does, then he can send her packing. No roof over her head, no back wages, not even her own children. She is a bad wife, who has given the body that is rightfully his to another man.'

She paused, and tucked her bottom lip under her top; there was the faintest of blushes on her cheeks, and she held her eyes wide. He could hardly have believed that she could be so positive, or that she could speak with such bitterness.

'So there you have it, dear Leo Lion. Is that a good enough party piece? Rose Quinlan doing a drunken striptease. What do you think of Maggoty Rose? You see, her petals are all chewed by caterpillars and earwigs? How do you feel about being the first person to see her laid bare?'

In silence, he rolled the mug between his hands, drank deeply from it, then placed it carefully centred on a tile. 'May I?' Rose nodded, not taking much notice. He picked up the 'phone and dialled.

'Mon? Sorry if I woke you. Rose and I are having a cup of tea. OK? Expect me when you see me. Night, love.' He put the 'phone back.

Rose lit a cigarette and, as an afterthought, offered him one which he took. 'You don't have to, Leo.'

'I know.'

'Poor Leo, Rose knows that all men are not like that, even if Maggoty doesn't.' She held a lighted taper to his cigarette. 'I've had way, way too much to drink tonight.' She waited as he drew the tobacco to life. 'Look at the time.'

He sighed. 'Rose, it's not chewed petals you've been hiding, it's just ordinary thorns. We all have them, they're nothing you should be ashamed to show. Come and sit here. Talk to me.' He moved to make room on the low couch. 'I refuse to admit to the existence of this Maggoty Rose . . . Briar Rose, yes.'

'I quite like that. Briar Rose . . . yes. I wish that I could live up to that.'

Although he didn't look the part, with his lean frame and intellectual appearance, Leo had always been a great one for hugging people. He hugged her now. 'You'll be OK, Rose. You need somebody to tell you what a very nice person you are. So I'll tell you. Rose Quinlan, you are the very nicest person. Monica and I think you are the best person we know, and that's the truth. It makes me feel terrific that you let me be the one to see you have thorns. They are great. Your arguments are legitimate: women do have a rotten deal.'

'I know. I suppose, if I'm absolutely honest, I'm not really ashamed of Maggoty. I used to be. Do you know a book called *Les Mandarins*?'

He nodded.

'I have it if you want to borrow it.'

'I'll have to wait for the translation.'

'Ah, of course. It led me to reading her earlier book, not a novel.' She gazed inwardly and said with a faint smile, '*The Second Sex*. It's huge . . . not just physically . . . the ideas. I couldn't put it down. It was a revelation. I felt quite frightened by it, but I began to feel strong.' She laughed. 'Not for long and I have to keep going back to it to renew my strength. I am going to send a copy to Becc and I think I shall give one as a present to every woman I know.'

'You usually tell me when you've got something new.'

'I know, but this wasn't like reading the latest novel; I couldn't grasp it well enough to talk about it. All the time I was reading it, I had the feeling that it was like owning an unexpurgated version of something. I didn't like to own up to you.'

'Because of the sexual politics?'

'Is that what it is?' She gave him a wry smile, 'No, because you're a man. I think it's a subversive book. If it ever becomes widely read, I mean *really* widely, it will attack our society in the way that the Bolsheviks attacked theirs.'

'Lend it to me? It sounds as though I'm going to have to study the enemy.'

'I can't let it go at the moment; I'm going to need it again when Ballard gets back.' She clasped her hand over his and turned her gaze away. 'It is so good to be able to talk to someone. Mon and I hardly ever see one another at the moment. I couldn't even mention it to Winifred until I'm better acquainted with my new ideas. She would be as shocked as if I joined the Communist Party.'

He held on to her hand and, if not shocked himself, was at least dumbfounded by Rose's assurance. 'What about Ballard?'

She seemed to brace herself. 'Nobody knows yet. Ballard and I are splitting up.'

For a long moment he was silenced. 'You mean divorcing?'

'That would jeopardize his political career, and I couldn't do that – and it would totally break up the family. And, on a purely selfish note, I have to find a way of earning my keep when I give up *this* job. Being married is the only job I've ever done.'

'What about the children?'

'Ballard would never keep them short of anything, and of course he would be here a lot of the time, just as he is now. It isn't their separation. The children have to know that there's a rift; Vee and Nora are old enough to understand that. But outside the family I shall only tell you and Monica. If and when things change, then we will divorce, but in the meantime I shall do my duty as the wife of a good MP. I'll go with him to meet Mr Khrushchev, attend the State Openings, and sit on the platform at election time. For a while, our face to the world will be as conventional as ever.'

'And all this is settled?'

'Sort of settled. It came to a head a couple of weeks before Christmas, and I had a confrontation with him in the London flat. I'm afraid neither of us behaved very well. Perhaps I should have waited, but I stormed up there with my little temper red hot.'

'Rose.' He looked painfully concerned. 'All this has been going on and you've been keeping up appearances, behaving as though he has just gone off with some trade delegation?'

'Oh he has.'

'Couldn't you have told us?'

'No, you would have been so kind and understanding that you would have gone treading around me as though on eggshells. I enjoyed my Christmas, the first time in years. And tonight was terrific.'

'It's going to be tough times, Rose.'

'I don't care.'

'You can rely on me and Mon, you know that.'

'I know.'

'Any time you want us, we're there for you. What brought it to a head?'

She was quiet, concentrating on drinking her tea, then she said, 'Because of what I just said about husbands having rights that their wives cannot refuse.' She drew deeply on her cigarette and blew out a straight stream, then said in a low voice, 'Women have those rights too; but have you ever wondered how a wife rapes her husband? I know that there is no such crime as rape within a marriage, but what else is it, Leo?'

Angrily, he crushed out his cigarette on the hearth. He didn't know what to do to comfort her, except hold both her hands as she poured herself out to him.

'He's done it before. I haven't always resisted him, it's easier . . . and less painful . . . fewer bruises. Afterwards he's always sorry and ashamed, and he's nice and tries to make up for it. I find this a bit embarrassing, but I want to tell you. Do you mind?'

He shook his head emphatically. 'Of course I *mind*. I could kill the sod . . .'

'When we were first married, I liked having sex so much that I couldn't understand why people ever got out of bed. I don't know what happened, but during the war he changed. It was as though he didn't want me unless he had to force me to have him. I didn't understand it then, and I don't now.'

'Get rid of him, Rose. Kick him out now. If you don't make a clean break, how are things going to be any different? Isn't it going to make it worse? Separate rooms are going to make you an even better challenge to him if he's like that. He'll have you in chains next.'

She took another cigarette and lit it from the first and said, almost casually, 'He has a mistress.'

'Oh, *Rose*.' He put his arm tenderly about her shoulders and ruffled her hair.

'He lays it all at my door. Maybe he's right.'

'He's a real sod.'

'He certainly didn't tell me to boost my morale: she's about half my age. It's the girl who's been running around after him for ages. You've met her.'

'That little up-market tart with the eager bosom who came to your garden party?'

'You think she's a tart?'

'You shouldn't let that accent fool you: she's delighted a few Deb's Delights or I'm no judge. I don't care if she is young enough to be the sod's daughter, she can't hold a candle to you, Rose. Don't let the bugger put you down.'

'I'm going to try not to.' She opened the door of the now hot stove. The heat from it flooded the room. 'I don't like keeping you like this after such a super evening. Anyway, thanks for the shoulder to weep on. I don't know what I'd do without you and Mon.'

'You'd do all right, believe me. Your old man might be the mouthpiece in your family, but you are the brains and heart of it. Your kids will stick by you.'

Standing up, he took her cigarette and drew on it thoughtfully before he threw it into the fire. He turned out the electric light, throwing the room into a red-lit darkness. 'Is this confessional couch for anyone's use?' He plumped the cushions and sat close to her.

She looked only slightly alarmed.

'Don't worry, I'm not about to make confession. Except . . . well, I've wanted to get this right.' He smiled disarmingly. 'It's been hovering on my lips for ages, so I might as well . . .'

He stopped what he was saying with his own mouth. The second member of the Wilkinson family that night to give an unexpected and passionate kiss to one of the Quinlans. But the kiss by the light of the Aga stove was by far the less chaste. Perhaps because it had its beginnings a long way back, sleeping in the unconscious, keeping itself alive by discussions about fictional lovers that were only creations of a novelist's imagination. Proxy kisses. Second-hand rapture.

This kiss was more thorough, more erotic and sensuous than that between Jon and Helen had been, or could be, until they too reached maturity. The kiss Leo gave Rose had years of experience and pent-up desire behind it; it was firm and gentle and loving. Knowingly erotic, lustful and ardent. It was a practised kiss that knew only too well what it was intended to do, which was to draw up to its highest pitch the latent desire of two people who had not until then realized what it was they felt for each other.

And the kiss did what was intended.

There were no crowds pushing, no cold spray, no noise except the crackle of the Aga and the tick of the pendulum clock, and no one watching.

He had taken her by surprise. Had he really? Her desire too was pent up, and she found herself responding as eagerly as she had once responded to Trevelyan. Returning his long, nuzzling kisses. Holding him as hungrily and tightly as she had held Trevelyan. Not resisting when he slipped the narrow straps of her party frock from her shoulders. Not pulling back when she felt his mouth cover first one breast and then the other.

When he did that, Rose knew that it was not Trevelyan himself that she had wanted, it was the attention of a tender and appreciative lover. When eventually he sat up and kissed her on the mouth, she saw a Leo she had never seen before. Other women had, but not Rose, though few had seen him so surprised by what was happening. His tie off and collar undone, his hair dishevelled and his whole face heavy with the knowledge that his long-suppressed desire just might run away with him. Rose had never seen him look as attractive as he did now, struggling with this electrifying situation.

'How did you ever come to give yourself to Ballard?'

Rose stiffened. 'Don't, Leo. I don't want to talk any more about him.'

He ran his hands over her smooth shoulders and down her bare back. 'God help us, Rose, I've been so bloody envious of that photographer.'

'Don't be.'

She was getting over Trevelyan, but she was not likely to get over the change that their affair had wrought in her.

When the telephone rang, Leo and Rose remained with their arms encircling like the kissing lovers in Rodin's statue, although the naked marble lovers did not look as though they were enjoying one another nearly as much as the warm-blooded, dishevelled, erotic composition on the couch.

'Let it ring,' he said.

'We must stop now; you must go home,' she said, kissing him again. 'We can't do this behind Mon's back. It's unforgivable.'

'You stop first then.'

Rose's libido was alive, ruling her actions, storing away the guilt for her. If she did have a choice, who would have her choose righteousness, when wickedness was the more pleasurable? What man would be an angel when he could be Pan? What woman would be the temple virgin when she could be high priestess?

The ringing continued.

'What if it is Monica?'

'Why on earth should it be when there's a whole world full of people out there. She'll be fast asleep.'

'It might be Jon and Becc.'

'They'll ring back.' He stroked the inside of her thigh tentatively and gave a mock groan of desire. 'For God's sake, Rose, let's do it. Come on, please. Just this once let's find out what it's like together. It could be fantastic. It will be; you know that, don't you? All that Lawrence, all that Zola we've talked about with all that intellectual dispassion.' His fingertips moved instinctively into the line of her groin and she did not make a move to stop them. 'Don't you think it's a wonder we didn't do it years ago? We've had enough opportunity.'

She guessed that it would be fantastic.

'At least give me as much as you'd been giving your photographer that day. You were high on him.'

'Don't push it, Leo. You've just had more . . . more than he ever had.'

'That's not enough.' His voice was low and whispering with desire which, unlike his groan, was not false. 'You want it too. Just give in to yourself; do what you want. Let's go upstairs.'

'We must be out of our heads even talking of it.'

'Then for once let's be out of our heads. Where's the harm? If we were sad we'd try to cheer one another up, wouldn't we? What's the difference if we want to satisfy one another when we want some sex?'

'You should go back to your own bed. We're not talking about cheering one another up, are we?'

He grinned and gave her a kiss. 'Want to bet? It would do it for me.'

'Doing it with you would ruin everything.'

The phone stopped ringing. During the minute when they had waited for it to cease, he had caressed her with the kind of tenderness that she had expected from Ballard and had imagined she would have had with Trevelyan.

Becc had said that every man/woman meeting was a sexual one. Did that mean that it was inevitable that long-standing friends were always potentially in danger of admitting to the sexual element in a relationship? Becc's youthful wisdom: 'Leave any man and woman together long enough and they'll end up in the sack.' If that were the case, then was there any point in fighting the inevitable?

Potential was not inevitable.

'Say something, Rose.'

'All right then, I'll admit I'd really like to be in bed with you just this minute. But over this last year, I've discovered at least one thing about myself. I'm not good when I drink too much.' She smiled, 'I'm not good in both senses . . . My Wife of Bath gets the upper hand.' She kissed Leo hard and long, as she had kissed Trevelyan, as she might have kissed some other presentable man at that moment. 'You see what I mean? But I'm not going to let her ruin what Mon and I have got. Get into bed with you, and it wouldn't survive. Just kiss me again and then go home.'

He bent over her, revelling in her response, the couch drawing them ever nearer to the prone position they must eventually reach. Her hair had fallen forward untidily, she was only half dressed and her lipstick was gone. Part temptress part angel. He thought that he had never seen her look more wonderful than she did now.

'I have the solution.' He got up and poured them a glass of red wine from the half-full bottle on the dresser. 'We'll drink up this nice Beaujolais, so that you will find it easier to send Rose away, and when she's gone, I'll take the Wife of Bath up to your guest room.'

'That's called getting the woman drunk, Leo. It's not your style.'

'For God's sake, Rose, the woman wants to.'

She sipped the wine and he licked the red juice from her lips. He grinned, knowing now that she would do it, seeing it in her eyes. 'You can throw out the wicked woman as soon as she's had her way with me. That way Rose's friendship with Monica will not be put at risk.' He knew just what to touch on a woman's body, and how. Not the obvious places, but the ones that did not make a woman feel threatened – her inner arm, her throat, her ears. 'Please, Rose, let's put one another out of our misery, and I'll die happy.'

She laughed, feeling the fruity wine course through her. He was so familiar, so reliable. So safe. She could hardly choose a better lover. It would be so easy, such a relief, they need not even take so positive an action as to go upstairs. A readjustment of positions now and they could satisfy each other. The temptation to do something against Ballard whilst satisfying her curiosity about Leo as a lover was almost overwhelming. Her subconscious suddenly let out Ballard's accusation. Prick-tease! She could not keep on doing this either to men or to herself. He kissed her repeatedly, wherever he could find bare skin, making his argument physical, and she did not want to make him stop.

The telephone bell shrilled out and they both jumped.

Leaping as though panic-stricken, Rose jumped up, hitching her straps into place. 'I must answer it. It must be somebody who knows I'm at home or they wouldn't let it ring like that.'

Leo straightened his clothes, lit two cigarettes, and gave one to

Rose, still caressing the inside of her thigh as she lifted the receiver.

'Gran! Goodness, I expected anyone but you.' She raised her eyebrows at Leo; he paused in his caress but did not let go. 'It's four in the morning, are you all right?'

Leo watched as her eyes showed her shock at what was obviously distressing news.

'Oh, Gran! When? I was only next door with the Wilkinsons . . . But you should have . . . being there all on your own . . . Are you all right? I'll be straight over. Leo's just here, I'm sure he'll come with me. Oh Gran, I'm so sorry. I'm really, really sorry. I'll be there in fifteen minutes.' She replaced the receiver and stood staring unbelievingly. 'It's Ballard's mother . . . Winifred's dead. She just died . . . like Papa did. Poor Gran. Where are my flat shoes? Oh God, I'm going to be sick.' She rushed out into the garden, and he held her as her shocked body ejected party punch, Napoleon brandy, and the Beaujolais. Any time up to when his hand had traced the line of her thigh, or when his lips had made contact with her breast, Rose would have been mortified to have had Leo hold her as she vomited, but they had gone beyond the bounds that had ruled them. He wiped her face with his handkerchief and helped find her shoes.

'I'll get your coat, and I'll ring Monica. We'll go in your car.'

As he talked to Monica, they held one another's gaze. Her body's sexual response to him had not subsided. That, and the dramatic news, her incipient awareness of something threatening approaching – as foreknowledge of a thunderstorm or an earthquake – pushed adrenalin into her bloodstream and made her breathless.

As he waited for the car engine to warm, he said hesitantly, 'Rose, I . . .'

'Don't, Leo. I'd hate you to say that you were sorry . . . and I'd hate it if you didn't.'

'No regrets, Rose. Go on, say it.'

'If I said I had regrets, it wouldn't be true – except about Monica.'

'Years ago, Monica and I promised that we would never break one another's hearts, but we would not try to keep one another in chains. We had old-fashioned ideas about free love. Maybe she thinks we did it years ago. If she flirts with a doctor or two, it doesn't hurt me . . . it's the marriage that is important.'

As he turned the car on to the road, Monica came dashing out, wearing Leo's sheepskin coat over her nightdress, her fantastic hair jumbled around her shoulders, making Rose wonder momentarily why Leo would want to try to complicate his life trying to make love to another woman. 'Anything I can do, Rose, you've only got to say.'

'Thanks, Mon. Just see to Vee and Nora.'

'Of course, of course. What about Ballard?'

'I've got a number for him, I'll ring from Gran's. If the others ring from London . . . I suppose you'd better tell them.'

'Stay with Rose, Leo.'

'As though I shouldn't, my darling.' He gave her a quite lingering kiss out of the car window. 'Now go and tuck yourself up and keep the bed warm.'

Before they reached Charlotte's he halted the car, dimmed the lights. 'I'll try to be patient until all this is over.'

She returned his kiss without showing him any of her earlier open-mouthed desire. 'Let's leave it there, Leo.'

'I don't think that's possible, Rose.'

When Rose was eventually put through to Senator Weissman, the line was amazingly clear. 'Mizz Quinlan. Hi. Walt Weissman here. Mizz Weissman says you wanted to get your husband in a hurry. I don't know what to say, he left here a couple'a days ago to go to the airport. Mrs Weissman wanted him to stop over for our New Year party, but I guess he had a real tight schedule. The roads weren't good, so Mizz Weissman made him promise to telephone that he arrived there OK. He said he made good time and was at the airport hotel. I did hear on the news that some flights have been delayed. Best thing is to check in to a hotel and wait for the weather to clear. We gave him the names of a couple'a good hotels. I'll get them checked out for you and then ring you. I wish I could help more. Hope it's not too urgent. OK, ring any time. Don't apologize . . . no problem. Ballard's a real friend, a great guy.'

In England it was now midday. Charlotte stood in the doorway listening to Rose's half of the trans-Atlantic conversation, Leo sat keeping himself awake with a mug of strong, black coffee and making notes that might help Rose until Ballard or Jonathan came. The doctor had come and gone, followed by the undertaker, who had taken Winifred's body to his Chapel of Rest.

Winifred's doctor had surprised Rose and Charlotte by signing a death certificate. She and Charlotte had expected an inquest, as there had been into Papa's death. He had said, 'I have no problem with stating the cause. I've been treating Mrs Quinlan for some time for a heart condition. I frequently suggested that she tell her family, but she could be a very determined woman, as you no doubt know. She had it fixed in her head that she was not old enough for the condition to be life-threatening. She did not take kindly to any mention of her age, did she? But it *was* her heart. I think she was not helped by the number of cigarettes she smoked. Do you smoke, Mrs Quinlan? As soon as this is over cut it down, my dear. You won't be sorry when you are seventy.'

'So he's not still at that Senator's then, Rose?'

'No, Gran. I can't understand it. He gave me an itinerary, but he must have changed it. I can't think what to do next. The Senator is going to try the airport hotels.'

Leo said, 'Would you like me to ring the airline? Who was he booked with? They'll be able to tell us if the flight was delayed and if he was transferred.'

In an American hotel, considerably more swish than the one with satin sheets and red lampshades that Helen had fancied, Ballard Quinlan, dressed only in an expensive silk dressing-gown which was a gift from Miriam Corder-Peake, returned the receiver to its rest, handling it as though it might break, and plumped heavily down on the bed. 'My mother's dead, Mimi. That was Rose. I can't believe it . . . She said it was like Papa, she simply stopped breathing.'

'Oh, my poor darling.' Miriam, in a wide-sleeved silk kimono with embroidered cherry-blossom, fell to her knees at her lover's feet and took his hand. 'And poor, poor Mrs Winifred. You must take some brandy.' She leapt up again, doing the only helpful thing she could think of at the moment. 'Of course you *must* go at once. Let me pack your case. Darling, how absolutely awful and dreadful, but there can be *absolutely* no connection with your grandfather . . . Would you like to be alone?'

He held out a hand and she came to him at once. Sitting on his lap, she put her arms about him and drew his head to her cherry-blossomed breast and stroked his wonderful head. 'No, not alone,' he said, 'the shock hasn't hit me yet. I need you . . . there are arrangements . . . You must travel back with me.' His beautiful dark, heavily-lashed eyes were just so awfully sad. She had never seen them wet with tears, and it pained her most dreadfully.

'Of course, my darling. Leave everything to me. Now you drink up all the brandy and I'll start things moving.'

If there was one thing that the Hon. Miriam could do, it was to get things moving along. People responded to the cut-glass of her voice, and her assumption that officials would do her bidding. Mostly they did. Inside an hour she had laid out travelling clothes for both of them and packed the rest, settled with the hotel, changed her flight so that she could travel with him, packed both their cases, ordered a light meal and a car to take them to the airport, and had the shower running ready for him to step into.

As he showered, she put up her hair and made up her face.

'Darling, is the cat out of the bag? I mean . . . Senator Weissman must have suspected something to get his secretary to ring here.'

'Absolutely not out of the bag. It was a guess on Walt Weissman's part: he thought my flight might have been held up.'

'Why don't you just tell her, darling?'

Why didn't he just tell Mimi that Rose already knew?

'The Party doesn't go a bundle on Members getting divorced.'

There had been many times, over the last two or three years, when Miriam would have liked to suggest that Ballard should tell the Party to jump in the lake. If they decided not to re-select him, then he would be able to devote all his efforts to hunting heads for his agency. They were sufficiently financially secure to do the right thing by his family. Miriam's own capital was pretty substantial and very well looked after. If it were not for the Party, he could tell his wife that he wished to marry another woman, and let her divorce him. It would not be pleasant, of course – Daddy and Mummy would loathe it – but they would survive as they had survived the birth of little Gerald. Giving up the baby still pained her. She had hated pretending that she was going out to Salisbury on a spree, and had been terribly afraid giving birth in a foreign clinic, however swish and modern it was. And she had felt sad that little Gerald would grow up to think of her as Aunt. But people like her own always rallied round. Daddy had been livid at Ballard, but Mummy had said enigmatically that history did tend to repeat itself, and Daddy had gone down like a deflated balloon. Miriam would have liked to know what history that was – Daddy surely wouldn't behave like that, but someone must have done. But one never asked questions. She felt guilty for even entertaining such a thought, but there were times when she particularly missed him and began to wonder whether there would ever be a suitable time for Ballard to divorce his wife and marry her. He was such a decisive and powerful man, so authoritative, and she did understand why he wanted to hold on to his seat. Men always wanted power, it was natural to them to want to rule. He saw his career leading directly into cabinet and then to the House of Lords. She was sure that he would do it. All this committee and delegation work he took on was to that purpose. He was admirable and she loved him terribly.

'But I can't bear it when you go back to her. I get the most frightful pictures of you and she . . . I mean, you *must* do it with her sometimes.'

'I've told you, we don't. Chance would be a fine thing; Rose is quite frigid. The only thing she is at all interested in is her bloody garden.'

'And your children: she is a good mother.'

'Well, of course, and the children.' He hated it when Miriam talked about children.

'And the house you share with her.'

'Miriam, I have just received the news that my mother is lying dead, and you are working yourself up into a state over something I cannot really help having – a wife, children, and a bloody house!' He came from the steaming shower and dripped his way through the sitting room of their suite and into the bedroom. She ran after him.

'Oh, I am *such* an absolute pig! A jealous and possessive pig. The thing is I adore you so much that I can't bear thinking that there is another woman who has any claim on you. Of course Mrs Winifred has. Oh! Had. But I mean *physical* claim. Let me do that for you.' She unpinned the new shirt she had laid out for him and, having helped him into it, buttoned it on him. 'You haven't a black tie with you, so I chose the dark navy, with your charcoal suit . . .'

Another thing she could not bear was being in his bad books.

Standing there, holding out his tie, she appeared so wraith-like and vulnerable in her white silk that he could not keep up his crossness. She was so young and pretty, and with her hair down and not wearing make-up, she looked like a schoolgirl. 'Come here, goose. Now listen, you might not think it from my manner, but I am really very cut up about Mother . . .'

'Of course you are, darling.'

'. . . and I may well be moody and fly off the handle when we get back. But you have to believe me, I love you. I love you very, very much, and if it were in my power to marry you, then I would do so. And the very moment I am in a secure enough position to do so, I shall be divorced in as discreet a way as I can arrange. You know the problem, if I get my hands on the new constituency or something equally secure, and get the worry of Covington being so marginal off my back, then it would all come right for us. We should be married. But until we can work all that out, then you and I must be patient and we must be very, very discreet indeed. All the time that I am home, I have to think before I speak: it's very nerve-wracking. And now that Rose has spoken to Walt Weissman, she must know that I left there a couple of days ago, and she'll want to know where I've been. It's a damned nuisance that I telephoned my grandmother yesterday and told her that I was still at Cape Cod. I shall have to think my story through very carefully. Quite apart from all the worry of the funeral, it will be a stressful few days. But in the corner of my mind I shall keep a picture of Mimi wearing her white silk.'

'Oh, darling, I know all that. I know you love me, and I love you – terribly – but I shall be excluded from everything you'll have to do when you get back to the terrible, terrible thing you have to face there, and I long to share it with you. I really liked Mrs Winifred.'

'I know you did, and she liked you. And when it is over, I shall return to London at once.'

'And you won't . . . with your wife . . . you won't *do* anything?'

'There's nothing to do. Because I can't keep my hands off you, doesn't mean that I cannot spend a couple of celibate nights in my own home. I have spent scores of celibate nights sleeping beside my wife. What can I say to make you understand?'

She blinked her large schoolgirl eyes at him. 'Just promise that you will not fuck with her, Ballard.'

He gave her bottom a slap. 'Language. All right, I promise faithfully that I shall not fuck with Rose. I have not fucked with Rose in ages. I do not want to fuck with Rose and shall never do so again. Does that satisfy you?'

Even though he and Rose had parted so acrimoniously after their meeting in the flat, he was stirred by thoughts of sleeping with her. God knows, he didn't want to be aroused by her. But several times since, his mind had gone back to the afternoon in Spain when she had taken over their love-making. It had been exciting, but unnerving. Perhaps he should have stayed on, but Miriam's desirable and obedient little body had called to him. If he had stayed on, he and Rose might have come to some new level of understanding of one another. On the other hand, he might never have found his way through to Walt Weissman and the important contact that he had made over the last few days.

He had a strange feeling of unreality. The last weeks had been stressful but exhilarating.

The gratification he got from his dealings with the Senator . . . the cloak and dagger in those dealings.

The relief – satisfaction – of telling Rose about Mimi . . . He should never have told her about young Gerald, but she had made him so blindingly mad that for a moment he almost hadn't cared about the consequences – just so long as he could hurt her and wipe that superior expression from her face.

And in the handshake of the ex-Senator he felt that he had been given the key to the vaults of the Bank of England.

Powerful. Keeping so many balls in the air whilst walking along a crumbling cliff edge had been exhilarating. That had made him feel powerful. He had reached firmer ground. It was all coming together. His overseas trips with trade delegations and House of Commons teams had paid off: he had at last made the right contacts. All that he now needed to do was to keep going. Rose's voice telling him that his mother had had a heart attack added to the unreality of the last days.

'Make a fuss of me, Mimi.' She kissed and caressed him. He kissed her and ran his warm hands over her dainty little body, sending a shiver through her. She was extraordinarily desirable. Pedigree from her mother. It was the appearance of breeding that had attracted him to Rose. Not a trace of coarseness; even at seventeen Rose had possessed an aloof beauty and restrained elegance that was the stuff of storybook princesses. But Miriam was the real thing. She had been 'finished', been presented at Court, and she rode to hounds. He himself was about to start riding to hounds. His first pink and the breeches hung in the London flat. She was class and she loved him. He moved an assured leg over her.

'Darling, should you? I *mean*, Mrs Winifred . . .'

'The one has nothing to do with the other.'

'You are quite *wicked*, Ballard.'

'Lie down and shut up.'

Which of course she did, because she did like it so much, and things were so much better now. There were times when she wished that he wouldn't be so quick; they could have made it last much longer if he had done it her way. It would be better once they were married; then they would not always be snatching at their love-making.

She went to take another quick shower and to re-do her hair and face. 'Darling?' she called, 'shall you mind if I don't come to the service for Mrs Winifred. It won't appear too frightfully uncaring?'

He called back, 'I shall mind, but best not come.'

'I shall hate not *being* with you.'

'I promised you, Mimi. I shall only walk behind the coffin with Rose, I shall not sleep with her.'

She smiled to herself as luxurious creamy lather slid from her body and swirled down the plug-hole. He had known exactly what was in her mind. He always did. Her time would come. For the first time he had said that he loved her. He had actually said, 'God forgive me, Mimi, I believe I've actually fallen in love with you.'

As the fifties decade ended, so the Quinlan family – in the form in which it had always been known – ended too.

In 1956, Winifred's funeral and memorial service had been a model of high church propriety.

Everyone, even Rebecca, was formally dressed in sober winter wool. Men wearing uniform black serge and either Homburg or bowler hats, and Winifred's women friends in good quality Jaeger or Windsmoor wool in grey or fashionable black with competitive hats.

It was all very British. Jonathan was not the only one to say, 'Wouldn't Nan have just loved it?'

When the family entered in procession behind the coffin, it must have been an unusual person who was not in the first instance drawn to watch Rose. Her naturally pale hair appeared paler against the black and white she wore, her youthful complexion brushing against the packed curlicues of Persian lamb, looked as perfect as a child's; the severity of her silvery hair, knotted into a netted and beaded chignon, emphasized the extraordinary serenity and beautifully balanced proportions of her profile.

Senator Weissman, being in the country, attended to acknowledge his new British partner's loss. A true Anglophile, he absorbed every detail of a service held in one of the greatest cathedrals on earth, and counted himself fortunate at having persuaded the Englishman to join him. Putting two and two together, he had supposed that there was something going on that maybe should not be, but that was the way of the world, and men in their prime – as his new partner so obviously was – must be made allowances for. But, when the Senator saw Mrs Quinlan, who he had supposed would be a comfortable housewife, he was confounded. The woman was every red-blooded American man's dream of a perfect English lady. She could have been a royal princess. One hell of a First Lady. One hell of a great lay, if he was any judge. An irreverent hard-on threatened, so he was forced to turn his attention to the 'programme'.

What Senator Weissman had been following was Rose and Ballard, presenting their usual united face, walking side by side behind the coffin. United for the last time, as the family now knew.

As he followed his mother's coffin down the aisle of Winchester cathedral, Ballard regretted that he had not been in more suitable circumstances when the news of his mother's death had reached him. He had felt disorganized, detected and hated it. He had other vague feelings of regret of things past, coupled with resentment at the unfairness that there were no second chances, no way of going back and doing things differently. Impressive and perfectly turned out, he followed the coffin down the aisle of Winchester cathedral with his chin lifted, presenting to the congregation his distinguished silver-haired temples and handsome profile. Part of him regretted that this would be the last time that people looking at him and Rose together would say, 'Have you ever seen a more handsome couple?' He had always gained great satisfaction in knowing that they impressed. Mimi, pretty as she was, would never elicit that same kind of admiration. But Mimi, young and fashionable and terribly sexy, was a pretty good exchange for a wife who, however stunning she might look, was cold.

Jonathan came alone, glad that this was the last time that the family would have to present themselves as a background for his father's career. No village church for Ballard Quinlan's mother, even though it meant a trek from Honeywood to Winchester and back to Honeywood churchyard again. He had, as his great-grandmother said he should try to, forgiven his grandmother, but he would find it difficult to forget the prejudice that had caused the rift between them. What he felt now was a real sadness that she had lived such a terribly narrow life.

He felt that he could never forgive his father, not only for his attitude to Elna, but for the entirely false front he presented . . . and now he was separating from their mother. They had exchanged scarcely a word since Jon had arrived at Gran's yesterday. What was the use? His mother had begged them all to stay out of it, and Jonathan was not sorry to have this excuse for avoiding the situation at home.

Rebecca, almost unrecognizable to her old friends now that her hair was cropped to one inch and bleached as white as her mother's, was not so much devastated at the impending break-up of her parents' marriage, as at the sudden understanding that with death there are no second chances. She would never now be able to tell her grandmother that she had grown to understand her. Nan's nature needed people to approve of her as much as Becc's own throve on being shocking. Rose's embargo on her children defaming their father did not stop Becc telling her, 'Sod him, Ma. You'll be well shot of him. When you are a free woman, you'll wonder how you ever stood all this domesticity.' To which Rose had replied merely that she wished everyone would stop using such ugly language.

Villette had grown as beautiful as her mother had been when, at about the same age, she had married Ballard. Only Ballard and Charlotte (being the only ones to have known Rose then) could have seen that the resemblance was only skin deep, for Vee was as worldly-wise as Rose had been naïve. Certainly she was no longer a virgin, nor had she been for ages. She had discovered sex for herself, enjoyed it, and saw no reason why she should not practise it – but always safely. She had surprised more than one casual and unprepared lover by producing a Durex sheath from her cigarette case. Nan's death appeared to leave her as unaffected as did the coming upheaval. 'I don't see why *he* should be the only one to shake off the dust of the village. I think that we all should. I *mean*, couldn't we all emigrate to Australia or something? That would be *t'rific*!'

Anoria was at a vulnerable age for sex and death to be playing such an important place in her life. Papa's death had seemed all right because he was a hundred, and had lived much longer than most people; he had nothing to complain of. But Nan hadn't really had her share of life. She was over sixty, but Anoria had never thought of Nan as being *that* old, not old enough to die, at any rate, because she had nice legs and wore high heels, and had tits that were higher and more pointy than Nora's own. Nan always made up her face so early in the morning that, even if it was oldish, you could never tell. It wasn't *fair*. She hated the idea that Great-Grandmother too must soon have to die, but at least that would be more fair because she *was* old.

She had switched off from the slow and dull ceremonial, as resentment had ground away inside her. Not only against unfairness, but against Her! And against Him! In a moment of weakness she had confided in Kate Wilkinson about things to do with Them. Kate, who to Nora's surprise had been terribly understanding and nice, had confided back to Nora that she had been going in for petting. 'Heavy?' enquired Nora, who was the school changing-room expert. Kate had not said, but had agreed with Nora that it was awful even to think that mothers and fathers did it. She! (Miriam) was not much older than Jon, yet her father had obviously been doing It to her otherwise there wouldn't be grounds for divorce.

As she observed her parents following Nan's coffin, she tried to place them in a situation similar to a scene from *The Constant Nymph*, bits of which she had read several times, and was presented with an image – herself with crumbling apple pie stuffed in her mouth, her mother with her hair tousled and a dark patch on her blue crêpe skirt; her father with his back to the room, pulling his braces on to his shoulder and combing his hair. She knew enough now to guess what they had been doing. It had given her a quite shameful feeling, but not much understanding.

She resented them all. Her father for letting them all down, and her mother for not making him want to stay. That '*No*, Ballard!' which had reached her whilst she had been cutting the apple pie, now took on significance.

If her mother had not let him do It to her, then he probably needed to do It to some other woman.

But why couldn't he have found somebody better than Miriam? He could have gone to a prostitute. Wasn't that what they were for? They were supposed to charge a lot, but Father was quite rich.

She couldn't help thinking about these things, even though it was Nan's funeral service; for months now her mind always seemed to be thinking about sex. She had known about it for ages, but it was only since her breasts had got these sensations and she kept getting these dreams about boys, even men, that she had begun to understand some of the complications of becoming a woman, and she was not sure that she wanted to. And yet there was *something*, something sort of splendid in the sensations one got, something that made her feel on the edge of sorting out the pieces of a puzzle. Her friends said that she was 'dotty'. The head of her school had called her 'as intelligent a student as I have ever had in the school, but your anti-authoritarian attitudes put you in danger of ruining the promise you show.'

Charlotte, glad that Sid was not here to know what was going on in his family, was helped by a protective shell that had begun to grow about her tender heart seventy years ago, in a childhood where nobody ever expected much of anybody, and assumed that nothing good ever lasted. On the arm of Jonathan, Charlotte followed behind Ballard and Rose. She had always said that she had been the luckiest woman alive. After she had helped Sid get over Honoria's death, and then Henry's death, Charlotte's life had been very good. All that she could hope for now was to do what little she could for each of them as they needed her. They all wanted something different, yet the same, from her. They wanted her to be on their side, not understanding that it was not possible for her to do that. All that she could do was to listen and comfort as best she could. Nora and Vee had not wanted to talk much, perhaps they thought a great-grandmother was too far removed from their own generation. Yet Nora had wanted something, a room with Charlotte if Shaft's Farm was to be sold.

Charlotte knew that it was her own fault for having been so

complacent all these years. She should have heeded what she had learned as a child, that nothing good lasts. If she had kept herself armed with that, then all this would not have been so devastating. It wasn't only Winnie's sudden death – Charlotte knew how to deal with death because you knew that it was always on the cards; it was these terrible injuries – that was it, injuries – to the family that they would never get over. Why was Ballard going to make all these changes at once? He wasn't a natural liberal thinker, she had always known that, but she had always thought that he was basically decent and was trying to make this a better country. And she had always known that he wasn't in Sid's league as a family man, but she had never even given it a thought that Ballard was the sort to go off with a girl young enough to be his daughter. The face of him! Ballard had been the light of hers and Sid's life; he had come along just as they were as low as they could be after Henry was killed. It was, if they had never known him, or as if he was about to be snuffed out just like Henry had been. No . . . Ballard was still alive, she must hold on to him, come what may. Hold on to all of them, one way or another.

Even now, Charlotte found it difficult to believe that Ballard was serious about going over to the Tories. To have gone over to the other side was one thing – he wasn't the first to have done that; but to break up the entire family for the sake of a spoilt and shallow bit of a thing who wasn't fit to shine Rose's shoes . . . It would have broken Sid's heart.

Sid had known all about the Corder-Peakes. Ballard had been pleased as Punch when he told them that they had some sort of débutante helping in the election. Sid had been sure that she was only there to find out what she could for the Tories. In Sid's opinion the Corder-Peakes were chancers from way back. They had made pyroxylin for the British army in the Boer war, at the same time supplying it to the Boers. By the time of the Great War they no longer bought in chemicals, but had their own plant to produce their gun-cotton. Between the wars they expanded into all kinds of explosives, and by 1945 were worldwide armaments' suppliers.

Charlotte had once lectured Sid on his prejudice. 'You can't hate the girl because of her parents and grandparents.'

And Sid in his sharp way had said, 'You want to make a bet on that, Lotte? She's a Corder-Peake and they got their money from making anything that will blow up another human being, and our Henry was blown up by dodgy explosives.'

Sid was a reasonable and level-headed man, except when he got something like that into his head.

* * *

Ballard Quinlan – Member of Parliament for the new constituency of Covington and Hillford – had once again in his career clung on to his seat. Covington and Hillford was the old Covington constituency but with its boundaries newly drawn to take in a lower middle-class area with the sole purpose of creating another seat for the Government. But it hadn't quite come off and, once again, because of Covington's unpredictability (or cussedness) in politics, Ballard had held on to his seat by his fingernails. He was giving serious thought to his future in politics.

There was no way that he could give it up: he was hooked in the way that some actors, having once stepped into the limelight, will do anything to stay there. What he got from rising to his feet and hearing his own rich voice ring out across the chamber, and from sitting on committees, commissions and enquiries, was what young people experimenting with LSD, hash and mescalin called 'a high'.

Of course, he had never been convinced of socialism, so he had no problems with his conscience; now that he had seen socialism in action, indeed, he found himself thinking actively against it. He began to resent the comrades who ran his constituency. A bunch of teachers and trades-unionists holding his future in their hands every five years or so when it was time for readoption. Too many times recently he had been questioned or rebuked by that cabal for bucking the Party line. Recently he had given an interview in which he made unfavourable comments about the coal industry and the nationalized section of road transport. He had only said openly what many were saying privately, but the 'brothers' had hauled him over the coals.

Miriam was sympathetic to his views: her own flirtation with the idea of a leftist rebellion against the traditions of the Corder-Peakes had long gone, and she was left now with a membership card and admiration for Ballard as a reason for the dogsbody work she did for the Labour Party. Like Ballard, she had never had a thing in common with the Covington Labour Party. She suspected that they suspected her of something – spying for the Conservatives, probably – which wasn't surprising seeing that the rest of the Corder-Peakes were dyed-in-the-wool blues, and she had never really got a hold on what socialism was all about. They talked about equal opportunity, when it was obvious (even to someone who knew so little of the way things worked as Miriam herself) that an insignificant teacher living by the packing plant, or a librarian, or a railway person, or one of union brothers, would never be equal to people born to better things with more money and good connections. They might be able to conduct a deep discussion about economics or internationalism, but with the best will in the world, one was forced to the obvious conclusion that the kind of influence and wealth a family such as her own possessed, would out-gun the comrades and the brothers every time.

She had joined the left for much the same reasons as some of her girl cousins hung about the harvest fields and building sites. Her own kind held power because they were prosperous; the 'real' people would demand power, take it. There was such virility in young men who had returned from war and were ready to stand up to the likes of her father and uncles, and when they sang 'The Red Flag', she shivered with a desire she had mistaken for political fervour. She had expected that they would be making plans to take over her father's bank account, put him and her mother into a council house, and use Brigland's Park as offices for one of the nationalized industries, but nothing of the kind had occurred. And by the time her father's party had returned to Government, Daddy had become more affluent than he had ever been. Had commandeering the land or turning over public schools to the state system suited the Conservatives, they would never have shilly-shallied in the way that the socialists had done.

Even after several years of involvement in the political world, poor Miriam was still confused: if an armaments' manufacturer and dealer such as her father could thrive as well under the socialists as under her father's Party, then Miriam felt that the entire political world was beyond her, so that she had no problems when Ballard said disloyal things about his own Party, and Miriam herself had nothing as troublesome as an ideal to grapple with.

She was more mature, quite grown out of her flirtation with rebellion. She was ready to return to the fold for, if the truth be known, she had, in her political phase (which had not only been unopposed, but had been maddeningly and terribly patronized by Daddy), badly missed the code by which she had been brought up, missed her own sort, missed the nouveau-riche flamboyance (although she did not recognize it as such) upon which she had been nurtured. She had missed the hunt, too, and once more longed for the hunt balls which – her father being MFH and still a great hunting man himself – were held at Brigland's Park.

Always with his eye to the main chance, ear to the wall, and a nose for an opportunity, at the time of his mother's death Ballard had begun making moves. Planning ahead, he sounded out, had discreet meetings, and had ambiguous, easily refutable discussions with men who were not on his own side of the political fence, and others who were on no side at all, but who owed their seats on the boards of nationalized companies, or places in higher management, to Ballard's agency. His involvement with Senator Walt Weissman hadn't gone unnoticed by a certain department of the Defence

Ministry tucked away in deepest Kent, nor by Sir Evelyn Corder-Peake's business colleagues. Suddenly, Ballard was not only in the money, but in favour with the Great, the Good and, more importantly, the Powerful.

When it all came together, it would seem the most natural thing in the world for him to ditch the Party which had so often beggared itself to get him returned, cross the floor of the House, and go to sit on the Tory benches.

First, he had to make an honest woman of Miriam, and thus truly join her set. With his usual slickness, he began the process of slipping out of his marriage to Rose. He provided her with the necessary evidence of his infidelity at an hotel in Jersey, with a total stranger recommended by a private investigation agency, whose one night sharing an assumed name and double room with him was sufficient evidence to end a long, unsuccessful marriage. Miriam was never involved.

With the same feelings of dejection and anger that she had felt when she had seen the Shaft's Farm 'For Sale' notice go up in the spring, Monica Wilkinson put a cup of tea for Leo on the bedside table and went to watch the Pickford's van, which had come to collect some of Ballard's things, manoeuvre into position.

Leo put down his paper and got out of bed to sit beside her, holding her against his lean chest with his sport-hardened arms. 'How is Rose?'

'Putting a good face on it. If it were me, I'd be throwing things,' she answered. 'Hatchets.'

'Rose has had more practice at putting a face on things. With a man like me, you've been cosseted.'

'And what's that supposed to mean?' She turned an aggressive face upon him and he felt the promise of his arousal disappear.

'A joke, Mon. You do get tetchy these days.'

'Meaning?'

'Meaning, you're working too hard.'

'It wouldn't hurt you to do a bit more.'

'I do what I can. Nobody expected a life of ease with us both working.'

Even though she was half aware that they were getting on the same verbal roundabout they had recently found themselves riding quite often, she didn't bite her tongue. 'You do enough to placate your conscience. At least you could play your part. Helen's the only one with a conscience, it's not right that she does more than her fair share.'

'You mustn't get so frantic about it all. It doesn't matter if Kate forgets to peel the potatoes, or James forgets to put his laundry in the basket.'

'It matters. It matters because if I don't do it myself then Jean ends up doing it and it's not what we pay her for.'

'Then let's have her in more hours.'

Monica banged the window shut against the sound of the removals men cheerfully talkative at the start of their day. 'Don't you listen, or what! Jean doesn't particularly want any more hours, and our kids are old enough to have common-or-garden family concern and be a bit more responsible for themselves. I had my chores to do right from when I was five.'

'And did you do them?'

'Of course I did.'

'Ah well, that's because you knew your place as a woman.'

She scowled at him.

'It's a joke.'

'I'm not in the mood.' She sat down heavily on the window seat. 'I'm sorry, you're right, I am tetchy. But I don't know how I'm going to stand it without Rose there.'

'Rose has had to stand it with you gone all day.'

'I've only been going out to work, not moving away. Why couldn't that little tart stay off her back; she must have known that Ballard's pants are always ready to fly open.'

Raising his eyebrows and pursing his mouth, Leo looked at Monica over the half glasses he had recently had to admit that he needed.

'All right, I know . . . pot calling the kettle . . . It was different for us, she was already cheating on you.'

'Come here and keep your crudenesses for the nurse's cubby-hole or wherever it is you go to drink tea and smoke yourselves to death.'

Pretending reluctance, she allowed herself to accept a bit of a hug. 'I really am miserable about it. I shall miss their kids terribly. I don't know what Kate will do without Vee, she's another one like a bear with a sore head. Poor Kate.'

'Well, don't press her too hard about not doing the chores. I'll see Jean if you like. I'm sure I can charm a few more hours out of her.'

'I'm sure you can, but it's not the kind of thing a good Marxist does, is it, to let some poor woman pick up behind a family who can afford to pay?'

'I never claim to be a good anything. The alternative is that you give up your job.'

'Or you could give up yours.'

He rubbed her shoulder affectionately. 'Come on, stop being daft.'

'What's happening to us, Leo?'

'Nothing's happening.'

'Are you sleeping around again?'

'What's that supposed to mean?'

'It's supposed to mean that I get patted and hugged and stroked, and that's bloody all. How long is it since we did it twice a day, or in the car . . . how long is it since we did it at all?'

'We aren't kids.'

'What is it, then?' adding sarcastically, 'Perhaps the magic has gone from our marriage.'

She'd hit the right button, for whatever it had been that had kept renewing their relationship wasn't working any more. Monica thought she knew what it was.

'You don't like seeing Mike running the team, do you?'

'That doesn't bother me, except that he's not much good at it. The women have slipped in the league table.'

'Perhaps he's not as good at keeping them happy as you were.'

'Pack it in, Mon.'

'Well, that's when all these funny moods started: New Year's day, when you decided to resign.'

She was right about when his introspective and withdrawn moods had started, but it wasn't giving up running the team that had brought about his spasmodic impotence, it was having Rose on his mind and Rose keeping her distance. Ballard's mother's death, and the problems with the Quinlan marriage, explained her avoidance to some extent. Leo felt quite bewildered. He didn't expect that she would have fallen into his arms at the first opportunity, but for God's sake, they had been within inches of making it with each other. She had been as worked up as he was – and then nothing.

He dreaded the thought of her not living next door. Even if he wasn't allowed to touch, she'd be there; they'd meet and have coffee in one another's kitchens as they had always done, see to one another's children just as they had always done. On the single occasion since New Year when he and Rose had been alone together, she had at first said that they must sell the house because it was a luxury she couldn't afford. Then she had said, 'The other reason is that I think I might fall for you, Leo, and that's the real luxury I can't afford. I've got Longmore, the house my aunt left to me years ago. It's in Bosham . . . you know, Chichester Harbour.'

'Of course I know Bosham,' he said testily.

'Good! I shall probably go there with Vee and Nora.'

It wasn't that he didn't want Monica in bed: he did, but something was different. A lot of things were different. The routine had gone from the house. Breakfast time was often a race around the table, and he too often had to eat dinner alone. All of their married life he had come home and had known that Mon was somewhere about; if not actually in the house, then next door. The kids weren't kids any more. Helen was bitchy as hell sometimes. Tom . . . God, what were they going to do about Tom? He wanted to write rock songs. Maybe a year from now it would all be sorted. He had at least taken one step in that direction.

'Mon, how would you feel about moving house?'

She felt his arousal and was surprised. 'Move away from Honeywood?'

'No. We could move next door.'

'You must be off your rails, Leo. That place is on the market for thirty thousand pounds.'

'I thought it was your dream house.'

'It is. Don't tease.'

He kissed her with the familiarity shared by any couple who have slept together for twenty years. They knew how to be fast or prolonged in their love-making, to pace themselves and one another, to make it as good as they could. It started off well, and Leo felt his old ardour return. Then his concentration lapsed; his mind wouldn't leave him alone. Shaft's Farm empty, Shaft's Farm without Rose, without the kids wandering through the fence, Rose living miles away . . .

He crashed on to his back. 'Sod it! Sod it! Sod it!'

Monica lay still for a few moments. 'Is that it then?'

With his eyes closed, he stretched out a hand to feel for hers. 'Darling, I'm sorry, I'm really sorry.'

'Well thank *you*.' Angry, she got out of bed and into the bathroom in a single movement, banging the door and locking it behind her. She not only felt frustrated because of their failures, she felt guilty. She was middle-aged. She had never been able to hit anything with a racket. She had grey hairs and her thighs were soft. She was overweight. She knew that if she had written to a women's magazine problems page she would be advised to change her style and surprise her man, to interest herself in his hobbies, to talk to her hairdresser and start a course of exercises and a slimming diet. But what if you had done all of those things? What if your man says he fancies your body? What then are you supposed to do when he can't keep going in bed?

When she returned, wrapped in a bath-robe, her hair wet from the shower, he was sitting on the edge of the bed drinking the lukewarm tea. He looked so dejected and vulnerable. She went and sat beside him. 'I'm sorry, darling, I just felt so . . .'

'I know, it's my fault. I can't do it, Mon. Even when I want to . . .'

'It's not the end of the world.'

'Oh no?'

'All men have bouts of impotence.'

'Christ, Mon! It's not impotence.'

'Don't get steamed up, it's just the proper term.'

He slammed down the cup. 'Oh right. Let's call a spade a spade. Give it the correct medical term. Leo Wilkinson, the great performer, has become *impotent*!'

Monica, not knowing what else to say and impatient at the dramatics, said nothing. Women were used to 'off' times – spells of frigidity, to use the correct medical term. Perhaps he was right, correct terms were stark. 'Off' times were built into a woman's cycle, but it sometimes appeared that men would as soon have their entire blood circulation fail than have it fail in the one place. She knew from the hospital how dejected they could be after surgery, and how they improved when their spirits rose along with everything else.

Having dressed and done her hair, she went back into the bedroom. Leo had put on linen slacks and a sports' shirt and was combing his long, fair hair. His reflection showed tears glistening on his lashes.

'Leo, darling, it isn't worth crying over.'

He put his arms round her, pressed his cheek against the top of her head and rocked gently. 'It's not that. It's that bloody removals van. We've been together a long time. It's going to leave a big hole. Maybe it's time for us to make a change too.'

'You weren't serious just now about moving?'

Releasing her, he went to his briefcase and drew out a sheaf of papers. 'I went to the estate agents.'

Monica glanced down at the details, then across at Leo who had gone to sit on the window seat and was watching her closely. 'You're joking.'

'No I'm not.'

'But it's thirty thousand pounds!'

'We could afford that with the automated warehouse contracts. But would you want to?'

She was scanning the details. 'I don't know why I'm even reading this. I know it as well as this place.' She read aloud. 'Shaft's Farm, a unique Elizabethan farmhouse, with some original stabling and outhouses. Large and well-maintained garden with many mature trees and shrubs, large vegetable garden, greenhouse . . . You're serious?'

He nodded. 'Could be. I've gone so far as to see my accountant and the bank manager: they're happy enough. I had never realized the kind of price our place would fetch. It will probably mean more Cheyne Walk people in the village, but it would mean that in any case – neither house is going to be affordable to Honeywood people. I hate to say it, Mon, but we're already living in a desirable property.'

The idea had not entered his head until Rose had said, 'I shall hate to think of strangers living here, but if we are going to sell up, it might as well be now: one upheaval will be less traumatic for Nora and Vee.'

The last ten years had been a good time for large-scale engineering projects, and now the age of automated distribution systems was here. Leo was one of the first in the field, as his new and thriving branch specializing in fine-tolerance engineering projects showed. When he had gone to see his accountant, Leo had really only been idling, but he had come out with a changed view of property being only a home: it could be a hedge against rainy days. 'Go after it, Leo,' the man had said. 'Listed property will always have a good resale value.'

Holding the sheaf of papers to her chest, Monica gazed out at the men carrying boxes to the van. What on earth could he be taking that he needed a van that size? Rose had said that he was not claiming any of the furniture. 'I think it's not stylish enough for Mistress Quinlan,' she had said.

Monica said, 'Wouldn't it seem that we're cashing in on Rose's bad luck, Leo?'

'It might if she were selling her fur coat, but the house will be sold whether it's to us or anyone else.' He paused, trying to evaluate her expression. There was still an edge in the voices of both of them. They had had years and years of good love-life, so it was not easy to accept difficulty. He had begun to want to own the house, and wanted Monica to want it too, but he didn't want to be accused of steam-rollering. Treading on eggshells. 'It would be great to have all those extra rooms.' Tentatively he took her fingers and fiddled with her rings. 'I suppose we shall be grandparents within the next ten years.'

'Don't be too sure, if this new contraceptive pill gets around, girls will be able to choose, and they might not choose babies.'

Trying light-heartedness. 'OK, we could grow mushrooms in the spare rooms.'

'Or we could have a room with mirrors on the ceiling.' She kissed him in a friendly sort of way. 'Come on, bath or shower?'

'Between the sheets,' he said.

Monica was not one for faking; not that he would have noticed anyhow in his relief that he could keep going. Another failure at that moment would have been too much to deal with, but the prospect of something happening to get them out of their rut excited him. If they were actually living in the Quinlans' house, it wasn't so likely that they would feel their absence. Afterwards, Leo lay back watching cigarette smoke curling upwards.

Monica, coming in from the bathroom, said, 'OK, let's buy it.'

'You're sure?'

'Go on, get up and go and see the estate agent.'

'They don't open till ten.'

'Jack Wilder's a friend of yours: surely you can ring him at home for a house with an asking price of thirty thousand.'

Leo reached for the phone. 'You're sure? We haven't even talked it over.'

'You don't talk over things like this, you just do them – like the first time we went away together, and when you decided to start up on your own. You either do it or you don't: you gamble on the big things; it's only the little ones get niggled over.'

When she heard the removals van start up, Monica reached the window in time to see Ballard's car going down the drive. 'He's gone! I'm going round to see Rose. I have to tell her. I don't feel good about it, you know.'

'Better us than some strangers. Bring her back with you. I'll make some scrambled eggs.'

'Wonders never cease, but don't do them for me . . . I'm going back on a diet.'

'Not again.'

'I need to be as slim and elegant as Rose if I'm going to be mistress of that place.'

'For heaven's sake, Mon, I married you for your curves.'

'I feel such a louse for getting so excited. But we are just the people for that house, I've always loved it. We'll make it a really happy place. What if Jon and Helen get together seriously . . . imagine me and Rose sharing our grandchildren. Rose could come and stay as much as she likes.'

Rose and Leo sharing grandchildren? The idea was pretty devastating.

Leo wondered how long it would be before Mon realized that there was no way that she could possibly continue nursing and run that great house. He would say nothing; she must discover that for herself. He had a picture of weekend tennis, and swimming . . . Ballard had planned a swimming pool: Leo's regular sub-contractors would put one in for a quarter of the price Ballard was considering . . .

* * *

Vee was, of all four children, the one who had grown up to most resemble Rose.

Her face was unexpressive as she attached the filter to the coffee-maker, but her mother knew that Ballard's leaving would have hurt Vee deeply. Rose had gone into the garden whilst Ballard had said whatever it was he felt able to say to a twenty-year-old daughter whom he had deserted for a mistress.

Rose came back into the house holding a few heavy-headed pink Bourbon roses. 'Look, Vee, your favourites.'

Vee took them and gave her mother a brief rocking hug, then unexpectedly and quite out of character said, 'Mum, I really love you. I don't know how to say these things . . . not like Becc. Not like Dad, he's good at all that.'

Rose, seeing Vee's mouth work and swallowing dryly as she tried to take control of herself, knew from her own way of dealing with emotions that she was afraid would get out of her control, that Vee was in trouble. It was easy for people like Becc and Nora, like Ballard: they had no problem when it came to expressing their anger or resentment.

Rose looked at her daughter almost shyly. 'But when *you* say something, it stays said.'

Vee nodded.

'It's all right for you to go on loving Ballard, you know. I told Nora the same thing. Because the marriage has broken down, it doesn't mean that the family is destroyed. He is still your father.'

'Oh yes, and he loves us dearly.' She sounded bitter. 'He just told me that. He even cried when he said how much he loves us all, and the last thing he wanted was to hurt us . . . the *last* thing.' Vee had not burst into tears since she was a child; like Rose she was afraid of letting anyone see that they could hurt her. Even so, tears began to stream down her face. 'God, Mum, how I hate him.'

Rose, who hadn't held a weeping Vee since she was a girl, felt a great wave of love for Vee envelop her as she did so. God forbid that Vee should grow up like herself, swallowing everything, hiding, not being the woman she longed to be. Getting to know 'Princess' Joffe, and coming to terms with Monica's decision to go back to nursing had, for the first time, made Rose see that it was not selfish to want things for oneself, to want to be oneself. Rose knew that she had still to find out what that was. 'It's all right to feel like that, Vee. He two-timed his wife and family and left us for another woman. Hatred isn't too strong an emotion in the circumstances. But try not to hang on to it; try good honest anger. If you like there's a great patch of briars growing up behind the garage; in your present frame of mind, I can recommend taking a scythe to them.'

Vee dried her eyes on a tea-towel and looked straight at her mother with a crooked smile. 'Is that how you've managed to keep so calm?'

Rose thought, she is so lovely. 'It is only my face that's calm. I could have murdered him for what he's done, especially to you children.'

Water hissed on to the coffee in the filter. Vee broke away from Rose and poured it. 'He should have taken up acting.'

'But that's just what he does. You've seen him in the House when he's putting on his high moral act.'

'He said, hurting us all was the last thing he wanted . . . I mean, did somebody force him to chuck us over for that . . . that crack-jawed cow!'

Monica was in the kitchen before she realized what was going on. 'Sorry! I'll come back later.'

'It's all right, Monica,' Vee said. 'Hand down one of those mugs, it's quite good coffee.' She smiled wryly. 'Charged with basic emotions, like homoeopathic remedies: you can't taste it but it works. Have a mug of hot and angry coffee.'

Rose and Monica exchanged glances.

Vee said, 'It's OK, Mum has given me permission to hate him for a while, she then recommends that I vent it on the weeds between the garages. Perhaps it will help sell the place.'

Monica said, 'Helen says you and she are planning to share a flat when you finish your course.'

'Don't you think it's a great idea?'

'Yeah . . . good,' Monica said.

'What's wrong? You don't sound very sure.'

'It's one of those crossroads.' She took her usual seat on a stool beside the Aga stove.

Rose, sitting opposite, said, 'We've just had a call from Wilder's. They've had an offer. Jack Wilder is coming round this afternoon . . . Can you imagine, estate agents working with such speed?'

Monica looked into her coffee. 'Do you still feel OK about going?'

'No, of course I don't, but I'm sure it's going to turn out all right.'

Vee said, 'It couldn't be turned into offices, could it? That lovely old place at Bishop's Waltham just died when that company bought it. The people who used to live there must feel really, really sick when they see all those bare windows.'

Rose said, 'I wouldn't want to sell to people like that, but we have to sell, Vee. Longmore's going to need it.'

'Listen, Rose,' Monica said, 'the call from Wilder's . . . it's Leo. It's Leo, us, *we've* made the offer. He . . . we want to buy Shaft's.'

'Auntie Mon, that's great! Perfect. It kind of stays in the family.'

'I didn't know you had even thought of it.'

'We hadn't. It never occurred to me that we could even afford it. It was you joking with Leo about buying it made him start thinking . . . He only told me about it just now, and I said yes straight away . . . Well, naturally I would, wouldn't I, but I wanted to see how you felt about it. I mean, people never really let go of the homes they've had . . . What do you think, Rose?'

'It's marvellous, Mon. Honestly, I'd be so pleased if you had it.'

'I wouldn't alter a hair of its head. I wouldn't let anybody touch the garden . . . you could ring me up and tell me what to do. I might even grow vegetables; I've always liked the idea.'

'If you do that I'll even leave you my bucket with the cushion.'

'It's awful talking money, but you know Leo's offered twenty-eight thousand pounds. He says if the agents are asking thirty, then Ballard will be expecting about twenty-five. It seems awful when it's your friends. Do you think Ballard will accept?'

Rose stood up, and with an expression Monica had not seen before, looked down at her with her arms folded tightly. 'As a matter of fact, the house is mine now. I took it as a settlement, providing a roof for the children and all that. I can't say that Ballard's been mean.'

Vee said, 'I shouldn't bloody think so. He's rolling in it, so is she. You should have taken him to the cleaners, Mum.'

'As long as he provides for you lot, I'd rather fend for myself. The trouble is, when I came to think how I could earn a living, the only thing I'm any good at is gardening. I've made up my mind to make a go of Longmore. If all this had happened next year, I wouldn't have had the option; the Longmore agent would have found new tenants.'

'But why not sell that place instead of going to live there?'

Rose could hardly say, 'Because I'm afraid if I go on living next door to your husband I shall finish up in bed with him.'

'Because Shaft's will fetch a good price and I will need the money to make a go of Longmore. And in any case Longmore has much more potential for making income – as a hotel: it's just an idea.'

Monica was more than a little surprised at the revelation. Rose, compliant, dominated Rose Quinlan, now owned not only the farmhouse, but the big old house at Chichester. She suddenly felt that the Rose she had known, the friend with whom she shared secrets and whom she loved, was changing. Impossible hereafter to think of her as the same vulnerable woman who, when Monica had come in a few minutes ago, had stabbed her with the pathos of her situation. 'Potential for making income.' Had that phrase been in the mind of the gardening Rose of the hand-rolled cigarettes and Wellington boots? Or was it Jonathan, the estate agent, talking?

Leo appeared. 'I thought you were bringing Rose round for my scrambled eggs. They're ruined.' He flashed a query at Monica which Rose did not miss. 'By the way, this letter's for you, it was in with ours.'

Rose took the envelope, opened it, but took no interest in the contents. 'I'll accept five hundred less than Wilder's price, Leo.'

It was not often that Leo was caught off-guard. He looked at Monica, floundering rather. 'Oh . . . Jack Wilder said that Ballard had gone back to London, and that he would ring me later.'

'He has,' Vee said, obviously finding the situation satisfying. 'Mum is quite happy to screw you down for more than she expected.'

Rose held out her hand. 'Deal, Leo? Don't look so shocked . . . Mr Wilder *would* think that he must ask Ballard's opinion, but this place is mine. Twenty-seven-and-a-half thousand and it is yours.'

When Leo, his face still expressing disbelief, said 'Deal', and kissed her in his old, friendly way, Rose wished that he had not.

Charlotte was the sort of person of whom people said, 'Isn't she marvellous?' And, compared to very many of her contemporaries, she was. She still kept her little Tin Lizzie on the road; not driving far, but enough to keep her hand in, recharge the batteries, and cling on to her independence. Much as she loved Ballard and always would, she could never forgive him for what he had done to his family. Rose had never been anything but a loyal and good wife who, although she hated anything to do with politicking, had never let him down. She had dressed the part and been charming wherever he had taken her.

The new one would do the same, but with her it was different: she actually wanted all that stuff. The trouble had always been that Rose had been too young when she married. To marry young you needed to have lived the kind of life Charlotte herself had lived. There wasn't much she hadn't seen by the time she had married Sid. Rose had hardly been out from behind those high walls of her auntie's house.

Charlotte would miss them. At least she would have Nora. It was agreed that Anoria should stay on in Honeywood, living with Charlotte until she was ready to change schools.

On the day when Leo and Rose exchanged contracts on Shaft's Farm, Jonathan turned up.

It was weeks since he had been home. Rose saw him come springing over the lawn, jumping dry-stone walls. He looked marvellous. 'I thought I was never going to see you again. Becc said you were both working this weekend.'

'Becc is. She's got some scheme about making blouses out of cheese-cloth, and you know what it's like when she and the Joffes get together; they'll be burning the midnight oil.'

'Well, come on in. Vee's here, Nora's down at Gran's. Your father was here first thing collecting his wardrobe and a few things he wants, but he's gone.'

'Gran told me. I'll get my bag. I . . . ah . . . Come on, I've got some news.'

Holding his arm as though not to let him go, Rose walked with him across the lawn towards his car. 'Oh, you brought Elna.'

'She's my news.'

Elna, a bit diffident and uncertain, walked a couple of steps then stopped, waiting to see how Jon's mother would receive her. She showed her relief in a generous smile when Rose welcomed her.

'Heavens, Jon, this is one of those days that makes you wonder what will happen next. It's really lovely to see you again after all this time, Elna.'

'I know it's not the best time to come, Mrs Quinlan, but Jon insisted it had to be today.'

'Of course it's the best time, any time is. I know what Jon's like when he gets something into his head. Can't wait, just like Becc.'

Rose saw the look they exchanged and wondered whether Becc was up to something.

'Mum. This is Mrs Jonathan Quinlan.'

Rose saw that the expression in Elna's dark eyes went deeper than anxiety: she was afraid, and put her hand in Jon's, seeking protection just like a small child. 'You're married?'

Jon nodded, grinning proudly at his wife. 'We got married in London, special licence, and came straight here.'

She laughed nervously, 'We did it quickly before my mother could put the law on to us.'

'This morning?'

Elna nodded. 'I hope you don't mind, we didn't want anything too . . . well, you know. For goodness' sake, Jon. Are you going to tell your mother the whole thing, or shall I?'

They had arrived at the terrace, where Jon flung himself happily down on a cruise-chair looking full of himself. 'We're pregnant! You are an expectant Granny.' He leapt up and crushed his mother to him. 'Oh Mum, isn't it the most marvellous thing that's ever happened? You see, El, look at her, I told you my mum would be pleased. I must go and find Vee. There's some bubbly in that bag, I'd better find some glasses. Show her your bump, El.'

Elna shook her head indulgently. 'How old are you, eight or twenty-eight?' she called after him. 'He's such a fool over all this, but I love him, Mrs Quinlan. Who can help it – he's the nicest thing that ever happened in my life. I'll make him happy, I know that. I wouldn't have agreed to marry him otherwise. I've hurt him once, I could never do it again. If it hadn't been for Mac, I might still be eating my heart out at home.'

Rose queried with her eyebrows.

'He's sort of my cousin. He came to visit at Christmas and my mother thought she could fix us up. She never asked me or Mac, she just assumed – because we were kin and he's a big, good-looking guy, to say nothing of him being West Indian – she just thought we would be sure to make a good match. She doesn't know that we're into the 1950s, girls like me are choosing their own husbands.'

'Not many are making it as difficult for themselves as you two. But Jon loves you . . . I mean really loves you.'

'I know. I'm sorry about the other girl, they've known one another since they were children; but I don't apologize for winning him back. It's not just because of the baby we've got married.' She was trying hard not to be tearful. 'My parents . . .'

When Jon came and enfolded her protectively, Rose thought, How mature and masculine he has suddenly become.

'Her parents would have accepted Elna and the baby, but they could not stomach me. Have you ever heard the term whitey? It's about as nice as saying nigger. And I'm a whitey.'

'Oh, Jon, they never . . .'

'I know, they never actually said it, but it is implicit in everything they say about me. Be honest, El, a white man with their daughter is distasteful, if not downright against nature. They're as colour-prejudiced as my father.'

'He's right, Mrs Quinlan. My mother set the family and the entire Bethesda congregation on to me. That's when my cousin said his piece to me. He's got this funny, jokey way of saying serious things. I think he doesn't like anybody to know that he's got a brain. He said: "Nobody ain't ever goin' eat a coconut if they believe the shell. You got to go smashing in if you ever goin' to get to the good bit inside."'

Jon grinned as he went indoors. 'So she came and smashed down my door and got me.'

Elna went on, 'Don't worry, we know what stuff we're up against.'

'I'm sure you do,' Rose said, 'but I promise you one thing, you'll never find any of it here.'

'Thank you, Mrs Quinlan. I wish my mother . . . She thinks she's such a good woman. It's because she leads such a narrow life. Home and church, church and home. That's no life for a woman of her age – she's still young enough to have another child, you know. And my father, he knows it's all wrong what she says, but he just buries his head.'

It came to Rose what the Birdhams would be missing in this happy, super couple and the expected baby. 'Wait till they see the baby: they'll come round. Nobody can resist a baby.'

Still young enough to have another child, you know . . . What would have happened if Rose had not had the abortion? She had no regrets, but she did see the strangeness of the situation where she might have been a new mother at the same time as being a grandmother at the same time as Trevelyan and Leo were on her mind.

A few days after Winifred's funeral, she had met Leo coming down their shared lane. Smiling, he had taken her hand and walked back with her. 'What about our unfinished business then, Rose?' Her heart had actually fluttered.

That was how it felt. They had been left in mid-air. Even now, when she could hear the cheerful sounds of Vee and Jon laughing inside the house, and she had just received the news of a grandchild, part of her mind was on Leo, the image of him earlier when he had come into the kitchen, his lean body moving athletically, tanned and healthy, as usual a wave of hair falling over one eye. She had wanted him then; she wanted him now. But then there had been moments when she had wanted Trevelyan. Moments? Yes . . . nothing more permanent; her need to experience sex with Leo was not as important as her need to keep her friendship with Monica.

Jon's laughter and Vee's squeals as the cork popped came from the house.

Rose said, 'It's wonderful to see him so happy. He's pretty good at putting a face on things, but I know when it's the real thing.'

'I've been very apprehensive at coming here and facing you.'

'Me?'

'You're used to all this –' she indicated the house and garden – 'whereas my family are working class. My father drives a train on the Underground.'

'I'm the one who gets apprehensive at meeting people. I'm glad that Jon didn't tell me you were coming, I'd have been fussing around for ages wondering whether everything was going to be all right.'

'When I met you before, I thought that I had never seen anyone who was so lovely and unruffled – I told Jon at the time.'

'It's something I put on before I get up in the morning and take off last thing at night. But . . . I've decided to take myself in hand. A bit late in the day, but I've given up putting a face on things.'

'You should take lessons from my mother: when things go wrong for her there's nobody who doesn't know it, I tell you. She never put a face on anything. I'll have to tell her soon.' Pulling her jacket aside, she said, 'There's precious little to show for it yet, but already it's been putting me off tea and coffee and making me want to pee six times a night.'

Tentatively, Rose laid a hand on the small mound beneath Elna's creamy linen dress. 'What is it, about four months . . . five?'

'Nearly five.'

'Do you feel it moving?'

'I don't know what it is supposed to feel like. Does it feel like a nerve quivering?'

Rose smiled, 'No woman who has carried ever forgets the feeling. Sometimes it can go on for a week before you realize that it's the baby and not the new bread you've been eating.'

'Jon said it was moving.'

Vee came out. 'You've made my big brother a very happy man. It's really, really good news. Wait till Nora hears. Jon's just trying to get Becc now.'

He came out with the champagne and enjoyed himself exuberantly. 'What's this, Mum? I wanted something to write a number on and wrote all over this. I'm sorry, but I started to read it to see if it was important.'

Rose took the letter. 'Oh, I was just about to read it. It's something that went to the Wilkinsons' by mistake.' She read. 'Good Lord.'

'Who's Miss T. E. Chaice?' he asked. 'I seem to remember the name.'

Vee said, 'That's your governess isn't it, Mum?'

Rose nodded and read the few lines over again, then handed it to Vee. 'It's from a solicitor wanting me to ring him.'

'Perhaps she's died and left you a fortune,' Jon said.

'Hardly likely. Poor Threnody was the eternal wronged woman –' to Elna – 'she was my . . . sort of carer. Her sweetheart had mysteriously vanished with her money and she had the idea that he would turn up, with dark secrets and a fortune.'

'Perhaps he did, and she wants to let you know.'

'Only one way to find out,' Jon said. 'Go and ring the guy.'

Jon said, 'Have you felt the bump yet, Vee?'

Rose said, 'My curiosity has got the better of me. I'm longing to know why Threnody should pop up again just as I'm about to move back to the place where we both spent ten years of our lives. Isn't it odd how things happen?'

All eyes were on her when she returned to the garden. 'You know Lorna Lammente, the romantic mystery writer?'

'Mystery?' Vee said. 'An excuse for writing about all that torrid sex.'

'Well,' Rose said, 'torrid or not, it was all written by Threnody, and she has died.'

Rose went to London. Threnody Elvena Chaice had left a very simple will. With the exception of a gift to Rose, all the considerable fortune and continuing income from Lorna Lammente's royalties were put into the hands of the Society of Authors for the institution of a 'Lorna Lammente Prize for a romantic mystery novel whose heroine must not be of tender years' – a phrase that she had refused to alter in spite of being warned by her solicitor of the difficulties such an imprecise phrase would impose on judges. And he was to be proved right. Over the years there has been more wrangling over how old a Lammente Prize heroine should be, than over the merits of the actual submissions for the award.

The gift to Rose was a generous sum of money to be used specifically by Rose to travel overseas, and Threnody's house in Sunningdale. With it went a letter, a file of cuttings. She hoped Rose would use the money to 'return annually to the place of her birth and drink at the wells of her childhood memories'.

Rebecca, sitting opposite Rose in one of the few restaurants in which she would eat these days now that she taken to a vegan diet, rolled her eyes heavenward. 'How can she write such stuff and get paid good money?'

'Oh, come on, you're like a lot of people who denigrate her: you have never read a word she's written.'

'I've seen the books.'

'To quote Gran, "Never judge a book by its cover." She doesn't write like that, she's really rather literate and she's always a good read. This "drink at the wells of her childhood memories" is a joke on me: it's the kind of thing that *I* was once prone to write when I was about twelve . . . I shouldn't be surprised if those aren't my actual words. I am really touched that she remembered. And look at all this . . .' She riffled through the file of magazine and newspaper cuttings. 'All stuff to do with your father and me: elections, that *Woman* interview, and the '55 election . . . just look at my hat! She must have been planning something like this for years and years. If only I'd known.'

'Actually, I like that hat, it's not bad. If it was to be turned round and worn level . . . I say, Ma, could I have that cutting?'

Rebecca was a good advertisement for a vegan lifestyle. She had become lithe and sinewy, and her carefully applied bare-faced complexion looked alive. She had, under Aze Joffe's tuition, and Sally's encouragement, turned into a good businesswoman. Because she liked people and was a good mixer at any level, she had not lost the knack of sensing the trends of fashion and would even press on with an idea that fashion writers had rejected, eventually being proved right. 'Ahead of its time' was the phrase often used about Rebecca Quinlan's style. Aze no longer had any of the fears that he had once had that the company they shared would come a cropper because of some whacky brain-child of hers. 'Trust me, Aze,' she would say, 'It will turn out OK.' Aze and most other people trusted her, and were susceptible to what Aze called 'Beccy's padded steam-rollering'. Ill-assorted partners though they appeared to be, they were successful, and it was the small corner of Aze's small empire which gave him more pleasure and satisfaction in business than any other.

Today she was wearing a black bias-cut skirt that flared at the hem and almost met with little black boots at her ankles. The glimpse of calf between was clad in the kind of black school stockings that she would at one time have done anything to avoid wearing. It was a combination of Edwardian and twenties style that unexpectedly worked in a striking way. She had grown so used to being stared at and commented upon that she was no longer aware of it happening. Her present style was certainly at odds with the thorough-going salad and bean bar, but she knew from the admiring expressions on the faces of young women that she had found another winner. Becc Quinlan was a recognizable Face. Her appearance would be quoted. 'In' women would announce that they had seen Becc Quinlan in Mario's or some such place, and report on what she was wearing.

'You know, Becc, this food is surprisingly good.'

'Probably because it didn't have to face the slaughter-house to get on to your plate. Well? Go on. What else about your odd-ball governess?'

By the time she died Threnody Chaice, in the person of Lorna Lammente, had written eighty-seven satisfactory resolutions to her Contessa series of mystery novels. Although these had a romantic element in that a man and a woman usually came together satisfactorily in the final chapter, they were not 'romantic' novels in the sense that they were love stories. She was, therefore, able to capture male and female readers.

Always a violent death, a missing person or missing body, always the same red-herring-strewn path for Miss Lammente's detective, the Contessa, to follow to a conclusion. How many times had Lorna Lammente speculated upon what happened to Threnody Chaice's lost lover? And how many times had she come up with a slightly different answer. Eighty-seven times. And all eighty-seven were reprinted with regularity and in several languages.

Hundreds of thousands of people saved their new Lammente or the latest Contessa novel for a sunny beach or Christmas hearth reading. Even quite literate people did not mind being seen reading a Lammente, because Miss Lammente herself was obviously well-versed in English literature and would drop in allusions to classics which didn't spoil the read but flattered literary types. *Wuthering Heights* was a favourite of hers, and a quote from it often gave a clue to the denouement. Several of her heroines were Catherines, or Kathys or Kates.

Over the years, Lorna Lammente had become her own creation. If people confused the character with her creator, or believed that Miss Lammente was a Contessa in real life, then it was not surprising. She adopted an imperious manner with journalists. She kept two shorthand-typists going, sometimes working on two books, one at each end of the room. She wore nothing that was not coloured dusky-pink or jade green, but never the two together. Even her many large rings and pieces of jewellery and her cigarettes in their long coloured holders were of these colours. She had rooms that were either entirely decorated in pink or entirely in jade green. She would never allow a close-up photograph or reveal anything about her early life. Although in gossip columns, and her name linked from time to time with other gossip column names, all that the public knew of her was what appeared in magazines. Most of these details were as true of Lorna as they were of the Contessa. Had she lived at a later date, she could not have got away with it, for enterprising members of the paparazzi would have zoomed in upon her, blown the gaffe, dug the dirt on the ex-companion-governess, and spoiled the fun. As it was she lived and died a glamorous, mysterious and romantic figure.

By the time Fredericka Weston died, Lorna Lammente and the Contessa already existed secretly, bringing in some royalties for Threnody, so that when she left Longmore she had had enough money to rent a small house in Slough. It was there, only a few miles from Longmore, that Threnody Chaice had worked on her fantasies and the mystery of her lover. As Threnody melded into Lorna and Lorna into the Contessa, she decided to ditch her Chaice past. Liking Berkshire, she didn't want to move far, so eventually bought herself a small house in Sunningdale which was then still functioning as an ordinary village. It was at this time that she decided she must lose touch entirely with her past, including Rose.

'Was she worth a mint?' Rebecca asked.

'I think she must have been. I never realized that cheap reads like that could make anyone a decent income.'

'Small profits on large volume sales – it's how Aze and I make our bread. Mmm, I could eat hummus all day.' As they were leaving the table, she wiped a finger around the bowl and licked it in a way that would have made Winifred shrivel with embarrassment. 'Let's walk through the Inns of Court where it's nice and peaceful.'

Rebecca linked arms with her mother, feeling, as she rarely did, very close to her and seeing, as she rarely did, how beautiful she was and how composed. Sally had said, 'Your mother always looks tranquil, untouchable. I can never believe she gets the Curse.'

She had been a good mother, a nice mother, but Jon and Vee had been her favourites. Oddly, that had never bothered Rebecca; in fact it was only since leaving home that she had come to see it. Jon and Vee were mother's, Nora was His, and Becc belonged to herself: a bit of her now belonged to the Joffes with whom she had a kind of family relationship. Somewhere on the verge of consciousness, Rebecca wished that she felt like this more often, more sensitive, not always so well tuned-in to her own creative station that she failed to pick up other things that were going on.

'Will you go? You know "drink at the wells" and all that?'

'To South Africa? Yes. I've always hoped that one day I should be able to go.'

'Have you really? I never realized. Why didn't you go before?'

'How could I?'

'You could have gone, the Old Man's never been exactly poor.'

Her mother turned a slightly puzzled look upon her, seeming not to make the connection.

'I mean, you should have told him that you wanted to go there. It wouldn't have been much to ask: he's been everywhere.'

'Mostly on expenses.'

'Oh, *Mum*! Stop making excuses for him.'

Her mother drew a deep breath. 'I said I wouldn't. You're right. The problem with me is that I've never known the rules of the game; I've had to pick them up as best I could whilst I was playing.' She laughed, her thin, bowed lips pulling back to reveal her small white teeth; then was at once serious again. 'I hope that I haven't done you all too much damage, Becc.'

'Damage? You?'

'I read somewhere that the children of divorced parents are – I don't know – five? maybe it's ten times more at risk of having their own marriage break up.'

'They are always trying to prove something with statistics. Your parents didn't divorce, neither did his. Anyway, you don't need to worry none about me . . . I like variety and moderation in all things – and that goes for men.' She stepped into the road, held her finger up, and a taxi stopped at once. 'I'll come with you to Waterloo.'

That was something Rebecca had always rather liked about her mother: she let you do things without making a fuss. Grandma never would. She would insist that no one was to make a fuss on her account, yet be vastly put out if one did not.

The Petersfield train was not due to leave for another thirty minutes, so Rebecca got two plastic beakers of coffee; but there were no seats available, several being occupied by people with cheap old bulging suitcases and paper parcels.

Her mother said quietly, 'Where do you think all these people with bundles are going?'

'To hell and back, probably. They're Waterloo's allocation of homeless people.'

'Allocation?'

'Just being facetious. Every station has some, and as long as there aren't too many or they don't beg or smell too badly, the station tolerates them.'

'A lot of them are women.'

'You think women can't be vagrants?'

'Do they sleep here?'

Rebecca felt a flash of antipathy: her mother was still as ignorant of the realities of life as she had ever been, hermiting away in her cabbage patch. It was no wonder that in middle age she looked as serene as a nun. 'You should come out with me and Sally one night: we do a stint doing the rounds with a van-load of food.' The line that appeared upon her mother's brow was hardly a furrow, but for her it was a recognizable sign of distress.

'I am so frighteningly ignorant, Becc, it makes me feel ashamed.'

Rebecca was sorry that her voice had come out sounding harsher than she had intended. 'Just so long as you don't stay that way now you know.'

'Should I give them some money?' The noticeboard indicating train departures clattered a new set of information as she pulled out her wallet. 'Oh look, "Portsmouth Harbour stopping at Petersfield". I've got ten minutes.' She had a fold of one-pound notes in her hand.

'No, Mum, not hand-outs. If you want you can give it to me and I'll get some woolly gloves and scarves or some tins of soup.' She took the notes and put them in her bag. Having reached the train, she found a First Class Smoker and opened the door. As her mother bent forward to kiss her cheek, Rebecca got a whiff of the Tweed perfume Rose always used.

I wish she loved me.

And was assailed by déjà vu.

Learning to ride Jon's two-wheeled fairy-cycle, not being tall enough to reach the saddle, whilst he was still too timid to leave his tricycle. 'You don't love me like you do *him*!' Her stage début at seven, as an elfin in a costume of paper leaves she had painted and pasted on herself. She had been the Wish fairy. 'I wish, I wish she loved me.'

For a city woman and a partner in a business that was known for its hard-nosed bargaining, this was really too childish. 'Still wearing the same old Tweed, Rosie? We're going to bring out a perfume to go with my new style. I'll send you a sample to try, if you like. If it works, we think we might go the whole hog and go into cosmetics as well.'

'What a good idea. Has it got a name?'

Rebecca wished that she could say, 'We're going to call it Rose.' 'It'll be called "Princess".' She laughed. 'What else, it was Sally's idea.' The guard's whistle shrilled as she slammed the carriage door.

The train jerked forward making her mother clutch at the open window. 'Becc?'

Such a tentative inflection; why is she always so bloody timid?

'I'm terribly proud of you, Becc . . . really terribly proud.'

Rebecca didn't know what to do about the tears that arose to blur her vision. God, don't let me bloody cry, she'll think she's said something wrong. Blessedly the train moved slowly forward; she walked with it. 'Oh, by the way, Trevelyan said to say "Hello".' Her mother opened her mouth to say something, but Rebecca stopped walking as the train picked up speed. She had thrown in the Trevelyan bit at the last minute, just as she had planned, with no time for a reply because she loathed the idea of becoming involved in any of her parents' complications. Trevelyan had been going to bare his soul to Rebecca, but she had made damned sure that he did not – no way! She waved once more and walked slowly along the platform towards the ticket barrier.

She and Aze had decided to go more up-market with the 'Princess' promotions, so they had decided to have Trevelyan do their brochure photography.

As always she felt disturbed by a visit from her mother. Elated. The phrase, still in her ears, pricking her tearducts: '. . . terribly proud of you.' The black ticket collector was about her father's age, and as white at the temples too. As he took her platform ticket he nodded and smiled. 'Nice. Tha's real nice t'ings you wearin'.'

She gave a little twirl for him, the skirt swirling like a half-open umbrella.

'Thanks,' she said, 'thanks a lot. You have great taste.'

'Ah know,' he said, tipping his hat to a jaunty angle.

Wow! Yes. Publicity shots of ageing black men – dozens of them – in British Rail uniforms; models with snow-white hair wearing the black gear. Something always came to her, something that was always there, but nobody saw until she saw it herself. Yeah! Great! That was the thing about London, you never knew what to expect. Thank God I had the sense to get away. She pictured her mother having to go back to Honeywood and begin the clearing-up process at the end of a big episode of her life. Honeywood! Ye gods and little fishes, talk about gingerbread houses.

Why *do* people get married?
Would she really go to South Africa?

On the steps of Caxton Hall, London's most favoured venue for top people's marriages, Ballard Quinlan, now a Conservative Member of Parliament, stood with his arm about his radiant new bride. They were a gift to the Sunday newspapers, offering as they did a wedding containing all the ingredients of a perfect Bank Holiday weekend story. 'Give him a kiss, Mrs Quinlan,' 'Pick her up, Mr Quinlan,'; 'A wave? Give us a wave, Mimi.' A slightly scandalous story of romance in high places: fame, wealth, and a difference of a quarter-century in the ages of the lovers. Although the press of both left and right had never much liked Ballard Quinlan, he was always newsworthy, so it was kind to him now . . . Well, it was Easter, and it had lost its great plum-pudding story of romance – that of Princess Margaret and her divorced lover – and there were still a couple of months to go before they could fill their columns with what would now be the Princess's 'Royal Fairytale Marriage' when she would marry the son of a Countess.

Ballard's life was about to change dramatically. He still ran his 'head-hunting' agency – not personally, as he had taken the extraordinary step of offering his secretary, Valerie, a partnership. He was astute enough to know that had he not had the foresight to tie her into the agency with a long-term contract, she might easily have set up on her own.

But the agency was small beer compared to the profitability of the armaments trade into which he had just arrived.

Fashion columnists dwelt upon the 'overwhelming femininity' of Miriam's dress, 'created for her by Yves Saint Laurent, enfant terrible' of fashion, who loved to dress female curves, whilst the social magazines indulged their readers with a spread of photographs of the 'glittering social occasion' and a sweet cameo picture of a 'wee page and a tiny flower-girl', identified as 'the bride's seven-year-old nephew Gerald Corder-Peake and his three-year-old sister Amanda'.

Anoria, a dark and serious-looking girl, was not recognized by the press. She stood slightly apart, as though dissociating herself from the crowd of ex-Debs and their ex-Delights, no less shrill and assertive now that they were married off than when they had 'come out' years ago. Nora had come, even though she was torn between her own unhappiness at the prospect of witnessing her father take part in the belittling ceremony. She felt hurt on his behalf because, except for Great-gran, there would not be a single member of the Quinlan family attending, whilst every Corder-Peake in England would be there. Jonathan and Rebecca had been incensed at the mere suggestion that they would attend. Villette was not so much put out for herself as for her mother, whom she saw as being ousted from her rightful position, even though Mother had protested that the Hon. Miriam Corder-Peake was welcome to take the Mrs Quinlan title. Vee had been barely civil to Nora for weeks, but had a sneaking admiration for her young sister's strength of mind to do what she thought she must do. 'He's still our father, Vee.'

None of them saw anything wrong with Great-gran wanting to attend. She was an old lady of over eighty, and their father's parents were both dead. So, unclaimed by the society photographers, Charlotte in a plain coat and hat from Quinlan's, Sid's old multiple store, leaning slightly on a black cane, appeared to have better breeding and more dignity than any of the Tharrup-hatted women and Moss Bros-suited men. She nudged Nora. 'Do you feel like an orphan of the storm too?'

Nora shrugged, 'I thought registry weddings only took a minute.'

Suddenly they were descended upon by Miriam who, Nora supposed, must now be her step-mother. 'How bloody dire,' she thought, 'bloody' being the extravagantly outrageous epithet now used by teenagers.

'Granny Quinlan, A*noria*. You absolutely must *not* hover in the background like that. Now come. Into the car you go with Mama and Daddy.' And so, steam-rollered in a new and commanding way that few people had noticed in Miriam in her spinster state, Nora and Charlotte found themselves very soon ushered into the deferential surroundings of the Savoy Hotel.

Anoria, in a pink bouffant-skirted frock and feathered head-band, too old for her but which she had chosen because (even though she really hated his bloody guts!) she desperately did not want to let her father down, felt larger and darker than her everyday large darkness that had come with her teen years. It was weeks since she had seen him; then, whilst waiting for Miriam to arrive, he had caught sight of her and Gran and had been about to come over and speak to them when he had been prevented by press cameras clicking like a thousand starling beaks, heralding the arrival of Miriam and Sir Evelyn.

Now he detached himself from a group of people and made his way across the room to where Charlotte was seated in a tub chair and Anoria was standing tasting the sharp champagne that a waiter had offered. 'Gran.' He kissed her cheek, 'I can't tell you how much it means . . .'

Charlotte nodded but did not commit her feelings to words. Although it was a good many years since she had attended his marriage to Rose, she remembered every detail. She and Sid had given Winnie *carte blanche* to get everything of the very best. And Winnie had done splendidly, probably because they had expected, as Sid had said, that Winnie would never be able to curb herself, and everywhere and everything would be decked out with ribbons like a pedlar's tray, but she had consulted books and done everything with unexpectedly good taste. Rose, at barely eighteen, had looked so perfectly beautiful. So pale and fragile in a creamy bias-cut heavy satin, with a long train and veil held in place with a bandeau of myrtle. So different from the new, hatless, and almost bare-shouldered Miriam.

Perhaps he too remembered. 'Ah well, Gran, none of us knows what's in store. The fifties has changed everything. Things will never be the same again.' Gran had always been there with a few pounds when he needed them, and with her love, no strings attached; but now he found it difficult to know where he was with her. It was hard to meet her eyes. 'Are these waiters looking after you? Anoria? Look, sweetheart, why don't you come and talk to some of Miriam's people. I'd like you to get to know them.' He squeezed her shoulder. 'Lots of lovely weekends in country houses. You'll love all that, won't you? Tell you a secret? You aren't to tell . . . a villa on the Costa del Sol. Sir Evelyn's wedding gift to Miriam. You will call her by her name, won't you? You can spend all your summer holidays there . . . I'm sure Villette will come round. Didn't we have some splendid days . . . remember those funny, pretty Spanish villages?'

Panic-stricken at the possibility of making a fool of herself, Anoria turned and looked out over the River Thames, but was unable to stop her eyes welling with tears.

'*Don't*, darling!' Pleading in a whisper, he took her hand. 'Don't do that, you'll spoil everything. I wanted you and Villette at least to be nice to Miriam. And you have been, darling. Today is the day of her life. She likes you, she really does want you to feel at home in her set. There will be hunt balls and Henley . . . I want you to have all that. It was never really an option before.'

'Leave her, Ballard,' Charlotte said. 'Let the fact that she came here do for now.'

He seated himself on a chair beside his grandmother, still holding the hand of Anoria who was looking hard at the river as she tried to make the tears syphon back into her tearducts. 'Listen, Gran. What is done, is done. There is no going back now. *This* is my future.' He gestured at the flowers, crystal, porcelain and silver, the fashionable guests and the all-pervading atmosphere of wealth and privilege displayed within the reception room of high ceilings, tall columns and plasterwork. 'I want my children to share it.'

Anoria, in control of her emotions now, said, 'Thank you, Daddy, but really I only want one thing. May I ask you now?' She gave him a tight smile. Even as a quite small child, she had known the right moment to strike home.

He looked relieved and grateful that tears and the possible display of some unpleasantness had passed. 'That's my girl. Let me guess, you want a paddock with a nice little horse to ride?'

For a moment, Nora looked as blank as though he had offered her a velocipede or a steam-engine. 'Not actually a *thing*, Daddy. But when I am eighteen I should like to go to university. Cambridge, in fact. I'm afraid I might not be clever enough, so you might have to pay, but I long to go there.'

A deal! She had not come here out of sentiment. She had come for a piece of the action . . . This he understood, admired even. He and Anoria understood one another. He became gay and smiling, giving her a playful punch. 'Cambridge, eh? Ah, all those picnics, lovely May balls and punts on the river . . . Cambridge it shall be, then. Now, I must do my duty. Don't run off without letting me know. Anything I can get you, Gran?'

'Thank you, no, Lad. I'll save room for a morsel of that cake when you cut it.'

He pecked her on the cheek and went to rise, but she restrained him for a moment. 'Who's the little page-boy?'

'Little Gerald? He belongs to Miriam's sister.'

His pause had been just long enough, and his expression just startled enough, to confirm what Charlotte already suspected. For Charlotte had no difficulty in remembering Ballard at seven years old, as she remembered Anoria too at that age – determined and solid, with black shiny hair and eyes as black and round as Pontefract cakes.

Charlotte had a stretch of years sufficiently long to see the whole genealogical picture. Honoria, Henry, Ballard, Anoria and Little Gerald the pageboy, all with the same striking black shiny hair and black round eyes fringed with thick lashes. They must all be blind as bats if they did not see the connection between Ballard, Anoria and the small boy.

At the time when Miriam Corder-Peake was laying claim to the title of Mrs Ballard Quinlan, Rose, testing the waters of domestic freedom and independence, was on a protest march against hydrogen-bomb testing, with people as far removed in style from the socialites at the Savoy reception as it was possible to be. Of the two women, it was probably Rose who was the happier.

Her children had underestimated her, not surprisingly: most children see themselves as the current generation, and their own lives as much more elegant than anything lived by their parents only twenty years before. Twenty years! Rose's children knew themselves to be Today's Generation, which was why they were so surprised when Rose went on her first protest march. And really rather pleased.

Her interest in the Peace Movement was new, and she was enthusiastic. It had been kindled at a meeting in London to which she had been persuaded to go by Princess Joffe. Princess had a lot of the same warmth and openness as Monica. She was a bundle of enthusiasm and generous spontaneity, so that when Rose moved to Longmore, which was not far from the Joffes' country cottage, Princess had included Rose in every possible event and occasion. Rose, missing Monica, had responded, and so began a new friendship that held the promise of enduring. The response of opposites who had a love of the talented Rebecca in common.

In the years since the Joffes had first seen the potential of Rebecca's flair for design, they had been through a succession of fashion styles together. Because of the transience of their cheap-and-cheerful lines, their joint venture was now a small rag-trade business with the label 'Mayfly'. Even as they prospered and developed, somehow Rebecca had always had her finger on the pulse, was always just ahead of street fashion. She had a sixth sense about what her own generation and that of Vee and Kate were after. Although she was now a woman in her mid-twenties, she was still avant-garde in her style, and a living model for the range.

Becc lived her chaotic life in a ground-floor flat of a crumbling house in what, in the early part of the century, had been a splendid square.

'Get your hands on city property, my dear,' had been Aze Joffe's advice when Rebecca's bank balance had begun to swell. 'Invest in the business a little, but believe me, get yourself a roof over your head and you won't regret it. Your brother is in the know, use your contacts, tell him to find you a bargain.'

Which was how Rebecca had come to have half-share, with Jonathan, in a large, five-floored London house. They each had a part which they were slowly bringing back to wholesomeness, and they let out the other rooms as furnished bed-sits.

One advantage of occupying such grand rooms was that there was always room to have people stay, which Rebecca loved. Most of her ideas for new designs were hatched in the company that assembled there. Which was how, on a particular visit to Rose's, when Princess Joffe was there flinging down lengths of fabric for Rebecca's approval in one corner, whilst a meeting about the Bomb was going on in another (neither activity being exclusive of the other), Rose found herself drawn into the company of people who were involved in a campaign to protest against the testing of the hydrogen bomb.

Rose at the beginning of the sixties was not the Rose who had taken her children to the opening of the Festival of Britain ten years earlier.

Now, her mind stimulated by Princess and others of Becc's leftish friends, Rose had become involved in the growing protest movement. She said to Sally, 'I was just thinking, all those years married to a paid-up socialist and I never knew what it was about.'

'This man who joins the Tory Party – you think he was a socialist? You know the saying, "It takes one to recognize one"? Aze and I, we met him a couple of times; he was always in the wrong party.' Her long red-enamelled nails gleaming, Sally Joffe carried a card on a stick painted with the drooping-cross symbol of the peace campaign as she trudged along singing, 'Ban, ban, ban the bloody H-Bomb', to the jazz band playing 'John Brown's Body'.

Rose, in her gardening corduroys and khaki jumper, strode out in a way she had not done since the children were little. She grinned at Sally. 'How are the shoes now?'

'To Hell with Aze and his "good quality hiking shoes": they weigh a ton. Next time I shall wear my gold kid courts. Light as a feather, soft as silk. You look quite at home in flats.'

'I garden a lot.'

'So Beccy says. She says you are an expert.'

Rose laughed. 'I don't know how Becc would know, I don't think she ever came into the garden after she was five years old.'

'She's a great girl. I wish she was mine.'

'You aren't old enough.'

Sally spread her hand expressively, 'What's old? Times when I feel a hundred, and times when Beccy seems old and wise enough for me to be her granddaughter.'

Rose nodded. 'I know what you mean. Girls know so much these days.'

They sang again for another mile or so until the column halted for a breather and a drink. Stretching back for what seemed to be miles, the column rested on the roadside grass. The jazz band had stopped playing, and there was again the sound that Rose had never heard until now, and would always associate with the early years of protest marches: hundreds of people laughing and enjoying talking to complete strangers. The first time they had stopped, Rose had wondered if columns of soldiers sounded like that. She took a flask of coffee from her haversack, and Sally a flask of spirits from hers.

'Bacardi. It disguises the taste of the vacuum.' She dashed a generous amount into Rose's beaker, and the fumes of the white rum evoked that summer, years ago. Brackish water, tar, and warm varnish, spicy food . . . She was over him now – her mad moment, her infatuation, her fling; she could not believe that she had ever really contemplated a serious affair. She was in love with the idea, his lifestyle, his manner, his awareness of her, his interest in her. In every way different from Ballard, even his long, non-conformist hair stated that he pleased himself.

He still phoned her occasionally; at Christmas he always sent an unsigned photographic calendar which she always hung in the kitchen. He now knew that she had not had the baby, and he had not given up trying to persuade her to meet him; but the knowledge that she had allowed Ballard to get her pregnant had been too hard for him to take. She smiled into her coffee. Now, if she so desired, she was free to do so. She no longer desired. Leo still lurked uneasily in her mind, and occasionally she awakened from a dream breathless, moist, her heart thudding, expecting to find him leaning over her as he had been the night Winifred died.

'Penny for them?' Sally Joffe broke into the rum fumes.

With a strange, distant smile, Rose considered for a moment. 'I'm not good with liquor.'

Princess raised her plucked, arched eyebrows.

'It's a joke. Not good.'

'Maybe you haven't had enough practice. Though I can't imagine you ever being out of control. Aze thinks that you are the perfect English Rose.'

Ah, there it was again: the face, the face that told lies about the kind of woman who would cheat on her best friend with her best friend's husband. The kind of woman who had to steer clear of him because she couldn't trust herself. 'He's not the first one. I can quite easily lose control.'

Sally put on a mock scandalized expression. 'What do you do when you do?'

'I'm a menace to anything in pants . . . can't keep my hands off them.'

Sally Joffe wondered how much truth there was in that. Some, she guessed; she had all the ingredients. 'Oh well,' she said, 'that's all right then. I wondered for a minute whether it was you who taught Beccy to jump into the Trafalgar Square fountain every single New Year.'

'Becc didn't inherit her tendency to show off from me but from . . .' And there it was again, that awkwardness that had thrust itself into so many conversations since Ballard had announced that he wanted to be rid of her.

After a pause that Sally Joffe knew wouldn't be filled by Rose, she said, 'You might as well finish the sentence. The more you practise, the easier it becomes. Being divorced is not so shocking.'

'People behave as though it is. Children suffer most from the gossip.'

'Attitudes are changing; the next generation won't think twice about changing partners. Children survive these things.'

'I hope that you're right.'

'I know I am. Didn't I survive what my parents did to me?'

'You're the epitome of normality. Did they divorce?'

'My real parents? Intellectual Jews from Munich. The first to go. People who think for themselves are dangerous. In a way they were divorced. They died, one in Auschwitz and one in the Buchenwald.' She tossed the information to Rose as though it was a rubber ball and not a grenade.

If normality existed, then Sally was, for Rose, its epitome. But Rose should have suspected something, she knew about stereotyping: her own wasn't the only face to tell lies to the world. She ought not to have assumed that there could not be a different Sally within the Princess, or that beneath the Paris chic was a natural duffel-coat wearer, or a head-scarf lurking within the false hair. She had taken the Joffes at face value, and found herself surprised to discover that they were thoughtful idealists. On the face of it they were the Joffes of the outrageous Rolls-Royce car, the Aze of the astrakhan collar and the Princess of the gold chains. A wealthy couple who enjoyed a good time and the good life.

Under it all were the real Joffes, needing to be picked out grain by grain. Until Rose had become interested in the campaign, most of what she knew of this serious side of them she heard through Rebecca. They encouraged trades unions in their workshops, Aze read the *New Statesman*, and they were visitors to every Labour Party conference.

'In the . . . in the gas chambers?'

Sally nodded. 'All of them. My entire family.'

Buchenwald. No person of Rose's generation would make any other association with that name than the horrifying 1945 newsreel images, films that were so shocking that warning notices were posted outside cinemas. Buchenwald. Mass graves, walking skeletons, mounds of decomposing bodies, some of which had been Sally's family.

'God . . . how terrible.'

'But you see me, don't you, as Princess Joffe? The papers I had when I arrived in England say that I was Sally White, aged eight. I survived what my parents did to me.'

'They saved you.'

Sending herself up, she said, 'Oy, oy, they gave me Jews for parents. In England, it was better they had been divorced.'

A line of cars, going in the opposite direction from the marchers, honked their horns and the passengers waved, raising the spirits of the protesters. Sally stepped out of line and, waving her placard, shouted 'Come and join us.' Laughing, she trotted back to her place beside Rose and took up where she had left off. 'What about yours? Were they blameless; didn't they make mistakes?'

'My mother died, my father remarried, my father died, my step-mother remarried, and I became Little Orphan Annie. I was packed off to England. At least, that's the story. I have no way of knowing whether it's all true. For all I know I could be a foundling child, or maybe my Aunt Fredericka kidnapped me in a fit of broodiness.'

'Was that your excuse for marrying the wrong man?'

'I had nothing else to go on. Aunt Fredericka was a recluse and a blue-stocking, and Miss Chaice and I lived in Never-Never Land. I believed that it would be like Hollywood films; I saw them all. Years and years of boy meeting girl and girl falling into his arms where she would be safe and he would cherish her and be so much in love that he would never harm a hair on her head.'

'And sleep in single beds. And you discovered sex all on your own on your wedding night.'

Rose smiled. 'It wasn't a bad discovery at the beginning.'

'Too much too soon.'

'I haven't done much better for my own kids, but at least I encouraged them to keep rabbits, and the farmer always put the bull with the herd at the back of our house, so they aren't really uneducated.'

'There's precious little wrong with Beccy. She thinks that your ex should be circumcised up to his groin. Now is that a healthy reaction, or is it a healthy reaction? Your kids will soon sort it out; just don't try to pretend that things aren't changed. They've changed. Being divorced is acceptable. I'm acceptable, you're acceptable. I talk like a grandmother. Hey, let's drink to that.' She tipped another nip into each of their thermos beakers. 'If the rum goes to your head, don't jump the jazzman with the trumpet: he's mine.'

Rose felt good. Walking with Sally, surrounded by people who needed no introduction before striking up a transient acquaintance-ship, she had a feeling of déjà vu. Then it came to her that this was how she used to feel during the war when Ballard was away for long periods overseas. Being answerable to no one, by herself, she had gone off whenever the mood took her, walking miles along country lanes or digging her allotment. Jon and Becc in their awful home-made little coats, carrying compost in their seaside buckets, herself in her old cords and flannel shirt, and Vee in her push-chair with her funny blanket knitted from odd bits of wool. Recalling how self-possessed and content she had felt then raised her spirits and her confidence now. She had been alone with the children, but not lonely. She had forgotten how capable she had once been. For fifteen years all that had been buried under Ballard's needs, Ballard's demands, Ballard's career, Ballard's ego. When he came out of the army, all that was left of those days of freedom was when she went into her garden in her faded shirt and the army sweater.

The column, having rested, began to move again. Soon they were on the last stretch of the fifty-mile march. Press photographers suddenly appeared as they had done at Aldermaston, walking backwards, pointing their lenses at beards and woolly hats, at clergymen and girls in blue-jeans, at famous faces and babies in push-chairs, and at anybody who would make a picture tell a story that suited the politics of a particular newspaper, all of them hoping that the Opposition might turn up again and get their van overturned by a posse of elderly Quakers.

Ahead, the bell-like music of steel drums tried to compete with the outer-London holiday traffic; behind, the hot jazz trumpet ripped above it. Five or six abreast, people linked arms and, spontaneously, as these things happen on such occasions, an entire section of the marchers began to do a kind of Palais-glide step in time to the jazz band. Sally, pushing back her duffel-coat hood and suddenly returning to her Princess Joffe persona, danced with her lollipop, dragging Rose to join her. Rose, still flushed from the tots of rum, felt herself released into a dance of wild carelessness; others joined, and there formed a kind of Greek circle-dance. The jazz band, seeing this, stopped marching and joined the dancers.

A gift to the pressmen, one of whom had once spent a week covering the controversy about the boundary changes when the newly created constituency of Covington and Hillford had held its first election. Even in corduroys and with her hair loose, he knew that he was not mistaken in that profile. 'Mrs Quinlan?' Automatically she turned her head, and he had his full-face shot. And another and another in quick succession.

'No. I'm not her. I'm quite somebody else,' Rose called as he disappeared into the crowd.

'Thanks, ma'am. I can see that;' he called back, waving a salute.

The intrusion of the photographer broke up the dancing, and the column went forward again.

'Who are you then?' Princess Joffe asked. 'Now is your chance to be anybody you like.'

Rose smiled, showing her small even white teeth.

She'll still be beautiful when she's ninety, Sally Joffe thought.

Rose said, 'I can, can't I? Little Miss Moneybags has taken my old name: she's welcome. What shall I choose, Sally? Nothing at all rosy. Prickly. Briar rosy. Rosa rugosa.' She smiled. 'Do you know Rosa rugosa: very sharp thorns . . . very difficult to eradicate.'

'Rosa Thorn?'

'Yes! Rosa Thorn. Christen me, Sally. No, I don't mean christen . . . what is it you do? Is it bar mitzvah?'

Sally shouted above the din, 'Are you circumcised?'

There were plenty of people around them who enjoyed seeing two women so obviously enjoying themselves. The feeling spread. It had been a great march. The greatest yet. They told one another that this was the turning point. Those first polite acts of civil disobedience by a few polite people were turning into a great movement. And those few – one of which was Sally Joffe, who a couple of years ago had politely trespassed, confronted the polite police, and spent Christmas in gaol – seeing the column swelling to thousands as it neared the centre of London, knew that their action had been justified.

And it dawned on people like Rose that collectively they had influence. It had been meeting Sally Joffe that had brought her to where she was now. Sally Joffe had roared through Rose's stagnant mind like a cleansing fire.

'It never occurred to me that there was any other way of doing things. I've always been so ignorant; I thought that matters like defence were for men like Ballard.'

Princess again now, wearing earrings and lipstick, gave Rose a sardonic smile. 'Men of integrity and honour?'

Rose nodded. 'Absolutely. "The man you can trust with your children's future!" I never even questioned him. Leo (Sally had noticed how often the name Leo cropped up, and the look on Rose's face when he said the name) and Ballard used to go at it hammer and tongs sometimes. If Ballard talked about "taking out", Leo insisted on calling it "killing people", and when Ballard argued about Mutually Assured Destruction being a deterrent, Leo would say "Mad, Ballard, can't you see that it's MAD?" It was all so boring, men droning on about the way things should be done. It went in one ear and out the other, I was really only interested in my kids, my garden and my books. Then one Sunday morning we were in our kitchen having a cup of coffee. It was just before . . . well, it was the last time we were all together . . . Leo and Ballard had started on again about the balance of power – you know how they do?'

'I know how they do.'

'All that stuff didn't mean a thing. Then Leo said, "What you're saying then is this: If I 'take out' Vee and Nora, you would retaliate and 'torch' Helen and Kate. You're prepared to risk their lives on the assumption that I shall always be sane and scared enough not to do it?" It was as though somebody had switched on a floodlight. Just after that I saw *On the Beach*, and then Becc took me to hear Michael Scott. I was probably primed and ready to go off by the time I met you.'

'And here you are.'

'Oh yes, and here I am.' Rose punched the air in an un-Rose-like gesture.

'You like this Leo.'

'He's super, so is Monica. Since I lost my Miss Chaice, I have never been able to talk to anyone except Monica. And now you.'

Sally gave her a shrewd look. 'You're a puzzle, Rosa, and no mistake. I'd love to know what goes on behind that placid face.'

'Very little actually. But I intend changing all that. I think that the sixties is going to be the time when I get rid of the Little Orphan Annie I've been dragging around for thirty years.'

'I hope I'm around to see what happens.'

'So do I. Is it too late to change?'

'"Life Begins at Forty",' she sang. 'It's my party piece: I'll do it for you some time.'

'God, I do hope that it does.'

'You know what Aze always says.' She hunched her shoulders and spread her palms in a droop-mouthed expression typical of Aze. 'You don't wanna worry, Princess.'

When the protesters ended their march in Trafalgar Square, Rose Quinlan had by no means entirely metamorphosed into Rosa Thorn, but, with a five-pointed star in lipstick emblazoned on one cheek, and a peace symbol on the other, the process had begun.

In Germany, on a commission to record on film the building of the Berlin Wall, Wes Trevelyan's eyes were riveted on an out-of-date English newspaper.

> On the day when the Russians exploded their 12th bomb, 3,000 police clashed violently with 15,000 protesters who staged a 'sit-down' and jammed Trafalgar Square. In the crowd were well-known figures: Bertrand Russell the philosopher, Canon Collins, chairman of the campaign, John Osborne the playwright, singer George Melly, actress Vanessa Redgrave, Princess Joffe and Rose Quinlan, recently divorced wife of MP arms dealer Ballard Quinlan. Eight hundred and fifty people were arrested.

Two photographs accompanied the piece, one showing Earl Russell in the 'sit-down' with two policemen looking on, and a close-up of Rose, with a symbol drawn on both cheeks, smiling and as beautiful as ever. That episode had been painful.

The caption read: 'Arms dealer's ex-wife protests against armaments.'

Trevelyan tore out the picture and put it between the pages of a notebook. He had often wanted to see her, but had so far not done so because he couldn't bear to be hurt again. He had found some small comforts here and there – pretty women and photographers were natural allies – but Rose . . . There were days when he could not get her out of his mind. Those were days when his work was terrific, inspired. He hated them.

Ballard, having parked his brand-new latest model Jaguar car in the underground car park of a tower of brand-new apartments, said, as he handed his car keys to the highly braided door attendant, 'Afternoon, Bates. Make sure my car gets washed and polished before six. My man's coming round to pick it up.'

'Will do, sir,' said the man. 'Front lift's working again, sir.'

'About time,' said Ballard, 'I shouldn't much like asking a Senator to take the back lift.'

Bates lowered his eyelids at the very idea.

The lift purred speedily to the top apartment. The most expensive one – with a roof garden.

'Darling! At last. I thought you had got lost.' Miriam kissed him delightedly. 'Come and see, darling. Doesn't it all look splendid? The cook they sent is a *woman*. It's all the thing now, women who do cordon bleu – and there's a maid. The butler will come *later*. You don't think a butler's a bit much, darling, do you? I know how Americans love all that kind of thing. They expect everyone to have a butler. And it will be quite fun.'

Ballard picked her up and kissed her. 'I am so lucky. How many men come home, climb to the sixteenth floor, and find a Mimi waiting?'

She added ice to drinks she had poured when she heard the lift bell. 'I do love it here. Everything so new and *stylish*. Nothing at all like Mummy's and Daddy's old antique stuff. There's such a lovely new smell. And it's all so *warm*, and no draughts. Sometimes I just sit on the balcony and *look*. It's like being in an eyrie or at the top of a castle: not a single soul in the world can see in. It's such a secret place. I feel *terribly* special.'

'And that's what we are.'

'You love it, too, don't you?'

'I adore it.'

'I don't ever want you to regret what you have given up for me, your children . . .'

'We have both done that . . . for each other.' She was so sweet and enthusiastic that he found pleasure in tantalizing her a little and then reassuring her. He had done so on the journey here, idling away a couple of hours so as to arrive home late – and now he would give her the tangible, physical reassurance that she wanted. And then he would sit opposite her whilst entertaining Walt Weissman to dinner, and she would be Mrs Quinlan in command of her dining table and servants. She played house and he loved to watch her. Life was all so easy and uncomplicated now.

In the early days when their relationship had been no more serious than a few one-night stands, and then had threatened to be entirely spoilt by her getting pregnant, he had not supposed that she would captivate him as she had done, or that he would actually fall in love with her. Over the years she had changed; she had listened to his wants and needs and made sure that he had them satisfied. He supposed that she had remodelled herself to please him. He looked forward to this evening: he couldn't remember a time when a dinner party at home had taken on such significance. This was an Occasion. If she knew nothing else, then she knew how to arrange an Occasion.

Playfully, he tossed her on the bed.

She landed lightly. 'I am so happy, darling. Are you happy?'

'I'm happy.'

'I want you to be happy. Let me undo your cuff-links. I love to watch you change out of your business clothes, it makes me feel so wifely.'

'No. Promise me that you will never be that.'

'Wifely?'

'I had wifeliness. A wife who could be relied upon to do nothing more exciting than exhibit vegetables at the local show.'

'Darling, you do exaggerate (face down so that I can massage your poor shoulder muscles, they are in absolute *knots*). Mrs Rose . . . she is much more beautiful than I am. And you say that she was cold, but I shall never actually *know*.'

'No, you won't, will you, my sweet? The only thing that you will know for sure on that front is that Mrs Mimi is not cold, and that I married her because she is fun and gay and does the things I like her to do, and knows the people I like to know, and frequents the places I like.'

'And don't forget that she is still in her twenties.'

Rolling on to his back, he pulled her down to give her a kiss. 'And quite capable of wearing an old man out.'

'Darling, *no*. I will not have you say that you are old. You are *not* old and you are *incredibly* fit. Women *adore* a tiny touch of white at the temples, it makes us think, Ah, here's a man of experience; there is nothing he has not seen or heard or done and he's probably been terribly bad in his time. I sometimes peek at your thing and wonder how many places it has visited. I don't mind, honestly I don't. Do you have any idea how that does so excite a woman?'

'And do you have any idea how it can excite a man to come back at the end of his day to a beautiful home, all glossy and fashionable, no boots in the hall, no light bulbs to replace, no dripping taps, to find a woman who has spent her day with her hairdresser and beautician –' he inspected and pecked her long, fuchsia-enamelled nails – 'and manicurist?'

'Yes, and fashion department . . . This is *new*, you know, and you are scrunching it.'

'Take it off, then.'

'Darling, the Senator's coming and there are domestics to see to . . . Ballard, not so rough.'

'If I had wanted to come home to a wife whose first thought was for the domestics when I wanted her' – a row of little buttons popped off – 'then I might as well not have gone through all the aggravation of the last years.'

The new Mrs Quinlan understood that she had much to make up to him for.

1963

The snow was at hedge height. Jon, unused to wearing the heavy, black-framed spectacles which he now needed for driving, peered through the clear fan the wipers made in the layer of fine freezing powder that was on the wind.

'Incredible!'

Aware that he must have said that a dozen times on this drive to Heathrow Airport, he wasn't deterred from saying it again. For England, especially the normally mild south, this depth of snow *was* incredible. 'They say it's the worst since the Thames froze over when Queen Victoria was on the throne.'

'Can you remember the first winter of the war?' Rose said. 'That was bad.'

'Of course I remember.' He chuckled with pleasure. 'You made me a brilliant sled.'

Rose laughed. She too was peering ahead, keeping a close watch on the rear lamps of the slowly moving car ahead. 'So I did. I used to be quite good at making things out of wood.'

'The shelves you put up at Longmore were a real job.'

'Maybe I should get an apprenticeship in carpentry: I might make a better living.'

'Ah, be patient. Longmore is going to do well once it takes off. The garden alone will draw guests to the place.'

Rose shook her head. 'I don't know, it's a mad scheme.'

'It can't lose. Shit!' The brake-lights of the car ahead were suddenly beneath the bonnet of Jon's car, which slewed to the sound of breaking glass. 'Don't get out. I don't think there's much damage done.'

She was glad to sit whilst he dealt with it. Her stomach was in knots, both at the prospect of taking off on an icy runway, and at the thought of landing alone at the other end. Last night she had lain awake – not for the first time since the re-entry into her life of Threnody Chaice – wondering what she had let herself in for. She half suspected herself of running away from the even more frightening prospect of what she was committed to in her future at Longmore.

Outside, Jon's breath snorted into the headlamp beams along with the other driver's as they inspected the damage. As soon as one moved away from any source of heat, the ice seemed to clamp one's muscles. As people had made allowances for one another during the bitter winters and deep snow of Britain in 1939 and 1940, so now, twenty years further on, they did the same: your mistake today, mine tomorrow. A feeling of camaraderie that would disappear with the thaw as it had with the peace.

The other driver had his wallet out, and Jon was waving the offer away. They exchanged anecdotes about road conditions they had encountered as they picked out odd bits of hanging glass. Jon looked up at Rose and winked. A Jon that she could never have imagined developing from the boy with the home-made sled. He wore his hair almost to his shoulders. It softened his face and, Rose thought, made him even better looking. But the changes were not only as superficial as that; no one could wish for a more successful marriage than his and Elna's.

The driver from the car behind gave a hand to disentangle the bumpers. Jon, laughing with the two men, was oblivious to his mother. He was now totally detached from her. He had a wife and a child. Sonia. Sonia. For Rose to think her name was to see her face – the most beautiful child ever born, and to Jon the most amazing. He adored her. Elna adored her. Rose and all her relations adored her. At three she had a milky-coffee complexion, pupils the colour of tiger-eye, and dark hair that glowed red in sunlight. When Jon had come down the ward holding the pink-wrapped baby and given her to Rose to hold, Rose had been overcome with an elation she had never experienced with any of her own babies. 'Oh, Jon, she breaks my heart,' and he had seemed to pulse with elation. She had never felt closer to him than at that moment; closer even than when she held him for the first time. He had given her something that no one else could ever give: her first grandchild.

'Doesn't she just?' He was quite unashamed of his overwhelming pride in Sonia, now affectionately known as Sunny. She had made him into a person who until then had never existed. He had wanted her to have everything, to be everything. He had worked hard, saved, studied, and had become the happy, confident man with the 'trendy' clothes and long wavy hair that he now was.

The front driver tried his engine, and Jon and the second driver held up their thumbs as the two cars parted company. Waving his thanks, Jon jumped back into his seat, saying there was not much damage done, rubbing his hands, his glasses steamed up.

'Christ! Who wouldn't be catching a VC10 to Johannesburg if they had a chance?' They moved away, but now keeping a good distance from the car ahead, now with only one working red lamp and a dented boot.

He had insisted on picking her up at Longmore, even though it had meant starting out from London in the early hours. 'You should have let me take a taxi.'

'You're safer with me: see how gracefully I crashed him? In any case, I want to see that you actually take off and don't find another excuse. We were beginning to think that you didn't want to go.'

'On the contrary, I may never want to come back.'

'You couldn't! It's a terrible place.'

'I was born there.'

The sky was beginning to lighten the snow-white landscape and, as they approached the road leading to the airport, the roads became churned by snow-chains turning snow and rock-salt into bow-waves of pinkish slush.

'I can't bring myself to think of you as South African.'

'Nevertheless . . .'

'It's not so long since you and the Princess were picketing the South African embassy . . .'

'I couldn't *not* go there now. You understand? Becc doesn't understand. I think Sally Joffe does. Becc says that to visit the place is tantamount to supporting segregation. Do you think so?'

'Mum, you don't have to explain yourself. Go. Becc never did understand how the rest of us tick. But I'm sure she would do the same as you if it was her home; she would want to go back.'

'It isn't my home, England is, but I do have such a curiosity . . . no, it's more than that, I have a *longing* to go there. If I don't go now, I may never go. I have this awful blank patch in my memory. I have this daft hope that, if I go there, I might be able to recall my early years.'

'Perhaps that's what your Miss Lammente thought. It was a clever idea of hers not to let you get your hands on the Sunningdale property until you had been to South Africa.' He laughed lightly, patting her hand. '"To drink at your wells"?'

Rose laughed too. 'That's right – "To drink at the wells of my childhood memories". But I expect in reality they are all dry: it's a long time since they put me on the boat.'

'Poor little thing. It's only since Sunny was born that I began to realize what a heartless thing it is to send your kids away.'

Rose rested her hand on his, 'I never wanted to do that.'

'I know.' He did know, but he could have wished for her to have been stronger when it had come to boarding school; his father must have known from his own experience how bloody those places were. He wouldn't mind if he and Elna had a dozen children: he would keep them all at home where he could keep an eye on what was happening to them.

'I've often thought how awful it would be if Elna hadn't stood up to her mother.'

'So have I. No Sunny.' He paused, taking short, uneven breaths as he always did when he was encouraging himself to say something difficult. 'Is Monica still miffed after all this time?'

'I don't suppose so, she's not like that. It's almost become a rift, but the truth is we simply haven't made a move to get together . . . the months slip by and then a year, and well . . . you know, it becomes a big thing.'

'Actually, it was Helen who came after *me*. I was never so surprised . . . I mean *Helen*! It was never going to be serious, we both knew that. I'm sure she wasn't really all that heartbroken . . . Monica should have left it alone, it was nothing to do with you.'

'I know that, but she had too much to deal with all at once: us leaving the village, her training, moving into Shaft's, and then Helen breaking her heart. When mothers see their kids in pain, they do tend to take against people.'

'Helen wasn't in pain over breaking with me. She's got a much bigger pain than that . . . and Monica must know.'

The regret and irritation in his tone made Rose turn to see what he meant, but he shook his head and gave a firm motion with his hand, leaving Rose even more puzzled as to why Monica should have been so upset when Jon had gone back to Elna.

They were now in a slow-moving line of traffic heading for the airport. The sun rose in a clear sky, reflecting brilliant pink and gold from the snowy surface of a field. Days and days of Arctic weather, a short midday thaw and an immediate refreezing, had given the snow the texture of soft icing. On the moors and downlands, sheep and cattle had perished from trusting an unfamiliar but solid-looking landscape. Villages were cut off, roads impassable, some people lost in snowdrifts and others surviving in unbelievable circumstances. Water pipes and graveyards froze solid, roads were treacherous, schools closed. Children, not caring and feeling no guilt at enjoying the weather, had the best time of their lives.

'The take-off will be OK in this weather. You don't need to worry.'

'Look, darling, I hate to say these things, but one must be sensible and practical. Everything I have is divided four ways, after a provision for Sonia which she will get when she is eighteen.'

'OK, OK.' He squeezed her hand again. 'But do come back, Mum, if it's only to claim your house at Sunningdale. It's a nice little property.'

Now he had gone. He had wanted to see her off, but Rose had insisted that he get back home. She wanted to be alone and anonymous, with her mental decks cleared so as to deal with her fears and misgivings. As she waited to board the aircraft, she looked at the scene below. The yellow lights of the airport cast an unpleasant light on the snow-covered fields around the starkly cleared runways. Aircraft bodies glittered, and lights winked and flashed. Little motors dragging trailers of luggage moved about like insects, and flight-buses moved off in a constant stream. She had never seen an airport, except in the summer months when travellers were flying to places like Tenerife and sunshine. She thought it appeared mysterious and dramatic, like the last scene in *Casablanca*.

Soon now the aircraft would taxi along the runway and, for the first time since she was a child, she would see the country where her mother and father married, Rose herself had been born, and where they had died and been buried. Although she was apprehensive, a prickle of excitement, even more intense than the excitement she used to feel when entering one of the big cinemas with Threnody Chaice, made her shiver. That same thrill of expectation now, in the airport waiting area, as years ago in any cinema foyer. Waiting for the unknown, anticipating the experience of anything, from *Ben Hur* and *The Gold Rush* to *All Quiet on the Western Front* and *Blackmail*. Until one had shown one's ticket for the seat and taken the step into the darkness, there was no clue as to how one would come out of the experience.

Now she had shown her flight ticket, and had been given a seat on the *Jetliner*. This time the experience was not a celluloid one, but would be her own. Never mind the outcome, it would be for real. And this time she was not stepping into darkness.

Tomorrow it would be high summer.

PART TWO

The Pill! • Beatles • Minis • Alabama
Dallas • Algeria • The Pill! • Beatles • Ronan
Point • Wind of change • 101 Dalmatians • Jets & Sharks
Breathalyser • Sharpeville • Paris riots • Brazilia • Psycho
Moors murders • Gemini • Aberfan • The Pill! • Beatles • Twiggy
Jagger • Hippies • Oz • Svetlana • Che Guevara • Neil Armstrong
Valentina Treshkova • Saigon • Profumo • James Bond • The Pill!
Beatles • Martin Luther King • Bobby Kennedy • Prague
Rome–Tokyo–Mexico Olympics • 'Hair' • Golda
Yoko • Bernadette Devlin • Judy Garland
Maxis • Yeah, yeah, yeah • The Pill!

Vee experienced the dual emotions of apprehension and elation at finding herself with the responsibility of running Longmore Health and Country Club whilst her mother was in South Africa. Having been established and in operation for only a short period of time, Longmore was still little more than a small private hotel offering a vegetarian menu and a large, romantically neglected garden.

The few staff they had were either enthusiasts for the health club philosophy and vegetarian cooking, or thought the others were all a lot of cranks but were OK to work with. Most of the rooms were usually occupied, though not by the kind of people they hoped eventually to attract; but at least it kept the place ticking over. Rebecca, who was to be taken seriously in anything to do with trends – now it was wholesome, beautifully cooked food – was sure that there was a place in the market for a good hotel of the kind she thought Longmore could become. As yet it was still teetering along, but it did at least provide an income and a home for Rose and her two daughters. Anoria (having had enough loving and smothering care, from Great-gran and from Aunt Ellie who was paying a long visit) moved to Longmore and had settled in a state school where she was working hard to get a place at university.

Villette, who had great faith in Becc's foresight, had plans for the place and longed to see it grow and become famous. What they needed was an input of cash. Even now, as she walked through checking things on her way to the kitchen, she made a mental note of the firms she must write to, information she must have, reps she must talk to – such as the 'Blue Lagoon' swimming-pool designer whom she had asked to do a survey whilst her mother was away. The South African trip had been put off and put off, but at last the need for the cash that the Threnody Chaice house in Sunningdale would bring, and the slow but sure expansion in the number of residents and dining-room clients, had made her mother see sense in going now before a hopefully busy season got under way in earnest.

As usual, Vee had been up since the early hours, and had driven the brake along the salt-strewn roads to London, where she had bought the best produce available at Covent Garden. The first time she had gone to the market she had been scared to death. Not only was she a newcomer, she was one of very few women in a very male world, and she had no idea how to bargain or banter with the sharp and knowing men. It went against the grain for her to do it, but in the early days she played upon her apparent fragility and asked for help. The hard-nosed dealers, pleased to be her patron, not only showed her the ropes but also how to select and buy the best. In six months she was able to walk confidently into the racket and rush and find exactly what she wanted.

Now she commanded respect, she knew what she wanted and would raise hell if anyone dared try to palm her off with second-class stuff. Amazingly in that man's world of dawn trading, she was admired for her knowledge and for being willing to try anything new. Now that they knew her, certain dealers would take a chance on something exotic, knowing that, if it was of top quality, she too would take a chance. She would snap up carambola, Cape gooseberries, plantains or yams without being sure how they would use them in the kitchens, but confident that Mac would know, reasoning that if these fruits and vegetables were popular in their country of origin, then they could become popular in the UK. And so it was that there were Barbadian dishes and what later became popular as star and kiwi fruits on Longmore menus at a time when such exotic items were still viewed with suspicion in larger kitchens than theirs.

Mac was the same Manley McKenzie of whom Mona Birdham had had such high hopes for Elna. A mountainous, brown-skinned man with a self-guying sense of humour and a relaxed attitude, Mac had carried them all through the traumas of the first days, and kept a level head in any crises that had since arisen. His 'Don't worry – they cain't shoot us for it,' had become the philosophy that saved Rose and Vee from going off their heads.

Jonathan had suggested Mac, at first sight the most unlikely candidate to take charge of the kitchens of a place like Longmore. 'I've found you the best cook in London. He's working as a sauce cook in the West End, but Mac is an anarchist when it comes to creating dishes – sauce-making cramps his style.'

Rose had been doubtful. 'Why would you come to a gimcrack place that hasn't even got a booking as yet?'

'Because I like to do things my way, and nobody in this country wants to take orders from a know-all nigra. In a place like this, I'll be great. Promise you the best cooking for miles.'

Know-all he might be, but he was indeed great in the domain of the high-ceilinged, old-fashioned kitchens. He was easy to get along with, he suited the Longmore set-up, and it suited him. He frequently put on a self-parodying accent that was part B-movie Uncle Tom, part West Indian on a base of London East End. His perfect Lancing College accent he used only as a put-down for certain uppity types.

When working, he was unconventional, noisy, and appeared to create havoc with utensils, but within thirty minutes of the last dish going into the dining room, order was restored and his domain was returned to its hygienic regimentation. Jon had been right: he *was* one of the great cooks. If he had recipes they were in his head and never quite the same twice. Vee, afraid that something extraordinary would be lost, had undertaken to write down his creations.

She went through the new swing-door into the white-painted kitchen, with its gradually expanding rows of pans and utensils and its shelves of assorted jars, bottles and boxes. Amey and Den – a middle-aged woman and a teenage boy who turned a hand to everything from washing up to stirring sauces – were washing and cutting long, bright-red sticks of rhubarb into inch pieces, treating them, as one did in January, as a rare delicacy. 'Nice and tender, Amey?' Vee asked, sampling a piece.

'Tender, not a lot of taste. It'll need a scrape of root ginger to make anything of. It wasn't meant to be ate in January.'

'That don't stop her eating it though,' Den said.

Ill-assorted pair that they were, Amey and Den were good workers and got on well together, and with the flamboyant Mac.

'What did you think of the red peppers, Mac? Super, aren't they?'

'Mm-mm, they look good enough t'eat . . . Pricey though, I reckon. I think I'll stuff them with them pine-seeds, like before. Make them into a main course? OK with you?'

'You're the boss.'

'Right! You remember that.'

Mac, in his usual starched white wrap-around and red bandana, laughed loudly, acknowledging that here, in this part of the house, that was precisely what he was.

In Rose's childhood days here with Threnody Chaice and Aunt Fredericka, the Longmore kitchens had been too large, but for the purpose of catering for guests and diners, the arrangement of rooms was ideal. Vee had plans for modernizing. Over Mac's dead body. He liked to have a wood fire under his pans and faggots in the bread-oven. Time and labour made Mac's style of cooking expensive, but to Rose's surprise there were plenty of people who were willing to pay the price.

'Right! I'm king o' the kitchen. Now you tell me what was in that pine-seed stuffing. No Vee, not out of no book . . . if you going to learn the Mac way, you can't rely on no book.'

'OK. Coarse oats, millet, pine-kernels, onion, a little cream. Right?'

He made a playful ear-cuffing gesture at Vee. 'You forgot the garlic and egg and the black pepper and the salt and the touch of molasses. Girl, I shan't never make nothing of you if you don't pay attention. And don't stand around, help me with these peppers.' And then, in his own more received English and cultured accent, 'Did the Boss Lady get off in good time?'

Vee started slicing and trimming, doing one to every three of his. 'Oh yes, Jon saw to that.'

'I never knew such a family of early risers. Elna says Jon always got up to see to the new baby in the middle of the night with no problem.'

'It used to be only Mum who was up with the lark in the old days, but we all seem be taking after her. Except Nora: she takes some waking.'

'She's still got problems to deal with.'

Vee looked up at him questioningly.

'Don't look so dozy. The girl has problems with her father and the new mother. Nora keeps her head down for as long as she can. It's the way human folks sometimes deal with their problems, shut them away.'

'She never talks about it. I think she had the idea that she would like being in with their set, but after her first holiday with them she never seemed to want to go again.'

'She talks to me, but she wouldn't thank me for telling you about it.'

'Fourteen is just the wrong age to discover that your father has been having an affair.'

'Isn't no age when it's good to discover that.'

'Well no, but one understands better as one grows up.'

'You're a better philosopher than a scullery maid. Give me that before you mash it to all hell.' He grimaced like a pantomime baddy and took the knife and pepper from her. 'Now, get out of my kitchen, or I shall put in a bad report on you when the Boss Lady gets back.'

Except for Elna, Mac was the first black person with whom Vee had ever had dealings of any kind. Initially she had been apprehensive at having to work so closely with him. He was not only black, but he was outspoken and loud and he sent up not only white people's airs and prejudices, but black people's too. When he was working he sang, clattered and talked to equipment and utensils. When he needed help he shouted for Amey or Den. But he was full of contradictions: his way of relaxing was to smoke a little dagga and sew strange and beautiful abstract appliquéd hangings about which he would be highly enthusiastic for the time they took to make and then give them away.

But the most outstanding thing about him was his size. He was large – in truth he was huge – but with the lightness and delicacy that is often found in big, bulky men. Light on their feet, surprisingly good dancers. He claimed to have been a heavyweight wrestler in his early years. Once when Vee had said, 'Heavyweight I believe, but I don't think I go for the other bit', he had picked her up and tossed her as easily as one would a child.

It had been a turn-on for Vee. But then a lot of things were.

It was about two years since he had come to Longmore, and Vee had lost her inhibitions when talking to him. She was glad now when she had an excuse to go into the kitchens. He was twenty years her senior, and although he was not a father-figure, he did in a way replace something strong and masculine that her father had removed when he abandoned them. Vee guessed that Nora felt much the same. Mac talked a lot of common sense and would never let anyone get away with a euphemism. As when Vee had bitterly referred to their father having 'left home', and he had said, 'Why don't you out with it and say that he abandoned his family and buggered off with a bird – it's what you mean . . . Say it?' And Vee, discovering that that was indeed what she meant, said, 'Actually, he buggered off with a tart!'

Mac had thought that funny. '"Tart"? Vee, honey, when you try to be shocking you don't know the words.'

That was then. This was now. Now she knew the words. But unlike her older sister, she got no pleasure from being overtly shocking. Vee, with her expression inherited from Rose, could be much more shocking in her own way.

Satisfied that the day was going well, Vee went off to see to the only two rooms that were at present occupied, and to make up the menus for the tables. This, she thought, is where I was always intended to be. How chancy it all is, finding a niche, discovering that one isn't the dim, pretty one of the family. It had been Jon and Becc who had persuaded Mother that this was the best possible use for Longmore, but it had turned out to be Vee who had seen the possibility of taking Longmore far and away beyond the kind of private hotel they had set out to make.

Monica Wilkinson, uprooting a dead row of last year's runner beans, tried to remember what it was that Rose had told her about beans.

Was it that one should leave the roots in the ground because of nitrogen . . . or was it nitrates? Or must they come out because of the next crop? It had all come so easily to Rose that Monica had thought that she only needed to place herself there and copy Rose's pattern of growing things to be able to slide into Rose's place.

Nitrogen or not, snapping off the sticks and yanking out the bean vines and setting fire to them was infinitely more suited to her irritable mood than good horticultural practices. Once the satisfying flare had died down, she abandoned the garden and went into the house where Jean was hands-and-knees waxing the hall.

'You wasn't long then.'

'It seemed long enough.'

'Wasn't never enough time out there for Mrs Cue.'

'Ah well, I shall never be Mrs Cue, shall I? Pack that up and I'll pour us some coffee.'

'You put plenty of milk in mine, then: that's been stewin' this last hour. I don't know how you can drink it like you do, makes my head spin.'

'That's why I like it strong-brewed.' Monica poured a full mug for herself and a quarter with four of sugar topped with hot milk for Jean.

'I suppose it won't be long now before she's off to South Africa.'

A small tweak at the buried hurt. She still missed Rose dreadfully at times. In the days when Rose had first left, there had been too much going on with the moving-in for Monica to notice too much how she was missing Rose at every turn.

Yet they had not visited one another. The longer it went on, the more difficult it became. Monica, unusually defensive about Helen's depressed mood had said, 'Honestly, Rose, I think Jon's behaviour was pretty shitty.'

The fact that Rose had left Honeywood without trying to heal the rift had been more hurtful to Monica. Of course Monica knew that Rose was not to blame for Jon's behaviour. Monica might easily have said that she was sorry, but she did not, and so they parted company in an atmosphere of disturbance. And so it had gone on and on until now there was an unadmitted rift between them. One that Monica wanted healed. But it never seemed to be quite the right time to do something about it.

Leo was no help. He got picky and resentful when she mentioned Rose. The last time he had said crossly, 'For God's sake, the Quinlans are history.'

As soon as it dawned on her that the changes in Leo were because he was lovesick for Rose, everything else fitted.

Living in her house, refusing to change her garden, entirely expunging Ballard's influence on the house, throwing himself into his work from morning to the early hours . . . It had started after that New Year party with the badminton crowd, when they had all had too much to drink and he had phoned to tell her not to wait up. She must have been blind not to wonder what they were up to till four in the morning in an empty house, with Rose in that black georgette dress that the men's doubles' had ogled all evening. It all went to make up the story Monica told herself to explain the changes that had taken place in Leo. This all added to the difficulty she had when it came to lifting the phone and dialling Rose's number.

'She's probably out there by now,' she said in a tone that didn't invite Jean to take it further.

'I shouldn't really,' Jean said, taking the cigarette Monica pushed across to her. 'Nor should you: you live off coffee and cigs and diet pills.'

'You forgot to mention my booze and the "Pro-Plus".' She sounded as tetchy as she felt. She hadn't mentioned the amphetamines that boosted her and gave her the slender figure she now had.

'You're never still taking them things? I read in my magazine: there's women in America that is hooked on them.'

'Next week they'll be telling us just the opposite. If they were that harmful, chemists wouldn't be allowed to sell them over the counter. They're not as dangerous as aspirin.'

'And I suppose nobody ever died from taking too much of that?'

'Oh, Jean, you're a real old woman sometimes.'

'If your man don't tell you, somebody has to.'

'Mind you don't say anything to him.'

'If I'd have been going to say something, I'd have said it long ago. But just look at you, thin as a wraith.'

'I'm *slim*, Jean, *slim*.'

'And your tits have gone.'

'For the first time in years I can wear a size ten.'

'And your man don't mind?'

Monica's gaze followed the cigarette smoke trailing upwards. Did Leo even notice? Why should he? He's got what he wanted – a hostess who can put on a good show when he's entertaining big contractors, instead of a working wife.

It was one thing being a gatherer and dispenser of gossip, it was another getting involved. Just as Jean Thompson had watched the break-up of the Quinlans and kept out of it, so now she listened to Monica Wilkinson's gripes, and kept out of the Wilkinsons' personal affairs. It wasn't all sweetness and light here.

In the red-brick close of council houses where Jean lived, people got things out in the open, at times literally out in the open, having shouting matches in the back yard; but these sorts of people in the big houses always put on a face. Like the Quinlans. All those years she was sitting alongside him at his elections, making out they were an ideal couple and making other people feel that they hadn't done so well. Him making speeches about falling standards, and all the time he was carrying on with that rich little bit of skirt. You saw it all the time on the telly and it didn't seem much better in real life.

The Wilkinsons didn't seem to be short of money. Stanley had always said he wouldn't want to win the pools because that much money turned people bad. Jean didn't think she'd go as far as that, but once you learned to read between the lines of moneyed people, you could see what he meant. If you asked Jean, she would say that Mr Wilkinson was making money hand over fist, but was having to work every hour God sent for it. The novelty of owning Shaft's Farm had worn off some time ago; Jean thought Mrs Wilkinson was getting bored with it. Not surprising, there wasn't often anybody here. All that slimming didn't help.

Then there had been the trouble with Helen. But Jean could have told anybody that Jon wasn't the sort to marry a girl like Helen. They had gone about together for a few months, but Jon was only having a bit of fun. It had knocked the stuffing out of Helen. There had been some sort of trouble, perhaps between the two mothers, though in Jean's opinion, parents ought to keep out of that kind of thing. Jean had learned that when her own boys were little: you could go rushing round somebody's house complaining they'd been bullied, and whilst the parents were falling out, the kids were back bosom pals again. Quiet little Helen was the exact opposite of that West Indian woman.

'Like father, like son,' Stanley had said when he heard who Jon had married.

'You can't say that,' Jean had said. 'The father's married blue blood, but this one Jon's marrying is working class.'

Stanley had said, 'I was talking about S-E-X. It don't strike me – though I have to admit I only saw either of them but the once, that time when Old Sid Quinlan got his cabinet telly and died – it don't strike me that the Wilkinson girl nor your Mrs Cue was very interested.'

'And you're an authority on it then?' Jean had said tartly, not being used to Stanley coming out with things like that except sometimes when he had taken a drop too much and was showing off what a devil he could be.

It might be the Swinging Sixties in England but, although she had lived here since Stanley brought her here as a bride, the soles of Jean's shoes were still nailed to the floor of the chapel in the Valleys.

'Well, I have to finish that hall if you've got people coming.'

Monica selected a couple of cookery books from the score displayed on the dresser. 'Another day, another dinner. One day I swear I shall serve up bangers and mash.'

'If it was Stanley coming round, he'd love bangers, he'd think it was Christmas and birthday rolled into one. I only give him sausages once a month. A couple of bangers wouldn't do you any harm.' She pushed a cloth into the well of the pungent Mansion polish, the advertisements for which she believed implicitly.

'Why is it that you won't allow Stanley to gain a pound, yet you're always trying to fatten me up?'

'Stanley runs to fat easy. And I don't try to fatten you up. It's none of my business, but I don't think all them diet pills and things can do anybody much good. Stanley don't starve, I just make him eat good, sensible meals.'

'And no booze?'

Monica couldn't see Jean's face, but she knew that the muscles around her mouth would have tightened. Jean knew that Monica drank, and Monica knew that Jean knew. The thing was, they liked one another. Monica never interfered with Jean's routine, and Jean liked being respected for the way she worked, so each made allowances for the other. Jean liked the way Mrs Wilkinson had treated their move into Shaft's. 'Sensitive', she had told Stanley.

It's nobody's business but her own. 'Rots your socks,' Jean said.

Monica knew that well enough. She had known anaesthetists who were hooked on their own stuff, and surgeons who couldn't incise without a long slug of something to steady their hands. Monica needed a little of the same to make life palatable. At least now she did not have the problem of making empty gin bottles disappear. Since she had discovered that slimming pills did a far better job than gin, and with none of the associated guilt, she always kept a large supply in the house, and in the evenings, when the effect tended to wear off, she had the choice of a few drinks if they were entertaining, or a couple of sleeping pills if her mind was on one of its merry-go-rounds.

As the effect of the coffee and her mid-morning pill took effect, she thought what a wonder modern pharmaceuticals were. Ideas for entertaining poured into her head. She would make a lobster bisque . . . she would make a coffee torte. She would . . . she would . . . God! There were times when these new pills after coffee had an aphrodisiac effect that was almost embarrassing. Why the hell was Leo never there when she wanted him? At night, when it suited him, he often didn't make a move until her Nembutal had calmed her down to sleepiness. If they could ever get it right, they could have such a time of it now that they no longer needed to worry about her getting pregnant.

What a wonder are modern pharmaceuticals.

She had read quite a lot about hashish and grass and LSD. On occasions, after dinner when the cigars and cigarettes were going round, somebody would say how much safer it was than these weeds. She suspected that they hoped they would be offered something. It made Monica feel that they probably thought the Wilkinsons not very 'hep'.

Monica would have been quite willing to have become hep if she had known where to go for the stuff. Certainly there was nobody in Honeywood whom she could ask. Tom would know, but she could hardly ask her son to find her a soft drugs' supplier. For the moment she would have to put up with the up-and-down side-effects of the slimming pills.

Leaving Jean to finish off, she jumped into her new, low sports car and drove off to the Portsmouth fish quay to see whether any lobsters had been landed.

She had gone miles before she remembered that this was not the season. But never mind, she loved this car, and when her brain was in gear as it was now, she could handle it like a professional, getting away from the lights leaving the Zephyrs and Zodiacs and Cortinas standing.

The light was going when the VC10 stopped for refuelling. Rose, whose lungs had felt seared by the icy air of Heathrow that morning, now felt stifled by the hot and humid evening air of Luanda. The moisture, the damp-flannel smell, the clear dark sky and the sound of crickets greeted her like a welcome as she stepped stiffly down the aircraft steps.

'Durban!' she thought. She must have been about seven; they had gone to Durban for a holiday. The sudden clear memory of it after all these years . . .

The airport facilities were primitive, but that was part of the adventure – for that was how she now thought of this journey back. The apprehension with which she boarded the aircraft had dropped away somewhere over the ocean. In comparison to the extravagant terror of the young mother who was in the next seat, Rose's fears were piddling. The woman's husband was across the gangway with a carry-cot and a toddler. The stewardesses were helping him feed and change the children, for the young woman herself was incapable in her dread of flying.

In the little waiting room, as she washed her babies' faces and hands, she smiled at Rose. 'I'm sorry, it must be awful for you sitting next to me.'

'You mustn't worry, I've been dozing most of the time.' Rose took the baby and bounced it to show that travelling beside a prostrate and quietly distraught woman in no way disturbed her.

'We're emigrating. Ron's got a chance that's too good to miss. A lot more money than he can get at home. He wanted to go to Australia, but it would have meant going by sea.' She shuddered. 'Days and days with hundreds of feet of water under you. I'd sooner put my head in the gas oven. My name's Bridgette, this one's Zara, the baby's Neil.'

The baby nestled its head in Rose's shoulder and fell asleep, sensuously burrowing into her neck.

'He's took to you all right; anybody can tell you're used to kids.'

'I've had four and I now have a little granddaughter.'

'Four? One was enough for me, we said we wouldn't have no more . . . Ron took precautions and everything, but something happened . . . you know how it is?' Rose knew. Precautions were never enough. Accidents happened. 'We shan't have no more. I'll make sure of that. Thank God for the Pill. Will you hold on to him for a minute while I take her into the Ladies?'

Lucky you. How easy the Pill had made it, a triumph for modern pharmaceuticals. One baby, six, none? And not to have to trust a man to be careful or to be prepared. No mistakes. No accidents. Even if a woman was forced into it and ended up bruised and hurt, at least there would be only half the damage done. Something – perhaps it was the total relaxation of the baby Neil in her arms, perhaps the feel and smell of hot air, made her think of that afternoon in the New Forest with Trevelyan. Had she been taking the Pill then, she might easily have made love with him, whether or not they had been interrupted by the ramblers. That had been a special kind of coitus interruptus. She could smile about it now.

But with Leo, she felt pretty sure, in retrospect, that Pill or no Pill, precautions or no precautions, she might not have been in a frame of mind to consider the consequences. Now, the Pill was woman's great protector. As for all women since Eve, from the time Rose had moved out of girlhood, her woman's body had always been lying in wait for her.

Nothing as simple as the single male hormone. Testosterone produced only a single effect, but women had a handful of hormones, rising and waning, coming and going, day to day, month to month, year to year, springing surprise after surprise, never a dull moment; tender budding nipples, menstruation, missed periods, pregnancy, morning sickness, lactation, desire, frigidity, menopause. Her body was primed to do certain things at certain times, and it did them whether Rose wanted it to or not. Even now, you see, even when the fertile years are almost over, she feels a baby's nose snuffling into her neck and her breasts react, her nipples grow hard, desire flickers. Even now, ages after her close encounter with Leo, she knows that her body is quite capable of springing that surprise upon her again.

It had done so last Christmas. Mac had kissed her beneath the mistletoe and they had both been surprised at their reaction. Just a kiss, but her body had reacted to the feel of his huge, warm body.

She looked down at the baby, who was not nearly as pretty as Sunny had been at that age. Sonia had been the idol of all the nurses. It was terrible that by the time she was twenty those same nurses would feel altogether differently should any son of theirs bring her home to meet the family . . .

She became aware that she was staring at a man's shoes. 'I thought you'd like a cuppa.' It was Ron, with three cups and an orange juice on a tray. 'Shall I take him now?' The baby didn't awaken but renestled into his father's neck.

'Your wife went off with the little girl.'

He nodded. 'Sugar?'

Rose refused. 'She'll be all right when she gets there.'

'I know. That's what I keep telling her. It's a marvellous life. Swimming pools, servants, plenty of money, plenty of sun. Nobody buys cigarettes except in boxes of two hundred, so they say. Cheap wine. You can get a bottle of brandy for a quid. Meat costs practically nothing. I told her, she can live like a lady out there. But it's not just that: there's plenty of work too.'

'It sounds like paradise.'

'It is, they need skilled workers.'

'Have you got a house to go to?'

'First off we shall be in accommodation. If you are going permanent, you get put up in family hostels. I expect they are pretty decent, it all sounded pretty good.'

Bridgette returned with a freshly wiped and changed Zara, and took the baby from Ron.

'All right now then?' he said. 'Shan't be long taking off now. Be there not long after breakfast.'

Rose saw all the blood drain from Bridgette's face. 'Tomorrow?'

Ron gave her a playful pat. 'Of course tomorrow, you lemon. Keep your pecker up, girl. Once we've had supper and they put the lights out, we'll be in clover.' To Rose, 'She's got some sleeping pills. I'll get the steward to fetch you a double gin, Bridge – knock you out flat.'

There was an announcement asking them to reboard the aircraft, and the cowboy-hatted bandoleered, rifle-toting police moved to guard various doors, presumably to see that none of them fled into the dark-blue night. Within minutes the jets were whining and Rose prepared herself for a night of sharing Bridgette's knocked-out dread.

As she stared out into the black and saw her own reflection, Rose wondered whether Bridgette and Ron had any idea of what life would be like, beyond their dream of a swimming pool in the sun and servants bringing trays of cheap booze. She wondered whether they had ever heard of the Sharpeville massacre. They quite likely supposed that it had nothing whatever to do with them, and were quite sure that they would never be unkind to their servants.

Even your mind springs surprises on you. Five years ago I wouldn't have given that two thoughts. I'm changing, thought Rose. Perhaps I'm growing up at last. She smiled at her own unchanging face, then put her arm around Bridgette who, sloshed and drugged, nestled just as baby Neil had done.

Angela Brazenose, sister-in-law to Threnody Chaice's London solicitor, stood where she could easily watch the passengers coming off the SAS flight from London. Angela was glad to have something useful to do, and it was great to be able to do something for Jack for a change. Jack always went out of his way to ferry them around London when they went home every couple of years. A third generation South African 'Brit', Angela still referred to herself as an 'ex-pat', and to England as 'home'.

Jack had said, 'You won't mistake her: baby blonde, beautiful as the very devil and walks like an empress.'

Laughing at his enthusiasm, Angela had said, 'Hey man, cool down.'

'Ah well, you wait until you introduce her to our Martin and you can tell him that. But don't let her appearance of utter sophistication and confidence fool you; she's as timid as a mouse. Be sweet to her, she's hoping to discover something about her childhood. She can't remember much . . . I don't think there's any great mystery; probably her mind blanking out when her mother died and she was sent to England. Anyhow, she wants to see if she can find her old home, and she wants to go to Durban. I'd be grateful if you'd keep an eye. Don't stint, there's plenty of lolly in the kitty.'

Amazingly, when the only woman who fitted Jack's very apt description of Mrs Quinlan did emerge, she was carrying a baby and appeared to be part of a family group. Angela held aloft a bunch of pink roses, and at once the woman responded with a wave and came across to the barrier. Man, what Angela wouldn't do for a complexion like that. 'Mrs Brazenose?' *And* the English accent – pure, natural Brit, unlike Angela's own, which was school-taught and obvious when in the company of real Overseas-spoken English.

'Hi. Mrs Quinlan?' she called.

'Yes. The roses were a good idea.'

'I'll be at the Exit.'

Rose felt damp and crumpled. Lord, the woman looked so groomed and tanned. She'll think I look a frump. She had seen that type on the aircraft: expensive-looking women with hair, face and nails groomed, legs polished, voices raised and confident, exchanging 'Jo'burg' gossip in sentences that flipped up at the end and vowels that sounded strange. Rose's nervousness was transmitted to the baby who began to whimper.

'I'll take him now.' Bridgette, transformed now that there was something more substantial than sheet metal beneath her feet, took Neil. 'Thanks for holding him. You must come and see us when we're settled in.'

'Thanks, I'd like that.'

'Right,' Ron said, 'we'll have a few drinks . . . You're stopping at the Cranbourne, aren't you?' With a peremptory smile and wave they hurried off to their new life and country. For ever, Rose assumed, for Ron would never again have anything as alluring as the promise of servants and sun with which to persuade Bridgette to leave terra firma.

The customs men were efficient and polite. Had she been through customs as a child? Presumably so. She had been in the charge of an elderly Scottish engineer and his wife, but she could remember hardly anything of them or the journey and arrival.

Angela Brazenose clicked her fingers and a uniformed black man appeared as if from nowhere. 'Denyel, collect the English medam's bags and wait for us in d' caw.'

The chauffeur took Rose's papers and went off.

'Look, Rose – OK if I call you Rose? I'm Angela. I thought you'd like to freshen up and maybe have a drink or something?'

'Oh nice,' Rose said, wanting to please Mrs Brazenose for putting herself out. 'Anything you say. It's really so kind of you to bother; it must be a real nuisance for you.'

'Don't bother about that, I just love it. I've couriered one or two of Jack's acquaintances before. It's always good fun.'

Angela guided the way to the door to the 'Ladies – Whites Only'. The room was cool and gleaming. An aproned black woman, in a beret worn like a pudding-cover, polished already shining surfaces. 'Mary, fetch the medam a box of tissues.' The black woman, without a look or expression that she had heard, handed Rose the box that was already at hand. Rose washed her face and hands, redid her eyebrows and lipstick, and combed her hair.

'A clothes-brush, Mary.' Mrs Brazenose, having had the brush placed into her hands, flicked the jacket of Rose's grey flannel suit.

In the bar they sipped long gin slings. 'We'll have to get you into something cooler than a suit.'

'I thought I would wait until I got here . . .'

'Great! I love shopping. How about tomorrow? Hey, Martha.' She waved at a woman who, with her carefully built and lacquered hair, beauty-parlour make-up and bronze skin, was almost a clone of Mrs Brazenose. 'Excuse me a minute? I just have to . . .' And she tripped away on her high sling-backs, her neat behind moving the tight short skirt of her sleeveless linen shift, leaving Rose to wonder whether she could get away with something like it. In her nervousness she had accepted a cigarette from a box the size of which one only ever bought for parties or as Christmas presents at home. Ron was right, nobody bought cigarettes in packets.

'Martha says you are invited to tea on Sunday. Her mother has come to live in Jo'burg, from England. Been here about a year; she likes to talk about home. Naah then, if you're ready, I'll get you to your hotel.'

The Cranbourne was slick, modern, international and four-star. Rose liked it for not being unfamiliar. The leggy receptionist in a linen shift and jacket had a trained smile and efficient manner. Having asked Rose if this was her first trip to Jo'burg, she'd said that Rose would love it; she had been here a year herself and wouldn't go back to Bolton for anything. She already spoke with the accent. 'Anything you need, Mrs Quinlan, awsk for me, Jinny. I still remember hah it feels not knowing d'ropes, you know?' She nodded at the discreet notices in two languages displayed about the foyer. 'Awfrikawns.' She rolled her eyes. 'Don't let it bother you.'

It had never occurred to Rose that she would be bothered by Afrikaners – it was the 'Whites Only', and 'No Blacks' notices on doors at the airport that she had found disturbing. She had never seen so many notices. Everything in two languages. Everything black or white. She wondered how long it would be before she made a mistake. Had it been like this when she was a child and she, like Jenny from Bolton, had not noticed?

'I've given you a really nice suite with a balcony – bedroom, sitting room and bathroom. Really spacious. I think we Overseas people need the space and air more than the locals, especially when we first arrive. I'll send a girl up to unpack for you. You don't need to tip her; if you do give her something, make sure it's not more than ten cents. Don't mind me saying so, but Brits tend to go over the top. It's only guilt. You get used to it.'

Only when the telephone in the sitting room of her two-room suite rang did she realize that she had fallen asleep. The voice of Jenny from Bolton. 'A call for you, Mrs Quinlan.'

'Rose? Angela Brazenose. Settled in? Look, I forgot to say a time for our shopping spree. Nine tomorrow morning suit you? You'll find it hot, so I thought I should take you out early and not go into the city. I have a lovely little boutique I use out at Rosebank. You'll love it. We'll have a great time.'

Having agreed and put down the phone, Rose had the uneasy feeling that providing a courier service was not entirely altruistic on Angela Brazenose's part. Or am I being ungrateful? Don't look a gift-horse in the mouth; where would she start looking for anything without at least one friendly face? Johannesburg, as far as she could gather from her journey from the airport, was a second New York. Talk about stranger in a strange land.

Looking round for her things, she realized that, whilst she had been asleep, Jenny must have sent up a 'girl', who had quietly unpacked and put everything neatly away in drawers and wardrobes, even to her toothbrush and make-up which was now in the bathroom. She had obviously gone away without disturbing her sleep for a tip. People were really nice.

The dining room and menu were ostentatious, but the food was good and the service terrific. When she was on her fruit course, a vaguely familiar couple stopped at her table, leaving the waiter who was guiding them to theirs hovering uncertainly. About fifty. Very English county. He gave a little bow, she said in the ringing accent of her class, 'Ah, so it is you. I said to Nigel I was sure it was you. There, Nige. I'm always telling him not to prejudge. He said that it wouldn't be you he saw being dropped off here. He thought that you were with the young couple with the children. But I said "no". I happened to glimpse you being met at the airport.' She made an expression Rose took to be a nod and a wink. 'No chauffeurs for your travelling companions. Oh, *what* a fuss . . . those poor stewards trying to cope with the baby . . . And poor you. But we mustn't keep you from your dinner.' She held out polite fingers. 'Kitty Pennington, my husband Nigel.'

Rose took the proffered fingers. 'Rose Quinlan.'

Nigel spoke. 'Quinlan? Unusual name. Met a chap with that name . . . MP. Suffolk, I think . . . four or five years ago now. No relation?'

Without a qualm, Rose said, 'None at all. I come from Berkshire.'
'Holiday?' The woman asked, unashamedly nosy.
'Sort of . . . business and pleasure.'
'First visit to Jo'burg?'
'Yes.' It wasn't a lie; not an actual visit, as such.
'If you want to know anything, just ask us. Second home, eh Nige?'
'Right. Only place to find any proper service these days. Mark my words, you won't want to go home. Come along, Kitty, the waiter's waiting.'
'Let him wait.' But with another instruction to Rose, 'Don't be afraid to ask us, my dear; we Brits must stick together,' the Penningtons took their places at a table for four which the waiter had obviously not intended for them.
Had Rose known of the subtle rather than the major differences between modern city life in Johannesburg compared to the UK, she might have taken them up on their offer. But she weathered them. Her naturally apologetic manner and her looks got her out of most predicaments, and when trying to find her way back from a short walk, she even elicited a civil reply from a regular policeman, not knowing that there were traffic cops to deal with the minutiae of the streets.
Her introduction to the sophisticated set and their ways came on the day following her arrival. Angela Brazenose, had decided that if she did not take her charge in hand she would quite likely turn up everywhere in the provincial, Overseas fashion she had arrived in. Not that she didn't look good; she simply didn't appear expensive enough.
Angela telephoned her brother-in-law.
'The sea froze? Hell, James, why do you stay on in a place like that. We were taught in school that England was temperate. Now, what I'm really ringing for is to ask how well breeched your Mrs Quinlan is . . .'
'. . . What is "not badly off" supposed to mean? Rich or filthy rich? I need to know, I'm taking her out to get some dresses, I want to pitch it right, not frighten her off: some of our boutiques can be pretty pricey. Is it a large inheritance coming to her? Oh, come on, you can't expect me to be her friend and guide if I don't know more than that. I thought I'd take her to Maudie. Yes, I thought you'd remember . . . Of *course* she's pricey. I just want to know that your Mrs Quinlan can afford her.'
Finally she gleaned from her brother-in-law (who gave the impression that it was all too trivial to be ringing at such an hour to talk about dresses) that, although Mrs Quinlan might be knocked

sideways by the Maudie price tags, she could actually afford them.

Maudie herself came to attend to them, and Maudie had to admit that this woman was a born clothes-horse. Put anything at all on her, and she looked as though it had been made for her.

Rose, who back home was used to searching the rails for herself and trying on clothes in cramped cubicles, was overwhelmed and initially embarrassed by the attention she received. She and Angela were seated in smart grey-and-pink, Swedish-looking armchairs, whilst frocks – no, *models* – were held up for their consideration by a beautiful coloured girl. In the open-plan fitting-room alongside other women, some of whom – quite naked apart from a G-string and high-heeled sandals – compared frocks with one another, Rose in her bra, pants and slip felt overdressed.

Eventually, after much coffee, serious discussion, and lulled by the quiet formality of Maudie and the attention of her assistants who came to admire the trying on and to wonder at the *fantastic*! complexion and the *superb*! profile of this beautiful new customer, Rose chose four frocks, a sundress, a rather glittery top and velvet skirt (which Angela said was an absolute *must* if Rose was to be visiting for more than a few days), two swimsuits and some cotton skirts and shirts which were boxed and made ready to send out by messenger boy.

'I've never been so extravagant in my entire life.'

'It is impossible to live in this city without some sort of a wardrobe. My sister-in-law never brings enough; she says that back home you have only two occasions, evening and the rest of the day; but here we have mornings in and mornings out, poolside afternoons and city afternoons, and then there's no end of variety for evenings: Brei, bioscope, bridge or just plain old sitting on the stoep with a sundowner. At least you have a start. Shoes aren't so bad: go for plain strappy things that take you most places, and you have some really nice city shoes already.'

At Maudie's desk Rose took out her wallet containing a wad of newly exchanged high-value rand notes and counted out four hundred rand, mentally calculated that must be about . . . ? Two hundred pounds! She was never quite sure whether she actually felt the air around her freeze, or whether it was the air-conditioning plus the expression on the faces of the manageress, but something told her that she had made a gaffe. Then Angela laughed gaily and gave Maudie a placatory smile. 'Oh, I should have *said*, Mrs Quinlan just yesterday flew in from Overseas . . . She simply hasn't had time to make her credit arrangements.'

Rose felt quite ill-at-ease under the sharp eyes that were now obviously weighing her up, not only herself but her hair, earrings, necklace, frock and shoes. She was quite glad her jewellery was gold. Angela Brazenose was sorting things out. 'But you know *me*,' Angela said. Maudie smiled as she patted the notes together like a pack of cards. 'It's perfectly all right, Mrs Brazenose, we are delighted to be able to suit Madam. She has a most beautiful figure.' She smiled, forgiving Rose now for whatever transgression of boutique etiquette Rose had perpetrated. 'And of course, *that* complexion could only just have arrived from Overseas.' She inclined the top half of her body in Rose's direction and handed her a pale pink card with a fountain and bunch of flowers logo. 'If you will be guided by one who has *the* most fine hair and complexion, *do* pay Emelda a visit at the very *earliest*. All the girls are London-trained. Do mention that Maudie recommended you.'

Rose thanked her for whatever advice it was that she was being given.

Angela said, 'Send everything round to the Cranbourne.'

'The Cranbourne! I did hear that it's about to be given a fifth star.' The name of the place obviously put Rose back in favour with Maudie and helped to smooth over the *faux pas* that had embarrassed Angela. 'A regular client of mine is there . . . Mrs Pennington? She telephoned yesterday to say that she would be in. The Penningtons have always used the Cranbourne.'

'We arrived on the same flight. I spoke with them in the restaurant.' Rose knew that to know the Penningtons was important to Maudie.

Maudie smiled expansively at Angela. 'Well, that's all right then.'

Angela, now back in Maudie's good books, said, 'Mrs Quinlan has one of those suites overlooking the new church.' Which obviously confirmed Rose's bona fides for the entrée as a Maudie client.

When they were seated in an architect's version of an Italian piazza, with waterfalls of purple bougainvillaea tumbling into pools and fountains of clear water, and waiting for iced tea, Rose said, 'Did I say something?'

Angela raised her eyebrows as she lit a long, long cigarette. 'Say?'

'Back in the shop when I was at the cash desk.'

'Oh you mustn't worry about that. That's just Maudie.'

'But what did I say? For heaven's sake tell me, or I might do it again. I should hate to put you in a spot.'

A black waiter with scarlet fez, breast-band and cummerbund served them with white-gloved hands.

'My dear, in this country, if a person shops in a place like Maudie's and has to pay with money, it means only one thing – un-creditworthy! Bankrupt.'

'They don't want your actual money?'

'Well, of course they will accept it, as Maudie did yours, but a person without credit is without any kind of social standing.'

Rose thought but did not say: This is Alice-in-Wonderland economics. 'I'm sorry, I had no idea. Surely people must pay with money?'

'Oh yes, of course. OK Stores, Woolworth's, Marks and Spencer kind of stores.'

'But not Maudie's?'

'Not if one hopes to be a respected client. I am. I can easily go three months ahead with my account. That's the kind of status most clients with one month's credit hope to get.'

'In England, that usually means one is strapped for cash. English stores rather like pounds and fivers.'

'Don't you have any accounts? I know my sister has a Derry's and a Wallis's account.'

'Oh yes, I have a couple of store accounts, but that's really to make it easier to order by 'phone.'

'But how does anyone know that you are really, *really* credit-worthy?'

Rose smiled, 'I suppose by seeing you always have the cash to pay on the nail and never need to buy on credit.'

Angela said, 'How long do you think you will be here?'

'A month? Five weeks? It depends.'

The black waiter came with fresh cups and another plate of biscuits, and removed the used cups and the crumbs.

'You really should open one or two accounts, Rose, if you don't mind me saying. I'll see to it if you like.'

'All right.'

'Much safer anyway than a wad of notes.' She pointed to the biscuits and half turned her head, raising her voice. 'I asked for *plain* biscuits. You understand "plain"?' Then, turning back to Rose and continuing as though she had not interrupted herself. 'You mustn't put temptation their way. All nigras are thieves. Take the gold fillings from your teeth if you fall asleep with your mouth open.'

The white-gloved hand removed the offending chocolate-covered biscuits.

Rose didn't know where to put herself, but neither Angela nor the waiter seemed aware of one another. She could see Angela's indifference to his presence, and would have liked to have known whether he too was as indifferent to her as he appeared. Certainly Angela was a likeable companion, but Rose felt that she must find some way of doing this thing on her own. Angela was obviously more than willing to give up her time to be helpful, but could she understand that Rose really did want to spend her time seeing whether she could find any trace of her old home and, if possible, of Ayah, and not look for invitations to an evening breifleish or Sunday tea. But she could not be stand-offish, because she really did not know her way about.

Too close to Johannesburg for peace of mind lay Alexandria Township: 'The Location'. Not as infamous as Sharpeville, nor as internationally notorious as South-West Township – Soweto – was to become. Alex was a vast spread of basic accommodation with few facilities, where thousands upon thousands of black workers were located.

For many of the inhabitants of the Location, this place was not home. Home was elsewhere, anywhere from Kimberley to the Orange Free State and the rest of Africa. Home was where aged parents had been sent when their work permits were withdrawn, and where the babies were brought up by grannies. Home was where their own tribal name awaited them, more difficult to the European tongue than Mary or Jim. Home was where the heart was; the Location was where their work permits allowed them to sleep at nights.

It was these thousands upon thousands of workers who serviced the city and made it the paradise which Bridgette had suffered months of anxiety and two days of terror to enter, and which Angela Brazenose had been brought up to accept as her birthright. To and from the Location every morning and night came and went train- and bus-loads of chauffeurs, clerks, shop-workers, errand-boys, window-cleaners, street-cleaners, refuse-collectors, bottle-scavengers, news-vendors, road-menders, scaffold-erectors, builders'-labourers, flat-'boys', steel-erectors, kitchen-maids, domestic cooks, hospital-cleaners, porters, loaders, swimming-pool cleaners and gardeners.

And there were the tsotsies. Gangs of youths who separated handbags from their owners by a razor applied to the handles and sometimes to the wrist, the most experienced of whom could slit a pocket or anything else with a skill that would have made the Artful Dodger appear amateur in comparison; they too were run by their Fagin equivalent. Tsotsies went back and forth with the daily migrant flow.

As well, there were thousands of other black workers who, although servicing the blue-skied paradise, did not (or were not permitted to) return to the Location except on one or two pre-arranged days a month. These were the 'girls'; domestic servants and nannies who lived on the premises – or rather in huts in the gardens or dormitories on the roofs of modern flat developments.

In their gingham aprons and white headsquares, the younger 'girls' tended to flaunt a vicarious kind of status that sprang from being nannies who were privileged to take white babies into the parks, where they frequently used the 'Whites Only' benches. On the occasions when they were in charge of some of the children of paradise, they were also permitted to travel upstairs at the back of a 'Whites Only' bus.

They carried permits which allowed them to be within the confines of the city at night. They worked long hours and were often 'not allowed to entertain any male person on the premises'. They were as alert to class status as any inhabitant of an English Shire.

Ron, reporting for work on his first day, had been shocked to discover that the firm had moved to the Cape without anybody telling him. He was offered a job there, but decided to stay and find something else in Jo'burg. They were pretty good about letting him stay on in the accommodation for a few weeks longer. Ron, who had been a good shop-steward back home, had a dad who was a union leader and interested in world affairs. Ron's dad had been dead against Ron coming here, and had tried to persuade him to choose any part of the old Commonwealth except this place. So Ron, having made the decision against his dad's wishes, wrote long letters explaining to his dad that it wasn't all Sharpeville and imprisonment without trial.

> There's your Bantu – that's your kaffirs (you know, Zulus and that kind of real black); then there's Asians (that's your Indians and your Chinese); and then there's Coloureds, which is like we'd say a touch of the tar-brush – you've never seen prettier girls anywhere. They came about when the Whites first arrived. The Afrikaners say they are the result of Hottentot women being raped by the first Brits, but the Brits say that there was a time when Blacks and Whites mixed and nobody thought anything of it.

He balked at telling him about the official classifications within mixed-race families, but Ron's father read newspapers and had seen reports of cases when two kids in the same family were given separate race classifications. Why hadn't Ron chosen Australia or Canada? That business about Bridgette was nonsense; if Ron had put his foot down she'd have gone all right. No, his only son had always hankered after things outside his own class. South Africa was a country of no-hopers who could only make it in a place where there was no real competition. Ron had said different, that it was a place where the talent went. Well, they would see.

Ron, with time on his hands whilst he waited to find something to suit his skills, wrote daily to his father, ignoring his Dad's admonitions to take up his situation with the unions.

> There's plenty of work about, I've been offered loads, but I can't see me working for Bata shoes, can you? There's not a lot of heavy factories: they import a lot of their stuff like machinery and equipment. The mines seem to be my best bet, and there's a lot of power-line contract work about, but I don't want to take anything away from home until Bridge and the little ones are settled. You'll be pleased to hear that I turned down three jobs (good ones with fantastic pay) because the places weren't unionized. All the managers had come out from England and had made it to the top quite easy. They said you have to forget unions if you want to get on, but I don't reckon I could bring myself to work in a place where workers don't have any say in things like health and safety. I reckon there's some dodgy practices going on. I've come to the conclusion that the best place is probably in the mines . . .

Ron thought that his Dad would be pleased. He wasn't; he could read between the lines.

Rose, with the same need as Ron to put things down so as to try to make some sense of the troubled country, wrote a detailed account to Sally Joffe as she had promised to.

> Japanese are classified non-White, and are not allowed into the Whites-only leisure resorts, yet there is one Japanese businessman staying in this hotel. I don't actually know where people such as Egyptians fit in . . . probably like the Portuguese, sort of honorary Whites who can be trusted not to overstep the boundaries and put themselves in a position where their dignity would be violated. If you're somebody like the Aga Khan, I guess that it wouldn't matter if you were blue with pink spots. It doesn't affect me, there is nobody more acceptable than a WASP (White Anglo-Saxon Protestant, but I expect you knew that). I can go anywhere I like; if I want to use a kaffir toilet, nobody will stop me. Not that anybody in their right minds would want to use one – even the White ones aren't brilliant – but it's the principle. Their thinking is so primitive that it makes even naïve me blush for their ignorance. I keep thinking that Germans in the thirties must have thought like these people do. But I must stay for a bit longer. Daily I feel closer and closer to the little girl I'm looking for. I just have to try to find out something if I can, and I feel certain, now that I am here, that the sights and sounds – and especially the smells – will bring

it back. I have seen the bank where my father worked – at least I have visited the site where it used to be; but like everything in the heart of the city, nothing old is left standing. There is a bank there, but it looks as though it has been transported from New York . . .

Bridgey sends her love. She moans about this immigrant accommodation (I have to admit it is a bit grim compared to what we were told), but it's not for long, and she's got the company of a whole lot of other women living in this building. I've got a nice little Ford just to get us about to look at property, but I shan't get a new car until we are settled. I thought I'd like one of the new Zodiacs. The women spend their days taking the kids to the parks and round the shops. The bus service in the city is pretty good.

Bridgette, not having been the one to decide to emigrate, was abl to paint a more truthful picture for her friend Sylvia.

It doesn't seem hardly fair to bitch about the state of the place when the weather is so smashing. It's just as well they have cleaning men ('boys') to come in to clean down the corridors, because none of the girls here want to do it; they can't wait to get places of their own so that they can get their own servants. They're always on about how many they will have, but when you work it out you'd have to be getting a pretty good screw to employ even one servant. You don't pay the servants much wages compared to what normal people get, but you have to give them somewhere to live and feed them, which all costs. These girls here don't think about that. Ron should easy get a good job, and I won't mind if we just have one servant to live in to do the cooking and cleaning and give a hand with the kids. Ron hired a car for a day and we went to have a look round the suburbs. You've never seen anything like the new houses. Fantastic! We looked over dozens of older-type bungalows; most have corrugated roofs. People say you get used to them after a while, but it still looks like a shanty town to me. You don't get swimming pools in those areas, but Ron says that in a year or two we would be able to move up-market a bit. There are some super places if you are in the manager or professional class. I told Ron he ought to try to qualify as a dentist or doctor. Four servants and a swimming pool and a chauffeur. I know that for a fact because I got talking to a woman in a coffee bar who had come from Essex, and she works as a receptionist. She had a nanny for her kids. If you get a nanny and you both work you can do quite well. Saturday is early closing. They say it's because the old Brits wanted it to be posh like Kensington, but I never knew that the Kensington shops close midday on Saturday. Ron says it's more like to have something to do with the Jewish Sabbath.

Ron always replied to his father by next post.

> What you said in your letter about fairness. Who said anything in this world was ever fair? I never found much fairness back home. You try getting into the Royal Enclosure at Ascot and you'll soon see. Nothing I can do about it out here (except go to some union meetings, which you'll be glad to know I've been doing): it's their way, and if that's how it is we just have to go along with it. I've got an interview for a job as senior electrician with the Witwatersrand Mining Company. We've been looking at some flats, but places in the city are pretty pricey. If I get this job, we'll probably go for something out in the suburbs.

It was in a stamped-mud yard in the Location, the more familiar name for Alexandria Township, that Fatima Kalim sat and watched over her daughter's children and her daughter's daughter's children. All of them blacker than she was herself, which was why she lived in Alex rather than in the Coloured area where she might have settled had her daughter, Mina, not compounded her own dark skin by taking a Swazi to father Trudy and their five sons upon her.

Trudy, although she had not been much more than a child at the time, had continued adding darkness to the pale Kalim colouring by allowing herself to be played about with by some black kaffir who kissed girls with his mouth like a white person and delivered fizzy pop to the back door of a very nice house in Dunkeld where Trudy had a good job as Nanny to just one child. History does tend to repeat itself. A kiss that turned out to be not just a kiss, but fat and beautiful Johannes who pushed a red plastic fire-engine back and forth at Fatima's feet.

Fatima did not fit in. She did not mix. She was different. Not that it mattered very much now: at almost seventy she was lucky to have a roof over her head at all. They all had work in the city; the Swazi was a good man, who rarely put his wages into the pocket of a shebeen queen, and he was kind to this old bag of bones who, thirty years earlier, had been brought to this country when it was easy to enter. She had worn a red and gold silk sari, a small remnant of which she still hung on to.

The Fatima Kalim of those far-off days, having found herself unwittingly abandoned by the death of her runaway soldier, who had not expected to die before he had the fortune in gold he had come here to find, had been taken on by the kindly Westons, who had also known tragedy. Ah, she could have told her grandchildren a tale, but although she had brought them up to be respectful and polite to their elders, she saw their eyes glaze over whenever she tried to tell them something of their own ancestry. They did not like to be reminded that the blood of their veins was not one hundred per cent black.

Lately, though, she had come to the conclusion that they were perhaps right to close their ears to her. Their history *should* be a black one. Mina was the result of Fatima's own lapse with a car driver. To this day, the smell of gas and engine oil never failed to admonish her for that one evening when they had been frivolous. But he had been a good man. Her job as nanny to the white child had come to an end just as Fatima discovered that she was pregnant, and that man of hers had taken on full responsibility for Mina and for the five sons. She had dreamed of a pale-skinned teacher falling in love with Mina, but it was fated not to be.

Mina's sons were black and rebellious, and made fists at one another. Since the trouble of Sharpeville they had become angry and secretive. What kind of a world would it be for Johannes – they tried to get her to call him Jo, but she always forgot – to grow up in if there was an uprising? White people would never give up their sweet life. Fatima had seen it, been part of it for years. She had seen old buildings knocked into the rubble upon which new, whiter, higher buildings grew, and in a short time these went the same way, until now when to walk through the city centre was to feel that one was walking through a canyon where the sun never shone. She had seen wood-ranges torn out and replaced by gas stoves, gas torn out and replaced by white ovens set into kitchen walls. Refrigerators replaced deliveries by ice-men and Kenwood mixers replaced bamboo whisks. Flats in the new blocks such as those where Mina and Trudy worked were Hollywood film sets in a Cary Grant film come to life. Why did her sons, and the men they mixed with, think that the Whites would ever give up all that without fighting to the death?

People said that there would be a blood-bath. Of course, how else could it end?

She popped a morsel of Milky Bar between Johannes' soft brown lips and received a smile that brought tears to her eyes. There were times when she wished that she could scoop him up and run away to a place where he would not be taught to make a fist as a greeting.

Leaving the baby to play within the wire-netted yard, Fatima went inside to put on the rice to steam. This was the one night of the month when Mina's day off coincided with her man, Sam's, shift-work, so that they could come to the Location, make a great fuss of their grandchild, Jo, with toys and clothes, and sleep under the same roof and the same blanket. Mina was fortunate: her Madam gave Mina plenty of packets of Durex lingam-sheaths. Give thanks for small mercies.

'Longmore, Bosham, Hampshire.' The impressive notepaper heading jumped out at Leo Wilkinson, seated in the office of his chief designer. A letter of enquiry to Blue Lagoon Pools, one of his subsidiary construction companies. He heart leapt at the sudden temptation. 'I could handle this one, Charlie.'

'You don't have to, Boss. I know you don't like nowt except steelwork.'

'It's all right, I know these people.'

'Oh . . . right. What is it, some kind o' fancy place for tired businessmen? I was hopin' I might get lucky.'

'Not up your street, Charlie. I believe they go in for vegetarian food.'

Charlie made a face. 'Oh well, you can tek it then. Theer opening up all over the shop; thank God for granting us a few steak houses and Wimpy bars. Eh, that's one thing I like about being Stateside: bloody great steaks weighing a pound or more, and that's just your breakfast. If this is a fibre and fart place, tek it and welcome. I spoke to some woman on t'phone. She said it were only a preliminary enquiry, but it weren't just a casual enquiry. They are going to install some watter, it's just a question of when and how much it will cost.'

Leo slipped the file into his case with a feeling of quiet satisfaction, even though, as Charlie said, he was happy enough with running the Blue Lagoon as another construction string to his diverse bow. After a lifetime of erecting high steel-towers, he could not get enthusiastic about holes in the ground and pouring concrete. Towers were the opposite of pools. Purposeful. Striding across the moors and downs. Charlie would roll his eyes at any such fancy notion: he liked the way that the pool business was taking off, because it demonstrated his belief that this country was taking off too. Success, affluence and pleasure; before too long it would be another US of A. The PM had said, 'You've never had it so good.'

Anoria Quinlan packed up her books, pulled on knee-length boots, and wrapped herself in the embroidered goat-skin coat, shaggy with hanging fleece-locks, which Becc had bought her last Christmas. If kept in a cupboard everything in that cupboard took on the smell of male goat from the Afghan. The goat-coat was a great fashion, and sold by the score from Becc's 'outlet' in Carnaby Street. As soon as she had seen the first batch of a few dozen, she had snapped up a whole consignment, knowing with her sure instinct that 'her' trade was just ready for something as casual, colourful and anti-establishment as this.

The billy-goat smell was not (in the new idiom) a 'turn-off'; if anything it added something to the two-fingers-up message to the conformists. Becc turned what might have been disadvantage into a positive statement by making a large cardboard cut-out randy billy-goat in frenzied psychedelic colours and standing him outside her shop. He bore the message, 'I smell, therefore I am!' Just the kind of 'in' joke enjoyed by many of the young people who crowded into Carnaby Street, which had become not only the centre of Swinging London, but the hub of the universe.

Those, like Anoria, who found goat a bit much, took to hanging their Afghans in a small cupboard with a bunch of smoking sticks and patchouli-soaked wads of cotton wool in the pockets. As she went through the kitchens on her way to the back door, she tossed her head at the loud tuneless humming that Mac, Amey and Den always greeted her with when she put on her Afghan.

'Don't you clowns ever get tired of that old joke?'

Amey rolled her eyes and Den giggled – actually he fancied both Anoria and her coat. Mac said in one of his Uncle Tom voices, 'Now hey, Mizz 'Noria, you done finished yo' homework?'

'Ah finished, Mo. And these little things are delicious. What are they?'

Mac became serious and stood beside her as she tasted, closing her eyes and rolling the filling around her tongue.

'Ambrosia tarts. Think they'll do?'

'You're a genius, old man. I'll take a dozen next time I go up to Becc's. Are they kosher? Mr Joffe loves sweet things, but Becc says he's taking up with orthodoxy again. Do you know what that means? I hope it doesn't mean he's going to get all serious like old Christians do when they catch religion.'

'Wouldn't do you no harm to talk to your Maker once in a while.'

'Mac! You're not serious?'

Mac just raised his eyes and shrugged his shoulders a little.

'I feel like making a snowman. Got time to help me?'

'Why not, it's time for my coffee break.' He abandoned the grating of orange zest and pulled an enormous jumper over his head, crammed his hair into a jelly-bag hat and followed her out into the garden.

Amey and Den watched from the window as Anoria and Mac rolled a small snowball until it was too bulky and heavy to move further, then piled on a head and smoothed and patted arms, added a pea-gravel grin and a couple of dried rose-hip eyes.

Amey said, as she watched Mac rolling snowballs and hurling them full-strength at Anoria, 'He's a bigger kid than she is, mucking about with cold snow like that.'

Den said, 'I expect he fancies her.'

''A course he don't fancy her, he's old enough to be her father.'

'Never made no difference to my old man: it was a ten-year-old girl that the police finally got him for.'

'Your old man was a pervert; Mac isn't no pervert.' She turned back to the preparation table. 'Come on, Mac will expect this lot done when he's had his break. You can't talk about your old man and Mac in the same breath. If he wasn't black you could say Mac was a perfect gentleman. And if you ask me, it's a pity he is black because he'd make just the right bloke to run this place alongside the boss. Several times I thought that. It would be a real family-run hotel. Her seeing to the upstairs, Mac running the kitchens, Vee doing the bookings and the menus and office. It'd be as nice a place to work as you could think.'

Den said, 'There's times when I wonder whether you are daft or just wants us all to think you are. Except for Mac and Mrs Rose not being married, it's all like you said.'

'But that's the whole point,' Amey said. 'Mrs Rose and Mac aren't married and never can be.'

'Isn't no law says they can't,' Den said.

Amey considered. 'Maybe there isn't no legal laws, but ladies like her don't marry black men.'

'Her son's married to Mac's cousin, isn't he?' He wetted his finger and marked himself a notional winning point.

'But she's a woman, and she isn't really hardly black at all.'

As he drove slowly along the salted drive of Longmore, Leo Wilkinson didn't know what to make of the scene. A young woman with long, heavy, flowing hair was trying to stuff snow down the neck of a tall black man wearing a flame-coloured jumper which did nothing to disguise his round belly and barrel chest. Leo couldn't help smiling as he watched; she clung on to the jumper as he twisted and turned, trying to scoop up snow, until eventually he tripped over something hidden in the snow and fell, whereupon she pelted him mercilessly.

Leo walked across what presumably must be a lawn, for there were no humps as there were in the deeply buried borders. The heavy hair, considerably longer now, and the flicking action to keep it clear of her eyes was familiar. 'Anoria?'

She stopped her attack on the big man, looked up and then hurled herself across the snow and against his chest. 'Uncle Leo! Oh, gosh, how marvellous. Where did you spring from?'

He hugged her and held her for a moment. 'I was looking for a little plum-pudding that used to be Anoria Quinlan. What on earth have you done with her?' Anoria looked so happy and well that he could scarcely believe that she was the same sour-faced, edgy girl who, when her parents divorced and Shaft's Farm was sold, had gritted her teeth and gone to live with old Mrs Quinlan rather than with Rose and Vee.

She pointed dramatically at Mac, who stood attempting to remove snow from the neck of his jumper. 'That man . . . he fed her baked fish and vegetables until the pudding melted away.' She took Leo's arm and guided him across the snow. She reminded him of Rebecca when she first came home from art college. Mock archness and wit. And 'that man' obviously held an important role in the Quinlan household.

Leo said, 'I think he left a very presentable replacement: you've grown into a very pretty young woman.'

'Uncle Leo, *please*! I never suspected you of sexism. Haven't you heard that kind of remark is out?' She was teasing him, showing that she was a woman with a mind.

He liked her. 'I never suspected you of sophistication. I'll bet James will never forgive himself for not snapping you up when you first asked him if he wanted to get married. What were you . . . five?'

'Probably, I was very into engagement rings at five. I got one in a Christmas cracker. This is Mac, who invented ambrosia. Mac, this is my best and only uncle, Leo Wilkinson.'

Leo took the man's hand. It was dry, firm and warm, the kind of hand that one naturally trusted.

'Nice to meet you, Anoria's uncle.'

'We used to live next door.'

'They bought our old house.'

'I remember, the Boss Lady told me.' His voice was deep-toned and pleasant.

'Take no notice, Uncle Leo. The man thinks he's Paul Robeson.'

Mac reverted to his received English. 'Actually, Uncle Leo, I'm in charge of this place whilst the Boss Lady is on her travels.'

Anoria brushed snow from him with his jelly-bag hat. 'Don't you let Vee hear you say that; she thinks she's running the place.'

'Ah, we aren't a bad team, though I say it myself. I'd better get back to the kitchen. You staying for lunch, Mr Wilkinson?'

'That would be nice. Actually, I've come about an enquiry my firm got about quoting for a swimming pool.'

'The Blue Lagoon man?' Mac said.

'I am actually. Blue Lagoon is my show; I thought I'd kill two birds . . . I didn't realize that your mother was away, Nora.'

'She's gone to South Africa, looking for her roots,' Anoria said.

'Will you be eating upstairs or with the family?' Mac asked.

'Family, of course,' Anoria answered for him. 'Hardly anybody more family than Uncle Leo. He taught me to play badminton.'

'Did a fine job there, Uncle Leo. She's not bad – for a woman.'

Anoria scooped up snow and threatened him; he cringed playfully. 'We have a court marked out in an old reception room. I can beat him easily when I want to. Maybe you could give him a few tips when he's finished dinner this evening.'

'This evening?'

'You are going to stay, aren't you? You have to, Vee's gone up to town to see about some new linen or something. She phoned Blue Lagoon to say it was no good coming because there was too much snow.'

'Sorry,' Mac said, 'but I have to work. Maybe see you later. Baked trout with almonds, calabrese from our own growing, fresh figs with cream. Sound good to you? Healthify you.'

'OK . . . ah . . .'

'Mac.'

'Right. See you later, nice to have met you.'

'Yeah. Great.' He disappeared in through the back door.

Leo had not missed the man's proprietorial use of 'our', and the implied invitation to join them for lunch.

'They'll be serving coffee in the lounge about now. Come on in.'

Anoria took his coat and left him to find the cloakroom, where he washed up and combed his hair. The hall and small reception area had been welcoming, with wood panelling, red rugs and brass light fittings; traditional and restrained, as was this cloakroom, with its deep old flowered handbasin and brass taps, and a wood-seated lavatory bowl covered inside and out with the same glazed orange chrysanthemums. Discreetly installed as they were, the only jarring note was a further cubical and a modern urinal. What he had so far seen of the place had Rose's instinctive touch and style. He and Monica had tried, but they never achieved in Shaft's Farm what they had set out to do, which was to replicate Rose's style with the rooms. Monica had never been able to – as she described it – 'dump an armful of flowers and bits of hedgerow into some old vase and make it look like a Dutch still life.' He had noticed in the hall an earthenware pot, crammed to capacity with hips and haws, old-man's-beard, holly, pink blossom . . . teasels, was it? and some kind of grassy plumes and bulrushes. An armful dumped in Rose's own style, they stood there elegantly and effortlessly arranged, which was how Rose herself always appeared to be.

How often these last long months had he pictured her as she was when she talked or listened, one ankle crossed lightly over the other, her knees covered but her slim legs arranged, not consciously or to arrest attention, but so that one could not help noticing them, one arm resting on the back of her chair so that the outline of her breasts showed, elbow bent as she fiddled with an earring or twisted a strand of hair round and round one finger: small, unobtrusive movements that drew one's eyes to her slender hands and fingers, which usually sported nails broken and blunt from gardening.

It had never occurred to him that she wouldn't be here. Anoria had been vague about why she had gone to South Africa. He had known that she had been born in that country, but Kate had said that she had met Aunt Rose on a 'demo' against the colour-bar. Had Monica known that she would be away? Although their friendship had cooled, Monica still seemed to get to know what was going on in the Quinlan family from Ballard's grandmother. Monica had become so scatty and vague: she was either in a world of her own or shining brilliantly. He had only offered to do the survey because it gave him an excuse for coming here. Rose had told him to stay away, but he had kidded himself that the enquiry about the pool meant that she had relented. As he drove, he had let his mind drift around things he wanted to tell her. Ask her. For one thing Rose was the only person he could talk to about Monica.

He replaced the white huckaback towel and went in search of the lounge, telling himself as he did quite often that he was a bloody fool for still hankering after Rose. His long-held image of her as ice and fire had been brought to life on that night when he had not been able to resist kissing her. He had wanted her so much and she had wanted him, he was sure of it.

Until then he and Monica had had twenty years of a really good relationship. She blamed the deterioration on the fact that she had been forced to give up her nursing job to look after the new house. Honest only to himself about it, he knew that the rot had set in when he had seen Rose in Chichester, when all his sublimated feelings for her had gushed into his conscious mind. He had been so bloody jealous of the photographer. Where might it all have led had Ballard's mother not died that night? To chaos; to another break-up for himself? Could such frantic passion as it promised to be survive on the rubble of two marriages and the complicated break-up of two families? Metaphorical grit in his mind's eye. One leg already over her, his fantasy of what the next move would have been . . .

As he walked along the corridor and across the hall, he could see through the glass-panelled door the red of an open fire. Logs. An extravagance, as he knew from the experience of keeping the open grate burning at Shaft's Farm, but he could afford it these days.

He had been thinking about that this morning. He'd been lucky. It was a good time to be in business. There were good contracts going in the steel construction industry and, although he was at present coining it in, he realized that there must come a slump at some time, which was why he was diversifying into fine-tolerance engineering, installation work, property conversions, and now this Blue Lagoon business. There were still times when he felt uneasy, though; if there was ever a deep recession, no amount of diversification would make much difference. What he needed to do was to take what he sensibly could from the business and try to make some wise investments. It wasn't *that* long since he had been a young engineer starting out on his own at twenty-five. It seemed such a short time ago, yet in another short stretch of twenty-five years he'd be an old man.

The waitress serving four people seated to one side of the fire looked up and came to him as he opened the door. 'Coffee, sir?' She showed him to a table in the other side of the hearth. 'Nice and warm here, sir. Dandelion or ground?'

'Maybe I'll try the dandelion. I think Miss Quinlan will be joining me.'

'Oh yes, sir, you must be the gentleman.' She poured and added a little cream. 'Miss Anoria's just gone to help Miss Vee to unload some things. She said she would only be five minutes. Oh, here she is.'

It wasn't Anoria who entered, however, but a raven-haired version of Rose as she had been when he had first set eyes on her. Villette had always taken after her mother. But now, with her hair parted to one side and dressed simply, and wearing just the plain kind of dress her mother might have worn when she wasn't in her old cords, she was Rose. His mouth dried. Rose twenty years ago. Cool and haughty, poised and extremely lovely.

He put his cup down, 'Villette.' He gave her the same kind of hug and kiss that he had always given her. But he felt awkward with her womanly form in the black woollen dress crushed against him. Although three years had certainly changed Anoria from a pubescent child to a young woman, that same time-span had transformed Villette. When he had last seen her on the day they had moved from Honeywood, she had still dressed in the same black pumps, jumper and black ski pants which Helen and most other teenage girls of the time wore, and she had seemed as sweet and vulnerable a girl as his own daughters were then. Here was a woman. But, as he saw from her bold, direct look, a much more dangerous and challenging woman than her mother.

'Uncle Leo.' Her voice was soft and clear, and her accent was what James would describe as 'posh' and Monica as 'up-market'. The kind of voice that sounded good on a telephone and made visiting Americans think of blue blood and family trees. She clasped his hand tightly, led him back to his seat and signalled to the waitress for coffee. 'Nora says that you are Blue Lagoon. Is that right?'

'It's my show, yes.'

'I had no idea. I said she must have got it wrong, because I had been dealing with a Mr Wilmslow.'

'Charlie Wilmslow. Blue Lagoon Pools, Ltd. The "Directors: C. Wilmslow and L. Wilkinson" is in very small print at the bottom of the page.'

'I'm sorry you came all this way for nothing. As you can see, the garden is feet deep in snow.'

'A bit of snow doesn't stop us. You only want an estimate, don't you? You weren't expecting us to turn up with JCBs and gangs of men? I came to give you an estimate, and that's what you'll get.'

'Did Nora ask you to stop over?'

'She did, but . . .'

'Please do. We couldn't bear it if you went rushing back. Why has it been such a long time, Uncle Leo? Surely you didn't stay away just because it didn't work out for Jon and Helen?'

'Of course not. I don't really know how it has come to be so long,' he lied. 'We are always intending to visit . . . I don't know. What with the house and my companies . . .'

'Companies?'

He grinned and shrugged deprecatingly. 'Big wheeler-dealer. I'm still the same old steel-tower erector, but I've got a few other things on the side these days. Such as swimming pools for the filthy rich.'

Vee put her hands up, palms out. 'Nobody like that here, sir. Honest.' She leaned back in her chair, crossed her legs at the ankles and twisted the gold loop in her ear. She could easily have aroused him doing that. Did she know? Did such mannerisms develop willy-nilly or were they copied?

'You've grown to look very like Rose.'

'I don't mind that. And if I look like her when I'm the age she is now, I shall be quite satisfied. I think my mother is a very beautiful lady.' He thought that she was sending him a message that he didn't really get.

'So do I, very beautiful.'

'But I don't have her timid nature.'

He smiled, 'No, I don't think you do.'

'But Mum is learning. You might not even know her these days. It was hard for us, but my father behaving like the tom-cat he undoubtedly is – and probably always has been – did us all a favour. It was time for us to leave anyway, don't you agree?' Again that penetrating look. She was suggesting something to him. Surely Rose had not told her?

She continued, 'I don't know whether Eliot was right to suggest lives measured in coffee spoons, but I do believe that our lives come in lumps. I think that I am right. We had a wartime lump, then the Honeywood lump. We were ready to start on this Longmore one.' She laughed, showing Rose's small, even teeth. 'I hope that this is a bloody great big lump. I love it here.'

The swearing rolled from her tongue as easily as it did from so many of this generation's. He wanted to say, 'Swearing doesn't suit you', as he would have done to Kate. Kate would have responded by rolling up her eyes. 'It's only a word, Dad: there are a lot of them about.'

'If the Honeywood lump hadn't come to an end because of my father, there would have been something else. We should have left. We were a very disturbed household, weren't we? You must have thought so.'

But Leo wouldn't be drawn. It was years since the Quinlans' break-up, yet within a few minutes she was trying to force him to plunge into a lake where there was who-knew-what hazard lurking.

'I think my mother wouldn't have stayed pinned down there for very much longer,' Vee continued. 'She is too intelligent to be satisfied with a vegetable patch and a flirtation or two.'

He drank coffee to prevent the need to take her up on any of that. 'The waitress says this is dandelion. It's very nice.'

She smiled, putting up the shutters against whatever was going on in her head. 'If you stayed with us for a few days, we could detoxify you a bit, send you back healthier than you came.'

'What on earth is detoxify?'

'Clean your blood, brush up your lungs. Like the old German spas, but without the sulphuric waters.'

He leaned back and laughed. 'What is this place? You want to purify me, Nora wants to run me around the badminton court, your . . . chef is he? He wants to feed me home-grown calabrese and fresh figs.'

'You met Mac? You should stay for his food alone. He's a genius . . . a wild man, a firecracker, but a magician when it comes to food. If we ever make anything of Longmore, it will be because of Mac.'

That same glowing reference that Anoria had given the big black man.

Monica answered the new trilling bell-call of the new stylish white telephone receiver. It was Leo. Jean, polishing mirrors, overheard Mrs Wilkinson's end . . .

'No, I don't mind if you stay.

'. . . Surely I must have told you that Rose was going to South Africa, Leo. I could have sworn that I did. Ballard's mother told me weeks ago . . .

'. . . Listen, Leo, I *would* like to see them. Could you just break the ice?

'. . . Of *course* there's a need. I can't just turn up. It's all gone on far too long, and the longer it does, the more difficult it becomes for me and Rose to meet. I can't see any way now but for each of us to bite the bullet and do it. Ask Vee, she was always the most sensible one.

'. . . Suggest Kew or somewhere like that. Kew's as good a place as any.

'. . . Oh, and Leo, find out how Jon is . . . and Becc.'

Jean was glad that she'd be able to tell Stanley that her two families were getting together again.

Monica crashed the receiver on to its rest. Selfish swine! What Leo wants Leo gets. He wants to stay, so he stays. And he never asked about Tom's injuries. The hand was healing well, but Leo wasn't to know that; for all he knew Tom might never be able to play a guitar again. Leo Wilkinson, who used to be a model father and good company, had gone the way of the stereotypical entrepreneur. They get their foot on the ladder, holding their wife's hand (or standing on their wife's shoulders), and as soon as they start moving fast they let go of the helping hand and leave the wife stranded. She knew that she wasn't alone because of all the *Nova* and *Guardian* articles she had read. She had never expected for a moment that Leo would become like that.

Since he had expanded his business, he was seldom at home, and if he was there then he was up in his 'playroom' building his toys. If he wanted to say that they were 'engineering models to scale', that was up to him, but if Monica were to sit for hours making doll-size dresses and hats, she'd at least be honest enough to say that she was making dolls' clothes. It wasn't as if she actually wanted him there all the time – she didn't – but she did at least wish that he would recognize that her life was a pretty thin one, and it was thin because she had given up her own career to service him and his house and the people he entertained because of business. And now she was growing old in their service.

Several times she had enrolled in evening classes, but it was no use studying anything serious and interesting if she had to skip classes because he needed her when he was entertaining somebody he was trying to get a contract out of. She had tried a few craft classes, but what grown-up woman with even half a brain makes pleated lampshades, or paints pastel-coloured flowers on old plates? Time-fillers! She had come to loathe time-filling courses. Yet she did them. It was at least in a higher league than the coffee-morning, fund-raising, bridge and Tupperware circuit so many other 'executive wives' were on. The other time-filler was having an affair. On the new private housing developments, site foremen and quantity surveyors were in great demand. Actually, an affair would be quite interesting, but she never seemed to come across any men she fancied.

She didn't mind him staying over – it was just great that they might get over this awful hiatus with Rose – but it was the sneakiness of him. He must have had the idea at the back of his mind when he said he would take a change of clothes in case the snows came back and he couldn't get home. He had done it on other occasions, but not when he was only going into the next county. She had joked with him about getting caught in snowdrifts on the bleak moors of Slough. It had seemed funny at the time. Now it didn't.

Sod him! It didn't help that she knew why she felt so put out. He had thought that Rose would be there. Serve him right, the devious bugger. She didn't particularly want him to come running home, but she didn't want him sounding so bloody pleased with himself. Being back herself with Rose in a state of their old intimacy was important to Monica. Vital. But she didn't want Leo's interest to be rekindled too. Rose was hers.

Sod Ballard! No matter what, Monica had to get back some of the old relationship with Rose. Why in hell's name had she had that sudden flash of suspicion about Rose and Leo? When she looked at it straight in the face, what was there to go on? Nothing more than there had ever been. They had always spent time together, trying to be the first one to get a new novel, then wrangling about it for hours. Why, on that one occasion, had she become suspicious and jealous?

She felt familiar symptoms rise up. Frustration, irritability and edginess. She wanted something – some bloody thing – but she did not know what.

Before the days of the new slimming pills, she would have gone off 'hunting' in an attempt to fill the void. She opened a packet of crisps and lit a cigarette. Leo should never have told her about seeing Rose with that photographer. He might have known that Monica would be hurt. She was hurt. Rose had been meeting that man and not told her closest friend, the friend who had helped get her out of a fix. She would never have dreamed that Rose could be devious. If Rose had kept that secret, had she kept others from Monica? A blight that weakened its vigour had settled on their long friendship, leaving it prone to attack. Resentment, jealousy and misunderstanding had each in turn had an effect. Self-inflicted injuries.

Fingering the bottle of amphetamines, she savoured its promise of a bit of a sparkle for a couple of hours. She still prodded at her irritable mood like a tongue in a tooth cavity.

Nobody had forced her to marry Leo. Leo had not tried to persuade her to take on little Tom, nor had he talked her into having Kate and Helen.

She had liked the idea of giving up nursing to become a wife and mother.

It was the thing that normal women wanted.

In the days when Monica was a young nurse, a woman had only to look around at the spinster professions to know that marriage was the better option, gave status to women, purpose, a reason for being. In the lives of members of the feminine professions, men, sexuality and children had no place; if a woman wanted them, she must get out.

Monica had seen Leo, wanted him and got him, and for a time she had felt herself to be liberated. Her hours were her own, she was her own mistress, until she thought it through and discovered that women were all in the same boat: domestic or working women, married or single – women lived in a man's world. At least Ballard never hid the fact that he was a tyrant, but Leo . . . Leo was the great liberal who talked up the feminist cause whilst he was probably servicing his Ladies' team.

She pushed the pills about, tempting herself.

Why do we do it? She had asked herself a thousand times. It wasn't as if women didn't know what married life was like: they could all see their mothers. Why didn't more mothers tell their daughters?

She had told Kate and Helen: If you are going to get married, do it when you are past forty. By then you'll probably be the envy of your married friends.

They thought she lived the life of Riley.

At the other end of the call, Leo rang off and stood for a moment in the little public telephone cubicle in Longmore's hall, a bit distracted because she had sounded . . . ? He couldn't put his finger on it, but she quite often appeared to be in that frame of mind these days. A peculiar kind of cheerfulness that he didn't believe. He didn't know which was worse: her sudden drop into the doldrums, her over-the-top enthusiasm, or the uncertainty of coming home not knowing which Monica he would find.

Damn! He hadn't remembered to ask whether Tom had had his stitches out.

Tom had had a drop too much on Christmas Eve and glanced his motor-cycle off a lamp-post. Not bad injuries, he had been lucky: cuts to his face, a nasty crack on his forehead, a cut across the back of his hand. Tom was old enough to know better: he'd be twenty-seven – eight? – this year, yet he was still as obsessed with guitar playing as he had been when he and Jon Quinlan had decided that they could outdo Tommy Steele. Now it was electric guitar and rock-and-roll. He was good, Leo had to admit that he liked his stuff, but where was the future? Jon Quinlan's start hadn't been that illustrious, but he had found himself a niche, established himself with a share in an estate agency, a house, a wife and family.

But was that what Leo wanted for his son? Tom had always been something of a free spirit, and it pleased Leo when kids showed a streak of unconventionality and liberal thinking. His son? It was only recently, since Tom's hairline had begun to recede leaving him with a peak that emphasized his long, straight nose, that he saw the likeness to Tom's biological father. Never mind. Tom was never going to look like Leo. Tom was a type just as Leo was a type. Different types. Leo loved Tom. Always had, always would.

Ballard's old study was now a television room furnished in modern Swedish-style furniture, plain blinds and a few uncluttered glass bowls and ashtrays. A steel-framed limited edition Green lithograph, which Leo called 'Holiday for Lavatory Seats', was the only picture hanging. Another – a large abstract oil in shades of rusty-iron bought from the artist only this morning – stood waiting to be hung. 'Links and Chains'. Monica felt pleased with her purchase because she knew the particular pile of rusty chains which had inspired it.

The only bit left of the previous Quinlan style was the fire-surround which, the interior decorator had said, was a perfect complement to the new Scandinavian style. A fire of coals, drawn up by the cold outside evening air, burned and glowed red on the walls. Monica turned the TV 'On' knob and sank into a chair that was more comfortable than its uncompromising bowl-like lines promised. She smiled as she contemplated the prospect of the LSD and pot. Sheer soaring pleasure.

In the event it had been so easy to come by. And of all people to have let her have it – Madeline Stringfellow.

She had gone down to the Portsmouth fish quay, a place she liked to drive to even when she wasn't expecting to buy fish. She had got to know a few of the skippers, some of the regular customers, and a couple of painters who set up easels there come rain or shine, and although the fish market seemed to be the coldest, wettest and most uninviting place on earth on a January morning, there was a kind of loud and echoing friendly air about the place. Yellow light from bare bulbs shone out of the sheds on to the wet quayside. Small fishing boats which seemed to be muddled and lacking any grace until one got to see what they were about, gently bumped their car-tyre sides against the wooden stanchions. She had got to like the bundled nets; the small wheelhouses; the sounds the wind made clattering their ropes and masts; the mix of smells – oil, fish, sea; the general air of purposefulness of the putt-putting engines; the rattling chains and squeaking winches; men's voices raised above the slap of heavy-headed codling being gutted and thrown into trays. There were no bodily comforts here, but she was usually able to find something to perch on and smoke a cigarette. Sometimes she would offer or accept one from somebody else. In that casual way she had a place where there were faces and people who belonged only in that one place. Nobody had a name, except a few picked up from shouts – Ben, Elkie, Boyo. And Stringfellow, who had long ago interviewed her for what had been going to be Monica's renewed profession.

Of all people to discover doing strong, heavy paintings that made one look with a new eye at rusting hooks and hawsers and green-slimed wood, Stringfellow had been the most unlikely. Although she had noticed her from a distance on other occasions, Monica had not recognized the woman in a scarf tied gypsy-fashion and arty clothes. It had been Stringfellow who had come and sat beside her one morning and said, 'I've just realized who you are; you've got slim.'

'Sister Stringfellow? Well! And you've got . . . ?' There seemed to be no polite way of saying 'a new image'.

Stringfellow had smiled, 'Yes – out of nursing.'

Today, Monica, in one of her moods of spontaneous enthusiasm, had asked Stringfellow whether she had any paintings for sale, and had been invited into Stringfellow's surprisingly conventional seafront house. There she bought 'Links and Chains' and went on an indescribably happy trip. An illegal substance it might have been but, as Monica said later, in a state of wonderful good humour, 'It beats all the rest to hell. You can keep the booze and the Pro-Plus and the Valium and Mogadon and amphetamines.'

Monica knew then that, if she could have just an occasional trip, her days would pass wonderfully. No more of the uppers and downers that had kept her muddling along for years.

It was no wonder that Stringfellow had become transformed. Mostly, she explained, because at the same time as her grandmother had died, leaving her the house but no money to keep it, Stringfellow had won the Pools. 'No joke, I actually won. I don't normally tell people, but I did win – the largest amount ever paid out up to then. So I was able to admit that I had made a huge mistake in thinking that nursing was to do with caring for sick people – I found it more to do with keeping time-sheets and seeing that if anybody is put out then it is not the man called Doctor, even if his brain is the size of a pea. Hope I haven't put you off, not that I think you're bothered any more about nursing, by the look of that car.'

Monica came away from Stringfellow's with the picture and her ticket to ride. No more black moods. Rainbows and psychedelic walls.

Tom Wilkinson, coming home to Honeywood in the early hours, discovered downstairs lights still burning at Shaft's Farm. Expecting his mother to be in bed and alone in the house, he picked up the kitchen poker before he moved cautiously through the house.

Tom was reckless, but he was not brave. Just that morning he had winced and complained as each of the fifty stitches that had been used to tack his nose and forehead back together had been removed. The surgeon had been pleased with the healing but had said, 'Come and see me in a year and we might be able to do something about that puckering.' Cringing at the thought, Tom hadn't been able to get out of the dressings room quickly enough.

The house seemed quiet enough. His face was bloody tender. The cocktail of painkillers and cider had worn off. One of the other patients waiting to see the surgeon had lost an eye. Christ! No way I could deal with that. Imagine stripping down to your eyepatch; it was bad enough that his hair was receding before he was even thirty.

He thought his mother must have gone on up without remembering the lights; then, in the new sitting room which they all still referred to as Ballard's, he found his mother stretched out on the new sofa, dead to the world. He got a car rug from the hall cupboard to put over her. She did not stir. Quietly he poured himself a really large Scotch and settled himself to watch the log smoulder. Its dry bark burst into flame, giving the room an air of gaiety and life. He spotted the Stringfellow picture. Nice. Strong stuff. Mum could be surprising. Goes to show that we are on our own, we don't even know our own mothers. Own mothers. Ha!

He sat back and watched the flicker on the walls. Monica stirred and sighed. She had changed. More since they had moved from the old house. She looked great these days: she wore a lot of ethnic stuff which suited her. She was the type: her big bones and strong face could get away with it and not look draggled. But she was restless and snappy. She had great enthusiasms, never the same thing from one of his visits home to the next. He'd ask how something was getting on and she'd say, 'Oh, *yoga*! I stopped going to yoga ages ago', or pottery, or archaeology, or architectural heritage. The Quinlans' old playroom was stuffed with things she had taken up and got tired of. The latest was golf: some guy called Ron was her latest guru. Ron gave golf lessons that meant her driving right out as far as Watham, but Ron was the best. Tom wondered which was the greater attraction, Ron or the golfcourse. She wasn't a bad looker for her age; he could see that an older guy who liked exuberant women would like Ma.

His dad didn't seem to have changed much – not in looks – unless it was that he had always appeared almost middle-aged. He'd always attracted the women. Those badminton groupies! Tom smiled to himself, remembering how grossly annoyed and embarrassed and, if he was honest, envious he used to be when he was about sixteen and he had taken up badminton and tennis seriously. Old Leo would come off the court and throw himself into a chair in what Tom later came to understand was a 'sexually available position', and the groupies in their tight-ass little white shorts would trip over themselves to give him a glass of Robinson's or find his towel. Leo had never realized that it was the boys who were most attracted to him. That wasn't a thing that would enter his head. He supposed.

He drained his Scotch and reached for a refill. Gradually he became aware of a strange smell about the room – not exactly strange, but out of place, as the smell of chips in a bedroom can be. A familiar smell in unusual surroundings. This was the smell that pervaded most of his friends' bed-sits, cars and vans; the smell of every party and gig and festival. Hashish. Somebody had been smoking hash in here. His eyes rested on the inert, quietly snoring figure of his mother.

On the side-table was a screw of paper, some Rizla papers.

He had put her moods down to her going through middle age: not that he wanted to know anything about all that kind of stuff. Women were all so bloody complicated. How great it had all been when this room had been Ballard Quinlan's old-fashioned study. 'Traditional', Ballard used to say it was. It was great when the two mothers were friends: if one was out, the other would give the kids their tea. The men hated each other's guts, but that made no difference to the simplicity of the set-up. The animals went in two-by-two.

That was the time when it was all dreams and plans, everything was ahead. You were sure then that somebody, somewhere, had a plan for you, and you had this idea that, even if you messed about for a bit, eventually it would all work out right. It always did for people like they were. The plan was that you faffed around for a few years, everybody tore out their hair because you wouldn't get your head down at school, but by the time you were twenty-five or so, you were beginning to sort out the pieces; and by the time you were thirty, you were beginning to make it. All you had to do was to see that you didn't get some girl pregnant, and you kept out of the hands of the police. Since his accident he had spent a lot of time thinking about himself. In a queer sort of way, the accident had been just what he needed – an excuse to call a halt and see if there was any way he could climb out of the rock-music scene.

Tom had obeyed the rules, but the plan hadn't worked.

It bloody hadn't.

All that had happened was that he had turned out not a bad guitar player. He didn't know what else to do. He wrote not bad songs, played pretty good classical guitar and pretty good rock 'n' roll. But the Donovans and Baezes of the world had the philosophy sewn up, and Tom didn't want to be a ten-a-penny ballad performer, doing pub gigs like the thousands of flash-in-the-pan Beatles' and Stones' clones. He did a lot of one-night gigs, but the time spent on the road practically living in the van with the group was beginning to hold fewer attractions for Tom. But he could do nothing else. Go into the firm with Leo? Christ, he'd have to be starving before he'd do that.

He reached across and helped himself to the makings of a joint.

Great!

Leo Wilkinson sat on after the other Longmore guests had left the comfortable lounge. First Anoria and Villette came in with fresh coffee, then Mac with a plate of warm biscuits. 'Help yourself, man. These you won't get in Fortnum's.' The way he settled in an armchair, and the manner in which Nora and Vee treated him, confirmed what Leo had supposed earlier: that Mac was something more than the Longmore chef; but he could not for one second imagine Rose had any personal involvement with him. The thought of all that huge mass of black enveloping Rose's whiteness . . . I must be mad, he thought. I shall go back with more trouble on my mind than I came with.

Mac asked, 'How'd it go, Villy?'

'I hate being called Villy, you know that.'

'OK, Mizz Villette, ma'am. How went the bookings and things in general?'

Vee said, 'We got a booking from the local Lodge for some annual "do". They've always been to the Berestede before, but this time they've chosen us. We have to knock them cold so that they'll drop the Berestede next year too.'

Mac saluted. 'No problem, ma'am!' To Leo, 'Did you like our menu?'

'I thought it was very good. I can't understand why people aren't tumbling over themselves to book in here.'

'They will,' Vee said. 'They will.'

She sat serenely, her hair falling forward, covering one eye. She was so much like her mother that his gaze was constantly drawn to her. As he watched her, he saw other traits that she had inherited or learned from Rose: the way she held her cup, the way she sat slightly sideways with one foot beneath the other, the way her head described an arc as she raised it to look at someone. Such triggers to his memory began a process that could easily have ended, as it often did, with renewed desire and the pain of unfulfilment. Perhaps if they had got further that night and satisfied their curiosity about one another, he would not keep finding himself speculating.

Mac, breaking into Leo's reverie, said, 'I think Leo's tired; we should let him go to bed.'

'No, I'm fine. I was just thinking how splendid this place will be, and what a pity it is that, when Longmore *is* successful, this comfortable scene will be a thing of the past.'

Nora said, 'We have a big family room upstairs. There's a lot of work to be done on it, but Mum says she will never give that up.'

Vee said, 'She has this way-out notion that you can somehow run a top-flight hotel but keep it as a family home at the same time.'

Leo said, 'Maybe she would settle for less than top-flight . . . a family hotel, isn't that what the seaside brochures call them?'

Vee said, 'B and B?'

'Not necessarily, but something of good quality that is still the family home,' Leo said.

'Mum will never settle for anything less than Longmore having a reputation for being the very best,' Nora said.

'She's ambitious,' said Vee.

'Rose?' Leo raised his eyebrows. 'I'd have said she hadn't an ambitious bone in her body.'

'Whoever sees Mum's bones?' Nora asked. 'You know she never lets people see beneath her skin. Her face is all anyone ever sees. They say "God, that woman's beautiful", and that's who she is to them. But that's not who she is.'

'That sounds very profound,' Leo said. He wanted them to go on talking about Rose.

'Nah, not really. If I said "Handsome is as handsome does", you wouldn't call that a very profound thought.'

Mac spoke. 'The thing is, Nora my chile, Boss Lady *does* handsome too.'

'I wasn't saying that she didn't *do* handsome, I was merely pointing out that, because she has this face, nobody ever thinks she can be anything but ladylike, elegant and serene. There might be an absolute witch and a nymphomaniac behind it, but who'd believe it?' And, pointing at Villette, '*She's* the same. Miss Frosty Knickers.' She laughed, flinging herself back in her chair. 'I mean, can you imagine Vee doing a can-can?' She tossed her own skirts about and kicked her legs as Vee smiled indulgently. 'Let me ask you this, Uncle Leo. If you heard a rumour about one of the Quinlan girls screwing the staff . . .'

'Hey, hey,' Mac said, 'watch the language, and don't forget I'm staff.'

Nora waved him down with imperious fingers. 'You're family . . . what I was saying was that Uncle Leo would guess Becc or me.'

Leo flicked a glance to see how Villette reacted. She still smiled faintly, enigmatically – Rose when listening to one of Ballard's bawdy jokes. Liberal and broad-minded as Leo always thought himself to be, he could not get used to the way young people felt that they had to bring sex into every conversation. The press said that they were the 'Swinging Generation'.

In theory Leo was in favour of being able to talk, even joke about sex with the same openness as one could talk and joke about politics or religion. In practice, it wasn't so easy to hear the language which had once been confined to changing rooms, élitist literature and brothels, used by one's nicely brought-up children. But they *were* teaching the world to sing, to open up, to be laid back and to let it all hang out. And they did. Leo had seen a couple inside one another's clothes, fondling quite openly near the Science Museum of all places, and he, like the rest, had passed on by – in London in the Swinging Sixties. Magazines fell over themselves to print photographs taken at rock music festivals of girls with daisies painted around their nipples, and of bearded men, not all of them young, pictured dancing in sunshine and flower-wreath crowns. There were moves to make 'full frontals' acceptable. Why not? Perhaps it was true that journalists had thought up the term 'Swinging Sixties' in a wine-bar, and were now fleshing it out with tales of countrywide wife-swapping, orgies of sex and drugs, and a general wildness and liberation. Truth or fiction, the idea of liberated sex was having its effect, and the idea of a 'Swinging' nation was becoming self-fulfilling. People, taking the opportunity whilst it was going, went in for a bit of outrage. Skirts went as high as the crotch and as low as the ankle. Subtlety in colour was out: those clear primary *House and Garden* colours that had so enraptured Rebecca and shocked Winifred in the early fifties were used in fantastic combinations. Psychedelic colour, conjured up in pot smoke and on LSD trips. Women's hair could be head-hugging and sculpted, or hanging in pre-Raphaelite tresses, whilst sons of men who had worn the military crop during their compulsory National Service, confronted their father's outrage with shoulder-length hair or pony-tails. And they all talked about sex. And Leo found it not so easy to appear laid back about it. At least the Quinlan girls did not seem to be setting out to shock. Nora used 'screwing' in company as naturally as Monica would have used 'making love'.

Vee said, 'You are getting to your vulgar stage again, Nora; have you been at Mac's cooking sherry?'

Nora, with a grin, put two fingers up at her sister. 'I can hear Uncle Leo's mind clicking like mad – does she does? or does she don't? Does she does or does she don't?'

Mac consumed a few more of his biscuits and held the plate out to Leo. 'Take no notice, man, they get like this round about midnight. Which reminds me, Vill. Aren't you up pretty late if you're going to market? I know, that's your affair. OK. I'm for bed.'

'Me too, I have some notes to finish,' Nora said. 'Can't we leave the pots for once, Vee?'

'I'll see to them. I want to talk to Leo for a while.'

'Thanks, Vee, you're sweet. I promise I won't tell them who it is you screw on Sunday afternoons in the vestry, or Wednesday mornings at the garage, or . . .'

'Go to bed, Nora, you're just jealous.'

'I'm saving myself.'

'Just watch you don't go off. You'll be twenty before you know it.'

Mac said. 'I don't know what young folks these days is coming to. Night.' He touched his brow at Leo, then pointed six-shooter fingers at the two girls. 'Nora, you write to the Lady Boss tomorrow like you promised. Villy, if you don't bring home half a dozen bulbs of fennel, I'll have your ass.'

Nora clasped his arm and propelled him through the door more quickly than he had expected so that they collided, laughing.

Vee began to straighten cushions and collect cups.

Leo emptied an ashtray. 'I'll give you a hand.'

She did not protest politely that he was a guest. 'Thank you, that'd be nice, but I think I'll have just one more cup to keep me awake. It's still nice and hot.'

Leo looked at her questioningly. 'To keep you awake?'

'I have to make a start for Covent Garden in a couple of hours; it would be fatal going to sleep now.'

'No sleep at all? How will you manage tomorrow?'

'Quite well, actually. I do much better sleeping the odd couple of hours here and there when I want it, instead of being dictated to by convention. Winston Churchill did it, you know . . . Went to bed in the afternoon, stayed up all night.'

'Alone, I assume.'

She laughed soundlessly in Rose's way. 'History doesn't say. For all we know, Winston might have been a double-dyed letch being serviced by a Downing Street harem.'

She leaned across the arm of the sofa where he was seated to put his coffee on the table beside him; her hair, Rose fashion, fell in a gentle wave over her eye. Then, without a flicker, she suddenly changed tack and he felt her arms about his neck and her warm, lipsticked mouth pushing against his own as she subsided on to his lap. He let out his breath and heard a soft groan. It might have been himself or Vee. It was a quiet groan of satisfaction, of pleasure, of delight.

If she had intended it as a playful kiss, which, from the way her body pressed against him, was not likely, her intention soon changed as he responded, his desire inflating him so quickly that he was forced to lift her weight from him. He opened his lips slightly to draw breath, and at once she was inside him, pressing him into action, urging him. He felt overwhelmed as desire surged through him. He could not resist her. Did not want to. Did not try. Every male's fantasy of being seduced by a young, beautiful, experienced girl or boy made real. She faced him now, kneeling across his lap, holding his head between her hands and kissing him with shocking ferocity, saying things that he could only half hear between the moving of her mouth from one part of his face to another. When he tentatively slid his hand further than the tops of her stockings, she moved her skirt and unfastened her cami-knickers. Her thighs were warm and firm and more silken than the stockings. She was selfish and assertive. He knew he was being used, but would any man in his situation care?

He had had a fair number of sexual encounters, but none like this. None where a woman had so purposefully and forcefully seduced him. She pulled off his tie and unbuttoned his shirt. He was in good shape, glad that he had not been tempted to wear the vest Monica had put out for him.

The only audible words between them were, 'Christ, Vee!' and, 'Now, Leo!'

Mac, after initially wondering whether he should have done a bit more to get Vee out of the situation he could see developing, decided against it in favour of standing under the shower and letting the day's cooking fumes and kitchen aches flow out of him in the hot water. Vee was old enough to know what she was about. At least she took the Pill. He guessed that she would knock the poor bastard for six. He grinned. Once – and only once – she had tentatively tried it out on him, but no way was he having any. No way! It would be like fuckin' your own daughter. She was one hungry madam. Poor bastard.

The warm water relaxed and aroused him and made him think of Rose. Boss Lady. She was a lady. Top to toe, inside and out. Not because she had that great face, though that was pretty good for a white woman, but she had Class with a capital C. She was really the first woman he had ever met – white woman that is – the first who really, honestly, was not race-conscious. There were plenty of white women who fancied him, plenty who would sleep with him – had slept with him – but they always made him think that they did it because they wanted to try it with a black man, to see if it was true what they said about black studs. Mostly he preferred women of his own kind, with larger lips than the Boss Lady's thin streaks; he liked round asses and large breasts with big dark discs.

But what he felt about Rose was nothing to do with her body, and it sure wasn't her face. He'd been pretty young when he had seen his first white girl in the buff. He hadn't liked it that much: she had appeared kind of unfinished. She had stood there probably thinking, as white girls do, that she was sending him wild, but she had made him think of the outlines of people in kids' colouring-in books. So it wasn't Boss Lady's chassis. It was herself. He'd never admit it to anyone but himself, but it had been a bit like rescuing a stray kitten. He had seen that she was floundering about lost, so he had started by taking her under his wing, and she had stayed there, so that he never thought past the days when they'd be getting this place on its feet. Nobody else seemed aware of what she was like (except maybe Nora a bit); that she was half scared to death. She faced everything that was thrown at her with the kind of bravery that he wished he had himself. He wished she was here.

Until he'd come to Longmore, whenever things got tough, he had packed his bags and moved on. He had come here on a whim, and she had brought him up short. He would stay. Nobody was going to move him. She needed him. Not to defend her, that would be insulting, but she needed somebody she could rely on, rely on absolutely, somebody who wouldn't leave her, wouldn't let her down.

He relaxed into his big bed.

He was a damn good cook: that wasn't boasting, that was fact. Not a chef; he would never let himself be called chef, would never want to be that. He cooked food he liked to eat himself, and the day he couldn't cook a dish from start to finish without employing a sauce-maker or a pastry cook, that would be the day he would pack his hand in. He would make Longmore – *they* would make Longmore a name that would be known by people who knew what quality meant . . . Not just people with money, but ones whose eyes would light up when they thought of visiting Longmore.

He heard Nora come out of the guests' shower. He wondered whether Vee was giving Leo the time of his life: she was a cat on a hot tin roof, always on the move. She'd have to be more careful now that they were getting regular guests. Guests tended to wander about at all hours. He had come down late one night, and there she'd been in the room they called a writing room, one arm and one leg draped quite elegantly over the armchair. She had looked over the man's shoulder and winked at Mac. The French businessman who, not surprisingly, always stayed at Longmore on his business trips, had continued moving, had never known that Mac had been there. She was a real little tramp. And what he liked about her was that she never pretended that she wasn't. If people mistook her for anything else, that was their problem.

In his room on the floor below Mac, Leo went back over those amazing minutes. Somehow they had slid the few inches from upright into the depths of the sofa whilst in the process of kissing, and whilst he had explored her and she had explored him, he had tried to slow himself for her; but it had been she who had quickened the pace. She was not a virgin, not even a novice. Her vigorous exhalations had sounded loud in the room. The softer panting had been his own. He had looked up at her and saw that she was open-eyed and looking directly at him, and she had held his eyes right to the end. Watched him as she dug her nails into his skin. Watched him as she held on to his shoulders. Watched him until she arched her back. He could still feel where her nails had run a sparkling soreness, the very thought of which aroused him.

She had let out a long hissing breath from the back of her throat and commanded, 'Now!' For a short while, Vee had kept him pinned down, watching him, smiling, her skirt still awry, yet somehow managing to retain the same look of imperturbability that Rose possessed. She said, 'Lucky old Monica. That was better than any of the fantasies I ever had about you when I was fifteen.'

She had stood up then and he remembered holding her and saying 'Good God, Vee! What possessed me?'

'I did. Good, aren't I?'

He had said, 'Bloody fantastic,' whilst being vaguely aware as he stood there that he should be feeling some sort of remorse or guilt.

It seemed such a short time since she had been that schoolgirl who had come to Uncle Leo for comfort when old Sid Quinlan had dropped dead. But he did not feel guilty. Helen's friend . . . but their schooldays were gone and now she was a woman who knew as much about love-making as he did himself. Maybe she did screw the vicar and the garage hands. He could believe it.

Sonia Quinlan, three years old, known as Sunny, and as pretty as the large framed picture of her hanging over Grandma Birdham's mantelpiece, sat at the breakfast table eating her egg and dippits, totally unaware that she was at the centre, and the cause, of a great heart-rending debate between her father and mother. Not that it sounded heart-rending, for her mummy and daddy were aware of the possible lasting effect that quarrelling parents can have upon a child. Even so, Sonia's parents' differences were fundamental, and in Elna's case she was experiencing that age-old dilemma within marriage when spouse and parents are in opposition.

As far as Sonia was concerned, she was surrounded by people who were totally loving; who had been put upon the earth to make her life as pleasant as possible. This wasn't far from the truth. The trouble, although Sonia did not know it yet, was that Grandma Birdham had come humbly to her daughter, begged her forgiveness, and cried at the idea of Sonia being denied the ultimate happiness of one day being with them all in paradise. But her daddy thought that she might achieve greater happiness in her earthly life if she was free of any guilt and repression – which he was convinced was all that she would receive if she was brought up within any of the religions.

'No!' Jonathan said. 'We're not going all through that again. I thought we had settled your mother's hash once and for all. It's that bloody old priest of hers. I'm not going to agree, so you may as well tell your mother to back off.'

'What harm can it do, Jon? She's trying very hard to make amends. You were baptized . . . I was.'

'I was christened, and just like pretty well everything else that was done to me in my childhood, I had no say in the matter. I was sent to any school they thought fit: nobody asked me what I wanted. I was never asked about my choice of clothes, or my name. And this from a father who was always sounding off about freedom of the individual. Sunny is an individual; she's going to make her own decisions.'

'OK, so you had parents like the rest of us. I sometimes wonder whether you believe you're the only child with an overbearing parent. Sunny can always reject religion if she wants to. You have. It's not as though they want her to be tattooed or circumcised or have a ring through her ear.'

'Elna, can you hear yourself?' She was putting on her lipstick ready for work, but he forced her to turn away from the mirror and face him. He suspected that Mrs Birdham had been visiting Elna far more often than he had been told of, and that Elna was being got at. 'That is precisely what they do want. They want her to grow up with her mind tattooed with their particular variety of God. It's not *their* particular religion I object to, it is every sort of religion. Sunny is not going to be baptized or christened or be admitted to a coven or join a sect or society until she knows a bit about it and is able to make up her own mind. I don't want her filled with mumbo-jumbo, her hands filled with beads, or her to be taught cannibalism with bits of bread and drops of wine. When she's old enough she can ask your mother and anyone else she likes why they do all this stuff, but Sunny is our child, and we've agreed that she should have the best we can give her. Giving her prejudices is not best.'

'It's just tradition, and wanting her to be part of something, part of a community.'

'The black community.'

'Not necessarily.'

'How many white people are there in Reverend Revelation's church?'

'She will grow up without roots, belonging nowhere.'

'My God, you've changed your tune. Can't you remember it was your bloody roots that split us up, and if it hadn't been for Mac we might have stayed split up. What if in the thirties your dad's roots had been in National Socialist movement?' He couldn't help smiling, his father-in-law Frank Birdham's colour was very dark. 'For sake of argument, would you have said it was all right for him to take her to meet his Nazi comrades?'

'And what about the kindergarten you want her to attend?'

'What about it?'

'How many children there were black?'

'For God's sake, Elna, what sort of a question is that?'

Without noticing that she had not rewound it, she jammed the cover back on to her lipstick and squashed it. 'Now look what you've done.'

He took the lipstick pieces from her and threw them into a waste-paper bin. 'Oh, come here.' He drew her, at first unwillingly, into his arms, and stood hugging and rocking her until she responded and gripped him tightly. 'Sweetheart, we must be nuts, getting daggers-drawn over our own baby. You remember? The one we said we would move heaven and earth for, to see she wasn't at a disadvantage because of other people's prejudice?'

Elna smiled wryly as she indicated that Jonathan should look at the solemn, yolk-smeared child who was earnestly engaged on the task of picking up bits of slippery white in her fingers and balancing them on her spoon before transferring them to her mouth, because she had been taught to use a spoon to eat her egg. 'Clever girl, Sunny. Look, Daddy.'

Jonathan said, 'I'll go and see them if you like. And I will tell them about the baptism thing . . . All right, I'll be nice and sensitive. How would it be if we let them take her to church at Easter, but not more often than that. She can even have a hat with flowers, and let's hope that Sunny can get it all in perspective. She can go to see Santa Claus in Hamley's and sing carols at Christmas; and see the preacher man and sing gospel at Easter.'

On his way to his office, through the thawing streets, Jonathan Quinlan went over in his mind what he would say to his in-laws. Why do I still feel that I am seven? There's a brave boy, Jon. It was a sad thing about modern, Western men: no rites of passage. Even so, he smiled to himself. He no more relished this interview than any in the past with his own father or his authoritarian housemaster – but I'm getting better at it. Not a lot, but better. Do old men still feel like little boys? Was that why they blustered and demanded their way through life? As he walked, he played over several possible scenes with Elna's mother. His thoughts returned to Elna: he wondered how she would feel about another baby. Perhaps it was too soon. He had been surprised to discover that babies were themselves, right from day one, and guessed that he might become a bit of a bore on the subject of how early human beings developed their own unique characteristics. If they had a lot of children . . .

He wished that he saw Tom more often these days. They had always been able to talk to one another. Tom was a good mate. Maybe he'd get him up for a weekend, have a few sessions like the old days, go to Ronnie Scott's and take Becc. Which reminded him . . . Becc had said that their father might be getting Petersfield, the safest seat the Tories had. Honeywood was in that constituency. Superman: with one mighty leap he went from Labour's smallest majority to one of the Tories' largest. Of course it might not be true, but their father certainly seemed to have pull these days.

That same day, Sally Joffe had visited the rambling workshop overlooking the cutting room where Rebecca's Mayfly range was made up. As she always did on her visits to Becc, she poured herself some coffee from the ever-ready electric filter, and perched on one of the draughtsman's stools. Rebecca recognized her friend's mood, which was one of excitement badly disguised as nonchalance. It usually meant ideas for expansion.

'OK, Princess, spill the beans.'

Sally sent signals indicating the girls who were pinning white muslin skirt-panels to a dressmaker's dummy.

'Put that stuff down, it's been stewing for hours. Come on, let's go. It's time for a bagel and chocolate.'

Sally slid off the stool and patted her own behind. 'Definitely no chocolate.'

It was ten in the morning; the little café was empty.

'Did you get a call from your mother?' Sally asked.

'No, but Jon did. She's fine. No problems. Nice hotel. People fussing over her, she says.'

'No luck with finding her old nanny?'

'She's probably dead ages ago. Mum should forget all that and get herself off down to Durban or the Cape and kick her heels for a few weeks.'

'I wish she had not gone. Those goons are devious, they probably have her name on some list.'

'Oh come *on*, Sally. Your goons aren't likely to see a middle-aged woman as a threat to their régime.'

'Middle age has nothing to do with it; woman has nothing to do with it. They put people away in that country.'

'Oh shut up, Sally, you'll give me the jitters if you go on like that. She's there! End of story. Now, what is so secret that you couldn't whisper it in front of my girls?'

'Everybody knows that there's no better place than Mayfly's design room for gossip.'

Becc took a flattened pack of Rothman's from her pants pocket, took out two crushed cigarettes, and handed one to Sally who waved it away. 'Wonders will never cease,' said Becc.

'I thought you had given up. Do you know how bad this is for your health? My doctor tells me it can shorten your life by five years.'

'She says bad for *my* health? Shorten *my* life? I should take Princess King-size Joffe's advice?' Becc had been in the company of Sally and Aze for so long that there were times when her gestures were totally Jewish.

'I have given it up. That is what I have come to tell you.'

'And this is what she could not say in front of my girls? I promise you they will not go spilling that secret to Marks and Sparks for their autumn range.'

Sally bit into a golden bagel with her large ivory teeth and said with her mouth full, 'I'm pregnant.'

Becc looked at her friend over her frothy chocolate. 'Don't talk with your mouth full: that last word sounded like "bun in the oven".'

'And like "up the spout" and "in the club", sweetheart.' Sally reached across and clasped Becc's hands, half closed her eyes, and looked like the cat that got the cream. 'He's the best gynae in Harley Street. He knows a bun when he feels one. I'm three months gone.'

Becc felt the cold dryness of Sally's clutching fingers, knowing well what lay behind that attempt at jocularity. 'Is one allowed to dance and shout and hire a plane to write it across the sky?'

Tears sparkled and threatened Princess's mascara and fashionable black eye-liner. 'Not until I've told Aze.'

'Aze doesn't know yet?'

'Of course Aze doesn't know. Do you hear the town-crier? Is it on the hoardings yet? He didn't believe he could do it. I wanted to tell you.'

'Oh, Sal.'

'I wanted to hear how it sounded. I just heard it the once so far. Doctor Grossman, that's my gynae, he said, "Nothing wrong with you, Mrs Joffe. Everything's fine; that's a baby you have in there." I said to him, "Are you sure?" He said, "You want a second opinion?" "No." I said, "but I'm thirty-three. Couldn't it be my age?" "Age?" he said, "you have time for six brothers and sisters." "Six?" I said, "Have a care for my poor Aisa, he is sixty almost." "Sixty is a good age to become a father," he said.'

Becc could only guess at the huge excitement that Sally was trying to hide with her flippancy. Sally and Aze had everything in the world except the one thing they really wanted. And now they would get it. Rebecca said, 'Sally Joffe is pregnant. Is that what you wanted to hear?'

Sally pressed her smiling lips together. 'Say it again.'

'Hey, have you heard the latest? The Princess is in the pudding club. OK, now go and find Aze.'

'He'll want to buy train sets and dolls' houses, and ponies and pedal-cars.'

'But no clothes. Absolutely no clothes. Auntie Becc will do the clothes.' Becc crushed out her half-smoked cigarette and straightened out another one, rolling it with restless fingers. 'Tell Aze, we are going into baby-wear.' She snapped her fingers and drew small outlines on the opened-out cigarette packet. 'What do you think? No whites and no blues or pinks. Primary colours! No buster suits, no tucks and frills. Look at this . . . lovely big, baggy things that open up everywhere. Wow! And what about a maternity range? Tell Aze . . .'

'I'll just tell Aze that he hit the right button, I'll leave you to tell him that his baby will wear a red dhoti.'

Rebecca laughed, because she felt glad about the baby, and because she always felt elated when a revolutionary idea burst upon her. She would make Sally stunning clothes, not to hide her pregnant shape, but to complement it.

Within a couple of months, a full-page picture of 'Princess Joffe, a golden-haired honey looking like a glamorous queen bee, wearing tapered trousers and an enormously baggy brushed angora sweater in yellow and black hoops', would appear in the *Daily Mirror*.

'Queen Bee' designs would create a look that would lift Rebecca out of the mainly London and Carnaby Street market and into the international league. Queen Bee would establish Becc Quinlan as one of the long-distance runners among the hundreds of creators of fashion that came and went in London in the Swinging Sixties. By the end of the year, in the USA, Queen Bee would have been featured in *Harper's Bazaar* and *Vogue* magazine. An article, 'Proud to be Pregnant', would begin a trend away from the generations of women who were expected to wear discreet camouflage. In her eighth month, Princess Joffe would hit the headlines again by appearing on the beach in Cannes in her full glory wearing a 'fantastic gold Lurex bathing suit by Queen Bee Fashions.'

Becc Quinlan would be the lasting fashion name of the Swinging Sixties.

Ballard stood looking down at his wife who was seated in one of the extraordinary-looking chairs in a glassy room full of plants, which the interior designer called an 'antre' which, as far as Ballard could recall, meant a kind of cave. There was nothing less cave-like. This was not the modern flat in town where they had lived when they were first married; this was a very pretty house at Richmond where they now lived most of the time . . . at least Miriam lived there most of the time; Ballard used the town flat for four nights a week when the House was in session. Miriam really felt more at home in Richmond. Lots of her chums were around, she rode in the park and kept a couple of dogs and, on the whole, it felt much more like home.

'But you can't be!'

When she put on that sassy look he often felt like slapping her. Rebecca used to do that. The look said: See if I care.

He had seen Rebecca recently. Quite accidentally in Regent Street. She had stopped and said, 'Hello, Dad, what are you doing out on the streets without your Roller? Slumming?' and stood waiting to see what would happen. They had both behaved very well, considering it was Becc, and considering that her eyes were made up to resemble a princess of ancient Egypt, plus her beige lips, and the extraordinary clothes she wore . . . He had enquired about her business and she had quoted the bottom line of her accounts, which was probably true if the collection of heavy gold bangles half-way up her arm was anything to go by. Ballard recognized the assurance that comes with prosperity. Becc was prosperous. He felt really quite proud that she had turned out to be a chip off the old block. She had asked if he liked being with the Conservatives and he had said that they weren't as stuffy as the other lot. She had laughed and said she knew what he meant, and that only Castro's men knew how to open up. He had not asked how she came to know that. He had offered to take her somewhere – lunch perhaps? but she had said no, that she had some fabrics to show to some shop in Bond Street. He had said how glad he was they'd bumped into one another like this, and she had said that she would tell the others and oh, did he know that Mum had inherited quite a lot of money and had gone off on a trip to South Africa and was having a whale of a time. 'Vee reckons Mum is having the time of her life screwing around in the sun. Maybe that's Vee's imagination because she'd like to do it. But still, you couldn't blame Mum: she knocks men cold when she comes up here.' Becc knew how to wind one up.

Now Miriam said, 'I can be and I *am*. I've been to my gynae and he says that I am five months' pregnant.'

'Five! But you said that you had missed your period because you had been on the starvation diet.'

'Apparently not. Actually I missed *four* and I missed because I'm expecting a *baby*.'

'I thought this Pill was supposed to be one hundred per cent . . .'

'Ninety-five.'

'And you are one of the five per cent. Oh right! Just my luck.'

'My *man* says I'm probably a very *fertile* type and that you are particularly *potent.*' She smiled up at him. 'I have always said that you are, and we do do it quite a lot; much, much more than my chums.'

'We don't want a baby. I've already reproduced myself four times; any more is irresponsible in a world that's already overpopulated.'

'Five times.'

He didn't respond.

'Ballard, I *want* this baby. If I don't have it I shall not be a very *nice* person to live with. You have your children and I want *mine*. It's not too much to ask, seeing what happened last time.'

But it was too much to ask. All that he had wanted was a simple, quiet life, with no problems about money or sex or winning elections. And he had got it all. His agency couldn't be more successful; the armaments consortium was a licence to print money; Mimi had been the best little sex-pot he had ever known; and, in crossing the floor of the House, he had negotiated for himself one of the Tory plum seats – not Petersfield, that would have been too much to hope for, but one with a majority large enough not to need constant nursing between elections.

Images of Rose absorbed in the life of the child, Rose tired from not sleeping, Rose with a child sucking breasts which had been his own pleasure. Chaos. Sleeplessness. No spur-of-the-moment sex.

It was too much to ask.

Was it any wonder he didn't want this baby?

Charlotte Quinlan thought how nice it was to have a man about the house again. He was a little younger than herself – about seventy-nine – and spry and clean. That was what she had always liked about Sid: he was always changing his socks and washing his hair. Well, Frank was like that. He had come canvassing and she had said, 'I thought you'd have finished with all that,' and he said, 'I shan't never finish fighting capitalism till the day I die.' So, finding a fellow liberal thinker (though a bit more to the left than herself), she had asked him in for a cup of coffee, and had been pleased when he had accepted her offer for a nip in it.

That had been weeks ago. They had been out for a trip or two together. He had pruned her privet-hedge and it was growing back lovely and young now. He lived in Petersfield, but he still drove his car, and one Sunday had come out to fetch her and had cooked her a roast beef lunch. He had no children; Charlotte showed him her photo albums and he had talked about his deceased wife and Lotte had talked about Sid and about all the old people there must be rattling around in great big houses (his wasn't as big as Lotte's, but big for a widower on his own). Lotte couldn't remember now how they really got down to deciding that it wouldn't be a bad idea to get together.

'A trial, say for about a month,' Frank had suggested.

'Like coming on holiday. A couple of months . . . it takes that to get settled in,' Lotte had said.

'Fair enough.'

And so it had come about. Frank did the man's work, the things Sid used to do – washers, oiling hinges, clearing out the duck-house – whilst Lotte went back to making nice pies and doing a decent-sized leg of lamb. And she helped him keep his membership books. They decided on Lotte's house because Frank had always fancied living a bit out in the country.

Frank Rogers knew all about Ballard: he had known him when he had had the gall to make his slogan at one election 'Man of the People'. Outside Lotte's presence, Frank would call him all the turn-coats under the sun, but he knew that Lotte had already been upset by that episode.

Frank, having lived alone for too long, had silent conversations with himself: it helped to sort things out. He would be civil enough to him if the turn-coat ever came to visit his grandmother which, according to Lotte, he didn't do much of these days. Quinlan's student daughter, Nora, had come to visit Lotte, and he had taken to her at once. A nice, practical girl who had got straight on with making the coffee and washing a salad. It was obvious she had come to tell Lotte something, so Frank had made himself scarce and went down the pub for an hour. As he walked along the winding road, he thought about how much he had got to love living in the village; as he kept saying to Lotte, he had found his spiritual home. He hoped that it would work out for them. He had never expected to get this much enjoyment out of life at his age. He certainly never expected to have the comfort of a nice warm soft body next to him at nights. He thought they might make a go of it. He quite liked being called Frank – his wife had always said Francis, which Frank thought didn't suit him at all.

He decided he'd ask her if she would like them to get married. They were old-fashioned. They weren't exactly living in sin, but there was more to it than being Lotte's lodger. It would be nice if they did. 'Commitment', that was the new word youngsters used a lot. And a good thing: too many running the country without any . . . He'd have to make it clear than he didn't want anything to do with Lotte's money: she was pretty comfortable by the seem of it, even though she passed on fair old amounts. She made him smile sometimes: 'We paid our taxes all our lives, me and Sid, and I think that's fair enough. I don't want to have to pay it all over again in death duties and that, so I shall pass it on while I can.'

Frank had a family now, the first one he'd ever had. Of course, he didn't have as much cash as Lotte, but what was left when he was gone he would leave to the little ones. All Jon's at the moment, none of the girls seemed keen to get themselves any babies. Funny old business that. Lotte didn't seem to see anything in it – Jon with a big family and the girls with none. 'Give them time, Frank,' she said. Frank didn't think she realized that they were all getting on now. But there, it'd be a queer world if everybody was the same.

Rose was in the third week of her visit to South Africa, and although she had scoured the city on foot and by car, she had still not seen much that she recognized from her childhood. But she had discovered a down-town shopping area that she recognized. It wasn't the kind of place her parents would have taken her – perhaps Ayah . . . ? She had tried every avenue Angela Brazenose had thought up.

Angela had worked hard at helping in what she would refer to as 'Rose's Quinlan's quest', and had introduced her to several contacts who had access to records; but the best lead had been given by the housemaid, Joyce, whose job it was to look after Rose's suite at the Cranbourne. Joyce, to whom Rose had related her story, said that if Fatima was Indian and had lived in Alexandria Township, then it might not be too difficult to discover her. Joyce, who had rarely been confided in by a guest, and who had never seen a white woman make a roll-up, gradually opened up to Rose and said that, if the medam would like, her boyfriend might help. She had a good boyfriend who worked in the records at the Jo'burg Bantu Office. With assurance she had said, 'Daniel will find, medam. He is a filing clerk. He is all day filing records. He will know where these records may be.'

In addition to Angela, Joyce, and Daniel the good boyfriend, those of Angela's friends who had access to information in any way, or were friends of someone who did, all took up what they saw as a romantic cause. Rose was a South African who had come home to discover her true origins and the mystery of her missing years of childhood, the secret of which was held by her old nanny.

Once Rose had made her daily telephone calls to any 'leads' she might have, there was little she could do except to explore the city or drive out from it in her hired car. She discovered – and in some cases rediscovered – the high veldt, and fell in love with its bleak grandeur. Over the days she had become more and more adventurous, going out into the sparsely inhabited veldtland, driving along the packed-earth roads, throwing up clouds of red dust in her wake.

It was the open veldt and the kopjes she remembered best, and her heart would leap when some well-buried memory sprang out.

Butcher-birds with their grisly larders, great bushes of protea flowers looking like artichokes which had been through Walt Disney's hands. Dust devils whirling across the flat earth, mirages of lakes and distant vehicles that appeared to hover a foot above hard-topped roads shimmering in the afternoon heat. And the sound of thunder and the deafening, torrential four o'clock rain, large drops hitting corrugated roofs, sounding like machine-guns firing. But the roads that gushed and flooded became dry within an hour.

She saw yoked oxen ploughing, and remembered being driven out by her father to a sight that would soon be history, yet was still not.

In Pretoria she saw families of Afrikaner farmers who seemed still set in the time of her own childhood, and probably even further back than that. Still dressing in best black on Sundays, the men in tall black hats, women with their hair covered by black squares and wearing long black dresses. At the new Voortrekker museum she saw them now as she had seen them then, picnicking as their ancestors had once laagered in large, close circles, eschewing the rustic picnic tables and benches, choosing the ground in preference. Now, though, it was mostly the middle-aged and old people who wore the best black; the younger element among the men had bare knees and the girls wore floral dresses. One thing she remembered was that her father had never referred to them as anything other than Damnboors.

She took reel after reel of photographs, and kept a rough notebook, and although so many sights that she had entirely forgotten flooded back, there was nothing that told her anything about herself. She might have been looking at a travel film for all the emotion she felt.

As a change from searching the older parts of the city and the tin-roofed suburbs, she took to looking around the new housing estates which were growing up on the perimeter of the city. She wondered where Ron and Bridgette would choose to settle: there was so much to choose from. The architecture was wonderful. Adventurous in the extreme, expansive glass and white walls, no two houses alike. The gardens were professionally designed and would have won medals at the summer show at Chelsea. Often she came across something – such as where a fine tree had been left standing and the house built around it – that caused her to wonder why it was that all architects did not have that same approach to building, which was to make everything as beautiful as possible. Most of the estates she looked at were middle-income houses, yet they were beautiful and affordable; Bridgette and Ron would be very happy here.

It was only after she had mulled it over on her long drives that she saw the reality of why luxury was so cheap compared to back home – cheap and plentiful labour which meant cheap and plentiful materials as well. Of course the architect could build a house around a tree.

She wondered how Ron was getting on in his new job. She had the address of the hotel where they were staying, except that it turned out not to be a hotel but a hostel where immigrants could stay whilst they looked around for accommodation. When Rose had asked Angela where Hillbrow was, Angela had raised her eyebrows and said, 'Half-way to hell – it's the place where there are flats where funny couples can live and no questions asked. They say it's the most densely populated area in the whole world.' And Ron had thought that it sounded like quite a nice part of the city, Hillbrow. Who wouldn't think that? Angela had said, 'If you really want to see them, why don't you say you'll meet them in one of the parks, or the zoo. Everybody goes to the zoo: there's a nice place to eat. I guess they might not be too happy you seeing where they are putting up.'

Rose put it off and put it off. She still meant to ring them to see how they were, but she seemed never to have a moment. Of course she had: she spent her days driving in all directions, Pretoria, Krugersdorp, the Hartebeestport Dam, Boksburg and many small places that reminded her of Hollywood frontierstowns, but not of anything to do with the blank years of her childhood. Her Johannesburg Handbook for January/February invited her to take a 'tour of Soweto any day of the week' by contacting the Non-European Affairs Department, but this she never had the courage to do.

She wrote home: '. . . if the city council wants tourists to visit Soweto, then I have a feeling that the townships about which I should like to know are those (like the one I saw on my way from the airport) we are *not* invited to see.' It was Mac who had replied, 'Maybe you ought to be a little more circumspect about what you write. Letters go astray, and you and Sally J. have been involved in one or two skirmishes, haven't you?'

She should have thought of that. Mac always knew what he was talking about. From then on she mostly wrote variations on, 'It's a great country. I'll tell you more when I get back.'

On most days when she got back from her outings, she had to change and go on to something Angela Brazenose had fixed. Sunday tea with some ex-pat, a visit to see *Cleopatra* at His Majesty's bioscope, bowling at the Moon, dancing at the Coconut, a Sunday visit to the Kyalami Grand Prix, music in the 'Wits' concert hall (that same Witwatersrand university against which she and Sally had joined in a protest when it had expelled its black undergraduates), or sundowners on somebody-or-other's stoep – 'bring your swimsuit' – the stoep often turning out to be blue terrazzo with matching mosaic pool and uniformed 'girl' or 'boy' to pour the drinks.

After a fortnight of this, instead of feeling part of a fast-living set, Rose began to feel as though she was back living in Honeywood, because she kept meeting the same group of people in different combinations. She was always asked, on meeting someone new, 'What do you think of South Africa?' The implication was that apartheid – or separate development, which was the preferred term – was not understood outside the country. She knew that the answer they expected was 'It's wonderful. Plenty of everything . . . and no tax on cigarettes and drink. And the sun. You're all so tanned and prosperous.' But she could not bring herself to say that. Even so, what would be the good of telling the truth, which was that it was all very much more difficult to take than she had expected it would be.

One evening Angela picked her up after a day during which Rose ended up with yet more white 'Maudie' boxes being delivered to the Cranbourne. 'It's simple: just a very friendly and laid-back evening brei at the Borgmans. They've just got back from a visit home to Sweden. He's my orthodontist, and she is so nice – and wooo, so sexy with it. Dr Pedr Borgman and Nana. I suppose where you come from they'd be called a "swinging" couple. Man, is our Pedr a looker? Just right for that new peachy number you bought today. He'll try to make out with you, you're his type. Wish I was.'

Rose, only half listening said, 'I'll wear the green. I can't think when I will wear it back home.'

Angela, who longed to know about the men in Rose's life said, 'It will make some man very happy,' but Rose was as clam-tight about any lovers as ever. Her brother-in-law was no help: all that Angela had been able to discover was that Rose had been married to somebody in their Government, there had been a bit of a scandal with his secretary, and now they were divorced. Angela thought it a crying shame that a woman like that should be on the market and not spoken for. For sure Pedr Borgman wouldn't let grass grow beneath his feet, but there was nothing to be gained there: he and Nana had such a good arrangement that there was no point in them ever changing it.

Neither Maudie nor Angela had understood why Rose had behaved so strangely and taken so strongly against that beautiful white Greek goddess gown with a swathed bodice and tiny buttons:

as Maudie had said, it had been made for just that classic type of face and figure.

There had been two other women in the fitting room, both of whom had succumbed to the latest 'bikini' treatment. Their hairless pubic areas looked incongruously pre-pubescent. Rose was so surprised by their giggling and the crudity with which they compared what the treatment had revealed, that Maudie had the gown on and fastened before Rose saw her own reflection. She had blenched and was momentarily confused as her mind was flung back almost twenty years. The crude words as Ballard told her of his intention, the unvarnished coarseness of what he thought he had a right to do, the brandy fumes on his breath, the popping of the tiny buttons, the tearing, the strong fabric biting into her flesh, and then his cruel, searing penetration.

'No!' She tried to unbutton buttons that did not undo because they were decoration. Panicking. 'No, I don't want anything at all like this.' Maudie, taken aback at the first assertive opinion this client had ever made, quickly unzipped her at the back before the gown was damaged.

The result of the embarrassing episode was that Rose had bought three expensive dresses, one of which was a piece of strange, greeny silk that was twisted and pleated into Maudie's most expensive model gown.

The Borgmans turned out, as Angela had promised, to be a handsome expatriate Swedish couple who lived in Houton, the greenest of the lush suburbs. Pedr was probably about forty, and Nana maybe five years younger. When he came to greet Rose, a thrill of shock caused her momentary confusion and shallow breath: not because of his reputed sexiness – which was apparent; nor because he was 'a looker' – he was that. Her first, fleeting impression was of Leo, so much so that she had a moment of confusion. Same height, same lean torso, hard brown legs, longish fair hair, fine, thin face. He and Leo had come from the same mould.

The barbecue was more like a Texan barbecue than a traditional breifleish. There was no bok or dik-dik slung over an open fire; instead the beefsteaks which dripped on to the charcoal burner were thick and heavy, as were the generously topped-up vodka glasses – the kind of thing, no doubt, that Ron and Bridgette expected. Any excuse for a party being the motto, this one was said to be given in honour of Rose having returned to the land that had given her birth, but Rose guessed that in this circle any other excuse would have served as well.

When Rose showed an interest, Nana took her on a tour of the house. Like many that she had seen on her drives, this was large, airy and the work of imaginative architects who had very few restraints put upon them in the way of plot-size, budget or labour.

'Somebody else who likes to read,' Rose said. 'This is the first house in Johannesburg that I've been into with any books with actual words: most people seem to like the big coffee-table ones.'

'People do read.' She made a moue and a good try at the loud South African voice of the Angela type. '"I rrillly like good 'tec mystery, man. Something you can get your teeth into, make you think." The story about your connection with the Contessa books makes them wild about you.'

Rose smiled at the send-up of the Angela types.

'I think it must be all this sun. Only three months of the year to curl up with a good long book.' The Borgmans' selection was so catholic that they could only have arrived on the shelves because somebody wanted to read them.

Nana went off to change into her swimsuit, handing Rose over to her husband's care with the remark, 'She *reads*, Pedr . . . I mean, *books with words*, man!' Angela had said that the Borgmans were faintly Pinko but their mild, side-swiping remarks about the local bureaucracy were pretty uncontentious. Even so, the conversation was open enough for Rose to answer the ubiquitous question, 'What do you think of things out here?' with a bit more honesty than usual, saying that she wondered how long this way of life could possibly last.

Back in the garden, where the lights were now alive with moths and bugs, Pedr said to his wife, 'Nana, when you've had your dip, why not show Rose your night garden.'

'Of course. But I have to see Oscar about the steaks just now . . . I thought you would like to, darling, there are some new windchimes you haven't heard. You'll love it, Rose, the moonflowers are at their peak just now. Show her, Pedr, show her.' She dived as straight and true as a professional, her long, slender body dividing the surface water smoothly.

Rose said, 'I wish that I could do that. So elegant.'

He laughed, picking up their two glasses and leading the way into the garden. 'Nana would take it as a compliment to hear you say that. The girls here think that it is you who are the tops when it comes to that. Your reputation goes before you.'

'As the Merchant said to Bassanio,' Rose said, only because nothing else came to mind.

'And a blue-stocking to boot.'

'Heavens no. That's the last thing. I never went to school, so it was probably Bassanio who said it to the Merchant.'

'Not any kind of school at all?'
'No.'
'How come you can throw a bit of Shakespeare around in such an off-handed manner?'
'I suppose it must be because I grew up with a lady whose head was always in a book, and she drew mine in with it.'
'You are out here on a quest to find your old nanny?'
'How did you know that?'
'Everyone knows. This is a village, and Angie is the town-crier.'
'Angela has been very good. She intends me to . . . I think she says "fulfil my quest".'
He laughed. 'Of course. Overseas visitors are the abiding interest. Tell me about this lady of yours who got you to enjoy having your head in a book so much.'
'Miss Chaice? I've never thought of it before, but I suppose she was another kind of ayah; at least she substituted for the mother I had lost.'
'Such tragedies always sound romantic in the telling.'
'Actually, Threnody was a romantic.'
'Ach, what a name.'
'It means "a lament". I have wondered whether that was her real name: she had a tragic lost love, and later she wrote books under the name Lammente.'
'Was she a good ayah?'
'She was much more than that; it was only in later years that I came to realize what an extraordinary woman she must have been. I landed up in my Aunt Fredericka's house, and Aunt Fredericka passed me over to Threnody Chaice. It was she who left me a bequest to come here.'
They stepped through a narrow gate made of iron. Just beyond it, water was being pumped in a lively flow over a pebble-bedded stream, over rocks that looked as though they had been part of the garden since time began, and into a small pool. By the light of concealed lamps shining through arching ferns, they paused to look. Rose said, 'This is really beautiful. The light seems to be natural daylight on the water, yet here it is quite dark. It reminds me of looking at a tank in an aquarium.'
'This is where Nana's night garden starts. This is her name for it.'
'She is obviously very creative.'
'Her substitute for children.'
'I should find it hard to be without mine.'
'We should like children. You must come again, in the daylight, and see the rest of the garden.'

'I thought she seemed reluctant to show me.'

'She was, but not reluctant for you to see it. Quite the reverse. You would not parade your children for others to approve, but you would wish them to see and to compliment you?'

'That is true.'

'Come.' He took her hand.

How comfortable she felt with a man who was a stranger to her until a couple of hours ago. Was it because he reminded her so much of Leo? A sensitive and relaxing man. Amiable, interested in her opinion, and apparently not eager to prove any male superiority. Like Trevelyan. Yes, rather like Trevelyan, too, with whom she had walked hand in hand beneath the trees of the New Forest. Very different trees from the ones in this garden. Pedr Borgman was the epitome of a Swede, had a body that had known a healthy childhood, good teeth and skin, clean-cut features and fine blond hair.

There were some very nice men. Leo, Trevelyan, Mac . . . McKenzie the gentle giant; and Pedr Borgman: she was sure he would prove to be nice. Why was it that she had fallen for Ballard's skin-deep charm? Why had she been so eager for the first man who came along? Inexperience because she was so young? Maybe. Perhaps in other circumstances, or with another woman, Ballard had another character, one that Rose had not been able to draw out. She had allowed him to dominate her without realizing that this was what he was doing – until it was too late. Perhaps he too was nice and she had brought out the worst in him.

They came to another patch of light, where he halted her by slipping his hand into the crook of her elbow and leaving it there, friendly and cool. These lights were bright, and directed towards a life-size classical statue of a woman set beneath an old and low-branched Indian bean tree. Her gauzy stone drapes, caught by the breeze, revealed the full breasts and belly of her figure; one foot lifted, her step springy and light, she looked as though she might just step towards them with the offering she held in a shawl.

'Nana's latest. "Flora". Isn't she a delight?'

'Ah . . .'

'She's new here.'

'One would hardly know.'

'Nana has some secret method of ageing stone. I believe it's yoghurt.'

'Yoghurt isn't easy to get in England. My secret with new brick-work or stone is to paint it with a solution of cow-dung.'

He laughed aloud. 'We don't have many cows in the northern suburbs.'

'You are not far from the zoo.'

'I somehow think that Nana will stick to her yoghurt.' He paused. 'You said, "Ah" when I called her Flora. You were going to say something, but you are much too English and well-mannered to tell me that I am wrong.'

'I was probably going to put my foot in it. I only ever have my rag-bag of bits of information to go on . . . no education, as I said.'

'But you do not agree that she is Flora?'

'She may be Pomona, but it's no big deal, most people call female garden statues Flora. I should stop myself from being picky and pedantic.'

'But since I asked, and she may not be Flora, and Nana would never forgive herself for getting her name wrong, we shall have to get it right, because she's really so delighted with this – she calls this "Flora's Grove". So whose grove is it?'

'I think, perhaps, Pomona's.'

He eagerly tugged her towards the statue. 'Tell me. Tell me why?'

'Well, if she *was* Flora, then she would not be bringing fruits. Flora was the goddess of spring blossom and flowering plants; she would be holding a bunch of flowers. But look at her, these are fruits.' He made her guide his hand over the shapes. He nodded, a faint smile on his mouth.

Ill-ease crept over her at the beginnings of the arousal he was causing in her. Brightly, she chattered on, 'Pomona, goddess of fruits, has been harvesting in the grove and filled her shawl with her pickings. See, they are about to tumble out, they are plentiful. A good omen. She's saying that there will be a good harvest.' Rose let her hand run up the woman's cool marble leg, along the drapes of her skirt, up to her shawl and the fruits, where she encountered Pedr's warm fingers, which clasped hers again as he stepped back and led the way on along the narrow path. Rose paused and looked back. 'Isn't that beautiful? Your wife is talented to set it right there.'

She felt his grip upon her fingers tighten slightly, as though he was about to say something, but he did not, and they walked on, sipping their drinks as they walked, she enjoying the male hand holding hers, the smell of swimming pool, his shaving lotion and fresh linen; he, practised in seduction, leaned only slightly in her direction, touched her only casually and lightly, listened and laughed, made intelligent, easy talk, walked slowly, paid attention.

Suddenly, still holding her hand, he raised it in a kind of salutation. 'I'm so glad good old Angie brought you. You are such a breath of fresh air. You must come often. Nana and I will probably keep you to ourselves. You have no idea how predictable the conversation is with the people we mix with. We see the same people month in, month out. Nana is the only woman who reads. They only go to a gallery if the exhibition is so scandalous that it hits the headlines with protests to close it down; and unless a film has some kind of racy reputation, nobody we know will bother with anything with sub-titles.'

'I was surprised to see *West Side Story* is showing here. I would have thought its theme is too anti-racist for your laws.'

'It's a musical: whoever heard of a musical with a message? If you were to ask any of our steak-eating friends back at the house, "What about *West Side Story*?" they would say, "Ach, man, didn't you just love that Maria, and that Officer Krupke, didn't that just kill you?" The keepers of our morals like something straightforward like banning *Black Beauty*.'

'Is that true?'

'Legendary, but it could easily be true: it's their style.'

'I like it.'

'The old jokes are the best. Ach, you are a drink of water in a cultural desert. Don't leave us.'

She had still not learned how to deal with the way these people were with their explicit compliments about her looks, and remarks made to one another as though she were not there: shops, hairdressers, parties; wherever she went, women ran a finger over her cheeks, 'Ah shame, man, will you just look at her cheekbones?' 'What wouldn't I give for a bone structure like that?' 'And her complexion.' 'Ach, English women and their complexions, don't you just hate them for it?'

She said, 'I am not here to stay, I have to go home quite soon.'

'Don't even mention it. This country is in need of more women with minds, to balance the Angie Brazenoses and her beauty-parlour maidens. Oh dear. Angie is a friend of yours. But you will not tell her. We love her really, but oh . . . oh, it is so difficult to hold a conversation.'

'She has been very kind to me.'

'She *is*, very very kind. She collects money for the little lost piccanins, and gives a shoulder blanket to any poor old Oom Jim who knocks at her door. Ah, but you beautiful English lady with brains, you are something else.' He squeezed her hand, 'Quite something else.'

Angela had said: He'll try to make it with you.

Forewarned is forearmed, so she enjoyed the touching and the attentiveness, more at ease than a few minutes ago.

Taking her elbow again, he led her along the winding path through trees and shrubs which were discreetly but delightfully lit for effect. On reaching a small shed or shelter of some kind, he felt around its walls until he found a hand-lantern and a wooden baton. 'That's better. This way.' He turned away from the path, holding aside low-growing shrubs with the baton. Soon they were clear of the branches, and he went ahead, holding the beam from the lantern for her to see her way along a narrow path of old brick, until ahead of them was a glow of light. The path widened here to a broad expanse of the same brick, from which arose an encircling wall in which was a moon-gate.

Pedr had to lower his head to get through, and held out a hand for Rose to take, but she could easily walk through upright. Suddenly they were in a clearing. From the leafy darkness along the brick path, directly into stark and bare brightness as floodlights came up. Of all Nana's extravagant and beautifully lit features that Rose had seen, this was the most dramatic and extraordinary.

An enclosed garden of large rocks, set in bare white gravel and sand, throwing black shapes. Spotlights set at ground level heightened the architectural shape of leathery aloes, and gave dramatic effect to groups of erect cactuses from which white, single blooms, looking like enormous shuttlecocks, flowered.

Pedr said, 'This is the moon garden. The lighting is tripped automatically. Not many people have seen it.'

'It's wonderful . . . I have never seen anything like it. Beautiful isn't the right word . . . it's awesome, powerful.' There was a faint movement of warm air, causing them to be enveloped in sweet, heady perfume, a blend of wild honeysuckle in the evening and fresh lavender at noon, and perhaps something sickly, on the edge of being corrupt. The flowers and their perfume were as impressive as the stark white rocks casting black silhouettes.

As the exotic scent hit her, Rose felt anxiety clutch briefly at her solar plexus, which made her tighten her grip on Pedr's hand just for a second or two.

Pedr turned, 'Something wrong?'

'No . . . no. What is that perfume?'

'That's from the moonflowers.'

He guided her to a wooden bench, batting everything around with his shoe to disturb any lurking scorpion beetles. He picked up her hand again and began straightening her fingers. 'Are you normally so tense?'

'Not at all. It was just a moment of déjà vu . . . you know how it is.'

'I thought you had been stung. Cigarette?'

Automatically she took one and began to relax, though she still felt puzzled about her reaction to the scent of the moonflowers.

'Tell me about the déjà vu.'

'Nothing much, but I suddenly remembered . . .' hesitating as she tried to draw out the memory. He was a good listener, quiet yet responsive. '. . . going to Durban as a child; perhaps we were on holiday. My father went swimming . . . something about his knees. Perhaps I had never seen him in anything except his bank manager's suit . . . That same perfume used to come into my bedroom at night . . . Ayah slept on the floor by my bed . . .' She inhaled on the long Rothman's, then exhaled a stream of smoke. 'I think she told me that it was the scent given off by a wonderful goddess who brought beautiful dreams. I had entirely forgotten about Durban.'

'I wonder why you got so jumpy; it seems to be a good memory.'

'I don't know.' She paused, trying to recall the moment when they entered through the moon-gate, but it was gone – or perhaps she preferred it gone. 'I'm sorry. This whole garden is so packed with ideas, I think I may steal some of them. Of course we don't have so much summer . . .'

'Are you a gardener?'

'Well, yes, I suppose I am. I'm at my best when I'm growing something.'

'Then perhaps you will decide to settle here; everything grows so well. Nine months of summer, hot days, and the four o'clock rains. You can't grow roses in England as well as we grow them here.'

'I have to admit that's true. And yet we think we are the experts. We don't expect to see them growing except in England.'

As his knuckles brushed lightly down her cheek from temple to chin, she felt a prickle of excitement. 'No one can grow this kind as well as in England, not even Sweden.'

She knew what he was doing. He would kiss her. She might even let him. But to show him she wasn't falling for it, she said lightly, 'When I divorced, I said I would choose a different name. I decided Rosa Thorne would be appropriate.' She stood up from the seat and took a few steps towards a group of large rocks.

'Can you see the significance?' he asked.

'Of the rocks?'

'No, of the whole garden.'

'I don't think so.' She considered. 'Secret. Enclosed. Circular.'

'Not circular . . . elliptical, pear-shaped . . . The shape of the womb.'

Rose didn't know how to respond to that. Monica had once said that Rose's spending all that time in her hideaway garden was an attempt to withdraw into the womb, to which Rose had retorted that it was an attempt to get away from a bunch of noisy kids. 'I suppose enclosed gardens are womb-like.'

'A garden as stark as this? This is Nana's, infertile. She isn't one for half-truths, it's an arid desert of a garden.'

'Isn't that a contradiction? A garden grows things.'

'Of course. Nana's garden is as barren as Nana.'

Elna, who was doing literature at evening classes, would have said that all this symbolism was good, it was 'meaningful'. But did the Borgmans really talk to one another about the womb/garden analogy? 'It might look and feel barren with all this white rock and stone and pebble, but look at how prolifically the moonflowers grow.'

'It's the perfect place for them. Significantly.'

'What is the significance?'

'One needs to watch them open. It takes time, but it is fascinating, one can almost see them move. Look, see, here is one that will be open in about one hour.'

The unopened flower, about the length of a man's handspan, attached to the plant by a bulbous base, swelling where the middle joint would be, still had dark red sepals around it.

'It swells as though the whole life-force of the plant is pumped into just this bud. As it prepares to open, it is lifted away from here.' As he indicated, she noticed how slim and delicate his fingers were, not like the sausage fingers of her own dentist. 'Then the sepals can no longer hold back the inner petals and –' he flung his clenched fingers apart – 'the petals open and the plant ejaculates its perfume. Much more slowly than that of course. It serves one purpose, to attract the night moths so that the species may be perpetuated. And in the morning there is nothing to show except the limp and slimy remains of that beautiful creation of the night. Sometimes they have the name fountains of the night.'

Rose saw the allusion.

'You see the allusion?'

'Yes. I think that your wife is hard on herself.'

'On her barrenness.'

'I've always thought that word is a kind of accusation. Women who are, must hate it, and often it's not the woman . . .' She trailed off, not having intended to sound sharp, but that is how it came out.

'This is true, of course, I could be at fault. I think perhaps women have a need to be the sin-eaters.'

'Sin?'

'No, I mean fault-eaters . . . guilt-eaters.'

Oh yes, Rose had been the guilt-eater of her own failed marriage, and having eaten her fill was only in the last year or two beginning to see that the fault wasn't entirely hers. Ballard had been a rotten husband, self-centred and unkind. 'Should you be saying these things?' Even to her own ears she sounded prissy; she liked his openness. 'I'm sorry, that didn't come out as I intended . . .'

'Nana sent me here as your guide . . . I guess she was impressed by your interest in our bookshelves. You may find it difficult to believe, but she is shy. She wants me to make friends with you so that she can share.'

Rose smiled. 'I don't find that at all difficult to believe.'

He shot her a quick glance. 'No, I don't believe that you do. You and Nana would be good friends. She sent me as your guide because I am not at all shy and she wants you to see her moon garden because you will understand what she is saying.'

'She is saying that she takes the blame for not having children.'

'And that the moonflowers are a celebration of all the phalluses that never bore her any fruit.'

Did the woman really go about making her garden a metaphor for her sex life? Did she talk about it as he suggested? *All* the phalluses? If there was meaning here, then what had there been in her own protected corner back in the Honeywood days, with its own rampant and tangled vines and cherished lily-pots. And what might one make of her prevarication over her neglected jungle at Longmore?

This was the kind of discussion, about metaphor and analogy in the text of a book, that she and Leo had enjoyed together – until sex had entered into their relationship. She had retreated from it with good reason, and before that, much as she had been tempted, had retreated from it with Trevelyan. She had never let it get further than the first shiver of desire with Mac.

Over the days and weeks that had followed her aroused feelings for Leo, heightened by emotions stimulated by Winifred's death, and by Ballard returning home and stating that he wanted a divorce, it had been revealed to Rose that she was to blame. For much of her adult life she had curbed her sexual hunger, sublimating it in the bringing up of four children, expressing it only in discussions strewn with words such as 'image', and 'allegory', repressing it in creating the beautiful Honeywood gardens.

At the time, the revelation had been disturbing, frightening.

She spent much of those first weeks of the break-up alone. Sorting, first through Winifred's neat and anonymous belongings, and then through the accumulation of fifteen years of living in Honeywood and, as she saw it then, sorting through the detritus of the major part of her married life, which had started out filled with passion and hope, and ended full of failure and resentment. It had happened like a tiny stone hitting a car windscreen; a minute crack appeared the first time Ballard forced her into submitting. She had felt herself to be expendable. When it had happened a second time, after all the pressures of the war, that original crack had become unstoppable, spreading until eventually there was nothing but cracks until the screen disintegrated.

Trevelyan had come along and made her aware of her hunger.

And then Leo.

Although there were times when she wished that she had been blessed with a more honest face than the sham coolness that disguised any rage and passion, unhappiness and insecurity, she sometimes felt that there were other times (as now when she felt out of her depth with the ejaculating moonflowers) when she was glad of its effect.

She said, 'I should like to walk back the way we came,' thus putting an end to his flirtatiousness, except that he put an arm lightly around her shoulder as he guided her along the pathway. It was a silent, companionable walk, during which she was aware of his arm, and of his warm fingers holding her bare shoulder. Several times, as they negotiated overhanging shrubs, she expected him to kiss her: the opportunity was there at every step, but he did not. She felt uneasy that she was disappointed. And a bit tense, like waiting for the second shoe to drop.

Back in the brei area of garden flares, searing steaks and splashing swimmers, Rose saw that the crowd was beginning to thin. She looked at her watch. 'Heavens, I had no idea it was so late.'

Nana came out of the house, slipped a glass of icy wine into Rose's hand, and indicated that they should sit in a group of wicker chairs. 'Did you show her, Pedr?'

'I did, my darling. Rose is a real gardener, who gets dirt under her fingernails.'

'You like my garden?'

Rose said, 'I think it is the most beautiful I have ever been in. You have real talent. You could be a professional designer.'

'Ach! I should hate to do it for a living. I could not bear to make it and then hand my darling creation over to someone else.'

'I am just starting out on renovating a really ancient garden . . .' but Nana wasn't listening.

'Which did you like the best?'

Not an idle question, nor was Nana searching for compliments.

'I think the grove. The moon garden.' Rose saw the briefest exchange of glances between husband and wife, and Nana's hint of a smile and raised eyebrow. Pedr had said that not many people had been there. '. . . Well, it is way out . . . way, way out; overwhelming and dramatic: I know that when I get back I shall keep thinking of it. But as for *like* . . . ? I like the grove with the statue. It's a perfect bit of romantic design – the right things in the right place – absolutely pleasurable. I should love to take photographs but it would seem crass to go in there with a camera.'

Nana nodded. 'You *are* a true gardener. Actually, I have some photographs I took myself. But of course, they are little more than illustrations.'

Rose nodded. 'No movement, no sounds or smells, no dimensions.' *Photography is poor substitute for reality* . . . Trevelyan in 1955.

'And no atmosphere of mystery in the surrounding darkness. But still, I will send them round to your hotel. Oh! I had forgotten. Angie. Pedr, she got stung on the mouth, terribly swollen. Mark took her off to Emergency. She didn't want to go, but I think he was right to insist: you never know what things lurk in the bushes in this country. At least at home we know which bugs are out to get us: they do not lie in wait in the dark. In Sweden we have only daytime bugs. Pedr will drive you when you are ready . . .'

When the party broke up, he took Rose to the Cranbourne in a car with electrically operated windows and an expensive-sounding engine. They sped through the city that was supposed never to sleep. It was well after midnight, yet everything was brightly lit and private cars were everywhere. Traffic cops cruised the streets around the city hall and the library, where meths drinkers gathered, but few people were out on foot.

When they reached the Cranbourne hotel, instead of drawing up to the main entrance, he drove into the car park and switched off the engine in the place reserved for the suite occupied by Rose. He turned to face her with his arm along the back of the bench seat in a relaxed manner, again as though he might have been going to kiss her goodnight. Instead, he said, 'Rose, you remember early in the evening when people were asking you what you thought of Johannesburg?'

'Yes. Did I say something I shouldn't have?'

'Not where Nana and I are concerned – we are dyed-in-the-wool liberals – and of course there's no reason why you shouldn't speak your mind; but . . .' He paused, as though searching for the right words.

'But I should keep my nose out of things that don't concern me.'

'No, no. These things *are* your concern . . . apartheid concerns us all. I was simply going to say to you that this is not Europe, don't ever believe that it is. Visitors are easily taken in by the sophistication of the city, and the talk about a more liberal society. Our mail is opened, our phone is bugged. Wherever you are, especially at a social occasion, even when you are with people who seem to be on your wavelength – maybe especially then – don't be lulled into thinking that people who ask you really do want to know what Overseas people think. People here have a saying: "Where three are gathered together, They are in our midst".'

'Who are?'

'BOSS. State Security. They keep an eye on people such as ourselves. The bureau people believe that Sweden is populated by Marxists, but that we are probably harmless; though they can't be certain, so they bug us and open our mail.'

'Are you involved in politics?'

He laughed. 'Not in the way a Swedish doctor or an English lady would think of politics, but Nana and I are Europeans, we travel a lot, we go to the theatre, we entertain, many of our guests are from Overseas. We – especially we Scandinavians and you Brits – we have known the delights of living under socialism.' He said this with a little irony.

'I can scarcely believe any government would go to such lengths.'

'Believe it, Rose. Oh, believe it!'

'I thought this was all left-wing propaganda.'

He laughed, 'The left doesn't need to invent. The Borgmans are suspect because in our household we read, and we encourage our servants to read. Books arrive from our families in Sweden. Friends bring us books. Books are touchy things; Pretoria thinks they are most dangerous.'

'And they are right. Books can be subversive, ideas can explode.' She laughed self-deprecatingly. 'You see, I know the jargon.'

He tucked a lock of her hair away from her eye and began to run his finger around her ear, idly playing with one of the green glass drops that hung from her lobes.

'You are so lovely, why do you feel that you must put yourself down?'

'I don't think that I do particularly.'

'You do. You apologize for having firm opinions. In the moon garden you wanted to put me down for the way I spoke of Nana's childlessness, but you retracted.'

'I'm not used to being argumentative with my host.'

'We agreed on guilt-eaters, didn't we?'

'No, I don't remember agreeing exactly.'

'You see, you can fight back.'

Vee's bitter dictum after her father left: 'We don't need men, Mum. Any patronizing from here on and we tell them to stick it.'

'That sounds rather patronizing.'

'I'm sorry.'

'You are right, I don't fight back enough, and when I do I end up sounding aggressive.'

'I can't believe it.'

'There you go again.'

'I'm sorry.'

'I was a wet for so long.'
'What is a "wet"?'
'A weakling. My daughters are helping me not to be.'
He fell silent, his warm fingers still idling with her earring, probably unaware that, by the way he breathed, his thoughts were giving him away. Short, quiet breaths, moist and close to her hair. When he had stood on the terrace pouring one-for-the-road drinks, athletic-looking bronzed limbs reminding her of Leo, she had felt the tension of arousal. As on the houseboat, as in the New Forest, as in Chichester, as with Leo, and as on her honeymoon and as on one occasion in Spain. Occasions when she felt at ease with herself. Why was it that a woman who doesn't want to cheapen herself, or lose respect, waits for the man to make the first move? She longed to be able to let her hand rest on his thigh and see what happened.
She swallowed on a dry mouth. 'I am trying to change. It is not easy having been married for a long time to a large ego stuffed with opinions.'
'Do I detect bitterness?'
She felt his knuckles lightly brush her cheek again, enticing her nerve-ends and muscles and glands into a reaction. Why didn't she go in? Why not open the car door and go? 'You should get back. Nana will wonder what has happened to you.'
'No. She will have gone to bed. She doesn't mind me being out late, nor do I mind her also.' Which is pretty much what Leo had said about Monica. My wife doesn't mind.
Rose wondered what it was like to have that kind of marriage. They seemed a very relaxed and happy couple. She had liked the way they looked at one another, each attending to what the other was saying. They smiled at one another a lot. What was their marriage really like? People had always supposed that she and Ballard got on well together.
'I've been hoping that you were going to invite me up for a nightcap.'
'I am sorry, I didn't think . . . I can't get used to living in a hotel.' She laughed, 'Which is ridiculous, because that is exactly where I do live back home.'
'It's all right, I wasn't serious.'
'Anyway, thank you for driving me.' She felt around for the door latch.
'You don't need to, it isn't often I get the opportunity to hold a conversation with a lovely woman who has something new to say . . . Ah-ah, now don't put yourself down. You are lovely and you are interesting. Before you arrived, Nana told me that Angie said that you looked like Marlene Dietrich. Nana likes to have beautiful

people around her. But you are not at all like Dietrich . . . absolutely not. Dietrich is always so self-aware, don't you think? She seems to say: Stop what you are doing, Dietrich is here, look at me, I am doing my stuff. Dietrich is so . . . *Kraut*! Did you hear Nana say to me, "Garbo", when we were meeting?'

'I've never been very good at accepting compliments about my looks. The thing is, I can never believe in them. I cannot ever see that I'm worth a second glance, and that's not false modesty . . . I see behind the mask, I know there isn't anybody very beautiful there. I really should go. Poor Angela, I'll ring in the morning to see if the sting was bad. Where is the lever on this door?'

'You will remember?'

'What?'

'"When two or three are gathered together" . . .'

'Of course.'

'Good. And –' he reached across her to get to the release knob – 'I hope you'll remember this too.'

As he pulled up the release knob, he moved his arms deftly about her. Again, her body – which had not returned to quiescence after her arousal in the moon garden – renewed its desire when he kissed her, and she returned the kiss, and again, in spite of the awkwardness of the steering wheel and gear lever. 'There is more room in the back.'

Without the slightest protest, Rose slid out of the front seat and into the back, where, in his warm, sinewy arms, she experienced his white teeth pressing his soft mouth against her own, felt his beard, smelled the swimming pool and citrus of mosquito oil on his skin. It was such an easy move to make here, in this country of space, grandeur, inhumanity and injustice; in this city of riches, of gold and diamonds, this place where she had been conceived, born and lived until she had been sent away, and to which she had now returned as a Stranger in a Strange Land.

It was not the elegant act that Jane Austen might have created for Elizabeth and her lover Darcy. Rather, due to the confined space, difficulty of free movement, the awkwardness, their urgency, and the slithering slope of the leather seats, it was coming together more in the manner of Lawrence's Lady Jane and John Thomas. It was only as the last wave subsided that Rose surfaced to hear herself gasp for breath.

Still clasping her painfully tightly, Pedr panted heavily, holding her close as though he would not release her, then, as he pulled away sufficiently to look at her in the dim light of a small moon, he said, 'Rose, you are quite spectacular. Can't I come up with you?'

A moment of panic at the suddenness and the strength of what had just happened prompted her to say no.

He had not pursued it, but when he left her in the foyer of the Cranbourne, she agreed to have dinner with him the following evening. 'Nana is going to a health spa in Lourenço Marques. She likes me to have fun when she is away.' He smiled. 'She feels not inhibited to have fun herself, and then she will not have to eat sins.'

Rose believed him, partly because she thought it must be the truth and partly because she wanted it to be. His long and lingering kiss before they left the Zodiac was still on her lips when she flung herself on to the big bed. She wanted to be fun for Pedr, and to have fun with him. Leaping from the bed to look at her reflection in the mirror, she almost expected to see some sign of decadence as in Dorian Gray's hidden portrait. The face that smiled out at her was tanned and smiling and surprisingly attractive.

Nana Borgman lay on top of the bed, an emperor-sized one she and Pedr sometimes shared, and wondered whether he would come home, or whether he would make a night of it with the English woman. She was just Pedr's type: bookish, classy and racially pure. Did she need to wear eye-glasses to read? He liked that: beautiful eyes looking out through large tortoiseshell frames, like the ones she wore herself. Nana knew him inside and out, as he knew her. He would have no peace until he had discovered what she was like in bed.

As soon as Angie had introduced her: 'This is Rose from Overseas. Isn't that great?' Nana had known, as Pedr had known, that sooner or later he would end up trying to get her into bed – more likely sooner than later. She sometimes said that she knew him better than he knew himself. As Pedr had told Rose, Nana didn't like going to Mozambique unless she knew that he too would be having some fun. Not that the vanilla with vanilla sauce affairs that satisfied Pedr were Nana's pleasure: her taste was for vanilla with dark chocolate.

She could never decide whether she really did find her black lovers wildly enjoyable, or whether her liberal ideals and cocking a snook at the race laws made them seem so. Pedr said that if they weren't living in such a mad country she would never have thought of taking a black or a woman as a lover.

The fact was, they were living in this mad country. Caught up in it and now involved in it.

They lived here making money – not being able to help making money; lots of it. They could take very little of it out of the country. Nana helped in the Bantu baby clinics, and was a member of the women's Black Sash movement, making her occasional silent protest against imprisonment without trial. Silent, respectable protest. When they went back for home visits, Sweden seemed chill and small and prissy.

As she drifted off into the reverie before sleep, she drew her mind away from the activities that had kept her and Pedr together, and thought of the fine, raw silk and lace mini nightdress that she had bought for Derina, and imagined her dark body moving within it. Last time they went to Lourenço Marques, Derina had brought body-paints with her and spent hours meticulously, deliciously decorating Nana's hands and feet and breasts.

Sleep didn't come. Unaccountably, the English woman had disturbed her. Many women had come and gone in Pedr's life, but none of them had mattered much. So why this English woman? She was not even young. She turned off the music player and looked at her watch. Pedr had been gone for a couple of hours; he would probably not be coming home. Then she heard his car and saw the sweep of his headlamps as he turned into the drive. If Rose had turned him down, Nana hoped that her own pleasure with Derina would not be spoiled. Pedr wasn't one for anything very unorthodox. Derina was. And Derina's cousin Tobias. She smiled at the prospect. Vanilla with double chocolate sauce. Pedr did not know the extent of Nana's fun.

Next morning Rose rang Nana to thank her for the marvellous brei, listening to herself talk to the wife of the man whom she had loved like an eager teenager on the back seat of his car. She phoned Angela, whose speech was distorted by apparently badly swollen lips. Rose sympathized and said that she mustn't think of making any plans for Rose's benefit. 'I have decided to go to Durban for a few days, and if I am no nearer finding Ayah when I get back, I shall have to start thinking about going home.'

Angela managed to give details of a hotel that she could recommend in Amanzimtoti just outside Durban. 'They know me there.' Then Angela rang Nana and heard that Nana was off to her health farm and Pedr was going to spend a few days in Natal. 'Durban?' Angela asked.

From her tone, Nana guessed that Angela knew that Rose was driving down to Durban. Angela was an open book. 'How lucky that Pedr had to go there too.' Nana could only reply, 'I think it's an excuse to put his new car through its paces.'

Pedr rang Rose very early. At the sound of his accent, her libido proved that last night was no temporary kindling.

'Are you still on for a ride down south?'

'Were you serious?'
'Of course. I have pulled a muscle in my arm – my experienced arm. You see, an orthodontist cannot work without it.'
'I didn't notice that it hurt you last night.'
He laughed. 'I wasn't working on your teeth.'
'Won't it be a strain driving all that way?'
He laughed again, 'Don't fuss, Rose. I learned the technique of one-armed driving when I was sixteen.'
She thought of being on the beach with him, of swimming in warm water with him, of dining, walking, talking, but most of all of making love again with him.
When he met her for dinner that night, it was all arranged. They would do the journey in two stages, stopping off at a motel in the Drakensbergs, a rest at Howick Falls and the Valley of a Thousand Hills. A week in Durban, and an unhurried drive back. He didn't even suggest going up to her room: in spite of the rest his doctor had ordered for his arm, he had a couple of emergencies to attend to at the clinic. 'An aperitif,' he said when he kissed her goodnight. 'Not that I need one, I am already terribly hungry.'
She felt free as a bird. What a cliché! But that was her mood. For the first time in her life she was answerable to no one but herself. She could do what she liked, be what she liked, go where she pleased. She had scarcely slept last night, instead she had sat out on the balcony of her suite into the early hours, smoking and sipping icy vodka-limes, no longer nearly as susceptible to alcohol as she had once been. She could not remember ever feeling so much at ease with herself. There was a sense of power in wanting to do something quite wild and then deciding to do it. She liked the feeling.
The sky above the orange glow of the city had looked soft purple, littered with chips of mirror that did not shimmer. A familiar sky under which she felt at ease, as though some of her childhood memories were perhaps within reach; if only she could find something to lever the log-jam then she felt sure that it would flow, and she would see her entire self from small child to grandmother. She would know Rose Quinlan.
The drums had been sounding as they had sounded on her first night here. Rolling out across the city from the mining compounds, she had caught the sound which she had then read as ominous. Tonight, only the sound of the largest reached her as she sat on her balcony. Not at all threatening now. Throbbing resonances, heavy vibrations, which evoked the rhythm of piston, heartbeat, pulse, and a man and woman making love on the back seat of a car.

* * *

They did the four-hundred-mile journey to Durban in one. Pedr had a new fast car, and the roads were deserted when compared with the English highways.

Before setting out, Rose had a call from Rebecca.

'Becc, darling, I can't tell you how much I need to talk to somebody from the twentieth century.'

'You sound as though you're ready for home.'

'People here think that's where I am.'

'*You* don't, do you?'

'Of course not, my heart isn't here. I'm glad that I came. Don't laugh at this, but I feel a real grown-up woman out here on my own.' Happening to catch sight of her reflection, Rose saw herself smiling self-satisfactorily.

'God spare us that, Ma.'

'What is that supposed to mean?'

'*I'm* grown up, Nora and Vee are grown up, so is the Old Man . . . *We're* all street-wise, but you and Jon still have your innocence.'

Innocent was the last thing Rose felt herself to be. She felt scarlet and experienced. 'Becc! You do say the wildest things. And all this long distance.'

Rebecca laughed. 'I know. It's all part of my artistic nature. I'm famous for it. Love you, Mum.'

'Listen, Becc, I can't believe I'm saying this, but I am having a really good time in spite of everything. But you need have no fears about me wanting to come here to live. I shan't stay here much longer, I just want to visit Durban before I come home. I have an idea that is where we were when my mother died.'

'Hope you're right. Have you heard from Longmore?'

'Not for a few days.'

'Then you don't know Uncle Leo's been there?'

'Leo? No, I didn't.'

'That's right. I don't know how he came to call in. Nora was a bit vague . . . you know.'

'Equivocal?'

'Well, you know how Nora can be. You haven't tracked down your old ayah?'

'No. I've got a couple more possible lines. I'm having to rely on other people. There's a whole new set of rules in this place. I don't hold out much hope. Now look, I don't want to ring off, but this call must be costing you a fortune.'

'It's OK, I'm about to make one.'

'One what?'

'Fortune.'

'You seem to be doing very nicely as it is.'

'Ah but this is "something else" . . . You'll never guess. Maternity and baby clothes.'

Rose's heart palpitated unevenly. 'Oh.'

Rebecca chuckled. 'Don't worry, Rosie, they're not for me. Rebecca knows what causes them. You'll never believe . . . it's Princess.'

'Sally?'

'Right on.'

'She's pregnant?'

'As a pomegranate.'

'I can't imagine it.'

'You should see her! She's not four months yet, but she's made this big announcement, and I'm designing all these terrific clothes . . . I mean, really pregnant styles. Pregnant women are such wonderful shapes. My idea is to show it all off. Sally looks really, really female . . . curves everywhere. And she's so radiant. Almost makes me want to try it myself.'

'But you won't.' Rose was torn between wanting other grandchildren and knowing that Becc was already on the sunny side of thirty and no husband in sight, and half hoping that she would go on being the unshackled, free spirit she was. If Rose had had it in her to envy anyone, then it would be Becc.

'I did say *almost* makes me want to try it. Listen, when you get to Durban, ring me from there. I just wanted to hear your voice. Oh, by the way, I met the Old Man . . . He's got slim. Perhaps the tart is wearing him to a frazzle. Anyway, just to give him a thrill, I told him you were out there fucking every man in sight. That made him think.'

Rose blushed.

Becc continued, 'So take your pills and go for it, Rosie.'

Rose was still smiling when Becc had gone. How had she managed to have a daughter like that?

Then Pedr had arrived and they were off into the city traffic, Pedr driving in true Jo'burg style: elbow out of window, revving, beating the red lights, jumping the amber, using gears to get ahead of the next driver, and then dicing with slower traffic at the many intersections of the suburban grid. Gradually everything cleared and slowed until, at the end of the white area, there were fewer and fewer vehicles. Then the wide open veldt, the vast red fields, shimmering mirages of spirit villages in an endless black-topped road that seemed to disappear into infinity: willy-winds dancing across fields; a changed conception of speed when ninety dragged; and driving space with few other cars for miles on end, so that one had the impression that it was a straight black line from the Rand to Natal Province.

Rose felt elated and happy. She was in a scene from any carefree Hollywood romance, or a Lorna Lammente novel where the Contessa is driven at speed across Europe. Time was suspended: she was somewhere, nowhere, anywhere, it did not matter. She wondered whether Ballard had believed Becc.

'Well? Share it.'

'I was just contemplating sending a postcard to my ex-husband who left me for a much younger woman.'

He turned, looking questioningly at her. 'Has he been certified yet?'

'She's rich too.'

'Money will not buy him what he has lost. You are one fantastic lady. What were the words you were writing to him?'

'"Met this handsome desirable young Swedish dentist. Had some super sex on the back seat of his car. Driving four hundred miles south to have some more".'

He laughed, throwing back his head exuberantly, and triumphantly picking up her hand, said, 'Four hundred miles? You have seen those small birds who live every moment on the wing? They know how to live; they never question, "Is this the right time?" "Is this the best place?" We shall be like them.'

'Living for the moment? The English believe you Swedes to be a gloomy people.'

'And we believe the English to be formal and unyielding.' He took her hand in his left one, driving at speed still with the other. 'Man! Were we ever wrong? Have you never done fuxing in the open under blue-gums?'

'Blue-gums aren't native to England.'

'And they are not native to Sweden, but one soon learns what is good in another country. You like fuxing in English fields?'

'Pedr!'

He grinned, 'Ah-ha, perhaps the English are a little formal after all.'

Wrenching the steering wheel, he turned sharply off the highway and squealed his tyres to a halt on the veldt. The only living thing in sight for what seemed endless miles was the clump of trees under which he had parked. 'These are native blue-gums.'

In the dappled shade of the silvery-blue, restless eucalyptus trees, they added thirty minutes to their itinerary, making love and then drinking icy post-coital orange juice from a large thermos he produced.

Back in the hot car, he gave her a quick, friendly kiss. 'Man, are we good together! We shall have a great time.'

'I know,' Rose said.

In spite of being bearded, he looked very young when he grinned. He was so wholesome, so desirable, that Rose felt she would not mind driving four thousand miles with him.

He said, 'Hold tight, I'm going to see how she holds flat out. Yell when you see any blue-gums. There are an awful lot of them between here and Durban.'

Rose stretched luxuriously as he put his foot down. 'Good,' she said.

Once or twice on the road south, Rose glanced sideways trying to catch herself off-guard, but she could not. He was cheating on his wife, even though he said that they had this open marriage and free love. She was doing what Miriam had done, but she could not shock herself or feel at all guilty, only feel delighted to have such an entertaining and attractive man wanting to drive all this way to the coast because he liked to be with her.

Several times he caught her glance and answered with a smile, his beautiful teeth revealed from within his blond beard. He wore his hair surprisingly long for a professional man, and this morning he had it tied back with a black string. Maybe he had the impression that she was an easy lay. With him that's just what she had been. Easy . . . eager back there in the shade of the blue-gums. Who would believe Rose Quinlan capable of that . . . ? Not that anyone would ever know. 'There was this English woman I remember, not that young either, with a look so icy you'd think your balls would freeze . . .' Perhaps he thought that she was Everyman's typical divorcée: starved of sex; having anything that came her way.

So?

It's what she was. This was the first time she had thought of herself as a divorcée or of the images attached. Grass Widow, Merry Widow, Unmarried Woman, Divorcée: all descriptions of a certain type – a certain type of *woman*. Their image of the predatory woman gave men permission to behave in a certain way. Fair game. They can't keep their hands off you. It was what one heard at any dinner party. What the hell did it matter? They were both enjoying it, and in a few weeks she would be gone.

Hundreds of miles went under their wheels whilst they exchanged frivolous bits of information about their lives and close families, jokes about themselves and their petty likes and dislikes, enough so as to know something of how they each spent their days, but insufficient for there to be any confessions. Very little about Ballard, nothing about Trevelyan or Leo. He talked a bit more openly about his life, so that Rose, sitting with the map on her lap, ostensibly path-finding, built up a picture of the man with whom she was planning to have a week of sex and sun. She liked the picture that was emerging.

From time to time they stopped at a filling-station in some small *dorp*, for gasoline, and for water to wash from their faces and hands the dust thrown up by traffic going in the opposite direction. The dust was terrible: with the car windows closed the air became unbearable in a few minutes, yet with them open the dust filmed everything. Only the windscreens kept free of the red film, for it was a matter of form that a black attendant polished them as the tank was filling. Mostly they pressed on because Pedr was the kind of driver who enjoyed his automobile, and this one was new and a purring, aggressive, speed-hungry model. And they wanted to reach Durban in time for dinner.

He asked her about her childhood and why she had gone to England. He was easy to talk to, not making much of her amnesia. 'Why should you feel embarrassed that your memory is on the blink, Rose?'

'I don't know. It's a flaw not having a past, not having parents or a childhood to refer to. I am never able to say, "When I was little I did this, or I hated that, or I was scared of cats", or something. I'm like some tree that looks perfectly healthy: it grows and bears its fruit, then it suddenly keels over and you see that it's entirely hollow; it's been living on its shell.'

When she confessed this, he pulled over and put his arms about her as though comforting a child. 'You are not hollow, and I shall see that you will never keel over.' He brought her more of the icy orange juice and, with cooling lints from the packs of them he carried, he smoothed her face and each of her fingers in turn. He was very practical and didn't fuss, but Rose thought it marvellous to have a man who showed such concern. As he wiped her fingers she had a sudden flash of memory of that same sensation. Thin brown fingers brushing her own plump pink ones. 'That reminds me of Ayah, cleaning me up after we had eaten popsicles.'

'Is this a new memory?'

Slowly, with her hand still in his, she said, puzzled, 'Yes, but it is as though I've always know it, but I just forgot for a moment.'

'Perhaps your lady who made you come here was right: you did need to come here. If your mother died and you were sent home to your aunt, it is not so surprising that you have separated this part from the English part. My mother made wonderful fruit preserves which she sealed with some waxy substance. In winter, at the light festival, she would pick off the wax and there was all the fruit just as whole as it had been in the fall.'

'You think this is removing some kind of preserving wax I poured over my early memory? I suppose it could be.' The thought of being suddenly confronted with those missing years was alarming. 'Didn't your mother ever open up a bad lot?'

He didn't answer at once. 'It's true, she did, but it was necessary to uncover them: a jar of bad plums is not useful. Are you scared that you may not like your memories?'

'If they were happy, then why should I have buried them?'

'All children have some happiness, don't they?'

'Of course, and even if I do not, then I shall at least know that I'm not hollow.'

'And you will not keel.'

She kissed him lightly on the cheek. 'You have no idea what keeling over means, have you?'

'Ach, Rose, there is so much I do not know . . . Most of it I will never care if I never know. About Rose Quinlan I must know everything.'

As they pushed further and further south, several scenes triggered small memories without much meaning. Again, as she had seen outside Jo'burg, a team of ten or a dozen yoked oxen flashed back to a time when she had looked through a car window from a kneeling position. Plodding in perpetual motion, they ploughed the rust-red earth of the fertile veldt. The car had black leather seats. Somebody said, 'You should not stop here, master, because of the poor whites.'

'Pedr? Who are the poor whites?'

'Travellers. Farm labourers mostly who travel around in beat-up old trucks with their women and a horde of kids. The blacks working on farms are poor, God knows, Rose, they are really dirt poor, but mostly they have homelands and they have their own tribes. But poor whites? Man, they are trouble. Poor devils, they belong nowhere. They despise blacks and if they ever get half a chance to be in charge of a gang, will soon show them the sjambok.'

'No one wants to be at the bottom of the pile.'

'Yet it is the bottom of the pile on which all the other rests. This country would go to the dogs if it wasn't for the poor labourers.'

'What about poor whites on this road?'

'Most people keep their windows up and their foot down, but they sometimes stand in the middle of the road holding their children. I keep a few rand and a couple of beers in the side pocket here. Like paying a toll. Or "discretion the better part of valour", is that what the English say?'

'Your English is good, even if you didn't know what keeling over means.'

He laughed. 'I try not to be mistaken for a Hollander.'

By the time they had passed through the Drakensberg range, past the Valley of a Thousand Hills, and beside the dramatic great fall of water at Howick, they had fallen into a pleasurable silence broken only when from time to time he asked, 'You OK?' and she replied, 'I'm loving it.'

At Howick they made a stop for some tea and a visit to the viewing area, where Rose stood silently watching the spectacle where a river ran out of river-bed and dropped suddenly, hundreds of feet down a ravine, where the river-water was transmuted into a curtain of ragged white net.

Pedr carried the plastic cups of tea to where he saw Rose, gazing down into the gully where the white fall became a pool and then a river once more. Even from a distance he sensed that to have approached her then would have been insensitive, so he put the tray down on one of the rough wooden picnic benches and drank his tea watching her. A spark of apprehension went through him, no more serious than static electricity; even so, the spark was sufficiently sharp to make him aware that he was feeling something for her that he never had for any of the other women he had taken on trips. Marriages didn't go on for ever.

It was only later that he saw the analogy: his and Nana's smooth-flowing marriage had hit upon a fault.

He and Nana had sometimes teased one another with that idea, but not too seriously. What would you do if we split up? Who would you have? There had been times during the last year or two when Nana had been going to her 'Health farms' when he had almost not made the effort to, as Nana said, 'bring something fresh into their relationship'. And recently it had not always been so fresh, because what Nana liked was for them to talk about how his woman performed, how Pedr performed, and how she and her partner – partners plural sometimes – performed. Before they married and lived casually with one or two casual lovers, their unpossessiveness had brought them close, because they fell romantically in love with one another and discovered that none of the lovers compared. And then when they married it appeared too outré, too conventional, too conformist for a free-living couple like the Borgmans to close up such a trusting relationship. Idealistically, they agreed that they must always feel free to take lovers outside marriage, 'for what it would bring to the marriage', and because the basis of their marriage was 'honesty and openness'. Once or twice it *had* occurred to Pedr that it might be merely a licence for Nana to indulge her increasing appetite for unconventional 'experiments'.

Until now there had never been any threat to their marriage. He preferred a conventional affair, a not very serious weekend here and there, Nana's penchant for black and female lovers was no real threat. He liked straight sex with women. Often. He looked at Rose standing poised and still, her sleeveless flowery silk frock moving slightly in the current of air from the falls; from here she appeared to be a slender woman perhaps in her late thirties? No longer so obviously from Overseas now that she was tanned. There was something about her . . . or was it just that, having found her so unexpectedly responsive, his mind was working overtime. She could drive a man crazy.

For a moment he felt quite unnerved. Although he had experienced her body, had caressed it, kissed it and known it as intimately as was possible, he had never even seen her without clothes. Maybe it was merely anticipation that was disturbing him: a fear that she might be disappointing, or that she might find him so . . .

She was unique, exciting.

And something else.

He could not have said what it was. She was classically beautiful and not conscious of the effect that had upon people . . . but when did he not have good-looking women around him? She was more than just that. Yet it was not only her looks, or her shapely, womanly figure. He knew that she was older than himself, but he had had women of all ages, and of different temperaments and many nationalities. Blonde, pale-eyed women whose bodies were as predictable as Barbie-dolls', and olive-skinned women with vivid mouths and dark bushes of hair. Short-term lovers who liked to lay submissively still and silent and lovers who shrieked and pounded.

Rose was like none of them. She was a still, calm woman; in some respects she was like Nana.

Mentally he undressed her, saw her as static as a Greek statue – the part that Nana sometimes played in the grove. To have two women like that: the dark and the fair, the barren and the fertile, the inexperienced and the mature. Nana would not like to be thought inexperienced, but compared to Rose she was. From what she had told him, of her life and her large family, and the man she had married, there could be no emotion she had not experienced.

Rose could have told him. Being in love. She had never experienced that.

When he saw her rouse herself from her reverie, he took the cups of tea and packets of biscuits to where she was standing. 'Rose! What is this?' She had trails of tears down her face. Putting the cups on the railings he drew her to him and rested his cheek on the top of her warm head. 'Who is it makes you so sad?'

They stood for several minutes gazing down at the water splashing the bedrock far below.

'I have been here before,' she said slowly, surprised, dragging the memory from some depths, her voice husky. 'It has been rather a shock. My father drove a Lancia. He came here: my father, my mother and Ayah. My mother wore a sort of long coat made of georgette, and it floated, but I can't remember her face. My father said that it was the air currents and that my mother should watch out or she would float away. I knew that it was all right because he made jokes. I don't know why I say it was my father, but I know that's who it was. Ayah wanted to get water from the bottom of the fall because of its healing power. My father said that sea-water from the big breakers was the strongest medicine. Oh dear, you will wish you had never volunteered to drive all this way with such a troublesome woman.' With the centre fingers of each hand, Rose dried her bottom lashes of tears. 'Am I smeared?' she asked.

'Man, you should just see yourself.' He moistened his handkerchief on his tongue and mopped up the mascara, then with his arm comfortingly about her, led her to his dusty car.

Mark Brazenose heard only his wife Angela's half of the conversation of a call to his brother in London.

'Say, man, thought you said that your lady was a country mouse from Berkshire?'

The handpiece quacked something and Mark heard his brother's laugh.

'. . . It's not what I am getting up to . . . not that I wouldn't mind getting up to it.' Angela raised her eyebrows at Mark.

'. . . You know very well what I mean. She's up to what all you Overseas types are up to when you get away from your tight little island and your skin starts to tan.

'. . . That might be the legal term for it, I call it a dirty weekend. Or a dirty week in the case of Rose . . .

'. . . Of course I'm sure. She's gone to Durban. Pedr Borgman's gone to Durban. He's driving. His wife's away . . .

'. . . No, Nana's not gone with them. These two are regular swingers, they do their own thing. You met them . . . that's right, he did the caps on my front teeth. Porcelain, cost Mark a bomb.'

Mark, now watching the porcelain flashing, thought that he wouldn't have minded if it had been just the one bomb. How many porcelain front teeth did it take to build a pool the size of the Borgmans'?

'. . . I thought I'd keep you posted. As you say, butter wouldn't melt in her mouth but, as Mark would say, she might do better sitting on it . . .

'. . . Of course not, I like her. Send me some more. I've been out of the house and had more trips since she arrived than for the last year. OK? I'll ring when I have more of the tasty details. Bye. Oh, hey, before you ring off. What's it really like in London these days? Is it all really swinging like they say in the magazines? All pot and hair and Beatles? Flower-power and let it all hang out – isn't that it? Lucky old you, right there in the heart of it all.'

Mark Brazenose raised his eyebrows, and when she replaced the receiver said, 'Christ, man, you can make such good fiction out of a little bit of fact that you should go in for writing books.'

'Maybe I should, then I could afford a month Overseas.' She bumped her hips at him. 'In swinging London.'

Joyce, the maidservant at the Cranbourne, makes her way along the dusty, pot-holed road. She knows the townships of Soweto and Alex as well as she once knew Sharpeville, where she used to live before it was bulldozed. But this part of Alexandria Township is new to her. It doesn't look so bad.

To Rose Quinlan it would have looked bad. But then Rose would not have known how very small a refinement it took to raise the status of one of the thousands of jerry-built shacks above another. Paint, a bit of fencing, hooks and nails on which to hang baths and brushes during the day, a pot with a geranium, a small shrub in the yard.

Joyce shows a youth the brief information she has on a scrap of paper: he frowns at it, then flicks his hand in the general direction in which she has been walking and resumes kicking an exhausted plastic soccer ball to another youth.

When she sees the old woman's colour and features, she hopes that she has found the one the madam had come to This Place to find. 'Where must I go to find Fatima Kalim? I am looking for her.' The old woman does not reply but looks suspiciously at Joyce with large, dark-brown eyes.

A grey, crimp-haired woman comes to the door. She is about the same age as Joyce's own mother. 'Who is this? Who wants Fatima Kalim?'

'I do not want her.' Joyce speaks with the dignity of an ambassadress, and with all the refinement of a domestic worker who has learned her languages well, distinguishing between one word and the next, hissing her esses, popping her dees and tees, rrrolling her arrs. 'I work at this hotel in the city. It is an Overseas madam who wishes to find her.'

'Why can an Overseas madam wish to find her?'

Joyce bridles a little: she has come not only for the money, but because it is a Christian act and Joyce is an active member of her church. 'I do not know everything! This madam has come from Overseas just now, she says the old one was her nanny but is lost now since many years.'

The old woman says, 'Tell her name.'

'Mrs Queenland.'

'Her *name.*'

Joyce takes another slip of paper from the breast pocket of her blouse. '"Any-one knowing the where-abouts of Fatima Kalim please no-tif-y Rose Queen-land." In the bracket it says "Rose Weston", you see?' She pronounces the name beautifully. 'Rrrawss Weysstone.'

Fatima takes the paper and peers at it closely, folds it and tucks it into the space between her flaccid breasts.

'I am Fatima. Selina, give the girl some fresh lemon. Come here, girl. Sit and tell me about your madam.' The old woman is suddenly alive.

They were not booked into a Durban hotel, but one in Scottburgh. Pedr had scorned Angela's recommendation of Amanzimtoti as too brash and Durban as having too many tourists, and had chosen Scottburgh, a small resort south of Durban.

Rose, standing on her balcony overlooking the bay, thought it delightful. 'I love it. Everything looks so clear and bright.'

Pedr was pleased. 'I knew you would, I come here quite often.' The question 'With whom?' that came to Rose's mind, was only in passing. She wondered whether he meant to this actual hotel. None of the staff had appeared to recognize him or take any notice of them obviously being together but not sharing a name. Perhaps they recognized him very well, but were discreet. Of course, a brother and sister could be holidaying together and insist on suites that were inter-connecting. Not that it mattered: Rose felt sure that one or other of the suites would not be used.

Scottburgh was a small resort relying almost entirely on indigenous holiday-makers rather than Overseas tourists, who preferred the long golden strand of Durban, with its beaded and feathered ricksha boys, its bead- and seed-weavers, fake-trophy sellers and wood-carvers. All that Scottburgh had by way of seafront entertainment was an open-fronted tea-house, a swimming pool, a curved bay with fine sand that was like cream-coloured castor sugar, and a lively, white-crested watchet-blue sea in which groupers lurked, sharks and marlins cruised and dolphins played. The sickle-shaped bay was netted across against sharks, and for extra security there was a look-out tower on an outcrop of rock. Hotel lawns and tennis courts were green and constantly tended by 'boys'. It was a perfect place for white couples who wanted nothing better than to leave the kids in the care of nursegirls, laze on the beach, rub Ambre Solaire into one another until they became dark-skinned, and return to their rooms whenever the fancy took them.

The permanently dark-skinned peoples were coralled in a bit of beach separated from the rest by the outflow of a small river. It was almost always empty of people. Pedr said that black people were reputed not to like to swim in the sea, and Rose said she wasn't surprised, seeing that there was no shark-net there.

Their rooms were large and airy and deeply shadowed by the overhang of the balcony. A porter had carried their bags, a housekeeper their keys, and two maids had unpacked their cases and hung up and put away their clothes. A white-jacketed waiter came and deposited a tray with sundowners on a wicker table on the balcony which faced the sea. Below their rooms was an old-style colonial garden with palm trees, avocados and frangipanis set in turf, whilst geraniums and the ubiquitous purple bougainvillaea tumbled about walls and pillars. Rose thought it heavenly.

It was now early evening, the sun was making its sudden drop down into the ocean.

Pedr said, 'Come and see.' He drew her out on to the balcony and down the steps, where they stood against a low wall, looking out to sea, their arms about each other's waists as though they had known one another for ages. 'Here is something else for you to remember – a real Natal sunset.' In a country of spectacular sunsets, this panorama, created by dust flung high in the atmosphere, and reflecting red, gold, burnt orange, pink and purple against the rolling sea, was astonishing.

'It is wonderful! Nature always beats anything we can do.'

'Nature! It had a little help from its friends. You Brits and your Woomera testing range. That's an atomic test sunset.' He was serious. 'Though the thing you *can* say is, if we ever go that way, we shall go in a blaze of glory.'

'Pedr, don't.'

'Give credit where it is due, Rose. Woomera Range has given Natal something to please their tourists.'

'Well, I *do* protest. I go on marches.'

He put a finger over her mouth. 'Out here anti-nuclear counts as "red".' Smiling.

'Where three or more . . .'
'Right.'
She suspected all people who lived in South Africa of being paranoid about the state police. 'But we are only two.'
'Only two. Yes. Enough. The perfect number. That is where Nana and I disagreed: she likes three.'
Rose thought she detected resentment in his tone, possibly jealousy. Perhaps open marriage was not so easy in practice.
'I wish you wouldn't keep mentioning your wife. It makes me feel well . . . *scarlet* or something.'
There was hardly any twilight, and soon, when the colour-glow followed the sun down into the sea, the sky would begin its quick deepening into the indigo of the night.
'I am sorry. Nana and I are such good friends, we never mind what the other . . .'
'I know. You said. But I'm not really up to taking all that on.'
His caressing hand tensed. 'You want to sleep with me, don't you?'
She encircled him with her arms and felt his vertebrae and ribs beneath his fine cotton shirt. His body was like Leo's. Athletic, hard, so little spare flesh.
'Why should you doubt it?'
'I wanted to be sure you were not disappointed.'
'Oh, Pedr, what an absolute idiot you are.'
'But I . . .'
After she had kissed him, he pressed his slim, hard body against her and said, 'I want you to remember me.'
'I shall.' How could she forget? Somewhere between Heathrow and Durban, bits of her old self had dropped off.
'And remember this' – he indicated the disappearing orange-red sunset over the orange-red sea – 'when you are back in your chilly island.'
'Not always chilly. It will soon be summer, and an English summer can be very hot.'
Standing behind her with his arms around her neck, he hugged her gently. 'I want you to miss this country. I want you to miss the Swedish dentist who fux with you in his car. I want you to remember this and wish to come back.'
Less than a month ago, she had come prepared to hate South Africa. If anything, now that she seen 'separate development' at work, she hated it – for that – more than ever. But the country itself was extraordinary. The more she saw, the more she found herself captivated by it. By the drama of its isolated cities, its desolate mountains, the grandeur of its landscape, the vastness of the high veldt and now, the lush greenness of Natal. The cities might be pushy

and brash, but they were but dots. The rest appeared unspoiled and beautiful.

'Things would need to change first.'

'They will change,' he said quietly, almost soberly. 'Mandela will not stay in prison for ever, Tambo won't always be exiled. This state of things cannot last. I promise you they will change soon.'

'How can you say that when even defending lawyers are arrested?'

Quietly, close to her ear, he said, 'I can say because I know these people. If you are meaning Braam Fischer . . . ?' For a moment he hesitated. 'Braam is a friend, Oliver Tambo is a friend, Nelson Mandela, Nat Nakasa is a friend.'

She turned, astonished when she realized what he implied. To know Fischer, Tambo and Mandela meant that he was not a harmless socialite with an expensive dental clinic in the city. These friends were the exiled, the rebels, the communists, the leading subversives. In Rose's short time of involvement with Sally Joffe in the various protest movements back home, these were names that inspired small acts of protest.

'Pedr! Why are you telling me this . . . this dangerous stuff?'

'I realized that I cannot *not* tell you. I have fallen in love with you, Rose. It is why I have tried to tell you about Nana. I love you and must have no secrets from you.'

'After two days?'

'After two hours, I knew it.'

This was the last thing she expected to hear. This was supposed to be a fling with a sexy young dentist. 'Is that the reason you stay in this country. Those friends?'

'Yes. They are the brave ones. These are the stars who show their faces. But we – Nana and I and others – are only foot-soldiers. We are necessary, though: we are the ones with the charity-box collecting money. Solicitors must be paid, children fed . . .'

She spent long moments sipping her drink.

'Don't go silent on me, Rose.'

'This isn't silence, I am trying to take it in. Haven't you virtually put your safety in my hands?'

'How else could I show you that I seriously love you?'

'A week ago you didn't know me.'

'What has that to do with it?'

'You hardly know me.'

'You weren't listening, I said that I seriously love you. Knowing has nothing to do with that.'

Footsteps sounded on the steps coming up from the beach. At once his tone changed. '. . . this is the terrible attraction of this place for Anglo-Saxon people like us. Until we come south, we never get enough time in the sun to be rid of our inhibitions.'

'Terrible attraction?'

'Perhaps "awesome", I don't always get the nuances of English. What I mean is that, when we arrive here, we are almost afraid of our instincts, our bodies. We are the most inhibited creatures. Our bodies tell us to do things and we don't know how to handle the sudden freedom of blue skies and warm sun. Some Europeans go mad, they are like drunks let loose in a distillery. They live under the sky because they cannot trust it to stay blue. They go barefoot and get jiggers, lie in the sun and get dehydrated, drink the cheap wine and forget why they came and how to enjoy themselves. Or they feel guilty about it all and become censorious.'

The returning guests said a friendly good evening and went on by.

Rose, not wanting immediately to return to the subject of his confidences said, 'You are very hard on the Anglo-Saxons.'

'Quite right. Think of what our countries have done. They clothed bodies that did not need protection, they tried to stop the joy of fuxing in the open air, and stop magic, and the talking to trees and singing with the wind. And then they frightened people with a God of retribution and foisted a Sado-masochist fetish upon races which were perfectly content with their old gods who had good cocks and full breasts.'

Rose suspected that he had made that speech before. She laughed lightly. 'In a nutshell, you're saying that Northerners have to learn to enjoy sex?'

He laughed too. 'You are such fun, Rose.' He pecked her cheek. 'Right. And at first it gives us a fright. All this sun. All the opportunities to uncover our flesh. Anglo-Saxon attitudes and inhibitions take a little time to change.' He wormed his hand under the strap of her dress and caressed the point of her breast.

She was happy. Happy that she was thought beautiful, happy that she had made love with him and would again, happy that by chance she now found herself in the arms of an uninhibited man to whom she could respond, happy that he loved pleasure and enjoyed giving it. She knew that she *ought* not to feel happy here, in this country, whose laws she had protested in London.

He tightened his grip about her, and slid his hand back into her sundress and into her armpit, stroking it softly. Again, as it had done on the night of the brei, a tide of desire for him swept everything else aside, leaving her with only sensation and the need to feel once again the moistness of his mouth, the heat of his skin and the contractions of his muscle and sinew, and to hear the sound of his panting breath close to her ear. 'Let's go in,' she said.

On the balcony they kissed, keeping their mouths in contact a long time whilst they caressed one another. 'You are wonderful, beautiful, exciting, and I am head-over-heels for you. I've been hit by a truck, a wall has fallen on me, I could take you to bed now and never get up for a week.'

Suddenly, the loud clang of the dinner-gong sounded right outside their door and went on sounding as its percussionist went on along the corridor and on to the next floor.

Pedr said, 'Ah, supper! Am I ready for that too?'

It being a holiday hotel, no one was expected to dress up. Rose put on her moon-garden frock at his request, and Pedr changed into cream flannel shorts and white, open-necked shirt. Watching his reflection as he combed his hair and beard, Rose thought: He's got everything, and for a moment wished that she could keep him.

As they were the dining-room newcomers, they were speculated upon. Both blond, both handsome, of an age. Europeans for sure. Dutch? Features too fine. German? Too slender. Scandinavian. Yes. Neither wore rings. So, brother and sister, there was the likeness, the same fairness.

Pedr enjoyed food. He was one of those people, like Leo, who seem to eat as they please and keep their flat bellies and tight bottoms. He looked up from his highly dressed watermelon and, catching her observing him, smiled. 'You were thinking things about me. Were they good things?'

She held his gaze. 'Absolutely not good . . . mad things. At home we say "A penny for them", and the person must sell their secret thoughts.'

'We shall do that all the time we are here. No, no, we shall do that for ever. You think I don't mean this about love? Angela has surely told you that I have a reputation with women, and you think this is Pedr's line.'

Rose laughed. 'To tell you the truth, since the blue-gums I don't really care.'

Sliding his hand between the glasses, silverware and flowers, he held her fingers briefly. 'I am beginning to wish that I had not been so quick to satisfy my gut hunger. We should have done something very quickly, and then I would not sit here in such discomfort. You blush quite often. I like that.'

The service was excellent. Having said that they would take coffee in their suite, a waiter arrived with it just as they stepped out of the lift. Rose poured, and Pedr hooked off his sandals and relaxed back into one of the white bowl-shaped wicker chairs, with his bare feet on the balustrade of the balcony. Like his hands, his feet were slender and bony.

As usual, the cool expression of her profile told lies about her true nature.

'Why don't we put out that glaring light, or the room will be full of beasts and bugs? There are candles here and the stars are bright. Do you have skies like this in England? We never do in Sweden. Ours are never so . . . so soft and sensuous as these. One can really imagine that there is a velvet canopy. Ah, Pedr, so poetic. In quite bad taste really, with all those bright bits of glitter, don't you think?'

'I don't have very good taste myself, which is probably why I like it.'

'Now you can tell me what it was that you were thinking when I asked.'

'You may not like it.'

'That is a chance one takes.'

'You look so much like a friend.'

'His name?'

'Leo.'

'Just a friend? Not your lover?'

'No!'

'Why so emphatic?'

'Because he wasn't.'

'And that is the truth?'

'You don't have to ask me twice.'

'Did you – *do* you – want Leo to be your lover?'

'I want you to be my lover.'

He laughed. 'Good, now I want to know about all of your lovers. Are you thinking of them now?'

'Of course not.'

'Ach! I will ask you when I have made love to you. Then you may be thinking of another lover.'

She thought of telling him that he was her first lover, but it would have sounded gauche to a man who obviously had had many affairs.

'What are you thinking now?'

'This scene would fit into one of my Miss Chaice's Lorna Lammente novels. I am here spending her money – a legacy; she left me money to come home. Home? . . . Two people together on a warm night, the bright stars in a velvet sky, the soft light, moths fluttering against the pink shade, the clink of spoons in the dark . . . truly Lammente.' Moving from her chair, she sat on the floor beside him, leant against his legs, and began caressing his foot whilst he rucked up her skirt and stroked her thigh with the other in a most gloriously sensuous way.

She tickled his feet which he couldn't stand, and said, 'That wasn't the truth I told you then. Nothing about Lorna Lammente's lovers except the candles. I was thinking that, if you don't move at once, I shall have to make love to you.'

He stretched languorously. 'Perhaps you have been used to quick men who don't play games first?'

'Did you play after the brei?'

'Of course, so did you, it is what we were doing the whole time. We were playing with one another from the time we met. I wanted to have you long before we looked at Pomona, also as we were looking at Pomona, and I wanted you on the path to the moon garden, and I wanted you very much in the moon garden.'

'I think I wanted you.'

He slid down to her level and idly caressed her skin. 'I did not want to take any chance that I had misjudged the moment. You flinched. I used the English wrong, and you flinched, so . . . we must have then more playtime to recover and be safe together.'

'I can't remember any flinches.'

'You remember. I was describing the flowers ejecting their perfume.' He turned her face so that she must look at him, and gave her an amused smile, 'I said ejaculating, but I intended to say ejecting, and you flinched and I sensed that you blushed. Perhaps it is then that I fell into love with you.'

'And so you played on until we reached the Cranbourne? You were not slow there.'

'I thought I must not make the wrong move. I did not want to scare you away. You are not easy to . . . to read, I could not read your messages. But you liked my kiss.'

Rose now wrapped her arms and her legs around him and drew him to her. 'I liked your kiss . . . very much, I liked your kiss.'

By the soft pink light of the single candle, he undid the ties of her summer frock, prolonging the action as one sometimes does in the opening of a tantalizing package. Not as practised as he in the preliminaries, she nevertheless unhurriedly removed his shirt and shorts.

If only Ballard had known that all she needed was time and his attention whenever she had to change roles from motherhood or domestic to the responsive lover he expected her to be and she had wanted to be. The weeks leading up to the marriage had been one long period of foreplay, so that sex in the first months of their life together had been marvellous. If only he hadn't been so concerned with his own needs that he had forgotten hers, they might have gone on and on like Charlotte and Papa.

But that was over, and she was glad to be where she was right now and with whom she was right now. He was lean and long where Ballard was thick and heavy, fair where Ballard was dark, silken-breasted where Ballard was hirsute. His body was slim and beautiful, Ballard's over-indulged. She did not feel inhibited. She liked the natural grace of his body, and the unselfconscious way he stood facing her, holding her hands.

'Well,' he said, 'will I do for you?'

'You will do extraordinarily well. The thing is, will I do for you?'

'Will you do for me? Rose, wonderful Rose, how can you doubt it? You are my ideal. I can never erect for shallow chatterboxes like Angela and the girls. You are sweet, ripe and experienced: I very much like that. I think you must be Pomona. Now I know how you came to know who she was. I think I should 'phone room service for a basket of fruit and take photographs of you. You are wonderful, totally, totally wonderful.'

'Truth, Pedr,' she said quietly, and seriously, 'honest truth? Do you really think that I am beautiful?'

Now, on the bed, he looked down at her and made a tender caress with his knuckles from her temple to her chin. 'I *really* think that you are exquisitely beautiful.' He ran his hands over her breasts, the mound of her belly and mount of Venus. 'A woman.' He gently lifted her breasts to where they had been before Jon was born, and ran his lips along a silvery line which any one of her four babies might have contributed. 'You carry the tokens of womanhood, this is truly very feminine. I find this exciting to me. It is what I love best in women.'

The image of Nana's sleek undamaged body slicing into the surface of the Borgmans' swimming pool, and the untouchable elements that composed her moon garden. The garden which was supposed to tell of a tragedy, failed to stimulate any compassion. Rose's emotions welled: she longed to compensate him for anything he missed in his marriage. At that moment, had she been able, she might have let him make her pregnant. 'I'm glad you think that.'

'I never before knew a woman who was so little aware of her looks. I think that you don't see yourself.' This was not said in a continuous flow, but was interspersed with short, tender kisses. 'Believe me, you are beautiful . . . beautiful and extremely sexy, with all these different things you possess that are saying woman, woman, woman. Does this sound corny?' He laughed. 'I am much better in my own language. I shall teach you Swedish and then tell you how beautiful and sexy you are.'

Running her hands over his back, this woman who had had such a clumsy love life, laughed lightly; this woman who had been called 'cold' so many times that she had almost begun to believe it, pulled her lover to her, kissed him and said, 'Until then I shall make beautiful and sexy love to you.'

She was not only a revelation to Pedr, but to herself also. She felt so free and liberated. So released from any constraints of *the* past, of *her* past, her failed marriage, her inhibitions, her disappointments, her insecurity. She felt valued, desirable, even beautiful. She wanted to be for him whatever it was he wanted. Perhaps it was a distillation of every love scene she had ever read or seen. Perhaps it was her naturalness, perhaps confidence in being the mature woman she was; perhaps it was that a virile lover, several years her junior, and with a body kept strong and fit, and whom she had known for only a couple of days, was overwhelmed with desire for her. Whatever it was, something gave her the instinct to give Pedr Borgman love that was more thrilling than he had ever known.

The night was humid and heavy, noisy with cicadas and distant music, and the inevitable drums, but Rose was scarcely aware of anything except his lean, warm, muscular body moving silkily with perspiration, his hands, surprisingly cool, roaming the contours of her own moist body, discovering her, murmuring sounds and declaring joy and ecstasy in the universal lovers' language which has no words.

In his desire he was lustful, his caresses erotic and full of understanding of women. He showed a sexual appetite which was as natural and eager and healthy as the appetite he had satisfied so zestfully at supper.

Rose's libido, which had lain almost comotose during Ballard's long and harsh reign, had not atrophied as might have been expected; possibly it had been sustained by fantasies and unremembered dreams, revived by Trevelyan and aroused by Leo. Or perhaps, fed by years of sitting with Threnody Chaice in the world of Hollywood fantasy, she felt that the Right Man had come along to share the kind of Scarlett and Rhett sexual gratification that had been left to the imagination of women of Rose's generation.

More likely, here was a very sexual woman, who had been inhibited one way or another for years, and was now away from home, in a romantic setting with a handsome and virile man who said he loved her, free and answerable to no one but herself.

So, on their first long, memorable night in Natal, Rose and Pedr believed they would never want to stop making love or to make love to anyone in the world but each other.

The following morning she looked down at him at first light, and wondered whether this could be love, or lust, or infatuation, or a holiday romance. Actually, she felt so joyful and happy that she didn't care very much. When she discovered him awake, dishevelled and smiling as he put a hand out to her, she thought it might be love, and decided not even to think of it, but to enjoy herself.

Young Gerald Hamilton sometimes wondered in later life – when he had become Gerry, even Good Old Gerry – how things might have panned out had he not, in that winter of 1963, been snowed up at home, bored and convalescing. But he had caught 'flu during the school vac., and the snow was above the hedges, and he was bored enough to go about idly opening and closing drawers and cupboards and looking through things which, in other circumstances, he would have been too occupied to have bothered with.

In his father's bureau, normally locked, he found a very ordinary pink manila folder of not many papers in which were various documents. 'Birth, Marr. Certs., Wills, Priv. Docts., etc.' was inscribed on the spine. It was only idle curiosity that caused him to open the folder, not ever having been curious to see a birth certificate until the words caught his eye. He was not even really interested in the details except that, having seen his own first name, he went on to read. It was his own document, at least a copy of it. And there were others: registration of a birth – his birth, not in this country – adoption papers and letters to Mums from Aunt Mimi, and one from Uncle Quin.

Gerald was a bright child, but in any case it did not need a bright child to realize within the space of a minute of finding the hoard that Mums was not his mother but his Aunt Pamela and Aunt Mi was his . . . his mother. Gerald's cheeks shrivelled and went icy.

His grandmother was fond of saying that eavesdroppers hear no good of themselves, and she would surely have something to say about the fact that snoopers fare no better. The story of Pandora opening her box of troubles suddenly had real meaning. He had known very well that everything in his father's study was out of bounds, yet like Pandora he had succumbed to temptation and curiosity. Once knowledge was gained it could never again be unknown. For his parents' sake, he had kept up the pretence of Santa Claus for years after he discovered the truth at the age of five. He must keep this too: this was much, much more important than a fairy story.

He had been born a bastard. And a German! His name was down for Lancing. Lancing wasn't the sort of college to accept German bastards.

That evening he was put to bed with milk and much fussing and cuddling because his fever had flared up again. And he didn't mind, not even when she kissed the top of his head; in fact he wished that she would kiss the top of his head a hundred times.

'Poor old chap,' his mother said.

She was his mother. *She* was his mother. She was his mother. Pamela was. Not little Aunt Mi. He cried inside himself at that awful truth and made his nose get all bunged up. Mother gave him a Vick's sniffer to put under his pillow. 'Just as well it snowed, eh? Else you would have had a spell in the sick bay.'

He wished that there was some way that he could let her know that he was glad that he was a Hamilton.

Tom Wilkinson, having once had to face pretty much the same problem as young Gerald Hamilton, decided once and for all to get the thing sorted. Even if it didn't bloody matter who his real father was, he wanted it sorted.

Somewhere, somewhere at the back of his mind was some bit of knowledge that had been festering away for years. He had always known that Monica was not his real mother: his mother had been Dad's first wife. But somehow, recently, the cankerous idea that Leo was not his real father was spreading bothersomely. Recently he had tried meditating and self-hypnosis to try to discover what it was that might account for his ambivalent feelings regarding Leo. Then, last night, when he had been on a minor trip with that good quality cannabis of his mother's, he had slipped back inside his three-year-old skin, and was holding on to the lavatory seat with both hands. He didn't remember the conversation, but he had absorbed the vital element. What he had overheard was Rose saying, 'Isn't he sweet, he insisted on going on the big toilet. He's losing his chub, he's going to be lean and athletic like Leo.' Monica, her hormones making her irritable, had said more loudly than she had intended, 'Oh Rose! Leo? He's never going to look like Leo. He's not Leo's.'

There was only one way to get the thing settled. He left a note to say, 'Didn't like to disturb you. Sleeping at Jeff's pad. See you at the weekend. Love you Ma. Tom.'

Monica was in the kitchen making tea when Jean Thompson arrived.

'Well, you're about bright and early. I seen you done the front steps already.'

'I just felt like it. Tom woke me. He's gone off on that motor-bike again. Wouldn't you think he'd had enough?'

Jean Thompson, unlike her usual self, did not comment, even though it was not often that Mrs Wilkinson felt like doing things such as the front steps. 'Look what I got. Came this morning. Look at all that beach, not hardly a soul on it, don't that make you wish you was somewhere like that? All this slush and muck everywhere. Walks all over the floor. It's the salt. Dries all white and sticky, you can't never seem to get rid of it. Durban. It don't say much: "Jean, This place is great. Ninety degrees. Have had a ride in a Zulu ricksha. Returning Eng. some time April. Love Stanley and boys. Rose Q. P.S. There is no TV in S. Africa." Here, you can look at it. Fancy, no telly. What do they do with themselves? It's all right having all that sun, but it don't shine in the evening.'

Monica too had received a card, but did not want to mention it. It had been a view of the Voortrekker Monument in Pretoria and was the reason for her buoyant mood. The cryptic message had read, 'All Passion Spent. Returning April. Promise to 'phone, Rose.' When their children were young and had quarrelled to the point of 'I hate her! Absolutely hate her. I shall never speak to her again!' – or 'him' as the case might have been – there came a point when their need for friendship, and a need to return to the old comfortable understanding of a close friend, far, far outweighed any indignation or hurt to the ego. Once Rose, as acting arbitrator in a serious rift between Vee and Helen, who were about eight, had phoned Monica to say that she was preparing the ground for Vee who wanted to come round to apologize, 'All passion spent.' It had remained a bit of shorthand that the two mothers understood.

'Mister Wilkinson still away?' Jean asked, trying to sound not too interested.

'He's gone down to Sussex. All this weather holds them up.'

'He might find time to drop in on the Cues then? It'd be nice if you all got together again, like in the old days.'

There were times when Jean asked quite innocent questions and Monica felt that a trap was being laid for her by some expert in winkling out the truth from a reluctant witness; or was it the sixth-sense of the Welsh that had given her a clue to Rose's message, 'All Passion Spent'?

Later Monica sat in the Cartwheel coffee-house, the place in Petersfield where she and Rose had often come together after doing the week's shopping. She felt cheated that those days were over, and that Rose was now part of other lives. She comforted herself with two of their most exotic pastries. And there, sitting and eating and drinking coffee and smoking, she decided that it was time she got herself sorted.

She would stop the Valium and the appetite reducers, a cocktail that sometimes made her so crazy that she couldn't keep up with either her brain or her moods.

She would allow herself some treats – why not? – and she would have them and enjoy them without dosing herself later with Epsom salts. It was crazy to live in a state of constant self-denial. Shaping herself to fit someone else's idea of a woman, shaping herself to standard sizes. It was all so crazy: it was obvious that fabric should be cut to fit women's bodies, not women's bodies trimmed to fit the clothes. She was sick to death of it all.

She would give up smoking, but not until she was over the other things.

And she would stop trying to be a fifty-year-old with a cover-girl figure. The hell with the women's magazines. They made you crazy. On one page they were telling you to be an aid to your man and comfort to your kids, on another they had a bloody great illustration of a Pavlova oozing with cream, and on the next a pull-out diet of bananas and milk and an exercise régime that got rid of seven pounds in a week. Crazy, crazy, crazy.

She would give it all up, get herself straightened out and . . . ? and . . . ?

She ordered one of the Italian ice-creams the coffee-house specialized in.

When she got back home, Jean had finished. The house was empty. She took mustard and water and sent the pastries and ice-cream out into the septic tank. Then she curled up on the sofa and had a good cry. No, not a *good* cry, a long cry. Anger, frustration, uselessness, loss, worthlessness.

At fifty, a male Cabinet Minister would be referred to as 'young', a male actor or news announcer with crows'-feet could easily be 'a dish', could be at the top of his profession, could receive acclaim for having maturity and wisdom. Could have a child. In an engineering magazine, in a profile on the expansion of Leo's company, WSE, Leo had been referred to as a successful entrepreneur at *only* fifty.

At that same age, whatever worth Monica had had was gone: it had lasted from twenty to forty at the outside. It had lasted whilst she had a flat backside and belly, perky breasts and an unlined face. It had lasted whilst her hormones kept going, whilst she still bore some resemblance to models and the girls in ads, who all had figures like youths. Women's clothes were all designed for women who looked like boys. What was wrong with a girl having breasts like melons? It was all crazy. Women had to wear the flat-chested clothes all day, and suddenly sprout melons at night when they were needed to aid and comfort the bloody men. If Leo went bust, no one would think twice of him starting another business. But let Monica try. That was quite another story.

She thought of Madeline Stringfellow's flat. There had been an air of serenity that Monica had found wonderful. Stringfellow had no man in her life. But she had a woman. In answer to Monica's question, she had said, 'Oh no, I couldn't bear living alone. My lover lives here when she's not away making her name in television.' She had smiled at Monica's rather gauche double-take. 'We've been together a long time and we're still in love. Her name's Felicity.' She had indicated a nude portrait of a mature woman with heavy legs, large breasts, and a strong face which was familiar to Monica. 'Felicity Pavoir? The actress? Of course, I remember her Lady Bracknell. She wasn't tempted to play up the "bag" scene, like so many Lady Bracknells do.'

Madeline Stringfellow had nodded, pleased at Monica's observation. Madeline and Felicity. Artist and actress, suiting themselves instead of suiting society. Did that account for Stringfellow's assurance? It probably accounted for her clothes and the unfashionable size and shape of Felicity's breasts. It had occurred to Monica as she had been sitting there drinking heavy cocoa and choosing the painting: why would any man want to sleep with something like Twiggy, that skinny model who looked like a playing card with hair, when there were soft women like Stringfellow and Felicity who had breasts and hips and bellies and asses.

In spite of their 'perverted' love, Monica thought that she had seldom seen two such feminine and real women. Who was it gave Madeline and Felicity permission to be women? Even if Monica had had their same proclivity, she knew that she was too conventional, too conformist to break ranks. That did not prevent her from envying them living by their definition of themselves rather than that imposed by other people.

There were times when Monica did not know who she was. The one thing that she did know was that she was not lesbian. Her orientation was plainly heterosexual, and her preference had always been for Leo. She felt that she was losing Leo. Since they had taken over Shaft's Farm, their lives had diverged. She told herself sometimes that the place was hexed. Before the Quinlans, Ted Wills' wife had run off with a migrant ploughman.

In Natal, Rose and Pedr walked for miles along the shoreline, swam within the safety of the shark nets, romping in the breakers; picked avocados and prickly pears. He took her to see bananas in bloom and showed her something of the shocking conditions of men labouring in the sugar fields, and the poverty of families who tried to make a living out of pot-making and bead work. He showed her the women basket-sellers eking out a miserable existence on the chance purchases of passing motorists.

The days were long and slow. They made love frequently, as often as not at Rose's instigation, sometimes quickly and daringly as they had done that first time in the car park of the Cranbourne, sometimes spending half the night discovering how next they could indulge one another. It was an episode in each of their lives which would stand apart from the rest: Pedr never mentioned Nana, and Rose, except for a couple of calls home, rejected everything she had left back there.

Pedr seemed always quite willing to listen patiently to her speculation about the childhood trip to Natal; Rose had convinced herself that something important had happened here because eventually she was able to drag back a memory, or at least an impression, of the return to Johannesburg. A car journey.

There was something that nagged at her about that journey home. 'Not my father driving, I feel sure . . . I just get the back of a man, black, wearing a peaked cap. I don't think it was our usual car: this one had red seats. Ayah sang to me, sad songs in a language I didn't know. I seem to remember it as a terribly sad occasion. My mother wasn't there, I'm sure. Do you think she might have eaten the infected watermelon? That is the story. You would think I would remember, I wasn't a baby.'

'Maybe we could find something. It might have been a news item in the local paper.'

And so, one morning on the second week of their idyll of sex and fun, they were drawn into looking for something that might tell Rose who she had once been when she was a child growing up in South Africa.

When Rose had explained to the archivist the unspecific nature of her enquiry, the woman had beamed, 'Oh, but we have the very thing for you: our compilations with index references. A wonderful person does this quite voluntarily. He is the kind of man who likes to see things tabulated and orderly. It's all cross-indexed, but it is best to choose your most substantial clue. Name, date or incident. Try "Name" for a start and see what comes up.'

The only likely items under Weston were a cluster all around the same time. With Pedr reading over her shoulder, Rose started with the first *Weston. Sddn. death. Dbl. tragy*. The item took most of the front page which Rose scanned lightly, but then her eye was caught by two names. 'My father was George and my real mother was May.'

They read on, Rose scarcely believing that the item was nothing more than a coincidence of these names.

SHARK ATTACK CHILD LOST –
DOUBLE TRAGEDY FOR JO'BURG VISITORS

Yesterday morning, little Derek George Weston (5) was the victim of a shark attack which took place within sight of picnicking families and a few yards of his father, George Weston, who had been teaching him to swim. By lunch-time, the boy's mother, May Weston, was found dying in her room at the Planet Hotel. She received hospital treatment for what appears was salicylic acid poisoning, but did not recover.

People who witnessed the scene at the beach were shocked and horrified. Natal-born Judy Ginster, also visiting from Jo'burg, said, 'We were all in the water. I'd noticed a little boy several times, because he was so fair and delicate. He looked like a puff of wind could blow him away.' Husband Martin Ginster said, 'I was trying to get my young daughter to take off, and said that that little chap could do it and he was just a baby. Last I saw, he was having a great old time, shrieking with laughter because he'd got the hang of it. His little arms and legs were going like the very devil.'

Mrs Ginster spoke for many. 'I'm very shocked. We have always felt this part of the beach was safe.'

A beach patrol volunteer told our reporter that in his opinion, more look-out towers should be erected because nets alone are not enough. 'An experienced look-out can spot the dorsal fin a long way out, and if there's only a suspicion of danger, we can clear the water almost in seconds.'

When asked how it was that such a tragedy could happen, a safety official said it was thought that the recent storm may have loosened a cable, but that the nets were regularly inspected after there had been big tides or storms. On the subject of attacks, he said that sharks were probably more attracted to a lot of splashing and flailing because it would appear that this was ailing or wounded prey.

An accompanying illustration was a library picture of a large dead shark, its huge jaws agape, its bare eyes staring out. Fleetingly, Rose wondered why would a reader of such a story need to be reminded of those jagged teeth? In the disturbing presence of the terrible predator, Pedr's presence – even though she heard his breath and saw his tanned fingers on the desk – seemed distant.

'Derek George,' she said. 'He was so fair and delicate.'

Because the shark jaws so dominated the page, the other picture did not immediately register with Rose. A man, wearing only bathing drawers and a straw hat, standing with his back to the camera. The caption read: 'The boy's father waiting for the divers to surface.'

'My father!'

The archivist looked up with interest.

'Look, Pedr', Rose said, 'this is my father. I've never seen him as a man. The only picture I've got of him was taken when he was about seventeen. He could be anybody.' This man was not just anybody. He was a father in the depths, with not a single particle of his anguish hidden, his head bowed in concentration, his draggled clothes, his hands dangling, holding his hat that was dragging in the water and seeming to weigh down his shoulders.

Subsequent reports gave up the whole story, simple and terrible. November. A summer holiday for Johannesburg bank official George Weston, who had taken his wife and their young son and daughter to stay in Natal. The little girl, Rose, who was older than the boy, could swim, but the boy could not. The boy wanted to surprise his sister and their nanny, who had gone to buy straw hats, by swimming unaided. The mother, who was on the beach at the time, was in a weakened state following a few days of indisposition from eating fruit from a roadside vendor. Friends returned with her to the hotel where they insisted she drink one or two large glasses of brandy. When her husband did not return at once, she went to her room, saying that she would rejoin her friends as soon as she had had a few minutes to compose herself. There she appears to have consumed more brandy, and an overlarge dose of aspirin. It was thought that in her exhausted state from the food-poisoning and what she had witnessed on the beach, she was in a state of severe shock, and not aware of what she was doing. She was discovered in a coma by the little girl and the nanny. Mrs Weston died in hospital.

Rose could feel Pedr's warm arm, and was aware of the archivist. Here, in these old files, was her missing memory. In all the movies she had seen, such a discovery would produce a sudden revelation. What should happen now, was that it should all come flooding back. The family which had been missing all these years would return and they would be hers.

Derek George. No one had ever said. Aunt Fredericka had thought it better for Rose not to have to face his death, than to have the chance of remembering his life. Derek. The name meant nothing.

She had no idea of the passage of time. Pedr sat quietly beside her. A discreet cough brought her back to the present. It was the archivist. 'I have found this. I am sorry, it isn't much, but it may be a bit of comfort. I could get copies made of' – she indicated the yellowed papers – but trailed off when she saw the front page jaws and teeth. The item she handed Rose was a close-up.

Pedr drove along the coast so that they could look for the tower. When they found it she said that he could leave her here for a while.

'You'll be all right alone?'

'Of course, but I need just a little time to be with this thing.'

It was a relief to be alone. To be free to sit in the hot sun staring at the one remaining weathered plaque which was attached to the ironwork of the tower by screws which had leached thirty years of rust into the concrete. No one would ever suppose that the small metal oval which looked like a manufacturer's plate had once been the source of local news, a sad little gathering, press photographer, a prayer, and George Weston, a sober young bank manager standing hat in hand.

There was no look-out or coast-guard on the tower which was set on some rocks against which the big waves broke. Her eye traced the line of markers showing the extent of the safe netted areas. But not so safe, for soon after they had arrived in Scottburgh she had seen warning notices posted up alongside publicity for films, tea-dances, the aquarium and night-spots. These warnings were savage with their illustrations of raw stumps, grisly wounds and deformed scar-tissue.

DEREK GEORGE WESTON

This plaque was placed
here to commemorate the life of
Derek George, the much-loved only
son of George and May Weston
of Berkshire, England.

Derek George. Had he been as fair-haired as herself? Had he, like his older sister, inherited the remote look and unreadable expression? Had he been called 'angelic' by neighbours and ayahs? Did black women stroke his cheek and say, 'Ah, sweet'? Had he slept in the same nursery? Sat at the same table? Been nursed by Rose's own ayah, played with the same toys as Rose? That did not seem to be feasible, yet for five years it must have been so. How much had Rose known, overheard perhaps, servant talk? People must have behaved strangely, for how did one talk to a child whose brother had been eaten by a shark?

It was so horrific and grisly, so tragic, so painfully sad, that she felt sick and wanted to weep, but she remained nauseous and dry-eyed. Without her tears, Derek George's only artefact was an old plaque with rusty fixings.

She withdraws, staring out to sea, not aware of the passage of time, until, along the tideline, a short black-haired man runs beside a bounding dog. In spite of the regular dual-language warning notices: '*Geen Hund* – No Dogs', the man is throwing a stick into the breakers which the dog fetches, lays at the man's feet, getting no reward except the one it wants, which is for the stick to be thrown back into the sea again, and again, and again. Rose watches them, following their progress. He is oriental. Japanese. Her thoughts drift towards the man and dog. It is strange – a Japanese man running a dog as though he wasn't Japanese but was a Honeywood villager. She has never thought of Japanese men owning dogs. Do they? Lap dogs, like the Chinese? She has never wanted to know, and now she does. As she now wants to know about Derek George. She sits there, and time gels, so that past – represented by the image of her tragic young father – and the present – the Japanese and the dog – are set for ever in her mind as one image.

That morning she had received a message from Jenny at the Cranbourne to say that the maid, Joyce, had a bit of information that might help – a woman named Kalim lived in Alex.

Rush and crash, rush and crash: the big rollers keep coming and breaking on the wide, beautiful strand which is almost empty because it is a 'Whites Only' beach and in Natal the overwhelming majority of people are not White. Derek. Derek. The more times she says the name, the stranger the sound becomes, until it holds no more meaning than the call of the seabirds. There are no Derek pictures, no artefacts. Who was it said that people are only the artefacts they leave behind? Or was that said of history . . . ? She feels bathed in exquisite sadness, an emotion that will not bear close examination. It is only a matter of hours since she has known of his existence: how can she mourn him, a baby brother she has never known? How can she not, for he is the black hole into which part of her life was sucked.

The beach here is wide. Early every morning it is sifted and cleaned by an army of Blacks, so that tyre-tread patterns give it the look of a Japanese gravel garden, and the first swimmer must violate it to reach the water. Behind her, Rose can hear the rattle of ricksha wheels and the rattle of the runner's leg-shells. 'Medem. Medem. Masta. Baas. Little Missee. Little Masta.' They try everybody who looks a likely tourist. 'Four rand. Only four rand. No charge for you to take the picture.'

Would her father have allowed Rose and Derek to ride with the ricksha boys? They had been on holiday: was he an indulgent father? Would Derek have wheedled as Vee had wheedled, demanded as Becc had done, asked as Jon used to ask, or soberly waited to see what happened like Nora? She closed her eyes and tried the trick of allowing her mind to go blank.

Nothing.

No déjà vu or sensation that gives her the slightest hope that she can give Derek George a breath of life. The image that appears to her is Monica. Suddenly she longs for Monica. Monica to whom she has been close for such a long time. What fools they've been! Rose had never told her about Trevelyan, then she had almost betrayed her with Leo . . . almost.

Rush . . . crash. Every seventh roller is the big one, which booms as it crashes; yet only feet below the turbulent surface the clear water is like liquid bottle-glass. She becomes aware of the smell of the sea; it reminds her of Spain so she turns her mind back to the present. Counting one to seven. The breakers are so long and powerful, gathering momentum from the swell far beyond the net-line, so that no wave is the lesser. Or is it that the tide is turning? Or perhaps the beginnings of a big blow? For the last two days the 'big blow' has been the favourite topic in the bar of the Blue Marlin.

If Leo was here she could say what had come into her mind . . . Leo wouldn't think her fanciful. 'This is how it's been for me for the last two years. Rush and crash. One experience following the other, with no rest between. You and me suddenly wanting one another; Winifred dying; Ballard's affair; that goddam awful divorce; selling Shaft's; Monica getting upset about Jon and Helen; moving; running up debts over Longmore; and then Sunny; and then Threnody's peculiar will. And now . . . ? Suddenly, Rose felt completely exhausted. Now poor little Derek, who has become a rusting plate on a look-out tower. Except that my bottle-glass calm has been on the surface and the turbulence going on below.

She wonders whether Threnody Chaice had known about Derek. It seemed likely: she had been Aunt Fredericka's companion; they would have talked before Rose arrived there. What had they thought when they began to realize that she had forgotten that period of her life? Had they agreed 'least said soonest mended'? That was like Aunt Fredericka: she never wanted anything to interrupt the easy flow of her days tending the Longmore grounds. Threnody must have loved Rose's mystery. Perhaps it was why she had always been so confiding about herself; she would have seen them as both in the same boat . . . Yes . . . Rose suddenly remembers one of the Lammente whodunnits – *Ship of Mysteries* – a murder at sea and no body . . . 'He must have gone overboard as food for the sharks.' It is the only

Lammente murder mystery that Rose had never finished, yet she has never thrown it away. Threnody *must* have known about Derek George. Was her insistence that Rose return to South Africa her way of trying to get Rose involved in unravelling her own past? That was very like her, and it made more sense of the conditions of her will than anything anyone else had come up with.

She lies on her back and stares at the astonishingly blue sky. She reaches for her camera and points it upwards so as to take home a square of blue associated with her Pedr days. Pedr, and days of wonderful sex, and fun, and abandonment, and not caring . . . These rollers she has ridden like a surfer, exhilarated, joyful, and not caring about anything except the pleasure of the moment. Joy is not something Rose has often experienced.

She catches herself thinking of Monica and Ballard raising their eyes to the ceiling on occasions when Leo and herself were involved in stretching some metaphor that had got them going.

What the hell, Monica, why must I always analyse? Pedr *has* been a great rolling breaker, and he's given me the time of my life.

Even so, she wonders how she can gracefully let him know that she would like to sleep in her own room tonight, in her own bed, alone. She doesn't want to hurt him: he has been so sensitive and concerned for her. Lucky Nana to have a man who cares.

It is a bit worrying, though, that he might yet prove to be a destructive tidal-wave, swamping this lovely affair they are sharing. Maybe it is just his way when he is involved in an affair, but several times during the last couple of days, when they were making love, he has grasped her passionately and begged her not to go home, saying that he could not bear it. What if he is serious? She hopes he is not.

She longs for calmness. The dark wood panels of the sitting room, the linenfold of the Longmore hallway, the big Edwardian coloured window on the first landing, with the morning sun behind it, scattering the dark red carpet with jewel colours. The old, thick lawns, still there since her childhood, and probably since her father's and Aunt Fredericka's childhood. The drooping cedar trees, and the crumbling walls held up by the twisted stems of Miss Bateman, Lord Mayo, Fair Rosamund and Edith Jackman who, Aunt Fredericka claimed, had been a schoolfriend.

The snows back home had gone now; there was so much to be done. Now that she had fulfilled the requirements of Threnody's will, the Sunningdale house could be sold and they could get on with the alterations to Longmore. The prospect was exciting. Neither Nora nor Vee was very forthcoming about Leo's visit, except to say that he said he could put in a good price to build a swimming pool. They spoke as though the decision had been made. Well, she'd see: too often she had been steam-rollered into making decisions that turned out to be mistakes. Jon's last letter was an outpouring against Elna's parents who wanted to have Sonia baptized into their church. He had sounded as though he wanted his mother on his side. Maybe he couldn't see that it didn't really matter, just so long as Sunny grew up in a family who cared, but if he and Elna felt strongly, then they had the right to have their way with Sunny, just as the Birdhams had had theirs with Elna.

Standing back from the people she loved – and from Ballard, with whom she had been involved for far too many years to ignore – she had been able to see the Quinlans as a kind of on-going saga, bits of the plot of which were under her control, provided she made the decisions that were hers to make and that she did not, like the Birdhams, try to mould lives that were not hers to mould.

There were very few stones on the beach, so her eye was caught by a flattened egg which she pocketed as being the only transportable memento mori. Having put her hand once on the plaque and photographed it, which was all that she could do for the lost relationship of Rose and Derek, she brushed the sand from her legs and pulled herself to her feet.

Raised voices entered her consciousness. She saw the Japanese man who had been playing with the dog being pushed in the back and jostled by three men wearing dark blue trousers, military-looking blue shirts and wide leather belts. A man walking the promenade went quickly down the beach towards the fracas, and she saw that it was Pedr. Their voices were raised and the dog ran away fast. Pedr was remonstrating with the uniformed men, then the Japanese man and Pedr were both shoved unceremoniously towards the promenade and taken away.

She recognized the situation: it was the one she had told Becc about. Unofficial patrols in unspecific uniforms, patrolling unspecified territory, warning off unauthorized users of white facilities. She had seen a family of Japanese tourists humiliated. The father pushed into his Mercedes-Benz car bearing diplomatic plates, whilst the wife and three children looked on at the man's shame.

Events that must be so commonplace that onlookers barely bothered to look. Perhaps they knew better than to do so. Don't get involved. Rose was surprised that liberals such as Pedr and Nana could bring themselves to remain living here, their presence in the country giving tacit support to the régime. She knew that if she remained here, she could not help but become involved. She longed for England.

Monica, immobile, dressed in a loose kaftan, was standing on the edge of the fish quay looking at the parakeets that were flying under the flopping swell of the sea as it hit the quay wall. On her walk from where she parked her car in the square near the cathedral, she had heard them squawking, a dozen of them flitting from branch to bud-bursting branch, following her progress through the streets of Old Portsmouth. She had come looking for Stringfellow and, not finding her on the fish quay, had gone to her house, only to be told by a cleaning lady that both of her ladies had gawn awf to France or somewhere. 'Be back in about a couple a three weeks.'

Monica had not anticipated this problem, which was why she was standing and staring down at the parakeets through the oily rainbows on the surface of the water, and why she was feeling anxiety, fear, and a desire to move move move and to rush in all directions at once, looking for an escape from the feeling of anxiety, fear, and the desire to rush in all directions looking for an escape from anxiety . . .

Awaking from her sweating, struggling, stifling, dream. The familiar comforting smell of Dettol. The familiar comforting sound of purposeful heels pounding stripped-wood ward floors, the rattle of screens and curtain rings. She was back on the ward. She smiled to herself without moving a muscle. Warm. Safe. Dettol-clean. Back on the wards.

Pedr was so concerned and attentive. Rose had not known him in a solemn mood. They talked to one another in a polite manner. After tea they walked along to the row of seafront shops where Rose bought a bagful of beaded bands, embroidered shoulder blankets, head-cloths and strange, hand-carved keepsakes that never had a tribal purpose but which tourists are expected to take back with them. The hotel manager had told the guests that a storm was brewing and suggested that they might like to spend the evening in the lounge bar where he had arranged some live entertainment. He had been smilingly reassuring, but Pedr said, 'What he is really saying is not to get caught in the open: if you thought the Jo'burg four o'clock storms were fierce, you haven't seen a thing until you see what hits this coast.'

He was right. In the event the storm was so fierce that Rose did not need to find a way of saying that she wished to sleep alone. Few people went to their rooms. The tornado blew the rain in horizontally, its whine almost drowning the sound of both band and singer. Lightning split the old avocado tree which was growing at the entrance and from which guests had picked fruits on their way to the beach, causing it to crash into the foyer, so that the internal doors of the hotel were constantly sucked open and crashed shut, taking curtains and flowers in the slipstream. Children were not put to bed, adults drank large quantities of mixtures invented for the occasion by the cocktail barman. Power and telephone lines were blown down so that the main rooms were lighted with candles and lamps. There was an atmosphere of England during the blitz. Pedr joined a large gathering of people they had only seen in passing during the week, and played cards for money. Rose, experiencing her usual problem of people thinking she was stand-offish, settled down with some sandwiches and drinks and a pile of Overseas and local newspapers. It seemed ages since she had given a second thought to what was going on in the world.

From time to time she gave Pedr a little of her attention, and was not too surprised to discover that he was not only a man who loved winning at cards, but was one who did not at all care to lose. But he was a good poker player, so that throughout the night his pile of chips slowly grew.

Despite the fact that the English newspapers were about a week out of date, she scanned them with growing interest after reading about the rumours of a sex scandal 'in the highest levels of Government' and wondered fleetingly whether Ballard could possibly be the 'unnamed' Conservative politician; but in the way of the 'respectable' press there was no hint to be had between the lines. Equally fleetingly she had a thrill of pleasure that it might be he. London police had attacked and broken up a protest meeting of four thousand jobless people . . . She wondered whether Tom Wilkinson had yet got employment.

Only ten or twelve years ago, when they had gone to the Festival together, the elder children had seemed so sure of their future. It was all so simple. Of the eight, only Becc and Nora had not drifted. By their early teens, those two had known what they wanted and had gone for it. James Wilkinson had always been an unknown quantity. His abiding enthusiasms had always been 'footer' and animals. Monica said that she would lay bets that he would be a vet who played soccer at weekends. Although Vee had thought she would like to 'manage something', she hadn't known what, or whether it was possible for a girl to manage anything. Longmore had given her the chance to prove how good she was. Jon had drifted around until he found himself in an estate agency, Helen and Kate had taken office jobs until the thing they would eventually do turned up – they didn't know what, but Rose suspected that it was marriage they hoped would turn up. Well, thank the Lord her own girls had not set a walk down the aisle as their goal. Perhaps though, thought Rose, it was not surprising that Helen and Kate had, with Monica and Leo illustrating to them how good a marriage could be.

At some point, in spite of the crashing thunder, Rose, like several of the other guests, dozed in her armchair, until at about four o'clock the sky got light, the wind dropped, the rain stopped, the poker school broke up and the sun rose in the bluest of skies.

Whilst the staff were trying to concoct breakfast, guests went out to look at what had happened to the avocado tree; what greeted them was a scene of the most terrible destruction. The banks of what yesterday had been a small inlet had been washed away by a great bore of floodwater pushing its way into the sea. People, still holding cocktails and cigarettes as though at a party, stood looking down at what had been the beach. There was no hint that there was any sand beneath the layers of vegetation deposited there like a great, coarse mat. Sugar cane, shrubs and trees, decorated by corpses of small animals, bright ripe mangoes and mangled avocados, bananas and prickly pears.

Out in the bay, the sun sparkled upon a now quiescent sea of small shivering waves and low rollers with creamy white plumes. Perhaps it was only Rose who saw the dolphins, for no one drew attention to them. A large school of them, their pneumatic curves of the same blue as the sea, could have been mistaken for bits of the sea itself, leaping and plunging. Why couldn't Derek George's encounter have been with one of them? The boy and the dolphin. What a chance it all is, whether we encounter the sharks or the dolphins. Briefly she speculated upon how different her life might have been had Derek George been nudged by the gentle dolphins in the bottle-glass sea. She would have remained a South African perhaps, accepting the conditions as normal and inevitable. Another Angela Brazenose. The idea was shocking.

She felt Pedr's arm slip gently round her shoulders.

'You're ready to leave here.' It wasn't a question.

Rose nodded.

'So am I,' he said.

* * *

Pedr drove at great speed: he appeared to be unable to drive any other way. Soon they were back at Howick Falls drinking coffee.

'You never did get your water from the breakers.'

Rose shrugged and smiled. 'I found better medicine.'

He squeezed her hand, looked at her closely, then turned away. 'I'm sorry I spoiled it for you.'

Puzzled she turned to him. 'You?'

'Being taken to the police. Having to account for myself.' He picked up a pebble, weighed it in his hand, and leaned over to look down into the ravine.

'You did the right thing.'

'You see, that man was treated dreadfully, he was just walking along. The damned beach was deserted, for God's sake.'

'I saw him, he was throwing a stick for the dog, the dog loved it.'

'Oh, it wasn't the dog. It was the disease.' The word hissed angrily from his tight mouth. 'It was yellow skin, slant eyes, the black of his hair. Two of us there, having to give account of ourselves: you and me both as much visitors here as Mr Amojo. But your hair is silver, mine is blond, Mr Amojo is yellow and black, is unacceptable. You could have thrown a stick for the dog, so could I.'

'Will this be . . . ah . . . at all dangerous for you?'

'It would have been wiser for me not to have become involved. Such things occur all the time; usually I do not become involved . . . The name Borgman should not be noticed too often.'

'Do they keep dossiers on all foreigners?' Since his confession on their first day in Scottburgh, neither of them had mentioned his involvement with . . . with what? Rose had no idea what, only that other people involved were already in prison or on the run.

'There will be a Borgman file. My presence in this country will be recorded somewhere. But, unless I do foolish things, as with the Japanese man, then I am merely a rich, playboy dentist who has a lot of dizzy friends.'

Rose was not assured.

'It wasn't even his dog.'

He gave a laugh. 'I know. Did you see how it hopped it when the trouble started?'

'You were right to intervene.'

'It ended our idyll. And here I am doing the same thing again. Forgive me, Rose.' Holding her face he kissed her warmly. 'Don't be angry with me.'

'Of course I'm not angry with you. I didn't come away because of that. It has nothing to do with you. I started thinking about home, and my hotel and all the problems I've left hanging there. And my children. And my friend, Monica – I have some bridges to repair there. It is the right time to leave. If we had stayed another couple of days we should only have been marking time. I don't think I could have enjoyed the beach after yesterday . . . Good Lord, was it only yesterday?' He squeezed her shoulders very hard.

'Tears? I never thought to see that. I've never met a woman so much in control of her tears.'

'I was brought up not to show myself up by crying.'

'You English. Was there ever such a nation as the English?'

'But I'm not.'

'My God, yes.' He took her hands and held them tightly. 'But you won't be proud of that.'

'No danger that I shall claim a South African heritage.'

Driving through the Drakensberg mountains, they suddenly hit fog. Rose, quite terrified of the long drop at the side of the highway, turned her face away from the edge of the road as they drove at a crawl and sat for long miles in silence. Rose withdrawn, Pedr excluded from whatever was going on inside her head; not at all like the amicable silence of their outward journey.

It was quite late when they arrived at the motel which was so new that the roads were not yet made up and many of the chalets were not finished. But the sight of the futuristic encampment of beautifully designed brick and tile tepees with cat-slide roofs settled around a brightly lit new architectural-style glass rotunda restaurant at once cheered Rose up.

They had dinner, trying to be cheerful for one another, and whilst Pedr went to fill up with gasoline and get the oil checked, Rose took their overnight bags into their 'tepee'. Sitting on a low couch, she slowly smoked a cigarette. She hadn't spent much time alone over the last days; her mind had never been clear because her emotions and her body were always clamouring. She couldn't bear this sudden downturn in their joy to continue: her discovery about her brother and Pedr's incident with the police must not be allowed to spoil their stay in Eden. There was nothing she could ever do about Derek George, and nothing to prevent anything that might happen as a result of the Japanese man and the dog.

When Pedr returned, she greeted him exuberantly. His face lit up at the sight of her holding out her hand to lead him. 'This place! Come with me.' She led him into the bathroom. 'Look. Isn't this wonderful? The whole room's a bath.'

Almost the entire floor area was a small sunken terrazzo'd pool which could have taken six or seven people with ease.

He laughed. 'Hollywood in the Drakensbergs. Do you like it?'

'I love it; it is exactly what we need.'

'Total immersion to wash away these last twenty-four hours.'

In a way last night's drama had come as a gift to Pedr because he had wanted space to think what to do. He had always found that he was able to think through a set of circumstances whilst playing poker. He must know whether she loved him. He did not want to continue his 'open marriage'. He wanted to commit himself and have commitment and he wanted it from Rose. 'I think this is intended for the "Springboks" team. What if they turn up?'

She reached out to touch him. 'With you here, I should never notice.'

Smiling now and tugging the point of his beard, she drew his face down and kissed him.

Baring his beautiful teeth at her, he pretended to snap. 'You gave the right answer.' She made a swollen-head sign at him. Slowly they returned to their earlier intimacy, joking and talking nonsense. He poured a bottle of scented bath oil into the gushing water inlet which foamed around them as they floated in the enormous Romanesque bath. As he was rubbing more oil into her shoulders, he said, 'I love you, Rose. I can't tell you how much. I could not even in my own language. Marry me. Nana wants her women, perhaps she will go back to Sweden and have what she wants. It is time for me to get out. If you'll marry me, I'll do anything. I'll go to England with you. Anything you like, but marry me. I love you. I think I have never before been in love. I know it. *This* is love.' Grasping her in an embrace with his legs and arms, his hands – under the warm water – moved gently over her skin. 'You are so marvellous to me and I want to possess you all the time. But not only to be within you – of course I do want to be inside you, it is wonderful inside you; but not only that. I want us to be always together. Am I sounding corny again? OK, so corny is the truth.'

But that wasn't what Rose wanted to hear.

Aroused, not only by his hands but as well by the tension of the previous twenty-four hours, it was not the ardent declaration of a romantic lover that she wanted to hear at that moment. What outwardly cool, enigmatic Rose desired was that he tell her, in stark uncompromising Anglo-Saxon words, what he wanted to do. And she – now that she had spent a week free of euphemisms and the language of Hollywood censors and modern English novels, and a week in which she had come to realize that words she had never said aloud were the only appropriate ones for the joyful, hedonistic lust they shared – she wanted to tell him the many ways she would bring him to climax. Their week of triumphant acts had made her cringe for her old Lorna Lammente heroines and wish to identify with gods and goddesses of Indian temples.

She felt adult and experienced. Whole. She had cried openly. She had uncovered the weaknesses and tragedies of her family and revealed to herself the stark reality that nobody had wanted her. Her mother had retreated into suicide. Her father had retreated into a new marriage and his own equivalent of Rose's secret garden bosks where, as she had herself, he pretended that everything in the world was fine. Her step-mother had soon got rid of Rose and abandoned her to her only living relative. Aunt Fredericka, having taken her into the Weston family home, had then handed her over to Threnody Chaice. Rose could not say that Threnody had entirely abandoned her, for, as she had lately learned, Threnody had kept herself informed of Rose over the years. She now understood something of why she had grabbed at the chance of marriage when Ballard had offered it.

They were all weak.

Rose now knew that she was stronger than all of them. She knew that, whatever happened, she had the backbone to deal with it. Last night, as the storm raged, she had, as Nora would say, got herself sorted. After she had done with thinking about the children and Monica, she had again turned her mind to the sensational newspaper report of the disappearance beneath the waves of her brother whilst their parents were looking on. The reporter's speculation about his death. The regurgitated stories of other shark attacks on that part of the coast. Then she imagined herself inside her mother's dreadful mind: what if she had seen Jon, or Becc, or any of them disappear before her eyes? How could any woman ever live after that? How could she bring herself to pretend to be a normal mother to her daughter having experienced that grotesque scene? Rose understood why her mother had done what she had done. Understood, but knew that she would have forced herself to have been there, to stay alive for her surviving children. She understood and forgave. And, although she would never again have the strange, numb blankness that had constituted her childhood memory for thirty years, she was glad to have herself whole.

In the way that she had dealt with Ballard's treachery, by looking it in the eye then going ahead to provide a home-base for her children, she had already proved herself not to be as weak and incapable as she had always supposed. Now she felt perfectly brave and strong. She had become so, alone.

Rose luxuriated in the deep foamy perfumed water. Pedr followed her, squatting down, his knees drawn up, his back to the wall. Kissing his wet knuckles warmly, she said, 'Pedr, you are one of the best things that ever happened to me. You are sheer pleasure and joy, just as Sonia is.' She laughed. 'It's funny, but that's quite true. I have no responsibility for Sunny, I enjoy her enormously, and then I hand her back. You are handsome enough to drive a woman to distraction. You have a wonderful body – and you have a wife. No, listen. You can't propose to me because you and Nana are still together; you've spent years together. You belong to her as much as Sunny belongs to Elna and Jon. I can enjoy you, but I cannot have you.'

'One of Nana's women has a child, and would probably be quite willing to have another to please Nana.'

'I don't want to marry.'

He swished the water, parting the foam, which re-formed, obsessively. 'This is not just an affair. You know that it is not. It is not casual. We are two people who should be together.'

'When we started out it was going to be five or six days of sun and sex whilst Nana was off having the same.'

'I never reckoned on falling in love, Rose. I shall soon be forty years, yet I have never known to be in love like this.'

'I never reckoned on you falling in love either. I'm sorry.' She knelt across him, massaging the oily foam over his chest. 'If I had guessed you would get serious, I would have gone down to Durban on my own. But I thought that all you wanted was to do the thing in more comfort than on the back seat of a car.'

They tried to make love in the water, but they were in too much of a hurry and the mosaic steps were slippery with oil and foam, causing them to slither and writhe. They trailed foam and wet footmarks across the polished pine floor to the low divan, emerging breathless from their fierce, cathartic exchanges. They were beginning to say farewell and there was so little time. She was glad to have had Pedr as a lover because he was uninhibited and generous. Even so, had her circumstances been different when she met Trevelyan or had her self-esteem been higher, then he could have been the one . . . or Leo, if Winifred had not died just at that moment. Oh Winifred, you saved me from losing Monica. Anyone can patch up friendship after a disagreement over children. But fucking your friend's husband leaves it beyond repair. She would tell Monica about Pedr.

Tomorrow Rose would ring Jonathan and arrange a day when he could pick her up at the airport.

'I think she's coming round. *Can you hear me?*'

A hand pats Monica's face. 'Wake up! Can you hear me? Wake up, wake up my dear.' A man's voice.

Thank God, the birth was over. Monica had forgotten that she was pregnant. How could she have forgotten?

'I'm sure she's there . . .'

Monica's eyelid is lifted. She leaves it open until it becomes dry. A white coat and a lace cap. Not a baby . . . she has had an operation? She opens the other eye.

'Ah. There we are, Sister.' The white coat nods and the lace cap smiles.

'Shall I raise her up a bit?' She does so.

He's a good-looking doctor. Nice and round and plump, comforting, it's always comforting to have a doctor with a belly. Monica smiles back at him.

'Now then, my dear, let us see what we can see.'

Sister straps Monica's arm and looks at the blood-pressure gauge as she pumps and lets out the air with a slow hiss.

The gauge reads one-twenty over seventy.

He says, 'You had a nasty accident. Do you remember what happened?'

Monica doesn't respond at once; she is calculating her options. Her mind feels as clear and clean as her stomach, except that her stomach feels sore. So does her throat. She suspects that she has been vomiting. 'No,' she says. 'Was I run over?'

'You fell off the quay.'

'The quay?' She is puzzled, for the last thing she can remember is following some parakeets.

'In Portsmouth.'

'Oh?'

'Don't you remember?'

'No. Where am I now then?'

'St Mary's.'

'Where?'

Nurse and doctor exchange brief glances.

'Well, never mind for now. You rest again. Sister will send a nurse to take your details, and we will get in touch with a member of your family as soon as we can.'

Fifteen minutes later, Sister takes incomplete forms to the duty doctor. 'She can't even remember her name.'

'Better get in touch with somebody at the local nick then.'

In the ward, Monica settles back into her propped-up pillows and lets her mind drift over her options. From her own experience of similar cases of trauma-induced memory loss, she guesses that she maybe has three days. No one will miss her until Thursday when Jean comes in, which gives Monica a couple of days in which to decide what she is actually going to do with the next twenty or thirty or more years of her life.

When Rose stepped off the bus outside the zoological gardens, the first chill of autumn on the high veldt made her glad that she had worn her cashmere cardigan. Her bare feet, having been in sandals for the three months since she arrived here in January at the height of summer, were brown and hardened to the weather.

The airy tea-house was much grander now than the place where Ayah brought her as a child. It was the only landmark she could think of where they could meet and Ayah not feel uncomfortable, which she would certainly have done at the Cranbourne, as would Rose in Alex Township.

Ayah was already there. Rose had passed one or two young women wearing saris but this one was old and sitting on the grass, erect and with her knees bent in the half-lotus that was typical of the Ayah Rose remembered. She was facing the main path, but Rose was approaching from the side. She slowed her pace so as to give herself time to take in the moment. She was thin, and she wore a most beautiful red sari banded in gold-thread embroidery. From time to time she plucked at the silk as the breeze threatened it. Suddenly she turned as though Rose had called to her and, leaping to her feet with agility, Fatima Kalim at first put out her hands and at once withdrew, rearranging them into a greeting or prayer position.

Rose took the hands in hers, but was unable to speak for the lump in her throat or see for the tears that filled her eyes until they overflowed and ran down her cheeks. After all these years, the same Ayah was still there, in the eyes, in the gentle upward curve of the mouth and, yes, in the small mole on her cheek that Ayah had said was a beauty spot and which Rose had forgotten. Her plumpness had dried into skinny folds and her hands felt like a bag of chopsticks.

'Ayah? Oh, Ayah.' A sight rare in public, a white madam embracing and kissing an old Asian woman. Fatima Kalim pulled quickly back, but Rose still held the bony hands. She thought she was saying, I'm sorry, I didn't think, but no words came out. Their eyes locked. It was a poignant and wonderful moment. Rose was quite unprepared for the depth of emotion that overwhelmed her.

Fatima didn't move, but stood staring, and with no show of emotion. She made a slight movement and became the one who was holding the other's hands; she opened Rose's cupped palms and looked into them as though she might see the answer to something there. Then she raised both palms to her lips and kissed each separately. Her thin brown lips were surprisingly soft and warm. Love mixed with painful emotions swamped Rose: it was as though a wave had hit her and she could not get her breath.

In only seconds of real time, Rose remembered sitting in the back of the hired car. Remembered herself and Ayah being driven home by the coloured driver. Remembered being enveloped within the folds of the white sari whilst Ayah kissed the palms of her hands. Remembered being allowed to hold the breasts that she had once been allowed secretly to suckle for comfort but was now too old to do so. Distress overwhelmed her now and she found it difficult not to cry to sobbing point.

Still without having spoken, Fatima Kalim drew Rose away from the curious eyes of coffee drinkers, and the idle eyes of gardeners and sweepers. Rose cried silently, wiping her dripping face, walking blindly until Ayah at last spoke.

'Sit here.'

Here was a peeling park bench, with no label to designate it as either European or Bantu. Now Rose looked around and saw that they had walked well away from the main area of the park, from which came distantly hollow-sounding belching lions; sharp, short canine barks; shrieking parakeets and macaws; and from further off the hoots and engine-revving of city dwellers in their cars. Building was going on here, high walls of red brick and a railed-off rocky bear-pit.

'This will be for elephants when it is finished building. I think new bear-pits will be behind this wall you can see, where the boys are taking bricks just now.'

Rose blew her nose and threw the sodden tissue on to a pile of builders' rubbish. 'I'm so sorry, Ayah. To make a fool of myself like that . . .'

'I could have made a better greeting. You have remembered me?'

'I have never forgotten. I can't remember much else, but I've always remembered you. I knew you at once.'

'Have you come home?'

'My home is in England, it always will be.'

'This is a good place for people . . .'

Rose supposed she meant 'people like you'. 'I have been here three months, I'm afraid that it is not my home.' She took the old, dry hand again. 'Much of that time I have been looking for you.'

For the first time, Fatima smiled. 'I have always been here.'

'I'm glad, or I would never have found you. I put notices in the newspapers.'

'I save my eyes for the women's magazines. I see colour very well . . . I like to look at the clothes; sometimes I make the recipes.'

'I always loved it when you wore your sari. I longed to be dressed like that.'

'You once wound yourself in a curtain the girl had washed. The girl was cross, but the madam laughed: she said you were a pudding ready for boiling.'

'Did I? I don't remember.'

The earlier touch of autumn had disappeared now. The stones and rubble grew hot, sending warm currents of air over their feet. The bench cracked a little as it expanded and shed flakes of old paint. Except for the distant animal sounds, and the chink of trowels as somewhere, out of sight, bricklayers worked on the elephant house, it was quiet, until some cleaning 'boys' came and leaned on their brushes, laughing when they saw that one great lumbering brown bear was in the act of mounting its mate.

As though this incident was not the cause of her wanting to leave, Fatima Kalim rose gracefully from the bench. 'Excuse me, I must pee.' She put up a hand as though to halt her problem. 'Waterworks! I am getting old.' Rose and her old Ayah walked easily across the grass, not saying anything until they reached the 'facilities' when Rose stepped aside to allow Ayah to go ahead. But Ayah too stepped to one side, and continued walking to another block which was at a little distance. In an instant Rose recovered and went into the European 'Women Only' block, her cheeks pink from her faux pas. When she came back out and saw Fatima waiting, she decided it was soonest mended to leave it without comment.

'Was it here that there was a lake?'

'A pond.' Fatima nodded in a general direction. 'Perhaps it seemed large to a small girl. You liked the water.'

'And you used to hold me? And let me put my bare feet in?'

'That is quite correct. And you can remember this?'

Rose shook her head. 'Not really: it is one of the snatches of memory I get sometimes. Could we just sit? I promise I shan't cry again.'

They sat on the warm grass, neatly edged and beautifully tended, but hard and prickly because lusher grasses did not thrive the daily baking for nine months of the year. 'Your name is Queenland now?'

'I am divorced.'

'It happens. My daughter has left her man. We live together.'

'I have two daughters living with me. And one older in London, and also a son, Jonathan. They are all grown up. Jon has a baby daughter, Sonia. Everybody calls her Sunny, because she is.'

'My Rose . . . you are a grandmother?'

Rose had promised not to cry, but she found it difficult when she saw Ayah's moist eyes.

'And you?'

'My man was black. He was a good man; even so we could not live in the place for coloured people, so I live where I live with the blacks. Mina is my daughter, Mina Rose. She was born one year after you were sent away . . . Mina Rose. Trudy is my granddaughter.' She beamed, showing that most of her teeth were still white and good; she had apparently not taken to smoking tobacco. 'Trudy's child is a boy . . . He has a church name, but he is "Big baas".' She clapped her hands at the joyful thought of 'Big baas'.

'How old is he?'

'Two years.'

'Sunny will be three this year.'

'Rose was not even one year when the first madam gave her to me.'

'What she was like?'

Fatima held her hands out, palms towards Rose, indicating the obvious. 'Like? Like you are.'

'But I am much older than she was when she died.'

'The face is the same . . . just the same. Everything. Your walk is like hers. She was the most beautiful white madam I have seen. Her face was perhaps solemn, but inside she was full of smiles and she was happy. I could think when I see you that my madam has returned from heaven.'

Rose was quiet for a few moments, taking it in.

'Would she have gone to heaven?'

'Of course. My first madam was a good Christian lady.'

'I know what happened.'

Now it was Fatima who paused before responding. 'What is it that you know?'

'I know that she did not die from contaminated watermelon.'

Fatima held a hand over her eyes, then she looked at Rose, shaking her head. 'Who can have told you? The English sister the new madam sent you to? Why? The masta said that it was not necessary for you to know. I think that my baas was right. You were very young.' She put her hand over Rose's. 'My masta died. It was too much . . . for all of us.'

'I remember that my father died, but I don't remember ever knowing anything else, which is why I came hoping to discover something for myself. I've got so few memories of my childhood. I came here to see if there was anything that would stir my memory. A few things I remembered; but this city has changed. Once I had started I felt that I must do whatever I could in the time I had. I am just back from Durban. Three days ago I saw the newspapers . . . I know everything that happened in Amanzimtoti. I know about Derek George.'

'Only just now?'

Rose nodded.

'It has been forty years for me. Time takes away some pain, but for you it is very close.'

'But I didn't know this. It is as though I had heard it happened to a stranger . . . my brother is a stranger to me.'

Fatima considered. 'Do you not remember you brother at all?'

'Until the other day I didn't even know that I had a brother.'

'Then my old masta was right: it was best that you were not told.'

'What was he like? Was he fair like me?'

'He looked so much like my old masta. No, he was not at all pretty, but he was strong . . .' She laughed faintly. 'He was mischief, always hiding things, hiding himself when he must come. This is why my old masta did not believe that he was lost. He thought that the boy had gone from the water and was hiding and giggling as he did at bed-time. The masta said, "He will come out when he is hungry." I think I shall not say any more.'

'I can't understand why I don't remember him at all.'

'When you were back at home, you were unwell: bad dreams, sleepwalking, very high fever . . . The doctor said that it was delirium because of shock. He said that it is good for people not to remember when they cannot do something to make the matter right. You understand that?'

'Yes, I know that it can be a symptom of shock. I have always assumed that I was suffering from some kind of mild amnesia, that my childish mind refused to admit that my mother was not coming back, and then when . . . when my father married again . . . Was I very mixed up?'

'You did not appear so. You accepted the new madam very well. She left you to me.' She frowned and turned her head, pinching her lips together. 'Please, I do not wish to bring those years back.'

Rose held on to Ayah's trembling hands. 'I'm sorry, Ayah. I am sorry to have brought it all back for you. It must have been terrible for you to be involved with the family. Not many would have wanted to stay. I don't suppose nannies were any better paid then than they are now.'

A breeze caught Ayah's vivid sari and flapped it across her face. With an elegant movement of a single finger she repositioned the fine silk. It had given her time to gather herself. 'I have called you "Rose". I hope that you do not mind?'

'But I am Rose. Of course I am Rose, what else could you possibly call me. Perhaps I should call you . . . Fatima?'

'Ayah. I was "Ayah" only to you. Rose, you must never think that I went with the old masta and madam because of money. Of course they paid me . . . The old masta was not very generous.' She hunched her shoulders a little and smiled apologetically. 'It is only the truth. Why I stayed was because of you. I had milk in my breasts and the first madam gave you to me. You were only some months old. The first madam was losing her milk because of weakness. I had full breasts: my child had died of pneumonia. I had no husband then . . . the first madam took me so kindly to feed her baby. She gave you to me, and you took to the breast as though you were mine. Until then I was ready to join my own baby and her father. Perhaps we saved one another, you for your Sunny and I for my "big baas".'

Quite a little crowd came to see her off at Jan Smuts airport: Angela and her husband, Nana Borgman and half a dozen of the Angela Set who Rose had met on several occasions. She guessed that Angela had organized the send-off and imagined that they would all meet up later for sundowners, or bridge now that the evenings were chillier. Nana had come, but not Pedr. Angela's people were probably quite disappointed to have been deprived of such a titillating parting, for she had known within a day of her return from Natal that the Rose and Pedr affair was the hot topic.

She and Pedr had taken leave of each other in her suite at the Cranbourne. A night of promises and tears and renewed passion. Pedr desperately trying to convince her that he could not go back to his previous existence with Nana; Rose trying to persuade him that he must do nothing precipitate; Pedr saying that he would not accept her refusal to marry him as soon as he was free.

At the airport, Rose had misgivings. She had been given the keys to a wonderful life with a man she had begun to fall in love with. She had not accepted them, but was already beginning to wonder how soon it would be before she changed her mind. If she was the cause of Pedr's marriage to Nana breaking up, then her behaviour would be as immoral as Ballard's had been, even though Pedr insisted that, long before Rose appeared on the scene, he and Nana had come to the conclusion that they had grown up and beyond the idea of their 'open' marriage, and had already discussed the possibility of divorce.

As Nana was giving her a parting gift of an album of photographs of her garden, and a memento rosebud from it preserved in a glass drop, Rose caught sight of Ron, who had travelled out on the same flight as herself. The stoned Bridgette and the children Zara and Neil. It seemed such a long time ago. Ron was just getting out of a car in the company of four men. She raised a hand to wave at him, but let it drop because she had a premonition that something was wrong. The men, close around Ron, hurried him through the concourse. Nana took the hesitant hand quite casually and said, 'Goodness, my dear Rose, what are we thinking of, you haven't a book to read. Come with me, or I shall be in trouble with Pedr: he particularly said that you must have something absorbing for the journey. No need for you all to come.'

As she spoke, she led Rose away from the Angela crowd who, at Nana's gracious command, were heading for the coffee-bar, and towards the airport bookshop. As soon as they were out of earshot, Nana said, 'You were watching those men, you know who they are?' Her face held a pleasant half-smile but her tone was serious.

'One of them. I travelled out with him and his family, they were emigrating from England.'

'Those men are State Security. The Englishman has been in trouble.'

'Ron?'

Nana picked up a paperback. 'Not quite like this,' and turned the jacket for Rose to see that it was one of the Le Carré spy series, 'but your man has been subversive. He has bitten the hand that was feeding him.'

'He's just an ordinary fellow, an electrician with a wife and two children. He was going to get them a swimming pool and a housemaid.'

'The bureau is very cross with him. He is being sent back to England with a bug in his ear.'

'I can't believe it.'

Nana bought two or three best-sellers for Rose, and when they were again on the concourse, said, 'Believe it, Rose. Migrants are not expected to involve themselves in trades unions. He has been speaking out at union meetings.'

'But unions are legal, aren't they?'

Nana raised an eyebrow. 'In this country one soon learns nuances, learns what a Joseph's coat the idea of freedom of speech can be.' She linked arms lightly in a friendly way. 'Pedr says that you are an . . . involved person yourself.' Her polite smile and conversational tone overlaid her meaning.

Rose was beginning to feel quite ill-at-ease. Twice Nana had mentioned Pedr's name. 'On a very superficial level. I'm no subversive. Not a political person at all.'

'Pedr says differently.'

For a brief second, Rose wondered what impression anyone seeing them might have. Two women of about the same height, fashionably and expensively dressed, slowly walking the concourse, idly conversing. Who would know that they shared a man, perhaps only last night (Pedr had said that he could not ever go back to Nana's bed, but he might have). Who could tell that the dark-haired woman regularly broke the morality laws, that her husband accepted that he was married to a woman who was 'AC/DC', as he had so unconcernedly said? Who could possibly have guessed that the blonde-haired one was actively considering telling him that, whatever the consequences, she wanted to continue their relationship? If she didn't say something now, then it would be too late. She drew Nana to a bench where they sat down.

'What else has Pedr said?'

Nana looked at her evenly and with a faint smile. 'My dear Rose, so much, it would take too long.'

'Look,' Rose said, 'I am going back to England, and I doubt that I shall ever come here again.'

'Does this mean that you are . . . you are really walking away?'

'I'm not "walking away", I am going home. I came here for a break and now I am going home to my family. I have a business to run.'

'You know what I mean. You will make him crazy . . . he is already making crazy plans. He would easily have booked a seat on this flight except that I think that it is not the kind of gesture that you would appreciate.' She shrugged a little. 'And you must know that there are other things here that he cannot walk away from.'

It came to Rose that this was a bizarre situation. She wanted to ask Nana: Don't you care? Don't you want him?

As though telepathic, Nana said, 'Pedr is very dear to me, we have been together for ten years. He and I, we respect one another. We are different people, and we have different needs and likes. You know that we have always taken lovers.' She flicked her hands. 'Stupid word, it is a book word, it is a word that needs enlargement, but you are going on an airplane. From always Pedr and I have these ideas that it is not important. He likes only women, I like both. He puts his fingers in a patient's mouth to mend her teeth or between her legs to make her aroused; a man will caress my breast or shampoo my hair . . . these are unimportant, people touching people matter only to the law.' She tapped her forehead. 'Sex is in the mind. Important to Pedr and me is that we have the same purpose, the same ideals: those things will not change for Nana and Pedr even if

Rose and Pedr are making earthquakes with their bodies in Scottburgh.'

I am beginning to feel out of my depth, Rose thought.

'Don't you care, Nana? Or don't you want Pedr?'

'I should not like to lose him as a comrade. You understand? He is needed here for as long as –' she laughed – 'for as long as we can keep up the swimming and sundowners. Ten years of so many Angelas.' She wagged her head, then she laughed. 'Can you imagine what they are guessing now? All kinds of hot gossip.' She handed over the bag of books and magazines she had bought.

'Thank you. Thank Pedr too.'

'Ach, you must thank Pedr. It will not be very many weeks before he will have a good reason to visit London. I think Chichester? Many dentists from all over the world.'

'Um . . . about Ron. Do you know what is happening to Bridgette, his wife, and the babies? Are they being expelled too?'

'I doubt it. The bureau doesn't concern itself with the domestic affairs of subversives. Once he is in the air, his file can be consigned to the archives at Pretoria.'

'She must be out of her mind with worry. She's terribly young, and petrified of flying. I can't see how she's going to get back without Ron; as it was he had to practically carry her here drugged. I wonder, perhaps I should cancel my flight . . . She hasn't anyone here, and the family is just working class: they'd find it hard to raise the money for one of them to come out and bring her home.'

She could cancel her flight. Here was her perfect excuse, and she wanted to take it. Nana laid a hand on her arm, and for a moment the two women looked at one another and saw behind the masks they each wore. 'No need to worry; it will be taken care of here.'

'Is there anything I could do at my end?'

Nana shook her head. 'Remind people of what is happening here. Tell them about Ron.' She hesitated. 'And the Japanese man and the dog.' She smiled wryly. 'I think he behaved unwisely being so open with you, but then he is very much in love. I think it is for the first time.'

Ballard had never really got used to being the son-in-law of Sir Evelyn Corder-Peake, and probably never would. Now, as he waited for him to arrive at the club, he lit an expensive Havana, the aroma of which always reminded Ballard that he was a wealthy and powerful man who need bow the knee to no man.

Surprisingly for such a self-indulgent man, Ballard had improved physically since Miriam had taken charge. He had not appreciated how an early swim can set a man up for the day, how a half-hour of isometric exercise and a simple thing like eating exotic fruits instead of pudding could reduce his weight. He had begun to prefer the fruits and the impressive ritual of silver knives and scoops for eating. He had gone beyond requesting easily available fruits, such as fresh brown Turkey figs or out-of-season alpine strawberries; no, one of Ballard's small pleasures was trying to discover a fruit that the restaurant could probably not provide. 'No carambolas? How disappointing. A nice edgy carambola is just what is needed after the duck. Paw-paw? All right then, I suppose I shall have to settle for the fresh lychees. I'll skin them myself.'

His hair was noticeably whiter, but in the most flattering areas just above his temples and in a fine streak running back from his forehead. The slimmer Ballard did not look younger, but he certainly appeared more attractive. His hand-finished suits hung well and announced discreetly, 'Wealth is here.' None of these changes affected his need to have an affair (and it did seem to be a need, for nobody could say that Miriam wasn't always ready, eager and able).

His current mistress was producer of one of the most popular children's TV programmes, which of course meant that they must both be discreet – and she especially: always a sensation-enhancer. She wasn't particularly good-looking, nor was she young – nearer Rose's age than Mimi's. But she had spent twenty years having discreet relationships and learning how to get maximum pleasure from the minimum of time. She liked the best of everything and was one of what at one time would have been called 'the fast set'. She had been married and wanted none of it. She had a career, and she was not backward at making her own desires known. She had no known origins and apparently no family or responsibilities. She was her own woman. She had certainly taught Ballard a thing or two, both in bed and out of it. She might have been the perfect mistress for Ballard Quinlan, except that there were members of that fast politico-media set who had, in journalese, 'improper associations with Soviet diplomats'.

Her name was Marsha Childs and, as Ballard well knew, she would not miss him half as much as he would miss her if the affair ended.

Sir Evelyn, knowing his daughter to be quite sound at bottom, had never been at all concerned at her flirtation with the red faction, but had never liked the idea of having a Socialist married to her, not even one who had crossed the floor of the House. Ever since that business over the boy . . . it had all been hushed up, as these things always can be: the Corder-Peakes had a sufficiency of skeletons; they could do without new ones. He had been persuading himself for so long that the history of his wife's family was that of his own, that the fact that he was the grandson of a corner-shop grocer was now entirely lost to him. In his entry in *Who's Who* he gave few checkable facts except, 'Born Sussex 1896, only son of a wine merchant.' One fact which would stand up under scrutiny, for his father had always stocked Algerian wine and sold sherry from the cask.

Although he had been born – Eric, not Evelyn – into generations of corner-shop trade, he had no intention of continuing in the tradition. He was not so much intelligent as clever, and blessed with a retentive memory. A scholarship to the great Souls grammar school and the good fortune of being given a commission in the '14–'18 war, started him on the road to obtaining the title by which he preferred to be known: 'MFH' or just 'Master'. The road turned out to be a primrose path.

Beautiful Margaret Peake (whose gowns were purchased, one might say, by the very ammunition that Evelyn fired off in France) had fallen in love with the officer who wore the uniform of the new and unique arm of the cavalry – the Tank Corps. On the eve of battle, she (as many young girls did for handsome officers) laid down her virginity and, not knowing how not to, became pregnant. He married her, linked his name to the illustrious Peakes, and the baby miscarried. He survived a dozen battles without injury and gained a reputation for being able to 'catch bullets in his teeth', and a row of medals which pleased Margaret's parents enormously. Having accepted that their daughter was one of the many casualties of war, the Peakes accepted the wine importer's son into their illustrious family, gave him a place in the family business, which was manufacturing and trading in the means of death. A business honourable and lucrative and rewarded by governments of all persuasions.

His history goes some way to explaining his attitude to Ballard and his entry into the family.

He stood still as his coat was slid from his arms by the porter, with the least amount of effort to either man.

'Mr Quinlan is in the Gough Room, sir. If you would care to follow me.'

If Sir Evelyn was at home anywhere it was in a gentleman's club. He sniffed the air. Roast beef, steamed puddings, pipe and cigar smoke and the general smell of dust and age and order. Male and serious, the fate of nations was planned in such places. He might not like Quinlan, but they at least understood one another in some respects, and they had in common the pursuit of wealth.

Ballard stood until his father-in-law was seated and a drink called for.

'Well, young man?' Sir Evelyn raised his ragged and bushy eyebrows and looked down his nose in the manner of a senior statesman.

'Before lunch, sir?'

'Always deal before you eat – always been my motto.'

'It's about Miriam, sir.' In the presence of Sir Evelyn, Ballard became a chameleon, easily falling into using the tone, accent and phrases of what at one time he would have referred to as 'bargain-basement county types'.

'What's the girl been up to this time?'

'Well, she's pregnant.'

'Wondered if she might be. Got a bit big in the buttock area lately.'

'What do you think, Sir Evelyn? I mean, she quite wants it, but there is already, you know, the boy. This is damned difficult. The thing is, I'm over fifty, and if I don't see another perambulator I shan't fret . . . I mean, I've been thinking about my will and that kind of thing.'

'Ah! What to do about young Gerald and your other . . . er.'

'Four children, right. Another baby would be a complication.'

'Well, forget young Gerald, he's a Hamilton now. The Hamiltons aren't short of a shilling, you know, but they aren't too hot on making heirs. Something amiss between their legs, if you ask me, a couple of them shirt-lifters . . . I sometimes wonder about Pamela's chap, but there, doesn't do to say these things. But still, it's an ill wind. Only young Gerald and the girl to inherit from the Hamiltons. You do what you like for your other . . . er . . . how many you say?'

'Four, sir.'

'Boys?'

'Only one.'

'Ah. Never mind, better than none. Bit depressing, y'know, not seeing the family name carried on. Man-to-man: Margaret lost all that bit down below . . . But there it is, always a good side to things, women are a great deal more fun if they think a chap's, you know, not going to put 'm in the club.'

Ballard nodded, gratified that his father-in-law was at last treating him like one of Them and not an interloper. Had Ballard known about the Algerian wine and the sherry cask, he might not have been so diffident. His own family's department store was classes higher than groceries and off-licences.

'Best thing as I see it, let Mimi have the child. It will do her good, settle her in that nice house. If she comes up with a boy, so much the better, if not . . . well, not much to be done about that. I'll see my solicitor gets something drawn up.'

Sir Evelyn downed his third G and T and slapped his knees. 'Right! Now that's out of the way.' He picked up the leather-bound menu.

And then casually, as though this had not been the prime reason for his wanting to see Mimi's husband, 'By the way, heard anything on the grapevine about dirty tricks in high places?'

Ballard of course had, from Marsha, but it didn't do to commit oneself, so he gave a jolly chuckle. 'Which ones . . . always dirty tricks there, Sir Evelyn.'

'No names, no packdrill.'

Ballard waited for the important message that was being signalled by this apparent tittle-tattle.

'Time you had a bit more time for your family . . . young baby and all that. Good time to go. Saw you with Marsha Childs, nice woman, very nice, does a lot for charity . . . President, aren't you? Well look, you know what I mean. Looks bad if a chap suddenly throws his hand in, but if you were thinking of spending a bit of quiet time in the country, now that Mimi's pregnant . . . don't have to wait till the next election. Have a chap in Harley Street look at your heart or something . . . get out gracefully . . . PDQ. You're a good chap in the Consortium, Quinlan . . . shouldn't like to lose you. Been to the races lately?'

Ballard shook his head and signed for another tray of G and Ts.

'Took Lady Margaret last week. Saw the Queen Ma there with that pretty actress wife of Profumo's. Nothing in that business, you know.'

Non-committally, Ballard nodded as his father-in-law continued.

'Profumo, he's straight as a die. PM won't have a word against him.' What Sir Evelyn didn't know about the shady side of politics and power wasn't worth knowing, and the signals were that the big scandal threatening was about to break.

Ballard knew that, in the interests of good manners and familial solidarity, he would today forget fine cuisine and eat rare beef with roast potatoes and Yorkshire pudding followed by spotted dick and heavy custard.

And he knew also that the rumours about Profumo, the Minister of War, were true. Sir Evelyn was warning him to distance himself before it was too late. If Marsha was involved, then Ballard and thus the Consortium might be under scrutiny. If the War Minister was in trouble, Ballard did not need telling twice to distance himself.

People stared at Becc as she swished her way through the concourse towards Arrivals. She *must* be Someone: who else except a pop singer or an actress would wear a dress like that as though it was quite normal to look as though it had been borrowed from a ten-year-old girl. Two bits of cloth linked at the shoulder and ending half-way up her thigh. With legs like that . . . She was very thin.

And people looked at Vee, particularly men. She had taken to wearing only black, the simplicity of which suited her. As she walked to where she was to meet Becc and the others, her hips moved provocatively beneath the closely fitting fine wool dress that reached her knees. She wore the finest black stockings and Italian shoes. Vee was not thin, she was curvaceous, with beautiful breasts and hips. With her chin raised, she looked straight into the middle-distance. With her features inherited from her mother, the only signal she gave that she was not ice-cool and untouchable was the full and sensual mouth she had inherited from her father; this she always outlined and painted carefully in vivid scarlet. She was a very confusing lady.

Nora and Jon arrived together. Jon in the formal dress of an estate agent wanting clients to have confidence in him; Nora, wanting everyone to know that she was a university student, wore linen trousers and her boyfriend's jacket with the sleeves rolled up to the elbow, and hugged to her chest a scruffy leather music-case bulging with books and papers.

'There's Becc at the bookstall!' Jon guided Nora in their sister's direction.

'Darling, just look!' She opened a glossy woman's magazine at a double spread showing very pregnant women wearing button-fronted flying suits in vivid colours.

Nora read aloud, '"New designs from Becc Quinlan". That's great, Becc.'

'The entire article is about *me*! Can you believe it?'

Jon hugged her shoulders and said laconically, 'I can believe it. Absolutely.'

She pulled away from him. 'Be anything you like, Jon, but don't be a bloody patronizing prick.'

He knew that whatever he said would be the wrong thing, so he shut up, and the three of them walked on to where they should meet Vee.

'God above!' said Vee. 'All the chicks come home to roost. I can't remember the last time the four of us were together. The plane's held up in Rome.'

'Winnie's funeral,' said Nora flatly.

'God, yes,' said Vee. 'What a bloody carry-on. I wouldn't want to do that one again. Anybody seen the old man lately?'

They went into a bar. Jon brought a tray of drinks to their table.

Becc, her skirt riding to her crotch when she was seated, said, 'Vee was asking if anybody had seen the Old Man.'

Nora said, 'He came up with some cash for me to supplement my grant. He phoned me and I met him. He didn't seem very happy. I felt sorry for him.'

'The posh dwarf has got a bun,' Becc said.

'Poor bloody cow,' said Vee.

Becc, not realizing that there was an association of ideas, said, 'How's Elna and the chick, Jon?'

'They're OK. We've got Sunny into a nice nursery school.'

'So I should think,' Becc said. 'Everything else all hunky-dory?'

Jon had no intention of telling any of them about the aggravation he had had from the Birdhams. They had even got their pastor to call and talk to Jon. He was fed up with it all. The Birdhams hadn't had anyone interfering in their early married life, why in hell's name couldn't they leave Elna to live as she wanted to? He didn't know which was the worst: families who smothered you, or those, like his own, who left you lying on whatever bed you'd made.

Vee said, 'When did any of you last hear from Ma, before she phoned me to say she was coming back?'

They shrugged and exchanged bits of information they had got from postcards and 'phone calls.

'Fancy her finding that old nanny she was always on about,' Jon said. 'I'll bet she was really chuffed.'

'She'll probably want to bring her across here,' Becc said.

'See anything of the Wilkinsons?' Nora said. 'I mean, since Uncle Leo turned up at Longmore.' Flicking a glance at Vee who sat coolly watching aircraft taxiing into position.

'Tom rang me,' Jon said. 'Monica's cleared off.'

All three of his sisters quickly fastened their attention on him. Vee said sharply, 'With a man?'

'I don't think so. I don't think anybody knows where she's gone.'

'A woman?' Becc said.

'Tom said that she was taking a sabbatical . . . you know, Tom. I think she was going off her rocker there at Shaft's.'

'That's no surprise,' Becc said. 'What a life! Imagine being stuck out there in the back of beyond and nothing except old Leo for company.'

'Does that mean that Leo is on his own there?' Nora asked.

'I don't know . . . you know Tom, he's always vague.'

'Excuse me,' Vee said, getting up, 'I'm just going to the . . .'

They watched her go.

Leo was in his office with two of his draughtsmen when the telephone rang. When his secretary said, 'It's the manager of the Longmore Hotel,' he said, 'Ah, I'll take it in my office.'

He said, 'Hello, Leo Wilkinson here.'

All she said was, 'Leo, I've just heard about Monica and I have to tell you that I think you're an absolute shit. She's a hundred times too good for you, and if I was married to you I'd have cleared off years ago. You promised to phone me and you didn't. You could at least have *phoned* me. Wham-bam, thank you, ma'am, like it's been with all those badminton types you've been fucking for years? Is that all I was, an optional extra, free at the point of purchase?'

He had no time even to reply, for the line went dead and he was left staring down into the handset. One thing was for sure, she was hurt and indignant. God, you never knew with women. She had behaved like a swinging tottie and he had laid her in that spirit.

Not so! He'd been quite knocked for six by her. He sank into his expensive hide-covered swivel chair. She had been *so* good, like Monica when he'd first met her; never afraid to say what she wanted from sex.

He should have phoned Vee, but there were always reasons not to. Getting James into Loughborough. Tom's accident, and Monica behaving very oddly lately. Thank God the girls were no trouble. The reason he had not gone any further with Vee, much as he would have liked it, was because he had thought about how he would feel if Helen was fucking around with Ballard. He hadn't phoned Vee because it was tempting fate. He had only got to let himself think about her and he found himself with an erection. Like now.

On the tarmac at Rome airport, Rose, streaming blood from a gash on her face, was rushed along with two other passengers and an interpreter to a first-aid room, where the attendant said her wound was too extensive to deal with there, it must be treated at once by a surgeon. One minute she had been on the little bus taking passengers from the VC10, and the next a part of another vehicle had penetrated the side of the bus, splintering the glass. She had felt a blow, but it was not until she saw the blood flowing down the front of her jacket that she knew that she had been hurt and realized from the expressions on the faces of people looking at her that it must be a bad wound. There was a lot of shouting and somebody questioned her in both English and Afrikaans.

Now, she was somewhere – she did not know where except that it was somewhere in Rome – and was looking into a haloed lamp and the masked face of the man who was concentrating on cleaning and treating the gash that went from her earlobe to the bridge of her nose. His English was quite good, but it was a one-way conversation in the way it is with a dentist at work.

'You must not worry, these sutures are fine . . . there will be no scar.'

Rose didn't like to think of what was going on just below her eye. She still didn't know what had happened. She had passed out. Now the surgeon was peeling off his gloves and a nurse was taking a sterile dressing out of its packet. He was not young, probably about her own age. As the nurse placed the dressing on, he pulled up a stool and sat beside her.

'I will tell you. It is a long wound. Quite deep, but clean. These are the best to deal with. I have made many, many sutures; in one year the scar will be invisible.' He smiled and squeezed her hand, assuring her that her eye was not damaged at all. 'Possibly an eyebrow pencil, that is all. Perhaps your own surgeon will send me photographs . . . or I may come to England and I shall boast of my handiwork.' He took her hand, 'It will be like restoring the Mona Lisa.'

Rose tried to smile, but the pain was too great; instead she squeezed his hand and mentally rolled her eyes at the Mona Lisa bit.

Becc said, 'What's up with Vee? Aren't you afraid you'll get frostbite on your balls, Jon? I don't think she likes men very much at the moment.'

Nora said, 'Hah!' and the other two looked at her.

'Well, go on,' Becc said. 'What the bloody hell is "hah!" supposed to mean?'

'If I tell you you'll only start picking at her.'

'Oh come on, Nora, I'm twenty-five, for God's sake.'

'Twenty-eight,' Nora said.

'I'll see Becc doesn't niggle her.'

'She had a fling with Leo and she's been mooning over him.'

'Vee?' Becc was incredulous. 'And Leo? Christ! She could find a thousand better men to screw than Leo – he must be fifty.'

Nora said, 'You two are like everybody else: you don't know Vee at all.' She crossed ankle over knee like a man and tapped a cigarette on the arm of her chair. 'Vee's a nympho.'

Jon laughed aloud.

Becc said, 'Don't be so bloody sexist, Nora.'

'Me? I'm a feminist!'

'What's the masculine equivalent of "nympho"?' Becc said. 'Think of it.'

Nora did. Becc was always two jumps ahead of anyone else. 'OK, she likes to sleep around. Shut up, she's coming back.'

Nora had another secret, but she didn't think that she would like to tell them. They didn't see one another for weeks and weeks, and then when they did they fell like vultures on any bit of gossip or information going. But she would tell them that she had a place at Leicester University.

'Leicester?' Becc said. 'That's the Swingers' university, isn't it? Don't they test your tolerance to LSD before they give you a place?'

'That's Sussex,' Nora said.

Jon said, 'Did you know James Wilkinson's going to Loughborough?'

'James?'

'That'll be great for you, Nora, right next door,' Becc said.

Jon said, 'Tom said James wasn't getting very good grades, but Leo paid for cramming.'

Vee said, 'The only thing James's good at is rugby; it's obvious why he chose Loughborough.'

Nora and James had already spent three weekends together. She was on the Pill and she and James thought they were in love. In the Midlands they would be well clear of the curiosity of the two families.

Becc had waited long enough. 'Where is that fucking plane?'

Jon said, 'Why does everybody have to use four-letter words?'

Vee said, 'Because there aren't any decent seven-letter equivalents. She could hardly get the same effect from "Where's that fornicating plane?"'

'"Fornicate" is nine letters,' Nora said. '"Screwed" is seven.'

Vee said, 'You should have gone for Cambridge, Nora.'

Jon said, 'Becc's right, that plane's very late. You'd think they'd come up with something better than "A hold-up in Rome".'

Becc said, 'I'm off to grab somebody's balls, and I won't let go until they tell me what's going on.'

She came back subdued and pale. There was another tray of drinks. She picked up a glass of spirit and took a mouthful, tossing it down her throat. 'It's Ma, she's had an accident, I've just seen the BOAC representative, they've been trying to call Jon. He says a luggage trailer crashed into the bus and she's been cut about the face. They're keeping her in hospital. Apparently some super-duper international plastic surgeon happens to be there and he's been asked to do the operation. They suggest we all go home and they'll let us know which flight she will be on. I gave them the Longmore number so that they can ring there.'

Becc's phrase, 'she's been cut about the face', seemed to linger around them, holding them together as a group as they had been held together as scared children.

Nora said, 'Hadn't somebody better ring Mac? He was preparing a celebration.'

Somebody had washed the clothes Monica had been wearing when she fell into the harbour, but there was still a faint odour of diesel oil about them. Her shoes had dried hard, but they were good leather so would soon walk in. The police had been to see her that morning and had told her not to worry, plenty of people lost their memories. She didn't seem to have any chequebook . . . ? Nothing in her pockets . . . ? Never mind, not to worry, best not try to remember. It would be only a matter of a day or two and she'd be as right as ninepins. So she knew that it was now or never. They had only to start by asking a few people at the fish quay and spread out from there, and by this evening they would have found Tom or James or traced Leo. The girls were away . . . it would probably be Leo. She hoped so. She hoped it wouldn't be Tom, although Tom would be the one most likely to understand. She would phone Tom.

She hoped that no busy-body living round the square where she had left her car had wondered why it was still there. It wasn't likely: people on holiday or going to the Isle of Wight left their cars parked for days on end in such places. The petrol tank was pretty full. She had checked her bag: it too smelled oily and she had had to throw away the bits of make-up she kept there; but the lipstick was all right, and her money-purse. She had already remembered that she had emptied her jumble of chequebook and charge cards into the glove compartment.

Afternoon visiting time would be the best time to go. She knew from experience that after the first half-hour when visitors were settled in, nursing staff went off for a quick cuppa and a quiet fag and then were back on the wards ready to field the questions always kept until just before the bell went for end of visiting.

There had been six taxis waiting. She did not direct the driver to where she had left her car, but asked to be dropped at the funfair on Southsea front. Straight from the hospital to the funfair? Taxi drivers had probably done odder drives than that.

It was only a matter of five minutes along the sea walk, and down the steps by the tower. The car started at once. She smiled to herself. That was the beauty of having money, wasn't it? Things got attended to even before they needed attention. She knew where she was going.

The drive from the square to the car ferry was a matter of five minutes. There was a space available. The ferry backed out only yards from the place where her cocktail of pep-pills, slimming-pills and hash had sent her diving off the quayside after the escaped parakeets. God above, what a bloody state to get into. One life, that's all you had, and hers was already half gone. She smiled at the seagulls dipping and diving around the ferry as it swung round and headed out of the harbour, past the fish quay . . . Leo was generous with cash, you could say that for him . . . past the Round Tower, past the Square Tower . . . she would have no worries about money because she had plenty in her own account . . . past the Hot Walls, the funfair, the long promenade where little groups of men fished with long beach-casting rods . . . she would soon get herself established, it was a haven for people wanting temporary work.

Once clear of the harbour the bar opened and, just to celebrate her new-found independence, she bought a single whisky. She hadn't smoked in hospital, so why start? She congratulated herself. That's a good start. Perhaps she wouldn't drink either. Right. So she left the bar and followed the arrow pointing to 'Teas, Coffees, Snacks'.

The tea tasted of nothing, but never mind. Established at what?

She didn't know, but she was no fool, if the worse came to the worse she could always get a job in a hotel or somewhere. The idea appealed. A room of her own. Scruffy. OK so it might be scruffy. Food. Food and a roof over your head and you could be your own mistress. She wasn't serious about working in a hotel. Maybe she'd just bum around for a bit and see what turned up. What was she best at? She smiled out of the murky porthole. Giving a man a good time?

A mature good-time girl? I could do that. Whatever happened from here on, she made herself a promise to keep it in mind that there were better things in life than popping pills and falling into harbours.

By the time she arrived, Monica decided that she would not take hotel work or become a good-time girl; instead she installed herself in a cliff-top hotel, having first purchased a suitcase and a few clothes suitable for a holiday. On foot she walked down the steep path towards the beach. They had had marvellous times here when the kids were young. Leo had said that the clocks here had stopped at half-past 1925, and from what she could see, no one had started them going. Except for a swimming pool, the hotel hadn't changed, and the seedy arcades and beach-junk shops were as gaudily inviting as ever.

Oh, but how useless these places seemed with no kids pestering for 'Pezz' dispensers, and double-hi bouncing balls, balls on elastic, black-eyed sunglasses, straw beachcomber hats, flip-flop sandals and endless frozen things on sticks.

When she went down for a drink before dinner, a quite nice man tried his luck. He only partly succeeded: in return for her letting him share his bottle of Médoc she let him share her table, but not her bed as he'd half hoped. He was quite good company. She told him a lot of lies. That she was a widow. That she had left her two lovers because there were occasions when they had almost forgotten that she was in bed with them. That she had been an entertainer and had appeared before the King of Egypt who had placed a large ruby in her navel when she had prostrated herself before him (on her back) at the end of her Dance of the Seven Veils. Actually, she was so slim now, and her expressions and mannerisms so outrageous, that this was not so difficult to believe.

He told her the story of his life as a rigger, which was something to do with oil-wells, which had taken him round the world almost. She was glad that he had not said that he was an oil-man: the temptation must have been there. And now he was not going round the world but to the god-forsaken places where the real people lived. He said would she like to go dancing? She doubted the likelihood of finding anywhere open in Shanklin out of season, so they settled for a walk and a drink in a pub overlooking the sea, and perhaps a dinner in . . . Ventnor? Tomorrow? Ventnor would be nice. She had liked walking with him. It didn't bother her that she had told him a fiction about herself. He enjoyed her much more than if she had said that she was a runaway nut-case, with an engineer husband and four grown-up children.

The next night they danced. She had forgotten how nice it was to have a man hold you in the small of your back. He got a bit excited when they rumba'd but men did; they got worked up over behinds moving to music. He kissed her when they walked home, and that was nice too.

Later, when she was creaming her face and brushing her bouncing hair, she wondered whether she might make a career out of this life. It was certainly pleasant. What would she need? Enough to keep her car on the road, enough for decent hotels and a few decent clothes. Lonely men in hotels didn't necessarily want sex – most of them did, but if they didn't get it then they would probably settle for the good company of a good woman.

She was wrong: if a man shares his bottle of Médoc and takes a woman dancing, he thinks he's OK to knock on her door at two in the morning wearing only his bath-robe and his assured smile. Realizing that they had been talking different languages, Monica asked him to go and fetch some decent glasses from the dining room, and when he came back his Médoc was his side of the door and an old-fashioned chest-of-drawers hers.

She didn't see him at breakfast, and by supper his table was being occupied by new guests.

After a day or two she decided she had better let somebody know where she was. She phoned the number Tom had given her – a friend's pad – and was surprised when Tom answered.

'Mum? For Christ's sake, where are you? The fuzz went to Dad's office, and he's been buzzing about like a blue-arsed fly.'

'I'm sorry, darling, I really am. I thought I'd have loads of time to tell everyone I was OK before the police discovered who I was. I just had to get away for a bit and it seemed to be such a good idea.'

'What about the amnesia?'

'Oh, well . . . you know.'

'You never had amnesia.' He laughed. 'You're a bugger, Monica.'

'Tom!'

'Well, you are.'

'I couldn't have got away with it any longer.'

'Did they actually fish you out of the harbour?'

'I experimented with substances, as they say.'

'I know that all right . . . you left it about. Good stuff, where'd you get it?'

'Tom, no. It's dreadful stuff.'

'You know what it was that did your head in, those fucking slimming pills. Don't do it. I don't know why you do: you've got better tits and ass than a good many birds half your age. You should be thankful; you shouldn't be trying to get yourself thin. D'you know what's wrong with you . . . ? For years you've been trying to be Rose . . . well, you aren't gonna. And in any case, we like you as you are.

'Are you there? Monica?'

'Yes.'

'Well then?'

'Why didn't somebody say so? Why wait until the only worthwhile experience in ages came from a bit of smouldering resin.'

He said nothing.

'Tom?'

'I'm still here.' There was something he wanted to tell her. Longed to tell her. To relieve himself of the confusion he'd been in for years. He knew perfectly well that there was nothing morally wrong in how he felt but, free and swinging as this society was supposed to be, it would be a big hurdle to get over.

'Tom, I'll tell you something I should have told you ages ago. You're the best thing ever happened to me.'

'Thanks, Monica.'

'Why have you stopped calling me "Mum"?'

Now was the time when he could have said. Safe distance. Telephone. 'I've been to see her.'

For a moment Monica thought that he meant he'd been to see Rose. 'Who?'

'The slag who got herself pregnant by some wandering Pole and then lumbered poor old Leo and Monica with me.'

Monica had thought the danger period for Tom would have been when he was about fourteen; but when his teens had passed with no great cataclysmic upheaval, she had assumed he had dealt with the circumstances of his birth. She didn't understand 'slag', which was a new word, but it sounded right for Wendy. 'The last thing you've ever been was lumber.'

'I know, that's great. But I was a cock-up in the slag's life.'

'Tom, it's not really good talking over the phone. Why don't you come and see me and talk it through?'

'I couldn't do that.'

'You could . . . you should. I know you're a big grown-up man and all that . . . just come for a day.'

'I can't.'

'Why?'

'Nobody knows where you are.'

Monica started to laugh.

'I don't know what's so funny.'

'Shanklin.'

'Shanklin? You never cleared off to *Shanklin*!' He laughed at such a ludicrous plan. 'Shanklin!'

'It seemed such a good idea.'

'It was. OK, I'll come and see you. I'll tell everybody to stop panicking but I won't say where you are – that OK?'

'And you'll come?'

'Tomorrow if you like.'

'Do, darling. You won't come on that bike will you?'

'Make a bargain.'

'Depends on what.'

'You stop popping pills and tipping the sauce and I'll sell my bike and come and see you.'

When he arrived at the hotel next day, he was wearing shorts and riding a sports cycle. When she saw him smiling and dripping sweat from his long hair, and looking so normal in spite of his still-swollen scars, she wondered what on earth she was doing living in a hotel when she had a perfectly good life of her own not thirty miles distant on the mainland, and three other children, a house, and a really decent husband . . .

'You look great,' he said as they descended the steep hill from the hotel to the seafront.

'Thank you, love. I feel great. I think it's been great actually doing something . . . driving my own life for a few days.'

He put an arm about her shoulder. 'You chose a bloody funny way of doing it. You scared the life out of us.'

'Us?'

'Yes. I don't think I've ever seen Dad so shaken.'

'Is he angry?'

'No. I think he's feeling guilt more than anything. Of course Helen was a bit "tut-tutty".'

'Poor Helen, she'd hate the police being involved.'

Now he had an opening . . .

But she stopped as they were passing a little shop selling hand-made trinkets, and when they came out, Monica having spent a small fortune on gifts of delicate silver tracery made into brooches, earrings and cufflinks, the moment was gone. There would be another. He had to get it right. He had made a plan of the order of things he had to tell her so that she wouldn't go flying off in all directions.

Rose had been given a tranquillizing jab. So, what with that, and the 6.45 p.m. flight out of Jan Smuts followed by the eleven-hour flight to Rome and then the shock of the accident and loss of blood, Rose had slept deeply. She had passed out fully dressed in the little operating theatre under the bright lights, and came to again in a small, white-painted room with morning sun streaming across the highly polished wood floor, remembering instantly what had happened. Distantly she heard people moving about, quiet voices, and rubber trolley-wheels.

Someone had undressed her and she was wearing thick woollen stockings and what felt like a flannelette nightgown. She lifted her head. That was painful. Her brain thudded, but worse was the sharp soreness across her face. There were two other beds in the room, both empty and precisely made up and covered in smooth white counterpanes. Beside each bed was a low wicker armchair with blue seatpad. A single table was placed centrally and a vase with a few tulips central to the table-top. Rose sank thankfully back into the pillows. The room was the epitome of tranquillity: she was reminded of a Hockney painting.

What a homecoming. Jon had been going to meet her at the airport, the BOAC official said that a message had got through to her family. She hoped that it hadn't sounded too dramatic.

A trolley rattled and a very young nun put her head round the door. A nun with a tea-tray.

Rose tried to struggle up and the little nun ran forward to give assistance, plumping the pillows and adding more until Rose could sit upright – all the while smiling and nodding – then helped her drink the tea through a straw. It was not very nice-tasting, probably chamomile, but anything was welcome. For the life of her Rose could not remember how to say 'thank you' in Italian, so she said it in English, to which the girl replied in a good American accent, 'You're welcome. Must fly.' Rose could have laughed except that it was too painful. 'Is this a hospital?' She discovered how difficult it was to talk.

'Not exactly. But we are nurses. Your embassy arranged for you to be brought here. I guess you are quite famous or something.'

The small effort exhausted Rose back into a doze in which her mind went into a turmoil of dreams and reality.

On the aircraft Rose remembered actually thinking clearly, almost as though she was saying it, 'I'm not the same Rose Quinlan who arrived here three months ago. Will the old one be waiting at the other end?'

Pedr had promised, 'I shall come to England in June. There is a conference in Chichester. You will come there with me? I shall stay for a month. I want to see "Swinging London". There are so many things we still have to do. I long to see your home. I want to see you whole, with your children.'

In the cool Hockney room, Rose sorted the recent events that led up to her being here: the steward who had been attentive during the flight, pressing on her magazines and drinks that she didn't really want, unable to stop himself using his charms on every woman he attended. Rose had enjoyed playing up to him. He was too young, of course, younger than Pedr. Ten years younger was fine, twelve . . . but this tanned and handsome hopeful was only about Jonathan's age. She smiled within her painful injuries. She shouldn't even have looked at him in that way. Women who looked at younger men in that way were called 'cradle-snatchers'.

She could remember the take-off and the crash. She let her thoughts drift, then slept again; when she reawakened the sun was shining from above. When she opened her eyes, she saw that the beaker had gone, and in its place was a covered jug and another beaker. As she became fully awake, she heard gentle breathing on her 'blind' side. The chair creaked.

'Hey, hey, Boss Lady, you're awake. Now don't you try to move.'

'Mac.' She put out her hand, feeling blindly for him. 'Oh, Mac.' She could have wept with relief and pleasure at the sound of his soft, deep voice.

He came round to her good side and stood looking down at her. 'Well, if you ain't a sight for sore eyes.'

She tried to smile but could only manage a wince. 'And so are you . . . you have no idea.'

He took the hand she was holding out to him, pressing it between his two great warm, gentle fists.

'Oh, Mac, don't let me cry – it hurts too much.'

Hiding as he always did behind his joviality, he put on one of his B-movie Blacks' voices, 'Well now, Boss, ain't no more than you deserve, going off like that and gitting your pretty face all messed up.'

She bit her lip. 'Don't, it's even worse when I smile.'

He raised the bed-rest and helped her to sit up, poured her some of the barley-water and slipped the straw between her lips; then he gave in to his own anxiety. 'My God, Rose, I've been in hell with not knowing. They said you were cut across your eye, but nobody would say whether your sight was damaged.'

'It's not.'

'I know that now, but I couldn't stand it, so I picked up my toothbrush and got on the first flight leaving for Rome. Don't worry, it's all arranged back home. Everybody's coping just fine. They all argued so long about which one of them should come out here, that I decided for them. So it was me came. What do you need . . . shall I go out and buy you some things? A nightdress? That one's a shroud. Toothpaste? Do you need to pee, want something nice to eat?'

'I don't even know where there's a bathroom.'

'I do. Come on.' He lifted her firmly but gently from the bed, and carried her out into the corridor where he met a tall nun wearing surgical gloves. 'Ah, Sister Mary-Joseph, I'm just taking the patient for a pee.'

'Mr McKenzie. That's not quite the way we do it here. I'll send for a wheelchair.' Another American, maybe Canadian.

'Don't worry, Sister. I don't plan on dropping her.'

'I'm sure, but you just pop Mrs Quinlan down here.'

Ablutions done, Mary-Joseph swished open the door and saw to it that Rose walked back to the white room. There, folding down the sheets, was the little nun. Mac lifted Rose on to the bed, arranged the pillows and sheets with great concern for her comfort, then sat down in the creaking wicker chair.

'My, my Mrs Quinlan, if you aren't the lucky one, great big strong man there, lift you like thistledown.' The little nun sounded so like Mac when he was sending himself up that Rose wasn't sure whether the nun wasn't doing the same. Rose asked her name. 'Sister Petroc.'

Sister Petroc stood, arms across her stomach, looking on benignly.

'You don't need to guard her, Sister. She's my Boss Lady.'

Sister Petroc's expression said, Oh go on with you. 'I have to stand by, Signor Berini is coming to see Mrs Quinlan's wound.'

'Then I can go?' Rose asked.

'You want to leave us so soon? We shall just have to see what Signor Berini says.'

'He's the big potato around here?' Mac asked.

'We think he is the best in the whole of Rome. His stitching is so fine he could embroider silk.'

When he did come to inspect his handiwork, Sister Mary-Joseph removed the dressing. Dr Mario declared himself satisfied that there would be no problems, and Sister Petroc re-dressed the wound. He would see his patient early next day.

Sister Petroc interpreted. 'Doctor Mario asks if Mr McKenzie would like to know of a good hotel with excellent Italian food?'

Mac touched his forehead in a salute. 'The excellent Italian food gets me every time. If you'll leave me the address . . .' He had no intention of leaving Rose to go out and eat excellent Italian food until she was asleep.

Not even the assertive Sister Mary-Joseph seemed up to trying to eject him. Most of the time he sat in the wicker chair and watched, and fed, and straightened sheets, and carried Rose to the bathroom. From time to time the nuns looked in or changed the jug and beaker and gave her pills. Rose slept fitfully.

Once when she awoke she watched him for ten minutes, asleep sitting up, breathing quietly as though listening. In the fragile room with its low white ceilings and curved archways, he appeared even more enormous than usual, his large hands, head and feet in proportion to his weight-lifter's chest. Every time he had carried her to the bathroom she had been aware of his soft, massive strength. One would have expected his presence to be at odds with the fragile, tranquil room, instead he enhanced it. She had often noticed that same quality at Longmore: his very presence could be sufficient to calm a fraught situation.

Wherever would they have been if he had not turned up, and wherever would they be if he left them?

Where would *she* be if he left *her*? That was nearer the truth.

She closed her eyes again. The nuns knew he was a good man. He hadn't a malicious bone in his body. Why had she not had the luck to have met a man like Mac when she was seventeen? She imagined what a great time kids would have growing up with a father like Mac: he stood no nonsense from Vee, yet always acknowledged the areas where she knew best and never interfered. He had time for Nora when she came home, and Nora always sought him out for company, standing in the kitchen willingly doing some job that she would have said was a chore if it had not been Mac who suggested she did it. Sunny adored him, treating him like a great teddy-bear, jumping on his comfortable belly whilst he made bear sounds, and watching intently as he taught her or helped her to discover some new skill.

If only . . . If only . . .

So much chance in everything. Yet it had been chance that had brought her and Pedr together. She had not intended to go out that night, but had gone on a whim because of the green dress.

How much did she know about Mac? She opened her eyes wider and tried to imagine him when he was about twenty. As often with the first generation of a mixed relationship, he had inherited the best genes of both races and thus – like the Cape Coloured girls she had seen serving on the beauty counters of the big Johannesburg stores – a kind of perfection. She smiled inwardly at the change in her attitude: without Ballard she now looked with appreciation at good-looking men. At almost forty, Mac's good oval skull, high cheek-bones, broad square brow and strong chin were the structure on which the symmetry of his looks hung.

But *would* the seventeen-year-old Rose have married a big, handsome coloured man?

No. She wouldn't have had the common sense. Young Rose Weston would still have chosen the glossy handsome veneer and not known that solid oak is the quality.

With her eyes closed, she felt him carefully catch hold of her hand. He caressed her knuckles with his thumb, humming a whole string of Beatles songs like lullabies, with a soft 'Yeah, yeah, yeah.'

Nora was the only one who knew the whole complicated story of the way their two families – the Quinlans and the Wilkinsons had become intertwined, and of the secrets and skeletons. She had known about Helen and Jon ages before it came out and caused the trouble between the two families. She had known about old Leo. About him and Vee screwing in the downstairs lounge – that wasn't too much of a surprise, Vee screwed everybody, and it must have been in the lounge because it was the only really warm room in the house and because Nora could always hear Vee's bedsprings when she had somebody in her room. Nora assumed that Vee must like the feeling of power it gave her to be able to get any man she chose to go to bed with her. But it hadn't worked on Mac. Nora would have loved to have been a fly on the wall when Vee tried it on Mac.

Vee intrigued Nora. Nora liked having sex, but not in the way Vee liked it. She sometimes wondered whether Vee *did* actually like it. It was as though she had always been hooked on it. Nora had first had it when she was still at school and living with Gran. She had needed somebody to tell about the secret about Gerald and had found James in his bedroom, the one that had been hers when they had lived at Shaft's. She and James had spent so many hours together in one another's bedrooms since they were children, that no one thought twice about it. She had told James what she had found out, and James had been very adult and comforting, and before they knew where they were they had done it and it had been great. Since then they had done it a good many times, more safely though since the first time. They were both responsible, and seeming not at all in tune with the spontaneity of the flower children and the Beatles' and Stones' fans of the era.

Nobody except Nora herself had known what a disaster Nora's visit to the Corder-Peakes had been. Disaster. Nora could scarcely bear to think of it even now. She had been having a splendid time. Old Sir Evelyn himself had taken her down to the stables and told her, 'See here, my gel, this little pinto is just the ride for you.' Nora's heart had leapt. He had been so kind. Miriam had kept saying to Nora's father, 'Have you seen them together, Ballard? Daddy has really *taken* to Anoria, he really-really *likes* her.' Nora had liked the two Hamilton children who were visiting their grandparents. Once she knew about Gerald she stopped visiting the Corder-Peakes, even though she had loved the park and the funny splendid way they lived, with croquet and tea on the lawn and there was a lake and a boat-house. It was like being in some old period film.

Nora had never been sly, nor had she ever been interested in spying or creeping about, nor had she been especially curious about what went on between people; yet it seemed that she was always in the wrong place at the wrong time, hearing or seeing something that she would rather not. She wished people would take more care to keep their secrets to themselves: when other people became involved it was a very hard thing. Like the time she had been getting apple pie and seen Mum run upstairs away from the Old Man; like the other time after Nan's funeral when, before she even realized what they were up to, she had heard Mum say, 'We can't, Leo, we can't, we can't . . . we must forget it ever happened', and he had said, 'We can never go back to where we were. We stopped being friends and neighbours that night. For God's sake, Rose, I can't stand it. I shall never want another woman.' Although she put her fingers in her ears, she was sure that Leo and her mother were kissing.

'Never' was apparently not too long – just the time between Nan's funeral and the day when he and Vee screwed at Longmore.

And she would have given anything not to have heard the diabolical conversations between Miriam and Miriam's mother, in which the old lady had told Miriam that it was not wise for Nora and Gerald to go romping around together. Romping! Nora had resented that word. The two Hamilton children and Nora had swum in the river, picked raspberries, gone to the pictures. 'It would be a very unpleasant thing if she and the boy became close and it fell to someone to have to explain their relationship,' to which Miriam had replied, 'I don't suppose they will. Nora is several years older and in any case they only have the same father; it is not as though they are fully brother and sister.'

And so the innocent friendship that she was beginning to enjoy with the boy Gerald and his little sister was damaged for ever. She came away and was determined never to go back. Almost as painful had been giving up the pretty pinto pony.

And she knew about Tom and Kate.

James had told her. Greatly daring because he was so conventional: a straight, testing her to see how she would take it. Nora took it very well, for her nature had changed very little from the day when she had been taken out for the first time into the wider world of London and the Festival of Britain. If she were ever to be described as impassive or phlegmatic, her sisters (although they would have understood why she was seen like this) would have defended her by saying no one should underestimate Nora, she was highly intelligent; it was just that she never went off in all directions at once. And it was true, she *was* intelligent, preferring to think first and act later. Although she could be as brash and coarse as the rest, especially when they were all together, Nora was quite unlike Becc and Vee. She had an air of quietude about her, which was perhaps why people did tend not to realize that she was there or to tell her things they wouldn't dream of telling Becc or Vee.

'I've got to tell you, Nora, our Kate and Tom have fallen for one another.' James, who strictly didn't smoke because of needing to keep himself fit, had lit a cigarette to cover his agitation at having committed such apparently prurient news to the public domain. 'Kate told me. She said she must tell someone. Poor old Kate, she was pretty upset, but I told her I didn't see why she should be.'

'If I were you I'd stop smoking before it gets a hold on you. Students can't afford to smoke, and it will ruin your lungs.'

James had stubbed out the cigarette. Nora had said after a moment or two to take in the momentous news, 'Well, it's not as though they are really brother and sister, is it? They aren't even related. And they're both nice people. And they know one another so well that they won't have to find out things they don't like after they're married.'

'I don't know about getting married.'

'Of course they will, Kate wouldn't want to be in love with anyone and not get married, Kate's not like that. Helen won't like it.'

'Why won't she?'

'Oh, James, because she's Helen and because no matter what anybody says she will see it as her brother and sister getting married.'

'I thought you were going to say because she'd be jealous.'

'Helen? She'd die of shame. Don't you remember the state she got in when everybody got to know your mother wasn't Tom's?'

'Tom still feels the same to me.'

'So he should.'

'You don't think it's . . . sort of queer.'

'It takes a bit of adjusting to, but it's not like Vee and Jon falling in love.'

'Or you and your Dad's other kid?'

'His name's Gerald, Gerald Hamilton.' Nora looked up from the jeans she was mending. 'James, most of the time you are really hep and great, but there are others when you are insensitive and as thick as two planks.'

So as to avoid her eyes, he looked at the ceiling which was pasted over entirely with posters of the Beatles. 'Does that mean I'm in the dog-house and you won't come to the game?'

Nora didn't reply. She would keep him waiting. Of course she would watch him even if it was not on the line. Nora loved watching rugby union. She loved watching James. He had grown as solid as his mother and as athletic as his father. It was one of Nora's pleasures to stand and watch James at the back of a line-out, leaping clear of the rest, one massive hand reaching, picking the ball out of mid-air and running hell-for-leather for the line. His grace, strength and athleticism stimulated her: if she liked James for any specific thing (which she didn't, she liked him for a whole lot of things, many of which went way back, but *if* she did), it was for his gift of thrillingly beautiful movement on the rugby field. She hoped that he would be an old man of forty before he stopped being able to leap for the ball.

Jean Thompson wasn't much of a one for writing letters just for the sake of it, only one to her mam sometimes, but when Mr Wilkinson said that Mrs Cue had been in an accident, she said to Stanley that she felt she wanted to write and tell her how sorry they all were, but her writing was so bad and she wouldn't know what to say except they were sorry. In the end she did as Stanley suggested and sent a nice card to Chichester and wrote on it, 'Please forward.'

In the normal course of things, Jean wouldn't have stayed on at Shaft's with things going on. She liked things straight, liked to know what was going on, but was there anybody who knew what was going on in the Wilkinsons' house these days? It had never been the same since the Cues moved. When she said to Stanley that she was being messed about, Stanley said why didn't she give notice, there was enough people wanting help in the village these days, but Jean said it was for the sake of the old house as much as anything. Well really, she felt sorry for all of them. Her mam had always said, money doesn't bring happiness, and she was right. Mr Cue was real money these days, and you couldn't hardly turn on the telly without seeing him fly-en off to some meet-ten or other – he must spend half his life going to meet-tens – what was the use of money if that's all you could do with it, answer me that? She was glad that she had chosen a really big card for Mrs Cue, because when she started to write she was surprised how much there was to say.

On the morning of the day when her stitches were removed, Rose received Jean's card redirected from Longmore to the nursing home. It read:

> 'Dear Mrs Q,
>
> Stanley and me are very sorry to hear that you were hurt. We hope there wasn't too much damage, it would be a shame. I have got the chance of a job in charge of school cleaners. It is full time, but now that the boys are grown up I can manage. Our Dai has got into the Tec. to do his HNC and wants to be a chemist. Not the sort that works in chemist shops. Our Mervyn is turning out clever. Who

would have thought it? We been up to the school and they say he should easy get three good A-levels which would get him into university and we should think serious about it. Stanley always thought that when they grew up they would all have a little plumbing business together because people always need plumbers, but as he said, it don't do to make plans. I hope if you ever come back to visit the village you will come and see us. I never missed anybody as much as I missed you those first weeks.

Yours very sincerely
Jean and Stanley.

The surgeon, who had been very attentive, visiting Rose almost daily, was himself going to give her a lift to the hospital. During her stay with the nuns she had learned from them of his great reputation with accident cases, how he had rebuilt faces and was frequently written about in magazines and medical journals. Rose felt quite guilty that she had not even heard of him until then. He had taken photographs of every stage of the mending process and asked her permission very graciously to use them in a book of case histories he was writing. Mac had seen the embassy and the travel agency and settled her mind with the news that her insurance covered her for everything.

Before Mac went back she made him go out and buy some cigarette tobacco, papers and matches – and a mirror. He hadn't wanted to buy the mirror. When she decided to look at the damage she was aware of his watchfulness. It did look a mess, but she could see that the antiseptic wash and the bruising contributed a great deal to that. The stitching was fascinating. Along the line of the gash, the surgeon had put in scores of small sutures, each one neatly tied. 'It looks like a little brown zip, doesn't it?' She hadn't thought of Trevelyan for ages, but now he came to mind. She wondered how he would react. She guessed his instinct would be to make an interesting comparative study.

It was an exquisite early spring morning as she waited for the car. She had a couple of hours to wait, but over the days here she had fallen in love with the tranquillity of the small garden which was tended with equal tranquillity by a grey-haired nun who seemed to do all her work kneeling on a piece of sacking. As she used to do at Shaft's, Rose went out into the garden very early, but never earlier than the gardening nun who would at once greet her with a broad smile and continue dead-heading or weeding or whatever chore she was about whilst Rose sat on a low stone wall and made herself a thin cigarette.

She had had two weeks of this and had loved it. It was now almost four months since she had left England on that dreadful snowy day in January. She longed to see her family, yet there was a kind of addictiveness about the quality of the life here. She had spent a great deal of this waiting time thinking about Longmore, and over the days vague ideas for the place had hardened into possible plans. She had made pages of notes, many of which analysed what it was that gave this place its quality, and how she could re-create it at Longmore.

As she idly watched, through the thin trail of cigarette smoke, the gardening nun shuffling forward from plant to plant, her attention was caught by a voice, or rather, a sound that reminded her of Monica. Of all people, Monica was the one she most wanted to see just now. Pedr? Yes, of course she wanted to see him, but for quite other reasons. The gardening nun too had heard the voices and stretched her neck to see over the rocks around which she was weeding. Sister Petroc appeared, looking thinner than ever in contrast to the tall, slim figure beside her, and pointed to where Rose was seated.

Rose, confused and not knowing what to do with her cigarette, took a step forward, tumbling her matches and papers on to the lawn.

'Monica? It *is* you. But you're so . . . Oh, Mon . . . What on earth . . . ?'

Monica. Rose went to envelop her in an emotional, tearful embrace but Monica halted, jerkily uncertain as she took in the damage to Rose's face. She was shocked at the sight of what looked like a strand of seaweed across Rose's face. It was impossible to keep the reaction from her expression.

'It's all right, Mon. I'm not going to break. If a tractor can only do this to me, you aren't going to do any worse.'

For long moments Monica was speechless, shaking her head and dashing away tears. 'I'm not really crying, Rose. Honestly. I'm not. It's just . . .'

'I know, you aren't crying. You don't cry, do you? I know. It's . . .'

They faced one another, gripping hands, too full of emotion for words. For almost twenty years the fabric of their lives and the lives of their families had been so interwoven that it would never be possible to unpick the woof and warp and be able to see the original separate strands.

Rose said, 'I'll have to get rid of this damned cigarette, it's burning my fingers,' and Monica burst out laughing, at which the gardening nun turned a broad smile upon them as Sister Petroc and Sister Adua brought out a rug and a tray of breakfast.

Seated on the grass, close, their hands searched for one another, in between trying to do justice to the scrambled eggs and orange juice. 'We have to eat it or we shall be in right stook.'

'That's OK, I've stopped dieting.'

Rose looked appraisingly at a slimness she had never before seen on Monica. 'You look good, Mon. Not much tits, but good.'

'I'm not putting on weight, but who cares, I've decided life's too short.'

Rose nodded, smiling lopsidedly. Holding her face in place had become an automatic reaction. 'I've come to the same conclusion. It's taken us long enough to find that out.'

'Don't be too hard on us, Rose, we've spent so much time giving away great chunks of our lives to . . .' She waved her hand vaguely, but Rose knew exactly who 'them' were.

'Do you think we can stop overnight?'

'I'm having a damn good try.' She scooped up scrambled egg and said conversationally, 'It was when I fell in Portsmouth Harbour, you know. They didn't know who I was when they fished me out . . . so I took the chance and ran away.' She began to giggle like a schoolgirl. 'To the Isle of Wight.'

Rose tried not to laugh, but she felt so elated that she had to hold her face with both hands. 'I'm not supposed to laugh yet.'

'Oh God, trust me to do something like that. Does it . . . ? Is it as painful as it looks?'

'Just irritating. It will soon be over, touch wood. Are you staying in Rome?'

'No, of course not. I came to see if you wanted company on the journey home.'

Rose's heart lifted. 'You came out specially?'

'Of course. I went to Longmore – part of making myself over. Of course I didn't know you wouldn't be there. Vee said you were due to come out any day. That guy Mac, who seems to be in charge there, said what did I think about coming to see you. Vee said she thought you'd like that. Vee's changed, hasn't she? She seems so capable . . . I wish I had half her self-assurance . . . Do you want me to stay and travel back with you, Rose?'

'It might not be for a couple of days.'

'I don't care if it's a couple of weeks.'

'Won't Leo mind?'

Monica had thought herself very sensible to have thought through her own reactions to the mention of Leo's name between them, and concluded that she must put those mad suspicions behind her or lose Rose for ever. 'Sod Leo,' she said, 'I've spent too much of my life wondering whether he would mind, or the kids would be put out, and sod-all good it's done me.'

His name passed between them and the ground did not shift.

'I'll have to go and change, a car's coming for me in about an hour.' She grasped Monica's fingers. 'I think I'd rather have you with me today than anyone.'

Rose, who was no longer in the white ward, but was using a visitor's room, put on the silk dress she had bought just before she left Johannesburg and fixed her hair up in a knot, watched by Monica who wandered about looking at the few possessions Rose had with her, possessions whose unfamiliarity made her realize how long the time was that they had wasted.

There was nothing here she recognized from when she had done this same thing in Rose's bedroom before she left Honeywood, not even a brush or comb or nightdress that was familiar. Even Rose herself was unfamiliar, not because of the terrible slash across her face, but the quality of Rose had changed. She seemed to have a more extrovert quality about her: she was tanned and her pale hair paler, and she had just put on what looked like a couture frock in a burnt-orange colour. The old Rose would never have chosen anything like that.

'These are proteas, aren't they?' She fingered the crisp texture of the large arrangement that had dried to a delicate paperiness in the dry Italian air. It was a bouquet that had been delivered just as they were about to take off, and the steward had taken charge of it.

'Yes, I didn't get them until a few days ago. They appeared here with my hand baggage.'

Monica thrust her fingers into the heart of the arrangement. 'Can I read the card?'

Rose looked out from the little washing cubicle. 'I didn't know there was one.'

'"Sparkling days, sublime nights and bubble baths in the mountains."'

Rose came quickly into the room. 'Where did you . . . ?'

Monica handed her the card. 'Hadn't you seen it?'

Rose shook her head. Monica said, 'I'm sorry.'

'It's nothing I shouldn't have got round to telling you.' She read aloud, '"Sparkling days, sublime nights and bubble baths in the mountains. I love you. More to follow in July. P."'

The old Monica would have come crashing in with something flip; instead she waited.

Rose said, 'I met him in Johannesburg. We were lovers . . . are lovers, I think. A tooth doctor. Young, handsome, Swedish, rich . . . and extremely virile.'

Monica let out a long silent whistle. 'No wonder you seem so different. Were they sublime, those nights?'

'What do you think?'

'Rose.'

'He's married.'

Rose waited, but the comment didn't come. It wasn't only that slimness made the face sit differently, she seemed edgy and had lost her confidence.

Had she *ever* known Rose? Monica wondered, or had Rose changed? Grown people don't change. During those months when she had suspected Leo of carrying a torch for Rose, Monica had tortured herself with the thought that the virtue she had always supposed Rose to possess was a front. Then when she had come to her senses again, she had decided that all such nonsense stemmed from the sense of abandonment she'd felt when Rose went away. But now? It was all topsy-turvy again. Rose *was* capable of having an affair with a married man. And sound careless about it – young, rich, virile.

After a pause Rose continued, 'We had a short, extraordinary affair. Nobody was hurt. His wife was having one somewhere else. It's rife in Johannesburg: they believe that everything they read about – wife-swopping, sex and drugs, and uninhibited, swinging London – is true, and they don't want to be left out.' A good enough explanation. Rose had just been swinging.

Monica soon realized that this was not going to be a simple reunion. If their friendship was to survive, and she most desperately wanted it to do so, then it would have to be rebuilt, trying to use some of the reclaimed stones of the old one. If Rose had changed or if – as seemed possible – Monica had never known Rose as well as she had supposed, then that too would have to be taken into the structure. And Monica's own facing of the truth about herself and Leo and the children would need to be accepted by Rose as well.

They had changed, it was no use pretending they had not. It came to Monica: we've swopped. I've become introvert and Rose is the extrovert.

Grown people *do* change . . . either that or we are all capable of a great variety of behaviour. She had been thinking about it during her sojourn on the Isle of Wight, when she had come to the conclusion that Leo hadn't suddenly changed from good-humoured and out-going to solemn and self-centred; all of it had always been there. What had happened was that he had allowed the worse traits to take over.

She said, 'I had always thought the sex thing was supposed to fade when women got to the menopause stage. It doesn't: it gets worse, doesn't it?' All we need, she thought, is the young, rich and virile bit to go with it.

Rose smiled, holding her stitches in place. 'Or better? Mine is definitely better. "Sublime" in fact.'

Oh yes, Monica thought, you've changed; and wondered briefly whether the oil-well rigger with the bottle of Médoc might have been sublime if she had given him half a chance.

'I'm glad for you, Rose. That doesn't mean to say I don't envy you. And I'm sorry you had to go through all this to push me into coming to see you; but I'm glad we're back again. My fault. I've had my punishment.'

'Oh Mon . . .' Rose lovingly hugged her friend. 'Have you ever heard of a "guilt-eater"? Well, you've got to stop being one.'

Monica took one of Rose's hands, squeezed it and smiled wryly, 'No more eating guilt? Damn, and I've just given up the amphetamines.'

When Sister Mary-Joseph came to say that the car was waiting, she discovered the two women sitting in silence, clasping hands. They had known suffering, it was there as it was with so many women. Why did the Good Lord give women such an unfair share of tender emotions to deal with? 'Signor Berini says that you may be with us a day or two after your stitches are gone. We'll find a corner somewhere for your friend.'

On that same morning, Sally Joffe, looking hugely more pregnant than her six months suggested, opened the door of the flamboyant Rolls to allow Rebecca to get in beside her.

'It's great, Becc. You have no idea. Aze says fine, it's my own money and so long as I promise to keep the weight off my legs he doesn't mind what I do. He's involved in this big protest rally. He's working twice as hard because he thinks if he doesn't then I might be tempted to.'

'You've got a man in a million there, Princess.'

'Don't I know it? You'll love this place. Twenties, still got the original chrome under the fifties plastic.'

Rebecca trusted Sally's judgement in premises, and Sally trusted Rebecca's in the design and style of clothes they produced. They had had a series of small shops dedicated to Rebecca's collections, but now they were investing everything they had between them in a much bigger venture. An old department store that had somehow not been torn down and replaced by some high-rise modern office block. 'The thing is,' Sally said, 'it's not really big enough and close enough to central London for the big developers, but Aze says land here is getting so scarce that it won't be long before they'll be snapping up everything you can reach by underground.'

'So he thinks it's an investment anyway.'

Sally laughed. 'You know Aze nearly as well as I do.'

Sally had been right: the decrepit old shop was perfect, even to the zig-zag push on the plate-glass revolving doors.

Rebecca said, 'You clever old thing. It might have been built for us.'

'Do you think we could be open by Christmas?'

'Don't doubt it. I've discovered a super lad. He calls himself "Malthus", but I don't think he's got anything to do with trying to keep down the population of the world – quite the reverse, the randy devil – but he is a super lad. Anyway, he's working on some really way-out plastic bags – black and silver on white. He's got *the* most terrific ideas.'

Sally well knew what Becc's 'super lad' would be like: there had been dozens over the years. They could be older or younger, black, white or brown and, like Becc herself, presenting an overt sexual image with great and shocking style. They were always in some way connected with the art and design world in which she functioned best. She 'discovered' them if there was something in their campness or pseudo-sado or military styles that sparked off against her own. One thing about Becc's lads, they were never dull.

Even as she spoke, the shop took shape in Rebecca's mind. White and mirrored, black and silver. Tango music, fringed fripperies, statuettes and lamps, everything to create a total style for their lives, for that generation of women who, starting as teenage girls, had followed Becc Quinlan wherever she led. Those first cheap adaptable blouses that she had been turning out in the house whilst she had thought her parents safely holidaying in Spain, through the more womanly Peephole and Mondriani fashions, the 'granny look', the 'soldier-soldier' fun, the 'titchy' and the bell-tent skirts, and now to the sophisticated 'vamp' look that she was planning.

'What do you think of "The Look" as a name, Sally?'

'Just "Look!" with an exclamation mark.'

'Right . . . right!' That's it exactly. I don't know whether we'd get away with it, but I've got this idea. Advertise with really really snotty-looking models, and they're looking down their noses at these blokes – or one bloke – and they've got balloons coming out of their mouths, like in cartoons, and they're saying things like, "Is that a gun you're carrying, or . . ."'

Sally joined in laughing, '. . . "are you just pleased to see me?" I love it!'

And so Rebecca was off on the great leap forward in the world of fashion that might easily either make or break her. Aze was not in on this venture and she would have preferred not to have had Sally's money in, but Rebecca knew how much Sally wanted to be part of the venture. She needed to show that, even though she was going to become a mother, it did not mean the 'Princess' era was gone. Rebecca was quite fearless in business. She had spent her growing years always pushing frontiers, trying to prise away the hold Paris had on the fashion world. Always living on the edge, the thrilling edge. If she ever stopped to ponder, she might just have wondered whether there had ever been a plan, or whether what appeared to have been planned was only a series of haphazard coincidences that had somehow made sense when seen in retrospect. But that kind of thinking she left to others: she had only to walk down a street and see the texture of a wall or the pattern of ironwork to have a dozen ideas jump at her.

Vee, driving back from Covent Garden, had finally made a decision about Longmore. She was going to leave. Not until Rose was properly back in control; but she *would* leave, it was all set up. She occasionally wished that she wasn't such a tart, but it was how she was. Probably took after the Old Man.

Vee had a real need for sex. Frequently and only with men. A couple of times she had been with women, but they had been too soft, too rounded, and probably too concerned and caring. Vee wasn't a woman to be languid and slowly warmed up: her attitude was pretty masculine. She seemed to start at just below boiling point and wanted quick gratification.

That's how she was, and she didn't see that there was anything she could do about that. Nor did she want to and, when she wished she wasn't such a tart, what she really meant was that she wished that women with a puissant libido were not seen as tarts. Men who liked to screw around were OK. Males with a strong sexual urge got a good press: they chased skirt, they were randy, or great studs. But women like Vee were easy lays, tarts who screwed around.

Marriage was an option, but not much of one. She knew from her own experience in the love game that there weren't many faithful men about, but they all expected their own women to be. *Own* women! Owned women was more appropriate. Even the swingers and ravers who threw their car-keys into the middle and swopped wives at the end of a party quite often took it out on their own wives later. There were times when she wondered why any woman at all would want to marry. Vee herself wouldn't. Becc wouldn't, and probably not Nora. Nora was the most intelligent feminist of them all.

God, she hoped Rose wouldn't.

Vee was pretty sure that poor old Mac was in love with Rose.

Well OK, let them get into bed, but Rose would be mad to take on another man. She was a different woman since the Old Man cleared off. She had sounded so happy and light-hearted when she had phoned from Johannesburg.

PART THREE

Hot pants • Belfast • Pakistan • IRA • Angry Brigade • Manson • Apollo • Vietnam • Butch & Sundance • Monty Python • Thatcher, Thatcher school-milk snatcher • Women's lib • Winnie Mandela • Germaine Greer • RIP Coco Chanel • Louis Armstrong

1971

Charlotte Quinlan was dead. She had died with no more fuss than Sid and Winifred. An influenza virus and her life was ended.

Rose, driving over to the funeral, wished she had not given in to the temptation of driving her new car but used the old Rover that practically drove itself. She could have done without the unfamiliar controls on a day that was bound to be a strain; and seeing Nora if only on a flying visit was bound to be emotional; plus time had run out for making a decision about Longmore. The offer to sell it to an hotel chain was tempting, but it would mean leaving the place she and Mac had built up and into which they had both put so much hard work. They had talked and talked, but in the end Mac had said that it must be Rose who should make the final decision. Then there was Ballard. But, having reached the last few miles of the journey which was a steep, bending climb out of Petersfield, she was forced to leave the confrontation with Ballard and concentrate on the unfamiliar gear-stick.

At the old Quinlan house, where Charlotte and Sid had lived for so long, and where later Frank had come to live, there for the first time since the divorce Rose was going to meet Ballard face to face. On most occasions where there was a chance of this happening, they could have made their excuses, but Charlotte's funeral was not such a one.

'Don't be sad, Rose,' Frank said. 'Lotte said I was to see that everybody had a good time. She reckoned that having had an extra twenty years after she'd had her four-score years and ten was pretty good.'

'It's difficult not to feel sad though. She's been part of my life for a long time.'

'She thought the world of you.'

'That makes me feel pretty rotten, I didn't pay her much attention after we left the village.'

'She wouldn't want you feeling that way. We've all got our own lives to lead. And you gave us some lovely weekends at the hotel. She couldn't abide old people who let themselves be fussed over. It was her independence I liked.'

Together they looked at a photograph of Lotte at their wedding, wearing a pretty frock and with a large outrageous hat covering her sparse hair. Her head was tilted and she was laughing as though she was twenty.

Jon, Elna and Sunny arrived in two cars. Sunny – who was trying hard to get everyone to call her Sonia – was at the stage of development when her legs were gangling, her chest was being transformed into a small bosom and yet, although her teeth were braced, one could see what a good-looking woman she would be.

'Sunny, sweetheart, give me a kiss.'

This was Sonia's first funeral and she was pleased with her new coat and shoes for the occasion.

'Where are the babies?' Rose asked. Jon and Elna had had four since Sonia. Shirley and John, twins, now five years old, Martinique who was three, and one-year-old Manley. When she became pregnant after the twins, Jon joked that Elna wanted to get as many in whilst she was able. There was a bit of truth in that. She had grown plump and comfortable and had every appearance of being pleased with life. She was two months pregnant again, but as yet she had kept the news to herself. Maybe she would stop at six.

It was as well that Jon was making good money these days. Not only was the housing market booming, but five years ago when Elna was preoccupied with the twins, causing Jon to feel excluded, he had discovered he had a talent for writing popular fiction. Rebecca used to say that Jon had read Daydreaming at university: a qualification in daydreams was what was required to be able create a character like Jon's fictional hero, Johnny Quest. Johnny Quest spy thrillers were a hit; he had no trouble in turning out two in a year. So far there were four novels in the bookshops and others in progress.

Sonia said, 'They are at Granny's and Grandpa's. Mum said she wouldn't bring them because they would only get bored and play around. Marti is very naughty, but what can you expect, she's only three.'

Elna sat sipping a Bacardi and coke looking over a pile of condolence cards with Frank; Jon settled down comfortably beside Rose. 'What's new then, Mum?'

'Nothing too exciting.'

Which was not strictly accurate. The eight years of restoration and refurbishment of Longmore were almost completed.

It was true that once Vee had gone, nobody had the same dedication for setting out at two in the morning for Covent Garden market, but she and Mac had found and trained a bored domestic science teacher who had some of Vee's imagination and flair. There were no stars or symbols, Longmore did not need or seek them.

Longmore was thriving.

Old money colonials, Indians who had been educated in English public schools, foreign diplomats, academics from Boston, and choosy actresses who had achieved Damehood were among the most regular of Longmore guests. Longmore did not go in for indulging one-day stopover American tourists. Its ambience was relaxed and tranquil: dishes to be savoured, meals that stretched to fill pleasant time. Although Mac allowed juniors to take a hand in making sauces and steaming vegetables, the preparation of dishes for the cold table was entirely his domain. And although the control and staff were still Rose's province, now that the accounting and managing had become more complex, she too had found it necessary to employ experts to do that work. Her great success was with the old garden though. She had turned down the idea of one of Leo's blue pools, and occasionally reviewed the possibility of installing one in the old stables some time in the future; the old squash court still existed, but somewhere along the line Longmore dropped the health and fitness idea they had started out with, and had settled for quiet and simple luxury.

The gardens were effective. Long-standing guests took a positive interest in their progress, often enquiring after them by long-distance call. A famous race-horse owner had donated a rare Indian bean tree, a French film actress had arranged for a mature Judas tree to be helicoptered in; an English woman judge's token of appreciation of Longmore ambience was a half-size Buddah in contemplation. As she had said she would, Rose used Nana Borgman's idea of creating a series of different gardens, each with its own character. But the Longmore gardens were not theatrical, as Nana's had been; Rose planned hers to give rest, to give perfume, to surprise with reds and shocking pinks, and to delight with crumbling walls and rambling plants.

Rose continued, 'They're going to do a TV gardening programme at Longmore.'

'That will push up the bookings.'

'If it does we shall have to build new kitchens in the old stables, and convert the present kitchens to more guest rooms. But I don't know whether it will come to that . . . it's a long story, I'll tell you later, when the girls are here. Becc says they're going to make a film of your last book, is that right?'

'Not just a film, a series for television.'

'That's wonderful. I only hope I shall be able to understand the film better than I understand the books. I find them as compulsive to read as I once did Threnody's Contessas, but I never know what all those undercover people are doing!'

Jon laughed, 'I don't think *they* know.'

'Is it really like that in the spy world?'

'Don't ask me, but it's what readers think it's like and that's what counts. It's a shame Vee can't get here, it would have been nice for us all to be together. Great-gran would have liked that.'

'She would, but it's that business about crews only flying so many hours at a stretch.'

'Nora has managed to get away.'

'She should be here soon. She's staying with Monica and Leo. I'm hoping she can come to Longmore for a couple of days before she has to get back.'

'James's not home though.'

'I don't think it's easy for them: this posting is so remote it all has to be organized ages in advance.'

'Is she OK?'

'I've only spoken to her on the phone, but she sounded fine,' she smiled. 'Uncommunicative, but fine.'

'How do she and James stick it? All those half-starved sickly kids, trying to work miracles with no proper equipment, no proper food. I couldn't do it.'

'Well, no, not many of us could.'

'Nora and James seemed the least like missionaries of anyone I ever knew.'

'Not missionaries, that sounds a bit . . .'

'I don't mean it to, I'm full of admiration, for what they do. They know they can't stop famine, they try to alleviate some of its effects – they make me feel decadent. But James and Nora . . .'

'You never can tell. I think it's a fascinating thing to see what your own children do with their lives. You'll find that with Sonia and the babies.'

For a long pause his gaze withdrew, then he said, 'I'll bet you don't remember, but that day when we all went to the Battersea Festival fun-fair, we stood and watched those two, hand in hand, ploughing their way along one of the boulevards. Monica said, "Startrite shoes." She was spot on.'

'I don't remember that, but I can see what she meant. They were a bit like that; two determined little children going off alone down a long, sunny road, absolutely sure of themselves.'

'Was it sunny? I always imagined the "Startrite" road was a long, lonely road.'

Rose, who found it difficult to stop taking the blame for her children's hang-ups, put a tentative hand over his. 'Oh Jon, I'm sorry about all that . . .'

Unexpectedly he gave her hand a quick squeeze and let it go. 'Come on, it's a bit early in the day for G and Ts, but what the Hell.'

A London cab slowed down in the lane outside the house. Frank said, 'That's a long way from home, I wonder who it is?'

'One guess,' Jon said.

Sonia said, 'Aunt Becc.'

Rebecca it was, of course. She never bothered with driving herself; if she wanted to travel, she would whenever feasible call a cab.

'Oh good,' said Frank, 'if Nora gets here soon, you can have a nice get-together before the outsiders come.'

Becc made her entrance: in her thirties now and, except for her father, much wealthier than any of the rest of her family. Her latest shops, designed to capture a new generation of young women but still remain beloved of her own sophisticated generation, were expected to be the high-street success story of the next decade. But, as was evidenced in her hollow eyes and much-starved body, the years of candles burned at both ends, with her art and ambition burning in the middle, had taken their toll. Seeing the two of them together, one might easily have believed that she and Rose were of the same generation.

She went round the room exclaiming to each in turn that it had been 'Simply ages!' She hugged Rose briefly and said, 'Love you, Rosie, you *must* come and look at my new boutique, really classy', then took Sonia to sit beside her.

Sonia fingered the complicated black beading on Becc's formal suit. 'Is this new?'

'Ages old. I wore it to Coco Chanel's memorial service.'

Sonia was impressed. Rebecca had intended her to be; she loved to thrill her niece.

'You went to *the* Coco Chanel's funeral?'

'Memorial service. Darling, she was a dead old woman who had been sitting on fashion for generations. Some of us went to make sure that she was gone.' Rebecca raised her eyebrows, trying to sound quite disgraceful, and thus re-stock her niece's store of gossip to be told to her girlfriends.

'Now, sweetheart, listen to me. I want your opinion. How does this grab you: a fashion shop only for the tens to fourteens?'

Sonia, who adored her aunt, who refused to be addressed as such, went pale with excitement at the prospect, then flushed with pleasure. 'Maybe ten's a bit young for fashion.'

'Right! You're absolutely right. Eleven to fourteen. You think it would go then?'

'You don't mean a department?'

'Absolutely not. A shop for girls over eleven.'

Sonia shot glances in the direction of her mother and father, particularly at her mother who didn't really approve of Becc. No, it wasn't that her mother *disapproved*, more that she took too much notice of Granny Birdham's opinions. Granny Birdham had this idea that fun people were sinful, but once Sonia had seen through Granny Birdham's ideas of sin, Sonia had come to the conclusion that Becc, beneath her way-out clothes and her way of talking which made people notice, was a nice person.

If Sonia wanted to be like anybody, it was Becc.

She said tentatively, 'Couldn't you could call the shop "Eleven Plus"?'

'Brilliant! Darling girl, you are a genius. I'll put you on a retainer straight away, and if Jon and your Ma say that you can, I'll take you along to the shop I'm thinking of leasing, and you can tell me exactly how it ought to be fitted out. You could do the official opening.'

'Will you ask today?'

'Best not today. Maybe we should work on Jon first.'

'Oh no, it's Mummy you have to get. Daddy just goes along with things.'

Becc felt a twinge of sadness and a little of guilt. Poor old Jon. She couldn't remember a time when he was not being told what to do by somebody. Maybe that's why there was such a lot of drugs and sex and violence in his books. He might like to believe that people read them for his characters and intricate plots, but it was Becc's opinion that Johnny Quests were popular because in every chapter somebody was sure to be taking or smuggling drugs, or using a gun, a guitar-string garotte, a knife; his characters bled, died, and screwed; there was a lot of screwing. She *must* remember to tell him how proud of him she was. He gave pleasure, which was what she did herself. She was proud that that was what she did.

Quite soon after Rebecca's arrival, Nora appeared quietly at the back door and came in without making an entrance. It wasn't that Nora was a retiring type of woman, it was just her way. When she needed her presence to be felt, it was felt all right. Rose was the first to notice her and went eagerly to greet this youngest of her children.

Frank Rogers ushered Nora eagerly into the room. 'Rebecca's only just arrived, and now here you are.'

'I know, she swished pass me in her taxi.'

'Darling!' Rebecca said, 'I did *that*? Where were you?'

'Walking along the lane.'

The two sisters clung to one another warmly but briefly. 'You walked! That's positively asking to be swished. People don't *walk* to funerals.'

She might have said, I do it all the time, but never would.

Nora. The one Rose admired so much but felt that she no longer knew. Did any of them know Nora? She appeared to be simple and uncomplicated, but Rose always thought that she saw guardedness in Nora's look, but then so she did in Jon's. Vee and Becc always wore their self-possessed public faces. Rose had never been able to get close to Nora since the cuddles had stopped. Rose had supposed that, because Nora was still a girl at the time of the divorce, she had been affected by it more than the others and that was her reason for going to live for a while with Charlotte; she had said that it was because she wanted to stay on at her local school, but that was only half the truth; just as it was only half the truth about the travelling-distance when she stopped visiting her father in spite of all his bribes and promises. By the time she had eventually come to have a room at Longmore she had seemed to have accustomed herself to the split. But who knew with Nora? Who really knew with any of them?

Only recently she had read a magazine article about a theory that there could be a subconscious awareness of conception which of course made her wonder about Vee and Nora. Had Ballard not forced her to have sex, then Vee and Nora might still be in whatever Limbo the unconceived inhabit. Rose liked and loved them both; life without them was as impossible to imagine as life *with* her unremembered brother was.

Nora looked marvellous. She had a hard, taut body; her face was suntanned with two panda-eyes from wearing sunglasses; much of her hair was bleached from wearing it hanging in a bunch from the back of a sun-hat. Every day she held hands with the poverty and disease of some southern nation, and had only days ago left a village where children had little flesh on their bones; now here she was in this village with her family who had every material thing possible. She smiled a confident and kind smile as Rose went to greet her. Confidence and kindliness were part of her stock-in-trade.

Rose, pressing her cheek to Nora's, said, 'Nora, at last. I was beginning to wonder whether you might have been recalled and would go flying off somewhere again and I should never see you.' Rose felt the same momentary awkwardness as always now that she was a woman.

'I wouldn't do that, Mum. Gran made me promise I would be here to see her off. I wouldn't have let her down.' She never said how difficult it had been to get away, but this was the last journey of the old lady who, more than anyone except James, had understood Nora.

Frank fetched some bottles of chilled wine which he and Jon served in generous glasses.

'*He's* not here then?' Nora said.

'Your father? Not yet. Frank says they're on their way.'

'He's bringing Miriam?'

'Well, she did know Charlotte.'

Jon, joining them, said, 'Are you all right about this, Mum?'

'Of course,' Rose smiled wryly. 'Actually, I think I'm more curious than anything; it's years since I last saw him . . . well, except in the papers.'

Blowing out a stream of cigarette smoke, Jon said, 'He's *always* in the papers.'

Nora opened her mouth to say something but was interrupted by a disturbance when yet again their attention was drawn to the lane outside. A shiny black Daimler had drawn up.

'Oh, good Lord,' said Frank, panicking a little, 'the funeral car's here! It's not supposed to come yet. Lotte's friends aren't even here.'

A uniformed driver got out with smart agility.

'Bloody Hell!' Rebecca said. 'Look, the Mafia's here,' as they saw Ballard emerge from the splendid motorcar.

Sonia wormed her way to the window. She was very curious to see this grandfather. She had seen him on TV but never for real. She could scarcely believe the poshness of the car. It had smoky windows and a long bonnet that was as shiny as a black mirror. She knew that he was over sixty, but he looked a lot younger than Grandpa Birdham who was the same age. He wore a black overcoat and was carrying a wreath, and looked just like Mr Heath had looked on Poppy Day. His wife had high heels that made her totter because they kept sinking into the gravel.

Frank went to the front door and there was a moment's delay as the wreath was dealt with and Miriam breathily said her condolences. Sonia perched herself on the window-sill where she steadfastly refused to see her mother's disapproval.

Her grandfather entered the big sitting room by himself, nodding at people, but not really looking to see who they were; he went straight to the big chiffonier where her Daddy had taken over the giving out of drinks. He said, 'Hello, Jon. Ah, Elna . . . are you well?'

Her Dad said didn't say Hello or anything like that; he said, 'Still drink straight whisky, Dad? It's Bowmore, or Old Paddy if you want Irish.'

'Just a shot of the Islay, Jon. I don't do much of it these days, but I do like the occasional tot.'

Sonia was amazed that there were no fireworks or anything, but she did notice her father's hand tremble a little as he upturned the glass. He looked jumpy, and spoke quickly as he sometimes did when Granny Birdham was laying down the law. Granny Birdham didn't scare Sonia. Nobody scared Sonia.

Ballard took the drink and said, 'One can hardly say "Cheers" on an occasion like this.'

Elna stood up and went to give Jon support. She knew that Jon found his father intimidating. She had an intimidating mother, so she knew how it could be. Jon was a good man, a thousand times better than his father would ever be.

Sipping his drink and being polite to Frank about his choice of Scotch gave Ballard a bit more time to adjust to the fact that he and Rose were under the same roof once again. The doors between three rooms had been opened and now that Charlotte's friends were beginning to arrive the place was becoming crowded. But he was pretty sure he knew where she would be. In the conservatory. To Elna he said, 'I hear you've given the Quinlan family a whole new branch. Have you pictures of them? You must show Miriam.'

Jon jumped in before Elna could reply, 'No, but if you are really interested in seeing them, Hampstead's not far out.'

Elna always carried pictures, she was proud of her children; anyone had only got to ask and she would bore them to death. She said, 'But Sonia's here. This is her sitting in the window like a hobbledehoy.'

Sonia, not wanting to put her mother and father at a disadvantage, took the hint and donned her parents' air of formality and politeness. Her grandfather put out his hand as he would to an adult. 'How do you do, Sonia.'

In the voice that had cost Jon fees for elocution, Sonia said, 'Hello, Grandfather Quinlan.'

He touched her cheek, 'You are a very pretty girl.'

'Thank you, I'll be better when my teeth are finished. I've been watching for you from the window. I suppose that was your wife who came with you?'

'Yes, that's Miriam.'

'She's terribly pretty.'

'You'll soon get in her good books then.'

'What do you think I should call her? She isn't my grandmother. I already have two.' Sonia thought that he was going to laugh. She would have quite liked that, because it wouldn't be the thing to do.

'No, no,' he said, 'she is not your grandmother.'

'Not anybody really to me, except she's your second wife.'

Now she saw that Daddy might smile, but Mummy gave him her 'Don't you dare!' look.

Ballard held out his glass for Jon to replenish.

'Could I call her "Miriam" then? Or Mrs Quinlan?'

'As you like.'

Jon said, 'That's enough for now.'

'But, Dad, I can't call her Mrs Quinlan, because that's who Grandma is.'

She pleased Ballard no end. She knew damned well what she was up to. He had lived with Rebecca and Villette for enough years to recognize a fake wide-eyed innocent. 'Call her Miriam. Why don't you slip up to the bedroom. She's up there changing her dress and doing something to her face.'

He turned and walked in the direction of the conservatory.

'Hello, Rose. I thought I'd find you here.'

There was only a brief pause before Rose moved but it was all the time in the world for him to take in everything about her. Oh how elegant she looked, her hair as simply dressed as ever, her black dress, equally simple, flowing over a figure which appeared as lithe as it had ever looked. Her only adornment were large round earrings and a fine gold chain that dipped into her modest cleavage. Not that he had expected to find her chasing fashion as Miriam did, but he had not expected to be so affected by the timelessness of the way she still looked, the way she had not been tempted to change her style. He could not think of anything she could do that would improve her.

Casually, slowly, she turned her head an inch in his direction. 'You're here then.'

It really did appear that they were running frame by frame through a home-movie editing machine. As he moved closer to her, he could see the faint hairline scars and a slightly crooked eyebrow. For the first time in ages he felt a surge of real emotion. What madness and desire she used to arouse with her faultless looks. He had once described her as 'Untouched by human hand', a cellophane-wrapped desirable gift that one longed to keep but at the same time longed to drag from its package. He must have been half-mad at those times. In his desire for her there had been occasions when he hadn't realized that she was seriously resisting him until later when he saw the bruises. Those had been bad times. Those had been the times when he had been mad. Losing self-control was frightening.

They shook hands. Such a polite greeting for two people who had lived for years putting a good public face on their troubled marriage. Now another man had access to her body. More than one for all he knew. He had known about the man from South Africa who came and went at intervals. It was not difficult for a man with Ballard's connections and pull to get information. When he discovered that she was having an affair, it had been hard to accept that a man like that should know her most intimate physical details; details which the first time Ballard had seen her completely undressed had been of such significance. The way her underarm hair spread out like a star. Did she still let it grow, or did the dentist like his women to have that pre-pubescent look; did he appreciate the amazing colour of her nipples and the texture and smell of her skin? No matter what any man knew of her now, only he himself had known Rose when she had truly been untouched by human hand, before Jon was born, when her breasts still tilted upwards.

They exchanged stilted clichés about Charlotte, her long life and easy death. He took in more detail. Her jawline was a bit looser and her throat creased, the outline of her lips not as clearly defined. She must know what he was thinking as he held her gaze; she had always known at once when he desired her.

She did not look away. Not a hint of a blush. Rose, who at one time could have won cups for blushing, neither coloured nor let her gaze drop, but continued to make conversation about a possible headstone for Charlotte.

'I was sorry to hear of your accident.' He traced the line, not touching.

'Oh, that's history.'

'A remarkable job. I heard you had Mario Berini.'

'Did you?' Without the slightest interest in how that was.

'He's expensive.'

'I didn't choose him. He happened to be the surgeon who happened to be working at the hospital I was taken to.'

'I would have been perfectly willing to have picked up the bill.'

'Why? It had nothing to do with you. The airport paid.'

He moved his head a fraction closer and searched her face. 'Only the faintest of lines, and a parting in the eyebrow.'

'Please, Ballard!'

'I'm sorry. But I *have* been concerned.'

'About me?' She looked scornful.

'Of course I was, and I am honestly relieved to see you looking so very much the same.'

'Really? I certainly don't *feel* the same, I'm pleased to say. Is Miriam well? I see she has given you a waistline and some cheekbones.'

'Oh yes, she is well. Spends a lot of time riding and hunting. A lot of dogs.'

Miriam was a very different woman from the girl who had thought it would be terribly thrilling to take up with Labour people. Women in general were changing. The Pill, careers, working, earning, buying cars, holidaying and going into restaurants, drinking in bars without men. She had plagued the life out of him lately. She wanted to *do* something. What was she supposed to do with the next thirty or forty years of her life? His own mother had been extremely happy living a very useful life as a wife and mother. 'Bollocks!' she had said. 'Your mother did *not* have a *useful* life – she had no life at *all*. All that she did with her life was to have you and then bore her friends to death talking about you. Had you become a postman, what *would* she have done with herself?'

'She's just freshening up. It's a fair old drive down. That bright young grand-daughter of ours has gone up to talk to her.' He wanted Rose to see, even in their separate lives, how much there was that still held them together. He wanted her to acknowledge them.

'*Ours?*'

'She is mine too.'

'Yours? You can't mean Sonia, who has a touch of the tar-brush? The baby whose black grandparents *you* said would cause the streets to run with blood?'

He was so taken aback by her fierceness that he did not even try to defend his position.

'Don't you dare lay claim to her; she's never been *your* grand-daughter, Ballard.'

After a moment of pause, he changed tack. 'Did you enjoy your stay in South Africa? I love the place,' he smiled. 'Quite the grand old style. No thoughts of marrying again? How about Dr Borgman? Or isn't he divorced yet?'

Now he was certain that he must have rocked her perplexing self-confidence. He waited for embarrassment to flush her cheeks.

It did not. She had often thought of things she would like to say to him, but never really imagined that she would do so. She said, 'Oh shut up, Ballard. Your information about Pedr Borgman isn't even up to date. If it hadn't been for the fact that I was curious, I wouldn't have exchanged half a dozen words with you. You can't *really* believe that I haven't changed? Did you suppose that I would still be intimidated by you? Of course the old Rose has changed. There's hardly a thing left of her. Her damaged ego has had large doses of independence; and as for her confidence . . . it has gone off the scale. A career, a nice income and good, enjoyable sex, Ballard. Really *really* enjoyable, lots of it. Why the Hell would any woman with all this want to marry?' She turned on her heel and returned to the house and the gathering of mourners who for the past five minutes had been consumed with curiosity about what was taking place in the conservatory.

It was late afternoon before Rose got away from Charlotte's. She and Jon, Becc and Nora had stayed on after the locally traditional sherry and cake at the house. Ballard had gone straight back to

London, as had Elna with Sonia. Now, driving back to Longmore, the new car went along as easily as Longmore's old Rover.

Catching a glimpse of herself in the car's interior mirror, she was surprised to see that she was smiling. Well, she had seen three of her children living lives they had chosen for themselves with all the signs of being satisfied with their choices. And, well, she had to admit, she had also had some small-minded moments of gratification, all of which had to do with Ballard. As Becc had described it, when Ballard had smoothed the lines of the flame-coloured MG longingly, he had assumed that the car was Becc's and that Jon's solid Rover belonged to Rose. 'I tell you, Rosie, he's sure you are going to Hell in a basket. I do *hope* he's right. Mind you, he's now quite at ease that he is not responsible for the way Vee and I have turned out.'

It had not been a sad day. Charlotte *would* have been pleased. It had had its poignant moments, of course. A lot had happened. Frank told them he thought he would get a small place; Monica had been in the Honeywood churchyard and they had made a definite date for lunch together. Perhaps this time neither of them would have reason to call off. Before she left them, she had told Jon, Becc and Nora about the offer by International Country Clubs to buy Longmore.

Mac's mother was dying, and whatever happened he was going home for a few months. He had been adamant that this should not influence her decision. She loved Longmore, yet if she turned down the ICC offer, what was left to do but live there?

But over the course of the day, a decision had become firm and she had already spoken to Mac.

Nora's reaction: 'Longmore without Mac in the kitchens, forget it, Mum. Take the money.'

Becc's, 'God, Rosie, you almost make me want to do the same. You should clear off and start a hotel on St Kitts or wherever it is.'

Jon said, 'If it were me, I'd sell it and then take some time. I'd go away and laze around on a warm beach for a few months.'

But she had made her decision before then. Seeing Ballard so stodgy and secure with his limo and the wealthy wife he would never be able to afford to shake off; Ballard still putting on a public face, and now too settled in the concrete of the Establishment to ever take a risk other than a bit of a gamble now and then on the Stock Exchange.

One by one her children had set her an example and until today she had never been able to see it. They had each in turn been confident enough to do what *they* knew was right for *them*.

The selling point in the advertising campaign for this low-slung wire-wheeled, sporty, scarlet convertible she was driving, read, 'Your Mother Wouldn't Like It.' She was delighted with the car. 'Going to Hell in a basket'. The young salesman, when he had realized that she was considering buying the car for herself, had said, 'There is a very classy dark green.'

'I don't think so,' she had said. 'I'm sure the scarlet is exactly right for me.'

He hadn't even smiled when she added, 'The thing is, now that I'm a grandmother I think it's time I started to grow old disgracefully.'

She put her foot down and felt the unsuitable car surge forward. She could but try.